PENGUIN

THE SECRET HISTORY

Christopher P. Atwood teaches Mongolian history and civilization at the University of Pennsylvania. He received his doctorate from Indiana University. He has travelled extensively in independent Mongolia and Inner Mongolia. Atwood's previous books include *The Rise of the Mongols: Five Chinese Sources* and the *Encyclopedia of Mongolia and the Mongol Empire*.

The Secret History
of the Mongols

Translated by Christopher P. Atwood

PENGUIN BOOKS

PENGUIN CLASSICS

UK | USA | Canada | Ireland | Australia
India | New Zealand | South Africa

Penguin Books is part of the Penguin Random House group of companies
whose addresses can be found at global.penguinrandomhouse.com

First published in Penguin Classics 2023
001

Translation copyright © Christopher P. Atwood, 2023

The moral rights of the translator have been asserted

Set in 10.25/12.25pt Sabon LT Pro
Typeset by Jouve (UK), Milton Keynes
Printed and bound in Great Britain by Clays Ltd, Elcograf S.p.A.

The authorized representative in the EEA is Penguin Random House Ireland,
Morrison Chambers, 32 Nassau Street, Dublin D02 YH68

A CIP catalogue record for this book is available from the British Library

ISBN: 978-0-241-19791-2

www.greenpenguin.co.uk

Penguin Random House is committed to a
sustainable future for our business, our readers
and our planet. This book is made from Forest
Stewardship Council® certified paper.

Contents

THE SECRET HISTORY OF THE MONGOLS

Acknowledgements

It has been my pleasure over the years to read *The Secret History of the Mongols* with students at Indiana University and the University of Pennsylvania, either in translation or in the original Mongolian. Many of their insights and questions about the text are reflected in the text that follows. Once I began working on a new translation, several students and colleagues assisted me with careful reading and criticism. Foremost among these readers was Nick Kapur, who put in painstaking efforts to improve this translation, pushing me throughout to prioritize readability in English. His intervention vastly improved the final version. Vito Acosta and Timothy May likewise read through the full text and offered valuable suggestions. My editor at Penguin, Simon Winder, was unfailingly wise and patient; Linden Lawson and the rest of the Penguin team did a superb job preparing the final text. Other readers and colleagues who offered valuable comments and suggestions include Sam Bass, Dotno Pount, Daniel Prior, David Robinson, Eiren Shea, David Sneath, Sangseraima Ujeed and Tsultemin Uranchimeg. I am grateful to them all. I am also grateful to Ruth Dunnell, Stephen West and Shao-yun Yang for allowing me to cite their soon to appear translation of Qiu Chuji's *Journey to the West*. All remaining errors and infelicities are mine alone.

My mentor in reading Middle Mongolian was György Kara. I was very much hoping to get his feedback on this translation, but he passed away while it was still in progress. My mother, Nancy C. Atwood, was very enthusiastic about this translation, but she also passed away during the final months of copy-editing. I dedicate this translation to their memory.

Introduction

The Mongol empire expanded faster and further than any other empire in world history. It was a measure of the scale of their conquest that it transformed Eurasia, creating the great countries we know there today. We often say that 'the Mongols conquered China, Russia and Iran', which is true – geographically. Yet before the Mongol conquests, China, Russia and Iran did not actually exist as unified countries, and the dominant tendency in their histories was to further disunity, not to unity. One could thus just as well say that the Mongol empire *created* China, Russia and Iran.

History views conquest ambivalently today. Not only is the cost to the conquered too often appalling, but telling the story of the conquerors is the kind of male-centred, ruling-class narrative that social history was intended to transcend. Yet it is conquest that has been the motor driving the connections between cultures and environments, transcending narrow national limits and generating globalization and hybridity. What would it be like to tell the story of conquest in a way that does not sugar-coat the violence and class dominance at its heart, but also locates that violence and class dominance in the domestic settings of the conquerors – not just the public personas of the male conquerors but also their private lives among their ladies and their children? Such is *The Secret History of the Mongols*, the pre-eminent story of Chinggis ('Genghis') Khan (1162?–1227),[1] his mother, his wives, his closest friends and his sons.

The Secret History of the Mongols (*Monġgol-un ni'uca tobci-yan*) is, as its first English translator, Frances W. Cleaves, said, 'not only the capital monument of thirteenth-century Mongolian literature', but also 'one of the great literary monuments of the world'. Its storyline begins with the distant genealogy and legendary past of the Mongol khans before their empire. It then gives a portrait of the young conqueror under his birth name Temujin, the sudden death of his father Yisukei, the dangers and hardships of his childhood and youth under his mother Ö'elun, and his gradual accumulation of friends and family. After alliances with a neighbouring khan, To'oril, and a sworn brother (*anda*) of his childhood named Jamuqa, Temujin eventually follows the advice of his wife Börte, strikes out on his own, gathers followers and is first elected as a petty khan, under the title Chinggis Khan.

What follows then are a series of battles with rivals in what is now eastern Mongolia and the adjacent parts of modern-day southern Siberia and China's Inner Mongolia. His rivals include the Yörkin house, headed by his cousins, the rival Tayici'ut princes, leading a more distantly related line of khans, and his old friend/rival Jamuqa. Backing him up in these conflicts, though, is To'oril, by this time known as Ong Khan, who rules the powerful Kereyit khanate, or kingdom, in central Mongolia.

Eventually, Chinggis Khan subdues his enemies in eastern Mongolia, finishing with a wholesale massacre of the Tatars who had killed his father and grandfathers. But as he rises to power, Jamuqa, who had also joined Ong Khan's entourage, begins to conspire with Ong Khan's son Ilqa Senggum and poisons the khan's mind against his eastern ally Chinggis Khan. In the end Ong Khan launches a treacherous attack on Chinggis Khan. The attack fails to kill or capture its target, but now Chinggis Khan is entirely on his own. After sending a lengthy indictment of Ong Khan's treachery, Chinggis Khan manages to catch Ong Khan feasting unawares, and drives him and his son Ilqa Senggum into exile, where Ong Khan is killed. The unification of the Mongolian plateau is concluded with two lengthy campaigns, first against the Naiman in western Mongolia, and then the Merkit in northern Mongolia. The last fugitive to be captured is Jamuqa; although Chinggis Khan offers to share the kingdom with him, Jamuqa knows it cannot be and accepts an honourable execution.

With that follows a lengthy description of the new regime.

Chinggis Khan organizes his people into the famous Central Eurasian 'decimal organization', assigning all the people into nested groups of tens, hundreds and thousands of households. To the thousands he appoints commanders from among those who assisted in his rise. He also designs a body of *keśikten*, a term meaning both 'fortunate ones' and 'those serving in shifts', as bodyguards. Around the borders of Mongolia, in Inner Mongolia, eastern Turkestan and the forests of Siberia, he marries his daughters to submissive rulers of nearby realms. Finally, he faces down a challenge from Teb-Tenggeri, a shaman who had initially announced Heaven and Earth's collaboration to enthrone Chinggis as the supreme Khan of all Mongolia, but who now seems to be aiming to replace Chinggis Khan's dynasty with his own. With Teb-Tenggeri killed, the unification of Mongolia and the stabilization of the new regime are complete.

Chinggis Khan now turns to the world beyond the Mongolian plateau. He first subdues the Golden Khan, the ruler of North China, who had previously conspired with the Tatars to hold down the early Mongol khans. The campaign begins in 1211 and concludes with the sacking of Zhongdu (present-day Beijing) in 1215. After that, Chinggis Khan responds in 1219 to a treacherous massacre of his merchants and envoys by attacking the Khwarazmian sultan of the Sarts (a general term for people of the Central Asian and Middle Eastern oases), campaigning as far as the Indus River. Finally, in 1226–7, he destroys the Tangut kingdom in what is now north-western China. In the midst of these campaigns, he makes his third son Ökodei his heir apparent, after a vicious family quarrel breaks out between his first son Joci and his second son Caġadai.

After Chinggis Khan dies during the last Tangut campaign, Ökodei is duly enthroned. With the help of his brother Caġadai (Joci had already passed away), Ökodei sets out to complete their father's legacy. First, he conquers the last Golden Khan in North China, who had fled south of the Yellow River. Then he dispatches Chinggis Khan's grandsons to conquer the western steppe as far as Hungary. But family troubles again intervene. During the campaign against the last Golden Khan, the spirits of North China's outraged Earth and Water had attacked the Mongol khan; only the willingness of Chinggis Khan's fourth son, Tolui, to drink an enchanted potion as ransom saves the khan's life. And on the great western campaign, another vicious quarrel breaks out between the cousins, pitting Ökodei and Caġadai's sons against Joci's son Batu. Despite these family conflicts, Ökodei confirms his father's organization of the *keśikten*, and institutes new policies designed to stabilize the empire and ease the lives of his Mongol subjects. The history closes with a testament in which Ökodei Khan reviews his four achievements and four demerits.

This story is told mostly in prose, but with lengthy passages of alliterative verse, sometimes presented as direct speech, sometimes presented in the voice of the narrator. Intimate scenes from Chinggis Khan's childhood, violent quarrels and bloody steppe battles are all pictured as if the author had witnessed them personally. Dates are given in the twelve-animal cycle, with the first one corresponding to 1201 during Chinggis Khan's early campaigns. Chinggis Khan himself passed away in 1227, and the history covers the period up to, but not quite including, the death of his son Ökodei Khan in 1241.

1. THE INFLUENCE OF THE *SECRET HISTORY* AND ITS PRESERVATION

Once told, the *Secret History* became, despite its secrecy (on which more below), the hidden mainspring of the narratives of the Mongol empire's rise. Under Chinggis Khan's grandson Qubilai (Kublai) Khan, who reigned from 1260 to 1294, the Mongol empire's capital was moved from Mongolia to the new twin capitals of Daidu and Shangdu – one the modern Beijing and the other now in ruins in Inner Mongolia. At the same time, Qubilai Khan decided to take the available Mongolian sources and re-edit them in a fashion shaped by Chinese historical conventions into an 'Authentic Chronicle of Chinggis Khan'. This was a bilingual text, with Mongolian as the primary version and an interlinear Chinese translation. The basic narrative was taken from the *Secret History*, but all the family conflicts and squabbles were purged to create a picture of Chinggis Khan as an uncomplicated and wise dynastic founder. Eventually, the Mongolian version was lost, but the Chinese text was combined with a similar 'Authentic Chronicle' of Chinggis's son Ökodei around 1319 to form the text now known as the *Campaigns of Chinggis Khan*, or *Shengwu qinzheng lu* in Chinese.

Meanwhile, a Mongolian copy of the 'Authentic Chronicle of Chinggis Khan' was taken to the court of the Ilkhans, the Mongol rulers in the Middle East. There it was translated into Persian and made the core of the monumental *Compendium of Chronicles* by the Persian vizier and polymath Rashiduddin, supplemented by a vast number of other Mongolian and Persian sources. This history was completed in 1304 and then folded into an even vaster world history.[2] Much of the *Secret History*'s text was thus preserved in more or less verbatim citation in the Chinese of the *Campaigns of Chinggis Khan* and the Persian of the *Compendium of Chronicles*, both sponsored by Chinggis Khan's descendants.

In China, the Mongol Yuan dynasty was overthrown by Chinese rebels and the Mongol court fled back into Mongolia in 1368. The new Ming dynasty gathered the materials on the former Mongol rulers and completed the *Yuanshi*, or 'History of the Yuan Dynasty', in 1370. This work was another monumental encyclopedia; the chapter on Chinggis Khan followed the 'Authentic Chronicle of Chinggis Khan' very closely and hence preserved at third hand much of the *Secret History*'s narrative line.[3] When Europe's Enlightenment thinkers like Gibbon and Voltaire became aware of Chinggis Khan in the eighteenth century, it was Rashiduddin's *Compendium of Chronicles* and the Ming dynasty's *Yuanshi* that were the sources of their knowledge, directly or indirectly – but behind both of them lay, unacknowledged, the *Secret History*.

Finally, in the nineteenth century, the once-secret *Secret History of the Mongols* began to emerge into the light of scholarship. The basis was a version of the text which in the Ming dynasty had been transcribed syllable by syllable into Chinese characters chosen solely for their sound value, and then glossed word by word into Chinese. This version of the text, the Hanlin recension,

thus preserved the Mongolian-language text with a complete
Chinese translation. It had been prepared in the 1380s as a tool
to help Ming-dynasty interpreters communicate with the Mon-
gols they had just expelled from China. Early in the fifteenth
century it was published in twelve-*juan* and fifteen-*juan* versions
(a *juan* is a Chinese textual division, longer than a chapter, shorter
than a volume). These editions no longer survive, but before they
were lost they were copied carefully in the eighteenth and nine-
teenth centuries by Chinese scholars; hence the text of the Hanlin
recension was preserved to the present. First Chinese, then Rus-
sian, Japanese, Mongolian, German, French and American
scholars began to use it to reconstruct the original Mongolian.

In the twentieth century, another version of the *Secret History*
surfaced in Mongolia itself, less complete but still very useful. As
the new government of the Mongolian People's Republic began
collecting manuscripts for its fledgling national library, scholars
found a copy of the *c.*1651 *Altan tobci* or 'Golden Chronicle',
compiled by the monk Lubsang-Danzin, which incorporated
verbatim about two-thirds of the *Secret History*. The text was
interlarded among other legendary and apocryphal materials
and frequently miscopied the now archaic *Secret History* lan-
guage, but it still proved invaluable for reconstructing the text.
The Lubsang-Danzin *Altan tobci* or *LAT* recension thus joined
the Hanlin recension as the second main resource for recon-
structing the Mongolian text of the *Secret History*, followed by
the parallel passages in the *Campaigns of Chinggis Khan*, the
Compendium of Chronicles and the *Yuanshi*.[4]

In the English language, three previous translators have
defined how the *Secret History* was read:

1. Francis Woodman Cleaves, whose translation was
   completed in 1956, but for personal reasons not
   published until 1982;
2. Igor de Rachewiltz, whose translation was first
   published in serial form from 1971 to 1985 and issued
   as a book with a massive commentary in 2004;
3. and Urgunge Onon, a Daur Mongol from Manchuria
   working in the tradition of his fellow Daur scholars

Duke Tsengde and his successors Eldengtai and
Ardajab (2001).

Along with the invaluable reference works produced by Hitoshi
Kuribayashi at Tohoku University in Sendai, these have been
my constant companions throughout this translation. The
transmission, recovery and translation of the text constitute
one of the great stories of modern scholarship; I have told this
story in the Afterword.

2. THE WORLD OF THE *SECRET HISTORY*

The *Secret History* gives us an insider view of a 'mobile coun-
try' unparalleled in its immediacy. But the Secret Historian
was not an ethnographer and took for granted the material,
social, political and spiritual background of Chinggis Khan's
youth and the early Mongol empire. Fortunately, many medi-
eval travellers, Chinese, French, Italian and Arab, visited this
exotic world and left us their impressions of this already
thousand-year-old civilization. A tour of how other Afro-
Eurasian writers saw the Secret Historian's world will orient
the reader to the unfamiliar lifeways of Central Eurasia's
mobile pastoralists and the institutions they built to live,
thrive and succeed in it.

Gers, hordes and *esuk*: dwellings and food

The fundamental technology for living in the steppe was the
mobile home made of felt coverings over a wooden trellis net-
work. In the *Secret History*, living in dwellings with walls of
felt defined the Mongolian people much more than the nomad-
ism that outsiders often fixed on. The *Secret History* describes
the people of Chinggis Khan as 'the felt-walled people' (*sisgei
tu'urğa-tan*), in contrast to the 'plank-door people' (*qabdasun
e'ude-ten*) of the conquered lands.[5] The Mongols at this time
did not label themselves as 'nomads' but they did view the Tan-
guts and others as being stuck in place with their 'ponderous

possessions and pounded-wall cities' (*nunji nuntuq-tan nödük-sen balaġasu-tan*).

This felt-covered trellis mobile home is called in its various forms 'yurt' in Russian and other European languages, but *ger* in Mongolian, pronounced roughly like English 'gear' but with a clipped 'ea' and a rolled 'r'. It is often described in other languages as a 'felt tent', but the Mongolian word *ger* contains none of the connotations of precarity and flimsiness that the word 'tent' brings up in English. Instead it was the regular, permanent residence which was supplemented by a wide variety of temporary, less solid dwellings, many of which are mentioned in the *Secret History*: the *nembüle* or grass-thatched hut, the *qoš* or *qośiliq*, a felt-covered tent made in the tepee shape widely used in Siberian and American boreal climates, and the cotton *cacir* or woollen *terme*, both much larger pavilion- or marquee-style tents used for grand political assemblies. To distinguish the *ger* from these more temporary structures, I use the Mongolian term.

Mobile felt dwellings have had a long history in the Central Eurasian steppe and have changed considerably since their first appearance, around 750 BC. Over time, the tendency has been to move from rectangular dwellings with a vaulted roof permanently fixed on wagons to ones with a perfectly round plan placed on the ground which can be disassembled, moved to a new location and reassembled. The modern *ger* as found in Mongolia, Kyrgyzstan and elsewhere is the culmination of this trend; it is never placed on wheels and is moved only by disassembly.

During the Mongol empire, however, this process was only halfway completed, and most people dwelled in non-disassemblable *gers* that were transported whole from place to place on wagons. Both a Chinese envoy, Xu Ting, and a Papal envoy, John of Plano Carpini, observed two types of felt dwellings. Some were round and disassemblable; these are the modern *gers* used today in Central Eurasia. The other type Xu described thus: 'The style on the steppe interweaves willow-wood to form a stiff and permanent enclosure, across which felt is beaten into place. This type cannot be folded up or opened out and must be loaded on to carts.'[6] These were the *gers* found in the empire's heartland and the ones known to the *Secret History*. The first type, the round, disassemblable *ger*s, were common on the frontiers of the empire and appear to have originally been a kind of special *ger* for campaigning.

Based on descriptions and surviving examples used in the shrine dedicated to the worship of the spirit of Chinggis Khan into the twentieth century, the non-disassemblable *ger*s had not a round plan but were formed in a rounded-off square with a projecting chimney-like neck for a smoke hole. Ibn Battutah, an Arabic jurist and traveller who visited the khanate ruled by the family of Chinggis Khan's eldest son Joci in 1332, described such wagons on the move:

> They [have] wagons with four large wheels, some of them drawn by two horses, and some drawn by more than two, and they are drawn also by oxen and camels, according to the weight or lightness of the wagon . . . There is placed upon the wagon a kind of cupola made of wooden laths tied together with thin strips of hide; this is light to carry, and covered with felt or blanket-cloth, and in it there are grilled windows. The person who is inside the tent can see [other] persons without their seeing him, and he can employ himself in it as he likes, sleeping or eating or reading or writing, while he is still journeying.[7]

The size of these *ger*s and their wagons differed greatly. William of Rubruck, a Flemish missionary who travelled the empire from 1253 to 1255, said he saw one such *ger* about thirty feet wide, placed on a cart twenty feet wide. Since modern *ger*s even for ordinary herders are 15 to 20 feet in diameter, such a size for an imperial *ger* is hardly surprising. But the vast majority of *ger*s were rather smaller.[8]

Within these *ger*s, whether of the round disassemblable type or the squarish fixed type, space was distributed by status and gender. William of Rubruck writes:

> After pitching the dwellings with the doorway towards the south, they place the master's couch at the northern end. The women's place is always on the eastern side, that is, to the left of the master of the house as he sits on his couch facing south; while the

men's place is on the western side, namely to his right. On enter-
ing the dwelling, the men would not in any circumstances hang
up their quivers on the women's side.[9]

Thus, status was determined by whether one was close to the
door (low) or opposite it (high), and gender by right (male) or
left (female). Right and left are always oriented as seen from
the high-status position looking towards the door.

William of Rubruck's first audience with Chinggis Khan's
grandson, Möngke Khan, on 4 January 1254 shows what the
inside of a large *ger* looked like to those entering. The guards first
told the missionary's party to wait 'in front of the door of the
residence'. The khan's steward 'lift[ed] up the felt which hung
before it' and had the missionary and his companions searched.

> Then we went in. At the entrance there was a bench with some
> *comos* [*esuk* or fermented mare's milk], near which they made
> the interpreter stand, but we were told to sit on a bench in front
> of the ladies [i.e. on the eastern side]. The interior of the dwelling
> was completely covered in cloth of gold, and in a little hearth in
> the middle there was a fire burning, made from twigs and the
> roots of wormwood . . . and also from cattle-dung.

The khan was seated on a couch or bed at the rear of the *ger*
with one of his wives beside him, and his children on a couch
behind the khan and his lady.[10]

Accompanying all such *ger*s were wagons to, as Ibn Battutah
said, 'carry the baggage, the provisions and the chests of eat-
ables' inside a felt-covered box on top 'with a lock on it' to guard
the provisions.[11] These wagons usually appear in the *Secret
History* as 'covered wagons' (*qara'utai terge[n]*). William of
Rubruck described the make of such locker-topped vehicles:

> this chest or miniature house is covered with black felt smeared
> with fat or ewe's milk, to render it rain-proof . . . In these chests
> they put all their bedding and their valuables, lashing them tightly
> on to high wagons which are drawn by camels, to enable them to
> ford rivers. These chests are never removed from the wagons.[12]

The contrast of these black-felt-covered wagons with the white-felt gers struck the imagination of the Daoist sage Changchun, who described the steppe as 'nothing but black carts and white tents, herders following the grass and water to pasture their animals'.[13] The 'chests or miniature houses', as Rubruck calls them, on top of the covered wagons were usually used for goods,[14] but they were big enough to hide a person in or to ride in. Both the young Temujin and later his wife Börte hid in such a wagon (§§ 85–6, §§100–101) and Mother Ö'elun rode through the night to the rescue of Temujin's brother Qasar in one (§244). In fact, these covered wagons seem to be the original form of Central Eurasian mobile residences, only later replaced by the gers placed on wagons, and finally by the round, disassemblable ger of today.

Another type of vehicle was the qasaq cart, with a single axle and two high wheels, pulled as a rule by a single horse or camel. Such carts were also used to load gers, both in medieval times and into modern times among the western Noġay Turkic nomads of the northern Caucasus and in the shrine dedicated to Chinggis Khan in Ordos.[15] In the Secret History, a ger mounted on such a wagon appears as the favoured conveyance to deliver a bride to her new family in style and comfort (§64). As John of Plano Carpini and William of Rubruck noticed, women were the usual ones driving these as well as other carts.[16] From the Secret History we can see that a 'girl on the front seat of a wagon' was as much a stock motif of medieval Mongol romance as the 'girl on a tractor' was in socialist-realist fiction.[17]

In modern Mongolia, nomad camps are as a rule fairly small – usually two to five gers, fifteen at most, with some associated carts. Each married couple would normally have its own ger. At least in modern times, camps are formed among family by diverse ties of birth, marriage or friendship.[18] The gers camp in a line facing roughly south to south-east, with the leader on the right as one faces south. Such small camps were probably always common in the steppe; the Secret History pictures Mother Ö'elun living in such a small camp after her husband Yisukei Ba'atur's death, together with Yisukei's other widow, an old servant named Granny Qo'aqcin, the two widows' children, and Temujin's wife and his two friends.

Once the empire was founded, however, Mongolian *ger*s would travel in vast groups. William of Rubruck describes how one major khan or prince might have up to a score of wives and each of his ladies had one main wagon-borne *ger*, many smaller *ger*-wagons for members of her entourage to sleep in, and one hundred or two hundred covered wagons for possessions. Ibn Battutah numbered the minor *ger*s behind a khan's lady's main *ger* at one hundred, each inhabited by four maids, and the covered wagons at three hundred, each also attended by a male slave.[19] Each chief lady would place her *ger* in the front rank, all facing south in order of seniority, from the senior right or west to the junior left or east, with her entourage stretching out in a line behind her and her covered wagons in rows between the *ger*s.

When moving on level ground, each lady in her main *ger*, placed on its wagon, would go first, with the lesser *ger*s and the covered wagons tied to each other in a line behind. A Chinese envoy, Peng Daya, says such columns of *ger*-wagons with their 'victual carts', as he called the covered wagons, 'look[ed] like columns of ants as they wind along, extending out for five miles, with the distance horizontally from left to right reaching half of that length'.[20]

To others these cities on the move gave a much grander impression. To William of Rubruck it was almost terrifying:

On sighting Batu's camp, I was struck with awe. His own dwellings had the appearance of a large city stretching far out lengthways and with inhabitants scattered around in every direction for a distance of three or four leagues. And just as every one of the people of Israel knew on which side of the Tabernacle to pitch their tent, so these people know on what side of the residence to station themselves when they are unloading the dwellings.[21]

Arriving among the Islamized Mongols of the fourteenth-century khanate of Joci, Ibn Battutah was likewise impressed:

Then the *mahalla* [camp] came up – they call it the *ordo* – and we saw a vast city on the move with its inhabitants, with mosques and bazaars in it, the smoke of the kitchens rising in the air (for they cook while on the march), and horse-drawn wagons transporting the people. On reaching the camping place they took down the tents [i.e. *gers*] from the wagons and set them on the ground, for they are light to carry, and so likewise they did with the mosques and shops.[22]

At the centre of this great portable city was the horde. This word is actually one of the few Mongolian words in English, derived from Mongolian *ordo*, which has a number of variant forms, such as *orda* or *hordu*. Far from being the chaotic rabble of the modern English 'horde', however, the true Mongol horde was the tightly organized nerve centre of the entire vast camp. As Peng Daya writes,

> Wherever the Tatar ruler's hunting tents are located is always called 'the *ordo*'. His Golden Tent (its pillars are made of gold, hence the name), where the . . . imperial ladies are amassed with the resident populace, is alone called 'the great *ordo*'.[23]

This particular Golden Tent, or Golden Horde, mentioned by Peng Daya is actually the same Golden Tent or *Altan terme* which in the *Secret History* Chinggis Khan seized from Ong Khan (§§184–5, 187) with its attached 'gold liquor services, bowls, and vessels' and staff.[24] Even larger was the Yellow Horde (*Śira Ordo*), with a dais and three grand entryways.[25]

This Yellow Horde, like others of the very largest tents used by the Mongols, were not *gers* for residence but pavilions for assemblies. Since horde was a social term – the horde was wherever a khan or head of one of the branches of the imperial family dwelled with his staff and court – not an architectural one, the term was equally applicable to such pavilions. One prince, Batu, in the middle of the frontmost southern line of his camp 'had a large pavilion set up, since his dwelling could not accommodate the number of men and women who had assembled'.[26] Only the most formal audiences would be held in such pavilions, with high thrones in place of couches, and their airy spaces able to seat several hundred people.[27] Apart from these formal occasions, emperors would spend more of their time in the *gers* of one or another of their ladies.[28] The Secret Historian's eye had relatively little interest in the great pavilions, seeing them only from the outside as sites of inopportune feasting (§§184–5) or quarrels (§275). Inside views, by contrast, are always of the khans' and their ladies' *ger*-wagons. Still less was the writer interested in the brick-and-wood palaces which the khans from Ökodei onwards began to build in their favourite spots to pitch camp; they appear only as storehouses for things (§279).

Such vast cities spread out in the steppe were obviously indefensible against armed attack. Yet even in the chaotic days before the unification of the empire and before the accumulation of colossal wealth, large assemblies took place. In troubled times, then, the *ger*s of minor rulers and their followers assembled not in an open line formation but in a circle. Such circles, called *küre'en* or *küriyen*, made the camp a mobile fortress, defensible on all sides. This practice of using wagons and *ger*s as mobile wooden palisades was a natural adaptation to warfare in steppe conditions. In southern Africa they were called 'laagers', on Europe's steppe frontier 'tabors', and in the North American prairie settlers would 'circle their wagons' to form 'corrals'. The Hanlin recension translators mostly render *küre'en~küriyen* as *juanzi*, 'corral; livestock pen', which identifies one aspect of the *küre'en*, the enclosure of livestock, but ignores the more important military aspect. Other medieval Chinese writings on the Mongol empire translate it, however, as *yi*, 'wing' (of a military formation), which highlights the military aspect but is somewhat misleading as to the form. In my translation, I have called these mobile fortified camps 'wagon-forts'.

Compared to dwellings, a rather less prominent position is occupied by food in the *Secret History*, particularly of the festive sort.[29] According to all accounts, feasting was an essential Mongolian political activity, with complex ritual rules.[30] As in many epic and saga traditions, these feasts commonly degenerated into quarrels, brawls and murder.[31]

The most distinctive and valued food among the Central Eurasian pastoralists at this time was fermented mare's milk. This drink, widely known in European languages as 'koumiss', from the Turkic version *qumïz*, is called *airag* or *cegee* in Mongolian

today, but in the *Secret History* was known as *esuk*, the term I
use in this translation. William of Rubruck, who grew to prefer
it to even the best Georgian wine, calls it *comos* and describes
how it was made: mares were milked and the milk placed in
skin sacks (*ituge* or *tüsurge*), where they were churned with
broad plungers (*bile'ur*) until the fermentation made a lightly
alcoholic drink.[32] Since alcohol played such a fundamental role
in Mongol feasting culture, great skin sacks (*yeke tüsurge*) were
prominently displayed in the *ger*s, serving the princes and com-
manders. Placed, as seen in a previous quotation, on a bench at
the 'foot' of the *ger*, that is, in the low-status area near the door,
the great skin sacks were handled by attendants who sat on the
doorward side of the bench facing the master and mistress.
Later, in the empire, other liquors were added to the menu:
grape wine, rice wine and mead.

Mongolian food, then as now, observed a seasonal distinc-
tion of a summer dairy-heavy diet and a winter meat-heavy
diet. This distinction is alluded to in a poetic couplet referring
to the inability to appreciate food, literally 'choke on the cheese
and gag on the grease' (§167). 'Cheese' here stands for the
'white' or dairy foods, and grease for the 'black' or meat foods.
Mongolian herders make an enormous variety of dairy prod-
ucts: the *Secret History* mentions *taraq* or a kind of kefir (§145)
and *tosun* or clarified butter (§254). As William of Rubruck
observed, 'In the summer . . . as long as their *comos* (that is,
mare's milk) holds out, they care for no other food.'[33] During
the winter, however, only the wealthy could have *esuk* at all,
and even they ate primarily meat. Mutton was then the staple
meat of the Mongols; horses were slaughtered only on special
occasions, and beef was eaten just as rarely.[34] Mutton was usu-
ally boiled, hence the repeated references in the *Secret History*
to the khan's 'soup' (*šülen*) as a way of saying food in general.
Porridges (*buda'a*) of boiled millet, with or without mutton,
were also part of the daily meal, but were deemed worthy only
of a single reference in the *Secret History* (§46).[35]

Although we think of the Mongols of the empire as being
primarily pastoralists like today, in those days hunting sup-
plied much of their food in winter. As can be seen in the vows

of loyalty made to Chinggis Khan at his first coronation (§§123, 179), serving the khan in the great ring hunts was just as essential a duty as serving him in war. The best illustration of these passages is the description by Ala'uddin Juvaini, the Persian historian and official in Mongol service. According to him, hunts were prepared for like campaigns, following initial reconnaissance of the state of game in each district. Then in the beginning of the winter season,

> [the khan] issues orders that the troops stationed around his headquarters and in the neighbourhood of the *ordus* shall make preparations for the chase, mounting several men from each company of ten . . . and distributing . . . arms . . . The right wing, left wing and centre of the army are drawn up and entrusted to the great emirs [commanders].[36]

And when all was ready, the khan and his ladies and court proceeded to hunt. The hunters were arranged in a vast circle and their beating the game lasted one to three months:

> they form a hunting ring and drive the game slowly and gradually before them, taking care lest any escape from the ring . . . Finally, when the ring has been contracted to a diameter of two or three parasangs [six to ten miles], they bind ropes together and cast felts over them; while the troops come to a halt all around the ring, standing shoulder to shoulder. The ring is now filled with the cries and commotion of every manner of game . . . When the ring has been so much contracted that the wild beasts are unable to stir, first the Khan rides in together with some of his retinue . . .[37]

Then the actual killing would commence, proceeding down the ranks from the khan to the common soldiers. The colossal amounts of game meat so gathered and frozen in the cold of the Mongolian winter were distributed as spoils of this war on the kingdom of beasts.

A very different way of securing food from the natural world is described in the *Secret History* as it praised Mother Ö'elun and her sons for their resourcefulness in making a living after they

were abandoned by their retinue. Mother Ö'elun gathered wild
crab apples and bird cherries and wild root crops: silverweed,
great burnet, garlic, onion, scarlet lily bulbs – all foods which are
still collected today in Mongolia for seasoning or medicinal pur-
poses. Her sons also fed her by fishing and hunting marmots and
jerboas. By the nineteenth century Mongols refused to eat fish,
but in the empire period observers noted they enjoyed the flesh of
the larger fish: hucho, or taimen salmon, and sturgeon.[38] Mother
Ö'elun's children fished, but they had to settle for smaller catches
like white fish and dace. Muslim and Christian travellers at the
time were repulsed by the Mongols' enjoyment of rodents, but
marmot meat is still considered a delicacy. The sons' hunting of it
was an example of *ang*, individual hunting, very different from
the *ab* or ring hunting described above, just as their small camp
of three to five *ger*s differed from the vast camps of the imperial
hordes.

Mongolia in the rise of Chinggis Khan: a storyline and its illusions

The narrative arc of the *Secret History* traces how a single
couple becomes a lineage, and how a lineage becomes first a
kingdom and then an empire. In this regard, the work is analo-
gous to the 'Primary History' in the Hebrew Bible – the
narrative that begins with the primeval couple in Genesis,
continues through the growth of Israel from Abraham, through
Moses, David and Solomon, down to the fall of the kingdom
and the exile.[39] And as with the Primary History, the *Secret
History*'s narrative structure of genealogy to empire has been
taken as a confirmation of social evolutionary schemes that
posit humanity evolving from family to band to tribe to chief-
dom to state.[40] However, in the *Secret History*, as in the Primary
History, this genealogical story takes place in a country where
states and empires had already existed for centuries, if not
millennia, and continued to exist throughout the period of the
story being told. Whatever we might make of the historicity of
Chinggis Khan's distant ancestors, such as Alan the Fair and
Bodoncar the Simple, it is crucial to realize that the impression

that they lived in a world with no states is an illusion created by the narrative structure of the work.

Historically, we know that a series of dynastic states and empires rose and fell in Mongolia for a thousand years before Chinggis Khan. The many institutions which the *Secret History* ascribes to Chinggis Khan's state-building – the decimal organization of the army into tens, hundreds and thousands, the horde system and the *kesikten* or imperial bodyguard structure that went with it, and the division into imperial and consort lineages – all of these find precedent in one or another of these earlier dynasties. Even the lineage myth of a wolf ancestor is well attested in earlier dynasties. In other words, what the *Secret History* presents as Chinggis Khan creating a state after a long period of familial incubation was historically a conquest and assimilation of a pre-existing dynastic state tradition by an outlying clan on the periphery of that dynastic world.

It is unclear how much the new Mongol dynasts after Chinggis Khan were aware of the earlier history of steppe empires. Inscriptions and other written monuments left by previous empires in Sogdian, Brahmi, Chinese, Runiform Turkish, Uyghur, Kitan and other languages and scripts were scattered around Mongolia, but the tradition of reading them had been lost. Uyghur scribes among the oases in eastern Turkestan did maintain a living memory of the more recent of these steppe empires and would join the Mongol entourage after 1204. But the primary conduits of institutional memory were the Kereyit and Naiman kingdoms, dynastic states that ruled over central and western Mongolia respectively, as young Temujin was growing up to become Chinggis Khan. The Naiman kingdom, at least, was already using Uyghur-script Turkic as its court language.

Although little is directly known about these kingdoms or khanates, from the accounts of the rise of the Mongols we can see that they were miniature prototypes for the kind of state that Chinggis Khan would later build. To take the Kereyit kingdom in particular:

- The khanate had been ruled by a single, albeit fractious, dynasty for several generations.

- The khan's horde, or political centre, and his core army followed separate but parallel tracks of nomadization from the southern Gobi or semi-desert in the winter to the northern Khangai or wooded forest in the summer.
- His Golden Tent or *Altan terme* was a vast mobile structure able to seat hundreds.
- The khan was advised by four chief commanders.
- His military core or centre (*ğool*) was organized around vanguard units numbering as many as a *tümen*, the Turco-Mongolian term for a unit nominally numbering ten thousand men and their families.
- When princesses of the ruling family married, they were accompanied to their new home by an *inje* or human dowry of up to two hundred Kereyit subjects so that her *ger* would become a kind of embassy of Kereyit dynastic power in her new husband's realm.

All of these institutions would be adopted by Chinggis Khan's new empire. (For a schematic representation of Chinggis Khan's new ruling class, see the tables in Appendix C.)

Despite being organized around single dynasties, the Kereyit and Naiman khanates were frequently split into separate courts by disagreement within the family. The Naiman khanate had similar institutions to the Kereyit, but while the Kereyit kingdom recovered its unity during Temujin's youth, the Naiman had split, seemingly permanently, into a Betegin, or more Mongolian-influenced eastern half in western Mongolia, and a purely Turkic Kücugut half in the Altai Mountains at the intersection of present-day Mongolia, Xinjiang, Kazakhstan and Russia. Two brothers, Tayang Khan in the Betegin east and Buyruq Khan in the Kücugut west, battled each other for supremacy. Buyruq Khan continued the Naiman's traditional anti-Kereyit policy, while Tayang Khan sought to tame his dynasty's traditional anti-Kereyit feelings in return for their assistance against his stronger, western brother.

It is unclear if writing was used at the Kereyit court, but we know that literate ambassadors from the Tangut Xi Xia, or Western Xia, kingdom in north-west China and the Jurchen Jin empire with its capital at Zhongdu attended regularly, rubbing

shoulders with ambitious client commanders from the king-
dom's lawless eastern fringe like Temujin and Jamuqa. The
court language of both Naiman khanates, however, was Turk-
ic; a Uyghur scribe in Tayang Khan's Betegin Naiman kingdom,
Tatar-Tong'a, later introduced writing to Chinggis Khan's court
when he was captured by Chinggis in 1204. It was these two
khanates, and above all the Kereyit, which served as the main
institutional vectors for the transmission of Central Eurasian
traditions of statehood to Chinggis Khan. This transmission
began when Chinggis Khan seized the Kereyit throne and drove
into exile the last Kereyit ruler, Ong Khan, in autumn 1203.
Although the Secret Historian dates the unification of Mongo-
lia from 1206, earlier Mongol historians tended to see 1203 as
the empire's founding date.

In sharp contrast to these two relatively large-scale, stable
dynastic kingdoms in central and western Mongolia, the east-
ern area of the plateau where the young Temujin grew up was
divided between scores of petty warlords. Corresponding to
the present-day areas of eastern Mongolia, Transbaikalia in
Russia, and the Hulun Buir and Üjumucin districts of Inner
Mongolia, these areas were a kind of troubled water in which
the Jurchen Jin empire in North China, the Kereyit kingdom in
central Mongolia and even the Kücugut Naiman all fished.

Retrospectively, historians of the Mongol empire, including
the Secret Historian, divided the people of this broad area into
Tatars, Merkit and Mongols. In reality, these groups were all
shifting coalitions of practically autonomous petty ruling houses,
whose ideas of consanguinity were determined more by their
outside allegiances than by unchanging genealogical writ. Chin-
ese records from the Jurchen Jin dynasty contemporary with the
rise of Chinggis Khan make little mention of these larger cat-
egories, instead referring to various subgroups by name such as
the Qonggirat, Bosqur, Jalayir, Salji'ut, Qatagin, Yörkin,
Me'uden and Küiden. The labels of later Mongolian historians
seem to be partly a reification of the particular coalition struc-
ture that attended Temujin's rise to become Chinggis Khan, and
partly a broad geographical shorthand. Here is how the broader
terms appear to have been understood:

- Merkit: This group, often seen as three allied houses, occupied the fertile valley of the lower Selenge River where it flowed through northern Mongolia and the southern part of Russia's Buryat Republic before emptying into Lake Baikal.
- Tatar: Before the rise of Chinggis Khan, this was actually the general term for all the Mongolic-speaking pastoralists of the plateau. After the rise of Chinggis Khan and the adoption of the term 'Mongol' for Mongolic-speaking pastoralists, the term Tatar was limited to those closest to the frontier with the Jurchen Jin dynasty. These Tatars were some of Chinggis Khan's most implacable enemies. They dwelled in south-eastern Mongolia and in south-western Hulun Buir and present-day Üjumucin districts in Inner Mongolia.[41]
- Mongol: The term 'Mongol' in the *Secret History* usually meant all those east of the Kereyit kingdom who were not Merkit or Tatars. Geographically, it thus included those in the Onon and Kherlen valleys and in the Hulun Buir area. One can see traces, however, of the much narrower usage that must have prevailed during Chinggis Khan's childhood: just those of the upper Onon and Kherlen valleys, near the sacred Burġan-Qaldun mountains (modern Khentii). Other groups alongside these 'Mongols' (in the narrow sense) were the Tayici'ut of the middle and lower Onon, the Yörkin of the middle Kherlen, the Jadaran of the Ergune (Argun') River valley, and the even more remote Qonggirat, Dörben, Salji'ut and Qatagin of the Hulun Buir area to the east.

It is in this context that the *Secret History*'s lengthy opening genealogy, with the division into groups 'with such and such surname', is to be understood. This genealogy has often been taken as the charter for a 'clan-patriarchal' or 'tribal' society, in which all were ranked within a hierarchy of senior and junior corporate clans and genealogies determined how these corporate clans behaved.[42] However, the genealogies we have are all retrospective and show major divergences about who is related to whom and how. In the Chinese summary of Jürcedei's Mongolian biography, for example, his own Uru'ut house is said to be one of the five sons of Nacin Ba'atur, along with the Manggut, the Jalayir, the Qonggirat and the Ikires.[43] In the *Secret History* genealogy, however, the Jalayir, Qonggirat and Ikires do not even appear, being seen as completely unrelated, and instead the Uru'ut and Manggut are paired with the Siju'ut and Doġulat.

As is well known from other societies, then, the genealogical connections were an idiom to talk about relationships. Houses that were politically and socially allied would be 'brothers'; those that were closely allied but of subordinate status might still be 'brothers', but with the lower-status ones being born from the common ancestor's lower-status wife. One way to undermine the reputation of a rival warlord would be to spread a story that his claimed ancestry in a high-status lineage was actually fake. Over time, as new political alliances were made, new stories would appear to justify them, making the genealogy a kind of palimpsest of turbulent political actions. All of these devices appear in the *Secret History*'s genealogies, which were only written down after the rise of Chinggis Khan had completely reset the genealogical structure and made such alliances of merely antiquarian interest. (See Appendix B for a late, schematic representation of the ranking of the Mongol clans.)

Nor must it be thought that all those of the 'such and such' surname were in fact of common ancestry – even in theory. For example, the *Secret History* writes that 'The sons of Caraqai Lingqu became Senggum-Bilge, Hambaġai, and so on, the ones with the Tayici'ut surname' (§47). But the Tayici'ut were a political group, not a kinship group. The leaders may have claimed common ancestry, but they led a diverse conglomeration of people. Those of the Besut surname fought with them; they were reckoned as Caraqai Lingqu's descendants by a junior wife. Other sources tell us that the Je'uriyet were also attached to the Tayici'ut, again with the idea that they were sons of a minor wife. And in the *Secret History*'s story itself, we learn that the Tayici'ut princes had many commoner subjects of the Suldus and

Hü'uśin surnames, who were too lowly to appear anywhere at all in the genealogy. In fact, the names listed in the *Secret History*'s genealogy did not include all in society, only those who were contenders for political power in the area that eventually gave rise to Chinggis Khan, and thus claimed their share in the 'heavenly-destined' pedigree.

Indeed, throughout the *Secret History*'s genealogical prologue, as a *yin* to the genealogical *yang*, is the ruling lineage's accumulation of unrelated subjects. Inequality was a fact of life, inherent in birth and ignored at one's peril. This fact is inculcated through formal didactic means: Grey Wolf is 'born with a destiny from Heaven above' (§1) and Alan the Fair's later three sons were born from a supernatural yellow dog (likely here a euphemism for a wolf) that entered 'with the beams of the sun and moon' (§21). But, as always, the *Secret History* inculcates a hard, realist lesson as well. One of these 'sons of Heaven', Bodoncar the Simple, eggs his brothers on to conquer a nameless, non-hierarchical people that had shared their food with him. 'They have no big or little, no bad or good, no head or hoof. They are all on a level. They would be easy folks to handle. Let's capture them,' he says, and so the brothers plundered them and 'got to live with herds and food, subjects and servants' (§§35, 39). Thus was illustrated the folly of equality.

Although they camped in ever-vigilant wagon-forts and had none of the panoply of monarchy deployed by the Kereyit and Naiman khans, the various Merkit, Mongols and Tatars of this eastern part of the Mongolian plateau had their own aspirations to rulership. One title held by those who claimed genealogical seniority and the priestly-shamanic functions that came with it was *beki*. This was the title of Toqto'a Beki among the Merkit, as well as Sece Beki among the Mongol kin of the later Chinggis Khan.

However, three or four generations before Chinggis Khan, a group of houses in the valley of the Onon and Kherlen Rivers, which run parallel through eastern Mongolia and the Transbaikal steppe, elevated one of their number as khan. The Secret Historian believed Qabul was the first khan in this Onon-Kherlen region, but most other Mongol empire histories accord his father

Tumbinai that title as well. Unlike among the Kereyit and Naiman, however, this title remained elective, not hereditary; after Qabul's death the title of 'khan' passed to a distantly related cousin named Hambaġai, of the Tayici'ut confederation.

Over the next few generations, into the time of Temujin of the Borjigin and Jamuqa of the Jadaran, the title of khan would be assumed by many of these Onon-Kherlen warlords, including several not mentioned in the *Secret History*. But the title never became hereditary, and none of the Onon-Kherlen leaders organized anything but the most rudimentary court in their wagon-forts. Judging from the career of Temujin and Jamuqa, the key issue blocking the formation of a hereditary dynasty was the power and attraction of two poles: the immensely wealthy Jurchen Jin dynasty to the south in North China, and the less wealthy but closer Kereyit khanate to the west. In fact, for Temujin, and quite possibly others as well, the title khan was at first less an assertion of independence and more the expression of an aspiration to be a viceroy for the Kereyit khans. The *Secret History* cites extensively from an earlier source, the 'Indictment of Ong Khan', but that source also had a telling passage which the Secret Historian chose to delete. In it, Temujin as Chinggis Khan compares himself to a falcon cast by the Kereyit ruler Ong Khan and views his early campaigns as being undertaken solely at the Kereyit khan's behest:

> Father Ong Khan, like a grey fledgling gyrfalcon I was once cast from Chiġurqï Mountain past the lake of Buir and took cranes with mottled feet to bring back to you, my lord. Who is this talking about? These are the Dörben and Tatar folk. Again, like a gyrfalcon on its first hunt I was once cast beyond the lake of Hulun and seized cranes with blue feet to bring back to you, my lord. Who is this talking about? These are the Qatagin, the Salji'ut and the Qonggirat folk.

Aspiring petty leaders in eastern Mongolia were subject to attack and speedy replacement by ever-ready rivals if they should outgrow the subordinate role planned for them by their patrons. Such would-be 'khans' were mere falcons on the wrists of Jurchen

Jin or Kereyit rulers – until Chinggis Khan turned against his handler, seized the throne of the Kereyit and eventually shattered the power of the Jurchen Jin.

The world beyond Mongolia

The author of the *Secret History* had no experience outside Mongolia, and hence the work's account of the foreign conquests after 1209 is confused and inaccurate. However, an understanding of the world around Mongolia during the time of Chinggis Khan and his son Ökodei Khan is necessary both to understand the narrative and to understand its elisions and illusions. Such a survey is all the more necessary because the kingdoms surrounding the Mongols were so remade by the Mongol empire that pre-Mongol Eurasia is very strange to those approaching it from the perspective of modern nation-states. Familiar countries like 'China', 'Russia' and 'Iran' were created out of the break-up of the Mongol empire and did not exist in anything like their post-Mongol form during its rise. The following section will thus sketch out what states and dynasties did exist during the rise of Chinggis Khan, in place of the ones we are more familiar with. For a detailed chronology of the foreign conquests see Appendix D.

The Jurchen Jin

The leading power in the world of Chinggis Khan's childhood was the Jurchen Jin dynasty (1115–1234) in North China. This was one of the many dynasties founded over the centuries by non-Chinese peoples from Mongolia, Manchuria or the Tibetan plateau but centred in traditionally Chinese territory. The Jin or 'Golden' dynasty was founded by the Jurchen people from the forest lands of Manchuria. The Jurchen forces were commanded by Aqudai (Chinese Aguda), who gave his name to the ruling family, at least in Mongolian usage. The Jurchens in turn had risen by overthrowing another ethnically non-Chinese 'conquest dynasty', the Liao dynasty (907–1125), founded by the Kitans from the steppe lands of south-eastern Inner Mongolia. From their homeland, the Kitans had conquered the Jurchen lands in Manchuria, the cities of present-day Beijing and Datong in

North China, and Mongolia. Kitan commanders held the upper hand in their relations with Korea, China's Song dynasty and the Tangut kingdom; their diplomatic influence extended to Central Asia and Afghanistan. After overthrowing their former Kitan overlords, the new Jurchen rulers quarrelled with the Song dynasty in central and southern China and in the ensuing war seized all of North China as well.

This meteoric rise of the Jurchen Jin dynasty had set the stage for the world of Chinggis Khan's youth. The Kitan Liao, themselves a nomadic people speaking a language fairly similar to Mongolian, had ruled central and eastern Mongolia, leaving behind inscriptions, cities, stupas and border walls, ruins of which have lasted to the present. The Kereyit and Naiman dynasties had already existed as tributaries on the frontier of the Kitan Liao territory; with the fall of the Kitan Liao dynasty in 1125, they then became the independent khanates that we see in the world of Chinggis Khan's rise.

Once stabilized, the Jurchen Jin dynasty set their capital in Zhongdu, present-day Beijing. Taking their dynastic name from Chinese *jin* for 'gold', the Jurchen Jin ruler was known in the Turco-Mongolian world as the *Altan Khan* or 'Golden Khan'. At its height, during the childhood of Chinggis Khan, the Golden Khan's Jin dynasty ruled over a population of more than 48 million. The vast majority of these people were Han or ethnic Chinese, but the Jurchens still formed the core of the army and the ruling dynasty's most reliable population; the Kitans of Inner Mongolia were the main cavalry force.

But when the Mongols looked south, they still named the country they saw there as the land of the *Kitat*, the Mongolian plural of the singular 'Kitan'. This term, which is still the Mongolian term for 'Chinese', was also used in Turkic and Persian in the form of *Khitay*, which became the 'Cathay' of Marco Polo. Another term that appears in the *Secret History* for China as a region or place is *Jauqut*. Both terms, however, included only China north of the Yellow River. The Song dynasty south of the Yellow River was seen as a different country.

The Mongols were well aware of the multi-ethnic nature of

the Golden Khan's armies. In the *Secret History*, the 'Chinese [*Kitat*] soldiers' are divided into several different groups:

- Ethnic Kitans, literally 'Black Kitans' (*Qara-Kitat*): Black was the colour associated with the ethnic Kitans, for whom it symbolized the direction north and the topographic element of rivers. 'Black Kitans' was thus used by the Mongols to designate ethnic Kitans wherever they lived. Most ethnic Kitans lived on the frontier in Inner Mongolia, where they also managed the Jin army's stud farms. Kitan soldiers were crack cavalry forces that the Golden Khan had to rely on, despite their frequent rebellions against the Jurchen ruler, inspired by memories of their own previous dynasty.
- The Jurchens: They were the ruling people of the dynasty, most of whom at this time lived in military communities attached to garrisons across the empire. Jurchens and Kitans in such communities, together with their slaves and dependants, numbered a little over six million, or about 15 per cent of the empire's total population.
- The Jüin or Jiün: With a name derived from the Kitan word *tiw-* or *diw-*, 'to collect, assemble',[44] the Jüin or Jiün is a Kitan term meaning the 'assembled ones'. The term designated mostly those Turco-Mongolian pastoralists along the frontier who served the Golden Khan as auxiliaries, policing their fellow Turco-Mongolian herders across the frontier on behalf of the emperor in Zhongdu. In fact, most of the Jüin/Jiün were the same people who were later referred to as Kitans or Tatars. Jin-dynasty figures give their total number, men, women, children and attached slaves, at about 137,000, but their military significance for the Jin border was far out of proportion to their numbers.
- The Öng'ut: They were often known as 'White Tatars', in contrast to the 'Black Tatars' to the north of the Gobi. Although the *Secret History* does not treat them

as part of the Jüin folk, they were one of the Jin
dynasty's key forces guarding the frontier. Of mixed
Turco-Sogdian ancestry, they were also distinctive in
having converted en masse to East Syriac Christianity
in 1007.

Although the *Secret History* told many secrets, there was one
secret it did not tell – that Chinggis Khan was enrolled, until
around 1210, among the tributaries of the Golden Khan. Every
year he would go to the Jurchen Jin's Inner Mongolian frontier
post at Jingzhou and bow towards the capital in Zhongdu as he
presented tribute. Nor was he alone: virtually all of the leaders
from the Kereyit, Mongols and Tatars had a history of paying
tribute to the Jin. Indeed, the rise of Chinggis Khan was con-
nected not just to serving Ong Khan, but beyond that to a major
restructuring of Jin frontier policy. The Mongolian historians
were happy to vent their grievances against the Jin dynasty's
frontier policing and their hatred of that policing's Tatar/Jüin
agents; but they remained quiet about the many years when
they docilely bent the knee to those very agents' masters.

The Golden Khan appears only twice in the stories in the
Secret History of the time before the Mongol invasion of 1211.
In both cases, we get a glimpse of what it meant to be on the
receiving end of the famous 'using barbarians to control barbar-
ians' policy. In §53, the Tayici'ut khan Hambaġai went to a
marriage arranged with some Tatar/Jüin allies, and in retali-
ation for past opposition his hosts handed him over to the
Golden Khan, who had him painfully put to death. In §§132–3,
the tables were turned and young Temujin and the Kereyit ruler
To'oril, soon to be titled Ong Khan, participated in a punitive
campaign against the Tatars undertaken at the behest of the
Golden Khan. In return, they were rewarded with new titles and
a share of the booty. This campaign is historically documented
both in a Sino-Jurchen inscription recently discovered in Mon-
golia and in the biography of the commanding general, Wongian
Xiang; it took place in the spring and summer of 1196.

These examples illustrate how the Jin dynasty originally dealt
with the frontier. Unable to administer Mongolia as the Kitan

Liao had, they managed the turbulent Tatars and Mongols by granting titles and the right to pay tribute to many petty rulers along their frontier. But they would also use punitive expeditions and spur on attacks from their rivals to take down any of these petty rulers who seemed to be accumulating too much power.

Soon after the 1196 expedition, however, Wongian Xiang concluded that the Jin needed a different policy. The constant low-level conflict was too expensive, so he advocated building a long border moat and wall, keeping Jin armies behind it. The wall was built far out into the Inner Mongolian steppe, along the present-day border of Mongolia and China, so the lands of the more tractable Jüin were south of it, behind its defensive screen. With the wall in place, the Jin would not need to undertake so active a management of the jostling petty rulers north of it.

Left unstated in the Chinese sources, quite possibly because the Mongols purged any such records when they later edited the Jin dynasty history, is that control of the frontier north of the wall was left to the Golden Khan's client ruler To'oril. He was the one who had received the title *Ong*, or 'King', Khan from the Jin and whose 'falcon' was Temujin, the young Chinggis Khan. Thus, Chinggis Khan's various campaigns from 1201 to 1202 against the coalition of the Qonggirat, Dörben, Salji'ut and Qatagin, against Jamuqa and against the Tatars, were undertaken not only under the overall command of Ong Khan, but were ultimately intended to make Ong Khan the regional protector of the Jin dynasty's peace. Even after Chinggis Khan had overthrown Ong Khan, the Jin dynasty continued to allow him to present tribute in Ong Khan's place. Not until he had already won over many of the Jüin and Öng'ut border people and was ready to attack North China did Chinggis Khan break off paying tribute to the Golden Khan.[45]

The Tangut

On the western border of the Jurchen Jin empire, in what is now the Gansu, Ningxia and south-western Inner Mongolian areas of China, was another hybrid 'conquest' dynasty, the Tangut Xia (982–1227). The Tangut people were originally from the Tibetan plateau, although their language is only very distantly related to Tibetan. Having migrated from there to the Ordos region of Inner Mongolia centuries earlier, they gradually rose to power and founded a new dynasty, titled the Xia, or Western Xia (also known as Xixia). Although the Tanguts were neither Turkic nor Mongolian in speech, they had much in common with Turco-Mongolian dynasties, and writers in the Mongol empire such as Rashiduddin treated them as just another Turco-Mongolian kingdom. Their land was mostly west of the Yellow River, so Chinese often called their kingdom Hexi; in the form of Qaśin, with the plural -n, this term is found in the *Secret History* as another word for the Tanguts. Since the Gansu-Ningxia area of China was only sparsely inhabited, the Tanguts were a much larger percentage of the population than Jurchens were in the Jin lands, maybe even a majority.[46]

The Tanguts had particularly close relations with the Kereyit khanate. Kereyit princes in trouble, whether due to Naiman or Mongol attacks, or due to court quarrels, were assured of a welcome in the Tangut kingdom. As a result, when Ong Khan and his son Ilqa Senggum were overthrown by Chinggis Khan, Ilqa Senggum fled to the Tangut kingdom. Harbouring him eventually made the Tangut kingdom a target for the Mongols, even after Ilqa Senggum moved on to Kucha, an oasis town in eastern Turkestan. There the local ruler executed him and sent his head to the Mongols.

The Tangut rulers were major patrons of Buddhism, first of Chinese-style Buddhism and then of Tibetan-style Buddhism. Tibetan gurus (lamas) were invited to the Tangut court and honoured as Dynastic and Imperial Preceptors. In turn, the Tangut ruler was glorified, in the words of an ode to the ruler, as a 'humane emperor-bodhisattva' and a 'Buddha Son of Heaven'.[47] The Tangut ruler appears in the *Secret History* as the 'Buddha Khan' (*Burqan Qan*) and 'the Victorious Buddha' (*Ilugu Burqan*) – 'Victorious' is a translation of the Sanskrit *Jina*, commonly used as an epithet of the Buddha to denote his victory over all limitations. This 'Victorious Buddha' is in fact the only appearance of terminology associated with a scripture-based world religion anywhere in the *Secret History*.

Siberia's Forest Folk

To the north of Mongolia were the vast taiga forests of Siberia that stretched to the tundra along the Arctic Ocean. The line between forest and steppe was not sharp; there were islands of taiga forest in the uplands of northern Mongolia and islands of steppe in the valleys of southern Siberia. The forest lands produced valuable commodities: sable and squirrel peltry, white gyrfalcons and, in one of those islands of steppe in the midst of the forest, the Minusa Basin, fine white geldings. Historically, both the ancient Turkic speakers and the immediate precursors of the Mongols have been thought to have migrated from forest lands into the Mongolian steppe – the former from the forests north and north-west of Mongolia in the second and third centuries AD, and the latter from the forests in the Amur River valley during the era of the Kitan Liao in the tenth to eleventh centuries.

These migrations from forest to steppe may be the historical background for the stories in the beginning of the *Secret History*, about Grey Wolf and Fallow Doe crossing 'the sea' (presumably Lake Baikal) to the headwaters of the Onon, and about the people who came up the Tüngkelik Stream: Barġu, Qori-Tumat, Uriyangqai (or Uriyangqan) and Baya'ut, all names associated with the forests. In the later, historical, sections of the work, forest peoples appear under generic names as Forest Folk (*Hoi-yin Irgen*) or Uriyangqai, as well as under particular ethnic designations. Of those distinct ethnonyms it was Oyirats under their ruler Qutuġa Beki who played the largest role in the politics of Chinggis Khan's rise.

To the Secret Historian, as to other steppe Mongols, forests were inhospitable lands. In describing the young Temujin taking refuge on the wooded Khentii, the author describes the 'clinging sands and tangled woods' with an image attested elsewhere: 'so tangled a glutted snake could not slither into them' (§102).[48] When a coalition hostile to Chinggis Khan and Ong Khan is defeated, we see the Oyirat ruler 'cutting his way through the forests' as he returns to his home in the taiga around Lake Khöwsgöl in the northernmost province of modern Mongolia

(§144). And when the Tumat rebel, the armies campaigning against them struggle to make their way 'by trails blindly in a thick forest' until Dörbei set them to 'hack and saw down the trees standing in the trails' made by bison (§240). The word for trail here, *horum*, is only used of trails made by forest animals – elk, moose and bison (see §§103, 240) – as opposed to the word *mör*, used for paths in the steppe made by people (see e.g. §§82–3, 90). The Forest Folk were conquered early on in the empire's expansion, but steppe Mongols still found their country an alien and even frightening one.

Qara-Khitai

When the Jurchens of Manchuria overthrew the Kitan Liao dynasty in 1125, not all the Kitans submitted. In line with their nomadic background and their distant kinship with the Mongols, one prince of the imperial line, Daiši Lemya (Kitan for 'Daiši the Scribe'), fled to Mongolia with a large band of Kitans. There he proclaimed himself the *Gür Khan*, a Kitan title meaning 'Universal Sovereign' (or possibly 'Sovereign of the Realm'), and tried to rally Qonggirats, Jadaran, Merkit, Tatars and many others to attack the Jurchens and restore Kitan rule. The attempt failed and eventually Daiši Lemya moved west to Central Asia, where in 1141 he defeated the rulers of the local Turkic Muslim dynasty. As a result of that victory, he created an empire that eventually ruled directly or indirectly the whole of oasis Central Asia from Samarkand and Bukhara in the west to the Uyghur kingdom in the east.

As was mentioned, Mongols called ethnic Kitans 'Black Kitans' (*Qara-Kitat*). This term followed a tradition of colour symbolism that paired northern river people, associated with military prowess and the colour black, with southern mountain people, associated with white and civilian culture.[49] Central Asian Turks pronounced the Mongolian *Qara-Kitat* or 'Black Kitans' as 'Qara-Khitai', and that is how the empire is known to history. But it is important to note that the term 'Black Kitans', whether pronounced *Qara-Kitat* or *Qara-Khitai*, designated ethnic Kitans everywhere, in the old homeland in eastern Inner Mongolia as well as in their new western empire. It was not, at least in origin, a special term for the Kitan realm built up in Central Asia, although that is how it is often used today.

The Qara-Khitai empire was a loose conglomeration of tributary kingdoms ruled by a core of Kitans, Tatars and other mostly Mongolic-speaking nomads brought from the east in Daiši Lemya's entourage. Like the later Mongol empire, they maintained a capital area that integrated walled cities with seasonal movements of armies which herded and hunted. The centre for the Qara-Khitai was the valley of the Chüy River in present-day Kyrgyzstan and Kazakhstan; within the Chüy valley, their movements centred on the city known as Balasaghun or Quz-Orda. In terms of their foreign policy, the Qara-Khitai maintained good relations with the Tangut Xia and through them with the Kereyit; for that reason, when driven off the throne by the Naiman ruler, the Kereyit monarch Ong Khan fled first to the Tangut kingdom, then to the Uyghur kingdom, and finally to the *Gür Khan* in the Chüy valley.

The *Secret History*'s account is very fragmentary, but other sources detail how Chinggis Khan's unification of Mongolia created shock waves that shattered the Qara-Khitai empire. Refugees from his conquests, Küculug Khan of the Naiman and Ilqa Senggum of the Kereyit, both ended up in Qara-Khitai territory with large bands of their followers. Küculug eventually married the *Gür Khan*'s daughter, usurped his father-in-law's throne and ruled the Qara-Khitai until he was killed by an expedition under the Mongol commander Jebe in 1218.

Even before the fall of the empire, two of the *Gür Khan*'s tributary kings had broken away and submitted directly to Chinggis Khan. As a result, their royal families received a princess and favour as an 'imperial son-in-law' family. One was the ruler of the Uyghurs, titled the Ïduqut or 'Holy Glory', and the other was the ruler of the Qarluqs, titled Arslan Khan or 'Lion Khan'. Both were Turkic-speaking dynasties with a long history – indeed, the first time the Qarluqs are mentioned, they are called *Ui'urtai Qarlu'ud*, 'the Uyghur-like Qarluqs' (§198). Despite the similarity of language, however, they differed in many other ways.

The Uyghur Ïduqut reckoned their ancestry back to the khans of the great Uyghur empire that had ruled Mongolia from centuries earlier. After the fall of that empire in 840, they fled to the Turpan and Besh-Baliq oases in eastern Turkestan (modern Xinjiang), where they settled down and became sedentary rulers of a Buddhist kingdom. The Qarluq rulers too had a long history, going back centuries; they lived to the north-west of the Uyghurs and had converted to Islam in the ninth century. They ruled over many sedentary Muslim and Christian farmers and city dwellers, but unlike the Uyghur Ïduqut, Arslan Khan and his Qarluqs still practised nomadism.

The Sarts and the Khwarazmian sultan

The Qara-Khitai realm and the Chüy River were the effective limits to the south-west of the young Chinggis Khan's world. Beyond it, the Khwarazmian empire had begun a meteoric rise only a few years earlier than that of Chinggis Khan, after a previous century of slow and steady growth. Eventually, as the Qara-Khitai empire fell apart, the Khwarazmian empire under its sultan Ala'uddin Muhammad (r. 1200–1220) joined with Küculug Khan of the Naiman to partition the Qara-Khitai lands in 1213. And in 1218, when Jebe captured Küculug Khan, the two new empires, Khwarazmian and Mongol, finally acquired a common frontier, roughly on a line from the Pamir Mountains north to Lake Balkhash.

But although the sultan's empire was new to the Mongols, the Sart people he ruled were not. Sarts, or *Sarta'ul* in the Mongolian plural form, was the Turco-Mongolian term for all the sedentary people of the Central Asian and Middle Eastern oases and cities. Derived from the ancient Sogdian word for 'caravaneer', such Sarts were still leading caravans from Khwarazm and other Central Asian cities into Mongolia during the time of Chinggis Khan. As late as the twentieth century the term was still used to designate the city and village dwellers of Central Asia, as opposed to the various pastoralist peoples nomadizing in the mountains and steppes around them. By the twentieth century the Sarts were all Muslim, but in the Mongol empire Mongols also applied *Sarta'ul* to the still-substantial populations of Christians and Jews in Central Asia and the Middle East as far as Baghdad, and even to the Hindus in India.

As oasis dwellers, the Sarts were well known to the Mongols as the subject people of the Qara-Khitai and as caravaneers. Such caravaneers regularly travelled through the Muslim oases to the Uyghur kingdom, and on to the Öng'uts of Inner Mongolia before heading into Mongolia proper. Chinggis Khan met one such Muslim caravaneer named Hasan 'driving a thousand wethers with a white camel down along the Ergune River in order to buy sables and squirrels' (§182). When Chinggis Khan acquired a border with the sultan's great empire, he naturally opened trade relations. These trade relations were, however, brutally interrupted when the sultan killed the merchants, seized their goods, and then killed the Mongol envoys sent to demand justice (§254). This famous Otrar massacre led to Chinggis Khan's equally famous expedition to crush the sultan.

Despite the use of identifiable written sources, the Secret Historian's account of this campaign is tremendously confused. But the Secret Historian's confusion was aided by some broader confusions common to all known Mongolian accounts of the campaign. One key confusion was that no known source of Mongolian origin shows awareness of the actual sultan who was in power at the time of the Otrar massacre and Chinggis Khan's first invasion, named Ala'uddin Muhammad. They all mention not him but his son Jalaluddin Mengburni, who picked up the flag of resistance and at the big battle at Parvan won fame by temporarily driving back the Mongol advance. But before then, right after the first campaign season, Chinggis Khan had dispatched an expedition under Jebe, Sübe'edei and Toqucar to hunt down Sultan Muhammad. (He died on an island in the Caspian Sea, and the expedition of Jebe and company was repurposed into a general attack on the far west.) But, unaware of Sultan Muhammad's existence, the Secret Historian, who was no military expert, assumed a different purpose for the expedition, one of circling around the whole Khwarazmian empire and then starting off the campaign by attacking it from the west.

But where did this assumption come from? Apparently from knowledge among the Mongols of one of Chinggis Khan's failed strategies. Surveying those Mongolian sources known from Persian and Chinese summaries, we can see that in addition to ignoring Sultan Ala'uddin Muhammad, they also ascribe a tremendous importance to a certain military governor in the Khwarazmian empire, Khan-Malik (also known as Malik Khan or Yamin Malik). This importance was related to a cleavage in the social structure of the Khwarazmian empire – a cleavage which Chinggis Khan attempted unsuccessfully to exploit.

The Khwarazmian empire was based in the oasis of Khwarazm and its main city of Urgench, territory today shared between north-west Uzbekistan and northern Turkmenistan. As such, its civilian base population was Turkic-speaking Muslim Sarts, that is, oasis-dwelling farmers and urbanites. This urban and agricultural civilian base vastly expanded as the empire conquered Persian-speaking Sart cities in eastern Iran and north-western Afghanistan. But the core of the empire's army was non-Muslim Turkic-speaking Qangli nomads from the area of modern Kazakhstan, recruited into Khwarazmian service in the entourage of Qangli princesses who married into the Khwarazmian dynasty. As one Persian historian who had been Jalaluddin Mengburni's personal secretary wrote, these Qangli were 'Turks ... people of the same race [as the Mongols], polytheists as they are'.[50]

Khan-Malik was one of these Qangli commanders, a nephew of Jalaluddin's Qangli mother, and the commander of a purely Qangli force. He was stationed as military governor of the city of Herat in present-day Afghanistan, and Chinggis Khan's early battle plan in fighting the Khwarazmian empire appears to have been to use cultural affinity to try to peel off him and other Qangli commanders from the Sart base of the Khwarazmian dynasty. This strategy of appealing to nomadic cultural affinity he had used successfully against the Jurchen Jin dynasty, winning over many ethnic Kitans in the Jin army and getting them to desert to his standard. This time the strategy failed miserably, probably for reasons larger than just Toqucar's opportunistic sacking of some of the towns in the area of Herat (§257). But the Secret Historian seems to have been aware of this idea of rallying Khan-Malik to the Mongol cause, and since Herat was in the south-western part of the Khwarazmian realm, guessed (plausibly, but incorrectly) that joining up with him was somehow connected with the original plan of Jebe, Sübe'edei and Toqucar's expedition.

The margins of the Secret Historian's world: Song China, the caliph and the far-western steppe

Around these empires which were well known to the Secret Historian, either through their previous interference in the Mongol steppe or through Chinggis Khan's campaigns, were shadowy realms which the Secret Historian appears to have known only by name.

About the time of Möngke Khan's coronation in 1251, when the *Secret History* was being first conceived, the kingdom of Hungary in the far west, the caliph of Baghdad in the south-west and the Song dynasty in South China were all still in opposition to Mongol power. In the *Secret History*, however, all three are presented as if they had either been satisfactorily subdued (Hungary and Baghdad) or else had never been hostile to the Mongol empire (Song China). In the latter case, how the Secret Historian misrepresented the death of the ambassador Jubqan is very telling. In reality, Jubqan's disappearance while on a mission from Ökodei Khan to the Song dynasty was one of the justifications for the Mongol declaration of war on the Song in 1234. In the *Secret History*, however, Jubqan is turned into a Mongol ambassador who was molested by the Jin on his way to the Song! Evidently the Secret Historian preferred to see the Song as a friendly power and was hoping that no further conquests would be needed.

A final aspect of the *Secret History*'s geographical viewpoint is the surprisingly limited knowledge of the Qïpchaq and Qangli nomads of the Kazakhstan, Caspian and Pontic (Black Sea) steppes. These Qïpchaq and Qangli were Turkic-speaking mobile pastoralists – indeed, they were often considered the best practitioners of the arts of pastoralism. Later on, in Qubilai Khan's reign, Qïpchaqs who had been deported to the east were organized into a special guards unit, one of whose tasks was to produce a kind of clarified *esuk* or clear fermented mare's milk for the khan's table. In the era of Chinggis Khan, neither the Qïpchaqs nor the Qangli had a unified state. Instead, like the Tatars, Merkit and Mongols of eastern Mongolia during Chinggis Khan's rise, they formed a large number of petty houses and small kingdoms that hired themselves out to stronger neighbours: the sultan of Khwarazm, the kings of Georgia and Hungary and princes of Ruthenia.

There are clear indications that the pre-Chinggisid Merkit rulers like Toqto'a Beki had connections with the Turkic-speaking nomads as far west as the Ölberli kingdom, in the Zhem (Emba) valley between the Ural Mountains and the Caspian Sea. But as far as the Secret Historian goes, even the Qïpchaq and Qangli nomads are just names, no better known than the Hungarians, Ruthenians, Ossetes, Kashmiris or Saxons who are listed as some of the eleven peoples conquered in the great western expedition. Evidently, the Secret Historian's community had not inherited these old Merkit networks and had no personal knowledge of the many Qïpchaq or Qangli prisoners of war. This could be read as evidence for the hypothesis (see below) that the Secret Historian served in the horde of Qasar and his descendants, who, like the other princely lines descended from Chinggis Khan's little brothers, had never participated in the western campaigns and had not accumulated prisoners of war there.[51]

Heaven and Earth, *jada* and *ja'arin*: spirits in the *Secret History*'s world

The supernatural plays a paradoxical role in the *Secret History*. On the one hand, the ruling house's destiny from Heaven is one of the primary themes of the work, announced in the very first line. On the other hand, the actual instances of Heaven speaking are often presented in a quite ambiguous way. Heaven in the *Secret History* is rather like Chinggis Khan himself: his action propels the story forward, but his motives are often lost in his cryptic silences, only to be interpreted by obscure signs and symbols.

The dominant role of Heaven (*Tenggeri*)[52] in the Mongolian imperial ideology is attested to by all sources on the Mongol empire. The Song envoy Peng Daya, after visiting Ökodei's court, wrote:

> In their everyday speech, they always say, 'Relying on the strength of immortal Heaven and the fortunate protection of the emperor.'

In all affairs that they desire to undertake, they say, 'Heaven wants it like that.' Regarding anything that people have already done, they say, 'Heaven is aware.' There is no affair that is not attributed to Heaven; from the lord of the Tatars to his common people, it is thus.[53]

'Relying on the strength of immortal Heaven and the fortunate protection of the emperor': this is the official Chinese translation of the Mongolian original *Möngke tngri-yin kücun-dur, yeke su jali-yin ibe'en-dur*, or 'By the Power of Eternal Heaven; by the Protection of the Majestic Imperial Fortune', which is cited verbatim once in the *Secret History* in a memorial of Batu to Öködei (§275) and paraphrased several times elsewhere. The Secret Historian's attribution of events to Heaven begins with the primordial ancestor Grey Wolf, 'born with a destiny from Heaven above' (§1), and continues throughout the work.

The key power of Heaven is to give success or failure, victory or defeat in political and military pursuits. As the Papal envoy John of Plano Carpini said, 'They believe in one God, and they believe that . . . it is He who is the giver of the good things of this world as well as the hardships.'[54] While John went on to claim that they had no custom of worship towards Heaven, Marco Polo, who actually lived among the Mongols in Qubilai Khan's bodyguard, described a ceremonial and its purpose: 'They say that there is a High God, supreme and heavenly, whom they worship every day with incense burned in censers, asking only to be sound of mind and strong in health.'[55] And on special occasions of military crisis, khans would take off their hats, hang their belts round their necks and beseech Heaven to grant victory (cf. §103).

This attribution of political power and military victory to Heaven has a long history in Central Eurasian political thought. The famous Old Turkic inscriptions, erected in central Mongolia in honour of Bilge Khan (r. 717–34), his brother Kül Tegin (684–731) and the great commander Toñuquq (c.646–726), make the same attribution of all success to Heaven.

But, as in those same inscriptions, Heaven is often paired with Earth. Thus the *Secret History* attributes success to 'Eternal

Heaven' fourteen times, but to 'Heaven and Earth' ten times. This pairing of Heaven and Earth is not found in other official texts from the time of the Mongol empire, but it is an inheritance from the formulae of the Old Turkic inscriptions. There 'the blue sky [*kök täng'ri*] above and the brown earth [*yaǧiz yer*] below' are the two governing elements of the world. The inscriptions tell how the 'Türk Heaven [*Türük täng'ri*] above and the Türk Holy Earth and Water [*iduq yir sub*]' called the Türk rulers to power. Another passage speaks of the 'Heaven and Umay and the Holy Earth and Water' placing the Türk rulers on the throne – *umay*, which in Mongolian means 'womb', is a kind of personified Mother Earth.[56] The Old Turkic inscriptions' reference to Holy Earth and Water likewise recalls the *Secret History*'s reference to the spiritual 'masters and rulers of the Earth and Water' (*ǧajar usun-u ejet qat*) of North China in §272.

What these references to Heaven and Earth reflect is a conviction that Heaven's favour is fundamentally mediated by holy land. In the Old Turkic inscriptions, this holy land is the area called Ötüken Mountain (*yiš*), meaning the present-day Khangai Mountains of central Mongolia. In the Old Turkic inscriptions, Ötüken's holiness is often expressed in naturalistic, almost geo-political, tones: 'A land better than the Ötüken mountains does not exist at all! The place from which the state [*il*] can best be controlled is the Ötüken mountains.'[57] But the *Secret History* illustrates more clearly the sacred valences of these holy lands. The word *ötüken* is also found in the *Secret History* as a common noun, *etugen* or 'earth', but with a special affinity for poetic and sacred contexts (for example, in §§201, 245) and is often paired with *eke*, 'mother' (§§113, 255).[58]

In the *Secret History*, however, the Khangai Mountain was no longer the sacred land. Instead the holy place was the Burǧan-Qaldun Mountains, the modern Great and Small Khen-tii Mountains, from which the Onon, Kherlen and Tuul Rivers flowed. The eastward-flowing Onon and Kherlen formed the Onon-Kherlen region, which, as William of Rubruck reported, the Mongols showed off to foreign envoys as 'their own particu-lar territory, in which lies the residence of Chingis Chan'.[59] The headwaters of the three rivers were forbidden to non-Mongols

(§179). The *Secret History* likewise records how, when Chinggis Khan fled from the Tayici'ut to Burġan-Qaldun, the supernatural protection he received there came from Heaven (§80). And after being harboured there a second time, Chinggis Khan prescribed for his descendants a daily ritual to Burġan-Qaldun in gratitude for its protection (§103); this ritual may well be the same kind as that mentioned by Marco Polo for Heaven.[60] The sacred land was thus a material conduit for receiving from and giving blessings to the immaterial Heaven.

The other way in which Heaven's destiny was accessed was through lineage. The genealogy with which the *Secret History* begins has a heavenly supernatural origin – whether that of Grey Wolf and Fallow Doe or that of Alan the Fair and the heavenly light in the form of a yellow dog that impregnated her. Alan the Fair's words, echoed in the praise of Mother Ö'elun, draw out explicitly the obvious implication that the descendants of this lineage will rule (§§20–22, 75). Ritually, the membership in this divinely destined lineage was re-affirmed by periodic sacrifices, including the *jügeli*, glossed as 'hanging meat on a pole to sacrifice to Heaven' (§§43–4), and the *ġajaru inaru* sacrifice, glossed as 'sacrifice to the ancestors' and 'sacrificing burnt food in the ground' (§70). The practice of burning sacrificial meat in a pit in the ground for the ancestors was widely practised both by the predecessors of the Mongol rulers and by the later Mongol khans in the Mongol Yuan dynasty in China.[61] The *Yuanshi* describes the 'burnt food' sacrifice as it was performed later on in the Mongol dynasty as follows:

> Every year, in Moon IX and after the 16th of Moon XII, in the Court of Burnt Food [*Shaofan yuan*], one horse, three sheep, mare's milk, ale, and three bolts each of red silk, gold weave, and silk tabby lining are used. And one Mongolian *darqan*,[62] together with one Mongolian shaman, is ordered to dig a pit in the ground to roast the meat, continuing to burn it with the ale, mare's milk, and the rest. The shaman in the dynastic language [i.e. Mongolian] calls aloud the imperial names of the reigns in sequence and performs the sacrifice.[63]

Apart from the meat that was burnt, some was evidently left over as *bile'ur* and it, along with the *sarqut* or sacrificial drink (probably a mare's milk-based liquor), was consumed by those attending. As we see from the stories in the *Secret History*, to be excluded from consuming the meat and milk-liquor of these sacrifices was to be excluded from the lineage, to be in effect excommunicated from the heavenly blessings that lineage ancestry imparted.

European writers describe a number of household cults that are not mentioned in the *Secret History*, most involving a family of felt images hung from the wall of the *ger* over the master and mistress's seat, and mare and cow udders placed by the door. As is still done today in Mongolia, drinking is preceded by sprinkling, first towards the felt images, and then outside to the cardinal directions.[64] Captains of a hundred households and captains of a thousand households also kept similar such families of images in a separate covered wagon, presumably for the worship of the entire people of the unit. For these images special worship was arranged on particular days, conducted not by the members of the household but by a body of religious professionals, the shamans (*bö'e*).[65]

Shamans (Mongolian *bö'e* or Turkic *qam*) among the Mongols played the role of priests, diviners and healers. As priests they presided over the ancestral sacrifices for the social groups larger than the individual household. The chief shaman in any social group camped in front of the *ger* of that group's secular head and normally indicated specific and auspicious times and directions for moving camp on to the next place.[66]

As diviners, shamans predicted the future in a number of ways, most of which are not specifically mentioned in the *Secret History*. Scapulimancy, for example, or the burning of sheep's shoulder blades and divining the future from the cracks, is remarked on by virtually all non-Mongol sources, but is never mentioned in the *Secret History*. Conversely, the examination of entrails (*abitla-*) used as a divination method by the shamans in §272 is not mentioned by the non-Mongol sources. Calendrical practices are, however, mentioned somewhat cagily as 'discourse on the year and on the month' (§§204, 216); that this discourse involved astronomical observations and predictions is confirmed by Chinese and European sources.[67]

On a day-to-day basis the most important function of the shamans was as healers, and in this sense they appear in the *Secret History*, diagnosing the illness of Ökodei Khan and considering sacrifices of prisoners, gold, silver and provisions, as ransom, before settling on the khan's little brother, Tolui, as the proper sacrifice (§272). Most likely it is not only modern or non-Mongol readers who would have sensed something amiss in this.[68] In the succession conflicts from Ökodei's death in 1241 onwards, accusations of witchcraft were frequently levelled by shamans against others, and by others against shamans who assisted political enemies.[69]

Another peculiar practice, in which forest peoples and the Turkic peoples from the western steppe excelled, was the use of weather-stones, called *yay* or *jay* (Turkic) or *jada* (Mongolian).[70] Such weather-magic to bring rain or snow is still practised today in various styles among Turkic and Mongolian peoples, with a variety of stones or stone-like items, including ancient Palaeolithic stone blades, gallstones or bezoars of livestock, or naturally smooth and triangular- or egg-shaped meteoritic stones with a reddish-brown, reddish-yellow or black colour. Dipped in water, they may be shaken or rubbed in combination with various songs or formulae to bring about the desired precipitation.[71] Militarily, *jada* stones could bring snowfall that could freeze unprepared armies; such a snowfall played a big role in the final Mongol victory over the Golden Khan's army at Sanfeng Mountain in February 1232. But such techniques were still subject to Heaven's will; when the Naiman and Oyirat rulers tried to use them against Chinggis Khan, the snowstorm fell on themselves instead and they realized that 'Heaven is not pleased with us' (§143).

The most characteristic form of shamanism described by ethnographers since the eighteenth century involves a trance and spirit possession or (in a different conceptualization) the shaman's journey to the spirit world. William of Rubruck gives the only known description of such practices from the empire period itself, as seen by a Christian who saw possession as the work of demons:

Some of [the shamans] also conjure up demons, and they gather in their dwelling at night those who want an answer from the demon, putting cooked meat in the centre of the dwelling. The *cam* [or *qam*, Turkic for shaman] who issues the summons begins uttering his incantations and holds a tambourine which he bangs heavily on the ground. At length he falls into a frenzy and has himself tied up; and then the demon appears in the darkness and gives [the shaman] meat to eat, and he utters oracles.

One Hungarian prisoner of war joined them in the shamanic session, but 'the demon made his appearance on top of the [*ger*] dwelling and cried out that he could not enter, since there was a Christian with them'.[72] The Persian historian Juvaini agrees that spirits entered through the smoke hole of the *ger*; he also claimed that such spirit possession was facilitated by homoeroticism.[73] Another, very hostile, Persian historian, Juzjani, claimed that Chinggis Khan could tell the future by means of spirit possession, in addition to scapulimancy. According to Juzjani, the khan had special clothes which, when worn, would induce a shamanic trance in which he would accurately predict the future and have his words taken down by a bystander to be read and followed later, when he recovered his senses.[74] If any of this is true, then the Secret Historian kept that secret as well.

In the *Secret History*, we find three instances of what seems like such shamanic foretelling. In each case, the word *ja'arin* (plural *ja'arit*) is associated with the episode. Two are related to the foretelling of Chinggis Khan's rise (§§121, 244); the other to foretelling a grand destiny for one of his great commanders, Muqali (§206). In modern Mongolian from the seventeenth century onwards, at least, *ja'arin* is a title of especially exalted shamans. In the Hanlin recension of the *Secret History*, it is glossed in Chinese as *shengao* or 'spiritual communication'. Previous English translators have rendered it 'heavenly foretoken' (Cleaves), 'heavenly sign' (de Rachewiltz, Onon), or 'omen' (Onon). Comparing the various usages, the original signification seems to be the spirit which first possesses and then gives visions or words to the medium; from that meaning it came to designate either the message spoken or the person being so possessed.

Yet while observers stress that the Mongols gave total obedience to their shamans, the *Secret History* seems to be less than fully committed to the revelations of such *ja'arit*-spirits. Certainly, the spirit that possessed Qorci and announced, 'Heaven and Earth have taken counsel saying "Let Temujin become master of the kingdom"' agreed with the historian's narrative; but Qorci's own demand for an extreme reward later sets in motion a train of events that leads to the death of Boroġul, one of Chinggis Khan's most cherished commanders. And then when Teb-Tenggeri announces the same Heaven and Earth's nomination of Temujin, he hedges his bets and says that Heaven is sometimes saying let Qasar, Chinggis Khan's brother, hold the kingdom, thus egging on Chinggis Khan against his brother. And while there is nothing so suspicious about the supposed spiritual signs that accompany Muqali's rise, the Secret Historian, in actually telling the story of Muqali joining young Temujin's camp, makes no mention of any such omens (§137). Thus, if not openly sceptical, the Secret Historian maintains a certain reserve or ironic distance from shamanic revelations.

3. DATE AND AUTHORSHIP

A Year of the Mouse – but which one?

The *Secret History* concludes in §282 with a clear statement of its date – or as clear as the usual dating system of Mongolian documents during the empire allowed.

> At the moment when the great *quriltai* was assembling, in the Roebuck Moon of the Year of the Mouse, and the hordes had been pitched at the Seven Hills of Köde'e Isle on the Kherlen . . . the writing was finished.

The *quriltai* was an assembly of the imperial elite of the empire. At the beginning of a reign, the members of the imperial family and the great commanders elected a new khan; after that coronation *quriltai*, regular assemblies would be called to plan great conquests and new policies. The Year of the Mouse (*Quluǧana jil*) is a year in the twelve-year animal cycle which had been used among the peoples of the steppe since long before the birth of Chinggis Khan: Mouse, Cow, Tiger, Hare, Dragon, Snake, Horse, Sheep, Monkey, Chicken, Dog, Pig. The Year of the Mouse is the first of the twelve animals in the cycle and among the plausible years corresponds to 1228, 1240, 1252 and 1264.

In trying to decide between these possibilities, scholars have focused on two questions: 1) which Year of the Mouse had a great *quriltai* along the Kherlen River? And 2) which Year of the Mouse post-dates the latest action reported in the *Secret History*? Since no 'great *quriltai*' is explicitly recorded in any of those years, let us take the second question first. The text of the *Secret History* in the Hanlin recension records the life of Chinggis Khan, who died in 1227, and then all but the conclusion of the reign of his son and successor Ökodei, who died in 1241. Thus, the most common view of earlier commentators was that the work was written in 1240. Later scholars pointed out two big problems with this view: 1) there is no mention of any *quriltai* in 1240; and 2) in fact, the text in §276 mentions how Güyuk had already returned from the campaign in eastern Europe, but an entry in the annals of Ökodei places his recall in the Moon XII of the Year of the Mouse, or between 15 December 1240 and 4 January 1241. The *Secret History* was finished, however, in the Roebuck Moon or Moon VII, which in 1240 would be July–August 1240. Thus, the *Secret History*'s narrative certainly extends beyond the 1240 Mouse Year. If this final note about the date of completion, commonly termed a 'colophon' by specialists in ancient and medieval studies, applies to the text as we have it, it must post-date 1240.

In fact, closer examination of the text we have shows that numerous items in it post-date the summer of 1240. The text in §263 states, for example, that Mahmud Yalavach the Khwarazmian was appointed as overseer or *daruǧaci* in Zhongdu; this, however, did not happen until November 1241.

More importantly, a partisan slant is deeply embedded in the text, favouring the family of Chinggis Khan's fourth son Tolui, and harshly critical both of Chinggis Khan's second son Caǧadai and of Chinggis Khan's grandson and second successor Güyuk.

(See the family tree of the empire.) The account of the debate over the succession to Chinggis Khan in §§254–5 and the quarrel between the grandsons of Chinggis Khan in §§275–7 treats Tolui and his son Möngke as always reasonable and right and Cağadai and his grandson Böri, along with Ökodei Khan's son Güyuk, as always arrogant and wrong.

This slant can be seen outside the narrative blocks as well in statements like that in §243, where Chinggis Khan is said to have singled out his second son for criticism: 'Cağadai is difficult; his character is narrow-minded.' To understand the significance of this statement, consider that Körguz, a Uyghur official who in a quarrel had spoken much less insulting words to a member of Cağadai's family, was executed by having his mouth stuffed with stones.[75] The *Secret History* author would have been liable to the same penalty for such a statement, unless in the meantime the politics had changed and Cağadai's character was now fair game. That change indeed happened in 1251, when Tolui's son Möngke seized the throne from Güyuk's sons and their key supporters among the Cağadaid family. The coup in 1251 resulted in the publication of a number of works attacking Cağadai as harsh and bigoted against Muslims; the *Secret History*'s treatment of him fits well into the same political climate. The *Secret History*'s text must thus post-date 1251.

Indeed, the 1252 Mouse Year is by far the best fit for the political and personal context of the *Secret History*. Although there is no specific mention of a 'great *quriltai*' on the Kherlen River in Moon VII of that Year of the Mouse, there is record of a plethora of important political decisions taken in that moon: plans for the invasion of the Dali kingdom in present-day Yunnan province of south-west China, the sultanate of Delhi in northern India, the Ismaili imamate in Iran, the Abbasid caliphate in Baghdad and the borders of the Song dynasty in southern China.[76] A large assembly of princes and commanders meeting to decide on a set of major campaigns that would define the whole empire's agenda for the next few years: that is still a 'great *quriltai*' by any other name.[77]

This same year also saw a major innovation in the cult of Chinggis Khan. Shortly after the Moon VII *quriltai*, the new khan

Möngke conducted the worship of his father and grandfather at the Kürelgu Mountain, near Köke Na'ur or 'Blue Lake', both of which are mentioned repeatedly in the *Secret History* as places of significance in the young Temujin's life. The worship had been planned with months of preparation by over fifty Chinese academicians and liturgists from Confucius's home province of Shandong, with a full programme of liturgical hymns and dancing and use of ritual utensils.[78] The ritual took place on the seventh to twelfth days of Moon VIII, during which sacrifices were offered to Heaven and Earth and to Möngke's grandfather, Chinggis Khan, and father, Tolui – but not to his uncle, Ökodei Khan, or cousin, Güyuk Khan. Spirit tablets were constructed for the ancestors being worshipped and Möngke was personally present, wearing a ritual crown and robe.[79]

This cultic context fits the contents of the *Secret History* perfectly. The worship of Heaven and Earth fits well with the *Secret History*, which departed from the usual Mongol formulae about the power of Eternal Heaven to speak of Heaven and Earth elevating Chinggis Khan. Moreover, the themes of the narrative reflect deeply the issues of the 1251 coup. Möngke Khan had been orphaned in 1232, when his father Tolui died after an obscure illness. His mother raised Möngke and his able brothers as a widow. The empire, however, after the ambivalent reign of Ökodei had somehow lost its way, with internal divisions, accusations of witchcraft and shamans (*bö'e*) interfering in politics, and the engine of conquest stalled for a decade. After a bloody purge of his cousins, the victorious son of a widow was attempting both to honour his grandfather Chinggis Khan and to prove that his harsh actions were fulfilling, not betraying, his legacy. A predestined heritage somehow gone wrong, a widow alone with able sons in a hostile world, conflict between brothers that should be united: readers will find all of these themes in the *Secret History*. For that reason, August 1252 may be taken as the date when at least a first draft, with the full basic conception of the *Secret History*, was completed.

The anonymous author

If the history was completed in 1252, who wrote it? The work is anonymous, and will undoubtedly remain so. The names of well-known persons that have been proposed as the author can all be easily excluded. Still, although we will probably never know the author's name, the work itself offers us many clues to the author's contacts, methods and social position.

Many of the names proposed for the author seem to assume that literacy was so rare in Mongolia that we only need to find the name of someone who could read and write and we have the author. The first person known as a literate official at the Mongol court was Tatar-Tong'a, a Uyghur scribe and keeper of the seal in Naiman service who was captured by Chinggis Khan, performed the same functions for him, and was granted great honours under Ökodei. Another name that has been proposed is that of Cinqai, a Christian of the Church of the East, who is variously called a Uyghur, a Kereyit or an Öng'ut and was the chief of the secretariat and keeper of the seal under Ökodei and Güyuk. Both of these, however, can easily be excluded: Tatar-Tong'a because he was not alive in 1252, and Cinqai because no one still alive would be less likely to support Möngke Khan's agenda; Cinqai barely escaped the 1251 purge with his life. In any case, both of them were likely native Turkic speakers, and it seems very hard to credit the work as having been written by anyone other than a native Mongolian speaker. In addition, Cinqai was far too familiar with the geography and history of North China to make the kinds of mistakes the Secret Historian did. Another figure proposed is Father Mönglik of the Qongqotan, who was married to Mother Ö'elun and thus became father-in-law to Chinggis Khan. The idea is that he would have had the access to know of the intimate scenes. However, he was undoubtedly deceased in 1252; indeed, he probably predeceased Chinggis Khan.

More credible as the author, although still impossible, is Qutuǧu Noyan, referred to throughout the *Secret History* by the familiar nickname 'Śiki' Qutuǧu.[80] He is credited as the empire's first chief scribe in *Secret History* §203 and hence was

certainly literate. He is also known to have lived through the
entire reign of Möngke Khan. However, the very passage of the
Secret History in which Qutuġu as scribe is granted special
supervision over 'the cities with earthen walls' years before the
Mongols had any such conquest in sedentary lands is but one
of the many anachronisms in the work; in fact, this assignment
to oversee the census occurred in 1234, not 1206. It is incon-
ceivable that Qutuġu Noyan could make such an egregious
mistake about his own biography – and that is by no means
the only such mistake relating to his biography in the *Secret
History* – if he was in fact the author.[81]

Clearly, simply finding famous people who could write or
were intimate members of the elite will not get us far. Instead,
it is important to look at how the work was written. As will be
discussed below, the Secret Historian combined extensive
quotation from written materials with a number of vivid stor-
ies that have no parallel in any written source, indeed many of
which seem far too intimate to have been easily written down.
Obviously, oral informants must have been consulted as well.
Once we assume that oral informants played a role, then those
informants may be tracked down in the same way journalists
track down the anonymous sources of a Washington insider
account: by seeing who among those chronicled comes out
looking unrealistically good and influential. So here the key to
identifying the Secret Historian's informants is to see who was
still alive in Möngke Khan's time and who is given an unreal-
istic share of goodness and power in the *Secret History*
narrative.

Among those figures from Chinggis Khan's childhood alive
during Möngke Khan's reign, three stand out:

1. Śiki Qutuġu: Rashiduddin reports that he lived to the
   age of eighty-two, and died during the khanate of
   Ariq-Böke in 1260–64; he was in attendance on
   Tolui's sons as well.[82]
2. The wives of Chinggis Khan's brother Qasar:
   Rashiduddin reports that during Möngke Khan's time
   several of them 'were still alive, and [the khan] held

them in great respect and honour'. At least one of
them is known to have been a Tatar.[83]

3. Naya'a: Rashiduddin reports that he lived to be over a
hundred, into the reign of Möngke Khan, yet still
remembered eating some of the food during the
marriage banquet at the wedding of young Temujin
and his first wife Börte.[84]

All these figures would have been excellent informants. The
Secret Historian clearly takes the side of Śiki Qutuġu and Naya'a
in disputed issues and grossly exaggerates their influence. Like-
wise, the Secret Historian treats Qasar as loyal throughout,
ignoring well-known stories that said he committed several
offences against Chinggis Khan.[85] And the Secret Historian's
account of Qasar's rather minor role in the conquest of North
China is, compared to the accounts of other parts of that con-
quest, unusually accurate and geographically coherent. It is thus
very probable that the Secret Historian used as informants Śiki
Qutuġu, Naya'a of the Ba'arin, and one or more of the wives of
Qasar who accompanied him on the campaign.

Moreover, the constant use of Qutuġu's nickname by the
Secret Historian indicates a relationship that had a certain
familiarity and affection in it. In Mongolian familial culture,
relationships between parents and children or teachers and
students are relatively strict, while ones between children and
those of the grandparent's generation are more relaxed and less
hierarchical. One may thus surmise from the use of the nick-
name Śiki rather than the title Noyan, which other histories
use, that the Secret Historian is more likely to be a family
member two generations below Qutuġu than to be a pupil or
a family member in the generation of Qutuġu's children.[86] Śiki
Qutuġu was a Tatar, and the story of the massacre of the Tatars
is one of the most unique and important in the work as a
whole; that one of Qasar's wives was a spared Tatar lady might
also point to a potential source for that story. So, although we
do not know exactly who wrote the work, we can pinpoint
certain of the author's allegiances: respectful of Naya'a of the
Ba'arin, affectionately devoted to Śiki Qutuġu of the Tatars as

a sort of grandfather figure, and attached to the entourage of Qasar's widows – perhaps in the service of one of his Tatar wives.

One may note a further, very important aspect of the Secret Historian's life. The literary critic M. M. Bakhtin has referred to the chronotope of a narrative – the time and space through which the narrator travels.[87] Much more could be said on this topic, but the main point here is that while Chinggis Khan and his sons and grandsons travel from Mongolia south to Henan in China, south-west to the banks of the Indus and west to the steppes of Ukraine, the narrator never accompanies them.

In other words, consider the scenes set in Mongolia, such as the Merkit's morning raid on Chinggis Khan's camp and the kidnapping of Börte in §§98–101, or the morning confrontation in Chinggis Khan's *ger* in §§245–6. The reader sees the day break and knows that the author has seen just such a camp and woken up under a quilt in just such a *ger*. But, however dramatic the scenes of Chinggis Khan's son Tolui's yielding to the shaman's incantation during the campaign in North China or the confrontation between the princes in Ukraine, one gets no sense of the environment around which these events occurred; the narrator has not actually witnessed the scene and makes no attempt to let us see it either. In other words, the author's visualized chronotope, the time and place where the narrator can describe places and spaces, not just dialogue, is limited to Mongolia. Outside Mongolia – and mostly central and eastern Mongolia at that – the places are just names, frequently confused.

In practical terms, this means that when the work was written, the Secret Historian had never left Mongolia. Nor is there evidence of the slightest interest on the part of the historian in the cities which Chinggis Khan and Ökodei had built on the steppe or the deported Sarts and Chinese who inhabited them, or the Buddhist, Daoist, Christian and Muslim clerics who ministered to these new inhabitants. The Secret Historian was, in Lev Gumilev's phrase, an 'old Mongol' following the ways of Möngke Khan, who ruled 'honouring the commandments of his ancestors; he did not slavishly copy the way things were done in other countries'.[88]

Close to the entourage of one of Qasar's widowed ladies, living only in Mongolia, highlighting the words and wisdom of women like no other writer in the Mongol empire, a genius whose name was not recorded in history: this profile suggests strongly the tantalizing possibility that the anonymous author was in fact a woman. Within the many vivid scenes of women in their domestic world, we see the ambivalent relationship of the Secret Historian to the patriarchal world. Even while praising Mother Ö'elun as 'born both womanly and wise', the author participates gleefully in the ridiculing and silencing of her rival, Belgutei's mother, the other wife of Yisukei, forgoing even to record her name. The writer records how the Mongol heroes build their empire on desire for

Foreign folk's
Chubby-cheeked
Lovely ladies and
Geldings good of rump (§123)

But then note the words the historian puts in Köke-Cos's mouth. The 'difficult' son Caġadai has attacked his big brother Joci by claiming that he was the son of his mother's Merkit captor, and hence a 'bastard foundling of the Merkit'. Köke-Cos points out that Caġadai's charges implicate his own mother as well, and calls on him not to ignore the cost that warfare took even on his own family or demand perfect chastity of his mother:

The starry heavens would spin about,
The wandering folk would raise a war.
Never slipping off to rest, they'd take each other prisoner.
The loamy earth would lurch about,
The kingdom whole would take to arms.
Never quiet in their quilts, they'd hunt each other down like game.

In that time,

We went not by our own desire;
It was all but by the combat's chance.

We fled not by our own desire;
It was all but by the conflict's chance.
We went not by our heart's desire;
It was all but by the killing's chance. (§254)

The historian records how Caġadai's grandson Böri and Öko-
dei's son Güyuk ridiculed Batu as an old woman:

'When grannies play wearing a quiver,
Wishing they were equal to us,
What's a heel for but to hurt them?
What's a sole for but to stomp them?'
Güyuk said, 'Let's flog with hot sticks the breasts of those
grannies with bow cases, you and me, all of them.' (§275)

But the shadow of these taunts is brute fact, known to the
Secret History's readers, that such savage, misogynistic
tortures – kicking to death, flogging the breasts with flaming
sticks – were applied to accused women of the Caġadaid and
Ökodeid families in Möngke Khan's coup of 1251. Is the work's
message thus to question the culture of macho sissy-shaming
and its attendant violence – or just that turn-about is fair play?

4. TITLE, GENRE, COMPOSITION

The title: why secret? And really a history?

Just as the author of the work has occasioned much contro-
versy, so too has the title. Since neither of the two versions in
which the work was preserved have the same format as the ori-
ginal, many questions about the work's original form remain.
In the seventeenth-century *LAT* recension there is no title, since
the work was incorporated into Lubsang-Danzin's larger work,
the *Altan tobci* or 'Golden Chronicle'. The Hanlin recension's
editors, working for the ethnic Chinese Ming dynasty in the
1380s, looked back on Mongol rule in China that lasted in one
part or another of the country for over a century and a half.

From 1271 on, the Mongol empire in China was known as the 'Yuan dynasty', a term that continued until the Mongols' expulsion from China in 1368.

The Hanlin recension starts off with three phrases, each of which has been taken as the work's title. At the top of the first line in all the editions are the words in Chinese 'Secret History of the Yuan Dynasty' (*Yuanchao mishi*) – for many scholars working in Chinese this is still the work's common title. Below that, the older twelve-*juan* recension writes in a transcription from Mongolian: 'Secret History of the Mongols' – *Monggol-un ni'uca tobciyan*. This second title was eliminated in the fifteen-*juan* version a few decades later, but it must be the original Mongolian from which the Chinese 'Secret History of the Yuan Dynasty' was taken. As such it has become the usual title of the work in non-Chinese scholarship.

But in the body of the text, as its very first words, is an independent phrase, one that seems to function as a heading or title: 'The Origin of Chinggis Khan' (*Cinggis Qa'an-u huja'ur*). Beginning with the Japanese scholar Naka Michiyo, some scholars have understood this to be the real title of the work. This theory builds on the fact that the twelve-*juan* recension of the Hanlin recension treats the text up to §247, or the beginning of Chinggis Khan's invasion of China in 1211, as the main text and all that came after as a continuation. In this theory, everything that happened in Mongolia was the 'origin' of Chinggis Khan and the original topic of the history; all the foreign conquests and the reign of his son Ökodei were simply later add-ons. However, such a division in the text ignores the pervasive continuity in language and themes between the 'main text' and its supposed continuation (see Appendix A). In reality, 'The Origin of Chinggis Khan' is likely simply a heading describing the genealogy that immediately follows; indeed, *huja'ur* could just as easily be translated as 'genealogy' or 'lineage' as 'origin'.

Some have raised doubts about whether the title 'Secret History of the Mongols' (*Monggol-un ni'uca tobciyan*) was there in the Hanlin recension's Mongolian original. But 'Secret History of the Mongols' seems hardly to be a title that the Ming-era transcribers would slap on a work which had not previously been titled as such. Since we know that the work was treated as secret during the time of the Mongol Yuan dynasty (for reasons I will discuss below), it makes sense that, formally or informally, it would have been referred to as such. Moreover, it is highly unlikely that the early Ming scholars and officials would create a Mongolian version of a title that was not there in the original. Most likely, then, the Mongolian manuscript that served as the basis for the Hanlin recension's transcription and translation did have 'Secret History of the Mongols' written at its head in Mongolian.

Whether that heading was a formal title given to the work by the author, or whether it was a kind of nickname attached to it by later scribes as the work was transmitted, the title 'Secret History of the Mongols' tells us several important things about how the work was read. First, there is the word 'Mongol'. Actually, the title could just as easily be translated as the 'Secret History of Mongolia' or 'of the Mongol Dynasty' as 'of the Mongols'. The word *Monggol* implies not just the Mongols as a people, but also the land of the Mongols, and the political entity founded by Chinggis Khan. Indeed, since the Ming translators translated it into Chinese as 'Secret History of the *Yuan Dynasty*' (emphasis mine), they evidently understood *Monggol* here as referring not to the Mongols as an ethnographic group but to the state and empire founded by Chinggis Khan in 1206, and which was renamed the Yuan dynasty by his grandson Qubilai Khan in 1271. This accords with the contents of the work, in which the focus is not on the Mongols as a people but rather on the story of state-building, of how the Mongol empire was founded.

The word 'Secret' is a key to the work's audience. That the work was indeed secret becomes apparent when we compare its contents with those of all the other histories written by historians under the Mongol empire or shortly thereafter. Upon such examination, we find that several shocking events detailed in the *Secret History* are either unknown anywhere else in the historical record or at best only alluded to in cryptic hints: the young Temujin killing his half-brother Bekter, the kidnapping of his young wife Börte, the subsequent doubts about the legitimacy of Chinggis Khan's first son Joci, the brawl between his sons during the debate on the succession question, and Öko-dei's savage rebuke of his own son Güyuk's arrogance. Had this history been widely known, such lurid events and statements could not have been kept hidden. One can only assume that they were not known and that the *Secret History* was indeed kept secret at least until the fall of the Mongol empire.

The secrecy of the work is alluded to in an event of 1330. Two scholar officials, one from southern China and one a Turkic-speaking Öng'ut from north-western China, had an imperial commission from the Mongol emperor Tuq-Temur Jaya'atu Khan (r. 1328–32) allowing them access to sources necessary for compiling an encyclopedia of Mongol Yuan institutions. But despite the imperial commission, two Mongolian Hanlin academicians, Yat-Buqa and Taš-Qaya, flatly denied their request to access the *Secret History*: 'The *Tobciyan* [History] concerns court secrets; it is not something that can be circulated in writing to outsiders. Your servants dare not accept the edict.' The emperor let the refusal stand.[89]

Why was the *Secret History* so secret? As the colophon (concluding note) of the history states, the work was first prepared during a great *quriltai* or assembly of the ruling class of the realm. And although non-Mongol envoys and officials were present in great numbers at such assemblies, the most important sessions excluded all but the Mongol ruling class.[90] One may presume that the initial audience was the Mongol ruling class attending such a *quriltai*. Why did they not let it circulate further? Certainly, the less than flattering stories about Chinggis Khan's childhood and youth and record of the often vicious conflicts within the family would have encouraged the princes and high commanders to prohibit wide dissemination of the work.

But the most important reason for the secrecy may have been the passages describing the early khans' institutions. The sections on the imperial bodyguard twice reiterate 'Let no one ask the number of the nightguards' and prescribe arrest and confiscation of all possessions for the person unwise enough to do so (§§229, 278) – yet that number is easily calculable from the surrounding passages in the material. Similarly, non-Mongols, even officials, were forbidden to learn the number of Mongol troops,[91] yet the list of captains of a thousand in the *Secret History* has been used by historians ever since to calculate that very number. It is likely that it was these military secrets, as much or more than the embarrassing stories, that led the Mongol authorities at the *quriltai* to label the whole history 'top-secret'.

On the other hand, although the work was not publicly accessible, it was not entirely unknown. As was discussed at the beginning of this Introduction, the *Secret History* exercised an obvious influence on the less secret history of Chinggis Khan compiled during the reign of Qubilai Khan. Even this latter history was not really public, but it did circulate outside the court and we know it from versions preserved in Chinese and Persian translations.[92] However, in the process of adding new material and revising the chronology to compile this less private version, the most sensitive stories of the *Secret History* were all deleted. The *Secret History*'s unique glimpse into women's lives and stories unfolding within the *ger*s and hordes of the Chinggisid rulers were almost all eliminated to make a purely public and official story.

Finally, the title shows that the *Secret History* was indeed seen as a 'history'. In later Mongolian, *teuke* or modern *tüükh* is the usual word for 'history', but in Middle Mongolian it is *tobciyan*. Even apart from the fact that the Hanlin recension's *tobciyan* is translated by Chinese *shi,* 'history', the meaning of 'history' is demonstrated by a bilingual Sino-Mongolian inscription of 1362 in which the court historian Wei Su talks about his 'curating of the *tobciyan*' (*tobciyan-i-e qadaǧalaqsan-aca*).[93] The Persian historian in Mongol service, Rashiduddin, described the Mongolian histories that needed such curation:

> However, from reign to reign, they have kept their authentic chronicles in Mongolian expression and script, unorganized and disarranged, chapter by chapter, scattered in treasuries, hidden from the gaze of strangers and specialists, and no one was allowed access to learn of it.[94]

With its label as a *tobciyan*, the *Secret History* was evidently seen as one work in this rather disorganized legacy of confidential dynastic history.

Genre: chronicle, epic, or something else?

So, from its title, the *Secret History* is a history – which is how readers, Mongolian or foreign, have always initially approached it. But in the twentieth century, as scholars compared the *Secret History*'s telling of the events more closely to the other histories, doubts began to arise, doubts crystallized in the title of a 1972 article by the Japanese scholar Hidehiro Okada: 'The Secret History of the Mongols: A Pseudo-Historical Novel'. Even more than the supernatural elements, the serious divergences in chronology between the *Secret History* and other sources and the large amount of vivid, domestic description and personal dialogue that could not possibly have been based on written official records all contributed to a sense that the seeming historicity of the work was an illusion. If it was history, it was very bad history, so scholars thought it more polite to insist that it was either a 'novel' or a chronicle mixed with 'epic' features. As Okada wrote, the *Secret History* is 'a masterpiece of historical fiction unsurpassed in literary value by any later work. It is not a chronicle, however. It is not intended to be. [It] is a good novel based on Chinggis Khan's life.'[95]

Such a view has won few takers. In the first case, as a genre, the novel, historical or otherwise, is not recorded anywhere in the lands of the Mongol empire at this time. (The closest thing would be the Chinese-language historical dramas in twelfth- to fourteenth-century North China.) By contrast, the *Secret History* does have measurable overlap with clearly historical-type texts. In fact, the Secret Historian cited numerous historical, biographical and administrative sources verbatim; the *Secret History* was, in turn, cited at length by the Qubilai Khan-era compilers of the 'Authentic Chronicle of Chinggis Khan'. The evidence of citation shows that the Secret Historian was thus known as a historian writing in a tradition of historical writing.

But if calling it a novel seemed far-fetched, the idea that it is an 'epic chronicle' won many more takers. Igor de Rachewiltz called it 'a literary masterpiece . . . in which epic poetry and narrative are so skilfully and indeed artistically blended with fictional and historical accounts'.[96] Since Vico and Hegel, the idea that national literatures begin with an era of oral epic, only later to yield to an 'age of prose', has become a commonplace.[97] The *Secret History* could thus be seen as a product of this metamorphosis frozen in the transition from oral epic to prose chronicle. Indeed, the widely used English adaptation by Paul Kahn (done originally from Francis Cleaves's hyper-literal translation) treated the entire work as poetry, a treatment authorized by speculations about how the text as we have it was the result of a comprehensive prose rewriting made in the ensuing era of Qubilai Khan.[98]

However, the *Secret History* bears very little resemblance to the actual epics found in Mongolia and neighbouring lands today: lengthy poems narrated extempore by bards to the accompaniment of a fiddle or lute. Such epics are sung in the winter, often as the prelude to hunting. To be sure, many themes, such as and the seizure or rescue of a bride, horse theft, blood brotherhood and wrestling competitions, are found in epics as well as the *Secret History*. Some of the descriptions of smashing in *gers* in §109 and §111 and the exaggerated renditions of martial prowess in §195 strongly recall passages in Turkic epics such as the Manas of the Kyrgyz.[99] Yet the way in which such events are narrated or the context in the story differs strikingly.

For example, the creation of blood brotherhood between Temujin and Jamuqa is focused in the *Secret History* on the exchange of gifts; in epics it is the outcome of an athletic contest and gifts are exchanged only in parting.[100] In epics, the hero enters the camp of the monstrous enemy, the *manġġas*, in disguise, like Odysseus returning home to Ithaca; and, just like Odysseus, it is during an athletic contest, whether archery, horse racing or wrestling, that the hero's true identity is revealed. Athletic contests thus reveal the truth. In the *Secret History*, however, there are two wrestling bouts and both are rigged.

Most strikingly, Mongolian epics are 1) non-historical; 2) cyclical, i.e. consisting of numerous repeated narrative motifs which can be connected to form repeatable episodes; 3) pervasively hyperbolic; and 4) bound by a small-scale social horizon, focused on family and local social relations. Indeed, one analyst has called them not epics at all, but 'heroic fairy tales'.[101] In all these ways they differ radically from the *Secret History*.

Of course, there is always the possibility that the epics of the *Secret History* times differed radically from those documented by ethnographers from the eighteenth century on. But to use the concept of an otherwise undocumented 'epic' to explain the *Secret History*'s deviations from the expectations of a chronicle hardly generates insight. And even in the more historically oriented epics of other peoples that have traditionally defined the genre, such as the *Iliad* and *Odyssey* or the *Song of Roland*, the monochronic absolute past and exteriority contrast sharply with the profound ironies, silences and interiority of the *Secret History*.[102]

Better than epics as a comparative tool for understanding the *Secret History* would be the saga, a genre of vernacular narrative produced in abundance in Iceland from the thirteenth to the fifteenth century. Almost without exception anonymous, sagas were written in prose but with a key role for skaldic poetry in alliterative verse. The sagas concerned identifiable persons, places and dates, and drew on previous written sources, yet at their best have a vividness and power that has seduced generations into treating them as virtually infallible. Thus, the kings' sagas (*konungasögur*) such as the famous *Heimskringla* of Snorri Sturluson (1179–1241), a history of the Norwegian kings completed around 1230, have played a similar role in defining our image of Norwegian and Icelandic history that the *Secret History* has played in modern images of the Mongol empire. Yet the notes for a modern translation of, for example, *King Harald's Saga*, one of the component epics in the *Heimskringla*, will contain numerous caveats such as 'The saga account of the battle, although immensely vivid, conflicts with the [considerably earlier] *Anglo-Saxon Chronicle*, which is clearly more reliable.'[103] The reader will find many such notes in this translation as well.

Despite such inconsistencies with other accounts, however, both these royal sagas and the family sagas (*Íslendinga sögur*, 'Sagas of the Icelanders'), which told the stories of settlers in Iceland, are clearly concerned with factuality. As part of that concern, they employed numerous 'authenticating devices' to 'give the impression that they relate events exactly as they happened, or at least as people have said they happened'.[104] These devices include reference to continuing physical objects, references to changes in customs between the narrative time and the saga writer's time, the explicit citation of poetry used on the occasion, and assurances that the author has read one of the acknowledged trustworthy sources, such as Ari Thorgilsson. And indeed, the 'fictional worlds' they create are 'largely consistent' with what can be documented through other sources or archaeology.[105]

As a work more contemporary to the events it narrates, the *Secret History* did not need to use devices to bridge the time-gap between writer and event, nor are there any explicitly cited sources. Instead the Secret Historian's main authenticating device was implicit: the use of extensive verbatim citation of other sources, in a wide range of genres. As a result, the *Secret History* came to share the nature of a comprehensive anthology of existing writings characteristic of other very pioneering histories, such as the *Records of the Grand Historian* (*Shiji*) in Chinese and the 'Primary History' in Hebrew. As in the *Records of the Grand Historian*, 'the multi-voiced nature of the work also serves to offer historical lessons, through an ironic interplay between quoted assertions and factual narrative'.[106] A similar such ironic distance can be found in the *Secret History*, for example in the contrast of the narration of the Jamuqa–Temujin split and the citation of Jamuqa's version of it (§§118–19, 127) or in the contrast between the quoted public record of Ökodei's good deeds and the covert secrecy of his bad deeds (§281).

Certain parallels with the 'Primary History' (the Genesis-to-Kings narrative of the Hebrew Bible) have already been noted, and more can be adduced. First, they share a similar prosimetric style, with most of the narrative being given in prose, but with numerous passages in poetry. Second, they share a similar set of diverse subgenres within the work: genealogy, biographical stories and dialogue, lengthy institutional regulations, lengthy lists of officials and persons, and personal last testaments. Third, both were composed through a process of weaving together existing documents covering particular stages of the story to create a work which was dramatically longer and more extensive than any known predecessor. This incorporation, however, resulted in abrupt transitions in style and left a number of 'loose ends' dangling.

Fourth, both are, despite the diversity in subgenres, character-ized by a strong narrative arc, repeated two or three times, of rise and fall, success and failure in realizing a heavenly-destined mis-sion. Families grow and expand into clans and peoples, but this progress is stymied by conflict and disobedience, until a new cha-rismatic ruler renews the polity's founding principles and there is revived growth. In both cases, the individual narratives are linked by a powerful sense of direction; history is going somewhere, and doing so under the impetus of a single supernatural driving force. The sense of characters in the grip of a 'vertical connection', pro-pelled from above to move towards their complex yet destined roles, which Erich Auerbach[107] saw as characteristic of biblical, rather than Homeric, narrative is powerfully present in the *Secret History*. Yet the distant, impersonal and almost entirely mute Heaven of the *Secret History* is radically different from the vol-uble, personal God of the Hebrew Bible.

In the *Secret History*'s case, we see an early kingdom or khanate rising from the heroic widow Alan the Fair and her son Bodoncar. This kingdom falls, however, with the poisoning of Yisukei Ba'atur and the abandonment of widows and chil-dren on the range. A new Chinggisid khanate then rises again from its cradle in the *ger* of the second heroic widow Ö'elun and her son Temujin until he finally assumes the title of Ching-gis Khan. Yet soon after his death, under his son and chosen successor Ökodei, the empire is once again divided under a ruler incapable of assuming a clear direction. Likewise, in the Primary History the first rise and fall arcs from the patriarchs to the bondage in Egypt, the second from the calling of Moses through the Exodus and conquest of Canaan to the last of the Judges, and the third from the calling of Samuel through Kings Saul, David and Solomon and the division of the kingdom and the exile in Babylon.

The problem of the 'historical value' of the *Secret History* is thus very similar to that of the historical value of the Norse royal sagas or of stories of Saul and David. It is also quite similar to the long-standing problem of the speeches in classic Graeco-Roman history. Did Pericles, for example, really make the oration which Thucydides cites at such length? Sceptics on this question abound. But the sceptical distaste which modern readers often show for the speeches of Thucydides, Herodotus or other classical historians is 'the special dilemma of our own traditional scholarship ... disoriented by *our* habituation to quotation marks and unsettled by the need to separate the Thucydidean element from the historical "document" ... our problem arises from our insistence on a clear-cut distinction between objective and subjective truth.'[108] With due adjustment for the different context, much the same could be said about the *Secret History*.

The real problem here is the conflation of 'history' and 'chronicle' and the assumption that if the *Secret History* is 'historical' it must be a 'chronicle'. In other words, the key thing that makes a work 'historical' is the accurate division, sequencing and dating of events, and the rejection of anything unrelated to that task. Indeed, the *Secret History* does not much fit that model of 'history'. Yet if it is assumed that what makes a work historical is that it is an argument made in narrative form that attempts to explain why the past situation changed into the present as it did, how it felt to live through that change, and what message that transformation holds for those living in the time of the historian, then the *Secret History* fits the definition of history in the fullest sense.[109]

The Secret Historian's aim to explain how present states came to be is flagged particularly by the phrase 'This [or that] was the way in which ...' (... *yosun [t]eyimu*). Used ten times by the Secret Historian, it usually concludes tales of pivotal events. Thus, it is used to flag

- key marriages (Dobun the Marksman and Alan the Fair, Yisukei Ba'atur and Madame Ö'elun, and Temujin rescuing his wife Madame Börte),
- key friendships (Bo'orcu, Jamuqa and Jebe with Temujin, and Böri the Brawny with the Yörkin princes),

- key quarrels and griefs (Mother Ö'elun's over Qasar, Tolui's over Ökodei, how Chinggis Khan's grandsons went on the campaign that would lead to their fateful quarrel).

In most of these cases, the Secret Historian's narrative follows lines not found elsewhere, presumably based on new investigations, of why certain well-known and pivotal events occurred. In other words, the Secret Historian uses the phrase to flag occasions where new and convincing explanations are offered for historical events that the readers probably knew had happened, but might find puzzling or unexplainable. Presenting such an explanation is an essentially historical task.

A related misunderstanding of the Secret Historian's purpose has lain in the confusion over the work's topic as a whole. If the Secret Historian aims not to date all the events exactly but to explain why something happened, what is that main thing that the historian thinks needs explaining? The usual answer is that

> The central theme of our epic chronicle is the *modus operandi* of one dominating figure [Chinggis Khan] who, together with the other leading characters – his family and retainers – skillfully manipulates the society of his time to achieve his one goal, viz. tribal supremacy for himself and his clan against innumerable odds.[110]

Yet this view can only be sustained if the section on Ökodei is treated as a tacked-on appendage – and the deep-seated, pervasive literary and narrative connections binding the Ökodei section to the Chinggis Khan section make such a reading of the work impossible.

It has also been argued that 'unity' – family, ethnic, political – is the work's key theme. Indeed, fraternal unity is proclaimed repeatedly as a virtue, from when Alan the Fair admonishes her five sons with the familiar motif of the unbreakable bundle of arrows (§§18–22) to Tolui's words of loyalty to his older brother Ökodei when he is declared Chinggis Khan's successor (§255). Yet if fraternal unity is the overt message, fraternal conflict, up to and including fratricide, is the covert reality – and the perpetrators, pre-eminently Chinggis Khan himself, seem to suffer little for it. When he kills his blood brother Jamuqa, the latter tells him, as long as the killing is done the right way, 'I will bring lasting, abiding protection unto the seed of your seed' (§201). So it is hardly surprising when the history's final dramatic narrative is one in which the grandsons of Chinggis Khan hurl insults at each other over lack of manliness and are in turn berated by their elder khan Ökodei. Finally, the work concludes not with reconciliation but with Ökodei confessing that his own rule has been a mixture of overt achievements and covert crimes. Clearly something has gone wrong, and family conflict seems to be central to it.

The answer provided by the Secret Historian, not directly but ironically, through the disjunction in what is said from what is meant, is neither the explicit moral of brothers agreeing nor what might seem a despairing cynicism of unending conflict. Instead the central truth is the disturbing secret that brothers sacrificing brothers, if done right, can restore the health of the empire.[111] The Secret Historian thus justified the purges of 1251, when the Möngke Khan seized power and made a clean sweep of his quarrelling cousins. As the son of the famous widow Sorġoqtani Beki, Möngke Khan was the unspoken third in a line of widows' sons, walking in the footsteps of Bodoncar the Simple, son of the widowed Alan the Fair, and of Chinggis Khan himself, son of the widowed Madame Ö'elun, who would use the techniques of blood-purge to restore the family and refound the empire.

Composition

So how was the *Secret History* composed? The most recent research suggests a threefold process:

1. Collection, arrangement, and citation of written sources of various genres;
2. Collection, writing down, and arrangement of narratives collected orally from Šiki Qutuġu, Naya'a, ladies of Qasar's hordes, and others;

3. Composition of additional alliterative poetry, partly on traditional models and partly original, to illustrate themes and heighten the effect.

Although these three stages were probably broadly successive, one should not imagine that they were strictly separated. Nor did the Secret Historian hesitate to alter or modify the existing sources, written or oral, that seemed not to make sense. From the perspective of a modern historian, the results of these changes were sometimes brilliant, at other times disastrous. But in any case, the alliterative verses were not, as Hegelian ideas about the primacy of verse or the idea of 'epic chronicle' might suggest, the basic stratum but actually, with few exceptions, the last stage of the composition. For that very reason, though, the alliterative verse is the best guide to the final text's structure and meaning.

For the basic narrative outline, the Secret Historian had two main types of documents: annotated genealogies and certain prose narratives, of greater or lesser elaboration. Numerous genealogies circulated during the Mongol empire, with major differences between them. For example, six different schemes for the ancestry of Temujin from Bodoncar the Simple and his mother Alan the Fair are known. In the shortest there were only seven ancestors between Temujin and Bodoncar; in the two longest, one of which is that of the *Secret History*, there are ten ancestors between them.

The *Secret History*, however, goes a step further to giving the origin of Bodoncar's mother Alan the Fair, who conceived from a heavenly light. This was done by using two other ancestral genealogies: one going back to an ancestral couple Master Borjigin the Marksman and Mistress Mongol the Fair, and the other going back to an ancestral couple, Grey Wolf and Fallow Doe. The Secret Historian harmonized these two different genealogies, each with their different ancestral couples, together with the genealogy of Alan the Fair as the ancestral matriarch, rather than choosing between them. As a result, the Secret Historian created a uniquely long genealogy. Similar such problems had to be resolved elsewhere in the genealogy, and harmonizing the various traditions was sometimes difficult. At times, as with the Yörkin, the Secret Historian is fairly explicit about having to resolve the issue with a new hypothesis.[112]

As for chronicle-style narratives, the Secret Historian used a few that are cited elsewhere and hence can be identified. The most important of these is a set of three documents focused on how Chinggis Khan conquered the Kereyit and Naiman khanates and unified Mongolia. The core of these three was the 'Indictment of Ong Khan', a lengthy document which Chinggis Khan is said to have sent to the Kereyit ruler Ong Khan in the spring of 1203. In it, Chinggis Khan enumerated the services he had rendered to Ong Khan and charged Ong Khan with betraying that loyal service. This 'Indictment' is cited mostly verbatim by the Secret Historian in §§177–81. On the basis of that 'Indictment' document, an 'Indictment Narrative' was later drawn up, sketching the geography of the Kereyit khanate, revealing Ong Khan's scandalous early days, offering more details on the enumerated incidents of Chinggis Khan's services to him, and finally describing how Chinggis Khan overthrew him and his envious son Ilqa Senggum in the autumn of 1203. A final 'Indictment Narrative Continuation' supplied a similar story about the declining Naiman Khanate in western Mongolia, how the khan plotted against Chinggis Khan and was defeated in the autumn of 1204. Together these three documents, all in strongly Turkic-influenced Mongolian prose, supplied the chronological framework and narrative skeleton for §150 to §196, more than a fifth of the whole work.[113]

When it came to the foreign conquests, the Secret Historian appears to have had no such basic document or set of documents. Because the author was forced to depend on orally transmitted anecdotes about countries and campaigns far beyond his or her personal experience, the tales of those campaigns are better on particular episodes than on the larger chronology or geography of the campaigns. But the Secret Historian did incorporate two documents describing the western campaigns in Central Asia that were also used by other historians; as cited in other sources, the documents appear to be quite reliable, if extremely dry. Unfortunately, the Secret Historian fundamentally misunderstood the logic of the campaign, and as a result pieced the two documents together in the wrong order, creating an upside-down narrative that is ironically not just the driest, but probably the least accurate of the history's stories about Chinggis Khan.

Once annotated genealogies and narratives had supplied the skeleton, biographies of great commanders helped flesh out the story with personal anecdotes. Many such biographies are found in Chinese or Persian summaries in the *Yuanshi* or the *Compendium of Chronicles*. In at least one case, that of Jürcedei, we can see that the Secret Historian quoted extensively from the Mongolian original of a biography whose Chinese summary is still extant. A biography of Jelme must also have been the source for many lengthy quotations, although no independent version of Jelme's biography has survived to confirm that fact. Other independently attested sources which the Secret Historian used include a narrated list of the errors and good deeds of Qasar and an encomium of Tolui, telling the story of his death for the sake of Ökodei Khan and praising him and his widow for their sacrifice.

The biography of Jürcedei just mentioned exemplifies a common structure of these biographies. First, the protagonist's deeds are recounted in the third person. This main body is followed by a concluding speech in which someone, usually Chinggis or a later khan, expresses appreciation of these deeds. Some of these later encomia were collected by the Secret Historian and introduced narratively as a set of speeches by Chinggis Khan giving rewards to his early friends in §§203–23.

The Secret Historian's orally collected stories also appear to have had a very strong biographical focus. Thus, integrating biographical material with the main narrative was a similar process whether with written or oral materials. The main problem was that most of this material had little or no dating for early events. Fitting these narratives into sequence thus created a 'lumper vs splitter' dilemma. For example, if a number of biographies have undated stories about battles with the Tayici'ut, all slightly different, should one be a 'lumper' and assume they all refer to one big battle? Or should one be a 'splitter' and assume that they refer to several different little battles? The Secret Historian's response to such questions was very much that of a 'lumper', turning, for example, what other sources consider to be three different battles of Chinggis Khan against a coalition in eastern Mongolia into one vast multi-staged battle in §§141–9.[114]

The result of sewing together so many written sources is some inconsistency in spellings and terms. Within the text there are many examples of variations that mark the citation from one source or another. For example:

- Yisukei Ba'atur (majority usage) vs Yisukei Khan (Indictment, Indictment Narrative)
- Qanġġai (modern Khangai) (Indictment Narrative Continuation) vs Qanġġar-Qan (Biography of Dödei Cerbi)
- e'ere-, 'besiege' (the Secret Historian's preferred usage) vs ba'u-, 'pitch camp' (C Source on Central Asian conquests) for 'to besiege'[115]
- Nišabur (S Source on Central Asia) vs Nicabur (C Source)
- daruġacin, 'overseers' (S Source) vs daruġas, 'overseers' (C Source or other Caġadaid Mongolian source).

In addition to these narrative sources, the Secret Historian also had access to official documents, edicts and decrees of the khans, which were cited liberally and often at great length. (The 'Indictment of Ong Khan', apart from its associated narratives, could also be considered such a document.) One such document is the list of captains of a thousand in §202, under the year 1206, which differs in order of precedence and orthography from how the Secret Historian refers to the commanders elsewhere.

Although the easiest way to add in such official documents and decrees would have been to put them in the mouth of the khan at the appropriate date, the Secret Historian did not take such a simple path. The most extensive citation is that of Ökodei Khan's decree on the rules and regulations of the keśikten or imperial bodyguard. Since that decree notes (rightly or wrongly) in its preamble that Ökodei is simply reiterating the regulations in effect under Chinggis Khan, the Secret Historian felt free to take the bulk of it and transfer it to the beginning of

Chinggis Khan's reign in 1206 (§§224–34), and then include only a summary of it under the reign of Ökodei (§278).

There are a number of other lengthy addresses placed in the mouths of the khans and princes which have every appearance of being cited from actual texts, such as:

- Chinggis Khan's two decrees to Sübe'edei on his expedition against the fugitive Merkit (§199);
- the Uyghur Íduqut's message of submission to Chinggis Khan (§238);
- Chinggis Khan's decree dividing the Golden Khan's Inner Mongolian auxiliaries between Muqali and Bo'orcu (§266);
- Batu's memorial describing the disrespectful behaviour of his cousins and requesting a decree from Ökodei (§275); and
- Ökodei Khan's decree on new measures (§279).

We know from surviving examples of decrees that they were dated only by the twelve-animal cycle. Thus, in some cases, the best explanation of their placement in the history is that the Secret Historian misdated the decree, putting, for example, the khan's decree to Muqali and Bo'orcu in the Dog Year of 1226, not the Dog Year of 1214 – unaware that Muqali had actually died in 1223.

One can trace a number of inconsistencies and stylistic flaws resulting from this insertion of verbatim material. For example, in the lengthy set of decrees about the imperial bodyguard or *keśikten*, the khan usually refers to himself with the imperial 'us' or 'we', but suddenly, in §233, the emperor begins to use 'me' and 'mine'. Evidently a less formal account was inserted into the citation of a court document, producing the inconsistency. Similarly, in §275 the Caġadaid prince Böri begins ridiculing his cousin Batu in the third person singular, but suddenly begins using plural verb forms. The best explanation is that what was originally an attack on Batu's whole branch of the Chinggisid family was inserted into the narrative and repurposed as a particular attack on Batu. And in §199, Chinggis Khan is speaking to

Sübe'edei about his campaign to begin in the Year of the Cow; suddenly, however, he speaks about the Year of the Cow in the past tense. In this case the author had a second decree, which was issued later, well after the multi-year campaign had begun, and was referring retrospectively to the campaign's beginning. At other points, a certain abruptness or repetitiveness seems to have also resulted from the process of editing or stitching together documents.[116] I have not attempted to smooth out these visible marks of editing, although the process of translation naturally makes them somewhat less evident.

A striking feature of these decrees is that many of them contain a couplet or two of alliterative poetry. Although no decrees with alliterative poetry have survived in the original Mongolian, one or two of these poems do have parallels in Chinese and Persian sources translated from Mongolian, demonstrating that they were common expressions and not creations of the Secret Historian.[117] And in one case, with the encomium of Tolui, we have Tolui vaunting his own suitability as a ransom for the khan in verse (see §272), in a passage that was also translated into (quite unpoetic) Persian, confirming that the poetry was in the source document, not created by the Secret Historian.

Such use of short couplets for emphasis, usually but not always alliterative, is also found in passages likely composed by the Secret Historian. 'No friend but a shadow, no whip but a tail' is a favourite way to picture loneliness, 'echoing the elders' words and pounding in the past times' words' describes how parents berate their children, and 'thrall of the threshold, property of the portal' describes chattel slavery. Although the Secret Historian favoured certain such proverbial expressions, there is no reason to think any of them are the historian's own creations.

Very different are the lengthy poetic passages, such as the praise of Mother Ö'elun (§74), Cilger the Brawny's lament (§111), Jamuqa's description of Chinggis Khan's warriors at the Battle of Naqu Qun (§195) and Chinggis Khan's praise of his keśikten (§230). These works are elaborate productions, written with a delight in using complex imagery and obscure vocabulary to make a powerful point. They also tend to cluster around those very passages and episodes that are the least corroborated in other sources, such as the theme of Mother Ö'elun and Madame Börte's wisdom and courage and that of Jamuqa and his ambivalent relationship with Chinggis Khan. Such passages are evidently summative expressions of the Secret Historian's vision of the empire's rise. As such they were logically, if not always temporally, the final capstone to the composition of the work.

Language and script

The *Secret History* was written in Middle Mongolian, in the dialect that was the court speech of Chinggis Khan and close to, if not exactly, the ancestor of the modern standard Khalkha dialect of modern Mongolia. The Mongolian language is the only major representative today of the Mongolic family. Minor Mongolic languages that survived into the modern era, such as Daur in Manchuria, Monguor and Yogur along the north-eastern edges of the Tibetan plateau, and Mogholi in Afghanistan, are also descended from Middle Mongolian, and frequently preserve archaic features lost in standard Mongolian. Kitan, a separate language of the Mongolic family, was still being spoken in eastern Inner Mongolia at the time of the *Secret History* but would soon disappear, assimilated by Middle Mongolian. Mongolian also had many similarities to the Turkic languages, including not just the Turkish of Turkey but also Uyghur and the languages that would become the Kazakh, Kyrgyz, Uzbek and Turkmen languages of today. Although the Turkic and Mongolian languages are probably not related in the sense of being derived from a common proto-language, they came to share through historical contact an immense amount of vocabulary, grammatical structures and idioms.[118]

For this reason, Turco-Mongolian is a useful term to describe the culture of the Mongol empire – actually, the Persian writers in Mongol service during the Mongol empire generally saw their masters as yet another kind of 'Turk'. Just as the Roman empire was ruled by a Latin-speaking elite whose language was deeply influenced by repeated waves of Greek speakers – farmers, merchants, scribes, philosophers, physicians and slaves – so the Mongolian empire was ruled by a Mongolian-speaking elite whose language was influenced by repeated waves of Turkic speakers: herders, caravaneers, merchants, scribes, poets, monks and prisoners of war.

The Mongolian language was already undergoing rapid change when the *Secret History* was written. Large numbers of archaic words appear in the text, never to be seen again in Mongolian; Mongolian texts written less than a hundred years later in the fourteenth century already seem noticeably closer to the classical Mongolian literary language that eventually emerged in the seventeenth century. The Mongolian plateau had been a mix of Turkic and Mongolic speakers for many centuries before Chinggis Khan's time, but with an increasing tendency in the two centuries before his birth for Turkic speakers to adopt Mongolian. As a result, the Mongolian of the Mongolian plateau became increasingly shot through with Turkic vocabularies and idioms, although Chinggis Khan himself is clearly stated to be monolingual, knowing Mongolian alone.[119] After the adoption of the Uyghur script to write Mongolian early in the empire, most scribes were thoroughly bilingual in the two languages, and Turkic-based terms of high culture came to prevade Mongolian vocabulary.

Turkic influence was also mediated by the adoption of the script of the Uyghurs. Most Turkic speakers had adopted Islam and with it the Perso-Arabic script, but the Uyghurs, as Buddhists, maintained their traditional script. It was in this Uyghur-Mongolian script that the *Secret History* was originally written. This script is an alphabet, written vertically in columns from left to right. Indeed, it is the only currently used alphabetic script written vertically – and is hence often called the 'vertical script' (*bosoo üseg*) in Mongolian. It came originally from the Aramaic script of the Middle East and was then adapted to write Sogdian, an Iranian language of early medieval Central Asia. The Sogdians became key merchant and clerical partners of the Uyghurs when the latter were a steppe empire in Mongolia (744–840).

These Uyghurs spoke a Turkic language; to write it they took over the Sogdian script of their intellectual mentors and adapted it to their Turkic language. When their empire was overthrown and large numbers of them fled to the oases of eastern Turkestan, they re-established a flourishing Buddhist Uyghur culture there, one that lasted up to the fifteenth century. Marco Polo noted that the Buddhist Uyghurs were 'very learned in their own laws and traditions and ... keen students of the liberal arts'.[120] In the *Secret History*, the Uyghurs appear as early adherents to the Mongol cause and, not coincidentally, purveyors of luxurious fabrics and elegant language. Thus, when the Mongols rose to power and adopted a script, it was to the Uyghurs that they turned. There is a story that when Chinggis Khan conquered the Naiman in 1204, he found a Uyghur scribe named Tatar-Tong'a in the entourage of Tayang Khan and took him into his service to run his secretariat and tutor his children in writing. Uyghur and Mongolian were fairly similar in their grammar and phonology, and the Uyghur script could easily be adapted to Mongolian.

Even further to the east in what is now Inner Mongolia was another Turkic-speaking people who surrendered early to the Mongols, the Öng'ut. They paid tribute to the Golden Khan of the Jin dynasty in North China until the rise of Chinggis Khan. Their dialect differed from Uyghur and their state religion was not Buddhism but East Syriac Christianity. Still, Uyghurs and Öng'ut easily understood each other and the two supplied a disproportionate amount of the scribal talent in the Mongol empire.

Probably the earliest known piece of writing in Mongolian is the so-called 'Stone of Chinggis Khan'; it is generally thought to have been inscribed on the occasion of an outstanding arrow-shot of 335 *alda* (over 1,700 feet!) fired by Chinggis Khan's nephew Yisungke in 1225. But there is no reason to doubt that Chinggis Khan's court was already using writing by 1204 at the latest; indeed, many scholars have suspected that the adaptation of the Uyghur alphabet to the Mongolian language may have occurred well before then, at the Naiman or Kereyit courts in central and western Mongolia.

Thus, the Uyghur alphabet had been used for writing Mongolian for almost fifty years at least when the Secret Historian first set 'pen' to paper (actually the Uyghur script at this time was written with a calamus, a hard, ink-dipped reed). Although not as developed as it would be after the reforms of the seventeenth to eighteenth centuries, the script was already reasonably stand-ardized. In the adaptation from Uyghur to Mongolian, however, numerous ambiguities had entered the alphabet. In the pairs of letters *t* and *d, q* and *ġ, k* and *g, o* and *u,* and *ö* and *ü* both were written identically with the same letter. The letter *n* could easily be missed at the beginning of a word, as its letter was the same as the extra 'crown' used when a vowel began the word. As for *j*, a sound that did not exist in Uyghur, it was written with the *y* letter at the beginning of a word and with the *c* letter in the mid-dle of a word. Various devices had been invented to resolve some of these ambiguities, but none were used consistently. As a result, the script was easy to write but hard to read, and particularly confusing when writing proper nouns.

5. MONGOLIAN TERMS AND THEIR TRANSLATION

One of the key issues of rendering into English a work from a world which is not (yet) familiar to English speakers is how far to go in translating specific institutional terms and titles. Here I will introduce certain terms and titles whose meaning might not be immediately obvious.

Khan

In Middle Mongolian, the title of supreme sovereignty, corres-ponding to English 'king' or 'emperor', was *qan* or *qa'an*, terms which are the origin of the English 'khan'. In later Mongolian, *qa'an* more or less completely replaced *qan*, which fell out of use. However, it is generally accepted that *qan* and *qa'an* were originally ranked, with a *qa'an* being higher in status than a *qan*. Whether by Chinggis Khan's time there was in fact a strictly drawn distinction between the two when used as a title, such that a *qan* was always subordinate to a *qa'an*, is currently in dispute among scholars; my own position is that there was wide variation in practice, and distinctions between the two titles are mostly conventional, with little political significance.

Thus, in the *Secret History*, the author worked with the following, not entirely consistent, paradigm:

- Pre-Chinggisid Mongol khans, §§1–71: *qa'an*
- Pre-Chinggisid Mongol khans, §§96–177: *qan*
- Pre-Chinggisid non-Mongol khans in Mongolia: *qan*
- Foreign rulers (outside Mongolia): *qan*
- Chinggis: *qa'an*
- Ökodei: *qa'an*.

Meanwhile, the author uses *qan* generally as a common noun meaning 'sovereign, ruler' in the indefinite form *qa*, 'a ruler', or the definite form *qan*, 'the ruler'.

But not only can exceptions be found for most of these categories in the *Secret History* itself, the exceptions seem to follow other paradigms used in sources used by the Secret Historian. And the reason there are such other paradigms is partly related to the fact that the Secret Historian's paradigm appears to have been historically inaccurate: in the author's own lifetime and in most inscriptions of the Mongolian empire afterwards, Chinggis was a *qan*, not a *qa'an*, for example.

Although, as a rule, when an author makes a mistake one should translate that as a mistake, in this case the familiarity of 'khan' in English as a version of the name makes pursuing an incorrect and purely conventional distinction seem pedantic. In line with this reality, I have largely eliminated the *Secret History*'s distinction of the two terms in this translation. *Qa'an* and *qan* as titles are both translated as 'khan'; the term *qa'an* as a common noun is also given as 'khan'. The term *qa(n)* as a common noun is translated throughout as 'ruler' or 'sovereign'.

Qatun and *üjin*: lady and madame

Etymologically associated with khan is the Turco-Mongolian *qatun*, often written in the Persian form as *khatun*. As used in the *Secret History*, however, it designates not just the wives of the khans but also all wives of high-ranking men. It is thus similar to 'lady' in English, and so I have translated it.

Another title of high-ranking women found in the *Secret History* is *üjin*. This word is a borrowing from Chinese *furen*, 'lady', and is found in a wide variety of forms in sources from the Mongol empire. With the *Secret History*'s *üjin* can be compared forms such as *wüšin*, *hüjin* and *fujin*, all attested during the Mongol empire and attempting to deal in different ways with the *f-* sound, which did not normally appear in Middle Mongolian. The variety of forms, as well as their relation to other forms found in Kitan, Jurchen and other languages spoken around Mongolia at the time, shows that the word was still perceived as foreign by Mongolian speakers in the Mongol empire. I have thus translated it with the title 'madame', which in English has a similar meaning as *üjin* and also shares the ongoing phonetic dependence on a neighbouring language of sophisticated urban culture (French in the case of 'madame', Chinese in the case of *üjin*).

Horde

As is discussed above in 'The World of the *Secret History*', the *ordo*, a mobile palace-cum-staff complex, was the centre of Mongolian imperial organization. This term actually became an English word, as 'horde' – but one which has come to have almost the opposite connotation of the Mongolian original. The famous 'Golden Horde', for example, designated one of several such Mongolian imperial or princely headquarters where the inside was richly decorated with gold. The associations it brought up in Mongolian minds were thus much more like those of the 'White House' or 'Kremlin', rather than the vague image of a disorganized mob obsessed with gold that it might connote in English today. Many translators have rendered it as 'palace tent', but this term is both clumsy and misleading, especially as 'tent' and the felt *ger* are quite different levels of structural solidity (see above). I have thus repurposed 'horde' by using it in the original sense of the Mongolian *ordo*.

Ba'atur

The word *ba'atur* or *baatar* in modern Mongolian means in general 'brave man, hero, valiant one'. The term is fairly well known in English, at least among those with some knowledge of Mongolia and the Central Eurasian steppe in general; it is used in familiar names such as Sübe'edei Ba'atur. But it is also a specific institution, involving those on political probation who are given a chance to prove their loyalty to the khan through front-line service. Thus, when Arqai-Qasar commands a unit of 1,000 *ba'atur*s, they are not simply brave men, but specifically brave men from various folk who until recently had been fighting against Chinggis Khan and thus were on probation. The usual practice has been to translate *ba'atur* as 'hero' but leave it untranslated when it is attached to a name as a title, such as Sübe'edei Ba'atur. Given the specific institutional meaning, however, and its relative familiarity, I have chosen to use simply *ba'atur*, with a note explaining it at first appearance.

Tümen

Tümen is the common Mongolian word, borrowed from Turkic, for 'ten thousand'. In the context of the Central Eurasian system of numbering people by households into units nominally of ten, one hundred, one thousand and ten thousand, *tümen* is also used to mean a military and social unit nominally of ten thousand households. Even at the beginning, however, *tümen*s were not normally a full ten thousand; the Mongol army classified *tümen*s into large, medium and small, with 7,000, 5,000 and 3,000 households respectively. And over time, *tümen* soon came to mean simply a large socio-political unit of no exact size. When used in that sense I transcribe it as *tümen*, rather than translate it as 'ten thousand'.

Keśikten

The *keśikten*, literally meaning both 'favoured ones' and 'one on a shift', designated the imperial bodyguard.[121] The Hanlin recension most commonly glosses the term by its function as *huwei*, 'bodyguard'. But from Marco Polo, who actually served in it during Qubilai Khan's time, to the present, historians and others describing the institution have generally just transcribed the Mongolian. Since that is the usual practice of those discussing it, in my translation too I have simply transcribed the term as *kesikten*.

Anda and *nökor*: various forms of friends or comrades

The notions of *anda* and *nökor* have proven difficult to translate. Igor de Rachewiltz translated *anda* as 'sworn friend'; *nökor* as 'companion' or occasionally 'friend'. Cleaves, however, chose just to transcribe *anda*, and translated *nökor* as 'companion'. The concept of *anda* indicates a sworn or contractual relationship that involves exchange of gifts and which then sets up a relationship of ongoing exchange between the two. Precisely because it is a relationship of exchange, two *anda* cannot belong to the same household or lineage. Although it certainly contains a strong element of trust and loyalty, that trust and loyalty is, as in a business partnership, oriented towards the mutual benefit of both sides.[122] Given the distinctive institutional context, I have followed Cleaves and simply transcribed as *anda*.

Nökor adds to the idea of trust and loyalty the common expectation of living together as companions. Given the authoritative structure of Mongolian households, however, friends living with their host in practice became more like trusted vassals. Thus Chinggis Khan says of Jelme, 'Ever since we befriended each other [*nökocekse'er*], [he] has been a thrall of the threshold and property of the portal' (§211). And indeed, the Persians, who borrowed the word *nūkar* from their Mongolian conquerors, used it to mean 'servant; dependant'. In Mongolian, however, *nökor* retained more of its more egalitarian sense and today means 'friend, companion; comrade; husband, spouse'. Claims that the *nökor* formed a legal status like 'housecarl' or 'thane' in Norse and Anglo-Saxon society are overstated. The real equivalent of the housecarl or thane was the *kesikten* of the imperial bodyguard, not *nökor*, and its use in what were obviously servant and master relations (i.e. Jamuqa and his groom Kökecu) was more about expressing affective ideals than about defining a particular class. I have generally translated it as 'friend' ('buddy' would be even better semantically, except for its overly colloquial sound), which has the added benefit of having a verb 'to befriend' which corresponds to the Mongolian verb *nökoce-*.

Aqa and *de'u*: elders, seniors, juniors, youngers

Like many languages, Mongolian has different words for brothers or sisters depending on whether they are older or younger than the speaker or narrative topic of reference. Thus in Middle Mongolian 'big brother' is *aqa* and 'little brother' is *de'u*, 'big sister' is *egeci* and 'little sister' is *döi*. Translators to date have generally used the formal-sounding 'elder brother' and 'younger brother' for *aqa* and *de'u*; I have preferred to use the less wordy and less formal English equivalents of 'big' and 'little' brother or sister.

But in many contexts it is wrong to assume that *aqa* or *de'u* are really 'brothers' at all. Translating *aqa* as 'big brother' or 'elder brother' implies that the sibling relationship and male sex are primary and the age difference is secondary. In fact, in *aqa* the age difference is primary, and the connotation of sibling and male is often secondary or even absent. And even where *aqa* and *de'u* are being used to designate close relatedness, that relatedness is often not specifically sons or daughters of the same father or mother, but membership in a larger genealogical or local community. Thus in many contexts an *aqa* is a 'senior' or an 'elder'; we even know that Tolui's very respected granddaughter was known as Kelmiš-Aqa. *De'u* similarly is primarily about being junior in age, and only secondarily about a sibling relationship and maleness (in fact, in modern Mongolian *de'u* replaced *döi* to become the usual word for younger siblings, male or female). So I translate it in many circumstances as 'junior' or (as an epithet) as 'young', as in 'Young Jamuqa'.

Kö'ut, ökit, küregen: status variations of kinship terms

In Middle Mongolian, family members in the next generation are called *kö'ut*, 'sons', *ökit*, 'daughters', and *küregen*, 'sons-in-law'. That much is simple and easy to translate. Over the course of the *Secret History*, however, the semantic range of these terms shifted as the history's focus changed from a family on the steppe to a khan in the court. By the end of the history, after the great conquests, *kö'ut* is used in ways that can only be translated as 'princes', *ökit* as 'princesses' and *küregen* as 'imperial sons-in-law'.

In certain borderline cases, it is hard to decide the valence; in the story of the capture and release of the Tayici'ut leader Fatty Kiriltuq in §149, *kö'ut*, 'sons', and *de'u*, 'little brothers; junior kinsmen' attempt to rescue their leader. In that passage I have translated them as 'sons' and 'junior kinsmen', but where the same paired *kö'ut de'u* appear in the institutions of Chinggis Khan, 'princes' and 'junior kinsmen' convey the meaning better.

In the opposite direction from its meaning as 'prince', *kö'ut* also carries the sense of child or minor status entirely apart from any familial or blood relation. In this sense it is 'boy', but with the same patronizing or contemptuous status derogation that calling an adult man 'boy' has in caste societies. *Ger-un kö'ut*, 'boys of the *ger*', was the Mongol empire's term for war captives, particularly those employed as craftsmen for their princely masters. In many cases, the *Secret History* uses *kö'ut* where 'son' is not the meaning, but rather 'boy' – in the sense of 'boy of the *ger*', that is, a slave or servant. Other terms used this way in the *Secret History* include *jala'u*, 'young man', and *de'u*, 'junior'.

Noyan: commander or captain

Noyan (plural *noyat*) is translated sometimes as 'commander', sometimes as 'captain'. When a *noyan* is ruling a separate people, or is being treated as one of the leading officers operating with considerable autonomy under a khan, then I translate it as 'commander'. When a *noyan* is being described as part of a hierarchy, down to the captains of ten, I translate it as 'captain'.

Since the units in the decimal hierarchy were as much peace-time administrative units as wartime military units, a *noyan* also had civilian functions; Chinese sources translate it as 'official' (*guan*). The equivalent in Turkic is *beg* and in Persian and Arabic sources it is *amir*, anglicized as 'emir'. Like *noyan*, both these titles are fairly fluid, covering a range of ranks from supreme commander to the captain of a company.

People, folk, fellows and minions

Mongolian contains several words to designate human beings in the singular or plural, without specification of male or female. *Kü'u(n)* does not distinguish status and can be well translated as 'person' or even just elided as '(some)one who . . .'. *Haran* by contrast does contain something of the sense of an ordinary or a lower-status person – in the plural in modern Mongolian as *ard*, it became the word for 'the people' as opposed to the ruling classes. I thus translate it sometimes as 'fellow', where the idea of an 'ordinary guy' seems dominant, sometimes as 'commoner' or 'common man' in legal contexts, and sometimes as 'minion' where a strong sense of class hierarchy is at play. In all these senses it carries a connotation of being the head of a taxpaying family and hence a connotation of a man of 'lower-middle-class' status. (The classically masculine word *ere* is translated sometimes as 'man' but more often as 'real man'.)

The word *irge(n)*, which in modern Mongolian means 'citizen; (legal) subject', in Middle Mongolian was a purely collective noun referring to the common people of a given place or political formation in a mass. As such, it was commonly modified explicitly or implicitly by a political or an ethnic name: Tangut, Kitat ('Chinese'), Sart, Tatar, Merkit, Kereyit, Naiman. Previous English translators like Cleaves and Onon followed the Chinese glosses in the Hanlin recension, in which it is translated as *baixing*, 'commoners; common people', to translate it most often as 'people'.

Translating both the strongly collective *irge(n)* and the individual *kü'u(n)* as 'people' obscures a crucial nuance of the Mongolian. Previous translations avoided this problem by rendering most of the non-collective plurals simply as 'men', but this creates a different inaccuracy in assuming that all the individual *kü'u* or people being mentioned were male.[123] Evidently sensing the insufficiently collective nature of 'people', de Rachewiltz sometimes translated irgen as 'tribe' or 'tribesmen', albeit only in contexts of people in Mongolia. Such a division into 'tribal' and 'non-tribal' societies is, however, problematic in itself and certainly not found in the text.[124] I have thus rendered *irgen* most often with the somewhat archaic English 'folk', which has a virtually identical set of meanings and strongly emphasizes the collectivity.

Ulus or kingdom

Another slightly unfamiliar translation is 'kingdom' for *ulus*. *Ulus* (modern *uls*) means 'country; state; nation; people' in modern Mongolian and is glossed in the Hanlin recension sometimes as *guo*, 'state; dynasty; empire' and sometimes as *baixing*, 'commoners; common people'. These meanings derive from the fundamental signification of a people, no matter how small, under a single ruler. From that basic meaning, which centred on people, came the modern meanings that stressed the 'single ruler' aspect, and thus came to mean the 'state' as an apparatus. The other aspect, which stressed the place where the people lived, was the origin of the modern meaning as 'country'.

Previous translators have followed the Chinese to render it as 'nation' or 'people'. 'Nation' tends to indicate only a large and fully sovereign collectivity, while 'people' suffers from imprecision and minimizes the top-down nature of the community. I have found that with a little adjustment of one's expectations to the context, 'kingdom' usually works perfectly. As has been noted about medieval Europe as well, the idea that kingdoms must be vast, country-sized entities is a modern one.[125] The *ulus* of the *Secret History* may be the whole Mongol empire, or it may be a few thousand people under the dominion of a petty ruler. An *ulus* may also be nested within another *ulus*; thus the Mongol empire as a whole is an *ulus*, but each of Chinggis Khan's sons and nephews themselves rules a little *ulus* within the empire as a whole.[126]

In the original Mongolian, such *ulus* are clearly mobile. As it was composed of a mobile pastoralist people, the *ulus*/kingdom can be on the move – thus we read that 'Aġucu Ba'atur . . . set his *ulus* in motion' in flight from Chinggis Khan. One could speak of 'kingdoms' being set in motion, but in this and similar cases the violence to usual English-language expectations is a little too severe and I have translated it instead as 'set his folk in motion'. Yet it should be remembered that the issue is not so much one of the nuance of language, but of the difference of ecological and political context. A Mongolian *ulus* or kingdom relied on subject people who paid regular taxes and did military service as nomads. The term *irge(n) orġo*, 'subject households', is a binome that refers precisely to such people, and is used in the *Secret History* for taxpaying subjects among both Kereyit and Merkit pastoralists as well as the peasants of China and Baghdad.[127] But because of the mobility of their pastoralist economic base, khans in Mongolia could have their taxpaying herders seized and deported, together with all their herds and homes and productive equipment, by hostile powers in a way that rulers of farming subjects did not have to worry about.

NOTES

Introduction

1. 'Chinggis Khan' is how his name is pronounced in Mongolia today, rather than 'Genghis'. This imperial name is of unclear etymology, but may be related either to Turkic *Teng'iz,* 'Sea' or to *cing'iz,* 'hard; fierce'. Whatever the etymology, Persian writers wrote his name as Chingiz. However, Persian frequently omits diacriticals, such as the extra dots that distinguish *ch-* from *j-,* and leaves the vowels unmarked. The scholars of the eighteenth century through whom Gibbon, Voltaire and other Europeans of the Enlightenment first learned about the conqueror read his name as Jengiz (with the g hard as in 'gift'). This spelling went through various changes to settle into 'Genghis' in English. How the first *g-* came to be pronounced hard in English when an 'h' was carefully added to make the second 'g' hard and the first soft is a philological mystery.

2. Tome I, containing the history of the Mongol empire up to Rashiduddin's time, has been completely translated by Wheeler Thackston.

3. This chapter is translated in Atwood 2017/18.

4. For the story of the recovery of the text, see the Afterword, 'The Transmission and Translation of the *Secret History*', and Figure 4, 'History of the Text'.

5. Today modern Mongolian *gers* have wooden doors, but in the time of the Mongol empire the doors were always made of hanging felt.

6. Atwood and Struve, p. 99; for John of Plano Carpini's account, see Dawson, p. 8.

7. Gibb, pp. 472–3.

8. William of Rubruck (Jackson and Morgan, p. 73); Gibb, p. 472; Dawson, p. 8. One way to measure the width of the *gers* is by the number of draft animals that pulled the wagons on which they were mounted. John of Plano Carpini gives a range of one to four or more. Ibn Battutah says two or more than two, while William of Rubruck mentions only the maximum case of a *ger* he saw drawn by twenty-two oxen.

9. Jackson and Morgan, pp. 74–5.

10. Ibid., pp. 177–8.

11. Gibb, p. 473.

12. Jackson and Morgan, p. 73.

13. Dunnell, West and Yang, p. 33.

14. Thus, one appears as a 'wool wagon' (*nungġasu-tu tergen*) in §§85–6 and another as a 'locker wagon' (*co'orġa-tai tergen*) in §124.

15. See Andrews. The early-thirteenth-century illuminated Radziwiłł Chronicle, surviving today in a copy from the 1490s, already shows 'Polovtsi' (that is, Qïpchaq) pastoralists in a *ger* mounted on a *qasaq* cart; see *Radzivilovskaia letopis'*, ed. M. V. Kukushkina and O. P. Likhacheva (St Petersburg and Moscow: Glagol and Iskusstvo, 1994), vol. 1, plate 237 ob., 242 ob., and vol. 2, pp. 247, 253.

16. Dawson, p. 18; Jackson and Morgan, p. 74.

17. See §§6, 54, 64.

18. Bruun, pp. 92–5.

19. Jackson and Morgan, p. 74; Gibb, p. 486. The entourages of non-imperial commanders were on the same model, but of course much smaller. Ibn Battutah, in Gibb, p. 480, described

how one lady, the wife of a commander, dwelled in a 'wagon [that] was covered with rich blue woollen cloth . . . Behind her were a number of wagons in which were girls belonging to her suite.'

20. Atwood and Struve, p. 97.

21. Jackson and Morgan, p. 131 (with 'Batu' for Rubruck's 'Baatu'). Three or four leagues is about four to five and a half miles – considering the difficulty of measuring, William of Rubruck's estimate of the size of Batu's camp is remarkably similar to Peng Daya's estimate of five by two and a half miles.

22. Gibb, p. 482.

23. Atwood and Struve, p. 97.

24. See the description of John of Plano Carpini, who saw it, Dawson, pp. 62–3.

25. John of Plano Carpini calls the Yellow Horde the largest of them, Dawson, p. 5; see also the description of Benedict the Pole on p. 82.

26. Jackson and Morgan, p. 131. The 'Golden Pavilion' described by Ibn Battutah, Gibb, pp. 483–4, may be the very same one seen by William of Rubruck. It may also be the *cacir* or cotton pavilion tent mentioned in §275 as the location of the great western campaign's victory celebration.

27. Atwood and Struve, p. 99.

28. William of Rubruck had his first interview with Möngke Khan while he was in one of his ladies' *ger*; see Jackson and Morgan, pp. 177–8. On the custom of choosing a lady to stay with, see Gibb, p. 483.

29. For food in the time of the Mongol empire, Paul Buell and Eugene Anderson's study of the fourteenth-century Chinese dietetic work, incorporating many Mongolian, Turkic and Persian recipes, is fundamental. See *A Soup for the Qan*, pp. 87–105.

30. See Atwood and Struve, pp. 92, 99–100, 118–19; Dawson, pp. 62, 63; Jackson and Morgan, pp. 75–85; Gibb, p. 477.

31. See the Tatar feast at which Yisukei was poisoned (§67), the brawl with the Yörkin (§§130–32) and the quarrel between Chinggis Khan's grandsons celebrating their victories in eastern Europe (§275).

32. Jackson and Morgan, pp. 81–2; see also Atwood and Struve, pp. 118–19.

33. Jackson and Morgan, p. 79.

34. Dawson, p. 17; Atwood and Struve, p. 100. A Chinese envoy said: 'I lived in the steppe for more than a month and never

observed the Tatars killing a cow for food' (Atwood and Struve, p. 100), but in §214 we see Jedei and Jelme killing a black ox for food behind the *ger*.

35. On millet, see Atwood and Struve, p. 83; Dawson, pp. 17, 56, 57–8; Jackson and Morgan, pp. 84, 110, 141, 221; Gibb, p. 474.

36. Juvaini/Boyle, p. 27.

37. Ibid., pp. 27–8.

38. See §272.

39. The concept of 'Primary History' is that of David Noel Freedman; see a recent survey by Richard S. Briggs, 'Reading the Historical Books as Part of the Primary History', in Brad E. Kelle and Brent A. Strawn (eds), *The Oxford Handbook of the Historical Books of the Hebrew Bible* (New York: Oxford University Press, 2020), DOI: 10.1093/oxfordhb/9780190261160.013.22). 'Primary History' contrasts with the 'Secondary History' of I and II Chronicles. In Jewish Bibles, the 'Primary History' comprises the *Torah* and 'Former Prophets' (*Nevi'im Rishonim*). In Christian Bibles, it comprises the books from Genesis to II Kings, but without Ruth.

40. On this evolutionary sequence, see (among many examples) Marshall D. Sahlins, 'The Segmentary Lineage: An Organization of Predatory Expansion', *American Anthropologist*, new series, vol. 63, no. 2, part 1 (1961), pp. 322–45. The pervasive influence of the Bible, meaning here the Primary History, on the origins of social-evolutionary thought is a major theme of Margaret T. Hodgen's *Early Anthropology in the Sixteenth and Seventeenth Centuries* (Philadelphia: University of Pennsylvania Press, 1964), e.g. pp. 222ff., 436ff.

41. The 'Tatars' of the *Secret History* are to be clearly distinguished from the 'Tatars' of foreign writers on the Mongol empire, and from the 'Tatars' of Russia from the sixteenth century on. In the twelfth century, before Chinggis Khan's unification of Mongolia, the term 'Tatar' was used in China and the Islamic world to designate *all* the Mongolian-speaking nomads. Thus, to outside observers around 1175, Mongols, Merkit and Kereyit were all just different sorts of Tatars. When Chinggis Khan unified the peoples of the Mongolian plateau he imposed the name 'Mongol' on the whole empire and discouraged the use of the word 'Tatar'. Chinese, Arabs and Slavs continued to call all Mongols 'Tatars', however. Thus, when the tsars of Moscow conquered the remnants of the Golden Horde and built the Russian empire,

they called all the subjects of the Horde 'Tatars'. By this time, the mid-sixteenth century, the people of the fragmented Golden Horde had become Muslim and Turkic-speaking and included many farmers and urbanites. Even so, these people of Kazan, Astrakhan, western Siberia, Crimea and the steppes in between were still called 'Tatars' by their Russian rulers, a name they eventually came to use for themselves. Thus, when the new rulers of Soviet Russia designated nationalities and autonomous republics after 1917, they naturally used the name 'Tatar' for the Muslim, Turkic-speaking farmers and urbanites of the republic of Tatarstan, centred on Kazan. Culturally and genetically, however, the inhabitants of this republic see themselves mostly as descendants of the *Secret History*'s (Volga) Bulgars (§§262, 270, 274) and have no special connection to the *Secret History*'s Tatars.

42. Classic authorities in this perspective are Boris Ya. Vladimirtsov and Elizabeth Bacon. See Boris Ya. Vladimirtsov, trans. Michel Carsow, *Le régime social des Mongols: le féodalisme nomade* (Paris: Adrien-Maisonneuve, 1948), and Elizabeth E. Bacon, *Obok: A Study of Social Structure in Eurasia* (New York: Wenner-Gren Foundation for Anthropological Research, 1958).

43. *Yuanshi*, p. 120.2962; cf. Atwood 2012, pp. 29–31; Atwood 2015b, pp. 167–70.

44. This word is cognate to Middle Mongolian *te'u-*, meaning 'to pick up scattered objects, to gather; to collect'.

45. For the details of this winning over the Jüin and breaking with the Jin dynasty, see the citation from the *Yuanshi* translated in Atwood 2017/18, p. 23, and the less official sources translated in Atwood and Struve, pp. 51, 63–4 and 84–5.

46. Shi Jinbo, pp. 17–18.

47. Dunnell 1992, p. 104.

48. This Mongolian metaphor is clearly the source for the Persian historian Juvaini's description of the Ossetian city of Magas in the Caucasus Mountains: 'they ... conquered ... as far as the city of Magas, the inhabitants of which were as numerous as ants or locusts, while its environs were entangled with woods and forests such that even a serpent could not penetrate them' (Juvaini/Boyle, p. 269).

49. See Atwood and Struve, pp. 12–13.

50. Nesawi/Houdas, p. 137.

51. However, the absence of references to the many campaigns in Manchuria and Korea after 1214, except for one very brief, quite

possibly interpolated, reference in §274, would argue against that possibility.

52. This word, probably of Hunnic ('Xiongnu' or Huna) origin, was borrowed into Turkic as *Tängri* and Mongolian as *Tenggeri*. Uyghur scribes wrote the word in an archaic orthography which omitted most vowels, thus spelling it as *Tngri*. This orthography was passed on to Mongolian scribes unchanged. The modern Mongolian pronunciation is *Tenger*.

53. Atwood and Struve, p. 109.

54. Dawson, p. 9.

55. Polo/Cliff, p. 72. The implicit identification of Heaven with the Christian God may seem a misunderstanding, but it is found consistently in Mongolian court translation practices and vocabularies. The Mongols evidently believed that the Heaven who gave Chinggis Khan his throne was not a uniquely Mongolian god, but rather the same supreme God of all the great literate religions around them: Christianity, Buddhism, Islam and Daoism.

56. See Tekin, pp. 263, 265, 288 for the translation, and pp. 232, 233, 252 for the Old Turkic text.

57. Ibid., p. 261 (translation) and p. 231 (text).

58. In §245, 'brown earth' or *dayir etugen* is found; *dayir* is exactly the cognate of *yaġïz*, 'brown', in the 'brown earth' phrase of the Turkic inscriptions.

59. Jackson and Morgan, p. 170; cf. p. 125.

60. It is likely that these rituals long pre-dated Chinggis Khan's time, and the attribution to him is only the first example of the later tendency in Mongolian texts to attribute all ritual activity to the charter example of Chinggis Khan and his family.

61. See Kesigtoġtaqu and Ma.

62. *Darqan* (plural *darqat*) refers to those granted special freedoms in return for unusually meritorious service to the imperial lineage. See §219 for a description of these 'free rights'.

63. *Yuanshi*, p. 77. The Court of Burnt Food was a court in Qubilai Khan's palace in Daidu (modern Beijing); Xiong Mengxiang, p. 115. I would like to thank Eiren Shea for her assistance with the cloth names.

64. See John of Plano Carpini (Dawson, p. 9) and William of Rubruck (Jackson and Morgan, pp. 75–6). The felt image corresponding to the master is called Naciġai; see Polo/Cliff, p. 72.

65. John of Plano Carpini (Dawson, p. 9) and William of Rubruck (Jackson and Morgan, pp. 156, 240).

66. William of Rubruck (Jackson and Morgan, p. 156).
67. *Yuanshi*, p. 3.43; William of Rubruck (Jackson and Morgan, pp. 240–41).
68. See, for example, William of Rubruck's jaded account (Jackson and Morgan, pp. 242–5).
69. See, for example, Möngke Khan's denunciation of Oġul-Qayimiš, Güyük's wife, as 'the worst of witches' (Jackson and Morgan, p. 249). The Persian historian Juvaini, writing in the late 1250s, and reflecting the tone at Möngke's court, where he had served, says Güyük's wife spent her time 'closeted with the *qam* carrying out their fantasies and absurdities' (Juvaini/Boyle, p. 265). *Qam* was the Turkic equivalent of Mongolian *bö'e*, 'shaman'.
70. These terms are all in fact cognate from one root.
71. See Molnár and Boldbaatar.
72. See Jackson and Morgan, p. 245.
73. Juvaini/Boyle, p. 59.
74. [Jūzjānī]/Raverty, pp. 1077–9.
75. Juvaini/Boyle, p. 505.
76. *Yuanshi*, p. 3.46.
77. The arguments given here are presented at greater length in Atwood 2007. For a consideration of other dates that have been proposed, particularly 1264 or 1228, see Appendix A.
78. Although the Chinese annals only tell us about the role of Confucian liturgists, comparison with later instances of imperial worship practices makes it virtually certain that native Mongolian *beki* (priest-shamans) and East Syriac Christian priests played an equally, if not more, prominent role in this worship programme.
79. See Atwood 2019/20, pp. 43–4 n. 146.
80. The meaning of Śiki is uncertain. It may be short for *śiki quru'u*, 'pinky finger'. However, Qutuġu Noyan seems to be referred to by the Persian historian Juvaini sometimes as Tekecuk; or at least, Tekecuk seems to be doing in the campaign in Central Asia exactly what Qutuġu Noyan is elsewhere said to do (Juvaini/Boyle, pp. 132–3, 405, 464–5). Tekecuk itself is a diminutive of 'billy goat' in Turkic, and *śiki* or *śikiken* ('little *śiki*'), as it appears, might be a Mongolian dialectal form of the same word.
81. See Ratchnevsky 1993.
82. Rashiduddin/Thackston, p. 34.
83. Ibid., pp. 33, 97.
84. Ibid., pp. 73–4, 116.

85. Ibid., p. 33.

86. Of course, such a nickname would be most likely to be used by someone *older* than Śiki Qutuġu – a grandmother, for example. Chronologically, however, the author must have been younger than him, in which case a grandchild (or one in that generation) is more plausible than one in the child's generation.

87. Bakhtin, pp. 84ff.

88. *Yuanshi*, p. 3.54.

89. *Yuanshi*, p. 181.4179, cf. p. 35.784.

90. This ruling class is carefully defined in §269: the descendants of Chinggis Khan and his brothers, both male and female, the wives of the princes and husbands of the princesses, and the commanders of a thousand and above. Chinese and European envoys both remark on non-Mongols being barred from all major decision-making sessions. See Atwood and Struve, pp. 107–8, and Dawson, p. 62.

91. Hsiao, p. 74.

92. This history compiled under Qubilai Khan was known as the 'Authentic Chronicle of Chinggis Khan' (sometimes translated as the 'Veritable Record'). The text translated into Chinese is preserved as part of the *Campaigns of Chinggis Khan (Shengwu qinzheng lu)* and translated into Persian as the basis for Rashiduddin's history of Chinggis Khan in his *Compendium of Chronicles*.

93. See the translation of lines 46–7 in Cleaves 1949.

94. Rashiduddin/Thackston, p. 13, with modifications following Allsen 2001, p. 100.

95. Okada, p. 67.

96. de Rachewiltz 2004, p. xxvi.

97. See the essay 'The Poet in the Age of Prose' in Erich Heller's *In the Age of Prose: Literary and Philosophical Essays* (Cambridge: Cambridge University Press, 1984).

98. Paul Kahn's *The Secret History of the Mongols: The Origin of Chingis Khan*. These speculations were connected with the 1228 theory of the *Secret History*'s original date, one which is untenable for many reasons. See Appendix A.

99. See, for example, Daniel Prior's translation of Saghïmbay's epic in the Manas cycle, *The Memorial Feast for Kökötöy Khan*.

100. See Birtalan.

101. See Chadwick and Zhirmunsky, pp. 312–14. For a translation of a major Mongolian epic, that of Khan Kharangui, see Hangin et al., 1989.

102. On epic time and classical exteriority, see Bakhtin, pp. 13–19, 133–40, and Auerbach, pp. 13–23.

103. See Snorri Sturluson, trans. Magnus Magnusson and Hermann Pálsson, *King Harald's Saga: Harald Hardradi of Norway* (Harmondsworth: Penguin, 1966), p. 154. The battle in question is the Battle of Stamford Bridge in 1066.

104. Robert Kellogg, 'Introduction', in *The Sagas of the Icelanders: A Selection* (New York: Penguin Books, 2001), p. xxvi.

105. Ibid., pp. xxvii–xxxi. The most dramatic such confirmation has been the excavations of the remains of 'Leif's Camp', previously known only from the *Vinland Sagas*, at the site of L'Anse aux Meadows in Newfoundland. See ibid., pp. 626–35.

106. Mark Edward Lewis, *The Early Chinese Empires: Qin and Han* (Cambridge, Mass.: Harvard University Press, 2007), p. 216.

107. Auerbach, pp. 17–18.

108. Fornara, p. 155.

109. This three-fold understanding of history as involving event, experience and myth comes from Paul A. Cohen's *History in Three Keys: The Boxers as Event, Experience, and Myth* (New York: Columbia University Press, 1997).

110. de Rachewiltz 2004, p. lxii.

111. Atwood 2008/9.

112. On the genealogies of the Mongol empire and their use by the Secret Historian, see Atwood 2012.

113. On the 'Indictment Narratives' and their use by the Secret Historian, see Atwood 2017a.

114. Historically, there were at least two battles, and it is possible the 'splitters' were right and there were three different battles.

115. The C Source and the S Source were two important Mongolian sources on Chinggis Khan's western expedition distinguished by their spelling of the Iranian city Nishapur as Nicabur vs Nišabur.

116. In §280, for example, it looks like a lengthy passage about the staffing of the post-roads (*jam*) was omitted, leaving only the introductory sentence and the almost identical concluding sentence. And in §260, two phrases both speak about the khan being appeased in slightly different wording. From the rest of the section it appears that two different decrees were stitched together and that, in stitching them together, the historian repeated the topic sentence that showed how they fit together.

117. See, for example, the couplet about the clouds clearing and ice melting in the Uyghur address to Chinggis Khan, which is also

found in a Chinese biography of Botu, one of Chinggis Khan's sons-in-law. Likewise, the description of a forest so deeply entangled that a glutted snake could not slither into it is also used by the Persian historian Juvaini to describe a forest being attacked by Mongol armies in the Caucasus. In both cases, the passages in the Chinese or Persian histories were obviously translated from the Mongolian.

118. As a comparison with European languages, one could say that the relation of Middle Mongolian with Kitan and Uyghur Turkic is somewhat like the relationship of English with German and French, respectively. These Asian languages are, however, rather less alike than the European ones.

119. See [Jūzjānī] /Raverty, pp. 1113–14.

120. Polo/Cliff, p. 62.

121. In Middle Mongolian this would actually be *keśik-ten*, with the suffix-*ten* being written separately. I have simplified the spelling to make it a single word.

122. In recent centuries, the term *anda* included partnerships between Ewenki or Orochen hunters and Daur Mongolian farmers in Manchuria, with the Daur Mongolian farmer supplying the muskets and ammunition and the Ewenki or Orochen hunter supplying the skills and labour.

123. Thus, in §240, Cleaves, de Rachewiltz and Onon all translated both *kü'u* and *ere* as 'man' when actually the text distinguishes the tasks assigned to the 'people' (*kü'u*) and to the 'men' (*ere*). These translations thus obscure the fact that, as we know from other sources, whole households participated in distant campaigns. Evidently the commander Dörbei the Fierce is assigning certain tasks to all adults in the camp, including women, while reserving others to men. This same contrast of people in the army (including noncombatants) vs fighting men is at work in §193, where 'every living soul' (*amitu ele kü'un tutum*) lights the fires, five for each fighting man (*ere-yin tabun anggida*). Here *kü'un*, 'person', or 'soul' contrasts directly with *ere*, 'male; real man', implicitly designating those fighting men numbered into military units.

124. On the manufacturing of 'tribes' and 'tribalism' by scholarly translations and research on Central Eurasian nomadic societies, see David Sneath's *The Headless State*. In reality, the complete absence of 'tribes' and tribal terminology in the *Secret History* is demonstrated in Atwood 2015a.

125. See, for example, Christian Raffensperger, *The Kingdom of Rus'* (Kalamazoo, Mich. and Bradford: Arc Humanities Press, 2017).

126. See §§269–70, where Ökodei Khan speaks of the 'kingdom of the centre' (*ğool-un ulus*) and distinguishes those 'princes who govern a kingdom' (*ulus medekün kö'ut*) within the empire and those who do not.

127. See §§150, 162–3 and 177 for the Kereyit, §197 for the Merkit, and §§260 and 272 for Baghdad and China.

Note on Spellings and Pronunciation

In this translation I use a simplified spelling of the Middle Mongolian, readable for non-specialists, but preserving all the information needed for specialists.

The vowels may be pronounced as follows:

A: as in 'father';

E: as in 'bed';

I: like *ea* as in 'beat' when stressed (first syllable), like *i* as in 'bit' when unstressed (second syllable on);

O: like the *aw* as in 'awesome';

U: like the *o* as in 'toll';

Ö: like the *oe* in German 'Goethe';

Ü: like the *oo* in 'tool'.

(These rough equivalences are based on American, rather than British, English.)

Modern Mongolian distinguishes short and long vowels (thus *zun*, 'summer', vs *zuun*, 'one hundred'). In Middle Mongolian, however, this distinction was not yet fully formed.

Most of the consonants are roughly as in English, although it should be noted that the *g* is always hard, and the *r* is rolled, as in Italian.

The following letters may need some explanation:

C: This letter was pronounced at the time of the Mongol empire, in Middle Mongolian, like English *ch* as in 'chalk'. In modern Mongolian this pronunciation is retained when followed by *i*. In front of other vowels, however, it becomes like the *ts* in English 'cat's eyes'. Thus, *Cinggis* is pronounced 'CHING-gihs' (with the second *g* hard) but *Caġadai* is pronounced 'Tsah-GHAH-day'.

Ġ: The ġ with a dot represents a sound like hard g but further back in the throat, similar to q (see below), but lightly voiced and without the aspiration. In between vowels it can be pronounced as a spirant, somewhat like the uvular ŕ of French, German or Hebrew.

J: In Middle Mongolian this is pronounced like English j as in 'jam'. In modern Mongolian this pronunciation is retained when followed by i. In front of other vowels, however, it becomes like the ds in English 'bird's eyes'. Thus Borjigin is pronounced 'BORE-jih-gin' (with the g hard and the r trilled), but Jelme is pronounced 'DZELL-meh'.

Q: This sound was pronounced in Middle Mongolian like a k, but further back in the throat. It corresponds to and is similar to the k of words like Kara Kuş in Turkish, although further back in the throat. In modern Mongolian it is pronounced more like the ch in German 'Bach' or Scottish 'loch'.

Ś and Š: These two sounds were written differently, and probably differed slightly in Middle Mongolian. They are identical in modern Mongolian, however, and may be pronounced like English sh as in 'shaggy'; ś is used before i and š in other positions and in non-Mongolian words.

Stress is generally on the first syllable.

The apostrophe (') represents a silent g or ġ, as found in the written Mongolian. When it separates two different vowels, the two vowels can be read as a diphthong and stressed; thus, Ca'ujin is pronounced roughly 'CHOW-jihn' in Middle Mongolian or 'TSOW-jin' in modern Mongolian. When it separates the same vowel that vowel becomes long, which in English can be represented by stress: thus Qada'an may be pronounced roughly 'Kah-DAHN'. The occasional ā can also be pronounced as a stressed vowel, thus Caġān may be pronounced 'Tsah-GHAHN'.

Mongolian, like many languages of northern Eurasia, is characterized by vowel harmony. In such a system vowels are divided into two or more classes, and each word, along with its case endings, can contain vowels of only one class. This class is determined by the first vowel in the word. Thus, once the first vowel is set, the possibilities for the later vowels are restricted.

In the Middle Mongolian system there are two classes and one neutral vowel:

'Masculine': A, O, U

'Feminine': E, Ö, Ü

Generally 'feminine' but can also be found in 'masculine' words: I.

Since they belong to different classes, the distinction between o and u and ö and ü thus needs to be marked only in the first syllable. The u in Temujin is necessarily a ü because it follows an e, while the u in Jamuqa is necessarily a u because it follows an a. Following the lead of the Mongolian script, after the first syllable I have thus used the single form without the umlauts for either.

Names in Middle Mongolian consisted of one or sometimes two meaningful elements. Titles or epithets were also frequently attached to names. To separate out such attached titles from multiple elements in a single name, I link actual name elements by a hyphen, but do not link titles to names. Thus 'Sübe'edei Ba'atur' and 'Ja'a Gambo' consist of a single-element name (Sübe'edei, Ja'a) followed by a title (Ba'atur, Gambo). However, 'Sorġan-Śira' and 'Erke-Qara' are each a single name formed of two elements ('Pockmark-Yellow' and 'Wilful-Black').

I make a few exceptions to the above rules. The first is for the great central figure; rather than the traditional English 'Genghis' or Cinggis, as one would expect from my system, I give his name as Chinggis, as is currently the overwhelmingly favoured spelling in English-language publications by Mongolians.

Second, for those rivers, mountains and other physical features whose name is still the same today (save for the usual gradual phonetic changes), I have used the modern forms, as can be found in atlases. Thus in place of Keluren, Qanġġai and Barġujin, I spell Kherlen, Khangai and Barguzin.

Third, the Uyghur-Mongolian script was also used for writing Uyghur Turkic in the Mongol empire, and such Turkic spellings for persons and places in the western part of the empire are common in the *Secret History*. The phonology and orthography of the script as used for Turkic languages differed slightly from that used by Mongolian; where such names clearly reflect Turkic features, I follow that orthography. Thus I write Qïzil-Baš, rather than following the Mongolian, which has no z and vacillates between Kisil-Baš and Kijil-Baš. The special 'back' i, written as ï and corresponding to the dotless ı in modern Turkish, is pronounced something like the 'oo' in English 'look'. Since the distinction of i and ï follows vowel harmony, it only needs to be marked in the first syllable.

Finally, where the *Secret History* mentions non-Mongolian persons or places, I have tried my best to preserve both familiarity and the impression of the Mongolian. In general, for place names I have tried to use familiar English names that are, however distantly, cognates to the Mongolian – where no such cognate term exists I have preferred to use the Mongolian. Thus Mongolian *Erdiš*, *Tunggon*, *Semizkent* and *Bajigit* are cognates of the more familiar English 'Irtysh', 'Tongguan', 'Samarkand' and 'Bashkir' and I have used those terms. In some cases, however, the Mongolian uses a special Mongolian term. For example, while China's Tongguan Pass is written Tunggon in Mongolian, Juyongguan Pass is written as Cabciyal, that is 'Canyon'. In that case, rather than confuse the reader with a new Mongolian term, which no longer exists anyway, I simply translate Cabciyal as 'the Canyon'. Similarly, with Altan Khan I follow Marco Polo's lead, who called him *Roi d'or* or 'Golden King', and call him the 'Golden Khan'.[1] For *Kitat*, however, I have made a concession to familiarity in using the non-cognate and somewhat inexact 'Chinese', while for *Qara-Kitat*, literally 'Black Kitans', I have followed usual practice and used either 'Qara-Khitai' for those in Central Asia or 'Kitans' for those in Inner Mongolia.

NOTE

1.   See Polo/Cliff, pp. 143–5.

Note on Chapter,
Sub-chapter and Section Divisions

The original editors of the Hanlin recension divided the work into twelve *juan*, and further into 282 small sections. The 282 section numbers have been universally adopted by scholars and readers as the most convenient way to cite quotations from the text; these section numbers are found in the margins of the text and referred to in citations with this symbol: §.

Previous translators have followed the *juan* divisions in the Hanlin recension. This division is based, however, purely on length and does not give any sense of the narrative flow. I have preferred, therefore, to divide the work into eight chapters and forty-four sub-chapters, all with new titles supplied to orient the reader as to the storyline.

Figures

GENEALOGY: GREY WOLF TO BODONCAR

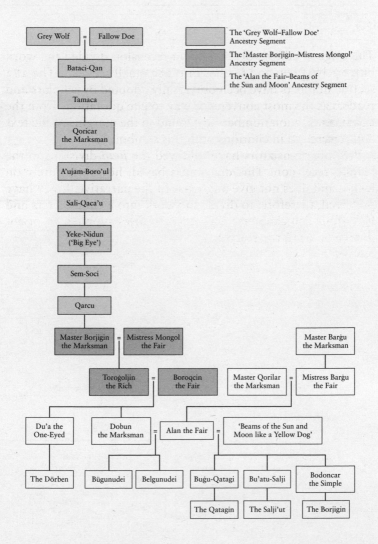

GENEALOGY:
ALAN THE FAIR TO CHINGGIS KHAN

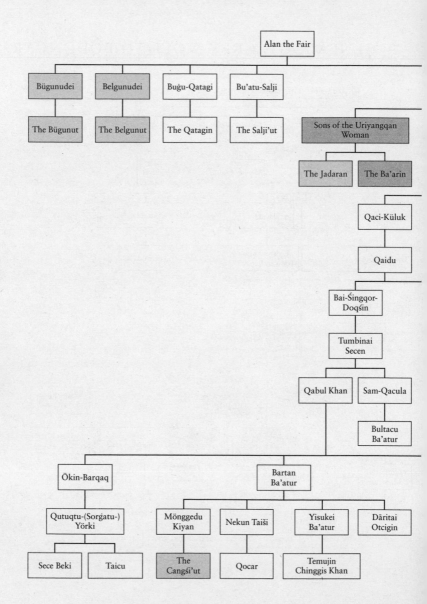

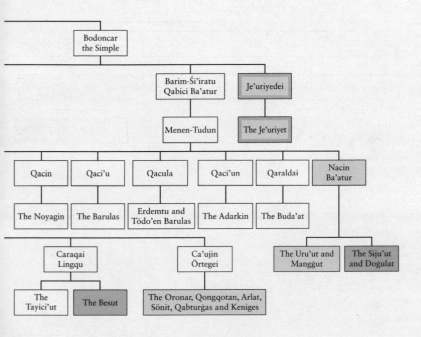

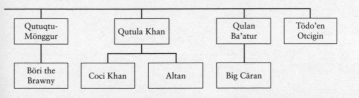

Light grey: of lower-ranked or disputed paternity
Dark grey: of lower-ranked maternity

GENEALOGY: THE IMPERIAL FAMILY

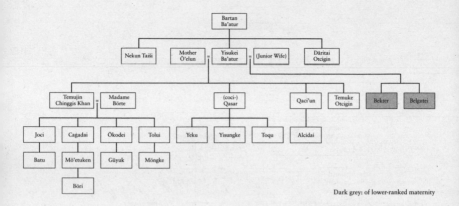

Dark grey: of lower-ranked maternity

HISTORY OF THE TEXT

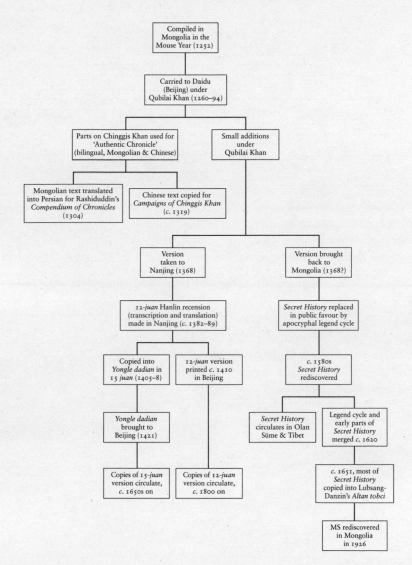

Compiled in Mongolia in the Mouse Year (1252)

Carried to Daidu (Beijing) under Qubilai Khan (1260–94)

Parts on Chinggis Khan used for 'Authentic Chronicle' (bilingual, Mongolian & Chinese)

Small additions under Qubilai Khan

Mongolian text translated into Persian for Rashiduddin's *Compendium of Chronicles* (1304)

Chinese text copied for *Campaigns of Chinggis Khan* (c. 1319)

Version taken to Nanjing (1368)

Version brought back to Mongolia (1368?)

12-*juan* Hanlin recension (transcription and translation) made in Nanjing (c. 1382–89)

Secret History replaced in public favour by apocryphal legend cycle

Copied into *Yongle dadian* in 15 *juan* (1405–8)

12-*juan* version printed c. 1410 in Beijing

c. 1580s *Secret History* rediscovered

Yongle dadian brought to Beijing (1421)

Secret History circulates in Olan Süme & Tibet

Legend cycle and early parts of *Secret History* merged c. 1620

Copies of 15-*juan* version circulate, c. 1650s on

Copies of 12-*juan* version circulate, c. 1800 on

c. 1651, most of *Secret History* copied into Lubsang-Danzin's *Altan tobci*

MS rediscovered in Mongolia in 1926

Maps

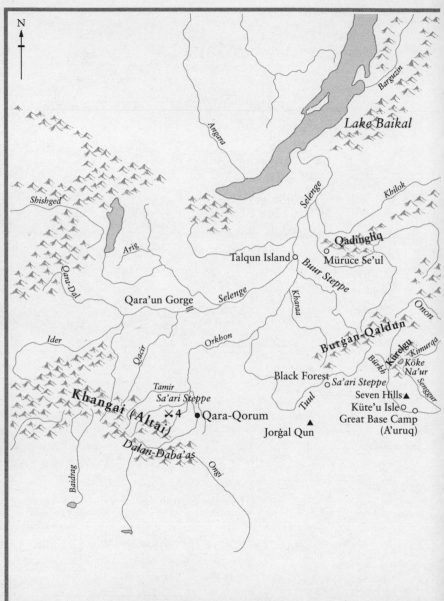

The Mongolian Heartland during the Childhood of Chinggis Khan

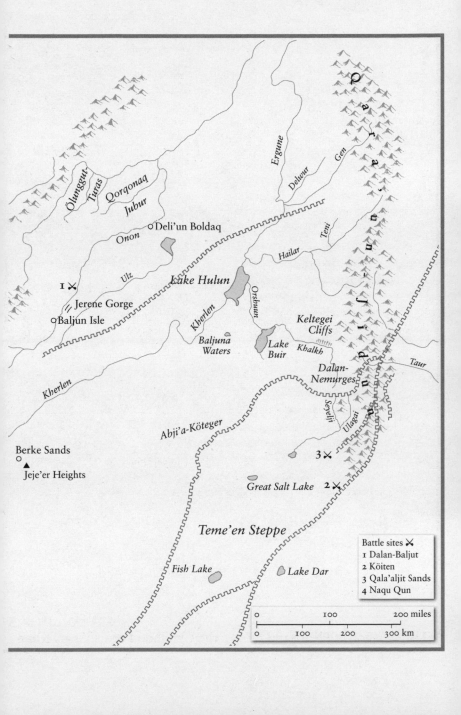

The Mongol Empire in 1210

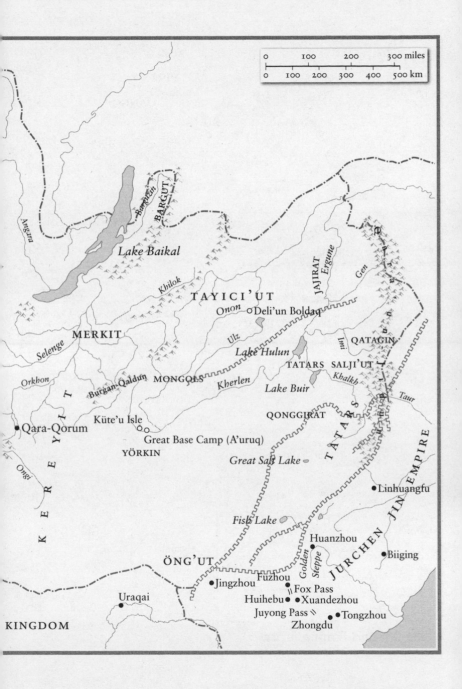

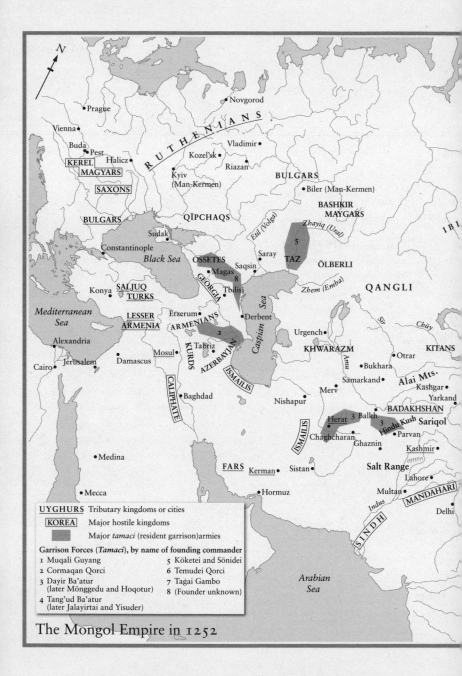

The Mongol Empire in 1252

Legend:

UYGHURS — Tributary kingdoms or cities

KOREA — Major hostile kingdoms

Major *tamaci* (resident garrison) armies

Garrison Forces (*Tamaci*), by name of founding commander

1 Muqali Guyang
2 Cormaqan Qorci
3 Dayir Ba'atur (later Mönggedu and Hoqotur)
4 Tang'ud Ba'atur (later Jalayirtai and Yisuder)
5 Köketei and Sönidei
6 Temudei Qorci
7 Tagai Gambo
8 (Founder unknown)

Map labels:

Prague • Novgorod • Vienna • Buda • Pest • Halicz • KEREL MAGYARS • SAXONS • BULGARS • RUTHENIANS • Vladimir • Kozel'sk • Riazan • Kyiv (Man-Kermen) • BULGARS • Biler (Man-Kermen) • BASHKIR MAYGARS • QÏPCHAQS • Etil (Volga) • Zhayiq (Ural) • 5 • TAZ • ÖLBERLI • IBI • Sudak • Constantinople • Black Sea • Saray • Saqsin • Zhem (Embal) • QANGLI • OSSETES • Magas • 8 • GEORGIA • Tbilisi • Caspian Sea • Konya • SALJUQ TURKS • Mediterranean Sea • LESSER ARMENIA • ARMENIANS • Erzerum • Derbent • Urgench • Sïr • Chüy • KHWARAZM • KITANS • Alexandria • 2 • Tabriz • AZERBAYJAN • KURDS • Amu • Merv • Samarkand • Otrar • Bukhara • Alai Mts. • Kashgar • Yarkand • Cairo • Jerusalem • Damascus • Mosul • ISMAILIS • Baghdad • CALIPHATE • Nishapur • BADAKHSHAN • ISMAILIS • Herat • 3 • Balkh • Sariqol • Hindu Kush • Chaghcharan • 3 • Parvan • Ghaznin • Kashmir • Medina • Sistan • Salt Range • Lahore • FARS • Kerman • Hormuz • Multan • MANDAHARI • Mecca • Indus • SINDH • Delhi • Arabian Sea

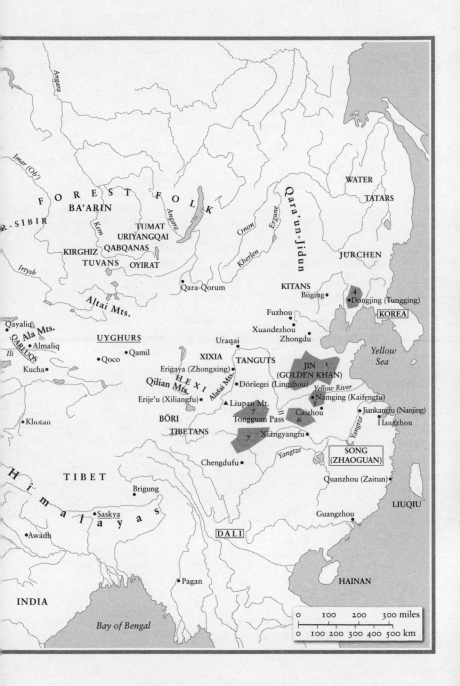

F O R E S T   F O L K

R - S I B I R

BA'ARIN

TUMAT
URIYANGQAI
QABQANAS
KIRGHIZ   QABQANAS
TUVANS   OYIRAT

Angara

Kem

Irtysh

Imar (Ob')

Ansara

Onon

Ergune

Kherlen

Qara'un-Jidun

WATER
TATARS

JURCHEN

Altai Mts.

KITANS   •
Biiging   •

Qayaliq   •
Ala Mts.
•Almaliq
Ili
Kucha•

QARLUQS

UYGHURS

•Qoco   •Qamil

Uraqai

Fuzhou   •
Xuandezhou   •
Zhongdu   •

Dongjing (Tungging)

KOREA

Yellow
Sea

•Khotan

XIXIA   TANGUTS
Erigaya (Zhongxing)•
Qilian Mts.   Dörsegei (Lingzhou)•
Erije'u (Xiliangfu)•
BÖRI
TIBETANS

H E X I   Alasai Mts.

▲Liupan Mt.
7
Tongguan Pass

JIN   1
(GOLDEN KHAN)

Yellow River
•Namging (Kaifengfu)

=   Caizhou
6
•Xiangyangfu   •

•Jiankangfu (Nanjing)
I Iangzhou

SONG
(ZHAOGUAN)

H
i
m
a
l
a
y
a
s

TIBET

•Brigung
•Saskya

•Awadh

•Pagan

Chengdufu•

Yangtze

DALI

Yangtze

Quanzhou (Zaitun)•

Guangzhou•

LIUQIU

INDIA

Bay of Bengal

HAINAN

| 0 | 100 | 200 | 300 miles |
| 0 | 100 200 | 300 400 | 500 km |

THE SECRET HISTORY
OF THE MONGOLS

1: THE ORIGIN OF CHINGGIS KHAN

LINEAGE OF CHINGGIS KHAN

The Origin of Chinggis Khan: there was Grey Wolf born with [1] a destiny from Heaven above. His wife was Fallow Doe.[1] They came crossing the sea.[2] And there was Bataci-Qan, born when they made their home at the headwaters of the Onon River, on Burġan-Qaldun.[3]

Bataci-Qan's son was Tamaca. [2]

Tamaca's son was Qoricar the Marksman.[4]

Qoricar the Marksman's son was A'ujam-Boro'ul.

A'ujam-Boro'ul's son was Sali-Qaca'u.

Sali-Qaca'u's son was Yeke-Nidun.[5]

Yeke-Nidun's son was Sem-Soci.

Sem-Soci's son was Qarcu.

Qarcu's son was Master Borjigin the Marksman, who was [3] born at the headwaters of Botoġan Bo'orji, which flows on the southern slope of Burġan-Qaldun;[6] his wife was Mistress Mongol the Fair.[7] Master Borjigin the Marksman's son was Toroġoljin the Rich; he had Boroqcin the Fair as wife, Boroldai Suyalbi as a young man,[8] and Dusky and Grey as fine geldings. Toroġoljin's sons were Du'a the One-Eyed and Dobun the Marksman.

Du'a the One-Eyed had a single eye in the middle of his fore- [4] head and saw for a distance of three days' march.[9] One day, [5] Du'a the One-Eyed went up on top of Burġan-Qaldun with his little brother Dobun the Marksman. Du'a the One-Eyed looked out from on top of Burġan-Qaldun, and saw a group of folk moving camp and coming down the Tüngkelik Stream. And he [6] said, 'Among those folks moving camp over here, on the driver's seat of a covered wagon,[10] there's a girl and she's fine. If she has not been given to any man, let us ask her for you, my little brother Dobun the Marksman.' And he sent his little brother Dobun

7 the Marksman to see. When Dobun the Marksman reached those folks, she was a girl with a truly fine and fair name and fame, named Alan the Fair, who had not been given to any man.

8 As for that group of folks, the daughter of Master Barġu the Marksman, lord of the Deep Barguzin Hollow,[11] named Mistress Barġu the Fair, had been given to Master Qorilar the Marksman, commander of the Qori-Tumat. The one born of Master Qorilar the Marksman's Mistress Barġu the Fair in the land of the Qori-Tumat at the Ariġ River, was her named Alan

9 the Fair. In his land of Qori-Tumat, they were banning each other and vexing each other over their lands filled with sable and squirrel peltry; Master Qorilar the Marksman's seed would become those with the surname Qorilar.[12] And thinking that the game of Burġan-Qaldun was very good for hunting and the land was fine, he came here moving his camp to that of the two Uriyangqai, Sets Up Willows and Śinci the Rich, the lords of Burġan-Qaldun.[13] That was the way in which the brothers sought there Alan the Fair, daughter of Master Qorilar the Marksman of the Qori-Tumat, born at the Ariġ River, and how she was taken by Dobun the Marksman.

10 Alan the Fair came to Dobun the Marksman and bore two
11 sons; their names were Bügünüdei and Belgünüdei. His big brother Du'a the One-Eyed had four sons. Once all that had happened, the big brother Du'a the One-Eyed passed away. After Du'a the One-Eyed had passed away, his four sons despised Uncle Dobun the Marksman as if he were not their kin, broke away and moved off. They became those with the surname Dörben and became the Dörben folk.

12 One day, after that happened, Dobun the Marksman went up the To'ocaq Heights to hunt. In the woods, he met an Uriyangqan man who had killed a three-year-old elk and was
13 roasting its flanks and its guts.[14] Dobun the Marksman said, 'Friend, that roast meat's fair game,' and the man said, 'I'll give you some.'[15] And he took off the hide of the half-severed chest together with the lung and gave all the other meat of that

three-year-old elk to Dobun the Marksman. As Dobun the 14
Marksman came down the road loaded down with the three-
year-old elk, he met a poor man who was leading his son by
the hand. When Dobun the Marksman asked, 'Who are you?' 15
he said, 'I am from the Ma'aliq Baya'ut. I can't go on. Give me
some of the meat of that game. I will give you this son of mine.'
With that, Dobun the Marksman broke off the pair of thighs, 16
gave that part of the carcass to him, and took away the boy; the
boy was a servant inside the *ger*.[16]

Once that had happened, Dobun the Marksman passed 17
away. After Dobun the Marksman had passed away, while
Alan the Fair was without a husband, she bore three sons. They
were named Buġu-Qatagi, Bu'atu-Salji and Bodoncar the Sim-
ple. Her sons Bügunudei and Belgunudei, who had been born 18
before from Dobun the Marksman, spoke to each other about
their mother behind her back: 'This mother of ours, while
without brother or cousins and without a husband, bore these
three sons. The only one in the *ger* is this Ma'aliq Baya'ut man.
The three sons must be his!' they said. Their mother Alan the Fair
found that they were talking about her behind her back and
one spring day, she boiled a sheep from the winter provisions 19
and sat her five sons Belgunudei, Bügunudei, Buġu-Qatagi, Bu'
atu-Salji and Bodoncar the Simple down in a row.[17] She gave
them each an arrow shaft and told them to break it. Each one
was broken – why would they not be? – and let fall. Again, she
bundled together five arrow shafts, gave the shafts to them and
told them to break them. All five of them one after another
took the five arrow shafts joined together but were unable to
do as she said and break it.

Then their mother Alan the Fair spoke,[18] 'You my sons Belgu- 20
nudei and Bügunudei were talking to each other with suspicion,
asking whose and what manner of sons are these three sons who
were born to me. Every night, a shining yellow man entered in 21
with a brilliant light through the smoke hole and lintel of the *ger*
and stroked my belly; his brilliance dissolved into my womb.
When he left, he would crawl out with the beams of the sun and
moon like a yellow dog. Why do you speak wildly? If you only
understood it, it is a sign that those three must be sons of Heaven!

How can you speak the way the black-headed people do?[19] When those three have become rulers over all, then crude commoners will understand it!'

22   Again, Alan the Fair spoke words of admonition to her five sons: 'You my five sons were born from a single womb; you are just like the five arrow shafts. If you are alone one by one, you will be easily broken by anyone like the single arrow shafts. If like the arrow shafts joined together you are joined in accord as one, then how could you be easily broken by anyone?'[20] Then Alan the Fair, their mother, passed away.

23   After their mother Alan the Fair had passed away, when the five brothers divided up their livestock and food, Belgunudei, Bügunudei, Buġu-Qatagi and Bu'atu-Salji took it all for themselves. Bodoncar they deemed foolish and simple and did not give

24 him his share as if they did not count him as kin. Bodoncar was not counted as kin and he thought, 'Why stay here?' He rode a pale-grey horse with a dorsal stripe and a saddle-sore spine and a bare-bones tail and he thought, 'If it dies, I die; if it lives, I live.' He went away down the Onon River. He went and arrived at the Isle of Baljun; he made a grass-thatched hut and there he lived, there he stayed.

25   While he was living there, he saw a female brown goshawk eating a black grouse.[21] Using the tail hairs of his pale-grey horse with a dorsal stripe and a saddle-sore spine and a bare-bones tail, he

26 trapped the goshawk and took care of it. Having no food to eat, he spied some game corralled by wolves against a bluff, shot it dead and ate as much of it as he could get. He scrabbled for what the wolves left over and ate it. He fed his goshawk from his own

27 gullet, and so passed the year. Spring came. When the ducks flew north, he starved his goshawk and released it. He hung out ducks and geese until they stank with stench on every snag and decay on every deadwood.

28   From the shady side of Düiren Mountain,[22] a group of folks came down, moving camp along the Tüngkelik Stream. Bodoncar would go to those folks and cast his goshawk. During the day, he would drink *esuk* and at night he would come back to

29 his grass-thatched hut and spend the night.[23] When those folks asked Bodoncar for his goshawk, he did not give it to them.

Those folks never asked Bodoncar 'Whose son are you? What folks do you belong to?' and Bodoncar too never asked 'Who are you folks?' and so they dealt with each other.

His big brother Buġu-Qatagi remembered that his little ³⁰ brother Bodoncar the Simple had gone away down the Onon River and came to look for him. When he asked among the folks who had come moving camp down along the Tüngkelik Stream about such and such a person with such and such a horse, those ³¹ folks said, 'There's a man and a horse that are just like the one you are asking about, and with a goshawk too. Every day he comes to us, drinks *esuk*, and goes away. Who knows where he spends the night? When the wind is in the north-west, the feathers and down of the ducks and geese hunted with his falcon blow by us scattered in the wind like swirling snow. It must be near here. Now is the hour when he arrives. Wait a few moments.'

In a moment, a man was coming up the Tüngkelik Stream ³² and when he arrived it was indeed Bodoncar. His big brother Buġu-Qatagi recognized him by sight and led him away, trotting off up the Onon River. Bodoncar went trotting along ³³ behind his big brother Buġu-Qatagi and said, 'Big brother, big brother, how happy for a body to have a head, and a coat to have a collar.' His big brother Buġu-Qatagi did not get what he meant by that.

When he said the very same thing again, his big brother did ³⁴ not get what he meant and made not a sound in reply. They went on and Bodoncar said the very same thing again. When he said the same thing, his big brother said, 'Just now, what was it you were saying over and over again?'

Then Bodoncar said, 'Those folks just now who were on the ³⁵ Tüngkelik Stream: they have no big or little, no bad or good, no head or hoof. They are all on a level. They would be easy folks to handle. Let's capture them.'

Then his big brother replied, 'Well, if that's the way it is, then ³⁶ let's get back to our home, plan it out together as brothers, and capture them.'

Having got back to their home, the brothers talked it over ³⁷ and rode off. They sent Bodoncar himself off as an outrider. Bodoncar went as an outrider and seized a woman early in her ³⁸ term; he asked her 'What kind of woman are you?' That woman said, 'I am a woman of the Jarci'ut's Adangqan Uriyangqan.'

39   Those folk were plundered by the five brothers together, who got to live with herds and food, subjects and servants.

40   That woman came to Bodoncar early in her term and gave birth to a boy. Since he was the son of some foreign [*jat*] folk Bodoncar called him Jajiradai. He was the ancestor of the Jadaran.

The son of Jajiradai was Tügu'udei.

Tügu'udei's son was Böri-Bulciru.

Böri-Bulciru's son was Qara-Qada'an.

Qara-Qada'an's son was Jamuqa.

They became the ones with the Jadaran surname.

41   That woman had another son with Bodoncar. Since she was a woman he had married by capture [*bariju*], he named that boy Ba'aridai. He was the ancestor of the Ba'arin.

Ba'aridai's son was Ciduqul the Brawny.

Ciduqul the Brawny had many women, and his sons seemed to be born incessantly [*mene*]. They became the ones with the Menen Ba'arin surname.

42   Belgunudei's sons became the ones with the Belgunut surname.

Bügunudei's sons became the ones with the Bügunut surname.

Buġu-Qatagi's sons became the ones with the Qatagin surname.

Bu'atu-Salji's sons became the ones with the Salji'ut surname.[24]

Bodoncar's sons became the ones with the Borjigin surname.[25]

43   The one born from Bodoncar's married wife was named Barim-Śi'iratu Qabici. Bodoncar took to himself one of the ones who came as the dowry servant of Qabici Ba'atur's mother and gave birth to a son. He was named Je'uriyedei. Je'uriyedei

44   originally participated in the *jügeli* sacrifice.[26] After Bodoncar passed away, they said about Je'uriyedei that since a man of the Adangqa Uriyangqan was ever in the *ger*, Je'uriyedei must be that man's child, and expelled him from the *jügeli*. They made

him one of the Je'uriyet surname, and he became the ancestor
of the Je'uriyet.

Qabici Ba'atur's son was Menen-Tudun. Menen-Tudun's sons 45
were Qaci-Küluk, Qacin, Qaci'u, Qacula, Qaci'un, Qaraldai
and Nacin Ba'atur.

Qaci-Küluk's son Qaidu was born from Mother Nomolun.[27] 46

Qacin's son was named Noyagidai. Because he had the
behaviour of acting the chief [noyamśiq], his sons became the
ones with the Noyagin surname.

Qaci'u's son was named Baruladai. With a big body, he was
greedy [baruq] for food; his sons became the ones with the
Barulas surname.

Because Qacula's sons were greedy for food, they were
named Big Barula and Little Barula, and they also became
the ones with the Barulas surname; they were the ones who
became the Erdemtu Barula, Tödo'en Barula and the other
Barulas.[28]

Because Qaraldai's sons did not have any headman to stir the
porridge [buda'an], it was they who became the ones with the
Buda'at surname.

Qaci'un's son was named Adarkidai. Because he was a tale-
bearer [adaruqci] among his big and little brothers, his sons
became the ones with the Adarkin surname.

The sons of Nacin Ba'atur were named Uru'udai and
Manggudai; their sons became the ones with the Uru'ut
and Manggut surnames.

The ones born from a woman Nacin Ba'atur took for himself
were named Siju'udai and Doguladai.

Qaidu's sons were Bai-Śingqor-Doqśin, Caraqai Lingqu and 47
Ca'ujin Örtegei.

Bai-Śingqor-Doqśin's son was Tumbinai Secen.

The sons of Caraqai Lingqu became Senggum-Bilge,
Hambagai, and so on, the ones with the Tayici'ut surname.

The one born from the woman Caraqai Lingqu inherited
from his big brother was named Besudei.[29] It was his sons who
became the ones with the Besut surname.

Ca'ujin Örtegei's sons became the ones with the Oronar,
Qongqotan, Arlat, Sönit, Qafburgas and Keniges surnames.

48   Tumbinai Secen's sons were Qabul Khan and Sam-Qacula.[30] Sam-Qacula's son was Bultacu Ba'atur.[31] Bultacu Ba'atur's son was Mergen Secen.[32]

Qabul Khan had seven sons. These were Ökin-Barqaq the eldest of them, Bartan Ba'atur, Qutuqtu-Mönggur, Qutula Khan, Qulan, Qada'an and Tödo'en Otcigin.

49   Ökin-Barqaq's son was Qutuqtu-Yörki.[33] Qutuqtu-Yörki's sons were Sece Beki and Taicu. They were the ones of the Yörkin surname.

50   The four sons of Bartan Ba'atur were Mönggedu Kiyan, Nekun Taiši, Yisukei Ba'atur and Dāritai Otcigin. They were born of Madame Süjigil; Madame Süjigil was the daughter of a Mongol Tarġut woman, a beautiful Tayici'ut girl.[34]

Qutuqtu-Mönggur's son was Böri the Brawny. He was the one who hacked open Belgutei's shoulder when there was feasting at the forest on the Onon.[35]

51   Qutula Khan's sons were Coci,[36] Girma'u and Altan.[37] They were the ones of the Üye'et surname.[38]

Qulan Ba'atur's son was Big Cāran. He was the captain of the two *darqat* Badai and Kišiliq.[39] Qada'an and Tödo'en had no offspring.

EARLY KHANS

52 Qabul Khan ruled all the Mongols.[40] After Qabul Khan, even though his seven sons were still alive, Senggum-Bilge's son Hambaġai Khan of the Tayici'ut ruled all the Mongols by

53 Qabul Khan's word. Hambaġai Khan gave a daughter as bride to some Ayiri'ut and Buyiri'ut Tatar folk[41] who lived at the Orshuun River between Lake Buir and Lake Hulun.[42] And as he was going to send his daughter to them in person, the Tatar Jüin folk seized Hambaġai Khan. When he was being taken away to the Golden Khan of the Chinese,[43] Hambaġai Khan sent word with the envoy, Balaġaci of the Besut, telling him, 'Among Qabul Khan's seven sons, speak to Qutula and among [my] ten sons, speak to Qada'an Taiši.' He sent word to them to say, 'I became khan of all and lord of the kingdom and sent

my daughter in person; take warning from how I have been seized by the Tatar folk. Until the nails of your five fingers are finally ground flat, until the tips of your ten fingers are beaten to the bone, strive to pay them back for me!'[44]

Around that time, when Bartan Ba'atur's son Yisukei Ba'atur 54 was hawking on the Onon River, he met Big Ciledu of the Merkit coming from the Olqunu'ut folk and escorting a new bride he had taken. Once he had taken a good look at her, he saw her beauty was different from that of other well-born girls and he hastened home to his *ger* and brought back his big brother Nekün Taiši and his little brother Dāritai Otcigin. When they got 55 there, Ciledu was afraid and riding a fast dun mare.[45] As he flogged the croup of his dun mare and fled beyond the ridge, the three chased him from behind. As Ciledu went back round about the mountain spur and came to his wagon, his bride Madame Ö'elun said to him,[46] 'You – have you understood what those three fellows are about? Their looks are not like other people's looks – their looks are like they want your life. As long as you have your life at least, there's a woman in every wagon and a damsel in every dray. As long as you have your life at least, you'll find a woman to wed. The one not named Ö'elun – name her Ö'elun too then! Save your life. Here is my scent to go with you.' As she took off her undershirt and he reached down from his horse to take it and as the three rounded the mountain spur and rode up together, then Ciledu flogged the croup of his fast dun mare; in a flash he got away and fled up the Onon River.

The three chased him from behind over seven ridges until 56 they drove him off. They came back and Yisukei Ba'atur took Madame Ö'elun by the tether of the beast yoked to the wagon, his big brother Nekün Taiši went in the lead, and his little brother Dāritai went by the wagon-shaft. Then Madame Ö'elun said, 'My Ciledu, like a brother to me, you have never had your forelocks fretted in the winds, your belly empty in the broad grasslands, have you? Now how will you do these two braids of yours as you go, one hanging down on your back and one hanging down on your chest, one behind and one forward – how?' And she wailed in a great voice until the Onon River echoed it and the wooded valley rang with it. Then Dāritai went beside her and dissuaded her: 'The one who kissed you has crossed over many passes, the one you wailed for went over many waters. Shout, but over his shoulder he will not see you. Track him but you will not find his traces. Be quiet!' Soon then Yisukei brought Madame Ö'elun to his *ger*. That was the way in which Madame Ö'elun was brought to Yisukei's *ger*.

57   Since Hambaġai Khan had named Qada'an and Qutula in sending the message, all the Mongols and Tayici'ut gathered in the Qorqonaq valley and made Qutula khan.[47] The joy of the Mongols was to make merry with dancing and feasting. Qutula was raised up as a ruler and then they danced around the Bushy Tree[48] of Qorqonaq until the rut was up to the ribs and the hole
58   was up to the haunches.[49] Qutula became khan and then he and Qada'an rode against the Tatar folk. They battled with Köten-Baraqa and Jali-Buqa of the Tatars thirteen times but were not able to give them hatred for the hatred and vengeance for the vengeance of Hambaġai Khan.

TEMUJIN'S BIRTH AND
YISUKEI BA'ATUR'S DEATH

59   Then, when Yisukei Ba'atur captured Temujin Öke, Qori-Buqa and other Tatars, and when Madame Ö'elun was big with child, just then, when they were at Deli'un Boldaq on the Onon, Chinggis Khan was born. When he was born, he was born clutching a clot of blood in his right hand the size of a knuckle-bone. Because he was born when Temujin Öke was brought as captive – that was why he was named Temujin.

60   Yisukei Ba'atur's wife Madame Ö'elun gave birth to four sons, Temujin, Coci-Qasar, Qaci'un and Temuke, and she gave birth to one daughter, named Temulun. When Temujin was nine years old, Coci-Qasar was seven years old, Qaci'un- Elci was five years old, Temuke Otcigin was three years old and Temulun was in the cradle.

61   When Temujin was nine years old, Yisukei Ba'atur, thinking to find a bride for him among his maternal uncles' people, took

Temujin and travelled to the Olqunu'ut folk, the birth home of Mother Ö'elun.[50] On the way there he met Deyi Secen of the Qonggirat between Cekcer and Ciġurqu.[51] Deyi Secen said, 62 'Whose place were you headed to as you came by?'

Yisukei said, 'I came by hoping to find a bride among the Olqunu'ut folk, the maternal uncles of this boy of mine.'

Deyi Secen said, 'This boy of yours is a boy with flame in his eyes and fire in his face. *Quda* Yisukei,[52] last night I dreamed a 63 dream. A white falcon flew towards me clutching the sun and the moon and alighted on my hand. I told this dream of mine to someone, saying, "The sun and the moon were visible before, but now this falcon clutching them brought them over and alighted on my hand. What good is this whiteness descending showing me?" *Quda* Yisukei, this dream of mine was showing me that you would come leading this boy of yours. It was a good dream to dream. What kind of dream was it? The *sülder* of your Kiyat folk came and foretold this.[53]

We Qonggirat folk from days of old   64
    with the faces of our fair ones
    and the graces of our girl children
have not struggled for the kingdom;
    yet if one of yours should reign as khan
    the daughter fair of cheek
    we seat in the *qasaq* cart,
    we harness the black bull camel to go trotting out,
    we have her sit among you
    in the seat of queens.
We do not struggle to rule the nation,
    we raise our daughters fair of face,
    we sit them on our wagon's seat,
    harnessing soot-hued bull camels;
    we send girls off and have them sit by your side
    on the high seat.
Of old we Qonggirat folk
    have lived by brides as our bucklers,
    by pretty ones as our petitioners,
    by the faces of our fair ones,
    by the graces of our girl children.

65   Our boy child's bounds are noted,
      our girl child's grace is gazed at.⁵⁴
Quda Yisukei, come to my *ger*. My daughter is little, but let my
quda see her.' So Deyi Secen led him to his *ger* and had him stay
there.

66   When Yisukei saw Deyi Secen's daughter, he saw a girl with
flame in her eyes and fire in her face, and he let her into his
mind. She was one year older than Temujin, ten years old, and
named Börte. Yisukei spent the night there and the next day,
when he had requested the girl for Temujin, Deyi Secen said,
'What if I let you ask many times? It might honour me to con-
sent. What if I let you ask a few times? It might humble me to
consent. But it is not a daughter's destiny to grow old at the
door. I will give my very own daughter to you; place your very
own son among us as a son-in-law.'⁵⁵ They agreed thus and
Yisukei Ba'atur said, 'I will place my son as a son-in-law. My
son is scared of dogs; *quda*, do not let my son be scared of
dogs.' Yisukei gave Deyi Secen his spare horse as a gift, left
67   Temujin as a son-in-law, and went on his way back. On the
way, as there were some Tatar folk feasting at Cekcer's Yellow
steppe, Yisukei Ba'atur met them, dismounted and drank at
the feast.

      Those Tatars recognized him. Thinking that Yisukei the
Kiyan had come, and remembering their earlier grudge over
being captured, they plotted murder and mixed in poison for
him.⁵⁶ Feeling sick on the way, he went for three days and
arrived at his *ger* and felt worse.

68   Yisukei Ba'atur said, 'My insides feel sick. Who is at hand?'
And when they said Mönglik, the son of Old Man Caraqa of
the Qongqotan, was at hand, he had him invited in and said,
'Mönglik my child, I have boys who are still small. On the way
when I was coming back from placing my son as a son-in-law,
I fell victim to the Tatar folk's plot and now I feel side inside. It
is up to you to take care of the small ones left behind, your little
brothers and your widowed sister-in-law.⁵⁷ Mönglik my child,
go quickly and bring back my son Temujin.' Having spoken, he
died.

Lest he nullify Yisukei Ba'atur's word, Mönglik went and   69
said to Deyi Secen, 'Big brother Yisukei misses Temujin very
much and his heart aches for him. I came to take Temujin.'
Deyi Secen said, 'If *quda* is missing his son, then let him go. But
once he's seen him, let him come back quickly.' Father Mönglik
brought Temujin back.

That spring, when Hambaġai Khan's ladies[58] Örbei and   70
Soqatai made the burnt offering 'Ġajaru Inaru' to the ances-
tors,[59] Madame Ö'elun went and got there late and was treated
as a latecomer. Madame Ö'elun said to Örbei and Soqatai, 'Is
it because you think Yisukei Ba'atur has died and that my sons
will not get bigger that you somehow made me too late for the
blessings of the ancestors, the sacrificial meat, and the sacrifi-
cial liquor?[60] Now that I see you, are you going to move camp
without calling me to eat?'

To these words, the ladies Örbei and Soqatai replied,   71
'Invited but not included is your sort,
Consuming whatever you come across is your way;
Arriving but not acknowledged is your sort,
Gobbling whatever you're given is your way.
Is it that she thinks Hambaġai Khan has died that we get
spoken to like this by Ö'elun? Better then, move camp! And   72
leave these women and children on the range.[61] Go on! And
we won't take you with us.' And, having spoken, the next day
the Tayici'ut's Fatty Kiriltuq and Töde'en Girte and the
Taiyic'ut moved down along the Onon River. With Madame
Ö'elun and the women and children left behind in the move,
when Old Man Caraqa of the Qongqotan went to dissuade
them, Töde'en Girte said, 'The deep water is dried up, the
smooth stone is smashed up' and moved camp. 'How dare Old
Man Caraqa dissuade us?' they said, and stabbed him in the
back with a spear.

Old Man Caraqa was wounded and came back to his *ger*.   73
When he lay down in pain, Temujin went to see him. There Old
Man Caraqa of the Qongqotan said, 'As the kingdom assem-
bled by your late father – our whole kingdom – was taken away
and moved camp, I went to dissuade them and this is what they

did to me.' Then Temujin wailed and so went out to go back. As for Madame Ö'elun, when she was left behind in the move, she took up the banner and rode out in person and returned half of the folk. But these returned folk were restless and moved camp after the Tayici'ut.

2: THE YOUTH OF CHINGGIS KHAN

KILLING BEKTER

The Tayici'ut brethren moved camp to leave behind on the range
Madame Ö'elun, the widow, the little ones and boys, the
mothers and children. Madame Ö'elun,

> Born both womanly and wise,
> Finding food for her small boys,
> Fastening on firm her *boqta* hat,[1]
> Fixing up her flowing skirts,
> Flying up and down the Onon's flood,
> Finding wild fruits, crab apples and cherries,
> Filled she night and day their famished throats.
> Motherly Madame born with gall,
> Majestic sons she aimed to raise,
> So clutching a fork of spruce, off
> She set digging up silverweed and burnet.
> Motherly Madame's boys,
> Well raised on wild garlic and onion,
> Were brought up to rulership.
> Noble Madame mother's sons,
> Reared on rangeland's lily bulbs,
> Would be right-minded rulers.
> Lovely Madame's hungry boys,
> Reared on leeks and onion leaves,
> Grew up into well-born lords.
> Launched as lordly well-born men
> They'd live out proud and manly lives.

75

Saying to each other we must feed our mother, they sat on

Mother Onon's muddy banks and
Mastered metal hooks and lures,
Catching maimed and motley fish.
Turning needles into hooks,
They trout and little whitefish hooked.
Sewing seines and nets up snug,
They sifted pools for silver minnows,
And so they served back Mother's love.

76   One day, when Temujin, Qasar, Bekter and Belgutei sat
together casting fish hooks, they caught a shiny dace.[2] Bekter
and Belgutei grabbed it away from Temujin and Qasar. Temujin
and Qasar came into the *ger* and said to the Madame Mother,
'We got a bite on our hook from a shiny dace and it got grabbed
away from us by Bekter and Belgutei.' The Madame Mother
said, 'No spiteful talk, please – stop it![3] Why do you big and
little brothers act so to each other? We have no friend but a
shadow, no whip but a tail. When we are wondering how to pay
their bitterness back to the Tayici'ut brethren, why are you so
little in accord, like Alan the Fair's five sons of old? Stop it!'

77   Temujin and Qasar were not pleased with that. 'Yesterday,
they grabbed a skylark that had just been downed with a knob-
headed arrow in the very same way,[4] and today they grabbed
something else the same way again! How can we stand to live
together?' they said, and went out on their way slapping aside
the felt door. Bekter was sitting on top of a lone hill and watch-
ing the nine horses, the isabelline geldings.[5] When Temujin was
creeping up from behind and Qasar creeping up from in front
and they were pulling out their arrows, Bekter saw them and
said, 'When we cannot put an end to the bitterness of the
Tayici'ut brethren and are wondering who will be able to pay
them back, why do you make me a lash in your eyes, a spine
in your craw? When we have no friend but a shadow, no whip
but a tail, how could you imagine this? Don't extinguish my
hearth,[6] don't forsake Belgutei!' He sat cross-legged and waited.
Temujin and Qasar, from behind and from in front, fired at
close range and went off.

78   When they came back into the *ger*, the Madame Mother under-
stood it all from the faces of her two children. 'Murderers!

When bursting out from my hot womb, he wielded in his
    hand a black clot.
Like a hound that devours its own heam,
Like a panther that pounces against a cliff,
Like a lion that cannot restrain its wrath,
Like a python that takes its prey alive,
Like a saker that stoops at its shadow,
Like a pike that swallows soundless,
Like a bull camel that bites its calf's heel,
Like a wolf that stalks in the whirling blizzard,
Like a drake that eats the ducklings it cannot direct,
Like a dhole that joins in league to defend its lair,[7]
Like a tiger that wastes no time to take its prey,
Like a cur that hunts with cunning cruelty, you killed.
When we have no friend but a shadow, no whip but a tail, when
we cannot put an end to the bitterness of the Tayici'ut brethren
and are wondering who will be able to pay them back, you tell
me how can we stand it and why you act this way to each other!'
Pounding in the past times' words and echoing the elders'
words, she accused them fiercely.

TEMUJIN CAPTURED BY THE TAYICI'UT[8]

Once all that had happened, Fatty Kiriltuq[9] of the Tayici'ut   79
arrived with his dayguards,[10] saying, 'The fledglings have grown
feathers, the droolers have developed.' Afraid, the women and
children, big and little brothers, barricaded themselves in the
deep forested woods. As Belgutei snapped the trees in half and
built a palisade and Qasar exchanged fire with them, and Qaci'un,
Temuke and Temulun were fighting with each other to get into a
crevasse,[11] the Tayici'ut called out to them, 'Send out your big
brother Temujin. We have no issue with the rest of you.'[12] Called
out, Temujin was put on a horse to flee; the Tayici'ut saw him
escape into the woods and gave chase. When he crawled into the
deep forest of the Tergune Heights, the Tayici'ut could not get in
after him and set a guard around the place.
Temujin spent three nights in the deep forest, and when he   80

led his horse towards the forest's edge, thinking to go out, the horse's saddle slipped and fell off behind. He went back to look and even with the saddle's breast strap still fastened and the girth still cinched it had slipped and fallen off behind. 'Not just the saddle girth, even the breast strap – how did it slip off? Is Heaven dissuading me?' he said, and went back and spent another three nights.

Again, when he was about to get out into the gap in the deep forest a white boulder the size of a tepee fell and stopped up the gap.[13] 'Is Heaven dissuading me?' he said, and went back and spent another three nights.

Even so, he spent nine days without food and said, 'Why die nameless? I'll go out.' The branches that made it impossible to get out around the white boulder the size of a tepee blocking off the gap he cut away with his knife for whittling arrows,[14] and as he gently guided his horse through, the Tayici'ut were there on guard. They seized him and bore him away.

81   Fatty Kiriltuq took Temujin away and, putting him under the control of his subject people,[15] had him spend one night in each camp.[16] While he was being rotated around, one night each, the Tayici'ut feasted on the Red Disk Day,[17] the sixteenth of the first moon of summer, on the banks of the Onon and broke up as the sun went down. A feeble youth brought Temujin to that feast. As the fellows at the feast were being sent away, he grabbed the cangue away from the feeble boy,[18] struck him on the head once with it, and ran. Thinking that he would be seen if he lay down in the groves by the Onon,[19] he lay down on his back in the river's edge and lay with his face visible, letting his cangue float downstream in the water.

82   When the person who had lost him cried out, shouting in a loud voice, 'Catch him! I've lost the man,' the Tayici'ut who had broken up gathered again and, in the moonlight as bright as day, searched the groves by the Onon in ranks. Sorġan-Śira of the Suldus happened right on where he was lying in the river's edge and saw him.[20] 'It is just because you have this right kind of trick that you're envied so much by the Tayici'iut brothers, who worry about the flame in your eyes and the fire in your face. Keep lying there; I will not tell.' He spoke and passed on by. When they said

to each other, 'Let's turn back and search the way we came,' Sorġan-Śira said, 'Let's go back and search the way we came, each on his same trail looking over the ground he had not looked over,' and they agreed with each other, 'Yes, let's.' And they searched the way they came each along the same trail and Sorġan-Śira passed by him again. He said, 'Your brethren are coming here with their lips pursed and their teeth grinding.[21] Keep lying like this. Be patient.' And he passed on by.

When they said to each other, 'Let's turn back and search the way we came,' Sorġan-Śira said again, 'Tayici'ut princes, you lost a whole man in the bright white daylight. Now how are we going to find him in the dark of night? Let's go back and search the way we came, each along the same trail looking over the ground he had not looked over, and then break up and get together again tomorrow to look for him. Where is this person in a cangue going to go?' 'Yes' they agreed, and they searched the way they came and Sorġan-Śira passed by him again. 'Once we've searched the same way again, they've agreed to look again tomorrow. Once we've all broken up for the night, go look for your mother and little brothers. Don't tell anyone about it, saying I saw you – if you are seen by someone – or saying you were seen.' So saying, he passed on. 83

Once they all had broken up for the night, he thought to himself, 'Yesterday when I was being rotated to spend the night among the camps and I spent the night at Sorġan-Śira's camp, his two sons Cimbai and Cila'un's hearts ached for me and when they saw me at night, they loosened my cangue and let me rest.[22] Now, Sorġan-Śira saw me again and passed by without telling. I know they will rescue me again the same way,' and went down the Onon looking for Sorġan-Śira's ger. 84

The signal of the ger was that the milk would be poured in and they would churn the esuk all night until the day dawned.[23] As he went listening for that signal he came to hear the sound of the plunger, and when he went into the ger Sorġan-Śira said, 'Didn't I tell you to go and find your mother and little brothers? Why have you come here?' His sons Cimbai and Cila'un said, 'When the sparrow took refuge from the tiercel in a bush, the bush protected it. Now that he's come to us, how can you talk to him like 85 that?' Not pleased by their father's words, they chopped up the cangue and burned it in the fire and had him sleep in the wool wagon behind the *ger*. Their little sister Qada'an was told to take care of him and not tell a living soul.

86   On the third day, 'Someone must have hidden him,' they said to each other. 'Let us turn the inspection on ourselves,' they said to each other and inspected among themselves. They inspected in the *ger*, and in the wagon and even below the bed of Sorġan-Śira and they climbed on to the wool wagon in the back and pulled out the wool in the opening. When they reached his feet, Sorġan-Śira said, 'How could he stand it in the wool in this heat?' and the inspections were called off and they left.

87   After the inspection left, Sorġan-Śira said, 'You almost made my ashes blow away in the wind. Now go and find your mother and little brothers.' They mounted him on a barren straw-yellow mare with a white mouth, boiled a *tel* lamb,[24] fitted out a small flask and a big leather pail and, without giving him a saddle or flint, they gave him a bow and gave him two arrows.[25] Thus equipped, they sent him off.

88   So Temujin went off and reached the place they had fortified with a wooden palisade. He tracked the bent grass up the Onon River and came upon Kimurqa Stream from the west. Tracing the trail upriver from that, he met his family at Qorcuqui Hill on the Beder Spur by Kimurqa Stream.

BO'ORCU AND THE THEFT OF THE ISABELLINE GELDINGS

89 When he rejoined them there, they all went on, and when they were camping on the range at the Qara-Jiruken's Köke Na'ur of Senggur Stream inside Kürelgu, on the southern slopes of Burġan-Qaldun,[26] they killed and ate marmots and jerboas.

90   One day, with the eight isabelline geldings standing next to their *ger*, bandits came and robbed them of the horses even as they looked on, and left. On foot they were left behind just watching. Belgutei had gone off to hunt marmots riding the

bob-tailed, short-haired chestnut. In the evening, after the sun set, Belgutei came back, leading the short-haired, bob-tailed chestnut on foot with marmots weighing it down until it staggered. When they told him, 'Bandits came and robbed us of the isabelline geldings,' Belgutei said, 'I'll go after them.'

Qasar said, 'You can't handle them; I'll go after them.'

Temujin said, 'Neither of you can handle them; I'll go after them.'

Temujin rode the short-haired chestnut and tracked the isabelline geldings by the bent grass. Spending three nights, on the trail early the next day he met a trim youth, milking mares among a large herd of horses. When he asked about the isabelline geldings, that boy said, 'This morning, before the sun rose, there were eight isabelline geldings being driven along near here. I will show you their trail.' He had the bob-tailed chestnut set aside and mounted Temujin on a pale-grey horse with a dorsal stripe. He himself rode his own fast dun mare.

Without even going back to his *ger*, he left his pail and bucket for milking in a covered spot on the steppe. Saying, 'As for you, friend, you came here in great trouble. You know, true men's troubles are all the same. I want to be your friend. My father is known as Naqu the Rich; I am his only son. My name is Bo'orcu,' they tracked the trail of the isabelline geldings for three nights.

And in the evening, when the sun was touching the hills, they came to a wagon-fort of folk.[27] They saw the isabelline geldings standing and grazing by the edge of that great wagon-fort.

Temujin said, 'Friend, you stay here, and I will drive out the isabelline geldings over there.'

Bo'orcu said, 'I said I want to be friends. Now that I have come this far how can I stand aside?' and they charged in together and drove off the isabelline geldings.

Behind them came out fellows in pursuit one after another. 91 One of them with a white horse and a red coat[28] and holding an *uurga* was catching up to them on his own.[29] Bo'orcu said, 'Friend, give me the bow and arrow; I'll trade shots with him.'

Temujin said, 'I worry you might get hurt on my behalf. I'll trade shots,' and turned behind and shot at him.[30] The one with the white horse and a red coat beckoned with his *uurga* and came to a halt. His friends came up from behind. The sun set. Dusk came on. Those fellows were lost in the shadows, came to a halt, and were left behind.

92   They rode on through the middle of that night, and then rode three days and three nights through without cease, and got back. Temujin said, 'If you hadn't been there, would I have got these horses? Let's share. Say how many you will take.' Bo'orcu said, 'Me? I've become friends with you because I knew that you, a good friend of mine, came to me in trouble, and because I intended to help a good friend. Would I take this as a reward? My father is named Naqu the Rich. The only son he has is me. What my father has gathered will fulfil my needs. I won't take any of them. What is this help that I helped you with? I won't take any of them.'

93   They came to Naqu the Rich's *ger*. His son Bo'orcu had disappeared and Naqu the Rich was blubbering in tears. Suddenly he showed up and, seeing his son, he cried for joy one time and he yelled at him one time. His son Bo'orcu said, 'What is the matter? My good friend came to me in trouble. I befriended him and went with him. And now I've come back.' He rushed out and fetched the pail and bucket he left in a covered spot on the steppe. They killed a *tel* lamb for Temujin and gave him provisions, filling up his pail, and provisioned him well. Naqu the Rich said, 'You are two young men. Keep seeing each other; ever after, do not abandon each other.' Temujin went off and, travelling for three days and three nights, reached his *ger* at Senggur Stream. Mother Ö'elun, Qasar and his little brothers had been worried and rejoiced to see him.

TEMUJIN'S CAMP GROWS

94   Then Temujin and Belgutei went down the Kherlen River to find Madame Börte – they had been separated since he was nine years old. Deyi Secen the Qonggirat was staying there between Cekcer and Ciġurqu. Deyi Secen saw Temujin and was

very happy indeed and said, 'Knowing that the Tayici'ut breth-
ren envied you I have been very worried and was about to lose
hope. Finally, I have seen you!' He united them in marriage and
then escorted them back. While escorting them, Deyi Secen
turned back halfway at the Uraq Desert on the bend of the
Kherlen. His wife, Madame Börte's mother, was named Cotan.
Cotan saw her daughter on her way and they arrived when
they were at Senggur Stream inside Kürelgu.

Cotan returned and then Belgutei was sent to Bo'orcu with 95
the idea of their becoming friends. Belgutei got there and
Bo'orcu, without telling his father, mounted a hump-back
chestnut and, throwing on it behind him a brown woollen
mantle, came back with Belgutei. Already friends, that was the
way in which they became even better friends.[31]

They moved camp from Senggur Stream and pitched camp at 96
the range on the banks of the Bürkh around the headwaters of
the Kherlen River. Mother Cotan had brought a black sable-fur
coat as a gift for the groom's mother.[32] That fur coat Temujin,
Qasar and Belgutei took away. Thinking that, long ago, Ong
Khan of the Kereyit folk had called himself *anda* with Father
Yisukei Khan,[33] and that one who had called himself *anda* with
Father must be like a father himself, they learned that Ong
Khan was at the Black Forest on the Tuul and they went off
there. Temujin came to Ong Khan and said, 'Long ago, you
called yourself *anda* with my father.[34] You are like a father
indeed!' And he said, 'I have taken a wife and have brought the
wedding gift of clothes to you,' and gave him the sable-fur
coat. Ong Khan was very happy and said,

'Due to the donation of the black fur coat
Boldly I'll bring together your broken-up kingdom.
Moved by the memory of the sable coat
Safely I'll secure your sundered kingdom.
Set closer than kidneys
More cherished than chest
Let this be to me.'[35]

Then they returned and when they were at the banks of the 97
Bürkh, Old Man Jarci'udai, a son of the Uriyangqan, came
from Burgan-Qaldun carrying his bellows on his back and

leading his son named Jelme. Jarci'udai said, 'When you were at Deli'un Boldaq on the Onon, when Temujin was born, I gave him sable swaddling clothes. I even gave him this boy of mine, Jelme. But because he was little I took him away. Now let Jelme dress your saddle and lift up your felt door.'[36] And he gave him to them.

BÖRTE KIDNAPPED AND
THE RAID ON THE MERKIT

98 When they had pitched their camp on the banks of the Bürkh around the headwaters of the Kherlen River one morning early when the light of day was breaking yellow, Granny Qo'aqcin, who did chores inside Mother Ö'elun's *ger*, got up and said, 'Mother, mother, get up quick! The ground is shaking, you can hear pounding. Are the terrible Tayici'ut coming? Mother, get 99 up quick!' Mother Ö'elun said, 'Wake up the boys, quick!' and then she got up quickly herself. Temujin and the other children got up immediately and saddled their horses: Temujin rode one horse. Mother Ö'elun rode one horse. Qasar rode one horse. Qaci'un rode one horse. Temuke Otcigin rode one horse. Belgutei rode one horse. Bo'orcu rode one horse. Jelme rode one horse. Mother Ö'elun carried Temulun at her bosom. One spare horse was readied. There was no horse for Madame Börte.

100 Temujin and the brothers rode and as it was early went off in the direction of Burġan. Granny Qo'aqcin thought, 'I must hide Madame Börte,' and made her ride in a high covered wagon,[37] yoked to it an ox with speckled loins and moved up the Tenggelik Stream.

As they were coming along, when it was still grey and the day was breaking, from ahead of them came some common soldiers trotting up on patrol. 'What are you up to?' they asked.

Granny Qo'aqcin said, 'I'm one of Temujin's. I came to the big *ger* to shear the sheep and am returning to my own *ger*.'

Then they asked, 'Is Temujin in the *ger*? Is the *ger* far?'

Granny Qo'aqcin said, 'As for the *ger*, it's near, but I didn't see if Temujin is there or not. I got up in the back of the camp and then came here.'

At that, those soldiers trotted away. Granny Qo'aqcin 101 whipped up the ox with speckled loins and immediately, as it was about to move, the axle cracked in two. With the axle broken, they said, 'Let's run into the woods on foot' – at that very moment, the same soldiers came trotting up with Belgutei's mother riding double behind one of them and her feet dangling back and forth.

'What are you carrying in this cart?' they said.

Granny Qo'aqcin said, 'I'm carrying wool.'

The senior soldiers said to the younger boys in the squad, 'Get down and take a look.' The younger boys got down and when they opened the shut wagon's door, it was a person – a lady! – sitting there. Dragging her out of the wagon, they made her and Qo'aqcin ride double and took off. They tracked the bent grass and followed Temujin up in the direction of Burġan.

Following Temujin they circled Burġan-Qaldun three times 102 but were unable to catch him up. Dodging this way and that in the clinging sands and tangled woods, in deep forests so tangled a glutted snake could not slither into them, they followed him but were not able to catch him up. They were the Three Merkit, these three: Toqto'a of the Uduyit Merkit, Dayir-Usun of the U'as Merkit and Qa'atai Tarmala of the Qa'at Merkit. Remembering that, long ago, Mother Ö'elun had been grabbed away from Ciledu, now they had come to repay hatred for hatred. The Merkit said to each other, 'Paying them back for Ö'elun, now we have taken their women. We have paid them back for what they did to us.' So they rode down from Burġan-Qaldun and returned to their homes.

Thinking, 'Have those Three Merkit really returned to their 103 homes, or are they hiding in ambush?' Temujin sent Belgutei, Bo'orcu and Jelme to follow after the Merkit for three nights on reconnaissance and make sure the Merkit had removed themselves far away.

Temujin descended from the heights of Burġan and, beating his chest, said, 'Because Mother Qo'aqcin,

Like a weasel kept her watch,
Like an ermine cocked her ear,
Hastily fleeing hale and whole,
A hobbled horse I led on trails of hinds;
Dwelling in a den of dense-tied willow laths,[38]
I hiked the heights of high Burġan
And hid my life, like a little louse, in Burġan-Qaldun.
Saving as much as my poor self,
One mere mount I led on moose's trails;
Watching from a home of plaited willow wands,
I made my way on wide Qaldun,
And kept my life, like a cricket's chirp, in Qaldun-Burġan.

I was very frightened. I will do anointing every morning,[39] I
will do remembrance every day to Burġan-Qaldun. Let the seed
of my seed see to this.' And, facing the sun, he hung his belt
around his neck and hung his hat in his hands and, beating his
chest, he bowed nine times in the direction of the sun and he
made libations and prayers.[40]

104   Speaking his piece, Temujin, along with Qasar and Belgutei,
went to where To'oril, the Ong Khan,[41] was at the Black Forest
on the Tuul River and said, 'We were surprised by the Three
Merkit who came and stripped me of my girl and we have
come to ask the Ruler-Father of mine to save my girl for me!'
In reply to these words, To'oril the Ong Khan said, 'Did I not
say it to you last year? When you brought to me a sable-fur
coat and said, "Ones who called themselves *anda* in Father's
time, must be like a father!" and you let me wear it, then did I
not say,

"Moved by the memory of the sable coat
Safely I'll secure your sundered kingdom.
Due to the donation of the black fur coat
Boldly I'll bring together your broken-up kingdom.
More cherished than chest let this be to me;
Set closer than kidneys let this be to me."

Now being true to my word,

Moved by the memory of the sable coat,
Massacred will the mass of Merkit be;
Madame Börte will be made safe for you.

Due to the donation of the black fur coat
Destruction will be done to all the Merkit;
Dame Börte will we duly draw home.
You send word to Young Jamuqa.[42] Young Jamuqa is surely
in the Qorqonaq valley. I will ride hence with two *tümen*s;[43]
I will form up as the right wing; let Young Jamuqa form
two *tümen*s and ride as the left wing. Let Jamuqa set the
rendezvous.'

When Temujin, Qasar and Belgutei came back from To'oril 105
Khan to their *ger*, Temujin sent Qasar and Belgutei to Jamuqa,
telling them to speak to Jamuqa *Anda*.[44] He sent them to say,
'The Three Merkit came, and
My bed was made bereft –
As siblings of a single stem,
Shall we study how to serve them back?
My chest was chopped asunder –
As single seed of separate stock,
Shall we not ponder how to pay them back?'
Such was what he sent them to say to Jamuqa *Anda*, and he
also sent them to say to Jamuqa the words that were said by
To'oril Khan of the Kereyit. 'Mindful of how in days of old I
was kindly helped by his Father Yisukei Khan, I will be a good
friend. Send to Young Jamuqa to tell him that I will form two
*tümen*s and ride as the right wing. Let Young Jamuqa ride with
two *tümen*s. Let Young Jamuqa set the rendezvous when we
shall meet.' When these words had all been spoken to the end,
Jamuqa said,
'When I heard that Temujin *Anda*'s
Bed was made bereft,
My heart was heavy.
When I heard the news that
His chest was chopped asunder,
My guts were wracked with grief.
As we study how to serve them back,
Undone will be the Uduyit and U'as Merkit.
And Lady Börte shall be liberated.
As we ponder how to pay them back,
Massacre awaits the Qa'at Merkit.

Now that
    Skittish Toqto'a, when we slap the saddle leather,
    Will say it's the sounds of the war drums,
    He'll surely stay at Buur steppe.
    And Rebel Dayir-Usun,
    Now we've rattled the recurved bow's case,[45]
    Rests at Talqun Island where rivers run together.[46]
    When the blowing tumbleweed bounds at him,
    Now burrowing in the black woods, I believe
    Qa'atai Tarmala must be on the Qaraji steppe.
Now we will make a shortcut across the Khilok River – just let
the *saqal-bayan* stalks be thick enough – we will lash together
rafts and cross. We will leap over the
    Smoke hole of that skittish Toqto'a
    And smash apart his *ger*'s solid frame,
    To seize his girls in a sudden swoop.
    We'll pull apart his blessed portal[47]
    And plunder his kingdom painfully.'

106   Jamuqa also said, 'And say to Temujin *Anda* and To'oril
Khan the Elder, "As for me", tell them,
    "A standard seen afar have I sprinkled
    A steer's black leather-clad war drum with its booming bel-
        low have I beaten
    A steed with swift steps have I saddled
    A steel shirt have I suited up in
    A solid spear have I seized
    A stinging arrow on my string have I strung
    To slaughter all the savage Qa'at Merkit I set out."
Tell them:
    "A high-flown standard with milk have I honoured
    A bull's hard leather-clad war drum with heavy beats have I
        beaten
    A horse with inky hide his reins I hold
    A hardened breastplate have I hitched with thongs
    A honed blade have I hefted
    A hurrying arrow is here in my hand
    To harm the lives of hostile Uduyit Merkit I hasten."
To'oril Khan the Elder, ride forth and come by the southern

slopes of Burgan-Qaldun and pass by Temujin *Anda*, and let us set the rendezvous at Botogan Bo'orji on the headwaters of the Onon River. Riding forth from here and coming up the Onon River – my *Anda*'s kingdom is there, so taking one *tümen* from my *Anda*'s kingdom and I taking another *tümen* from here, we will form up two *tümen*s.[48] So going up the Onon River, let us come together at Botogan Bo'orji, the place of rendezvous.'

These words of Jamuqa's Qasar and Belgutei took to Temujin, who passed them on to To'oril Khan. Once these words of Jamuqa were delivered to him, To'oril Khan rode off with two *tümen*s. When To'oril Khan rode off, Temujin heard they were aiming for the banks of the Bürkh around the Kherlen on the southern slopes of Burgan-Qaldun and – himself being on the banks of the Bürkh – Temujin was thinking he would be in the way and so decamped and moved camp up the Tüngkelik, pitching camp at Tana Stream on the southern slopes of Burgan-Qaldun. Then as Temujin escorted his soldiers and as To'oril Khan's one *tümen* and To'oril Khan's younger brother Ja'a Gambo's one *tümen*,[49] that is, two *tümen*s in all, pitched camp at Ayil Qaragana on Kimurqa Stream, they all pitched camp together.

Temujin, To'oril Khan and Ja'a Gambo joined up and set out from there. When they reached Botogan Bo'orji at the headwaters of the Onon, Jamuqa had already reached the place of rendezvous three days earlier. Jamuqa saw the soldiers of Temujin, To'oril and Ja'a Gambo and formed his two *tümen*s up in ranks at attention. Temujin, To'oril and Ja'a Gambo dressed the ranks of their soldiers as well; then they approached and hailed each other. Jamuqa said, 'Did we not say to each other, "Rains may rage, but to the rendezvous – gales may blow, but to the gathering let us not be late"? As Mongols, are we not ones whose word "yes" is an oath? Did we not agree, "He whose promised 'yes' was not achieved, him we will prohibit joining our assembled arms"?'

To Jamuqa's words To'oril Khan said, 'We pulled up three days late to the place of rendezvous. Let Young Jamuqa decide the crime and the blame.' That was all that they said of the blame for the rendezvous.

109   They moved off from Botoġan Bo'orji, reached the Khilok River, lashed together rafts, and crossed. Then at Toqto'a Beki's they[50]
  Swarmed over the smoke hole
  And smashed up his *ger*'s solid frame,
  To seize his girls in a sudden swoop.
  They pulled apart his blessed portal
  And plundered his kingdom pitilessly.
As Toqto'a Beki was sleeping, the fishermen, sable-trappers and hunters who were on the Khilok River went travelling through the night to give word, saying, 'The enemies' outriders are coming.' After this word had been received, Toqto'a joined up with Dayir-Usun of the U'as Merkit and escaped into hiding down the Selenge and into Barguzin with a few persons.

110   As the Merkit folk fled down the Selenge in the night, as our soldiers dogged the heels of the fugitive Merkit through the night, plundering and looting, and as Temujin called out 'Börte, Börte!' to the fugitive people rushing on, then they met. Madame Börte was there among the fugitives. She recognized Temujin's voice, got down from the wagon and ran towards him. Börte and Mother Qo'aqcin seized Temujin's reins and tether in the night – it was bright moonlight. When he saw Madame Börte, he recognized her and they hugged each other in welcome.

Then Temujin sent word that night to To'oril Khan and Jamuqa *Anda* in a message, saying, 'I have found what I sought; let us not move through the night, let us pitch camp here.' As the Merkit folk were rushing on in flight, they pitched camp right there in the dark in the middle of those rushing on in a panic and so spent the night. That was the way in which he met Madame Börte and rescued her from the Merkit kingdom.

111   The beginning of it all was that Toqto'a Beki of the Uduyit Merkit, Dayir-Usun of the U'as Merkit and Qa'atai Tarmala [of the Qa'at Merkit], these three Merkits and the three hundred Merkit fellows, recalled how a long time ago Toqto'a's junior kinsman Big Ciledu had Mother Ö'elun snatched away from him by Yisukei Ba'atur,[51] and they went to take vengeance for that. They made Temujin circle Burġan-Qaldun three times and caught up with Madame Börte and gave her into the care of

Ciledu's little brother Cilger the Brawny. While she was in his care, Cilger the Brawny ran away as a rebel and said,

'A ghastly crow who gorged on scraps
Got up desire to dine on goose;
The gross and gory Cilger, me,
Did muster blessed Madame's majesty
And woe did bring to Merkit ones.
It came upon the craven head
Of crude and common Cilger, me.
Concerned but for my paltry corpse
I'm creeping through a covert canyon;
Who can be my comfort now?
A mangy bird who mangled mice
Made eyes to dine on meat of swan;
The thieving thrall-born Cilger, me,
Did think to touch a lady's thigh,
A madame of majestic mien,
And misery brought to Merkit men.
It fell upon the filthy head
Of vaunting vile Cilger, me.
My life as small as turds of sheep
I saved by scaling shadowed rills;
My life as small as turds of sheep
Who can shelter now for me?'

So he said as he fled.

They caught up with Qa'atai Tarmala. They brought him back and made him wear a plank cangue and sent him off to Qaldun-Burġan. [112]

Belgutei was told that his mother was in a camp over there – and Belgutei went to get his mother. And as Belgutei went into her *ger* by the western door, his mother left by the eastern door in a tattered sheep-skin coat and said to the other people outside, 'I was told my sons have become rulers. Here I am mated to a base man; how can I look my sons in the face?' and ran off to crawl into the woods. He sought her just then but did not find her. Belgutei Noyan fired off knob-headed arrows at every one of the Merkit lineage and said, 'Bring me my mother!'[52]

The three hundred Merkit who rode around Burġan were

exterminated unto the seed of the seed until their ashes blew away. Of the girls who remained, the ones good for the bed were got in bed, the ones good to go in the door were got in the door.[53]

113   To To'oril Khan and Jamuqa Temujin said gratefully, 'Made friends by my Ruler-Father and Jamuqa *Anda*, made mighty by Heaven and Earth

> Named aright by mighty Heaven,
> Nurtured well by our Mother Earth,
> Manly, we deprived of bed mates
> The ill-deserving Merkit folk.
> Their bowels we battered in
> And their beds we broke up
> And their boys we butchered,
> Their very remnants we have spoiled!
> With the Merkit routed, we retraced our steps.'

114   As the Uduyit Merkit were fleeing our soldiers picked up a five-year-old child with flame in his eyes named Kücu, left behind on the range, with sable hat, boots of the skin of doe's feet and a coat sewn of mink skin with the hair removed.[54] They brought him to Mother Ö'elun and gave him to her as a *sauġa* prize.[55]

115   Temujin, To'oril Khan and Jamuqa joined up and ripped open the wagon-fort's locked carts and ravished the ladies with lovely looks. On withdrawal from Talqun Island between the Orkhon and Selenge, Temujin and Jamuqa joined up and went back to Qorqonaq valley. To'oril Khan in withdrawing went by the Hökortu valley along the shady side[56] of Burġan-Qaldun and, going through passes of spruce and passes of aspen,[57] he did a ring hunt of its game and went back to the Black Forest on the Tuul.[58]

FRIENDSHIP AND
QUARREL OF TEMUJIN AND JAMUQA

Temujin and Jamuqa pitched camp together in the Qorqonaq   116
valley and, remembering together how they had become *anda*
before, they said, 'Let us renew our love for each other.'

The first time when they became *anda* was when Temujin
was eleven years old; Jamuqa gave Temujin the knucklebone
of a roe deer and with Temujin's copper-weighted knuckle-
bone given in return they became *anda*.[59] And they agreed to
be *anda* with each other when they were playing knucklebones
on the ice of the Onon River;[60] it was there they agreed to
be *anda*. After that, in the spring, when they were competing
with each other in archery with wooden bows, Jamuqa glued
together two horns of a two-year-old calf and drilled holes in
it and gave the whistling arrowhead to Temujin. He exchanged
it for Temujin's cypress-tipped knob-headed arrow and they
became *anda*. That was the way in which they agreed to be
anda the second time.

They said, 'If we listen to the words of the elders and ancients,   117
this is the way in which *anda* love each other: people who are
anda are as if they have one life without any separation and
are lifelong saviours to each other. Now let us renew our love.'
Temujin girt Jamuqa *Anda* about with the gold belt which he
had got by despoiling Toqto'a of the Merkit and mounted
Jamuqa *Anda* on Toqto'a's whitish-yellow barren mare with a
black spine. Jamuqa *Anda* girt Temujin *Anda* with the gold belt
which he had got by despoiling Dayir-Usun of the U'as Merkit
and mounted Temujin *Anda* on Dayir-Usun's very own kid-
white horned horse.[61] At the Bushy Tree, by the south face of
the Quldaqar Cliff, they called each other *anda* and loved each
other. They rejoiced with feasting and ceremony and at night
they slept together alone under the quilt.

As for Temujin and Jamuqa loving each other, they loved each   118
other for one year and half of the next year. And when they
agreed together one day to move camp from that range where

they were, on the Red Disk Day, on the sixteenth of the first moon of summer, they moved camp. As Temujin and Jamuqa went along together in front of the wagons, Jamuqa said, 'Temujin, *anda*, *anda*,

> Let us have our camp up against the high mountains
> And wranglers for our horses will have huts enough;
> Let us set our camp down against the swirling brook
> And shepherds for our sheep and lambs will share a bite.'

Temujin could not understand these words of Jamuqa and stood there silently and fell behind and waited for the wagons in the middle of the march – the caravan had formed up – and Temujin told Mother Ö'elun, 'Jamuqa *Anda* is saying something. He is saying,

> "Let us have our camp up against the high mountains
> And wranglers for our horses will have huts enough;
> Let us set our camp down against the swirling brook
> And shepherds for our sheep and lambs will share a bite."

I could not understand these words and not knowing what to reply I said nothing. I have come to ask my mother.' Before Mother Ö'elun could make a sound, Madame Börte said, 'Jamuqa *Anda* is said to be a person who easily gets tired of things. Now the time has come that he has become tired of us. The speech that Jamuqa *Anda* said to us just now is one that is aimed straight at us. Let us not pitch camp. As we have begun moving this way, let us make a clean break and move through the night.' So she said.

119   He approved Madame Börte's words and moved through the night without pitching camp. And as they were advancing they came across the Tayici'ut on the road. Now the Tayici'ut, they were skittish, and even though it was night, they moved the opposite way in the direction of Jamuqa. On the range of the Tayici'ut's Besut,[62] our people took up a little boy named Kökecu, someone who had been left behind on the range, and gave him to Mother Ö'elun. Mother Ö'elun raised him.

GATHERING A PEOPLE
AND THE FIRST CORONATION

We went through the night and when the day broke, lo:[63]   120

Qaci'un-Toġura'un, Qarġai-Toġura'un and Qaraldai-Toġura'un, these three Toġura'un brothers, had also gone through the night together to arrive.

And Qada'an-Daldurqan of the Tarġut and the five Tarġut brothers arrived as well.

And Mönggedu Kiyan's boy Önggur with his Cangśi'ut and Baya'ut arrived as well.

From the Barulas the brothers Qubilai and Qutus came.

From the Manġġut, two brothers Jedei and Doqolqu Cerbi came.[64]

Bo'orcu's little brother Ögolei Cerbi broke away from the Arlat and came to join his big brother Bo'orcu as well.

Jelme's little brothers Ca'urqan and Sübe'edei Ba'atur broke away from the Uriyangqan and came to join Jelme.

From the Besut, the two brothers Degei and Kücugur also came.

From the Suldus, Cilgutei and Taġai, the Tayici'ut brothers, came as well.

Sece-Domoq of the Jalayir with his two sons Arqai-Qasar and Bala came as well.

From the Qongqotan, Söiketu Cerbi came as well.

Jegei-Qongtaġar's son Sö'ekei Je'un of the Sö'eken came as well.

Caġan-Quwa of the Negus came as well.

Kinggiyadai of the Olqunu'ut, Sece'ur from the Ġorulas and Moci-Bedu'un from the Dörben came as well.

Botu of the Ikires, acting as son-in-law, came as well.

From the Noyagin, Jungšoi came as well.

From the Oronar, Jirġo'an came as well.

From the Barulas, Suġu Secen came with his son Qaracar as well.

And Qorci, Old Man Üsun and Köke-Cos with their whole wagon-fort of Menen Ba'arin came as well. Qorci came and   121

said, 'We were born from the woman that Bodoncar the Holy
seized. We were born of a single womb, burst from the same
water. We did not break away from Jamuqa. A *ja'arin*-spirit
came and showed it to me before my very eyes:[65] a fallow cow
came and circled around Jamuqa and butted up against his *ger*-
wagon. It butted Jamuqa and broke one of its horns and its
horns became uneven. Saying, "Bring me my horn" again and
again, it was mooing and mooing in the direction of Jamuqa
and pawing and pawing the dirt. A polled fallow ox with a
great *ger*[66] lifted it high and was pulling it in harness and as it
advanced behind Temujin on the great wagon road it was moo-
ing and mooing, "Heaven and Earth have taken counsel saying,
'Let Temujin become master of the kingdom; I am delivering
the kingdom to him.'"[67] The *ja'arit*-spirits show things before
my eyes, and explain them to me. Temujin, if you become
master of the kingdom, what joy will you bring me for having
explained them to you?'

Temujin said, 'If the kingdom is truly put under my rule, I
will make you a ruler of a *tümen*.' He said, 'For me, a person
who has shown you such a great sovereign sway, where is the
joy in being a commander of a *tümen*? When I have become a
commander of a *tümen* let me have free rights to choose from
among the kingdom's beauties and lovely daughters and make
me a man with thirty women. And listen with attention to
whatever else I say to your face.'

122   The wagon-fort of the Keniges, headed by Gunan, came
as well.

And the wagon-fort of Dāritai Otcigin came as well.

Mulqalqu came from the Jadaran as well.

And the wagon-fort of the Nünjin and Saġayit came as well.

After that many people broke away from Jamuqa, and when
camp had been pitched at Ayil Qaraġana on Kimurqa Stream,
Sece Beki and Taicu the sons of Sorġatu-Yörki of the Yörkin as
one wagon-fort, together with Nekun Taiši's son Qocar Beki as
one wagon-fort and Qutula Khan's son Altan Otcigin as one
wagon-fort – these also broke off and moved away from Jamuqa.
So when Temujin had pitched camp at Ayil Qaraġana on
Kimurqa Stream, they came and pitched camp together.

From there they moved camp and pitched camp at Qara-Jiruken's Köke Na'ur of Senggur Stream inside Kürelgu. It was 123 Altan, Qocar and Sece Beki who took counsel together and said to Temujin, 'Let us make you ruler. If Temujin becomes ruler,

Galloping as an outrider against gathered foes,
Fair of face
Goodly girls,
Palace-tents, pavilions,
Foreign folk's
Chubby-cheeked
Lovely ladies and
Geldings good of rump
Trotting wc will take for you.
When hunting wily game,
Bushes we will beat for you.
When hunting wild beasts,
Cram them close will we for you.
When corralling game by crags,
Press them till they pant will we for you.
If day of drawing swords has come
And commands of yours are countered,
Strip from us our household stock,
Separate sweet ladies from our side
And cast aside our coal-black heads
On brown and soiled beds.
If hours of peace are here
And harmony of yours is harmed,
Bear away our bondsmen,
Wrest from us our wife and child
And dump our bodies in a desert place.'
Professing many promises,
Owning many oaths,

They made Temujin a ruler, naming him Chinggis Khan.

After Temujin became Chinggis Khan, Bo'orcu's little brother 124 Ögolei Cerbi bore a quiver on his belt. Qaci'un-Toġura'un bore a quiver on his belt. The brothers Jedei and Doqolqu Cerbi bore quivers on their belts. Önggur, Söiketu Cerbi and Qada'an-Daldurqan said, 'Never will your morning drink be meagre;

never will your noon drink be neglected' and were made stewards. Degei said,

'Making soup of a second-year wether,
In the morning it shall never be meagre
And by day it shall not be delayed.
Herding the mottled sheep,
I will hold them under the cart.
Corralling the yellow sheep,
I will fill the camp with them.
Greedy and base am I;
Gathering all the sheep,
Guts are what I will eat.'

Degei herded the sheep. His little brother Kücugur said,

'The linchpins on the locker wagons –
I will not let them come loose;
The axles on the advancing wagons,
I will not let break asunder.

And will manage the *ger*-wagons.' Dödei Cerbi said that he would provision the maids and butlers. Qubilai, Cilgutei and Qarġai-Toġura'un together with Qasar were told to 'Bear the sword and hew asunder high and haughty necks; slash apart all strong and self-willed shoulders.' Of Belgutei and Qaraldai-Toġura'un he said, 'Let them handle the geldings; let them become grooms.' Of Ġodu of the Tayici'ut, Morici and Mulqalqu he said, 'Let them herd the horses.' Of Arqai-Qasar, Taġai, Sö'ekei and Ca'urqan he said, 'Aim as my *qo'ocaq* arrows, shoot as my *odora* shafts.'[68]

Sübe'edei Ba'atur said,
'Turning into a mouse,
Driving them into muster,
Becoming a crow,
Herding them into conclave,
All those outside I will gather.
Serving as a saddle felt
Shield I shall try to be
Screening a curtain felt
Shelter for your *ger* I shall try to be.'[69]

125   So Temujin became Chinggis Khan and said to Bo'orcu and

Jelme, 'When I had no friend but a shadow, it was you two who became my shadow and eased my soul. Let this remain in my soul. When I had no whip but a tail, you became my tail and eased my heart. Let this be ever in my heart. Going before the others, shall you not preside over all of them?'[70]

And Chinggis Khan said to them all, 'When I was made mighty and protected by Heaven and Earth, you were the elders who preferred me as companion over Jamuqa *Anda* and came to me. Shall you not be my fortunate friends? I have named you each to your positions.'[71]

Taġai and Sö'ekei were sent as envoys to To'oril Khan of the Kereyit to say that Chinggis Khan had been made the ruler. To'oril Khan sent back to say, 'It is most right that my son Temujin has been made a ruler; how can the Mongols be without a ruler? Do not crack this counsel of yours; do not loosen this league of yours; do not cut up this coat of yours.' 126

When Chinggis Khan sent Arqai-Qasar and Ca'urqan to Jamuqa as envoys, Jamuqa sent back to say, 'Tell this to Altan and Qocar,' and said, 'Altan and Qocar, how did you two separate Temujin *Anda* and me with a sting in the stomach and goad in the gut? When my *anda* and I were still together, why didn't you make Temujin *Anda* ruler without separating us then? What are you thinking now that you have thought to make him ruler? Altan and Qocar, you two, ease *Anda*'s soul by living up to your words and serve him well.'[72] 127

3 : THE EARLY BATTLES OF CHINGGIS KHAN

FIRST BATTLE WITH JAMUQA

128 After that, while Jamuqa's younger cousin Taicar was at Ölegei Spring on the southern slope of Jalama, he went to steal the horses of our Coci-Tarmala at Sa'ari steppe. Taicar stole the horses of Coci-Tarmala and got away. Coci-Tarmala's horses had been stolen; the hearts of his friends failed and Coci-Darmala went after them all by himself. He got to the edge of the herd at night and lay with his belly over his horse's mane. He fired a shot to snap Taicar's spine and killed him, before bringing back his herd.

129 Learning that his younger cousin had been killed, Jamuqa with the Jadaran made alliance with thirteen different peoples and formed up into three *tümen*s, crossed over the Ala'ut-Turġa'ut and rode against Chinggis Khan. Mülke-Totaq and Boroldai of the Ikires came to give news to Chinggis Khan while he was in Kürelgu that they were coming. When he learned this news, he had thirteen wagon-forts. They formed up into three *tümen*s as well, rode against Jamuqa, and gave battle at Dalan-Baljut.[1] Chinggis Khan was forced back then by Jamuqa and escaped into the Jerene Gorge on the Onon. Jamuqa said, 'We let him escape into Jerene on the Onon,' and as he was returning he boiled the princes of the Cinoas in seventy cauldrons. He cut off the head of Caġān-Quwa of the Negus and dragged it away by his horse's tail.[2]

130 Then after we had let Jamuqa get away, first Jürcedei of the Uru'ut leading his Uru'ut, and then Quyildar of the Manġġut leading his Manġġut broke away from Jamuqa and came to

Chinggis Khan.[3] Father Mönglik of the Qongqotan was there with Jamuqa and with his seven sons broke away from Jamuqa and came to join Chinggis Khan.

BRAWL WITH THE YÖRKIN

When so many different peoples had come from Jamuqa, Chinggis Khan rejoiced that indeed a whole kingdom's worth had come to him, and Chinggis Khan, Madame Ö'elun, Qasar and Sece Beki and Taicu of the Yörkin agreed to hold a feast together in the forest on the Onon. As they were feasting, one skin of *esuk* was poured in the first rank for Chinggis Khan, for Madame Ö'elun, for Qasar and for Sece Beki and others.[4] Because one skin had been poured in the first rank for Sece Beki's little mother Ebegei,[5] Lady Qorijin and Lady Qu'urcin each said, 'How could they pour for Ebegei in the first rank without pouring for me in the first rank?' and they slapped the steward Śiki'ur. On being slapped, the steward Śiki'ur wailed in a loud voice, 'Because Yisukei Ba'atur and Nekun Taiši are dead, is that why I have been slapped like this?'

That feast was overseen from our side by Belgutei, who stood holding Chinggis Khan's geldings. On the Yörkin side Böri the Brawny oversaw the feast. A Qatagin man was seized as a thief for stealing a tether from our hitching post.[6] Böri the Brawny came to that person's defence. For his whole life when Belgutei would wrestle he would tuck his sleeve under his right arm and go around with it bare.[7] And Böri the Brawny slashed open with a sword his shoulder that had been bared naked like that. Even though Belgutei had been slashed at like that, he went about letting the blood flow without making anything of it and without paying it any heed. Chinggis Khan was sitting in the shade and saw it from inside the feast. He came out and said, 'How did this happen to us?' When he said that, Belgutei said, 'The wound is hardly anything – I worry we might create a stink with those brothers on my behalf. I am not in pain; I am getting over it. When we have just been getting on nicely with those brothers, big brother, stop – hold on for a few seconds.'[8]

132   Chinggis Khan, without heeding Belgutei's words of dissuasion, ripped some branches from the trees clean off and pulled the plungers out of the leather sacks and they started beating each other up.[9] The Yörkin lost and Lady Qorijin and Lady Qu'urcin were grabbed and taken away. But then the next moment they said, 'Let's be reconciled.'

And while envoys were being sent back and forth saying, 'Hand back Lady Qorijin and Lady Qu'urcin and let's be reconciled,' they learned the news: that since Me'ujin-Se'ultu and the rest had not obeyed their treaty, the Golden Khan of the Chinese had sent Ongging *Chengxiang*[10] to marshal the troops without delay.[11] Ongging *Chengxiang* was advancing, driving Me'ujin-Se'ultu and the other Tatars up the Ulz with their herds and provisions.

EXPEDITION AGAINST THE TATARS

133 When he learned the news, Chinggis Khan said, 'From days of old, the Tatars have been a hateful folk who murdered the grandfathers and fathers. In this opportunity, let us join in on this attack.' So he then sent envoys to deliver word to To'oril Khan that 'They are saying that the Golden Khan's Ongging *Chengxiang* is advancing, driving Me'ujin-Se'ultu and the other Tatars up the Ulz. Let us join in on the attack against the Tatars who murdered our grandfathers and fathers. Let Father To'oril Khan come quickly!'

When this news had been delivered, To'oril Khan said, 'My son has done right in sending me this news. Let us join in on the attack.' Then on the third day, Chinggis Khan gathered his army and the army set out and To'oril Khan hastened to assist him.

Chinggis Khan and To'oril Khan sent the news to Sece Beki, Taicu and the other Yörkin, saying, 'Now in this opportunity, let us ride together and join in on the attack against the Tatars who from days of old have murdered our grandfathers and fathers.'

They were held up for six days by the Yörkin. Unable to wait any longer, Chinggis Khan and To'oril Khan led the army down the Ulz. As they were coming to join in on the attack with

Ongging *Chengxiang*, Me'ujin-Se'ultu and the other Tatars had built forts there at Qusutu-Śitu'en and Naratu-Śitu'en on the Ulz.[12] Chinggis Khan and To'oril Khan took prisoner Me'ujin-Se'ultu and those who had fortified themselves in the forts and killed Me'ujin-Se'ultu there. Chinggis Khan took from there a silver cradle with a quilt sewn with *tana*-pearls.[13]

Since they had killed Me'ujin-Se'ultu, Chinggis Khan and To'oril Khan went to meet Ongging *Chengxiang* face to face.[14] Ongging *Chengxiang* learned that they had killed Me'ujin-Se'ultu and was very happy and gave the title *Ca'ut-Quri* to Chinggis Khan.[15] To To'oril of the Kereyit he gave the title *Ong*.[16] The title Ong Khan came from his being so named by Ongging *Chengxiang*. Ongging *Chengxiang* said, 'Your joining in on the attack on Me'ujin-Se'ultu and killing him was a very great service that you two did for the Golden Khan. I will report this help to the Golden Khan. The Golden Khan shall decide if a greater title than this is to be added for Chinggis Khan and the title *Zhaotao* be given.'[17] So happy then was Ongging *Chengxiang* before he withdrew. Chinggis Khan and Ong Khan then plundered the Tatars and shared everything out and returned to dismount at their homes.

When they were rifling through the rangeland that the Tatars had fortified and where they had pitched camp at Naratu Śitu'en, our soldiers picked up from the range a little boy who had been abandoned. They brought the little boy with a golden round nose ring and a gold-stitched silk- and sable-lined stomacher and gave him as a *sauġa* prize to Chinggis Khan and Mother Ö'elun.[18] Mother Ö'elun said, 'He must be the son of a fine person; he must be the seed of a person with a fine ancestry.' Making him the sixth son and little brother to her five sons, Mother named him Little Śiki Qutuġu and took care of him.[19]

ANNIHILATION OF THE YÖRKIN

Chinggis Khan's base camp was at Lake Hariltu.[20] The Yörkin looted the clothes off fifty fellows who had been left behind in the base camps. They killed ten fellows. When he heard the news that those left behind in our base camps told Chinggis Khan about how they had been treated by the Yörkin, Chinggis Khan was very angry and said, 'Why have we been treated like this by the Yörkin? When we were feasting in the forest on the Onon, the very same ones slapped the steward Śiki'ur. The very same ones slashed Belgutei's shoulder. "Let's make up", we were told, and we handed Lady Qorijin and Lady Qu'urcin back to them. After that, saying "Let us ride and join in on the attack against the hateful and spiteful Tatars who murdered our grandfathers and fathers," we waited for the Yörkin six days; once again we were held up. And now, since they are relying on an enemy, then they themselves shall be the enemy too!' So saying, he rode against the Yörkin.

When the Yörkin were at the Seven Hills of the Küte'u Isle on the Kherlen,[21] their folk were plundered. Sece Beki and Taicu fled with a few souls. Chasing them down, we caught up with them at Tele'etu Pass and captured Sece Beki and Taicu. We captured them and Chinggis Khan said to Sece and Taicu, 'What did we say to each other in olden days?' Sece and Taicu said, 'We did not live up to the words we spoke. Hold us to our word!' Then, recalling their words, they bowed themselves forward for him. He recalled their words for them and held them resolutely to their words and right there cast them away.

137 Sece and Taicu having finally been sorted out, we came back. When the Yörkin had been forced into flight, Kü'un-Quwa, the son of Telegetu the Rich, and Scissors Cila'un and Jebke, all of the Jalayir, were among the Yörkin.[22] Kü'un-Quwa paid homage with his two sons Muqali and Buqa and said,

'Let them be thralls of your threshold;
If they flee your threshold,
Hew their hamstrings.
Let them be property of your portal;
If they quit your portal,
Slice open their stomachs,
And cast them away.'[23]

So saying, he gave them to him. Scissors Cila'un also paid homage to Chinggis Khan with his two sons Tüngge and Qaśi and said,

'I give them on grounds that they

Guard your golden threshold; if they
Separate from your golden threshold
Separate them from their sweet life
And cast them away.
I offer them with an obligation that they
Elevate the felt of your entryway; if they
Ever from your service extricate themselves
Kick them in the kidneys
And cast them away.'

Jebke was given to Qasar. Jebke brought a little child named Boroġul from the range of the Yörkin and gave him in homage to Mother Ö'elun.[24]

When Mother Ö'elun raised these four in her *ger* – the child 138 named Kücu got from the Merkit range, the child named Kökecu got from the Besut range among the Tayici'ut, the child named Little Śiki Qutuġu got from the Tatar range, and the child named Boroġul got from the Yörkin range – she raised them thinking, 'Who else would be eyes to see in the day and ears to hear in the night for my sons?'

The way in which these Yörkin folk became Yörkin was thus: 139 the eldest of Qabul Khan's seven sons was Ökin-Barqaq. His son was Sorġatu-Yörki.[25] As he was the eldest of Qabul Khan's sons, he selected from among his subjects those with

Gall in their gut,
Thrust in their thumbs,
Spirit in their lungs,
Swagger on their lips.

He selected for himself every man who had skills and all the brawny and powerful ones. And because they had spirit, gall and pride, and were wilful [*yorgimaq*],[26] that was the way in which they were called Yörkin. Such proud folk Chinggis Khan brought low; he exterminated those of the Yörkin surname. Their folk and their kingdom Chinggis Khan made into his own private subjects.

One day, Chinggis Khan said, 'Let's have Böri the Brawny 140 and Belgutei wrestle.' Böri the Brawny was one of the Yörkin. Before,[27] Böri the Brawny would seize Belgutei with a hand on one side and push with his other foot and make him fall, pushing him down without letting him move; Böri the Brawny was the brawniest in the kingdom. And then Belgutei and Böri the Brawny were made to wrestle. Böri the Brawny, a man who could not be beaten, took a fall for him. Belgutei, unable to pin him, held him by the shoulder and got on to his butt. Belgutei looked back, and just as he looked at Chinggis Khan, the khan bit his lower lip. Belgutei understood and moved up on his back, pulled the two sides of his collar in a firm crosswise grip, and put his knee on his spine until it cracked.[28] Böri the Brawny knew his spine was broken and said, 'I would not have been beaten by Belgutei. I was afraid of the khan and took the fall, hesitated and lost my life.' Just then he died. Having snapped his spine asunder, Belgutei dragged him off and threw him away.

The eldest of Qabul Khan's seven sons was Ökin-Barqaq. The next was Bartan Ba'atur. His son was Yisukei Ba'atur. The next son was Qutuqtu-Möngler.[29] His son was Böri. Instead of the adjacent Bartan Ba'atur's sons, by becoming friends with the proud sons of the more distant Barqaq, Böri the Brawny, the brawniest in the kingdom, had his back broken by Belgutei and died.

SECOND BATTLE WITH JAMUQA[30]

141 After that, in the Year of the Chicken [1201] the Qatagin and the Salji'ut joined together, the Qatagin led by Baqu-Corogi and the Salji'ut led by Irkidei Ba'atur;[31]

The Dörben and the Tatars reconciled, the Dörben led by Qaci'un Beki and the Tatars led by Jalin-Buqa of the Alci Tatar;[32]

The Ikires led by Tüge-Maqa;

Dergei Amal and Alġui of the Qonggirat;

The Ġorulas led by Co'os-Caġān;

The Naiman led by Buyruq Khan of the Kücugut Naiman;

Ġodu, son of Toqto'a Beki of the Merkit;

Qutuġa Beki of the Oyirat; and

Fatty Kiriltuq, Ġodun-Hürceng and Aġucu Ba'atur of the Tayici'ut – the Tayici'ut and that many other peoples gathered at Alġui Spring and, intending to make Jamuqa of the Jajirat a *Gür Khan*,[33] they chopped asunder a stallion and a mare and took an oath together. From there they moved camp down the Ergune River to the broad meadow in the peninsula where the Gen River flows into the Ergune. There they elevated Jamuqa as *Gür Khan*. Having raised him up as *Gür Khan*, they agreed with each other to ride off against Chinggis Khan and Ong Khan.[34] Qoridai of the Ġorulas heard that they had agreed to ride against them and sent off this news to Chinggis Khan while he was at Kürelgu. After this news was delivered, Chinggis Khan sent this news off to Ong Khan. Once the news reached Ong Khan, he mobilized his army and came quickly to Chinggis Khan.

Once he knew that Ong Khan had come, Chinggis Khan and 142 Ong Khan joined together and agreed to ride against Jamuqa. Chinggis Khan sent Altan, Qocar and Dāritai as his vanguard as they rode down the Kherlen; Ong Khan sent Senggum, Ja'a Gambo and Bilge Beki as his vanguard. Ahead of these vanguards, scouts were dispatched; one scout detachment camped on Enegen Güiletu. Beyond that, they had one scout detachment camp on Cekcer. Beyond that, they had one scout detachment camp on Ciġurqu. When our vanguards Altan, Qocar and Senggum had reached Utkiya and were thinking to camp there, a man came hastening from the scouts placed on Ciġurqu and delivered the news that the enemy was coming.

When that news came, they went on without pitching camp, intending to get intelligence while facing the enemy. They approached them to get some intelligence and when they asked who they were, it was Jamuqa's vanguard. It was these four, Aġucu Ba'atur of the Mongols, Buyruq Khan of the Naiman, Toqto'a Beki's son Ġodu of the Merkit and Qutuġa Beki of the Oyirat, who were advancing as Jamuqa's vanguard. Our vanguard exchanged calls with them, crying out, 'Dusk is falling on us, let us give battle tomorrow morning,' and withdrew and spent the night with the centre.

The next morning, they were unleashed and came together 143 and gave battle at Köiten. When they were pushing each other back and forth, up and down the slope, and re-forming their own ranks, at that very moment – Buyruq Khan and Qutuġa knew how to use the weather-stone – they performed the weather-stone magic. But the weather-magic reversed and the magic fell

on themselves.[35] Unable to advance, it was they themselves who
tumbled into the ditches; then, saying to each other, 'Heaven is
not pleased with us,' they scattered.

144   Buyruq Khan of the Naiman split away and made off
towards Uluġ Taġ on the southern slopes of the Altai. Toqto'a's
son Ġodu made off towards the Selenge. Qutuġa Beki of the
Oyirat, cutting his way through the forests, made off towards
the Shishged.[36] Aġucu Ba'atur of the Tayici'ut made off towards
the Onon.

Jamuqa plundered his own folk who had elevated him as a
ruler[37] and made off to return down the Ergune. Once they were
scattered, Ong Khan pursued Jamuqa down the Ergune; Ching-
gis Khan pursued Aġucu Ba'atur of the Tayici'ut in the direction
of the Onon.[38]

ANNIHILATION OF THE TAYICI'UT

When Aġucu Ba'atur returned to his kingdom, he set his folk in
motion in a panicked flight. Meanwhile on the banks beyond
the Onon, at the Ölenggut-Turas, the Tayici'uts Aġucu Ba'atur
and Ġodun-Hürceng marshalled their soldiers and stood in
ranks, thinking to give battle. When Chinggis Khan arrived, he
gave battle to the Tayici'ut. They battled back and forth, back
and forth, repeatedly, until dusk fell on them. They spent the
night leaning on each other in the very spot where they had
been battling. And as even more of the people came fleeing in
panic, they made a wagon-fort together there with their sol-
diers and spent the night propped up against each other.

145   In that battle Chinggis Khan had been wounded in his jugu-
lar vein and, agitated that the blood could not be staunched, he
let the sun go down. Right there, where they were leaning on
each other, Jelme stained his mouth with blood as he sucked
and sucked the clotted blood. Jelme sat guarding him half the
night without trusting any other person and half the night
through he would swallow the clotted blood until his mouth
was full and then spit it out.[39] And when the night was passing,
Chinggis Khan revived and said, 'The blood has finally clotted.

I am thirsty.' Then Jelme stripped his hat, boots, coat and clothes off completely and, wearing only his breeches, he ran in all but naked among the enemy who stood there propped up against each other. He climbed on to the wagon of the people who had set up a wagon-fort beyond and, looking for any kind of *esuk*, failed to find it – in their flight, they had put their mares out to pasture without milking them. Having failed to find *esuk*, he came back carrying a large covered pitcher of kefir on his back. The whole time, no one spied him come or go – was he not protected by Heaven?

Having brought the kefir in a covered pitcher, Jelme went right back to find water before returning. He mixed it with the kefir and made the khan drink it. Thrice the khan drank a mouthful and then said, 'My mind's eye is clearing up'; as he sat up, the day broke and it became bright. And when he looked around where he was sitting, where Jelme had sucked and sucked the clotted blood and spat it out had become muddy all over. Chinggis Khan saw it and said, 'What is this about? Why not spit it out further away?'

Then Jelme said, 'Since you were so restless, I was afraid that if I wandered off you would be worried and in a rush I swallowed what I swallowed and spat out what I spat out; agitated myself, how much must have gone into my own belly!'

Chinggis Khan said again, 'When I was lying down in a state like this, how could you have run around among them half-naked? If you had been caught, wouldn't you have betrayed the state I was in?'

Jelme said, 'My idea going in half-naked was that if somehow I was seized, I would say, "They realized that I wanted to go over to you, sirs,[40] and seized me to kill me; they stripped off all my clothes and with only my pants left on me I stealthily gave them the slip and even so came rushing off to you, sirs," and they would think it true and give me clothes and take care of me. But once I'd mounted a horse, in that very moment, as they were watching, wouldn't I get back here? With that idea in mind, and thinking to relieve the khan's nagging thirst, I went there with my eyes open and this idea in mind.'

Chinggis Khan said, 'What shall I say now? In a bygone day,

when the Three Merkit came and made me circle the Burġan three times, you saved my life once. Now the clotted blood you sucked with your own mouth and so delivered my life. And also, when I was restless with thirst, you put aside your own life and went into the enemy with your eyes open, satisfied my thirst, and brought me back to life. Let these three services of yours remain in my mind.' So it was decreed.[41]

146   When the day had fully broken, behold! The soldiers who had settled down for the night propped up against each other had scattered during the night. But the folk camped in a wagon-fort, thinking that they would be unable to take flight, did not move away from the place where they had camped. Thinking to retrieve the fugitive people, Chinggis Khan rode off from the place where he had spent the night. While he was retrieving the fugitives, Chinggis Khan himself heard a woman in a red coat on the pass weeping and crying in a loud voice 'Temujin!'

He sent someone to ask, 'What man's wife is weeping like that?'

When that person went and asked her, the woman said, 'I am Sorġan-Śira's daughter; my name is Qada'an. The soldiers seized my man and killed him; as my man was being killed, I called out to Temujin, weeping and crying, so that he might save my man.'

When the person came back and said these words to Chinggis Khan, Chinggis Khan heard it all and came up at a trot; he dismounted by Qada'an and they hugged each other. As for her man, our soldiers had already killed him. Having retrieved some of the Tayici'ut folk, Chinggis Khan camped at that very spot and spent the night. He invited Qada'an to come and sat her next to him.

The next morning, Sorġan-Śira and Jebe, both of whom had been Tödo'e of the Tayici'ut's minions, also appeared in person.

Chinggis Khan said to Sorġan-Śira, 'The heavy wood weighing on my head you splintered on the soil; the cumbersome cangue chaffing my collar you freed from my frame. Indeed, you all, both parents and children, helped me. Why did you tarry so long?'

Sorġan-Śira said, 'I was thinking to myself about the one

who would be ever reliable; how could I have hurried over? If I had hurried over to you earlier, my Tayici'ut commanders would have been just waiting to make the wife, children, herds and food I left behind blow away in the wind like ashes. Now, without being too hasty, we have finally rushed over here to join the khan.' When he had finished speaking, the khan said what he said was right.

Again, Chinggis Khan spoke: 'When we were fighting at Köiten 147 and pushing each other back and forth and re-forming our ranks, an arrow came from high up on the ridge; it snapped the atlas bone in the neck of my white-mouthed straw-yellow armoured charger – who fired it from on top of the mountain?'

To those words Jebe said, 'I fired it from on top of the mountain. If I receive death from the khan, I will stay behind fouling a piece of ground the size of a palm. If I should be favoured, in front of the khan, I will charge for him, driving through the deep water, smashing through the smooth stone. Whatever place he says to get to, wherever he says to attack, there I will charge for him, breaking apart the blue boulder, beating to bits the black boulder.'

Chinggis Khan said, 'Someone who has been an enemy hides his killing, his hostility and himself, and denies his words in fear. But as for this one, instead he does not deny his killing and his hostility, instead he openly admits it. He is one fit to befriend. He was named Jirġo'adai. Here and now, because he shot the atlas bone in the neck of my white-mouthed straw-yellow armoured charger, I name him Jebe and shall make him a weapon (*jebe*).'[42] He named him Jebe and he said, 'He will go by my side.' So it was decreed. That was the way in which Jebe came from the Tayici'ut and was befriended.

Chinggis Khan then plundered the Tayici'ut and slaughtered 148 the men of the Tayici'ut lineage, Tayici'uts like Aġucu Ba'atur, Ġodun-Hürceng and Qudu'udar, making them blow away in the wind like ashes unto the seed of the seed.

Moving his nation from there, Chinggis Khan wintered at Quba-Qaya.

When the Tayici'ut commander Fatty Kiriltuq was going 149 into the woods,[43] Old Man Śirgu'etu of the Naked Ba'arin with his sons Alaq and Naya'a thought that he was a man very much hated and they seized Fatty, who could not ride, and made him ride on their wagon.[44] When Old Man Śirgu'etu with his sons Alaq and Naya'a were coming back with Fatty Kiriltuq in their hands, Fatty Kiriltuq's sons and junior kinsmen caught up with them,[45] thinking to snatch him away.

Just as the sons and junior kinsmen caught up with them, Old Man Śirgu'etu got on to the cart and straddled this Fatty so he was unable to get up. Śirgu'etu took out a knife and said, 'Your sons and junior kinsmen have come to snatch you out of my hands. Now I've laid hands on you, my ruler; even if I don't kill you, they will kill me since I laid hands on my own ruler. And if I do kill you, all the same, I'll be killed. So right now, as I die, I will take a pillow with me to die on.'[46]

Straddling him as he spoke, Śirgu'etu was about to slit his throat with his big knife when Fatty Kiriltuq bawled out in a loud voice to his junior kinsmen and sons, saying, 'Śirgu'etu is going to kill me! When he's done killing me, will it do any good to rescue my dead lifeless body? Get back this instant before he kills me! Temujin won't kill me. When Temujin was small, thinking he was one with flame in his eyes and fire in his face, thinking he had been left behind on the deserted range, I went in order to fetch him. I thought, "If I train him, it seems he learns," and I tried to give him instruction, like training a fresh colt or foal. If I had thought, "I will put him to death," would I have been unable to put him to death? Now, they say his wits are waxing, his mind is maturing; Temujin will not put me to death. You, my sons and junior kinsmen, get back this instant, or do you want Śirgu'etu to kill me dead?' This he bawled out in a loud voice.

His sons and junior kinsmen said to each other, 'We came here to save Father's life. If Śirgu'etu actually puts an end to his life, what will we do with his body, empty and lifeless? Instead, let's get back this instant while he still hasn't killed him.' They agreed and went back.

Once his sons had come back to Śirgu'etu – Alaq and Naya'a, Śirgu'etu's sons, had run off and now came back – Śirgu'etu had them come hence. Father and sons then set out. On the way, when they arrived at the Qutuqul Meadow,[47] Naya'a said at that point, 'When we get there with this Fatty in our hands, Chinggis Khan will think that we have laid hands on our own proper ruler, and the khan will say of us, "They have laid hands on their own; how trustworthy can these minions be? And how could they be fit for us to befriend? Minions not fit to befriend, minions who have laid their hands on their own proper ruler – they are to be executed." And won't we be executed? Instead, let us let Fatty go free here and we can go on by ourselves. Let us say to Chinggis Khan, "We set out thinking to come and devote our strength to you, and we were coming here with Fatty in our hands, but we could not forsake our own proper ruler and thought, 'How can we look on and let him die?' So we let him go free. Filled with gratitude, we have come hoping to devote our strength to you."'

So he said, and fathers and sons approved these words of Naya'a. They released Fatty Kiriltuq at the Qutuqul Meadow and let him go. Right when Old Man Śirgu'etu with his sons Alaq and Naya'a arrived and were asked, 'Why have you come?', Old Man Śirgu'etu said to Chinggis Khan: 'Just as we came with Fatty Kiriltuq in our hands we said, "How can we look on and let our own ruler die?" We were unable to forsake him and so we let him go free. We came hoping to devote our strength to Chinggis Khan.' To that Chinggis Khan said, 'If you had come from laying hands on your ruler Fatty Kiriltuq, as minions who had laid hands on your own proper ruler, you would all have been executed down to the offspring. Your idea that you were unable to forsake your own proper ruler was right,' and he favoured Naya'a.

4: CHINGGIS KHAN AND ONG KHAN

BECOMING *ANDA*

150 After that, Ja'a Gambo of the Kereyit came to befriend Chinggis Khan when he was at Tersut. At the time he arrived, the Merkit came to give battle; Chinggis Khan, Ja'a Gambo and others gave battle and pushed them back. Then the Kereyit folk of the Ten Thousand Tübe'en and the teeming Donggayit who were scattered about came in submission to Chinggis Khan.

As for Ong Khan of the Kereyit, long before, when he had just lost his dominion in the time of Yisukei Khan,[1] he called himself *anda* with Yisukei Khan. This is the way in which they called themselves *anda*: because Ong Khan had killed the younger brothers of his father Qurjaqus Buyiruq Khan, he had gone into revolt against his paternal uncle Gür-Khan.[2] He had to crawl through Qara'un Gorge; a mere one hundred men escaped to Yisukei Khan. When they got there, Yisukei Khan himself let him in and rode out with his soldiers in person; he drove Gür-Khan off in the direction of Hexi and delivered Ong Khan's subject households back to him.[3] It was for that reason that they became *anda*.

151 After that, Ong Khan's little brother Erke-Qara fled and submitted to Ïnanc Khan of the Naiman, lest he be killed by his big brother Ong Khan. Ïnanc Khan sent his soldiers, but Ong Khan travelled around three walled cities and went to the *Gür Khan* of the Qara-Khitai.[4] Then he went into revolt again, and after passing by the Uyghur and Tangut walled cities he was reduced to nothing, penning up five goats with pointed sticks and milking

them and pricking camel's blood to drink. When Ong Khan had
come as far as Lake Küse'ur, Chinggis Khan sent Taġai Ba'atur
and Sö'ekei Je'un as envoys, so that in the same way as Ong
Khan had once called himself *anda* with Yisukei Khan, they
could do so as well. Chinggis Khan then went from the head-
waters of the Kherlen to meet up with him. Since Ong Khan
came hungry and gaunt, Chinggis Khan levied requisitions for
him,[5] brought him into his own wagon-fort and nourished him.

That winter, the two moved camp in ranks and Chinggis
Khan wintered at Quba-Qaya.

Then Ong Khan's juniors, his commanders and others spoke   152
to each other, 'This Elder-Ruler of ours acts worthlessly and ever
harbours foul feelings inside.[6] He has killed off his elder and jun-
ior kin. He even submitted to the Qara-Khitai, and moreover he
torments the kingdom. Now what are we to do with him?

'To speak of early days, the Merkit folk took him away at
seven years old as plunder and made him wear a black and mot-
tled kid-skin jacket and at the Buur steppe on the Selenge he
even pounded away at a Merkit mortar. When his father Qur-
jaqus Buyiruq Khan in turn raided the Merkit folk and rescued
his son from there, the Tatar Ajai Khan also took him away at
thirteen years old with his mother together as plunder too.
When they made him herd the camels he took some of Ajai
Khan's shepherds and home he fled! And also, after that, he fled
in fear of the Naiman and went to the Sarts' country,[7] to the
Chüy River, to the *Gür Khan* of the Qara-Khitai. Then before a
year was up, he rose up in rebellion and when he passed by the
Uyghurs' and the Tanguts' lands, he was reduced to nothing and
penned up five goats with pointed sticks and milked them and
pricked camel's blood to drink. And when he came to Prince
Temujin with nothing but a whitish-yellow barren horse with
a black spine, Temujin levied requisitions and nourished him!
Now he has forgotten how he is living off Prince Temujin and
ever harbours foul feelings inside; what are we to do with him?'
they said to each other.

These words they had said to each other were reported to
Ong Khan by Altun-Ašuq. Altun-Ašuq said, 'I entered into this
conclave as well, but I could not forsake my ruler.' Then Ong

Khan had those of his juniors and his commanders who had
spoken so seized: El-Qotor, Qul-Bari and Alin Taiši. Of his
juniors, Ja'a Gambo fled and submitted to the Naiman.[8] The
others were brought all bound and tied into the *ger* and Ong
Khan said, 'What did we say to each other when we came from
the Uyghurs' and the Tanguts' lands? But how could I think
like you do?'[9] and spat in their faces and released their bonds.
As soon as they had been spat upon by the ruler, all his minions
in the *ger* got up together and spat on them.

THE ANNIHILATION OF THE TATARS

153   After camping that winter, in the autumn of the Year of the Dog
[1202], Chinggis Khan gave battle to those Tatars at Dalan-
Nemurges: the White Tatars, the Alci Tatars, the Tota'ut Tatars
and the Aluqai Tatars. Before they fought, Chinggis Khan took
counsel and they all pronounced an ordinance together:[10] 'When
we beat down the enemy let us not stop for any booty. When we
have finished beating them down, the booty will be ours! It will
be shared! If we are driven back by the enemy, let us return to
the place we charged from in the first place. Let us execute the
people who have not returned to the place of the first charge.'
    Fighting at Dalan-Nemurges, the Tatars were pushed back.
They were beaten down and we took over and plundered their
kingdom at Ulagai-Seyelji. The leading folk, White Tatars, Alci
Tatars, Tota'ut Tatars and Aluqai Tatars, were wiped out there
and Altan, Qocar and Dāritai stopped for some booty, not
living up to the words of the ordinance they had pronounced
together. Since they had not lived up to their words, Jebe and
Qubilai were sent, and all the horses that they had captured
and whatever they had taken were taken away from them.

154   The Tatars were wiped out and the plundering of them was
finished. Saying, 'What shall we do with their nation?' Ching-
gis Khan went into a single *ger* to take counsel with our own
kin. They convened a great council[11] and discussed how 'From
days of old, the Tatar folk murdered our grandfathers and
fathers. Let us give them hatred for hatred and vengeance for

vengeance, measure them against a linchpin,[12] and slaughter them. Let us slaughter them till they are exterminated. Let us enslave the remnants. Let us divide them up unit by unit.' When they finished taking counsel and left the *ger*, Big Cāran of the Tatars asked Belgutei: 'What counsel did you take?' Belgutei said, 'We said we would measure you all against a linchpin and slaughter you.'[13] At this word of Belgutei's, Big Cāran spread the announcement among his Tatars and they built a fort.

When our soldiers surrounded the fortified Tatars and attacked, they suffered many losses. When we had subdued the fortified Tatars with great losses to ourselves and compared them to a linchpin to slaughter them utterly, the Tatars said to each other, 'Each person hide a knife up his sleeve and as we die let us take a pillow with us'; great losses were suffered even then, too. The slaughter of the Tatars compared to a linchpin was finished and then Chinggis Khan decreed, 'Because Belgutei revealed what we had concluded within our own kin as a great council, our soldiers suffered many losses. From this time on, Belgutei shall not be allowed to enter into the great council. Until the council ends, let him keep order over everything outside, and, having kept order, let him judge quarrels and those who commit theft and lies.[14] When the council has finished and after the *ötok* has been drunk,[15] then let Belgutei and Dāritai enter.' So it was decreed.

Then Chinggis Khan took Lady Yisuken, the daughter of Big Cāran the Tatar. Since he was pleased with her, she said, 'If it please the khan, he will take care of me like I am a worthy person and a fine body. My sister Yisui, who is older than me, is better than me and suitable indeed for a ruler! Our family had just taken in a son-in-law for her; now who knows in these troubles where she has gone?'

Chinggis Khan said, 'If your big sister is better than you, then we will have her sought. If your big sister is brought, will you give your place to her?'

Lady Yisuken said, 'If it please the khan, as soon as I see my big sister, I shall give way.'

At this word, Chinggis Khan had a decree issued publicly. When she was being sought, our soldiers ran into her as she was going into the forest together with the son-in-law to whom she had been given. Her man fled. They then brought in Lady Yisui. When Lady Yisuken saw her big sister, then living up to what she had said earlier, she got up and had her sit in her seat where she had been sitting and herself sat below her. She was just as Lady Yisuken had said and Chinggis Khan let her into his heart; he took Lady Yisui and had her sit next to him.

156   One day after the plunder of the Tatar folk had finished, Chinggis Khan was sitting outside to drink. As he sat between Lady Yisui and Lady Yisuken, drinking together with them, Lady Yisui gasped loudly. Then Chinggis Khan considered this silently and summoned the commanders Bo'orcu and Muqali.[16] He decreed: 'You two: the common men gathered here are to stand unit by unit. Set apart on his own the person who is from a different unit.' When they were thus standing each unit by unit, one fine, trim young man was standing separate from the units.

When they said, 'What person are you?', that man said, 'I am that son-in-law to whom Big Cāran's girl Yisui was given. Since we were being plundered by the enemy, I fled in fear. Now thinking that things must have calmed down, I came back. I thought, "How could I be recognized among so many fellows?"'

These words were reported to Chinggis Khan and he decreed: 'He thought exactly as an enemy would and was living as an outlaw; now what has he come to spy out? The likes of him were compared to a linchpin. What doubt can there be? Cast him out of my sight.' And so he was executed.

ESTRANGEMENT

157   In the same Year of the Dog, when Chinggis Khan rode against the Tatar folk, Ong Khan rode against the Merkit folk and drove Toqto'a Beki off in the direction of Barguzin Hollow. He killed Toqto'a's eldest son, Tegus Beki, seized Toqto'a's two women, Qutuqtai and Ca'alun, his daughter and his lady, and plundered his two sons Godu and Cila'un together with their folk; he gave nothing whatsoever to Chinggis Khan.

After that, Chinggis Khan and Ong Khan rode against Buyruq 158
Khan of the Kücugut half of the Naiman;[17] they arrived when
Buyruq Khan was at the Sogog River of Uluġ Taġ,[18] and he was
unable to fight them and removed himself across the Altai. They
chased Buyruq Khan away from the Sogog River, and by forcing
him to cross the Altai they drove him down the Ulungur of
Qum-Seng'ir. A commander of his named Yeti-Tobluq was serv-
ing there as a scout and was driven off by our scout; as he was
fleeing up a mountain, his saddle-girth snapped on him and he
was captured. Driving him down the Ulungur Chinggis Khan
and Ong Khan caught up with Buyruq Khan at Qïzil-Baš and
wiped him out there.[19]

When Chinggis Khan and Ong Khan came back home, the 159
Naiman warrior Kökse'u-Sabraq marshalled soldiers at the
Baidrag Belcir and made ready to give battle.[20] Chinggis Khan
and Ong Khan thought to give battle and marshalled soldiers.
They approached and dusk fell on them. They thought to give
battle the following day and spent the night in ranks. Ong
Khan had fires lit along his lines but then when night fell he
moved up the Qara-Se'ul.[21]

Then, as Jamuqa went along with Ong Khan, he said to Ong 160
Khan, 'My *anda* Temujin previously exchanged envoys with the
Naiman; now he has not come with us. O ruler, ruler! The
white-tailed lark that stays with you: that is me! The skylark is
my *anda*.[22] He must have gone over to the Naiman. He stayed
behind ready to surrender.' To those words of Jamuqa, Kürin
Ba'atur of the Obciq said, 'How can you be so sly and speak
such slanders and falsehoods about your upright brother?'

Chinggis Khan spent the night in place, eager to give battle 161
early the next day when the morning broke. But when he looked
at Ong Khan's position, he saw he had been abandoned and
said, 'They have treated us just like a burnt offering.'[23] Ching-
gis Khan then moved on from there across the Ider-Altai
valley and, moving on and on through it, pitched camp on the
Sa'ari steppe.

From then on Chinggis Khan and Qasar understood the
troubles of the Naiman, nor were the Naiman considered of
much account by anyone else.[24]

162   Kökse'u-Sabraq chased after Ong Khan and stripped Seng-gum of his women and children, as well as his subject households. And he stripped Ong Khan of the half of his folk, herds and food that were at Tele'etu Pass before returning. In that moment,[25] Toqto'a's two sons of the Merkit, Godu and Cila'un, took all their folk who were there and split off and joined with their father moving down the Selenge.

163   Plundered by Kökse'u-Sabraq, Ong Khan sent envoys to Chinggis Khan. He sent an envoy to say, 'I have been stripped of my subjects and my women and children by the Naiman. I am sending this message to ask my son for his four champions.[26] May he save my subjects for me!' Then Chinggis Khan marshalled soldiers and sent these four champions: Bo'orcu, Muqali, Boroġul and Cila'un Ba'atur. Before these four champions arrived, Senggum had been fighting at Hula'an-Qut and his horse's croup had been hit by an arrow and he was about to be captured. At that moment, these four champions arrived to rescue him and rescued all his subject households, women and children for him. Then Ong Khan spoke, 'Long ago, my lost kingdom had been rescued for me by his late father. Now, my lost kingdom had been rescued for me by my son sending his four champions. May the return of this gracious kindness be committed in trust to Heaven and Earth!'

164   Again, Ong Khan spoke, 'My *anda* Yisukei Ba'atur once rescued my lost kingdom for me. Prince Temujin has also rescued my lost kingdom. When these two, father and son, reassembled my lost kingdom for me, who were they suffering for as they reassembled it? As for me, I am old now. When I ascend to the heights,[27] I will expire. When I expire and ascend to the craggy heights, who will govern my whole kingdom? My little brothers act worthlessly. My sole son is just Senggum, which is like having no son at all. I will make Prince Temujin Senggum's elder brother and so I will have two sons.'[28]

       And Ong Khan gathered with Chinggis Khan at the Black Forest on the Tuul and they became father and son. The way they became father and son was that he was like a father, just as before in days of old Yisukei Khan had become *anda* with Ong Khan. The way they became father and son was that they spoke as follows: 'When we tackle teeming enemies, let us take them in a trap together. When we corral the cunning game, let us catch them in a ring together.'

Again, Chinggis Khan and Ong Khan pledged to each other, 'If in envy of us,

A snake with teeth should try to provoke
By trying words we'll not be tempted,
But talking in person, we will truly believe.
Or if a snake with fangs should slander the other
By slanderous thoughts we will not be swindled,
But speaking in person we'll sincerely believe.'

Such words they pledged and lived together lovingly.

Then Chinggis Khan thought: 'Over and above our love, let 165 us double our love,' and he made a proposal: 'Let Senggum's little sister be engaged to Joci, and in exchange we will give our Qoajin Beki to Senggum's son Tusaġa.' But Senggum, who thought very highly of himself, said, 'If our child goes to them, she will always be standing by the door and looking up towards the head of the *ger*. If their child comes to us, she will sit at the head of the *ger* while looking down at the door.'[29] He thought highly of himself, spoke scornfully to us, and was not pleased to give us Ca'ur Beki. With those words, Chinggis Khan quietly lost all affection for Ong Khan and Ilqa Senggum.

ILQA SENGGUM'S PLOT

Jamuqa understood how he had lost all affection and in the 166 spring of the Year of the Pig [1203] Jamuqa, Altan, Qocar, Hartagidai,[30] Ebugejin Noyagin,[31] To'oril of the Sö'eken and Qaci'un Beki formed a league and moved off to camp; they went to Ilqa Senggum at the Berke Sands on the shady side of Jeje'er Heights.[32]

Jamuqa said maliciously, 'My *anda* Temujin has envoys going to Tayang Khan of the Naiman with news. His lips are saying "Father, son" – his behaviour is different. Can you rely on him? If you do not take him by surprise, what will become of you? If you ride against Temujin *Anda*, I will charge in from the side.'

Altan and Qocar said, 'Mother Ö'elun's sons: the elders we will eliminate, the juniors we will exterminate for you.'

Ebugejin Noyagin and Hartagidai said, 'His hands we will hold tight for you, his feet we will fetter for you.'

To'oril said, 'Better yet, let us go and take away Temujin's kingdom; when his kingdom has been taken away and is all gone, what can they do?'

Qaci'un Beki said, 'Prince Senggum, whatever you are thinking, let us follow it to the furthermost and utter it to the uttermost.'

167   Touched off by these words, Ilqa Senggum sent those very words to his father Ong Khan by sending Pretty Tödo'en.[33] Touched off by those very words, Ong Khan said, 'How can you all think that way about my son Temujin? He has been our mainstay,[34] so if we think badly about my son like this, Heaven will not be pleased with us. Jamuqa's tongue is always moving. Is what he is saying really true? Or does it just look like it's true?' And he sent back to say that he was not pleased.

Again, Senggum sent to say, 'When someone with a mouth and a tongue speaks, why isn't he believed?' And after sending word twice or thrice, he had no other way but to make the effort and came himself. He said, 'Even at a time when you are still around, why are you treating us as if we were not? When you, his Ruler-Father, choke on the cheese and gag on the grease will he really leave in our keeping the kingdom assembled with such labour by your father Qurjaqus Buyiruq Khan?[35] Will he leave it in the keeping of any of us?'

Ong Khan said, 'How can I abandon my baby, my son? He has been our mainstay, and would it be right if we thought badly about him? Heaven will not be pleased with us.' His son Ilqa Senggum was disgusted by these words and went out slapping aside the felt door. Yet, cherishing his son Senggum's affections, Ong Khan invited him back in. 'Maybe Heaven will be pleased with us. You all say, "Let us abandon the prince." You do whatever you can. You take charge of it,' he said.

168   Then Senggum said, 'Those same ones were seeking an engagement with Ca'ur Beki. Now, by saying, "Come to eat the betrothal

feast"[36] we will fix a day and invite him to come and then we will catch him.' When he proposed this, they all said, 'Indeed!' and came to an agreement. They sent to say, 'We will give you Ca'ur Beki; come to eat the betrothal feast.'

Having been invited, Chinggis Khan was coming along with ten of his followers. On the way he spent the night in the *ger* of Father Mönglik. Father Mönglik spoke to him then: 'When we sought Ca'ur Beki those same ones scorned us and wouldn't give her to us. Now why have they about-faced and invited you to eat the betrothal feast? Why should fellows who think so highly of themselves turn about face and invite us with the idea of giving her to us? Is this desire really true? Or does it just look like it's true? Son, find out what's happening before you go any further. Let us send to them and make an excuse saying, "It is spring; our horse herds are thin; we have to take care of our horses."' So he spoke, and instead of going they sent Buqadai and Kiratai, telling them to eat the betrothal feast; Chinggis Khan returned from Father Mönglik's *ger*.

As soon as Buqadai and Kiratai got there, Senggum and his men said to each other, 'We've been discovered; we will surround them all early tomorrow morning and catch him.'

Altan's little brother Big Cāran came home and told his family that they had thus agreed to surround him and catch him.[37] He said, 'They're saying they will catch Temujin early tomorrow morning. I really wonder how someone who went to tell Temujin what they said might be rewarded?'

When she heard him talking like this, his woman Alaq-It said, 'What do you mean by that crazy talk? You better watch out lest some fellow even think it's true!'

As they were speaking, his wrangler Badai came in to deliver the mare's milk, heard what they had said, and went out. Badai went off and told his partner wrangler Kiśiliq what Cāran had said. Kiśiliq said, 'I will go as well and find out what's happening' and went to the big *ger*.

Cāran's son Slim Ke'en was sitting outside it, whetting his arrows as he sat. He said, 'What did you say just now? Until our tongues are cut off, whose trap can we keep shut?' Then

169

Slim Ke'en spoke as well to his wrangler, to Kiśiliq, 'Go catch Merkit White and White-Muzzle Bay and tether them here;[38] we ride early, while it is still dark.'

Kiśiliq went off and said to Badai, 'I looked into the news just now. It turned out to be true. Now, let us go to take the news to Temujin.' So saying, they agreed and went to catch Merkit White and White-Muzzle Bay and bring them back to tether. Once it had become dark, they killed a lamb in their tent and boiled it with [the wood from] their bedstead.[39] They mounted Merkit White and White-Muzzle Bay, who were tethered and waiting there.

They travelled by night and got to Chinggis Khan's one night.[40] From the northern side of the *ger*,[41] Badai and Kiśiliq told him all the news: what Big Cāran said, what his son Slim Ke'en said while whetting his arrows, and the words 'Catch the geldings Merkit White and White-Muzzle Bay and tether them.'

Badai and Kiśiliq said, 'Should Chinggis Khan deign to believe us, there is no need for hesitation. They have agreed to surround you and catch you.'

170   Shaken by these words, Chinggis Khan believed what they had told him. It being still night, he told the news to all those he trusted who were nearby. Lightening their loads, they abandoned everything and set off in flight, while it was still dark.

BATTLE OF QALA'ALJIT SANDS

They were moving along the shady side of Mau-Ündur,[42] and that shady side of Mau-Ündur had been entrusted to Jelme Quwa of the Uriyangqan; he was set as sentry to act as rearguard while the rest moved on. Moving forward, the next day they reached Qala'aljit Sands at noon, as the sun was beginning to go down from its zenith, and pitched camp for lunch. While they were having their lunch, Cikidei and Yatir, the ones who wrangled Alcidai's riding horses, were pasturing their geldings on the green here and there, when they saw behind them the dust of the enemy rising by way of Hula'an-Burġat,[43] along the southern slopes of Mau-Ündur. And they said, 'The enemy is here' and came up driving their geldings on. When Chinggis Khan had been told the enemy was here and looked, he could make out the dust along the southern slopes of Mau-Ündur, by way of Hula'an-Burġat, and knew that he, Ong Khan, had caught up with them. Once Chinggis Khan had seen the dust, he had his geldings fetched and loaded up and then rode off. Had he not seen it at that point, they would have been caught unprepared.

As they were coming towards us, Jamuqa was coming up along with Ong Khan. Then Ong Khan questioned Jamuqa. 'Who are the ones likely to fight for Prince Temujin?' he asked. Jamuqa said, 'They say his Uru'ut and Manġġut folk are there. Those people of his will fight! Every time they turn a flank, their training holds; every time they double about, their drill holds. They are a people familiar since childhood with spears and swords. They have black and mottled standards. They are a folk worth guarding against!'

To these words Ong Khan replied, 'If that is the way it is, then we will make our Jirkin *ba'atur*s charge, setting our Jirkin *ba'atur*s and Qadaq against them. As backup for the Jirkin, we will make Aciq-Širun of the Ten Thousand Tübe'en charge. As backup for the Tübe'en we will make the Teeming Dongġayit *ba'atur*s charge. As backup for the Dongġayit let Qori-Šilemun Taiši lead Ong Khan's thousand dayguards into the charge. As backup for the thousand dayguards, we and the great centre will charge!'

And Ong Khan also said, 'Young Jamuqa, marshal our army.'

At that Jamuqa went and stood off a little way from the rest and said to his friends, 'Ong Khan told me to marshal this army of his. I have never been able to give battle with *Anda*. Ong Khan says to me, "Marshal this army." He falls even shorter than I do; as a contender he doesn't make the grade. I will deliver a word to *Anda*. May *Anda* be patient!' And Jamuqa secretly sent word to Chinggis Khan: 'Ong Khan asked me a question. When he asked me, "Who are the ones likely to fight for Prince Temujin?" I mentioned first of all the Uru'ut and Manġġut. Having said this, he mentioned his own Jirkin first of all and we marshalled them as vanguard. We decided on the Aciq-Širun of the Ten Thousand Tübe'en as the backup for the Jirkin. We decided on the Teeming Donġayit as the backup for the Tübe'en. We decided on Qori-Silemun Taiši, captain of the thousand dayguards of Ong Khan, as the backup for the Teeming Donġayit. We decided to let Ong Khan's own great centre army be his backup. Ong Khan also said, "Young Jamuqa, you marshal this army" and entrusted it to me. From this you can understand that he is a contender who doesn't make the grade. What good are we at marshalling our army? Long ago I was never able to give battle with *Anda*. Ong Khan falls even shorter than I do. *Anda*, do not be afraid, but be patient!'

171   When Chinggis Khan had received these words, he said, 'What do you say, Uncle Jürcedei of the Uru'ut?[44] I will make you the vanguard.' Before Jürcedei made any sound, Quyildar Secen of the Manġġut said, 'I will give battle in front of *Anda*. *Anda* shall know how to take care of my orphaned children ever after.' Jürcedei said, 'We Uru'ut and Manġġut will give battle in the vanguard before Chinggis Khan.' When he had spoken thus Jürcedei and Quyildar marshalled their Uru'ut and Manġġut to stand up before Chinggis Khan.

As they were standing there, the enemies came on and the Jirkin were in the vanguard. As they were coming on, the Uru'ut and the Manġġut charged against them and crushed the Jirkin. In response to their crushing onset, Aciq-Sirun of the Ten Thousand Tübe'en charged against the Uru'ut and the Manġġut. He charged and Aciq-Sirun battled Quyildar and unhorsed him. The Manġġut whirled around to cover Quyildar.

Jürcedei charged with his Uru'ut and crushed the Ten Thousand Tübe'en, and as his crushing force was pushing them back, the Teeming Donġayit charged against him. Jürcedei crushed the Donġayit as well, and in response to that crushing onset Qori-Silemun Taiši charged with the thousand dayguards. Jürcedei drove Qori-Silemun Taiši into retreat as well. Even without any approval from Ong Khan, Senggum was about to charge in response to Jürcedei's crushing onset when Senggum's rouge-red cheek was struck by an arrow and he fell right there.[45] Senggum was felled and all the Kereyit whirled around to stand guard over him. They were crushed, and when the setting sun smote the hills, our side whirled around and carried back Quyildar, fallen and wounded, and Chinggis Khan pulled our side away from Ong Khan and from the place where we had given battle and, moving through the evening, spent the night at a distance.

AFTERMATH

We spent the night on our feet, and when the roll was called as the day was breaking, Ökodei, Boroǧul and Bo'orcu were not there. Chinggis Khan said, 'Ökodei was entrusted to Bo'orcu and Boroǧul. They got left behind with him, but whether living or dead, surely they could not have lost him?' That evening, our side brought in the geldings and we spent the night; Chinggis Khan said, 'Should someone come up against us from behind, we will have to give battle,' and dressed the ranks. We waited until the day grew brighter and when we looked, just one person was coming up from behind. When he came up, it turned out to be Bo'orcu. After we let Bo'orcu join us, Chinggis Khan said, 'May Eternal Heaven decide!' and he beat his breast.

Bo'orcu said, 'In the charge, my horse had been hit so hard it fell and I was running on foot. In that moment of pause when the Kereyit turned back to stand guard over Senggum, a pack-horse was letting its load list to the side, so I cut its load off and rode out of there on the pack saddle.[46] Tracking the path our side took in breaking away, I eventually found you.' So he said.

Again, after waiting a few minutes more, another person came up. As he came up, a pair of feet were dangling below. When we looked, it was like a single person. When he had finally arrived, there it was: Boroǧul riding double behind Ökodei, with blood trickling from the corners of his mouth. Ökodei had been struck by an arrow in his jugular vein, and as his blood was clotting Boroǧul was sucking with his mouth and the clotted blood was trickling from the corners of his mouth.

Chinggis Khan saw it; tears trickled from his eyes, and his heart ached. He had a fire kindled straight away and had heat applied [to the wound] and had some drink sought for Ökodei,

172

173

and he kept saying, 'When the enemy arrives we will give battle.'

Boroġul said, 'The dust of the enemy is off yonder – by the southern side of Mau-Ündur the dust is rising up in a long line in the direction of Hula'an-Burġat; they've travelled away yonder.'

To these words of Boroġul Chinggis Khan replied, 'If they had come we would have given battle. But as we have been given berth by the enemy, let us re-form our army's ranks and fight!' They then moved on, moving up the Ulagai-Seyelji into the Dalan-Nemurges country.

174 Then, Qada'an-Daldurqan came up from behind them, separated from his woman and child. Qada'an-Daldurqan arrived and recounted Ong Khan's words, saying, 'His son Senggum was hit hard enough to fall by an *ucumaq* arrow on his rouge-red cheek and they whirled around to cover him.[47] Then Ong Khan said, "When the issue was 'Provoke Temujin or not?' he was provoked, when the issue was 'Attack Temujin or not?' he was attacked. My dear boy has had a nail driven into his cheek. Let us charge them as we deliver the boy's life." Then in reply, Aciq-Śirun said, "Ruler, ruler, stop! When we sought a son yet in the loins we beseeched with prayer, making enchanted ribbons[48] and crying *abui babui*.[49] He's a boy who could only get born in that way – let us care for Senggum. Most of the Mongols are with us, with Jamuqa, with Altan and Qocar. Where will those Mongols go who fled in rebellion with Temujin? Now they are ones who go only by their geldings and are sheltered only by the shade.[50] If they do not come to us, we will go and tuck them in our skirts like dried horse pats and take them home – all of them!"[51] To these words of Aciq-Śirun, Ong Khan said, "Yes! Since that's the way it is, let not the boy be in pain. Take care of the boy without jostling him." And they withdrew from the place where the battle had been.'

175 Then Chinggis Khan moved down the Khalkh River from the Dalan-Nemurges and numbered his subjects. So numbered, there were 2,600 of them in all: 1,300 under Chinggis Khan moved camp along the western bank of the Khalkh; 1,300 of the Uru'ut and Manġġut moved camp along the eastern bank of the Khalkh.[52] As they moved forward, they ring-hunted for

provisions. Quyildar, with his wounds not yet healed, did not heed Chinggis Khan's attempt at dissuasion and charged in on the game, ripping his wounds open afresh, and so passed away. Chinggis Khan laid his bones to rest on the Keltegei Cliffs over Or Meadow on the Khalkh.[53]

Chinggis Khan learned that Dergei Amal and others of the 176 Qonggirat were at the end just where the Khalkh flows into Lake Buir and he sent Jürcedei with his Uru'ut there.[54] He sent him to say, 'If they say how from days of old, the Qonggirat folk have lived by the faces of the fair ones and by the graces of the girl children, then take their surrender! If the same say that they are in revolt, then we will give battle to them!' Once Jürcedei was sent to them, they surrendered to him. He brought them to surrender and Chinggis Khan touched not a single thing of theirs.

THE INDICTMENT OF ONG KHAN

Having subdued the Qonggirat, Chinggis Khan went and 177 pitched camp east of Tüngke Stream and delivered a message by Arqai-Qasar and Sö'ekei Je'un:

'Say to my Ruler-Father: "I have pitched camp east of Tüngke Stream. The grass there is good now. Our geldings have rested their joints."

'And say: "My Ruler-Father, why do you frighten me with your accusations? If you have to frighten me, why do you not let your stupid sons and stupid daughters-in-law get their fill of sleep and not frighten them? Why do you frighten them so that the bed where they sit in ranks is pushed down and the smoke that rises up is waved away?[55]

"My Ruler-Father, were you provoked by a person with a prejudiced heart, were you stirred up by a person standing athwart us? What was it that we had said to each other? Did we not say it to each other at the Red Hills of Jorġal Qun?

If a snake with teeth should try to provoke,
By his trying words we'll not be tempted,
But talking in person we will truly believe.

"Was this not what we said to each other? Now, my

Ruler-Father, did you talk to me in person before you broke with me?

If a snake with fangs should slander the other
By slanderous thoughts we will not be swindled,
But speaking in person we'll sincerely believe.

"Was this not what we said to each other? Now, my Ruler-Father, did you speak with me in person before you went away from me?

"My Ruler-Father, although I had but a few men with me, I was not such as to make you look for a more numerous band of men. Although I was stupid, I was not such as to make you look for a better one than me.

"On a wagon with two axles, if you break one of the axles, the oxen cannot pull forward. Was it not I who was like that other axle? On a wagon with two wheels, if you break one of the wheels, you cannot move camp. Was it not I who was like that other wheel?

"Thinking back to days of old, your father Qurjaqus Buyiruq Khan said that you were the elder of the following forty sons and you became the ruler.

"Once you had managed to become ruler, you killed your younger brothers, Tai-Temur Taiši and Buqa-Temur.

"When he was about to be killed, your younger brother Erke-Qara fled to save his life and as a rebel surrendered to Ïnanc Bilge Khan of the Naiman.

"When your paternal uncle Gür-Khan rode against you since you had become the murderer of your little brothers, you rebelled and to save your life fled down the Selenge and crawled along Qara'un Gorge.

"Moreover, as you went out from there, you gave your daughter Madame Huja'ur to Toqto'a of the Merkit to oblige him, and when you left Qara'un Gorge and came to my father Yisukei Khan, you said to him, 'Rescue my kingdom for me from Uncle Gür-Khan.' Since you came to him speaking this way, when my father Yisukei Khan heard this, he marshalled an army and set out, intending to lead Gunan and Baġaci of the Tayici'ut and rescue your kingdom. And he drove off Gür-Khan and the twenty or thirty people who were at

Gurban-Talasut in the direction of Hexi and rescued your kingdom for you.

"You came thence and at the Black Forest on the Tuul my Ruler-Father became *anda* with Yisukei Khan, and there my father Ong Khan said with gratitude, 'The grace of this help of yours – may the return of this grace to the seed of your seed be committed in trust to Heaven above and Earth!' And you were grateful.

"After that, when Erke-Qara asked for some soldiers from İnanc Bilge Khan of the Naiman and rode against you, you abandoned your kingdom to save your life, and fled with a few people to the *Gür Khan* of the Qara-Khitai, to the Chüy River, to the Sarts' country.

"Before a year was up you rebelled against the *Gür Khan*, and when you passed by the Uyghurs' and the Tanguts' lands you were reduced to nothing and penned up five goats with pointed sticks and milked them to drink and pricked camel's blood to drink. And you came to Prince Temujin with only a whitish-yellow barren horse with a black spine.

"Knowing that you, Ruler-Father, came reduced to nothing and thinking about how you had called yourself *anda* with my father Yisukei Khan, I first sent Taġai and Sö'ekei as envoys to greet you and then I myself also travelled from the banks of the Bürkh to meet you and we met at Lake Küse'ur.

"Since you had come reduced to nothing, I first levied requisitions and gave them to you. Was it not in the same way that you had called yourself *anda* with my father, that we called each other father and son at the Black Forest of the Tuul? That winter I brought you into my wagon-fort and nourished you. After wintering and summering together, that autumn I rode against Toqto'a Beki of the Merkit folk, gave battle at Müruce Se'ul of the Qadingliq Mountains, and drove off Toqto'a Beki in the direction of Barguzin Hollow. And I stripped the Merkit folk and all their teeming horses, hordes and *gers* and all their harvest I took and gave to the Ruler-Father.

"Your hunger I did not let last till midday, your gauntness I did not let last to mid-moon.

"And we also drove Buyruq Khan of the Kücugur from

Sogog River of Uluġ Taġ away over the Altai and, following the Ulungur we wiped them all out at Lake Qïzil-Baš.

"When we were returning from there, when we were marshalling our soldiers to give battle to Kökse'u-Sabraq of the Naiman at Baidrag Belcir, the dusk of evening fell on us and, intending to give battle early the next day, we dressed ranks and spent the night. As we did, my Ruler-Father, you had fires lit among your ranks and that night you moved up along the Qara-Se'ul.

"Early next morning when I looked, you had disappeared from your position and moved away on us. I said, 'They have treated us just like a burnt offering,' and I for my part, crossing by way of the Ider-Altai valley, came and pitched camp at Sa'ari steppe.

"Then Kökse'u-Sabraq chased you down and, having taken all of Senggum's women and children, as well as his subject households, he stripped you, Ruler-Father, of the half of your folk, herds and food that were at Tele'etu Pass and went back. And at just that moment when he was doing so,[56] Ġodu and Cila'un, the sons of Toqto'a of the Merkit, took all their own subject people with which they had joined you and rebelled, joining their father and moving off to the Barguzin country.

"Then, Ruler-Father of mine, you sent word to me to say, 'I have been stripped of my subjects by Kökse'u-Sabraq. My son, send me your four champions.' When you said that, then I, without thinking the way you had, marshalled soldiers under these four champions of mine, Bo'orcu, Muqali, Boroġul and Cila'un Ba'atur. And so, when Senggum had earlier been giving battle at Hula'an-Qut and his horse's croup had been hit by an arrow and he was about to be captured, at just that time these four champions of mine arrived and rescued him and all his women and children together with his subject households. And when they had, my Ruler-Father, you said gratefully, 'My son! For his sake Temujin sent his four champions to rescue the subjects he had already lost.'

"Now, Ruler-Father of mine, for what fault of mine do you indict me? As is customary with an indictment, send envoys to deliver it. If you do, send Qul-Bari Quri and Iturgen. Or if you do not send both of them, send the second.'"

To these words which had been sent to him, Ong Khan 178
said, 'Alas, how culpable of me![57] Was I to separate from my
son? I have separated from the right. Was I to part from him?
I have parted from my duty.' His heart ached and he said,
'Should I now see my son and think evil of him, let my blood
be spilled like this!' Swearing this oath, he pricked the ball of
his little finger with an *onubci* knife and let the blood drip
into a little bucket of birch bark.[58] 'Give it to my son,' he said,
and sent it off.

Again, Chinggis Khan spoke, 'Say this to Jamuqa *Anda*,' and 179
declared: 'You loathed me and separated me from my Ruler-
Father. Before, the one who got up first would drink from our
Ruler-Father's blue chalice.[59] You envied me when I got up ear-
lier and it was drunk by me. Now have your fill of Ruler-Father's
blue chalice – how much of it can you finish off?'

Again, Chinggis Khan spoke, 'Say this to Altan and Qocar,'
and declared: 'You two would do away with me – do you want
to dispose of me in the open or do you want to dispose of me
in some nice way? Qocar, when I said to you, "As son of Nekün
Taiši you, ahead of any of us, should be the ruler," you would
not do it. Altan, when I said to you, "It was Qutula Khan
indeed who was in authority; and as your father used to be in
authority, you be the ruler," even less would you do it. Since
long ago, Sece and Taicu were Bartan Ba'atur's sons;[60] I said to
them, "You be the rulers" but I failed to persuade them. I failed
when I said, "You be the rulers" and only gained any authority
when you all told me "You be the ruler." If I had been able to
make you the rulers, if I had been made to gallop as outrider
against gathered foes, if I were to be so protected by Heaven,
then when plundering your enemies,

Goodly girls,
Fair of face,
And geldings good of rump
Trotting I would have taken for you.
When sent to hunt for wily game,
Rousting game by rocks,
Hemming them in till they huffed would I have done for you;
Corralling game by crags,

Pressing them in till they panted would I have done for you;
Hunting wild beasts
Cramming them close would I have done for you.

'Now, be a good friend to my Ruler-Father. You are said to be easily bored. Do not let it be said you were only propped up by the Ca'ut-Quri.[61] Do not let anyone, whosoever they may be, pitch camp at the headwaters of the Three Rivers.'[62] So he sent to say to them.

180   Again, Chinggis Khan spoke, 'Say this to Boy To'oril,' and declared: 'The reason I call you "boy" is that Tumbinai and Caraqai Lingqu brought back Slave Noqta as spoils.[63] Slave Noqta's son was Slave Sö'ekei.[64] Slave Sö'ekei's son was Kökecu-Kirsaqan. Kökecu-Kirsaqan's son was Jegei-Qongtaġar. Jegei-Qongtaġar's son was you, To'oril. Whose kingdom are you sneaking around thinking someone will give you? My kingdom Altan and Qocar will never allow anyone else to govern. The reason I call you "boy" is that you are the thrall of my forefather's threshold, the property of my paternal ancestor's portal.[65] Such is my message to you.'

181   Again, Chinggis Khan spoke: 'Say this to Senggum *Anda*,' and declared: 'I was the son born with clothes, you were the son born naked. The Ruler-Father cared for us both equally. You were jealous, Senggum *Anda*, and lest a rift might develop [between you and your Ruler-Father], you drove me out. Now, go in and out night and day and comfort him, without worrying our Ruler-Father. As long as the Ruler-Father is alive, do not worry our Ruler-Father by persisting in your old way of thinking and by saying, "I shall be the ruler."'

Having said that, he sent further word to him, saying, 'Senggum *Anda*, send me some envoys. When you send them, send the friends Bilge Beki and Tödo'en.'

He said, 'When you send envoys to me, Ruler-Father, send two envoys. Senggum *Anda*, send two envoys too. Jamuqa *Anda*, send two envoys too. Altan, send two envoys too. Qocar, send two envoys too. Aciq-Širun, send two envoys too. Qaci'un,[66] send two envoys too.'

So saying, he sent Arqai-Qasar and Sö'ekei Je'un to carry all of these messages.

CONQUEST OF THE KEREYIT

When these words had been thus spoken to Senggum, he said, 'When did he ever talk about you as "Ruler-Father"? Didn't he just talk about you as the "Bloody Old Man"? When did he ever call me *anda*? Didn't he just talk about me as "Shaman Toqto'a goes around with a Sart sheep's tail pinned on"?[67] The schemes behind these words are not hard to figure out. These are the opening words of battle. Bilge Beki and Tödo'en, raise the battle flag; fatten the geldings – there is no doubt!'[68]

At that point, Arqai-Qasar returned home from Ong Khan, but Sö'ekei Je'un's wife and children were there at To'oril's.[69] His heart for leaving failed him and Sö'ekei Je'un lagged behind Arqai. Arqai came and said all those words to Chinggis Khan.

With that done, Chinggis Khan left and pitched camp at 182 Lake Baljuna. When he was pitching camp there, he ran across Co'os-Caġān and the Ġorulas right there. Those Ġorulas submitted without rebelling.

Hasan, a Sart, was coming up from Ala-Quš Digit-Quri of the Öng'ut and driving a thousand wethers with a white camel down along the Ergune River in order to buy sables and squirrels. When he was watering them at Baljuna, he met Chinggis Khan.

While Chinggis Khan himself was watering at Baljuna, Qasar 183 abandoned his wife and children and his sons Yeku, Yisungke and Toqu at Ong Khan's and left with a few of his friends. Longing for his big brother and looking for Chinggis Khan, he skirted the ridges of the Qara'un-Jidun without finding him,[70] and was eating leather and thongs by the time he joined Chinggis Khan at Baljuna.

Chinggis Khan was delighted that Qasar had come and took his counsel, intending to send envoys to Ong Khan. He spoke to Qali'udar of the Je'uriyet and Ca'urqan of the Uriyangqan, sending them to say, 'Say this to the Ruler-Father, saying it is Qasar's words. Say that he sent you to say, "Gazing at my big brother, my view of him vanished, following him, his footsteps were lost, and shouting aloud my voice was not heard. Gazing at the stars, I lie with a knoll as my pillow. My wife and children are with my Ruler-Father. If, as I hope, I should get a surety,[71] I shall go to the Ruler-Father." '

Along with that, he set a rendezvous, saying, 'We shall be advancing behind you; let us rendezvous at Argal-Geugi on the Kherlen. Go there!' And, having thus sent Qali'udar and Ca'urqan, they reached Argal-Geugi on the Kherlen while Jürcedei and Arqai went as outriders and Chinggis Khan set us in motion from Lake Baljuna and rode out to advance behind them.

184 Qali'udar and Ca'urqan reached Ong Khan and said the words which they had been sent from us to say, saying they were Qasar's words. Ong Khan had set up the Golden Tent[72] and was feasting entirely without a care. To Qali'udar and Ca'urqan's words, Ong Khan replied, 'If that's the way it is, then let Qasar come here.' As a surety, he sent Iturgen; he sent them back together. So they went and then when they arrived at the place of rendezvous, Argal-Geugi, they saw how big the pall of dust was and Iturgen and the envoys turned back in flight.

Qali'udar's horse was faster. Qali'udar caught up with Iturgen but his heart to grapple with him failed, and so instead he kept cutting him off from in front and from behind, as Ca'urqan's horse fell behind. At the furthest point where an arrow could hit him from behind, Ca'urqan fired one such that it lodged in the rump of Iturgen's golden-saddled black gelding. Only then was Iturgen captured by Qali'udar and Ca'urqan and they brought him to Chinggis Khan. Without saying a word to Iturgen, Chinggis Khan said, 'Take him to Qasar; let Qasar decide.' When they brought him to Qasar, without saying a word to Iturgen Qasar cut him down right there and cast him away.

185 Qali'udar and Ca'urqan said to Chinggis Khan, 'Ong Khan is entirely without a care. He has set up the Golden Tent and is feasting. Let us force a quick march, switching mounts and riding through the nights, and surround them to take them by surprise.' He approved their words, and sending Jürcedei and Arqai as outriders they travelled through the nights until they arrived and surrounded them while they were at the opening of Jer Gully in Jeje'er Heights. For three nights and three days the fight went against them as we surrounded them in ranks, until

on the third day they gave up and surrendered. How Ong Khan and Senggum escaped during the night no one knew.

Among those who fought was Qadaq Ba'atur of the Jirkin. Qadaq Ba'atur came and surrendered and said, 'For three nights and three days while fighting with you, I was thinking "How can I look on and let my own ruler be taken and killed?" and could not bear to forsake him. Thinking, "Let me sacrifice my life so he escapes," I drew the struggle on myself as I fought with you. Now if you put me to death with them, then let me die; if I am favoured by Chinggis Khan, then let me devote my strength to him.'

Chinggis Khan approved Qadaq Ba'atur's words and decreed, 'Unable to forsake his own ruler and fighting with us with the thought of sacrificing his life so his ruler could escape – that's a true man, is it not? He is a person fit to be befriended.' Thus he showed him favour and, without putting him to death, issued a decree in his favour that said, 'Let Qadaq Ba'atur and the one hundred Jirkin devote their strength to Quyildar's women and children for the sake of Quyildar's life. When a boy child is born, let him follow and devote his strength unto the seed of the seed of Quyildar. When a girl child is born, let her father and mother not marry her off according to their own pleasure, but let her serve before and behind the daughters of Quyildar.'[73]

Because Quyildar Secen had opened his mouth first, Chinggis Khan favoured him with a decree, a decree that said, 'Unto the seed of the seed of Quyildar, for the sake of Quyildar's service, let them receive the endowment for orphans.'[74]

And thus he brought low the Kereyit folk and divided them 186 up here and there, stripping them bare.[75]

Due to his service, Taġai Ba'atur of the Suldus was given the one hundred Jirkin.

Again, Chinggis Khan decreed, 'Ong Khan's younger brother Ja'a Gambo has two daughters'; while Chinggis Khan took the older sister of the two, Ibaqa Beki, for himself, the younger sister, Sorġoqtani Beki, he gave to Tolui. For that reason he favoured Ja'a Gambo by leaving his property and folk whole; calling him the other axle,[76] he did not strip them bare.

Again, Chinggis Khan issued a decree that said, 'Due to the 187 service of Badai and Kiśiliq, let the Onggojit Kereyit be their *kesikten*[77] together with the minions who had been taking care of the gold liquor services, bowls and vessels of Ong Khan's Golden Tent. With them serving them as quiver-bearers and cup-bearers, let them rejoice as ones with free rights, unto the seed of the seed. When they rush against the teeming enemies, let them take as much booty as they can get. When they kill wild game, let them take as much as they can kill.'

Again, Chinggis Khan issued a decree that said, 'Due to the service which Badai and Kiśiliq delivered at a moment of life and death, protected by Eternal Heaven, we brought low the Kereyit folk and ascended the high throne. For ever after, to the seed of my seed, as we sit on the throne let each of us, one after the other, be mindful of the service which they rendered.'[78]

When the Kereyit folk were plundered, whoever there was who was lacking something, he received a share. The Ten Thousand Tübe'en were divided up among us until everyone was able to get some of them. The Teeming Donggayit were stripped bare for less than a full day. The Jirkin *ba'atur*s who would take the enemy's bloody gear were divided up into shares, but there was not enough of them for all to get some.

The Kereyit folk having been thus abolished, that winter we wintered at Abji'a-Köteger.

188   Ong Khan and Senggum themselves had fled away in revolt, and Ong Khan was thirsty; to get into the Nekun River of Titik Ša'al he surrendered to the Naiman scout Qori the border guard. Border guard Qori seized Ong Khan. Ong Khan said, 'I am Ong Khan'; but not recognizing him, Qori the border guard did not believe him and killed him there.

Senggum skirted around the Nekun River of Titik Ša'al and went into the desert.[79] As he and his groom were seeking water, some khulans were standing there bothered by the gnats;[80] Senggum dismounted and was stealing up on them.

Senggum's friend Kökecu the groom and his woman were there together with Senggum. He left his horse in the groom Kökecu's hands. The groom Kökecu led his gelding back at a trot. His woman said, 'When he swathed you in the satiny, when he delighted you with dainties, he called you "My Kökecu".

How can you forsake your ruler Senggum like this and go off and leave him behind?' And his woman stood there hanging back.

Kökecu said, 'You just want to make Senggum your man.'

To that, his woman said, 'A woman said to have a dog's face – that's me. At least give me his golden goblet. At least let him scoop water with it to drink.'

Then the groom Kökecu, saying, 'Take his golden goblet,' tossed it behind him and trotted off.

After the groom Kökecu had arrived alone at Chinggis Khan's, people were talking to each other about how the groom Kökecu had come in and said, 'I came here leaving Senggum behind in the desert.' When all these words were reported in full to Chinggis Khan, he issued a decree favouring the woman over him: 'That groom Kökecu forsook his own ruler like that and came here. If anyone befriended such a man could he be trusted?' And he cut him down and cast him away.[81]

5: COMPLETING THE
UNIFICATION OF
MONGOLIA

THE NAIMAN PLOT

189 Mother Gürbesu of Tayang Khan of the Naiman said, 'Ong Khan was an aged great ruler of old. Bring his head.[1] If it is indeed his, let us sacrifice to it.' An envoy was sent to Qori the border guard and his head was cut off and brought to her. She recognized it and placed it on a white *toloq* spread.[2] Her daughters-in-law she had do the rites of the daughter-in-law, offering the *ötok* liquor, and playing the fiddle. She took up a bowl and sacrificed. Then, as the head was being sacrificed to in this way, it laughed. Since it had laughed, Tayang Khan had them trample it to pieces.

Kökse'u-Sabraq spoke. 'Since it was you who cut off and brought the head of the dead ruler, and since it was you who then again trampled it, how could that be right? The sound of the barking of our bitches[3] has turned evil. İnanc Bilge Khan used to say, "The woman is young and I, the man, have grown old. I begat this Tayang through enchantment. Alas, son of mine born debilitated, can you take in hand the care of my teeming, bad, lowly kingdom in its debilitation?"[4] So he used to speak. Now the noise of the bitches barking is an ominous one. The ordinances of our lady Gürbesu have turned cruel. You, my debilitated ruler Tayang, are soft. You have no thought or skill except for hawking and hunting.'

So were they talking about Tayang Khan when he said, 'It is said that there are a few Mongols to the east of here. With their quivers those people gave fright to and put to flight the aged great Ong Khan of old and drove him to death. Now they are the ones who say, "We will be the ruler." Let us say that above in Heaven the sun and moon are both brightly shining – indeed, there are the sun and moon there! How can it be that there are two rulers on earth? We will go and bring back those few Mongols.'

His stepmother Gürbesu said, 'What would you do with them? The Mongol folk have an evil odour and their clothes have dark stains; keep them far away! Maybe bring in the noblest of their daughters and daughters-in-law, wash their hands, and maybe they might be set to milk the cows and sheep.'

Tayang Khan said to her, 'If that's the way it is, what issue is there? We will go to those Mongols and maybe we will bring back their quiver.'[5]

To these words Kökse'u-Sabraq said, 'Alas, you speak so grandly! Alas, debilitated ruler, is it right? Keep this secret!' 190

Despite Kökse'u-Sabraq's words of dissuasion, an envoy named Törbi-Taš was sent to Ala-Quš Digit-Quri of the Öng'ut to say, 'It is said that there are a few Mongols to the east of here. You take the right wing; I will join in with you from here and we will take the quiver of those Mongols.'

To those words, Ala-Quš Digit-Quri sent to reply that 'I cannot take the right wing.' Ala-Quš Digit-Quri then sent an envoy named Yoqunan to say to Chinggis Khan: 'The Naiman and Tayang Khan are coming to take your quiver. Word came telling me to take the right wing; I wouldn't do it. Now I have sent to warn you. Beware lest your quiver be taken!'

THE MONGOLS MUSTER

At that moment, Chinggis Khan was hunting on the Teme'en steppe. Just as the ring was closing in at Tülkin-Ce'ut, envoy Yoqunan came from Ala-Quš Digit-Quri to deliver his message.

Since the message came when they were on the hunting exercises, they talked to each other about what to do. Many people said to each other, 'Our geldings are lean; what can we do now?'[6]

To that Otcigin Noyan said, 'Why do you make excuses that

the geldings are lean? My geldings are fat. How can we take such words sitting down?'

Also Belgutei Noyan said, 'Even if we remain alive, what use would it be if our quiver has been taken by another contender? For someone born a true man, even if he died, wouldn't it be fine so long as his quiver and bow lie together with his bones? The Naiman folk are saying grand words, that they have a great kingdom and a teeming people. If we ride up and push against these grand words, would it be so hard to take their quiver? If we get there, won't they have to watch lest their teeming horse herds be resting and get left behind? Won't they have to watch lest their hordes and *ger*s get left behind as they load them up? Won't they have to watch lest their teeming kingdom be gone to hide away in the high places? How can we let such grand words be said to us sitting down? Let us ride!'

191   Approving these words of Belgutei Noyan, Chinggis Khan broke off the ring hunt and then moved off from Abji'a-Köteger and pitched camp around the Keltegei Cliffs over Or Meadow on the Khalkh. And he had them count their numbers and numbered them there by thousands. There he appointed captains of each thousand, captains of each hundred and captains of each ten. He appointed chamberlains there as well.[7] He appointed the six chamberlains, Dödei Cerbi, Doqolqu Cerbi, Ögelei Cerbi, Tolun Cerbi, Bucaran Cerbi and Söiketu Cerbi there.

Once the numbering into thousands, numbering into hundreds and numbering into tens was completed, he selected eighty nightguards and seventy dayguards for enrolment. He enrolled the sons and junior kinsmen of the captains of a thousand or a hundred and the sons and junior kinsmen of the common people, selecting for enrolment those with skills and a handsome body and face. Favouring Arqai-Qasar, he decreed, 'Let him select *ba'atur*s to the number of a thousand. On the day of battle, let them give battle standing in front of me. Let them be dayguard *keśikten* for many days.' He said, 'Let Ögelei Cerbi preside over the seventy dayguards. Let him take counsel with Qutus-Qaljan.'[8]

192   Again, Chinggis Khan decreed: 'Quiver-bearers, dayguards, *keśikten*, stewards, door wardens and grooms shall go on day

shift duty, and before the sun sets they shall give way to the nightguards and go out to their geldings to spend the night. Some nightguards at night shall lie down in their recumbent position around the *ger*, and some shall be set to stand in shifts in their upright position at the door.

'When we have our soup in the morning, let the quiver-bearers and dayguards report to the nightguards; let the quiver-bearers, dayguards, stewards and door wardens each go in in their several ranks and let them each sit in their own seats. Let them finish the three nights and three days of their shift, spending three nights together. Then let them exchange shifts, and be nightguards during the night; let them lie down surrounding us.'

BATTLE OF NAQU QUN

Thus he completed numbering the thousands, appointed chamberlains, enrolled eighty nightguards and seventy dayguards, and had Arqai-Qasar select the *ba'atur*s. Then they rode from the Keltegei Cliffs over Or Meadow on the Khalkh against the Naiman folk. Having sprinkled libations on the banners at the Red Disk Day, the sixteenth of the first moon of summer of the Year of the Mouse [1204], Jebe and Qubilai went upstream along the Kherlen as outriders. When they reached the Sa'ari steppe, the Naiman scouts were there on the peaks of the Qanggar-Qan.[9]

Driving forward against our scouts, the Naiman guards captured a single white horse with a bad saddle from our guards. Taking this horse as evidence, the Naiman scouts said to each other, 'The Mongols' geldings are lean.'

When our side reached the Sa'ari steppe, they halted there and said to each other, 'What shall we do?' Dödei Cerbi proposed to Chinggis Khan: 'Those ones here with us are few, and, over and above being few, they have arrived exhausted. Thus, let us halt and pitch camp all over this Sa'ari steppe until the geldings are well fed. And every living soul will light five separate fires for every fighting man, and panic them with the fires. The Naiman are said to be many; their ruler is said to be a weakling who doesn't leave his *ger*. While we confuse them with the fires, it is our geldings who will be well fed. Driving back the Naiman scouts with our well-fed geldings, we shall press on their heels and push them back into their centre, and if we give battle while they are in confusion, that would work, wouldn't it?'

Chinggis Khan approved these words and decreed, 'Let it be so; have the fires lit'; this ordinance was proclaimed to the soldiers. Thus, they pitched camp over the Sa'ari steppe and had each living soul light five separate fires for every fighting man. At night the scouts of the Naiman from the peaks of Qanggar-Qan saw many fires in the dark. And saying, 'Weren't they saying the Mongols were very few? They have more fires than there are stars,' they sent up the pale-white horse with its very bad saddle to Tayang Khan and they sent to say, 'The soldiers of the Mongols have pitched camp enough to cover Sa'ari steppe; they're surging beyond what they were during the day, aren't they? They have more fires than there are stars.'

194   When this word from the scouts was delivered, Tayang Khan was at the Qacir River of the Khangai. Once this message was delivered to him, he sent a message to his son Küculug Khan. 'The Mongols' geldings are lean; they have more fires than there are stars, they say. The Mongols are many. Now

If we're big enough to battle,
It will be brutal to break it up, no?
If we're big enough to battle,
Their black eyes will barely blink.
When bearded cheeks are battered in,
When the black blood is bleeding out,
The brutal Mongols will not back down;
Will battle do, do you think?

The Mongol geldings are lean, it's said. Let us remove our folk, rolling them back across the Altai,[10] re-form our army's ranks, keep luring them on and keep touching off dogfights down to the sunny side of the Altai – our geldings are fat – and so after wearying the Mongol geldings and pulling in their bellies, then let us pour out into their faces!'

To these words Küculug Khan said, 'The same old woman Tayang's heart failed him so he said this. Where could all these teeming Mongols have come from? Most of the Mongols are here with Jamuqa and are ours.[11] That woman Tayang, who won't plod out as far as a pregnant woman goes to piss, who won't putter out as far as a puling calf goes to pasture – his heart failed him so he sent to say this, didn't he?' So saying, he spoke through envoys until he pained, until he wounded his own father.

To these words, being talked about as if he were a woman, Tayang Khan replied personally, 'Powerful, proud Küculug – on the day of killing each other in the fray, let's hope he won't drop this pride of his, maybe. When he's finally joined in the fray, he'll find it hard to break it off, maybe.'

To those words, the great commander with authority under Tayang Khan, Qori the border guard, said, 'Your father, Ïnanc Bilge Khan, would never let a fighting man's back or a gelding's croup be seen by an equal contender. Now, why does your heart fail you, while the morning is still early? Had I known that your heart would fail you like this, even though she is but a lady, I would have brought your stepmother Gürbesu to marshal the army, wouldn't I have? Alas, what a pity! Why do we pay like this for Kökse'u-Sabraq's ageing? Our army's drill has become negligent. It is the destined day of the Mongols.[12] It is no good! Alas, debilitated Tayang, you look just like you will fail.' And then he struck his quiver and trotted off in the other direction.

At this, Tayang Khan was angry and said, 'Lives die, bodies hurt: it's the same for all! Since that's the way it is, let us join battle.' He then moved from the Qacir River, and went down the Tamir before crossing the Orkhon, and, rounding the eastern skirts of Naqu Qun, they came to the Cakirma'ut. 195

Then Chinggis Khan's scouts saw them and sent a message: 'The Naiman are coming.' In reply to the message, Chinggis Khan decreed: 'More men just means more losses for them and fewer men just means fewer for us,' and then rode against them. He first drove their scouts back and then marshalled the troops, telling them, 'March in a caragana-style march, form up in a lake formation, and go to battle with a chisel battle array.'[13] So saying, Chinggis Khan went personally as an outrider, leaving Qasar to marshal the centre and Otcigin to marshal the reserves.

The Naiman withdrew from the Cakirma'ut and stood lining

the skirts of the southern slopes of Naqu Qun. The Naiman
scouts were driven back by our scouts and we pushed them back
until they merged with their great centre on the southern slopes
of Naqu Qun. Tayang Khan saw how they were being driven
back; Jamuqa was there, riding in the army with the Naiman,
and Tayang Khan asked Jamuqa about this. 'Who are they, these
fellows who drive them up here like wolves driving teeming
sheep, driving them into a corral?'

Jamuqa said, 'My *anda* Temujin raised four dogs on man's
flesh and keeps them shackled in chains. That's them, the ones
driving our scouts back here! Those four dogs have

Bronze as their foreheads
Borers as their tongues
Chisels as their snouts
Steel as their hearts
Swords as their whips
They drink the dew and ride the wind.
At the scenes of slaughter, they swallow human flesh;
On the day of dealing death, they devour the flesh of men.
They have slipped their chains now, haven't they? The shackled
ones are happy and they come on slavering.'

When he asked who the four dogs were, Jamuqa said they
were Jebe and Qubilai, Jelme and Sübe'edei. Tayang Khan,
said, 'Let us stay well away from these vile men,' and he stepped
backwards up the mountain and stood there.

He saw some of the men coming on gambolling around the
Naiman in a circle, and again questioned Jamuqa. 'Who are
they, those ones gambolling around us in a circle, like foals let
off the line early while suckling from their dams, like foals run-
ning wildly about their dams?' he asked.

Jamuqa said, 'They are called the Uru'ut and Manggut, who
Storm the serried spear-clad ranks
And gather all the gory gear,
Who smite the soldiers bearing swords
And send them sprawling, killing them,
And get their goods and gear.
Isn't that them now, gambolling happily towards us?'

Then Tayang Khan said, 'If that's the way it is, let us stay well away from these vile men,' and again he climbed back-wards up the mountain and stood there.

'Who are the ones moving up behind them, coming on like rav-enous raptors slavering, coming out in the lead?' he asked Jamuqa. Jamuqa said, 'This *anda* of mine Temujin who approaches, his whole body is cast of bronze with no gap through which you could pierce him with a borer, hammered of iron with no gap through which you could pierce him with an auger.[14] Have you seen how my *anda* Temujin comes up here now, slavering so, like a ravenous raptor? You Naiman friends were always going on about how, when you saw the Mongols, you wouldn't leave as much as a kid's hoof's skin. Now, look!'

To these words Tayang Khan said, 'Appalling indeed! Let us climb up the mountain,' and he climbed up the mountain and stood there.

Again, Tayang Khan asked Jamuqa, 'Who is that one coming up behind like a hulk?'

Jamuqa said, 'Mother Ö'elun used to feed one of her sons on man's flesh:
With a body full three fathoms long,
With a meal of a three-year-old steer,
With a breastplate of three-ply metal,
With a cart hauled by three bulls, here he comes!
When man and sword he swallows whole,
It doesn't stick going down.
When man and gear he gobbles down,
It never slakes his greed.
When in an angry rage
His *anggu'a* arrow he draws to fire,[15]
He'll rend asunder all ten or twenty men
On alpine ranges too distant to discern
With his shot.
When in a skirmish,
His swift *keyibur* arrow he draws to fire,[16]
He'll stick them fast and split them through
On steppes that barely can be seen
With his shot.
When he draws to fire mightily

Full nine hundred fathoms he'll maybe reach;
When he draws to fire holding back
Five hundred fathoms he'll hardly reach.
Poles apart from other men,
Born a python in powerful coils,[17]
he is called Coci-Qasar;
that's him!' he said.

Then, Tayang Khan said, 'If that's how it is indeed, let us push on up to the mountain heights; climb higher!' and climbed the mountain and stood there.

Again, Tayang Khan asked Jamuqa, 'Who is the one coming up from behind him?'

Jamuqa said, 'That is Mother Ö'elun's baby boy, called Easy-Going Otcigin. He's one who sleeps early; he's one who gets up late. But he won't hang back from the looming melee, he won't hang back from the fray.'

Tayang Khan said, 'If that's the way it is, then let us get up to the mountain peak.'

196   Jamuqa, having spoken these words thus to Tayang Khan, broke away from the Naiman and went off alone. He sent a message to Chinggis Khan, saying, 'Tell this to *Anda*.' His message said, 'Tayang Khan was killed by my comparisons; in dread he's clambered up the cliffs. He was murdered by my mouth, and in fear he's mounted up the massif. *Anda*, be patient! These same ones have gone up the mountain; there's no fight in their faces. As for me, I've broken away from the Naiman.'

The sun was going down on Chinggis Khan and he spent the night standing in ranks surrounding Naqu Qun. That night, as the Naiman tried to go into hiding, they tumbled down the Naqu and fell on each other with smashed bones and matted hair, all in a heap one on top of the other. They died crushing each other until they stood like rotten snags.[18] The next day, they wiped out Tayang Khan completely. Küculug Khan was elsewhere, and moved off in revolt with a few people. Upon being chased down, they made a wagon-fort on the Tamir. But they were unable to stand in that wagon-fort and moved off, escaping away in flight.

The nation of the Naiman, gathered together on the sunny side of the Altai,[19] was wiped out. The Jadaran, Qatagin, Salji'ut,

Dörben, Tayici'ut and Qonggirat who had been with Jamuqa sur-
rendered there too. As for Tayang Khan's stepmother Gürbesu,
they brought her to Chinggis Khan and he said, 'Weren't you talk-
ing about the evil odour of the Mongols? Now what brought you
here?' And Chinggis Khan took her for himself.

CONQUEST OF THE MERKIT

In the autumn of that same Year of the Mouse [1204], at the 197
Qara-Dal confluence, Chinggis Khan fought with Toqto'a Beki,
drove him off and plundered his kingdom's subjects. Toqto'a fled
away with his sons Godu and Cila'un and a few of his people.

As the Merkit folk were thus being plundered, Dayir-Usun of
the U'as Merkit brought his daughter Lady Qulan with him,
hoping to present her to Chinggis Khan. On the way he was
held up by the soldiers; Dayir-Usun met Naya'a Noyan of the
Ba'arin, and said, 'I am coming, hoping to present this girl to
Chinggis Khan.' Naya'a Noyan replied, 'Lct us present your
daughter to him together,' and detained them. The reason he
detained them was that, as he said, 'If you go on alone in this
chaotic time, Dayir-Usun, on the way the soldiers won't let you
live and moreover your daughter will be molested.' He detained
them for three days and three nights. Then, taking Dayir-Usun
and Lady Qulan, Naya'a Noyan delivered them together to
Chinggis Khan.

Chinggis Khan became very angry, saying, 'How dared you
hinder them?' As he was about to interrogate him, saying, 'Let the
interrogation be merciless and thorough, and let a binding ordin-
ance be made,'[20] then Lady Qulan testified, saying, 'Naya'a spoke
to us. He dissuaded us from going further, saying, "I am a great
commander of the Chinggis Khan; let us present your daughter
to the khan together. On the way, the soldiers would molest
her." Now if we had met soldiers other than Naya'a, would not
we have run into lawlessness, or obstacles? Maybe it was good
that we met this Naya'a. Now, if it would please the khan, while
interrogating Naya'a, would he not examine this flesh begotten
to my father and mother by a destiny from Heaven?'

When Naya'a was interrogated, he said, 'I look to no one but the khan! When I meet,

Foreign folk's
Chubby cheeked
Lovely ladies and
Geldings good of rump

then "They are the khan's" I say! If I have ever thought differently, then may I die!'

Chinggis Khan approved Lady Qulan's testimony and on that same day, when a trial was conducted, the result turned out identical to Lady Qulan's testimony and Chinggis Khan was pleased to favour Lady Qulan. Considering that Naya'a's words were validated completely and that he was one who spoke the truth, he favoured him as one who could be trusted with great matters.

198   After the plundering of the Merkit folk, of the two ladies of Toqto'a Beki's eldest son Ġodu, Tügei and Töregene, Töregene was given to Ökodei Khan.[21]

Half of the Merkit rebelled and fortified themselves in Tayiġal Fort. Chinggis Khan decreed that Sorġan-Śira's son Cimbai be sent in command of the left-wing soldiers to besiege the Merkit who had fortified themselves.

Chinggis Khan pursued Toqto'a and his sons Ġodu and Cila'un and those few persons who had left in revolt, and wintered on the southern slopes of the Altai.[22] As Chinggis Khan crossed over the Alai in the spring of the Year of the Cow [1205],[23] Küculug Khan of the Naiman, who had lost his kingdom and fled in revolt with a few people, allied with Toqto'a of the Merkit. They joined forces and marshalled their armies at the confluence of the Buqtyrma and the Irtysh. When Chinggis Khan arrived to fight, Toqto'a was struck there in the shower of arrows and fell.[24] His sons were unable either to collect his bones or to take away his body; they cut off his head and journeyed on with it.

The Naiman and Merkit had joined forces there but were unable to fight. Fording the Irtysh as they fled, they sank under and most of them met their deaths. A few of the Naiman and Merkit who managed to ford the Irtysh escaped and moved off separately. Küculug Khan of the Naiman, passing by the Uyghur-like Qarluqs, went to ally with the *Gür Khan* of the Qara-Khitai off in the Sarts' country, along the Chüy River. The sons of Toqto'a of the Merkit, Godu, Gal, Cila'un and such, journeyed on, passing by the Qangli and the Qïpchaqs.[25] Then Chinggis Khan returned and crossed over the Alai and dismounted at his base camps.[26]

Cimbai had wiped out the Merkit who had fortified Tayigal Fort. Chinggis Khan decreed that those who should be butchered were to be butchered and the remainder be stripped bare by the soldiers.

Moreover, the Merkit who had surrendered before rose up from the base camps in revolt and our servants who were in the base camps put them down. Then Chinggis Khan decreed, 'We had intended to keep them whole, but these same ones have revolted,' and had the Merkit divided up until they were wiped out.

CHASING DOWN THE FUGITIVES

In the same Year of the Cow [1205],[27] Chinggis Khan decreed that Sübe'edei, he of the cart with iron-shod wheels, be sent to pursue Toqto'a's leading sons Godu, Gal and Cila'un. Chinggis Khan issued a decree and had it recited to Sübe'edei:[28]

'Godu, Gal and Cila'un, the leading sons of Toqto'a fled in fright, firing behind them, and ran off like a khulan carrying off an *uurga*[29] or an elk bearing away an arrow.[30] If they have wings and fly up into heaven, then you, Sübe'edei, will you not become a falcon and fly to catch them? If they become marmots and dig with their claws into the earth, will you not become a spade sounding them out and reaching down to strike them? If they become fish and slip into the oceans and seas, then you, Sübe'edei, will you not become a cast net or a dragnet and entangle them?

'Moreover, I send you to cross high passes and ford broad rivers. Be mindful of how distant the lands are to which I send you and spare the army remounts before they waste away. Be

199

frugal with your provisions lest they should be exhausted. It will do you no good to spare your geldings after they have wasted away with exhaustion; it will do you no good to be frugal with your provisions after they are already exhausted. There will be teeming game on your route, but think far ahead and do not let your soldiers and people rush after the game. Do not ring hunt immoderately. If you ring hunt, thinking to add something to the provisions for your people in the army, ring hunt in moderation.

'Aside from moderate ring hunts, do not let your army people crupper their saddles; ride with the bit out of the horse's mouth and without throwing on the bridle. If such orders are followed, how can the people in the army rush forward? Once such an ordinance has been made, let those who break the ordinance be seized and beaten. As for those who have broken our decrees, should they seem like ones known to us, send them back to us. Should they be one of the many who are unknown to us, execute them there.[31]

'When split into squads beyond the river may you still drive on in this way;[32] when all alone beyond the mountain, may you not allow distracting thoughts. If your power is mightily increased by Eternal Heaven and Toqto'a's sons fall into your hands, what need would there be to bring them back to me? Cast them away there.'[33]

Again, Chinggis Khan spoke to Sübe'edei, and decreed: 'I sent you on this expedition because when I was small, I was made to circle Burġan-Qaldun in terror three times by the Uduyit of the Three Merkit. Such a hateful people have now escaped yet again, swearing [not to submit]. Intending you to go to the frontier of the far off, to the uttermost of the unfathomable, making you pursue them utterly, I had iron hammered on to your carts and sent you to wage war in the Year of the Cow. If when we are absent you think of us as present and when we are far as near, then you will be protected by Heaven above.'[34]

200   When wiping out the Naiman and Merkit had been achieved, and when those of Jamuqa's folk who were with the Naiman were taken, that same Jamuqa went up the Tannu-Ola with five

friends and became an outlaw. They had killed an argali ram and were roasting and eating it when Jamuqa said to his friends, 'Whose sons kill and eat argali like this today?'[35] In the middle of eating that argali meat, those five friends laid hands on Jamuqa and brought him bound to Chinggis Khan.

Jamuqa was brought bound by his own friends, and he said, 'Tell the Khan-*Anda*,

Black crows have clutched a colourful duck[36]

Black slaves have seized their own sovereign

In murky matters let the khan my *anda* not misjudge.

Brown harriers have harassed a high-flown drake[37]

Base slaves have banded together to jump their born master

In heavy matters let my holy *anda* not hesitate.'

At those words from Jamuqa, Chinggis Khan decreed, 'People who laid hands on their own ruler – how can they be allowed to live? Who would befriend such people? Minions who laid hands on their own ruler – execute them all down to their offspring!' In open view of that same Jamuqa, he had executed for him the minions who had raised hands against him.

Chinggis Khan sent a message saying, 'Tell this to Jamuqa.' The message was: 'Now we have come together – let us be friends. When we should have become the other axle for each other, you thought differently and went your own way. Now that we are together again as one, let us,

Advise the other of what he's forgotten,

Awake the other when he's been sleeping.

Even separated, when you were apart,

Still you were my spirit's fortunate, blessed *anda*.

At the second when slaughter would soon begin

Your heart was hurting for me here.

Even apart, when you were separate,

When the killing affray would soon arise,

Always your affections were in agony for me.

Should you ask when this was, it was the help you gave at the Battle of Qala'aljit Sands with the Kereyit folk, when you sent a message relaying what words you'd said to Ong Khan. Also, it was the help you gave when you sent your dreadful message that

you had killed the Naiman folk with your comparisons and mur-
dered them with your mouth and said, "Believe it to be true!"'[38]

201   When he spoke thus, Jamuqa said, 'In days of old, when we
were small, in the Qorqonaq valley, by calling myself *anda*
with the ruler-*anda*, we ate together food that would never be
digested[39] and spoke together words that would never be for-
gotten and lived life sharing one quilt between us.

Stirred up by someone standing athwart us,
Provoked by a person with prejudiced heart,
He managed to make us part.
Vital words we voiced as vows
But my vile visage
Being peeled for shame,
I failed in faith and
The familiar face
Of my fine *anda*
I forbore to follow.
Memorable words we mouthed in pledge,
But my raw mug
Being flayed for shame,
The faithful face
Of my faultless *anda*
I failed to find.

'Now the ruler-*anda* favours me and says, "Let us be friends."
At the time to become friends, I was not a friend of his. Now,
the surrounding kingdom is all subdued, the alien peoples are
all allied. You have pointed at the ruler's throne for me. Now
when the world has become ready, what would be the use of us
becoming friends? Indeed, I would enter your dreams in the
dark night, I would torment your thoughts in the bright day. I
would be a louse in your lining, a thorn against your throat.

'I had ample grannies.[40] In thinking to go much further than
Anda, I was enticed. Now in this birth, that of *Anda* and myself,
my name reached from the sun's rising to the sun's setting. *Anda*
was born as a champion, inheriting a wise mother, and gained
his skilful little brothers and peerless friends, and his seventy-
three geldings; I was surpassed by *Anda*. As for me, I was left
behind by my mother and father as a small child, I had no little

brothers, my woman was a blatherer and I had faithless friends; in all those things I was surpassed by *Anda*, who was born with a heavenly destiny. If *Anda* should show favour, if he should dispatch me quickly, his heart would be set at ease. *Anda*, if you would favour me in how you put me to death, put me to death without shedding any blood.[41] If, while lying in death, my bare bones be in lofty earth,[42] I will bring lasting, abiding protection unto the seed of your seed.

A blessing will I become for you.

My birth was from some other bounds;

The *sülder* of my *anda*'s better birth did beat me down.[43] Do not set aside the words I have spoken; recite them to each other evening and morning. Now deal with me quickly!'

When he had spoken, Chinggis Khan replied to these words, 'My *anda* was staying separate indeed, but I had not heard that his mouth was full of me behind my back or that his heart was set on slaying me. He is a person who has something to teach, yet this same one will not do it. If I were to say, "Put him to death," it would not be confirmed by divination. And it is not right to slay someone without a reason. He is a man who cut a broad path in this life.

'Tell him that this is the possible reason for it: because Coci-Tarmala and Taicar had been stealing each other's horse herds, you, Jamuqa *Anda*, about-faced and plotted rebellion. And we fought at Dalan-Baljut, and there you frightened me into escaping into Jerene Gorge, didn't you? Now if I were to say, "Let us be friends," it would not do. If I were to spare your life, it would not be all right. Say that! Now, in accordance with your request, tell them, "Let him be dispatched without shedding his blood."'

Having spoken, he decreed, 'Dispatch him without shedding blood and do not leave his bones visible; bury them well!' Jamuqa was dispatched there and his bones were buried.

6: THE NEW REGIME

CAPTAINS OF A THOUSAND

202 And so they set aright the felt-walled kingdom and in the Year of the Tiger [1206] assembled at the headwaters of the Onon. They planted the nine-tailed white banner, and gave the title of ruler to Chinggis Khan there.[1] They also gave there the title of *Guyang* to Muqali.[2] Jebe was made there to pursue Küculug Khan and wage war on him as well. To manage the reorganization of the Mongol kingdom, Chinggis Khan issued a decree: 'For those who helped establish the kingdom, I shall number it into thousands and appoint you each captain of a thousand, and speak words of favour.' The captains of a thousand were appointed as follows:[3]

1. Father Mönglik
2. Bo'orcu
3. Muqali *Guyang*
4. Qorci
5. Ilugei
6. Jürcedei
7. Gunan
8. Qubilai
9. Jelme
10. Tüge
11. Degei
12. Tolun
13. Önggur
14. Cülgetei

15. Boroġul
16. Śiki Qutuġu
17. Kücu
18. Kökecu
19. Qorġasun
20. Üsun
21. Quyildar
22. Śiluqai
23. Jedei
24. Taġai
25. Caġān-Quwa
26. Alaq
27. Sorġan-Śira
28. Buluġan
29. Qaracar
30. Köke-Cos
31. Söiketu
32. Naya'a
33. Jungšoi
34. Kücugur
35. Bala
36. Oronartai
37. Dayir
38. Müge
39. Bujir
40. Mönggu'ur
41. Dolo'adai
42. Böken
43. Qutus
44. Maral
45. Jebke
46. Yuruqan
47. Köke
48. Jebe
49. Udutai
50. Bala Cerbi
51. Kete
52. Sübe'edei

53. Möngge-Qalja
54. Qurjaqus
55. Geuki
56. Badai
57. Kiśiliq
58. Ketei
59. Ca'urqai
60. Qonggiran
61. Toġon-Temur
62. Megetu
63. Qada'an
64. Moroqa
65. Dori-Buqa
66. Idoġadai
67. Śiraqul
68. Da'un
69. Tamaci
70. Qauran
71. Alci
72. Dobsaqa
73. Tungquidai
74. Tobuqa
75. Ajinai
76. Tüideger
77. Sece'ur
78. Jeder
79. Olar Küregen[4]
80. Kinggiyadai
81. Buqa Küregen
82. Quril
83. Aśiq Küregen
84. Qatai Küregen
85. Ciku Küregen
86.–88. Alci Küregen and three thousands of the Qonggirat
89.–90. Botu Küregen and two thousands of the Ikires
91.–95. Ala-Quš Digit-Quri Küregen of the Öng'ut and
     five thousands of the Öng'ut.

Excluding the Forest Folk, these were the captains of the ninety-five thousands that Chinggis Khan named as the captains of a thousand of the Mongol kingdom.

GRANTS FOR SERVICE[5]

Chinggis Khan decreed that these ninety-five captains of thousands just named be assigned to thousands, at the same time as the sons-in-law as well. Among them, Chinggis Khan decreed, 'I shall grant favours to those who served me well.' When he said, 'Let the leading commanders Bo'orcu and Muqali approach,' Śiki Qutuġu was inside the *ger*.

He told Śiki Qutuġu, 'Go and bring them in,' but Śiki Qutuġu said, 'Muqali and Bo'orcu have served better than whom? They devoted their strength more than whom? "Favours shall be granted" – in what way was my service lacking? In what way was the strength I devoted lacking? From when
I was lodged in the cradle,
until at your lofty threshold
I lived to have long whiskers on my lips,
I have never had second thoughts.
Since they placed a piss-pot at my crotch
until at your golden portal
I passed my days, till whiskers framed my face,
I made no false step.
Laying me down by her legs
She raised me up to be like a little brother; [6]
Setting me down by her side
She raised me up to serve like her own son.
Now what favour will you grant me?'[7]

In reply to these words, Chinggis Khan issued a decree to Śiki Qutuġu: 'You are the sixth little brother, are you not? To you, my late-born little brother, join with the others in the favour of a share as a little brother![8] Moreover, because of your services, let no one hold you guilty for up to nine offences.'[9]

And he decreed, 'Now when protected by Eternal Heaven we

203

are rectifying the entire kingdom, you have become eyes for see-
ing and ears for hearing. And give shares in the whole kingdom
to Mother, to us, to the junior kinsmen, and to the princes,[10]
and for each separate folk by name sort out allotments of the
felt-walled people and divide up assignments of the plank-door
people.[11] Let not your word be nullified by anyone, whoever
they may be.'

Also, he appointed Śiki Qutuġu as the supreme judge of the
whole kingdom, to chastise theft and expose lies, to put to
death those whose ways are worthy of death, and to hold guilty
those whose ways are worthy of guilt.

Also, he decreed: 'Write out in the Blue Registries a record of
the shares distributed and the judgments judged for the whole
kingdom.[12] And in this way unto the seed of the seed, take counsel
with me and let no one alter what has been recorded in blue letters
on white paper. Let any commoner who alters it be held guilty.'

Śiki Qutuġu said, 'How could I as a late-born little brother
receive entirely equal shares? If the khan favours me, let him
entrust to me a grant from among the cities with earthen walls.'[13]

To these words, Chinggis Khan said in reply, 'You have
limited your own claim yourself; you see to it!'

Śiki Qutuġu, having managed thus to secure such favour for
himself, went out to invite in the commanders Bo'orcu and
Muqali.

204   Then Chinggis Khan decreed to Father Mönglik, 'You, born
together as I was born, growing together as I grew up, fortu-
nate, blessed – how great was your service and protection!
Among them was the time when Father Ong Khan and Seng-
gum *Anda* invited me as a ruse, when I was on the road thence
and spent the night in Father Mönglik's *ger*. If you, Father
Mönglik, had not dissuaded me, would I not have fallen into a
cascading flood and a carmine flame? That service I still remem-
ber and how could it ever be forgotten unto the seed of the
seed? Remembering that service, I shall let you sit in the seat at
the head on this side[14] and as you discourse on the year and on
the month,[15] gifts and favours I will give you. I shall attend to
you, unto the seed of the seed.'

205   Also, Chinggis Khan issued a decree to Bo'orcu, saying, 'When

I was small, we were robbed of the isabelline geldings, eight mounts, and on the way, when I was chasing them down for three nights, we met. Then you said, "I will become friends with a friend who comes to me in trouble," and without saying a word to your father in the *ger* you covered up on the steppe your pail and bucket for milking your mares, had me set aside my bob-tailed chestnut and mounted me on a pale-grey horse with a dorsal stripe and yourself rode your fast dun mare. You left your own horse herd ownerless and hurried off to make friends with me on the steppe itself, and we chased them for another three nights.

'And when we came to the wagon-fort of the one who had robbed us of the isabelline geldings, we found the geldings standing at the edge of the wagon-fort, and stealing them in turn drove them off, and escaped back home. Your father was Naqu the Rich; you were his only son; what did you see that made you become friends with me? You became friends out of your heart-felt heroism.

'After that, when I missed you and I sent Belgutei, thinking to become friends, you mounted a hump-backed chestnut, threw on it behind you a brown woollen mantle, and came as a friend. And then when the Three Merkit came to us and made me circle Burġan three times you circled it with me.

'After that as well, when we were challenging the Tatar folk at Dalan-Nemurges while the rain continued to pour down day and night, that night, thinking to let me sleep, you stood until the night ended holding out your cloak to shield me lest any rain drip on me, shifting but once to the other foot. That was a sign of your heroism.

'With what other heroism than that shall I finish? Bo'orcu and Muqali, the right in me they pulled out until it proceeded, the wrong in me they held off until it halted and I reached this throne. Now let their seat be the highest of all and let them not be held guilty for up to nine offences. Let Bo'orcu govern the right-wing *tümen* that makes its pillow on the Altai.'[16]

Also, Chinggis Khan said to Muqali, 'When we pitched camp at the Bushy Tree of Qorqonaq valley where Qutula Khan danced, I remembered [the service of] Kü'un-Quwa and pledged my 206 word to [his son] Muqali because of the word and sign which the *ja'arin*-spirit of Heaven showed there.[17] For that reason, let Muqali sit in the supreme seat and let him be the *Guyang* unto the seed of Muqali's seed.' So saying, he gave him the title of *Guyang* and he issued a decree: 'Let Muqali *Guyang* govern the left-wing *tümen* that makes its pillow on the Qara'un-Jidun.'[18]

207   Chinggis Khan issued a decree to Qorci, saying, 'You prophesied it all and from when I was small, you were my mainstay,[19] wet through with me when I was wet, chilled through with me when I was cold, a spirit of blessing. In that time, Qorci, you said, "If this prophecy proves correct and if by Heaven you arrive at what you wish for, then make me a man with thirty women." Now because that was correct, I favour you; look through the fine women and fine girls among these people who have surrendered and choose thirty women for yourself.'

Also, it was decreed that in addition to Qorci's three Ba'arin thousands, let the Adarkin's Cinoas, the Tölös and the Telengut be added to fill up a *tümen*;[20] let Qorci govern them, together with Taġai and Aśiq. And let them have free rights to the territory along the Irtysh as far as the Forest Folk; garrisoning the Forest Folk, Qorci shall govern the *tümen*. 'No one shall go hither and yon through the Forest Folk without the leave of Qorci. If they go there without his leave, why should he hesitate [to deal with them]?' So it was decreed.

208   Also, Chinggis Khan said to Jürcedei,[21] 'Your supreme service: it was when I was worried about the fight with the Kereyit at Qala'aljit Sands and Quyildar *Anda* made his promise. But his action you, Jürcedei, performed. The performance was this: that you, Jürcedei, charged in and crushed all the Jirkin, the Tübe'en, the Dongġayit, Qori-Śilemun, the thousand day-guards and the crack soldiers, reached the great centre and shot an *ucumaq* arrow at Senggum's rouge-red cheek, so that the door was opened and the reins slackened for Eternal Heaven. If you had not wounded Senggum what would have become of us? That was Jürcedei's supreme service. Breaking off from there and moving down the Khalkh, I would think of you, Jürcedei, as like the shelter of a high mountain. Leaving there, we came to water ourselves at Lake Baljuna.'

What is more, it was there from Lake Baljuna that Jürcedei rode out against the Kereyit as an outrider and, made mighty by Heaven and Earth, plundered the Kereyit folk until they were wiped out. Leader and kingdom alike were cut off, the faces of the Naiman and the Merkit fell, they could not fight, and were scattered. When the Merkit and Naiman scattered, as for Ja'a Gambo of the Kereyit, he retained his own kingdom under him intact on account of his two daughters.[22] When he broke away and became our enemy a second time, Jürcedei lured him out with a ruse, thus managing to isolate Ja'a Gambo and capture him alive. This second time, we slaughtered and plundered the kingdom of Ja'a Gambo.[23] This was the other service of Jürcedei. At the scene of the slaughter he set aside survival, on the cusp of the killing he closed in mortal combat.

So Chinggis Khan favoured Jürcedei with Ibaqa Beki.

In giving her away, he said to Ibaqa, 'I never said your heart and mind fell short or your beauty and charm were bad. When I favoured Jürcedei with you, who had alighted into the ranks of my ladies, into the ranks of those whose breasts and whose legs I came between, I was remembering the grand principle, and Jürcedei and his services by which he

Was a shield in the savage skirmish,

Was a hide-away from the hostile foe; he

Reunited a folk that had removed itself,

Bound up a kingdom that had broken apart;

I remembered them, and by that principle I gave you away. Ever after, as my seed sits on our throne and remembers the principle of such service rendered, may they never nullify my word and unto the seed of the seed, let them not sever Ibaqa's throne.'[24] So he decreed.[25]

Also, Chinggis Khan said to Ibaqa, 'Your father Ja'a Gambo gave you two hundreds of dowry servants (*injes*) and the steward Aśiq-Temur and the steward Alciq. Now as you are going off to the Uru'ut folk, leave me your steward Aśiq-Temur and one of the hundreds as a memorial from your dowry servants before you go.' And he took them.

Also, Chinggis Khan favoured Jürcedei with a decree: 'I have given my Ibaqa to you. Are not the four thousands of Uru'ut yours to govern?'

209   Also, Chinggis Khan issued a decree to Qubilai, saying, 'Scruffs of the sinewy and butts of the brawny you pinned for me. When I sent you, the four dogs of mine, Qubilai, Jelme, Jebe and Sübe'edei, towards a purpose I had planned,

By the time I said to get there
The boulder you ground to grit;
Before I said to attack there
The cliff you crushed apart,
Shattering through the smooth stone,
Diving through the deep water.

If I sent you, my four commanders, Qubilai, Jelme, Jebe and Sübe'edei, towards some country I aimed at and if these four champions of mine, Bo'orcu, Muqali, Boroġul and Cila'un Ba'atur, went beside you, and if when the day of battle arrived I made Jürcedei and Quyildar fight in the lead with their Uru'ut and Manggut, my mind would be entirely at ease.'

He favoured him with a decree: 'You, Qubilai, shall you not preside over all the affairs of the army?'

Also, he said, 'Because of Bedu'un's intransigence, I was disgusted with him and did not give him a thousand. You are the right one for him. He shall number a thousand with you and shall ever take counsel with you.'

Also, he said, 'Let us keep a close watch on Bedu'un ever after.'[26]

210   Also Chinggis Khan said to Ġunan of the Keniges, 'For you, leading commanders Bo'orcu and Muqali, for you chamberlains Dödei and Doqolqu, this Ġunan was a dog wolf in the black night, a black crow in the bright day. Do not act without counsel from Ġunan and Köke-Cos who when moving did not halt, and when halting did not move, on whom the seditious never saw smiling faces, and the treacherous never traced two faces. Take counsel with Ġunan and Köke-Cos and act.

'The eldest of my sons is Joci; let Ġunan lead his Keniges and become commander of a *tümen* under Joci,' he decreed. 'These four, Ġunan, Köke-Cos, Degei and Old Man Üsun – these are the four who without hiding what they have seen would not stifle what they have heard.'

Also, Chinggis Khan issued a decree to Jelme, saying, 'When 211
Old Man Jarci'udai came down from Burġan-Qaldun carrying
his bellows on his back and with Jelme just out of the cradle, I
had just been born at Deli'un Boldaq on the Onon and he gave
me sable swaddling clothes. Ever since we befriended each
other, Jelme has been a thrall of the threshold and property of
the portal; his services have been many. Born together as I was
born, growing together as I grew up, stemming from sable
swaddling clothes, fortunate, blessed Jelme: let him not be
convicted for up to nine offences he may commit.'

Also, Chinggis Khan issued a decree to Tolun, saying, 'How 212
can it be that a father and son govern separate thousands?
Because of the little kingdom you had assembled, with your
father being the other wing of the little kingdom you gathered
together, I gave you the title chamberlain. Now, as you make
up your own thousand out of those whom you tracked down
and gathered up for yourself, will not you take counsel with
Toruqan?'[27]

Also, Chinggis Khan said to Önggur Ba'urci, 'Three Toġura'ut, 213
five Tarġut, and you, Önggur, Mönggedu Kiyan's boy, with the
Cangsi'ut and Baya'ut: you all formed one wagon-fort for me.
You, Önggur, never strayed away in the mist; you never sun-
dered yourself in a mutiny; you were wet through with me when
I was wet, chilled through with me when I was cold. Now what
favour will you claim?'

When he spoke, Önggur replied, 'Should I be allowed to
choose my grant of favour, my Baya'ut brethren are hither and
yon among all the different alien people. Should I be so favoured,
let me be allowed to gather together the Baya'ut brethren.'

When he spoke, a decree was issued: 'Indeed! Gather your
Baya'ut brethren and govern them well, the thousand!'

Also, Chinggis Khan decreed, 'Önggur and Boroġul, when you
two stewards issued provisions on the right and the left sides
and when you two issued meals, letting neither those ranked in
seats on the right side feel ravenous nor those lined up in lines
on the left side feel overlooked, then my gullet would not gag
and my heart would be at ease. Now, Önggur and Boroġul ride
off and issue food for all the other people.'[28] So he decreed.

'When you take your seats, sit so as to be ready to serve provisions to the right and left side of the great skins; sit with Tolun and the others in the centre,' he said, and pointed out their seats to them.[29]

214   Also, Chinggis Khan said to Boroġul, 'My mother took you four, Śiki Qutuġu, Boroġul, Kücu and Kökecu, from other folk's rangelands; she.

> Found you on the ground
> Got you on your feet
> Fed you like a son
> Grabbed you by your neck
> Fostered up a human child
> Seized you by your shoulder
> Raised you as a real man

And fostered you as friends shadowing us, her sons. Indeed, with so much kindness and service have you repaid Mother's gracious kindness in raising you! Boroġul, you made friends with me and

> On the rapid marches
> In the rain and in the dark,
> Never did you let me rest unfilled.
> Faced against the hostile soldiers
> Fast engaged in savage battle,
> Never did you let my soup be cold.

'Also, there was the time when the hateful and spiteful Tatar folk who murdered our grandfathers and fathers were brought low, when the Tatar folk were measured against a linchpin of a wagon to give them hatred for hatred and vengeance for vengeance and we slaughtered them all until they were exterminated. Then Qargil-Śira of the Tatars went off as an outlaw as they were being killed. But, broken by hunger, he came back and went into Mother's *ger*, and he said, "I am just looking for a little something tasty."

'"If you're looking for something tasty, sit over there," he was told. And when he was sitting on the corner of the bed on the western side, behind the door, Tolui, five years old, came in from outside. But as soon as he turned to run out again, Qargil-Śira got up and, tucking the boy under his armpit, left with him. As he groped for his knife and was drawing it out, Boroġul's wife Altani was sitting on the east side of Mother's *ger*. Mother screamed, "The boy is done for!" As soon as she heard the scream, Altani ran out chasing Qargil-Śira and caught up with him and grabbed one of his braids. With her other hand, she grabbed the hand that was drawing the knife; as she pulled it away, he dropped the knife.

'North of the *ger*, Jedei and Jelme were killing a polled black ox for food; at Altani's cry, Jedei and Jelme grabbed an axe and ran up with their fists all red with blood, and right then and there they killed Qargil-Śira with their axe and their knife. When Altani, Jedei and Jelme were feuding with each other over who deserved the pluck for saving the boy's life,[30] Jedei and Jelme said, "If we hadn't been there and hadn't run up quickly and killed him, what would Altani, a woman, have done? The boy would have been slain. The pluck is ours!"

'Altani said, "If you hadn't heard my cry, why would you have come over? If I hadn't run and caught up with him and grabbed his braid and pulled away the hand that was drawing his knife and he hadn't dropped his knife, by the time Jedei and Jelme had got there, wouldn't the boy have been slain?" Once she finished speaking, the pluck went to Altani. Boroġul's wife, as the other axle for Boroġul, saved Tolui's life.

'Also, at the time when we were fighting with the Kereyit at Qala'aljit Sands, when Ökodei was hit by an arrow in his jugular vein and fell, Boroġul dismounted with him and sucked his clotted blood with his own mouth and spent the night. The next day, he mounted him up and, as Ökodei couldn't keep his seat, rode double and hugged Ökodei from behind. The corners of his mouth were reddened with blood as he sucked and sucked the clotted blood; he delivered Ökodei back alive.

'The gracious kindness my mother suffered in taking care of him turned into a service to two of my sons' lives! Boroġul became friends with me and he did not hang back from the eager summons, from the echoing shout. Let Boroġul not be held guilty even if he should commit up to nine offences.' So he decreed.

Also, he said, 'Let us grant favours to our daughters' offspring.'[31]   215

216   Also, Chinggis Khan issued a decree to Old Man Üsun: 'These four, Üsun, Gunan, Köke-Cos and Degei, pointed out what they have seen and what they have heard without hiding it or stifling it. They spoke up about what they learned and thought.

'In the Mongol principles and in the way of command there is the custom of becoming a *beki*.[32] He is the offspring of the Ba'arin elder. According to the way of the *beki*, let Old Man Üsun be the *beki* from among us and [with confirmation] from above. Having raised him up as *beki*, let him wear a white coat, ride a white gelding, sit in the supreme seat, and serve [the spirits], and also let him discourse thus yearly and monthly.'[33]

217   Also, Chinggis Khan decreed, 'As for Quyildar *Anda*, because of the service by which he offered his life in battle and was the first to open his mouth, let him receive the endowment for orphans unto the seed of the seed.'

218   Also, Chinggis Khan said to Cagān-Quwa's son Slim To'oril, 'Your father Cagān-Quwa would eagerly go into the battle before me and in the battle at Dalan-Baljut he was killed by Jamuqa. Now let To'oril be given the endowment for orphans for the sake of his father's service.'

When this was said to him, To'oril said, 'Should I be favoured, my Negus brethren are hither and yon among every alien people.[34] Should I be favoured, may I be allowed to gather my Negus brethren?'

When he spoke, Chinggis Khan issued a decree: 'If that is the way it is, you may gather your Negus brethren; will you not govern them unto the seed of the seed?'

219   Also, Chinggis Khan said to Sorgan-Sira, 'When I was small, when I was seized out of envy by Fatty Kirultuq and the Tayici'ut brethren, you, Sorgan-Sira, then thought, "He is just envied by the brethren" and had me hidden, and with your sons Cila'un and Cimbai you had your daughter Qada'an hide and take care of me and then you set me free. I remember this service and kindness in my dreams in the dark night and in my heart in the bright day. It was you who did it, even if you only came over belatedly from the Tayici'ut. Now if I were to favour you, what grant of favour would please you?'

Sorgan-Sira with his sons Cila'un and Cimbai said, 'Should

we be favoured, let us have free rights to make our territory in the Merkit country, on the Selenge. As for any other grants of favour, let Chinggis Khan decide.'

To this Chinggis Khan issued a decree, saying, 'Make the Merkit country on the Selenge your territory and have free rights to the territory as well![35] Unto the seed of the seed, let them bear the quiver, take the *ötok*,[36] and enjoy free rights! Let them not be convicted for up to nine offences.'

Also, as Chinggis Khan favoured Cila'un and Cimbai, he decreed, 'I remember the words you, Cila'un and Cimbai, said long ago; how shall you be satisfied? When you, Cila'un and Cimbai, speak what you are thinking and request what you are lacking, do not tell it to some middleman. In your own person and with your own mouth, tell me yourselves what you are thinking! Request yourselves what you are lacking!'

Also, he decreed: 'Sorġan-Śira, Badai and Kišiliq, you are ones with free rights. As those enjoying free rights,

When you storm the teeming enemy
Seize of the spoil as much as you can take;
When you circle all the stalking beasts
Grab of the game as much as you can kill.

To speak of Sorġan-Śira, he was Tödo'e of the Tayici'ut's minion; to speak of Badai and Kišliq, they were Cāran's wranglers. Now, you are my mainstays; may you all bear the quiver, take the *ötok*, enjoy free rights and rejoice!' So he decreed.

Also, Chinggis Khan decreed to Naya'a, 'As Old Man 220 Śirgu'etu, with you two, his sons Alaq and Naya'a, was bringing Fatty Kiriltuq to me, on the way you arrived at Qutuqul Meadow. There Naya'a said, "How could we forsake our own proper ruler and carry him off?" And, unable to forsake him, they let him go free. When Old Man Śirgu'etu arrived with his sons Alaq and Naya'a, Skylark Naya'a said,[37] "We came laying hands on our own proper ruler Fatty Kiriltuq, yet we could not forsake him and let him go free. We have come to devote our strength to Chinggis Khan. If we had come laying hands on our ruler, we would be told, 'How could minions like them who laid their hands on their own proper ruler be trusted ever after?' "

'When they said that they had been unable to forsake their

own ruler, then we remembered the custom and great principle of not abandoning one's own proper ruler and approved their words, and said they shall be appointed to some task. Now I have said, "Let Bo'orcu govern the right *tümen*" and I have given Muqali the title *Guyang* and have let him govern the left *tümen*.[38] Now let Naya'a govern the central *tümen*.'

221   Also, he said, 'Let Jebe and Sübe'edei form into thousands those they have tracked down and gathered up for themselves.'

222   Also, Shepherd Degei was allowed to collect census evaders and govern a thousand.

223   Also, as sufficient subjects were missing for Carpenter Kücugur, they were levied from here and there and – Mulqalqu alone of the Jadaran had been a proper companion – Chinggis Khan said, 'Kücugur and Mulqalqu, take counsel with each other and form a single thousand.'

THE REGULATIONS
FOR THE BODYGUARD

224   Those who had joined in establishing the kingdom and who had suffered together for it he made captains of a thousand. He numbered the kingdom into thousands, he appointed captains of thousands, of hundreds and of tens. He numbered them into ten thousands and appointed captains of ten thousand.[39] To those captains of a thousand worthy of being given grants of favour he gave favour, and decrees of favour were confirmed.

Then Chinggis Khan issued a decree: 'Previously, we had eighty nightguards and *kesikten* with seventy dayguards. Now, when by the power of Eternal Heaven we have been made immensely mighty by Heaven and Earth, the whole kingdom has been set aright, and has been broken in under one pair of reins, select and enrol for me *kesikten* and dayguards from every thousand. In enrolling them for me, enrol enough nightguards, quiver-bearers and dayguards that a full ten thousand may be filled with the enrolments.'

Also, Chinggis Khan decreed: 'As the decree on selecting and enrolling *kešikten* is published in every thousand, as *kešikten* are enrolled for us, as sons of the captains of ten thousands, thousands and hundreds, and sons of private persons enrol, let ones with skills, handsome, goodly and worthy to be by our side, be enrolled. As the sons of captains of a thousand are enrolled, let them come with ten friends and one of their junior kinsmen in their train. As the sons of captains of a hundred are enrolled, let them come with five friends and one junior kinsman in their train. As sons of captains of ten are enrolled and as sons of private persons are enrolled, let them come with three friends and just one junior kinsman in their train and from their unit of origin let a team of remounts be arranged. As the number of those by our side is built up, let ten friends be levied for the sons of the captains of a thousand from their thousand and hundred of origin. Should he have any share of inheritance given by his father or should he have however many men or geldings that he has tracked down and gathered up on his account, let the levy be in the amount set by us, without regard to his personal property, and let the levy be so arranged for him. In the very same fashion, let five friends for the sons of captains of a hundred and three friends for the sons of captains of ten or the sons of private persons be so levied for them without regard to their personal property.'

He decreed: 'Once our decree has been brought to the hearing of the captains of thousands, hundreds and tens, and to the teeming people, let any commoner who breaks it be held guilty. Should any commoner enrolled for us as a *kešik* try to evade his duty and any unacceptable commoner treat being by our side as a hardship, submit a different one, and, punishing that first person,[40] banish him from our sight to a faraway place.'

He said: 'Let no one dissuade a commoner who comes to us saying, "I wish to learn together with those by our side in domestic service."'

As Chinggis Khan issued the decrees, they selected men from 225 the thousands, and by that very same decree they selected out sons of the captains of hundreds and tens and, where previously there were eighty nightguards, they became eight hundred. He said: 'But over and above the eight hundred, a full thousand should be filled.'

He decreed: 'Do not dissuade those who would enrol in the nightguards.'

He decreed: 'Let Big Ne'urin preside over the nightguards and govern a thousand.'

Previously, four hundreds of quiver-bearers had been selected. He said: 'Select them and let Jelme's son Yisun-Tö'e preside over the quiver-bearers and let him take counsel with Tüge's son Bükidei.'

He decreed: 'As the quiver-bearers go on duty with the dayguards shift by shift, let Yisun-Tö'e go on duty and preside over one shift of quiver-bearers. Let Bükidei go on duty and preside over one shift of quiver-bearers. Let Horqudaq go on duty and preside over one shift of quiver-bearers. Let Lablaqa go on duty and preside over one shift of quiver-bearers. While bearing quivers on their belts, let them thus preside over their quiver-bearers on each dayguard shift. Mustering a thousand quiver-bearers, let Yisun-Tö'e preside over them.'[41]

226 He said: 'Over and above the dayguards who had enrolled previously with Ögelei Cerbi, let the thousand be filled up and let Ögelei Cerbi from the seed of Bo'orcu govern them.'

He said: 'As for one shift of the dayguards,[42] let Buqa from the seed of Muqali govern one thousand of the dayguards.'

He said: 'Let Alcidai from the seed of Ilugei govern one thousand of the dayguards.'

He said: 'One thousand of dayguards let Dödei Cerbi govern and one thousand of the dayguards let Doqolqu Cerbi govern.'

He decreed: 'One thousand of the dayguards let Canai from the seed of Jürcedei govern, one thousand of the dayguards let Aqudai from the seed of Alci govern, and as for one [final] thousand of the dayguards, the one thousand chosen ba'aturs, let Arqai-Qasar govern them and let them be dayguards on the common days, but on the day of battle let them stand in the front and become ba'aturs.'

He decreed: 'Those select ones who came from every thousand made up the eight thousand dayguards. The nightguards and the quiver-bearers made up two thousands as well; they made up a full ten thousand of *kešikten*.'

Chinggis Khan issued a decree, as follows: 'Let the ten thousand *kešikten* next to me be built up and become the great centre.'

Also, Chinggis Khan issued a decree to appoint those who would serve as elders for the four shifts of dayguards, as follows:[43] 'Let Buqa go on one shift duty, governing the *kešikten* and dressing the ranks of the *kešikten*. Let Alcidai go on one shift duty, governing the *kešikten* and dressing the ranks of the *kešikten*. Let Dödei Cerbi go on one shift duty, governing the *kešikten* and dressing the ranks of the *kešikten*. Let Doqolqu Cerbi go on one shift duty, governing the *kešikten* and dressing the ranks of the *kešikten*.' 227

And as he appointed the elders of the four shifts and published the decrees on the shifts going on duty, he decreed: 'As the shifts go on duty, let the shift captains verify the *kešikten* assigned to their shift, go on shift duty, spend three nights together, and transfer their shift. Should a person on a shift neglect that shift, let that person on shift who has neglected his shift be admonished with three blows of the cane. Should the same one on a shift again neglect the shift a second time, let him be admonished with seven blows of the cane. Should the same person, without any illness in his own person, and without the approval of the shift captain, and again on that same shift neglect that shift for a third time let him be admonished with thirty-seven blows of the cane and, as he has treated being by our side as a hardship, banish him from our sight to a faraway place.'

He decreed: 'Elders of the shifts, sound this decree in the ears of your *kešikten* on every third shift. If it has not been sounded in their ears, the elders of the shift shall be guilty. Once the decree has been sounded in their ears, should they break it, should they neglect the shift in the manner given in the decree, let them be found guilty.'

He said: 'Shift elders, do not rebuke without my approval my *kešikten* who were enrolled on an equal basis with you, simply because you think, "They are less senior than I am!" Should an ordinance be violated, point it out to me. Those whose ways are worthy of execution we will execute. Those whose ways are worthy of being beaten we will lay down on the ground and beat. If anyone should think, "I am more senior!" and therefore raise his own hand or foot against my *keśikten* equal to him or give blows with the cane, then in reply to the blow will be a blow and in reply to a fist will be a fist.'

228   Also, Chinggis Khan issued a decree: 'My *keśikten* are above the outside captains of a thousand.[44] The servants of my *keśikten* are above the outside captains of a hundred or a ten. If one in the outside thousands should quarrel with my *keśikten* as if they were entirely equal, we will punish the person in the thousands.'

229   Also, Chinggis Khan issued a decree, a decree to be published to the captains of every shift, as follows: 'Let the quiver-bearers and dayguards go on shift duty, let the day's service be conducted by each in their separate ways and in their separate tasks, and at the flaming sunset let them give way to the nightguards and go out to spend the night. Let the nightguards spend the night with us. Let the quiver-bearers hand over the quivers and the stewards hand over the bowls and vessels to the nightguards and leave.

'Let the quiver-bearers, dayguards and stewards who spent the night outside sit at the hitching post until we shall have eaten our soup, let them report to the nightguards, and when we have finished eating our soup, let the quiver-bearers return to their quivers, the dayguards to their seats, and the stewards to their bowls and vessels. Those going on every shift shall in their same ways respectively act according to this regulation.'

He said: 'After the sun has set, let any person who passes back and forth along the rear or along the front of the horde be seized, let the nightguards seize and hold him overnight, and in the morning let the nightguards interrogate him as to his intentions. As the nightguards transfer the shift, let their badges be handed over as they come in on duty. Let the dayguards who are leaving in the transfer hand them over indeed as they go out.'

He said: 'The nightguards shall lie down around the horde at night and the nightguards who stand covering the door[45] shall chop off the heads of any commoners coming in at night so that they fall clean off the shoulders and toss them away. If any commoner with an urgent message comes at night, he shall report to the nightguards and they shall have him stand with the nightguard to the north of the *ger* and report.'[46]

He said: 'Let no one sit in a seat superior to that of the nightguards.[47] Let no one enter without speaking to the nightguards. Let no one pass by behind the nightguards. Let no one pass by along the rows of the nightguards. Let no one ask the number of the nightguards. Let the nightguards arrest the commoner passing by behind the nightguards. Let the nightguards arrest the commoner passing by along the rows of the nightguards. The person who has asked the numbers of them, the nightguards – let the nightguards seize that person together with the horse he rode in on that very day, and his saddle and bridle, and the clothes he was wearing.'

Although Eljigidei was trusted, he used to pass by behind the nightguards in the dark; was that not why he was arrested by the nightguards?[48]

Chinggis Khan said:

'My felted *ger* with smoke-hole flap,
On cloudy nights they compass round
To let my rest bring calm relief –
My elder watch who ease my fears.

My horde of felt 'neath Heaven's stars,
Encircled round they ease my sleep;
My blessed night watch who now have
Me raised up to this rightful rank.

Sodden in the snowy storm,
Chattering in the chilly air,
Dripping in the downpour's damp,
Ranged about a reed-girt *ger*,[49]
Napping never where they stand,
Steadfast watch who soothes my heart,
You've hied me to this happy rank.

Staving off the spoiling foe,
Set about my swaddled *ger*,[50]

230

Stand athwart, my true night watch,
Who scorn to drowse.

Wide awake my wary watch,
Who stand prepared and will not slack,
When birch-bark quivers barely shake;
Fast of foot my fortuned watch,
Who stand to fore with none in front,
When willow quivers first resound –

Blessed night watch of mine,
Be named now the elder watch.'

He decreed: 'The seventy dayguards who enrolled with Ögolei Cerbi shall be named the great dayguards. Let the *ba'atur*s of Arqai be named the elder *ba'atur*s. Let Yisun-Tö'e, Bükidei and the quiver-bearers be named the great quiver-bearers.'

231   He said: 'My private ten thousand *keśikten*, who were selected from the ninety-five thousands to be my property next to my person – may the princes who sit on my throne for ever after remember these *keśikten* of mine as a legacy and care for them well, without vexing them. Have these ten thousand *keśikten* of mine not been called spirits of blessing?'

232   Also, Chinggis Khan said: 'Let the nightguards provision the horde's chamberlain girls, houseboys, cameleers and cowherds and let them see to the *ger*-wagons of the horde. Let the nightguards stow the spears under the banners and drums; let the nightguards stow the bowls and vessels as well. Let the nightguards take charge of our food and drink. Let the nightguards be placed in charge of the food, both the freshly butchered and the ready to cook.[51] If the food and drink fall short it will be the very nightguards who were placed in charge whom I will look to.'

He said: 'When the quiver-bearers distribute the food and drink, let them not distribute anything without the approval of the nightguards who have been placed in charge. When the provisions are distributed, let the distribution begin with the nightguards first.'

He said: 'Let the nightguards keep order over the entry to

and exit from the horde and *gers*. Let door wardens from the nightguards be nearest to the *ger*'s door. Let two of the night-guards enter and carry in the great skins of *esuk*.'

He said: 'Let surveyors from the nightguards go out and direct the pitching of camp for the horde and *gers*.'[52]

He said: 'When we hawk and ring hunt, let the nightguards go out with us hawking and hunting. Let them count out half of their number and have them stay at the wagons.'

Again Chinggis Khan said: 'If our person should not go to war, let not the nightguards go out to war apart from us.' 233

He decreed: 'You have been told so; now let those chamber-lains in position to govern the army who out of envy of the nightguards break this ordinance by sending them out to war be held guilty.'

He said: 'Indeed, they will say, "How can the soldiers of the nightguard not go out to war?" You nightguards alone guard my golden life! When I go out to hawk and ring hunt, you will suffer along with me. You will keep the horde under your supervision and you will take care of it, whether it is in motion or is at rest. Is it so easy to guard my person overnight? Is it so easy to take care of the *ger*-wagons and the Great Base Camp, whether on the move or being set down? I am thinking of how you have to go out, some here, some there, on such duties one on top of another – that indeed is why I say, "Let them not go out to war apart from us."'[53]

Also, he decreed: 'Let a judge from the nightguards hear all lawsuits together with Śiki Qutuġu.' 234

He said: 'Let some from the nightguards stow and distribute the quivers, bows, breastplates and weapons. Let them take in hand some of the geldings, load them with nets, and go out.'[54]

He said: 'Let some from the nightguards distribute the fabrics with the chamberlains.'[55]

He said: 'As for assigning rangeland for the quiver-bearers and dayguards, let Yisun-Tö'e, Bükidci and their quiver-bearers and Alcidai, Ögelei and Aqudai and their dayguards go on the right side of the horde.'

He said: 'Let Buqa, Dödei Cerbi, Doqolqu Cerbi and Canai go on the left side of the horde.'

He said: 'Let Arqai's *ba'atur*s go in front of the horde.'

He said: 'Let the nightguards keep well the horde's *ger*-wagons and so go at the side of the horde on the left side.'

He appointed Dödei Cerbi, saying, 'As all the dayguards among the *keśikten* surround the horde, let Dödei Cerbi be ever aware of the horde and the horde's houseboys, wranglers, shepherds, cameleers and cowherds.'

He decreed: 'Let Dödei Cerbi always be to the rear of the horde, let him eat what the herds leave, let him burn what the horses drop.'[56]

PACIFYING MONGOLIA'S NEIGHBOURS[57]

235 Qubilai Noyan was sent to wage war on the Qarluqs.[58] Arslan Khan of the Qarluqs submitted to Qubilai. Qubilai brought Arslan Khan to pay homage to Chinggis Khan. Seeing that he had not rebelled,[59] Chinggis Khan favoured Arslan Khan and decreed, 'I will give him a daughter.'

236 Sübe'edei Ba'atur of the cart with iron-shod wheels went to wage war in pursuit of Ġodu, Cila'un and the other sons of Toqto'a of the Merkit; he caught up with them on the Chüy River and wiped them out before returning.[60]

237 Jebe pursued Küçulug Khan of the Naiman; he caught up with him at Sariġ-Qol and wiped out Küçulug before returning.[61]

238 The Ïduqut of the Uyghurs sent envoys to Chinggis Khan.[62] The envoys sent to deliver the message, Adġiraq and Tarbai, addressed him as follows: 'As when clouds clear and mother sun appears, as when ice thaws and river water is drawn,[63] I heard of the glorious fame of Chinggis Khan and rejoiced greatly. Should Chinggis Khan favour me and I obtain but a ring hung on his golden belt or a rag cut from his glittering robe, I shall become a fifth son and devote my strength to him.'

Chinggis Khan showed favour to these words and sent a reply, saying, 'I will give him a daughter. Let him be a fifth son. Let the Ïduqut come hither, bringing gold, silver, *subut*-pearls, *tana*-pearls,[64] *naśiś*-brocades,[65] *darda*-brocades[66] and silks.'

When the message was received, the Ïduqut rejoiced that he

had been favoured and, bringing gold, silver, *subut*-pearls, *tana*-pearls, silks, *našiš*-brocades and *darda*-brocades, the Ïduqut came and paid homage to Chinggis Khan. Chinggis Khan favoured the Ïduqut and gave him Al-Altun.

In the Year of the Hare [1207], Joci was sent with the armies of the right hand to ride against the Forest Folk.[67] He went with Buqa as his guide. Qutuġa Beki of the Oyirat first came to surrender out in front of the Oyirat *tümen*. He came and escorted Joci; he served as a guide to his Oyirat *tümen* and brought him in peace to the Shishged. Joci first pacified the Oyirats, Buryats, Barġut, Ursut, Qabqanas, Qangqas and Tuvans.[68] Then, when he arrived at the Kïrghiz *tümen*,[69] the commanders of the Kïrghiz, the Yeti-Orun and Urus Ïnal, the Alti-Er and Öre Beg-Tegin – the commanders of the Kïrghiz[70] – surrendered and, bringing white falcons, white geldings and black sables, paid homage to Joci.

The Forest Folk in a circuit as far out as the Sibir, Keštimi, Bayit, Tuqas, Telengut, Tölös, Taz[71] and Bashkirs[72] were pacified by Joci and he brought the captains of a thousand of the Kïrghiz *tümen* and the captains of a thousand of the Forest Folk to Chinggis Khan and had them pay homage with white falcons, white geldings and black sables. Because Qutuġa Beki of the Oyirat had met Joci submissively at first and escorted him to his Oyirat *tümen*, Chinggis Khan favoured him and gave [his own daughter] Seceyiken to Qutuġa Beki's son Inalci. He gave Joci's daughter Qoluyiqan to Inalci's big brother Törolci.

He gave Alaqa Beki to the Öng'ut.[73]

Chinggis Khan favoured Joci, and decreed, 'Eldest of my sons, you have only just come out from the *ger* and in a country where the roads need luck to be travelled you pacified the blessed Forest Folk without straining or tormenting the men or geldings before coming back. I will give the Forest Folk to you.'

Also, Boroġul Noyan had gone to wage war on the Qori-Tumat folk. After the commander of the Tumat, Tayidu'ul the One-Eyed, died, his wife Botoqui the Fat governed the Tumat folk.[74] Boroġul reached the place with three common soldiers going ahead in front of the great army. Late in the evening, as they were going by trails blindly in a thick forest, they were ambushed from behind by Tumat scouts, the trail was cut off, and Boroġul Noyan was captured and killed.

When he learned that the Tumat had killed Boroġul, Chinggis Khan was very angry. He was preparing to ride off himself, but Bo'orcu and Muqali dissuaded him and he pulled up. Instead, hc appointed Dörbei the Fierce of the Dörben, decreeing, 'Marshal the soldiers sternly, pray to Eternal Heaven, and take on the challenge to subdue the Tumat.'

Once Dörbei had marshalled the soldiers, he first made empty feints at the paths and passes where the army might go and which the scouts might be guarding. But he issued ordinances for the soldiers to go along trails made by bison;[75] as for the people numbered in the army, each man was made to bear [blows of] ten switches as a lash when hearts failed.[76] They were to be trained at the axe, adze, saw and chisel, and at men's weapons,[77] and they were to hack and saw down the trees standing in the trails, along the trails made by bison. When they had made a road and gone up into the mountains, they suddenly came down through the smoke holes of the Tumat folk, plundering them while they were seated at a feast.

241   Previously Qorci Noyan and Qutuġa Beki had been seized by the Tumat; Botoqui the Fat was there as well. The way in which Qorci had been seized was this: in accordance with the decree saying, 'Let him take thirty women from among the beautiful girls of the Tumat folk,' he went to take some girls of the Tumat. And as he was doing so, the previously submissive folk rose up in revolt and seized Qorci.

Chinggis Khan learned that Qorci had been seized by the Tumat and said, 'Qutuġa Beki must understand the affairs of the Forest Folk!', but when he sent him, Qutuġa Beki was also seized. When they had managed to subdue the Tumat folk, Chinggis Khan for the sake of Boroġul's bones gave [his heirs] one hundred Tumat. Qorci got thirty girls; Chinggis Khan gave Botoqui the Fat to Qutuġa Beki.

242   Chinggis Khan decreed, 'I shall divide up some of the subject folk for Mother, for the princes and for the junior kinsmen';

as he was dividing them up he thought: 'The one who suffered most in the gathering together of the kingdom was Mother, the eldest of my sons is Joci and the baby of my little brothers is Otcigin.' And he made over Otcigin's share to Mother and gave them a *tümen* of folk. Mother was unhappy but did not raise her voice.

To Joci he gave nine thousands of folk.

To Caġadai he gave eight thousands of folk.

To Ökodei he gave five thousands of folk.

To Tolui he gave five thousands of folk.

To Qasar he gave four thousands of folk.

To Alcidai he gave two thousands of folk.

To Belgutei he gave one thousand and five hundreds of folk. Because Dāritai had been in agreement with the Kereyit, he said, 'I will put an end to him somewhere out of my sight.'

When he said that, Bo'orcu, Muqali and Śiki Qutuġu said, 'It would be like putting out your own fire; it would be like breaking up your own *ger*. As a legacy of your late father is left this uncle only; how can you forsake him? He didn't understand what he was doing, so don't do it! Let the camp and smoke of your late father's baby brother still whirl up.' So was Chinggis Khan spoken to, and he snuffled as if he had smoke in his nose as he was being lectured. 'Enough of that!' he said, and remembered his late father.[78] And in reply to Bo'orcu, Muqali and Śiki Qutuġu [he said], 'I have calmed down.'[79]

He gave a *tümen* of folk to Mother and to Otcigin and appointed for them Kücu, Kökecu, Jungšoi and Qorġasun from among the captains.

For Joci, he appointed Ġunan, Mönggu'ur and Kete.

For Caġadai, he appointed Qaracar, Möngke[80] and Idoġadai. Chinggis Khan also decreed, 'Caġadai is difficult; his character is narrow-minded. Let Köke-Cos be by his side evening and morning, and tell him what he has been thinking.'

For Ökodei, he appointed Ilugei and Degei.

For Tolui, he appointed Jedei and Bala.

For Qasar, he appointed Jebke.

For Alcidai, he appointed Ca'urqai.

THE END OF TEB-TENGGERI

244 Father Mönglik of the Qongqotan had seven sons. The middle one of the seven was Kökecu Teb-Tenggeri.[81] Those seven Qongqotan ganged up and thrashed Qasar. Qasar kneeled before Chinggis Khan, saying, 'The Seven Qongqotan ganged up and thrashed me,' but when he told him this, Chinggis Khan was in the midst of being angry about something else.

And so Chinggis Khan in his anger said to Qasar, 'Never defeated as long as you were alive – that was you. So how have you been defeated now?' At these words, Qasar first shed tears, then got up and went out; Qasar was disgusted and did not come back for three days.

Then Teb-Tenggeri said to Chinggis Khan, 'A decree of Eternal Heaven the sovereign *ja'arit*-spirits speak. Sometimes they say, "Let Temujin rule the kingdom" and other times they say Qasar. If you don't take Qasar by surprise, who knows what will happen?'

That being said, Chinggis Khan rode off that very night to seize Qasar; Kücu and Kökecu alerted Mother that he had gone to seize Qasar. Mother learned of it during the night and she immediately harnessed a white camel and travelled all night in a covered wagon. She arrived as the sun rose, and just as Chinggis Khan had tied up Qasar's sleeves and taken off his hat and belt and was questioning him about his intentions, Mother showed up; he was shocked and terrified of Mother.

Mother arrived in anger and, having got down from the cart, she first undid his tied-up sleeves and then gave him back his hat and belt. Mother was so angry; unable to hold back her fury, she sat cross-legged and took out her two tits and draped them over her knees and said, 'See? These are the tits you both sucked – you who bite your own afterbirth, you who gnaw your own navel, pounding, pursuing. What did Qasar do? Temujin would suck dry this one tit. Qaci'un and Otcigin together wouldn't suck dry one tit. But as for Qasar, he sucked them both dry, and with my bosom relaxed he calmed me down. He made my bosom relax and so,

By that telling of talent
My Temujin's is one bosom's talent,
My Qasar has a marksman's mighty talent.
Those who fled while shooting back,
His swift shots have now all subdued;
Those who fled away in fear,
His far-flung arrows brought to fall.
Now thinking you have wiped out all the enemy people, you
loathe Qasar!'

When he had finally got Mother to calm down, Chinggis Khan
said, 'Mother was angered and I was frightened; yes, frightened!
I was ashamed; yes, ashamed!' He said, 'Let us back down' and
he backed down.

Without letting Mother know, he took away Qasar's subjects
behind his back and gave just one thousand and four hundreds
of folk to Qasar. Mother learned about this and thus, brooding
over it, she went into a swift decline.

Then Jebke of the Jalayir was dismayed and fled away into
the Barguzin.

After that, the Nine-Tongued Folk gathered around Teb-   245
Tenggeri and those gathered at Teb-Tenggeri's hitching post
became more than those gathered at Chinggis Khan's.[82] As they
were gathering thus, the folk who were attached to Temuke
Otcigin went to Teb-Tenggeri. Otcigin Noyan sent an envoy
named Soqor to ask for those of his subjects back who had run
away. To this envoy Soqor Teb-Tenggeri said, 'I am in debt to
you and Otcigin [for the gift of your horse]'; he beat up Soqor
and sent him back home on foot, carrying his saddle.

Otcigin's envoy Soqor having been beaten up and sent back
on foot, the next day Otcigin went to Teb-Tenggeri himself and
said, 'When I sent my envoy Soqor, you beat him up and sent
him back on foot. Now I am coming to ask for my folk back.'

That said, the Seven Qongqotan barred Otcigin's way out on
this side and that, and said, 'How right you were to send your
envoy Soqor.'

And, afraid that he might even end up seized and beaten,
Otcigin said, 'I was wrong to send an envoy.'

And the Seven Qongqotan said, 'If you were wrong, then

kneel down and confess it,' and he was forced to his knees behind Teb-Tenggeri, yet they did not give him back his folk.

And early the next day, when Chinggis Khan had not yet got up and was still in his bed, Otcigin went in weeping, kneeled down and said, 'The Nine-Tongued Folk have assembled with Teb-Tenggeri; I sent an envoy named Soqor to ask Teb-Tenggeri to give back the folk who were attached to me. They beat up my envoy Soqor and he was sent back on foot carrying his saddle. And when I went to ask them myself, the Seven Qongqotan barred my way out on this side and that and made me confess my mistake and forced me to my knees behind Teb-Tenggeri.' So he wept.

Before Chinggis Khan had raised his voice, Madame Börte sat up in the bed and shielded her chest with the edge of her quilt; she watched Otcigin weeping and shed tears herself before saying, 'What are they doing, those Qongqotan? A while ago it was them ganging together and thrashing Qasar. Now they dare to make this Otcigin kneel down behind him? What sort of way is this?

'They plot like this even against these little brothers like junipers and pines. Truth! From now on,
When your body like a towering tree tumbles into ruin,
Your kingdom like a hempen halter
Who else would they allow to govern?
When your body like a firm foundation falls into ruin,
Your kingdom like a feathered flock
Who else would they allow to govern?
'Minions who plot like this against your little brothers like junipers and pines, would they let my three or four little brats govern anything when they're raised up? What are the Qongqotan doing? How can you keep watching and let your little brothers be done so by them?' So saying, Madame Börte shed tears.

At these words from Madame Börte, Chinggis Khan spoke to Otcigin: 'Should Teb-Tenggeri come, whatever you might be able to do, you decide.' At that Otcigin got up and wiped away his tears and then went out and prepared three brawny men.

After a little while, Father Mönglik with his seven sons arrived and all seven came in, and as soon as Teb-Tenggeri had sat down on the right side of the skins of *esuk*, Otcigin grabbed Teb-Tenggeri's collar and said, 'Yesterday you took my confession; now I challenge you,' and pulled him towards the door by his collar. Teb-Tenggeri grabbed at Otcigin's collar in turn and they grappled with each other. As they were grappling with each other, Teb-Tenggeri's hat fell at the head of the hearth. Father Mönglik picked up the hat, sniffed it and placed it in his lap.

Chinggis Khan said, 'Go out and test your brawn and strength.' Then Otcigin dragged Teb-Tenggeri out into the space between the door and the threshold, where the three previously prepared wrestlers were waiting for Teb-Tenggeri. They grabbed him and dragged him outside, broke his back and tossed his body away at the far end of the wagons on the left hand. And Otcigin came in and said, 'That Teb-Tenggeri, when I said, "You took my confession; now I challenge you" – he shammed in some no-good way and lay down. As a contender he didn't make the grade.'

When he heard that, Father Mönglik understood and shed tears, saying, 'From when the brown earth was no more than a bit of dirt, from when the broad sea was no more than a creek, I was a friend to the khan.'[83] As soon as he said that, his six Qongqotan sons rose up in the doorway, stood in a circle about the hearth, and rolled up their sleeves. Chinggis Khan grew anxious and, feeling hemmed in, he said, 'Give way! I am leaving.' And as soon as he left, the quiver-bearers and the dayguards surrounded Chinggis Khan and stood in a circle.

Chinggis Khan saw the place where Teb-Tenggeri's body had been tossed aside at the far end of the wagons on the left hand; he had a plain felt tepee brought from the rear and placed on top of it.[84] And he said, 'Harness the wagons; let us move camp,' and they moved on from there.

They covered the smoke hole of the felt tepee placed over 246 Teb's body, lowered the door flap, and had a some fellow guard it. Towards the third night, in the sunset's golden glow, the smoke hole of the tent opened and he went up out of it together with his body. When they checked, it was confirmed to be certainly Teb's body there above it. Chinggis Khan said, 'Because Teb-Tenggeri laid hands and feet on my little brothers and because he spread baseless slanders among my little brothers, Heaven was not pleased with him and took him away together with his body.'

Chinggis Khan then berated Father Mönglik, yelling, 'It was by not dissuading your sons from their behaviour and in thinking yourself equal to me that you lost Teb-Tenggeri his head. If I had realized this behaviour of yours, then you would have ended up in the same way just like Jamuqa, Altan and Qocar.' But when he finished telling him off, he favoured him yet again, saying, 'If you tear apart in the evening what you said in the morning, or if you tear apart in the morning what you said at night, you will certainly be talked about to your shame. What was said before is done with, enough of that!' So he relented once again and said, 'If they had reined in their ambitious behaviour, who would have equalled the seed of Father Mönglik?'

As for the Qongqotan, once Teb-Tenggeri was done away with, their faces fell.

7: THE FOREIGN
CONQUESTS

SUBDUING THE GOLDEN KHAN AND
RAVAGING THE CHINESE[1]

After that, in the Year of the Sheep [1211] Chinggis Khan rode against the Chinese folk. He took Fuzhou, crossed Fox Pass and took Xuandezhou,[2] sending Jebe and Küikunek Ba'atur forward as the vanguard. They reached the Canyon and the Canyon Pass was fortified against them;[3] then Jebe said, 'Let us try and lure them on so that they move towards us,' and withdrew. When he had withdrawn from them, the Chinese soldiers said, 'Let's pursue them!' and came on in pursuit until they covered the highways and ridges. When they came to the spur of Huanrzui, Jebe swung round rearward in an about-face, charged the enemies coming on one after another, and crushed them. Chinggis Khan's main army followed up, threw back the Chinese and crushed the manly and spirited soldiers of the Kitans,[4] the Jurchens and the Jüin; he slaughtered them until they stood like rotten snags all the way back to the Canyon.[5] And Jebe took the Canyon Gate; having seized the passes, he passed through them and Chinggis Khan pitched camp at Yellow Terrace.[6]

He besieged Zhongdu and sent armies to every town and walled city to besiege them.[7] He sent Jebe to besiege Tungging city. He came to Tungging and laid siege to it but was unable to take it. He withdrew up to six days' march away, such that the enemy no longer expected him, before swinging round to go back. He then marched his men leading mounts by the reins through the night, arrived when he was not expected, and took the city of Tungging.

248   Jebe came back from taking Tungging city and rejoined Chinggis Khan. As Zhongdu fell under siege, the Golden Khan's high official Ongging *Chengxiang* proposed to the Golden Khan,[8] 'A time destined by Heaven and Earth – maybe even a time of transferring the imperial mandate? – has arrived. The Mongols came in great force, crushed the crack soldiers of the manly and spirited Kitans, the Jurchens and the Jüin, and slaughtered them until they were extinguished. They have seized for themselves the Canyon we relied upon. Now if we marshal troops and send them out again, and if they are again crushed by the Mongols, then inevitably they will all scatter, each to his own city. In that case, if we tried to reassemble them, rather than doing us any good, they would turn hostile to us; they cannot be relied on to be friendly.

'If the Golden Khan should deign to agree, let us surrender and make peace for the present time with the Mongol ruler. If they agree to this counsel and we get the Mongols to withdraw, after they have withdrawn, then again let us take counsel together but with a different aim. Neither the men nor the geldings of the Mongols are adapted to the land and they are suffering pestilence, it is said. Let us give their ruler a daughter; let us issue gifts of gold, silver, fabrics and goods in great amounts to the people in their army. Who knows if they will not be taken in by this counsel?'

When he made such a proposal, the Golden Khan approved these words of Ongging *Chengxiang*, saying, 'If that is how it is, let it be so,' and sent a daughter named Gongzhu in submission to Chinggis Khan.[9] And he sent from Zhongdu gold, silver, fabrics, goods and possessions to the people of the army, to each as much as he had power to requisition cartage for. Ongging *Chengxiang* delivered the princess to Chinggis Khan. When they had arrived in submission, Chinggis Khan fell in with their counsels, and recalled the soldiers that had been pitched in siege at the various cities. Ongging *Chengxiang* escorted Chinggis Khan home as far as the spur named Maor-yuzui. Our soldiers carried off as many fabrics and goods as they had cartage for and left with them all tied up in heavy silk.

Continuing that campaign, they rode on against the folk of   249
Hexi. When they arrived there, the Buddha of the Hexi people submitted,[10] saying, 'I shall become your right hand and devote my strength to you,' and sent his daughter named Caqa as a gift to Chinggis Khan.[11]

Again, the Buddha Khan addressed him, saying, 'We have heard with fear of the glorious fame of Chinggis Khan. Now your *sülder*-bearing person has arrived here against us, we are in fear of your *sülder*.[12] We, the Tangut folk, were afraid and said, "We will become your right hand and devote our strength to you." While devoting our strength to you, we are a people with ponderous possessions and pounded-wall cities. We will partner with you but

When faring on the fast campaigns,
When fighting with the fierce rebellions,
On the fast campaigns, we cannot keep up!
In the fierce rebellions, we cannot fight!

If Chinggis Khan should deign to agree, we Tangut folk will send abundant camels raised in the shelter of the high feather grass and give them to you as sovereign wealth.[13] We will weave woollens and give them to you as fabrics.[14] We will gather and train hawks for casting and deliver the best of them to you.' Living up to his words, he levied camels from his Tanguts and brought us even more than we could drive.

By riding to war that time, Chinggis Khan brought the Golden   250
Khan of the Chinese folk into submission and received abundant fabrics. He brought the Buddha of the Hexi folk into submission and received abundant camels. By riding to war in the Year of the Sheep [1211], Chinggis Khan brought the Chinese folk's Golden Khan, named Aqudai, into submission and brought the Victorious Buddha of the Tangut folk into submission. He then returned home and pitched camp at the Sa'ari steppe.

After that, however, Jubqan and his envoys who had been   251
sent to make peace with the Zhaoguan[15] were held up by the Golden Khan Aqudai, and Chinggis Khan again rode against the Chinese folk in the Year of the Dog [1214]. Thinking, 'They

had managed to make peace; how can they hold up the envoys sent to the Zhaoguan?' Chinggis Khan set out for the Tong-guan Pass and sent Jebe to the Canyon.

When the Golden Khan learned that Chinggis Khan was coming by way of the Tongguan Pass, he put the armies under the command of Ila, Qada and Qu the Hunchback.[16] 'The armics will block the way, and muster the Red Jackets as the vanguard.[17] Fight hard at Tongguan Pass and do not let them get through the pass!' he said and sent Ila, Qada and Qu the Hunchback and some armies off in a rush. When Chinggis Khan arrived at Tongguan Pass, the Chinese soldiers had already arrived and were holding it as their land. Chinggis Khan gave battle with Ila, Qada and Qu the Hunchback and pushed Ila and Qada back. Tolui and Ciku Küregen charged in from the flank and made the Red Jackets retreat. They forced Ila and Qada back, and slaughtered the Chinese until they stood like rotten snags.

Learning that his Chinese soldiers had been wiped out in the slaughter, the Golden Khan left Zhongdu and escaped into the city of Namging.[18] As the soldiers whom he had left behind were dying of hunger they turned cannibal, eating each other's flesh. Saying, 'Tolui and Ciku Küregen have done well,' Chinggis Khan greatly favoured both of them.

252   Chinggis Khan pitched camp first at Huihebu and then pitched camp at the Yellow steppe of Zhongdu. Jebe broke down the Canyon Gate, forced back the soldiers holding the Canyon, and passed through to join up with Chinggis Khan.

When the Golden Khan left Zhongdu, he appointed Qada as the *Liushou*[19] in Zhongdu before setting out.[20]

Chinggis Khan sent Önggur Ba'urci, Arqai-Qasar and Śiki Qutuġu to count up everything there was of Zhongdu's gold, silver, goods and fabrics. When these three arrived, Qada came out to greet them face to face, bearing fabrics with brocaded gold threads,[21] and so welcomed them to Zhongdu. Śiki Qutuġu said to Qada, 'Before, the goods of this Zhongdu, and Zhongdu itself, really were the Golden Khan's! But now Zhongdu is Chinggis Khan's! How can you steal Chinggis Khan's goods and fabrics behind his back and give them to us? I won't accept them.' While Śiki Qutuġu would not accept them, Önggur Ba'urci and Arqai did accept them.

They counted up everything there was of the goods in Zhongdu and then these three came back. Chinggis Khan asked Önggur, Arqai and Qutuġu, 'What did Qada give you?'

Śiki Qutuġu said, 'He brought fabrics with brocaded gold threads for us. I said, "Before, this Zhongdu really was the Golden Khan's! But now it has become Chinggis Khan's! How can you, Qada, steal Chinggis Khan's goods behind his back and give them to us?" and I wouldn't accept them. Önggur and Arqai accepted what he had given them.'

Chinggis Khan then rebuked Önggur and Arqai very severely. He praised Śiki Qutuġu greatly, saying, 'He remembered the great way,' and decreed, 'Will you not be my eyes for seeing and my ears for hearing?'

After the Golden Khan entered Namging, he personally ²⁵³ submitted and paid obeisance. He sent his son named Tenggeri with a hundred companions, saying, 'Let him be a dayguard for Chinggis Khan.' Since he had received the Golden Khan's submission, Chinggis Khan decided to withdraw.[22]

As he was withdrawing through the Canyon, he dispatched Qasar with the soldiers of the left hand to march along the ocean. As he sent him off he said, 'Pitch camp at Biiging city.[23] Bring Biiging city into submission, go further and pass by Wu'anu of the Jurchens, and if Wu'anu intends rebellion, capture him. If he submits, then, passing by his border cities, march along the Ula and Naun Rivers and up the Taur River over the passes and come to join me at the Great Base Camp.'[24] From among the captains, he sent Jürcedei, Alci and Tolun Cerbi to go with Qasar.

Qasar made Biiging city surrender, secured Wu'anu's submission, and made all the cities on his route surrender before he came up along the Taur River and dismounted at the Great Base Camp.

THE SUCCESSION DEBATE

254 After that, Uquna and one hundred of Chinggis Khan's envoys were held up and killed by the Sart folk; Chinggis Khan said, 'Why have the Sart folk cut my golden halter?'[25] Then he said, 'Let us ride to give the Sarts hatred for hatred and vengeance for vengeance on behalf of Uquna and the hundred envoys,' and was about to ride when Yisui addressed him with a proposal:

'The khan intends to cross high passes, ford wide rivers, wage a long war and re-form his teeming kingdom's ranks. Nothing born into this life is eternal.

When your body like a towering tree tumbles into ruin,
To whom will you hand your kingdom like a hempen halter?
When your body like a firm foundation falls into ruin,
To whom will it fall, your kingdom, like a feathered flock?
Your four champions, the princes you gave birth to, which one of them will you name? What we have all been thinking about – the princes, the junior kinsmen, the teeming crude commoners and even myself, a wretch – this I have formed into this proposal. Let there be a decree to decide!'

Receiving her proposal, Chinggis Khan decreed, 'Even though she is but a lady, Yisui's words are righter than right. Why didn't any one of you, my little brothers, sons, or Bo'orcu and Muqali, make such a proposal? Forgetting I would not fare longer than my fathers, I was heedless. Dreaming I would not be doomed by death, I slept. The eldest of my sons is Joci. What do you say? Tell me!'

Before Joci could raise his voice Cagadai said, 'When you said, "Tell me" to Joci, are you saying it is Joci you are appointing? How could we be governed by this bastard foundling of the Merkit?'[26]

Joci stood up and, fastening on Cagadai's collar, said, 'I was never treated by the ruler as different from you; how can you despise me? What skills do you have more than me? Only in being difficult, maybe, are you better than me. If I were ever beaten by you in distance shooting, I'd cut off my thumb and throw it away. If I were ever defeated by you in wrestling, I wouldn't get up from where I'd fallen. Let the Ruler-Father make a decision.' As Joci and Caġadai stood there grabbing each other's collars, with Bo'orcu tugging at Joci's arms and Muqali tugging at Caġadai's arms, Chinggis Khan sat silent, listening.

Then Köke-Cos, standing on the left side, said, 'Caġadai, how can you be so rash? Your Ruler-Father placed hopes on you among his sons. Before you all were born,

The starry heavens would spin about,
The wandering folk would raise a war.
Never slipping off to rest, they'd take each other prisoner.
The loamy earth would lurch about,
The kingdom whole would take to arms.
Never quiet in their quilts, they'd hunt each other down like
game.
In that time,
We went not by our own desire;
It was all but by the combat's chance.
We fled not by our own desire;
It was all but by the conflict's chance.
We went not by our heart's desire;
It was all but by the killing's chance.[27]
You speak and you clot your holy mother's buttery affection,
you curdle your mother's milky heart.
From a warm body – was it not the same womb? – you all
burst out in birth;
From a hot flesh – was it not a single heam? – you all came
fiercely forth.
Hurt your mother whose heart gave you birth –
Her care will cool and your comfort she'll not allow.
Wound your mother whose womb gave you birth –
Her resentment to relent she'll not allow.
When your sovereign father
Was founding all the kingdom,
He tied his black head to the saddle,
He shed his black blood in buckets.
Not blinking his black eyes,
Not setting his flat ears to pillow,
He bunched his sleeves for a pillow,

> He spread his skirt for a bed,
> He slaked his thirst with naught but spit,
> He gnawed his gums for nourishment.

As he moved forward arduously, until the sweat from his brow ran to his soles, the sweat from his soles rose to his brow, at that time, your mother was toiling with him:

> She laced closely her *boqta* crown,
> She fixed up her flowing skirts,
> She tied tightly her *boqta* hat,
> She belted up her billowing skirts.

To raise you all,

> Pausing as she swallowed,
> She gave her half to you.
> Blocking up her throat,
> She gave her all to you,
> And empty went away herself.
> She seized you by your shoulder,
> She raised you as a man.
> She grabbed you by your neck,
> She fostered up a human child.
> She cleansed your figure,[28]
> She trained your feet,
> She brought you up,
> To a real man's shoulders,
> To a gelding's crupper;

She aimed only to see what was best for you now, did she not? Our holy lady had an aim as splendid as the sun, as spacious as a lake.'

255   Then Chinggis Khan decreed, 'How dare you all speak about Joci like that? Joci is the eldest of my sons, is he not? Never speak like that again.'

To these words, Caġadai sneered and said, 'Without speaking of Joci's strength or giving any answer about his skills – if "she" brings home what was bagged with a boast it won't do, if "she" skins what was stalked just in speech it won't do.[29] The older of the princes are Joci and me; we will jointly devote our strength to the Ruler-Father. We will cleave asunder those who dodge the arrow; we will cleave the heels of those who lag behind. Ökodei indeed is broad-minded; let us consider Ökodei. Ökodei is by the side of the Ruler-Father; if he were to be familiarized with the great training of the hat,[30] it would do.'

To these words, Chinggis Khan said, 'Joci, what do you say? Tell me!'

Joci said, 'That Caġadai said it. Caġadai and I shall jointly devote our strength to you. Let us consider Ökodei.'

Chinggis Khan decreed, 'To act jointly – what [merit] is that? Mother Earth is vast. The rivers and creeks are many. I have decided, "As the divisible rangelands are expanded and as the alien peoples are garrisoned, let me split you up," so, Joci and Caġadai, live up to your words! Do not let yourselves be mocked by the masses! Do not let yourselves be hooted at by the herders! Previously, Altan and Qocar pledged such words, but instead, because they could not live up to them, what was done to them? How were they dealt with? Now I will split off for you two some of the seed of Altan and Qocar and as you look at them [in their degradation], how could you be careless?'[31]

Then he said, 'Ökodei, what do you say? Tell me!'

Ökodei said, 'When I have been told to speak at the Khan-Father's pleasure, what shall I say? How could I speak as if I couldn't do it? I will harden myself to be able to do it! Sometime from now, there might be born among my seed something that would not be eaten by a cow if you rolled it up in fresh grass and would not be eaten by a dog if you rolled it up in rich fat; in that case, wouldn't they miss a moose breadthwise or a mouse lengthwise? That is as much as I can say for myself. What else should I say?'

To these words, Chinggis Khan decreed, 'If Ökodei speaks this way, it will be well.'

Again, he said, 'Tolui, what do you say? Tell me!'

Tolui said, 'I will be beside the elder brother whom my Khan-Father has named; for him, I will

Advise him of what he's forgotten,

Awake him when he's been sleeping.

For him, I will be,

The friend whose word is "yes, sir!"

The flaxen horse's scourge.

For him, I will,
    The spoken word of mine not keep undone,
    The space where I should stand not leave unfilled.
For him, I will
    Wage a lengthy war,
    Win over a short revolt.'

When he said that, Chinggis Khan decreed in approval, 'Seed of Qasar, let one of you govern yourselves. Seed of Alcidai, let one of you govern yourselves. Seed of Otcigin, let one of you govern yourselves. Seed of Belgutei, let one of you govern yourselves. I have intended similarly to let one of each seed govern; if you all do not tear down my decree to nullify it, you will not misjudge, you will not be guilty. If there should be born among Ökodei's seed something that would not be eaten by a cow if you rolled it up in fresh grass and that would not be eaten by a dog if you rolled it up in rich fat; will not at least one born among my seed be good?'[32]

So it was decreed.

256   As Chinggis Khan rode off, he sent envoys to the Buddha of the Tangut folk, telling him, 'You said you would become my right hand. My golden halter has been cut by the Sart folk and I have mounted up to confront them in person. Ride as my right hand.'

Before the Buddha raised his voice, Aša Gambo replied to Chinggis Khan: 'Why did you ever become ruler if your strength was insufficient?' and, speaking these arrogant words, refused to supply troops.

Then Chinggis Khan said, 'How can we let Aša Gambo speak to us like this?' And he said, 'Among the options, there is this: how difficult would it be to send out men against them on a detour, even as we are heading against completely different people. But enough of that! If we are protected by Eternal Heaven, when we return and have drawn in tight the golden reins,[33] maybe we can do it then.'

CONQUERING THE
SULTAN AND THE SARTS[34]

In the Year of the Hare [1219], Chinggis Khan crossed the Alai 257
and rode against the Sart folk. He took Lady Qulan from among
his ladies to go with him on campaign and appointed Otcigin
Noyan from among his little brothers to oversee the Great Base
Camp.[35]

He sent Jebe as the vanguard. He sent Sübe'edei as Jebe's
backup. He sent Toqucar as Sübe'edei's backup. As he sent the
three out, he said, 'Go around the outside, get into the rear of
the sultan,[36] and join in with us as we drive him back.'

First Jebe bypassed the cities of Khan-Malik without touching
them and moved on.[37] Behind him, Sübe'edei in the same way
moved on by without touching them. Behind him, Toqucar cap-
tured Khan-Malik's frontier cities and plundered his farmers.
Saying that his cities had been captured, Khan-Malik moved out
in rebellion and joined up with Jalaluddin Sultan.

Jalaluddin Sultan and Khan-Malik rode against Chinggis
Khan. Chinggis Khan had previously sent Śiki Qutuġu as
vanguard; giving battle with Śiki Qutuġu, Jalaluddin Sultan and
Khan-Malik crushed Śiki Qutuġu. And just as they crushed
him, coming up all the way to Chinggis Khan, then Jebe,
Sübe'edei and Toqucar came in on to Jalaluddin and Khan-
Malik's rear and instead crushed them in a slaughter. Having
crushed Jalaluddin and Khan-Malik, they drove them back as
far as the Indus River, without letting them link up with the
cities of Bukhara, Samarkand and Otrar. As they hurled them-
selves into the Indus River, many of their Sarts were lost in the
Indus River. Jalaluddin Sultan and Khan-Malik escaped with
their lives and fled up the Indus River.

Chinggis Khan journeyed up the Indus River and plundered
Badakhshan; arriving at Eke Stream and Ge'un Stream, he pitched
camp on the Parvan steppe and dispatched Bala of the Jalayir to
pursue Jalaluddin Sultan and Khan-Malik. He greatly favoured

Jebe and Sübe'edei: 'Jebe, you were named Jirġo'adai. You came
from the Tayici'ut and became a weapon [*jebe*]!'[38]

He said, 'Toqucar captured the frontier cities of Khan-Malik
on his own initiative and turned Khan-Malik into an enemy. I
will make it a binding ordinance and execute him.'[39] Yet he
ended up by rebuking him very severely without executing him
and punished him with dismissal from his command.

258   At that point, Chinggis Khan came back from the Parvan
steppe and sent Joci, Caġadai and Ökodei out with the army of
the right wing, telling them to cross the Amu River and pitch
camp at Urgench city.[40] He sent out Tolui, telling him to pitch
camp at Herat, Nishapur and many other cities. Chinggis Khan
himself pitched camp at Otrar city.

Then Joci, Caġadai and Ökodei sent to address him, saying,
'Our armies are complete and have arrived at Urgench. Whose
word should we follow?' They addressed him thus and Chinggis
Khan sent word to them, decreeing, 'Follow Ökodei's word.'

259   At that point, Chinggis Khan made Otrar city surrender and
he moved on from Otrar and pitched camp at Samarkand city.
He moved on from Samarkand and pitched camp at Bukhara
city. Then while Chinggis Khan was awaiting Bala he summered
at the ridge of the Golden Fort, the sultan's summer camp, and
sent envoys to Tolui. 'The season has got hot.[41] The other troops
have pitched camp. You join us.' When he sent word to tell him
that, Tolui had already taken Herat, Nishapur and other cities,
sacked Sistan city, and was sacking Chaghcharan city. When
the envoys delivered these words, Tolui first sacked Chagh-
charan city and then returned to pitch his camp and joined up
with Chinggis Khan.

260   The three princes Joci, Caġadai and Ökodei made Urgench
city surrender and divided up the city folk between themselves;
they did not set aside a share for Chinggis Khan. When these
three sons came to pitch camp, Chinggis Khan was unhappy
with the three princes Joci, Caġadai and Ökodei and for three
days did not let them pay homage.

Then Bo'orcu, Muqali and Śiki Qutuġu addressed him: 'The
sultan of the Sart folk who had been casting challenging eyes[42] at
you has been brought low and his city folk have been taken. The

Urgench city which we divided up among ourselves, and the princes who did the dividing up for themselves, are all Chinggis Khan's. Just when we have been made mighty by Heaven and Earth, have brought low the Sarts like this, and our teeming men and geldings are happy and smiling,[43] how can the khan be so angry? The princes understand their mistake and are afraid. May they take a lesson from this for the future. We worry, though, lest the princes might let their behaviour go slack. If you were to deign to allow them to pay homage, wouldn't it do?'

When they addressed him thus, Chinggis Khan relented and let the three princes, Joci, Caġadai and Ökodei, pay homage. He rebuked them so that he echoed the elders' words and pounded in the past times' words, until they were set to sink into the soil where they stood, until they could barely mop the muck sweat from their brows.

As he was expostulating and explaining to them with resentful admonitions, the three quiver-bearers, Qongqai Qorci, Qongtaġar Qorci and Cormaqan Qorci, addressed Chinggis Khan: 'Like a raw hawk that has gone into training, as the princes are just learning to go on campaign, how can you rebuke the princes like this, incessantly wearing them down? We worry lest the princes be afraid and let their ambition grow slack.

'From the rising of the sun to its setting there are enemy folk. If you send us, your Tibetan dogs,[44] against the hostile folk, we made mighty by Heaven and Earth will bring back gold, silver, goods and subject households for you. If you ask which people, we say there is someone called the caliph sultan of the Baghdad folk here in the west. We will go on campaign against him.'

The khan was appeased and relented at these words; the three quiver-bearers Qongqai, Qongtaġar and Cormaqan were favoured with a decree of approval from Chinggis Khan: 'Let Qongqai of the Adarkin and Qongtaġar of the Dolonggir be by my side.' Cormaqan of the Ötegen he sent on campaign against the Baghdad folk and the caliph sultan.[45]

Also, Dörbei the Fierce of the Dörben he sent on campaign 261 against Herat, Merv and Awadh of the Mandahari folk between the Hindu and Baghdad folk.

Also, Sübe'edei Ba'atur he sent northward as far as eleven 262 races of foreign folk: the Qangli and Qïpchaqs,[46] the Bashkirs[47] and Ruthenians, the Magyars, the Ossetes and Saxons, the Circassians, Kashmiris, Bulgars and Kerel;[48] fording the Etil and the Zhayiq Rivers,[49] reaching as far as Kyiv and Man-Kermen[50] – Sübe'edei Ba'atur was sent to ride against them.

263   Also, as he finished up conquering the Sart folk, Chinggis Khan decreed that overseers be left in every city.[51] And two Sarts of the Khwarazm surname, a father and son named Yalavach and Mas'ud, from Urgench city, came and talked about the ways and laws of cities with Chinggis Khan, who by this talk came to master those ways as well. And the son, Mas'ud Khwarazmi, Chinggis Khan appointed to govern the cities such as Bukhara, Samarkand, Urgench, Khotan, Kashgar, Yarkand and Kucha-Tarim with our overseers; the father, Yalavach, he brought back to govern Zhongdu of the Chinese. Because Yalavach and Mas'ud were the most able among the Sart people in the laws and ways of cities, Yalavach was appointed to govern the Chinese folk together with the overseers.[52]

264   Chinggis Khan had travelled seven years among the Sart folk and was now awaiting the return of Bala of the Jalayir. Bala forded the Indus River and chased Jalaluddin Sultan and Khan-Malik into the Hindu country. But he lost track of Jalaluddin and Khan-Malik and, unable to find them among the Hindus, he turned back. On the way back, he plundered the Hindus' frontier folk and brought back many camels and wethers.

Then Chinggis Khan returned and on the way back summered on the Irtysh. And in the seventh year,[53] in the autumn of the Year of the Chicken [1225], he pitched camp at the hordes in the Black Forest of the Tuul.

CONQUERING THE TANGUTS AND THE DEATH OF CHINGGIS KHAN

265   Chinggis Khan wintered there, and as he wished to ride against the Tangut people, he numbered the units anew; in the autumn of the Year of the Dog [1226], Chinggis Khan rode against the

Tangut folk. Of the ladies he took Lady Yisui with him. On the way, when he hunted the teeming khulans of Arbuqa, Chinggis Khan was riding Red-Earth Grey. When the khulans came on, Red-Earth Grey was terrified, and when Chinggis Khan fell from the horse his flesh was deeply damaged and he pitched camp at Co'orġat.[54]

After they spent the night, Lady Yisui said the next day, 'Princes and commanders, let everyone know that last night the khan spent the evening with a fever in his flesh.' When the princes and commanders assembled there, Tolun Cerbi of the Qongqotan proposed, 'The Tangut folk are

A people with pounded-wall cities
and ponderous possessions.
Their pounded-wall cities they will not
Pick up and move away.
Their ponderous possessions they will not
Pitch aside to move away.

Let us withdraw. But then when the khan's flesh has cooled, let us ride!' When he spoke, all the princes and commanders approved these words.

When they proposed this to Chinggis Khan, the khan said, 'The Tangut folk will say we have withdrawn because our hearts failed us. Maybe we should send envoys and wait out the illness here at this Co'orġat. If we see what words they have in response, and only then withdraw, it might do.'

So they sent envoys to bear this charge against them: 'Last year, you, Buddha, said, "We Tangut folk will become your right hand." So you said, and the Sart folk had not obeyed their treaty, yet when I sent to you asking you to ride with us, you, Buddha, without living up to your words, still less giving us any troops, lashed back at me with words. Thinking to confront you in person only after we had headed in a different direction, we rode against the Sart folk. And we were protected by Eternal Heaven and everything in the direction of the Sarts was brought into submission; now we intend to come and confront the Buddha about his words.'

When the envoys spoke, Buddha said, 'I never spoke any words of ridicule.'

Aša Gambo sent word saying, 'I spoke words of ridicule. Now, if you Mongols have studied warfare and wish to give battle, I myself have land in the Alašai Mountains, woollen tents,[55] and camel loads, so head this way to me at Alašai and let us give battle. And if you need gold, silver, fabrics or possessions, head over to Eriġaya or Erije'u.'

Whcn these words were conveyed to Chinggis Khan he said, with his flesh feverish, 'That's enough! How can we stand to withdraw and let him speak such arrogant words! Even if I should die, I would still be sustained by these arrogant words. Let us go!'

Saying, 'Eternal Heaven, you decide!', Chinggis Khan headed towards Alašai to battle with Aša Gambo. When he got there he crushed Aša Gambo, and made him take refuge high up in the Alašai. He then captured Aša Gambo and stripped bare his folk with their woollen tents and camel loads until their ashes blew away in the wind. It was decreed, 'Slaughter the manly and spirited men and the best ones of the Tanguts and let this and that other Tangut be seized and borne away by the people in the army.'[56] Chinggis Khan spent the summer on Snowy Mountain,[57] and sent troops against those Tanguts with woollen tents and camel loads who had gone into rebellion in the mountains with Aša Gambo; as planned they were stripped bare until they were exterminated.

Then he decreed as a favour to Bo'orcu and Muqali, 'Let them take as much as they think they have strength for.' Again Chinggis Khan decreed, granting favour to Bo'orcu and Muqali: 'Because I have not given any of the Chinese folk to you, divide up for yourselves the Jüin of the Chinese folk equally between you two. Let the best of their boys hold your hawks and follow along after you. Raise up the best of their girls and let them dress the skirts of your women. The trusted and beloved ones of the Golden Khan of the Chinese were the Kitan Jüin folk who murdered the grandfathers and fathers of the Mongols. Now are not you, Bo'orcu and Muqali, my trusted and beloved ones?'[58]

Chinggis Khan moved on from Snowy Mountain and pitched camp at Uraqai city; he moved on from Uraqai city and, when

Döršegei city was being sacked,[59] Buddha came out to pay homage to Chinggis Khan. As Buddha was paying homage, he displayed golden buddha images and other gold and silver bowls and vessels – nine each; boy and girl children – nine each; geldings and camels – nine each; and sundry other things – nine each; when he came to pay homage, he was made to do so with the door sealed.

As Buddha was paying homage, Chinggis Khan's feelings revolted within him. On the third day, Chinggis Khan made a decree – the Victorious Buddha had been given the byname 'Honest' and the Victorious Buddha 'Honest' had arrived – so Chinggis Khan then said, 'Dispatch this "Victorious".' And he decreed, 'Let him be dispatched by Tolun Cerbi's hand.'

When it was reported that the Victorious had been finished off by Tolun Cerbi's hand, Chinggis Khan decreed, 'As we came to the Tangut folk to confront them about their words, when we were hunting the khulans of Arbuqa on the way, it was Tolun who made a proposal, saying "Let his damaged flesh be healed," and spared my living body. Heading against the poisonous words of a peer contender, but made mighty by Eternal Heaven, we have brought him into our hands and taken vengeance on him. Let Tolun take this travelling palace which the Victorious brought with him together with its bowls and vessels.'[60]

The Tangut folk were plundered, the Victorious Buddha was 268 made 'Honest', and he was finished off. And the mothers and the fathers of the Tangut folk unto the seed of the seed were maimed and tamed[61] and done away with. It was decreed, 'During the times you eat your meal, while wishing to maim and tame and do away with them, continue to speak about putting them all to death.' Because the Tangut folk made speeches but could not live up to their words, Chinggis Khan campaigned against the Tanguts a second time. He destroyed the Tangut folk and in the Year of the Pig [1227], Chinggis Khan went up to Heaven. After he went up, very many of the Tanguts were given to Lady Yisui.

8: THE REIGN OF
ÖKODEI KHAN

ENTHRONEMENT

269 In the Year of the Mouse [1228],[1] Caġadai, Batu and the other princes of the right hand, Otcigin Noyan, Yeku, Yisungke and the other princes of the left hand, Tolui and the princes, princesses and sons-in-law of the centre, and the commanders of ten thousands and thousands all assembled as a whole at Küte'u Isle of the Kherlen and raised up Ökodei Khan as ruler just as he had been named in Chinggis Khan's decree.[2] Caġadai the Elder raised up his younger brother Ökodei Khan as ruler, and Caġadai the Elder and Tolui handed over to Ökodei Khan the nightguards, the quiver-bearers and the eight thousand dayguards who had been guarding the golden life of their father Chinggis Khan, his private ten thousand of *keśikten* who had been going alongside the person of my Ruler-Father.[3] In the same way, they handed over to him the kingdom of the centre.

270 Ökodei Khan achieved the raising of himself up as ruler and had both the ten thousand *keśikten* who came and went in the privy presence and the kingdom of the centre made over to himself. And he first took counsel with Caġadai the Elder, and sent Hoqotur and Mönggedu on campaign as backup for Cormaqan Qorci, who had been sent on campaign against the caliph sultan of Baghdad whom their father Chinggis Khan had left unconquered.[4]

Also, as for Sübe'edei Ba'atur, he had campaigned as far as the Qangli, Qïpchaq, Bashkir, Ruthenian, Ossete, Saxon, Magyar, Kashmir, Circassian, Bulgar and Kerel folk, crossed the Etil and Zhayïq Rivers, and went against the cities of

Magas, Man-Kermen and Kyiv.[5] Sübe'edei Ba'atur found him-
self in difficulties among these people, and Batu, Böri, Güyuk,
Möngke and many other princes were sent to ride off as
backup for Sübe'edei.[6]

Okodei Khan decreed, 'Let Batu be the senior of all these
princes on campaign.'

He decreed, 'Let Güyuk be the senior of all those starting out
from the centre.'

He decreed, 'As for these campaigns, let each of the princes
who govern a kingdom send the eldest son of their own sons on
campaign.[7] Let even the princes who do not govern a kingdom,
and the captains of ten thousands, thousands, hundreds and
tens, all the teeming people, send the eldest of their sons, as
long as there is at least one, on campaign. Let the princesses
and imperial sons-in-law in the same way send the eldest of
their own sons on campaign.'

And also, Ökodei Khan said, 'This way of sending the eldest
of every prince on campaign came from Caġadai the Elder.
Caġadai the Elder said, "I shall send the eldest of my sons,
Böri, on campaign as backup for Sübe'edei. If the senior princes
go on campaign, the troops will be ample; if the troops issuing
out are many, then we will advance with our faces held high
and mighty. The enemy people yonder – they are teeming for-
eigners. They are a difficult people to the very end. They are a
people who if they get angry die on their own swords – and
their swords are sharp, it is said." '

Ökodei Khan said, 'Given those words, and by the eager
might indeed of our Caġadai the Elder, we will dispatch the
elder princes,' and issued the order publicly. This must have
been the way in which Batu, Böri, Güyuk, Möngke and the
princes were sent on campaign.[8]

CONQUEST OF THE GOLDEN KHAN,
AND THE DEATH OF TOLUI

271 Also, Ökodei Khan sent to take counsel with Caġadai the Elder, saying, 'I have reigned with everything readied by my father Chinggis Khan. Won't they ask me, "By what skill have you reigned?" If Caġadai the Elder should approve, the Khan-Father left for us unconquered the Golden Khan of the Chinese folk. Now I will ride against the Chinese.' Caġadai approved, and sent to say, 'What worries could there be with that? Appoint a good person for the base camp and ride! I will dispatch soldiers from here.'

Olda'ur Qorci was appointed to oversee the great hordes
272 and in the Year of the Hare [1231],[9] Ökodei Khan rode against the Chinese folk and sent Jebe as the vanguard.[10] Having crushed as many Chinese soldiers as there were until they stood like rotten snags, he crossed the Canyon and sent soldiers in every direction to besiege the towns and cities; Ökodei Khan pitched camp at Yellow Terrace.[11]

There Ökodei Khan came down with an illness and was so sick that he lost the use of his tongue. So when they had all the shamans and the diviners do divination, the masters and rulers of the Earth and Water of the Chinese folk were raging restlessly, as their subject households had been plundered and their cities and towns had been sacked. When the shamans said, 'We will give subjects, gold and silver, cattle and provisions as a ransom,' and examined the entrails,[12] the disease did not relent, and raged all the more restlessly.

When they said, 'How would someone of the blood do?' and examined the entrails, the khan opened his eyes, asked for water and drank. And when he asked, 'What is happening?'[13] the shamans reported, 'The masters and rulers of the Earth and Water of the Chinese folk have been raging restlessly as their Earth and Water had been sacked and their subject households had been plundered. When we asked, "What else can we give as a ransom?" and examined the entrails, they became all the more restlessly violent. When we said, "How would someone of the blood do?" the disease relented. Now we await a decree.'

When he decreed, 'Who of the princes is by my side?' Prince Tolui was by his side.

Tolui said, 'When there were elders above and juniors below, the majestic[14] father Chinggis Khan chose you, elder brother, like a gelding, felt you like a wether, pointed out his great throne for yourself and loaded the teeming kingdom on you! While I am alive and by the side of my Khan-Elder I was told to advise him of what he has forgotten, and awaken him when he has been sleeping. Now if I lose you, my Khan-Elder, whom will I advise when he has forgotten and whom will I awaken when he has been sleeping? Truly, if you my Khan-Elder pass away,[15] the teeming Mongol kingdom will be orphaned and the Chinese will rejoice in their luck. I will take the place of my Khan-Elder.

The salmon's spine I slashed
The sturgeon's spine I shattered
The vanguard men I vanquished
The flanking ones I fought.
Him fair of face
Him firm of frame
Is me!
Shamans, chant! Conjure!'

He spoke and then, when the shamans conjured, Prince Tolui drank the water they had conjured. He sat for a moment and said, 'I am drunk. When my drunkenness is relieved, and as your orphaned little ones and juniors and your widowed little sister-in-law Berude come to mind,[16] let the Khan-Elder decide how he will take care of them. Whatever I have to say, I have spoken. I am drunk.' Having spoken, he went away, and that was the way in which he passed away.

And so it was that the Golden Khan was wiped out and given the name Slave Boy,[17] and the Chinese folk's gold, silver, fabrics with brocaded gold threads, possessions, piebald horses and slave boys were plundered. The khan left outriders and resident garrison troops there,[18] and left overseers in Namging, Zhongdu and other cities in every direction. And, hale and whole, he came back and pitched his camp at Qara-Qorum.[19]

CONQUESTS IN THE WEST AND
CONFLICT AMONG THE PRINCES

274 Cormaqan Qorci brought the Baghdad folk to surrender. He
learned that the best possessions of that land were said to be
good, and Ökodei Khan decreed, 'Cormaqan, stay there as a resi-
dent garrison[20] and continue every year to deliver yellow gold,
naq-silk with gold-gilt thread,[21] *našiš*-brocades, *darda*-brocades,
subut-pearls, *tana*-pearls,[22] Arabian thoroughbreds long of neck
and high of step, dark-brown, low-humped and humpbacked
dromedaries,[23] draft mules and riding mules.'

Batu, Böri, Güyük, Möngke and all the other princes who
had gone on campaign as backup to Sübe'edei Ba'atur first
subdued the Qangli, Qïpchaqs and Bashkirs, then sacked the
cities of Etil, Zhayiq and Magas,[24] and, slaughtering the Ruthe-
nians, stripped them bare until they were exterminated. They
plundered and made the folk of the cities of Ossetia, Saxony,
Bulgar, Man-Kermen and Kyiv surrender; they left overseers
and resident garrison soldiers before coming home.

Yisuder Qorci was sent to campaign as backup for Jalayirtai
Qorci, who had previously campaigned against the Jurchens
and the Koreans. There was a decree: 'Stay there as a resident
garrison.'[25]

275 Batu sent envoys to report to Ökodei Khan from the Qïp-
chaq campaign: 'By the power of Eternal Heaven, by the
Majesty of the Khan-Uncle, we sacked Magas, plundered the
Ruthenian folk, and subdued those in the direction of the
eleven foreign folk, before drawing in the golden reins.[26] We
agreed, "Let us enjoy a feast of parting ways" and set up a
great pavilion.[27] When the feasting began and I said, "I am now
somewhat senior among the princes here and am used to taking
one or two bowls of the *ötok* first,"[28] Böri and Güyuk were
disgusted, and they rode off on me without feasting.

'Riding along, Böri said, "So, if Batu is on the same level as
us, how can [the Jocids] be the ones to drink first?[29]
When grannies play wearing a quiver,

Wishing they were equal to us,
What's a heel for but to hurt them?
What's a sole for but to stomp them?"[30]

'Güyuk said, "Let's flog with hot sticks the breasts of those grannies with bow cases,[31] you and me, all of them." Eljigidei's son Harġasun said, "Let's pin a wooden tail on them."[32]

'We were all sent to campaign against various rebellious folk whose innermost feelings are alien,[33] but just when we were considering if it had been done rightly, done well, I was spoken to like this by Böri and Güyuk. And now they have scattered on me without approval.

'Now let a decree of the Khan-Uncle be issued to decide the matter.'

At these words from Batu, the khan was very angry and without letting Güyuk pay homage he said,[34] 'By whose words was this wretch led astray to fill his mouth up with talk against a person senior to him? Let the egg rot all on its own! He is full of hate towards the heart of the very person senior to him. 276

Send him as a scout
To slither up walls into soaring cities
Until all ten fingertips are beaten to the bone;
Take him off for ever as a garrison fighter
To get up walls of well-packed soil
Until his five fingernails are finally ground flat!
You! Crude, vile, wretched Harġasun: who were you following to fill your mouth up with arrogant words against our seed?[35] Let us send Güyuk and Harġasun off together.[36] Harġasun should be executed; but you are all saying I am biased.

'And what about Böri? Say this to Batu, let him send word about this to Caġadai the Elder. Let Caġadai the Elder decide.'

Möngke[37] of the princes and Alcidai, Qongqortai and Janggi of the captains proposed in a memorial, 'It was the decree of your father Chinggis Khan that matters of the field are to be settled in the field; matters of the home are to be settled in the home. If it please the khan, the khan is angry with Güyuk; it is a matter of the field. Wouldn't it do to send him off and entrust it to Batu?' 277

Approving these words, the khan relented, allowed Güyuk to

pay homage, and rebuked him with words of admonition: 'It is said about you that while you were still on your way to the campaign, you didn't leave unbeaten the butt of any man with a butt to beat. It is said about you that you smashed the faces of the common soldiers in the army. Were the Ruthenian folk being forced into submission by the fear of that furious rage of yours? Was it from thinking that you alone could subdue the Ruthenian folk that you held on to that fierce feeling and advanced full of hate towards a person senior to you?

'It is in the decree of our father Chinggis Khan – didn't he used to say that what's many is fearsome and what's deep is fatal? While talking as if you alone were prepared, you went hiding behind Sübe'edei and Böcek, among so many others. And teaming up with Böri you subdued the Ruthenians and Qïpchaqs and captured one or two Ruthenians and Qïpchaqs, feeling manly when you hadn't yet carried off for yourself so much as a kid's shank.[38] And when you had just started out from the *ger*, what was the reason you were still howling out words as if you alone were prepared? We will let Möngke, Alcidai, Qongqortai and Janggi be to him a bosom soul to curb the heart's provoking, and a big, broad spoon to cool the kettle's boiling. That's enough! The matter of the field has been spoken about to Batu. Let Batu decide about Güyuk and Harġasun', and so saying, he sent word. 'Let Caġadai the Elder decide about Böri,' he said.[39]

ÖKODEI KHAN'S REGULATIONS
FOR THE BODYGUARD[40]

278 Also, Ökodei Khan decreed: 'Proclaiming publicly a decree to announce anew the service of the nightguards, quiver-bearers and dayguards and all the *keśikten* who had served my father Chinggis Khan:

'Howsoever they were serving before by the decree of the Khan-Father, now let them serve in the same way.'

So it was decreed, 'Let the quiver-bearers and dayguards

serve in the previous way each in their tasks by day and, while the sun is still up, let them give way to the nightguards and then spend the night outside.'

He decreed, 'At night let the nightguards spend the night with us. Let the quiver-bearers and nightguards of the *ger* stand at the door. Let the nightguards walk the rounds along the rear and along the front of the horde. After the sun has set, let the nightguards seize and hold overnight any commoners who go by night. After the crowds have dispersed, let the nightguards take any commoners, other than the nightguards spending the night there, who have entered in violation into the inner chambers and been seized; chop their heads clean off and toss them away. If any person with an urgent message comes at night, he shall report to the nightguards and shall stand making a report with the nightguard to the north of the *ger*.

'Let Qongqortai and Śiraqan keep order over the entry to and exit from the horde and *ger* together with the orderlies and nightguards. Considering that "Although Eljigidei was trusted, he used to pass by above the nightguards in the dark and was arrested by the nightguards,"[41] it was decreed that only nightguards who do not allow any decree to be nullified are to be truly trusted.'[42]

And 'Let no one ask the number of the nightguards. Let no one pass by behind the seat of the nightguards. Let no one pass by the rows of the nightguards. Let the nightguards arrest the commoners passing by behind or alongside the nightguards. The person who asks the numbers of the nightguards, let the nightguards seize that person together with the horse he rode in on that day, and his saddle and bridle and the clothes he was wearing. Let no one sit in a seat even a little superior to that of the nightguards. Let the nightguards stow the spears, bowls and vessels under the banners and drums. Let the nightguards take charge of our food and drink, both the freshly butchered and the ready to cook.'

He decreed, 'Let the nightguards see to the *ger*-wagons of the horde. If our person should not go to war, let no other nightguards go out to war apart from us. When we hawk and ring hunt, let them count out half of their number at the *ger*-wagons of the horde and let them stay behind; let half of the night-guards go with us.[43] Let surveyors from the nightguards go out and direct the pitching of camp for the horde. Let the night-guard door wardens be nearest to the door. Let all the nightguards be governed as a thousand by Qada'an.'

Also, as for the appointment of the captains to each shift of the nightguards, he decreed, 'Let Qada'an and Bulġadar make up one shift, take counsel with each other, go on one shift duty, and dress ranks as they sit separately on the right and left sides of the horde.

'Let Amal and Canai take counsel with each other and make up one shift,[44] go on one shift duty and dress ranks as they sit separately on the right and left sides of the horde.

'Let Qadai and Qori-Qacar take counsel with each other, go on one shift duty, and dress ranks as they sit separately on the right and left sides of the horde.

'Let Yalbaq and Qara'udar take counsel with each other and make up one shift, go on one shift duty, and dress ranks as they sit separately on the right and left sides of the horde.

'Also, let the shift of Qada'an and Bulġadar and the shift of Amal and Canai, these two shifts, go on shift duty as they camp on the range to the left of the horde.

'Let the shift of Qadai and Qori-Qacar and the shift of Yal-baq and Qara'udar, these two shifts, go on shift duty as they camp on the range to the right of the horde.

'Let Qada'an govern the nightguards in these four shifts.

'Also, let the nightguards stand around the horde next to my person and lie down covering the door.[45] Let two common men from the nightguard enter the horde and carry the skins of *esuk*.'

Also, he decreed, 'Let Yisun-Tö'e, Bükidei, Horqudaq and Lablaqa form one shift of quiver-bearers each.[46] While bearing quivers on their belts, let them dress the ranks of their quiver-bearer cadets[47] during each of the four dayguard shifts, and let them rotate shifts.'

Also, as for the appointment of the elders of the dayguards' shifts from the seed of those who had been previously govern-ing them, 'Let Alcidai and Qongqortai who had previously been governing take counsel together and go on one shift duty of dayguards, dressing their ranks.[48]

'Let Temuder and Yeku take counsel together and go on one shift duty of dayguards, dressing their ranks.

'Let Manggudai, having governed those assigned to the rearguard, go on one shift duty of dayguards, dressing their ranks.'

Also, the khan decreed, 'As for all the captains, Eljigidei shall preside and they shall serve according to Eljigidei's word.'

And he also decreed, 'When a person on a shift is to go on shift duty, should he neglect the shift let him be admonished according to the decree with three blows of the cane.[49] Should the same person on a shift neglect the shift a second time, let him be admonished with seven blows of the cane. Should the same person, without any illness or excuse, and without the approval of the shift elder, neglect the shift for a third time, as he has treated serving by our side as a hardship, let him be admonished with thirty-seven blows of the cane and be banished from our sight to a faraway place.

'Also, should the elders of the shift, without verifying the kesikten assigned to their shifts, allow neglect on the shift, we will punish the elders of the shift.

'Also, as the elders of the shifts go on shift duty once every three times, when they transfer the shift to each other, let this decree be sounded in their ears. Once they have heard the decree, if the kesikten neglect the shift we will punish them according to the decree. If this decree is not sounded in the ears of the kesikten, the elders of the shifts shall be guilty.

'Also, shift elders, do not rebuke without approval those on my shifts who were enrolled on an equal basis with you, simply because you think, "They are less senior than I am!" Should an ordinance be violated, point it out to us. Anyone whose ways are worthy of death we will execute. Anyone whose ways are worthy to be chastised, we will admonish. Should someone think others are less senior and, without pointing it out to us, raise his own hand or foot against them, in reply to a fist let there be a fist, in reply to a blow let there be a blow.'

Also, he decreed, 'My kesikten are above the outside captains of a thousand. The servants of my kesikten are above the outside captains of a hundred or a ten. If one in the outside thousands should quarrel with my *keśikten* we will punish the one in the thousands.'

ÖKODEI KHAN'S NEW MEASURES

279   Also, Ökodei Khan sent to say: 'Let me not burden the kingdom that my father Chinggis Khan established with such trouble. Let me set their soles on the soil and their grip on the ground and make them happy.

'I reign with all readied by my Khan-Father and so, without burdening any folk, let one second-year sheep be given from the flocks of these kingdoms for my soup. Let one sheep out of a hundred sheep be issued and be given to the poor and destitute among themselves.

'Also, when the elders and juniors, men, geldings and *keśikten* assemble, how could drink be levied from the folk each time for that? Let mares be issued from the thousands in every direction and milked as they are herded by the mare-milkers, and then let the surveyors steadily issue replacements, and let there be mare-herders.[50]

'Also, when the elders and juniors assemble, we will give awards and grants of favour. We will pour out fabrics, ingots,[51] quivers, bows, breastplates and tax grain, and shall have the cities guarded. Let city sentries and granary sentries be selected and set to guard them in every direction.

'Also, we have shared out to the nation the rangelands and the waters.[52] For assigning the rangelands, would it not do to select surveyors from every thousand?

'Also, in the deep desert country,[53] nothing lives other than game animals. It would be a very wide space for the folk [to dwell in]; let Canai and Ui'urtai lead the surveyors and excavate wells in the desert with brick walls.

'Also, as the envoys ride post-haste, they are dispatched to roam throughout the kingdom [without any fixed routes]. So the business of the envoys as they ride post-haste is still too slow; there is still suffering among the nation. Now, to settle

this once and for all, would it not be best to select post-staff
and relay riders from every thousand in every direction, set up
post-stations in every settlement and dispatch the envoys via
the post-stations without letting them roam through the king-
dom without cause?[54]

'I think that Canai and Bulġadar understand these matters;
would it not be right for them to make proposals about them?
Let Caġadai the Elder decide if these matters which have been
raised are proper; if he approves, let Caġadai the Elder ratify
them.'

When he sent to ask Caġadai the Elder, he approved all these
matters about which he had been asked, and sent back to say,
'Let it be so done.'

Again, word came from Caġadai the Elder, 'I will link up my
post-stations with yours from here. Also, I will send envoys to
Batu from here to say, "Let Batu as well link up his post-
stations with yours."'

Again, word came from him, saying, 'The proposal on the
matter of everyone setting up post-stations is the rightest of all
of them.'

Then Ökodei Khan said, 'Caġadai the Elder, Batu and all the
princes, senior and junior, of the right hand; Otcigin Noyan,
Yeku and all those senior and junior of the left hand; all the
princes and the princesses, sons-in-law, and all the captains of
ten thousands, thousands, hundreds and tens approved. They
said in approval, "To take one second-year wether a year from
each flock for the soup of the world sovereign,[55] what burden
is that? To take one yearling from every hundred sheep and
give it to the poor and destitute would be good. To set up post-
stations and choose post-staff and relay riders would make
for the tranquillity of the teeming kingdom and the conveni-
ence of the envoys on their business as well."'

'They approved it all together.'

So saying, he consulted about the khan's decree with Caġadai
the Elder and it was approved by Caġadai the Elder and by the
kingdom as a whole; for every thousand in every direction, by
the imperial decree, one second-year wether from every flock
and one yearling sheep from every hundred sheep were taken

280

every year. Mares were taken and mare-herders were stationed. Mare-herders, city sentries and granary sentries were chosen. Post-staff and relay riders were chosen, the miles of every settlement measured, and post-stations were set up; Arazen and Toqucar were made to supervise them.[56] On the post-roads in a single settlement twenty relay riders were set; in every settlement, about twenty relay riders were set.[57]

It was decreed, 'The geldings for the relay, sheep for the board, mares for milking, oxen hitched to the carts and wagons: compared to the amounts set in our regulations,
If a short string is wanting
Let him forfeit half by the noggin;
If a spoon or a spoke is wanting
Let him forfeit half by the nose.'[58]

ÖKODEI KHAN'S FINAL
SELF-ASSESSMENT[59]

281 Ökodei Khan said, 'I have sat on the great throne of my Khan-Father and what I have accomplished after the Khan-Father is:

'I campaigned against the people of China and wiped out China's folk[60] – an additional deed.

'I set up post-stations so that my envoys would swiftly ride between us post-haste and also transport needs and necessities – another additional deed.

'In lands with no water, I had wells dug out and provided water and grass for the nation.

'Also, I left outriders and permanent garrison soldiers over the city folk in every direction, and made the nation live with their soles on the soil and their grip on the ground.

'These four deeds I added since the time of my Khan-Father.

'Yet, although I was seated on a great throne by my Khan-Father and carried forward on my back the teeming kingdom, it was an error of mine to be defeated by grape wine. This was one of my errors.[61]

'The second error was my weakness in being taken in by the

words of a wayward woman, and taking over the girls of Otci-gin the Elder Uncle's kingdom. To be led astray into a wayward and weak affair while I was the Lord-Khan of the kingdom: this was one of my errors.[62]

'Also, to hold a grudge against Doqolqu was an error. If you ask why it was an error, to hold a grudge against Doqolqu who had charged forward on behalf of my Ruler-Father was an error and a weakness; who now will charge forward for me like that? I myself confess my error in plotting against Doqolqu, not understanding the man who had been more eager than any-one in adhering to the principles of the Khan-Father.[63]

'Also, worrying lest the game born by a destiny from Heaven and Earth should go in the direction of the elders and juniors, I was greedy. By building fences and walls and hemming them in, I listened to words of resentment against the elder and younger brothers. This too was an error.[64]

'Since the time of my Khan-Father, I added these four deeds; four other deeds turned out to be errors.'

Colophon[1]

At the moment when the great *quriltai* was assembling, in the Roebuck Moon[2] of the Year of the Mouse [August 1252],[3] and the hordes had been pitched at the Seven Hills of Köde'e Isle on the Kherlen, between Śilgincek and ...,[4] the writing was finished.

Afterword: The Transmission and Translation of the *Secret History*

Almost as surprising as the *Secret History* itself is the story of how it came to be preserved to the present. The story involves both rare manuscripts being preserved in the *ger*s of Mongolia and the monasteries of Tibet as well as language textbooks blockprinted in imperial China. Both streams of transmission came together in the twentieth century, as scholars throughout the world rediscovered the *Secret History*. This transmission has also influenced how commentators and translators have understood the text. Transmission and translation must thus be understood together.

THE TEXT IN MONGOLIA (TO 1900)

In 1900, the *Secret History* was mostly unknown in Mongolia. The lengthy genealogy and a few of the stories of Chinggis Khan's childhood had been incorporated, verbatim or in para-phrase, into the chronicles that formed how literate Mongols, nobles, officials, scribes and Buddhist clergy, viewed their past. But Chinggis Khan had not been forgotten – far from it. Instead, the frighteningly harsh and realistic story told by the Secret Historian had been replaced over the course of the fif-teenth and sixteenth centuries with the magically endowed, yet much less personal, Chinggis Khan of apocryphal texts.

This apocryphal image of Chinggis Khan was recreated during Mongolia's 'dark ages', the period that began with the disintegra-tion of the Mongol empire in the continent-wide fourteenth-century crisis and ended in the late sixteenth century with the renewed conversion to Tibetan-style Buddhism and the revival of Mongolian letters and scholarship. During these dark ages, the shrine of Chinggis Khan became the religious, cultural and political centre of the Mongols. Around this shrine, a new body of literature was created in which Chinggis Khan was an all-knowing, all-wise figure in a supernatural world, where dogs prophesied, and rival khans engaged in shape-shifting contests. Chinggis Khan's right to rule was attested by the jade seal he was born with in his hands (not the *Secret History*'s clot of blood) and confirmed when he, unlike his brothers, was able to quaff the goblet of holy water descended from Heaven.

Where was the *Secret History* during this time? Certainly, manuscripts of the text still existed, since they would be copied again in the late 1500s. Evidently, however, they were no longer being read amid the general decline in literacy, opening the way for new texts, such as the 'Golden Chronicle of Chinggis Khan' (*Cinggis Qa'an-u altan tobci*), that canonized this apocryphal and magical Chinggis Khan. In the late 1500s, however, the conversion of the Mongols to the dynamic new Gelug ('Yellow Hat') school of Tibetan-style Buddhism led to an explosion of literacy. Rare and obscure old texts from the empire period were rediscovered and copied anew, even as new Buddhist translations from the Tibetan were also flooding the market.

The *Secret History* was brought back to life in this new literary revival. Fragmentary texts have been discovered at Olan Süme in Inner Mongolia, alongside translated Buddhist texts. In Toling monastery in western Tibet, thirteen leaves from a manuscript of the *Secret History* running from §90 to §120 were recently discovered and published (see Sarengaowa's study). The paper format, ductus or writing style, and the leaves' very existence in Tibet, with which the Mongols established strong ties only in the third quarter of the sixteenth century, all place this manuscript somewhere in the late sixteenth or early seventeenth century. But although the *Secret History* was becoming more popular, the apocryphal and magical Chinggis Khan by no means lost his hold on the Mongolian imagination. With two versions of Chinggis Khan's story circulating, the urge to harmonize them must have been strong.

Sometime in the 1620s, then, a new 'Golden Chronicle' or *Altan tobci* was created combining the early parts of the *Secret History* with the apocryphal legend cycle of Chinggis Khan as embedded in the 'Golden Chronicle of Chinggis Khan', and a vast amount of other material about him and his successors. The anonymous compiler created a history that begins with the Buddhist story of how the world coalesced and came under the first legendary monarch in India, Maha-Sammata, through the religious kings of Tibet, all the way to the second conversion of the Mongols to Buddhism.

This Buddhist narrative was expanded in 1651 by a Buddhist monk named Lubsang-Danzin to include the fall of Chinggis Khan's descendant Ligdan Khan in 1634 and the submission of Inner Mongolia to the rising Manchu Qing dynasty. Aiming to tell the full story of Chinggis Khan, Lubsang-Danzin quoted all sorts of manuscripts about the great founder of Mongolian kingship; most importantly for our purposes, he included not just the early parts, but a full two-thirds of the *Secret History*. Lubsang-Danzin entitled his version of the Mongolian chronicles 'The Golden Chronicle that Briefly Compiles the Deeds of State Established by the Ancient Khans';[1] today it is usually known as Lubsang-Danzin's *Altan tobci* or *LAT*, for short.

Following the recently invented tradition, Lubsang-Danzin tied Chinggis Khan to Buddhist history by making his genealogy as told in the *Secret History* an offshoot of the partly historical and partly mythical genealogy of Buddhist monarchs of India and Tibet. He also grafted the story of young Temujin, taken purely from the *Secret History*, on to a history of Chinggis Khan as ruler that placed episodes from the apocryphal legend cycle alongside most of the *Secret History* and many other fragmentary stories and sayings attributed to Chinggis Khan. Unfortunately, the new literary language of the Mongols differed substantially from the Middle Mongolian of the *Secret History*, and over the centuries many of the words had been considerably corrupted. For many now obscure words, Lubsang-Danzin inserted interlinear synonyms, some correct, others quite wrong. It is also unclear whether the manuscript of the *Secret History* used by Lubsang-Danzin was complete. In Lubsang-Danzin's own text, the passages copied from the *Secret History* have a vast gap covering from §176 to §208, get increasingly patchy towards the end of the khan's life, and finally omit the entire section on Ökodei Khan. It is difficult to tell if these gaps were already there in the manuscript he used or whether Lubsang-Danzin omitted the material, either deliberately or accidentally. In any case, Lubsang-Danzin's 'Golden Chronicle' did preserve for the future two-thirds of the *Secret History* text along with passages from many other, now lost documents of widely varying dates.

The chroniclers' idea of merging all the existing material on Chinggis Khan into an expanded text that covered Mongolia from the dawn of history to the Manchu Qing conquest of Mongolia was a popular one in general. Works like Lubsang-Danzin's *Altan tobci* became the model for a genre of chronicles that continued into the early twentieth century. But the juxtaposition of the *Secret History* with apocryphal legends created a tension – the two types of work were so radically different in language, tone and focus that it was evidently jarring for readers to jump from one to the other. In the end, all of the other chronicles in this genre chose to delete most of the *Secret History*. A seventeenth-century chronicle, called the 'Concise Golden Chronicle' (*Quriyangġui altan tobci*), ended citation from the *Secret History* at the point when young Temujin recovers his stolen horses in §93, and that became the general practice, followed by the particularly popular and widely copied 'Precious Chronicle' (*Erdeni-yin tobci*) of Saġang Secen (see Johan Elverskog's new translation). By contrast, Lubsang-Danzin's *Altan tobci* version again fell out of circulation.

From then on, the *Secret History* text known in Mongolia consisted solely of this initial one-eighth or so of the text. The rediscovery of the full text would not come until the twentieth century.

THE HANLIN RECENSION

The recovery of the *Secret History* in international scholarship began not with the text embedded in Lubsang-Danzin's *Altan tobci* but with an entirely different version of the *Secret History*. This version owed its existence to its use as a textbook in China for training Mongolian interpreters. With the expulsion of the Mongol Yuan emperors from China in 1368, the new Ming dynasty in China aimed to use carrots and sticks to pacify those Mongols in Mongolia who still paid allegiance to Chinggis Khan's family. It thus pursued an active military and diplomatic policy in Mongolia, and to do that it needed both translators, who worked with written texts, and interpreters, who handled oral communication only.

In 1382, the Ming court in Nanjing ordered two scholars in the Hanlin Academy, one named Huo Yuanjie – which might be the Chinese name of a Mongol named Qonici – and the Muslim Ma Shaykh-Muhammad, to create a handbook for training Mongolian-language interpreters: the 'Sino-Barbarian Glossaries' (*Hua-Yi yiyu*). But since this vocabulary was for training interpreters, not translators, they were not expected to master the Uyghur-Mongolian alphabet in which the *Secret History* was written. Thus, the Mongolian words would have to be written using Chinese graphs (characters) for sound.

Fortunately, Chinese-speaking scribes had long experience in turning Mongolian into Chinese, and vice versa. During the Mongol empire, scribes in conquered China developed a technique of using Chinese graphs purely for sound so that they could represent the sounds of Mongolian, Uyghur, Jurchen, Persian and other languages of importance in the Mongol empire. Diacritical graphs were used both to distinguish letters such as *l* and *r*, which were hard to distinguish in Chinese, and also to represent the *b*, *t*, *k*, *q* and other consonants at the end of a syllable. (Chinese syllables at this time could only end in a vowel or else in *n*, *ng*, or *m*.) Already a number of glossaries had been created using this system to represent Mongolian sounds fairly exactly with Chinese graphs and then defining the words in Chinese. Even conventions for representing Mongolian conjugations and declensions with specified Chinese graphs had been worked out.[2]

But the Ming emperor envisioned a larger, more comprehensive project. Further improvements had been made in the system for using Chinese graphs to represent Mongolian, but a larger vocabulary base was needed. The compilers then turned to a text which they had at hand, one with an extraordinarily rich variety of Mongolian words and phrases: *The Secret History of the Mongols*. A copy of this text had been discovered in the Mongol imperial capital of Daidu (modern Beijing), when the Ming armies captured the city from the last Mongol khan in China in 1368. In 1369, as the Ming court began to compile its encyclopedic history of the Mongol Yuan dynasty, the *Yuanshi*, officials assembled all the documents and histories they could find in Nanjing, the new capital of the Ming dynasty. The *Secret History* had not actually been used for compiling the *Yuanshi* ('History of the Yuan Dynasty'), but now it was singled out as being a good source for the compilers of the Mongolian section of the 'Sino-Barbarian Glossaries'.

The scholars in the translation and interpreting offices thus began to transcribe and translate the *Secret History*, a process that probably lasted for several years. The 'Sino-Barbarian Glossaries' was completed in 1389, and by that time a draft manuscript of the *Secret History* in Chinese graphs probably existed. This work consisted of three different levels:

1. A complete transcription of the Mongolian text, syllable by syllable, into Chinese graphs chosen for their phonetic value.
2. An interlinear translation, glossing almost every Mongolian word into Chinese and using the established system to mark the Mongolian's grammatical particles, declensions and conjugations with standard Chinese equivalents.
3. A running translation, sometimes abridging the more complex or technical passages.

The text was divided purely on the basis of length into twelve parts (*juan* in Chinese) and 282 sections. The running translation was inserted after the transcription and interlinear translation at the end of each section. The pronunciation the scribes used for the transcription was based on the Mongolian language as spoken in the former Mongol capital of Daidu, where scores of thousands of Mongols still dwelled. From the *Secret History* as thus prepared, the compilers of the 'Sino-Barbarian Glossaries' could derive a sense of what words in Mongolian were most common and important and so were able to make the glossary quite accurate and comprehensive.

Although the Ming empire was ruled by an ethnic Chinese dynasty, almost all the translators doing this work were Mongolian, speakers of Turkic languages such as Uyghur, or else Mongolized immigrants from the Middle East, just as they had been during the Mongol Yuan dynasty before. Indeed, probably most of the Ming dynasty's interpreters and translators were descendants of the Mongol Yuan-era translators and interpreters who had stayed in China and not followed the Mongol khans back to Mongolia. Their transcription and translation of the *Secret History* was, despite the occasional inevitable lapse, a tremendous feat of scholarship without which the Middle Mongolian language of the work would be much less well understood than it is today.

This transcribed and translated word-by-word *Secret History* was eventually included in a massive imperial encyclopedia covering China's vast body of classics, philosophy, science, history and literature. This work, called the 'Yongle Encyclopedia' (*Yongle dadian*) from the name of the reigning Ming emperor's era,[3] was completed in 1408 in 11,095 manuscript volumes. The *Secret History*'s twelve *juan* were redivided into fifteen *juan*, but otherwise the text was copied without much change. As one might imagine, very few copies of this massive handwritten encyclopedia were ever made, but the master copy was brought in 1421 from Nanjing to Beijing, where the Yongle emperor had fixed his new capital. Meanwhile, around 1410, the original twelve-book manuscript version was printed in Beijing, probably for the use of the interpreters who now had Beijing, not Nanjing, as their base. Thus, from then on, the transcribed *Secret History* – what we may call the Hanlin recension of the text – existed in two sub-recensions, one in twelve *juan* and one in fifteen *juan*, but otherwise virtually identical. Although published, neither was available outside the government offices in Beijing.

THE RECOVERY OF THE TEXT

The rise of the Manchu Qing dynasty (1636–1912) influenced history writing in both Mongolia and China. In Mongolia, the Manchus ruled through a native Mongolian aristocracy descended from Chinggis Khan or his brothers. After submitting to the Manchu empire, Chinggisid aristocrats and Buddhist lamas like Lubsang-Danzin wished to enshrine Chinggis Khan's legacy in history and preserve the genealogy of the nobles. And as China found itself part of an empire that grew to include all of Mongolia, Tibet and the eastern part of Turkestan (present-day Xinjiang), scholars were inspired to investigate the Mongol Yuan dynasty, the last time when China had been the centre of such an expansive empire.

As part of these investigations, those with special access began to make copies of both the fifteen-*juan* recension in the 'Yongle Encyclopedia' and then the twelve-*juan* printed recension. Chinese scholars could not read the Mongolian transcription, but they could easily read the running translation and puzzle through the interlinear translation. Over the course of the eighteenth century references to the work grew, and several scholars made complete copies of the two versions. Of these the oldest dated copy, made in 1805, is that of Gu Guangqi of the twelve-*juan* recension.[4] Another copy, this time of the fifteen-*juan* recension, was made by Bao Tingbo around the same time.[5]

It is very fortunate that such copies were made since none of the original Ming editions have been preserved. The last complete copy of the 'Yongle Encyclopedia' was destroyed when Anglo-French forces burned the Summer Palace in Beijing during the Second Opium War in 1860. In the 1930s, a copy of a manuscript dating to 1404 used in the production of the 'Yongle Encyclopedia' edition of the *Secret History* surfaced, but it included only the running translation, and not the more important transcription or interlinear translation. As for the *c.*1410 twelve-*juan* printed edition, it too was lost sometime in the nineteenth century. A copy was found in 1933 in the former imperial storehouses in Beijing, but it had only forty-one of the 610 original pages. Fortunately, however, these partial remains do confirm that the nineteenth-century MS copies are very accurate. From 1908, when Ye Dehui made the first modern printing of the text, based on Gu Guangqi's copy, the remaining minor discrepancies in the editions of the Hanlin recension have been gradually cleared up, and scholars can now rely on highly accurate editions, such as that of Professor Ulaan (Wulan) of Minzu University published in 2012.

The nineteenth century brought interest in the Hanlin recension of the *Secret History* beyond just China. In 1866, the Russian monk-scholar Archimandrite Palladius (Petr I. Kafarov), working from the Bao Tingbo copy, published a translation of the Chinese running translation. Since then, many translations have been made from the Chinese version. The most widely read translation from the Chinese into English is that of Arthur Waley, first published in 1963. Such translations, of course, miss much of the distinctive character of the *Secret History* since the Chinese running translation is quite free, usually abridging the text, and often more of a paraphrase than an accurate translation. The technical passages, often of special interest to historians, were summarized especially briefly.

Needless to say, serious translations must be made directly from the Mongolian, not from the old Chinese translation. But as long as the *LAT* recension of the *Secret History* was still unknown to scholarship this could only be done by reconstructing the Mongolian original from the Chinese transcription. This demanded, of course, a solid knowledge of Middle Mongolian. It also demanded a good knowledge of Early Mandarin, the name for the Chinese of the thirteenth to fifteenth centuries, one that differed substantially from contemporary Mandarin. The earliest attempt to reconstruct the Mongolian was done in 1917 by Duke Tsengde, an official of the Daur Mongol people from Hulun Buir in Inner Mongolia. Able to read Chinese and standard Mongolian as well as his own very archaic Daur dialect of Mongolian, Tsengde was in many ways well prepared.

His reconstruction was only made in manuscript, however, and was not published in facsimile until 1996.

The first published reconstruction of the Mongolian text and translation directly from the Mongolian into a modern language was that of Erich Haenisch into German, which was published in Leipzig in 1935. The Russian scholar Sergei Andreevich Kozin published another reconstruction in 1941 along with a highly influential Russian translation, based heavily on Palladius's text. Paul Pelliot, the famous French Sinologist and Mongolist, worked on the text for decades; his complete reconstruction and partial translation into French were published posthumously in 1949.

Kozin and Pelliot's reconstructions also benefited from finally being able to compare the Hanlin recension with the one preserved in Lubsang-Danzin's *Altan tobci*. Thus, for the first time, the two divergent strands of transmission were brought back together. The sole surviving manuscript of Lubsang-Danzin's chronicle had been discovered by the scholar-official Duke Jamyang in 1926 in eastern Mongolia as part of the Mongolian People's Republic's academic and cultural revival. The copy was deposited in the Mongolian National Library, where it is still kept today, and copies were written out by hand for both Kozin and Pelliot. A typeset version was also published in 1934 in Ulaanbaatar, but divergences between this published version and Kozin and Pelliot's transcriptions made from their copies caused doubt about the accuracy of the published edition. Still, Pelliot in particular used the *LAT* text at several points to correct the Hanlin recension, although he still treated the Hanlin recension as the base text.

Meanwhile, Mongolian authors began to bring this work to the attention of ethnic Mongols both in independent Mongolia (so-called 'Outer Mongolia') and in Inner Mongolia, still under China. In 1941, two Inner Mongolian authors, Altan-Ochir and Bökekeśig, independently published their own reconstructions of the Mongolian text as well, as part of the Inner Mongolian national revival under Japanese patronage. But the most influential figure in taking the *Secret History* back to the Mongolian people was Tsendiin Damdinsüren. One of the great scholars of the Mongolian People's Republic, noted both for his fiction and poetry as well as his later work on the Mongolian *Geser* epic and literary history generally, in 1947 he published an adaptation of the *Secret History* into modern literary Mongolian. Although Damdinsüren did not read Chinese, he was able to use the existing scholarship to understand the text well. He worked primarily from Kozin's 1941 edition, while also consulting Lubsang-Danzin's *Altan tobci*, Archimandrite Palladius's Russian translation of the Chinese translation, Duke Tsengde and Altan-Ochir's Mongolian versions, Haenisch's edition, and the voluminous general scholarship on the Mongol empire. The combined literary and scholarly quality of his rendition in modern Mongolian was such that it became an instant classic. Transcribed into Mongolia's new Cyrillic script in the second edition of 1957, in that form it became a staple of Mongolian literary education up to the present. For most Mongolians today, it is Damdinsüren's brilliant adaptation which is *the* 'Secret History of the Mongols'.

This Afterword is not the place to review the whole story of the subsequent scholarly history of the *Secret History*. The lines set out by Haenisch's 1935 German edition and associated dictionary of the *Secret History* language, together with Pelliot and Kozin's integration of Lubsang-Danzin's *Altan tobci* material into the mix, have defined the subsequent scholarship. The only new piece of source material revealed since the 1930s has been the thirteen leaves of the c.1600 Toling monastery manuscript; these help us to understand the origins of the *LAT* recension, but are not in themselves of tremendous significance.

TRANSLATING THE *SECRET HISTORY*: FIGURING OUT WHAT IT'S SAYING

The peculiar way that the *Secret History* was transmitted to today is of tremendous importance to its translation. As one of the oldest, and uniquely rich, samples of Middle Mongolian, the language of the *Secret History* presents numerous difficulties for scholars and translators. The existence of the Hanlin recension, with its word-by-word translation, has thus been an invaluable resource in understanding the work. Without it, the *LAT* recension on its own would frequently be almost incomprehensible. Yet the very centrality of the Hanlin recension has often led scholars, almost subconsciously, to confuse it with the *Secret History* itself. It is not the *Secret History*, but rather a reading of the text undertaken by a team of translators, Mongolian and not, working under radically different conditions from the original author of the text almost 150 years after the *Secret History* was written.

As an example of the importance of the Hanlin recension, let us take a passage near the end of the *Secret History*, in §281:

> *Basa Doqolqu-yi kegesuleku niken buru'u .. ker buru'u ke'esu . qan ecige-yin minu tus-u'an emun-e ölumleku Doqolqu-yi kegesuleku buru'u aljiyas .. edo'e minu emun-e ken teyin ölumleju ökku .. Qa'an ecige-yin minu bürin-u emun-e töro kici'eku kü' un-i ülu uqan öisuleduksen-iyen ö'er-iyen buru'ušiyaba bi ..*

My translation reads:

> Also, to hold a grudge against Doqolqu was an error. If you ask why it was an error, to hold a grudge against Doqolqu who had charged forward on behalf of my Ruler-Father was an error and a weakness; who now will charge forward for me like that? I myself confess my error in plotting against Doqolqu, not understanding the man who had been more eager than anyone in adhering to the principles of the Khan-Father.

This is one of the passages missing in the *LAT* text, so the Hanlin recension is our only source. The passage contains two verbs found nowhere else, at least in that exact form. One is *kegesule-* (translated here as 'hold a grudge') and the other is *öisuledu-* (translated here as 'plotting'). Both are glossed identically in the Chinese of the interlinear translation, however, as *yinhai,* 'secretly kill/harm'. Without that gloss, scholars might have struggled to make sense of *kegesule-*; the only similar modern verb is a homonym meaning 'to furnish with spokes'. And *öisuledu-* would have remained just a puzzle; indeed, even the sequence of *öi-* is impossible in modern Mongolian. If we trust the gloss, however, we can be sure of the basic meaning.

But they are two quite different words, used in close proximity; is there any difference in nuance between them? Fortunately, once the general meaning is given, plausible cognates suggest themselves. A root noun *kegesu* in the sense required (i.e. not as the spoke of a wheel) is found one place else in Mongolian, in the *Secret History* §67, where it is glossed in Chinese as *yuan-chou*, 'rancour, enmity, hatred resulting from past grievances'. *Kegesule-* would be a regular verb form from that noun, with an expected meaning of 'to hold a grudge'. Such a translation might be corroborated by the running Chinese translation, which renders the entire passage as 'To have the loyal Doqolqu secretly harmed due to a private grudge was yet another instance [of my mistakes]', thus bringing in the idea of an old private grudge (*sihen* in Chinese).

As for *öisuledu-*, it may be related to the verb found in §§67–8 and §245 in the Hanlin recension as *oyisula-* or *oyisulaldu-* and in the corresponding *LAT* text as *öseldu-* or *ösleldu-*. *Ösleldu-* is found in modern Mongolian as 'to hate each other; to take vengeance on each other', while the *oyisula-* family of verbs in the *Secret History* are glossed in the Hanlin recension's Chinese as *anhuai* or *yinhai*, 'secretly harm' or 'secretly kill'. These verbs are used for the poisoning of Chinggis Khan's father, Yisukei, and the Qongqotan brothers' plotting against Chinggis Khan's little brothers. However, scholars are not certain if the well-known family of verbs with the root *ös-* (itself a Mongolian noun meaning 'hatred; vengeance') is actually related to those with the root *oyisu-* or *öisu-*, found only in the *Secret History*. Indeed it is possible that one or more of these forms might be simply a slip of the pen in writing. My translation has proceeded on the idea that *oyisu-* and *öisu-* are the same, both meaning 'to plot (against someone's life)'; as can be seen from this explanation, my translation places considerable trust in the Hanlin recension translators.

Such confidence is generally merited, but not always. One

example where the Hanlin recension's translators almost certainly made a mistake can be found in §70. There, Chinggis Khan's mother, having been excluded from one of the ancestral sacrifices that defined community membership, cries out:

Yisukei Ba'atur-i ükube-'u ke'eju kö'ud-i minu yeke ülu bolquy-aca yekes-un keśig-ece bile'ur-ece sarqud-aca yekin qojida'ulumui ta.

This I translate as follows: 'Is it because you think [my late husband] Yisukei Ba'atur has died and that my sons will not get bigger that you somehow made me too late for the blessings of the ancestors, the sacrificial meat, and the sacrificial liquor?' Here there are two technical terms, *bile'ur* and *sarqut*. The Hanlin recension translators gloss *bile'ur* as *yuzuo*, 'left-over sacrificial meat', and *sarqut* as *zuo*, 'sacrificial meat'. The whole sentence is translated in the running translation as 'Saying that Yisukei has died and my sons you fear will not get bigger in the future, you go so far as to not give me any share of the sacrificial meat of the great ones'; the translators did not understand the difference between *bile'ur* and *sarqut* and merged the two into 'sacrificial meat' (Ch. *zuo*). But while *bile'ur* is not otherwise attested in Mongolian, and can thus only be understood in the way given by the translators, *sarqut* is well known in later Mongolian as a word for sacrificial liquor, and that is how I and most other translators have taken it.

More frequent than such errors in terminology are errors in proper nouns – names of persons, places, dominant families and ethnic groups. Already by the time of the early Ming interpreters, many such names had been forgotten or were no longer used. And, once forgotten, the ambiguities of the Uyghur-Mongolian script meant that such names were also frequently misread, blocking the possibility of further identification. One example of this is the name Nünjin, belonging to a family that joined Chinggis Khan's standard in §122. In the older forms of the Uyghur Mongolian script, an *n-* at the beginning of the word and the 'crown' marking a word that begins with a vowel were not consistently distinguished. (In later Mongolian, a dot would be added to mark the *n-*.) Thus the Hanlin recension read what should have been 'Nünjin' as 'Ünjin', a mistake that unfortunately was followed by all previous translators.

In this translation, by contrast, my aim has not been to translate the Hanlin recension itself, but rather the Mongol empire-era *Secret History* that lay behind it, the common ancestor of the Hanlin and *LAT* versions. Thus in disambiguating the Mongolian readings I do not necessarily follow the Hanlin recension, but rather what in the light of modern scholarship seems to be the most correct reading.

Let us take a few examples. Among the ambiguities in Middle Mongolian is the fact that some words have an initial *h-* that disappears in later Mongolian. It is found, however, in Persian and Chinese transcriptions of Mongolian names, as well as in the Hanlin recension's transcription. Thus we know that what is written Arġasun and Ula'an-Qut was actually pronounced as Harġasun and Hula'an-Qut in Middle Mongolian. In some cases, however, the Hanlin translators disagree with how other translators read the name. The Hanlin translators, for example, read one of the early pre-Chinggisid khans as Ambaġai and Chinggis Khan's mother as Hö'elun. But the Chinese translators at Qubilai Khan's court and the Persian translators at Ghazan Khan's court, both working under the close supervision of Mongolian rulers, read these names as Hambaġai and Ö'elun respectively. Translators actually working on histories under the patronage of Mongolian rulers would seem obviously more authoritative than those working on language textbooks under a Chinese ruler who had displaced the Mongols. For that reason, where the readings of proper nouns in the Hanlin recension conflict with those found in the *Campaigns of Chinggis Khan* or the *Compendium of Chronicles*, I have followed those non-Hanlin recension readings as being earlier, at least semi-official, and hence probably better informed.

Adding to the oddities of the Hanlin recension transcriptions, in both the *Secret History* and the 'Sino-Barbarian Glossaries', was the peculiar dialect that was being spoken by the Mongols in China proper by the 1380s. In this dialect there was a strong tendency for *kö-* or *kü-* at the beginning of a word to become *gö-* or *gü-* respectively. Thus *ködel-*, 'to move', they consistently read as *gödel-*, and *kür-*, 'to arrive, to reach', they consistently read as *gür-*. No trace of this sound change is found in sources from before 1350 or so. There is thus no reason to follow the Hanlin transcribers when they write 'Güculug' for 'Küculug' or 'Güregen' for 'Küregen', '(imperial) son-in-law', using a dialect that did not yet exist when the *Secret History* was actually written and that disappeared in the following centuries when those Mongols living in Nanjing and Beijing lost their language and began speaking Chinese.

Another tendency of the transcribers is to 'soften' consonants in between vowels, thus reading *-utu-* as *-udu-* and *-uke-* as *-uge-*.[6] This feature is not peculiar to the Mongols in late-fourteenth-century China proper; it was in fact a common feature of Chinese transcriptions of Mongolian even in the thirteenth century. Due to it, the common noun *qutuq* or the name Qutuġa is often read as Quduq or Quduġa. It is under this influence that what comparison with other readings and modern usage showed to be best read as Yisukei (Chinggis Khan's father) and Ökodei (his son and successor) came to be generally transcribed as Yisugei and Ögodei.[7] Here I follow what comparative data indicate to be the correct usage, not simply how the Hanlin translators rendered the names in the 1380s.

TRANSLATING THE *SECRET HISTORY*: CRAFTING AN ENGLISH VOICE

The language of the *Secret History* is of extraordinary richness, concision and vigour. Although our corpus of Middle Mongolian is small compared to that of New Mongolian, still it is astonishing how many words there are in the *Secret History* that are found nowhere else in Middle Mongolian. Much of this language consists of concrete words and terms reflecting the pastoral lifestyle, including an abundance of finely distinguished terms for horse pelages. However, there is also a wide vocabulary of fairly abstract terms as well. In that regard it is striking how many more or less synonymous words for verbs or concepts may be found in the *Secret History*'s vocabulary; this can be seen by looking at the index of Chinese interlinear translations, in which we find that Chinese 'heart' (*xin*) translates four different Mongolian words: not just *jüruke*, but also *öre, setkil* and *duran*.

At the same time, the richness of the *Secret History* vocabulary seems to have developed mostly out of internal resources. To a certain extent this may be an optical illusion produced by our lack of knowledge of the previous languages influencing Middle Mongolian. (The one exception is Middle Turkish, about which I will say a bit more below.) But one can say that, unlike modern English or Japanese, for example, one does not get the impression of two or more coherent vocabulary sources, such as Germanic, French and Latin in English, or native Japanese, Sinitic and English in Japanese. Instead, the extraordinarily rich vocabulary seems to be built from a vast number of roots that are equally 'Mongolian' and developed through a process of agglutination and suffixation.[8]

Of course, the historical influence of Turkic on Mongolian was certainly profound. However, regardless of one's position on the languages' ultimate relationship, Turkic loan words seem phonologically and grammatically more 'dissolved' than in the examples cited above – more like the mix of Anglo-Saxon and Norse in modern English, for example, than the mix of Anglo-Saxon and French. This merger of the two source languages was advanced by the widespread Mongolian assimilation of Turkic agglutinating elements, such as the suffix -*la*-, which forms verbs out of nouns. Still, there are certain passages, particularly relevant to the Kereyit, in which a strong, intrusive Turkic vocabulary appears. And later, Middle Mongolian works of the fourteenth century would show a much heavier influence of Uyghur Turkic 'culture words'. But these passages are exceptional and stand out as such.

My choice of vocabulary for this English translation has been shaped by this understanding of the work's Mongolian vocabulary. The vocabulary is nuanced yet grounded, complex yet consistent in derivation and phonology, capable of great abstraction yet constantly coming back to the concrete. I have tried to reproduce such a language. Readers will notice a general attempt to create a language that attempts to build a complex and nuanced language out of mostly vernacular English resources, without conducting any mechanical 'purge' of Latinate terms and constructions.

As has been noted by many linguists, the language of the *Secret History* is based heavily on varieties of paratactic concatenation, in which phrases are simply placed next to each other. As an example of parataxis in English, consider the following passage from Ernest Hemingway: 'Nick drove another big nail and hung up the bucket full of water. He dipped the coffee pot half full, put some more chips under the grill on to the fire and put the pot on.'[9] In contrast, relatively little use is made of hypotactic concatenation, in which the logical connections governing the clauses are made explicit. Here is an English example from Jane Austen: 'However little known the feelings or views of such a man may be on his first entering a neighbourhood, this truth is so well fixed in the minds of the surrounding families, that he is considered as the rightful property of some one or other of their daughters.'[10]

My translation stands out among those produced so far in attempting to reproduce this character of the *Secret History* language. Such parataxis can indeed be found quite often in English, but more often in a vernacular speech or certain fictional voices, rather than in an academic prose, where hypotaxis is seen as the very emblem of careful thought. Ernest Hemingway's famous voice, which I cited above, has been explained as a triumph of parataxis.[11]

Another pervasive feature of the language of the *Secret History* is the use of direct quotation in situations where indirect quotation would be more often used in modern Mongolian. Not just words, but thoughts, aims and intentions are reported with a complex apparatus of open- and close-quote verbs. In many cases, this usage is simply conventional and need not be reproduced further than would sound natural in English. Yet it also recalls what has been characterized as 'epic exteriority', the way in which epic characters do not have thoughts or ideas which they do not openly enunciate.[12] In line with this epic sensibility, the *Secret History* characters do a tremendous amount of talking – or at least sub-vocalizing – and yet fairly little observing or voicing fine shades of feeling. (The observing is left to the narrator, who is extraordinarily good at sketching a scene with a few telling details.)

At the same time, the Secret Historian is actually anti-epic in the relationship of speech to intention. Achilles might boldly claim that 'as I detest the doorways of Death, I detest that man, who hides one thing in the depths of his heart, and speaks forth another'[13] – but he would not have got on at all well at the court of Chinggis Khan. To be sure, personages in the *Secret History* also express the epic ideal of a perfect match between speech and deed – 'As Mongols, are we not ones whose word "yes" is an oath?' (§108) – yet the *Secret History* displays the disjunction between this ideal and the real practice of heavenly-destined leaders just as it does with the oft-enunciated ideal of fraternal unity. Indeed, one may say that in the *Secret History* what is most important is never spoken, and the incessant vocalizing and sub-vocalizing never quite reveal the real intentions. This is true at the level of higher characterization – what did Jamuqa really mean with his poetic suggestion about horse herds and sheep flocks to Chinggis Khan? What really prompted Chinggis Khan at the moment of total victory to offer to share his throne with his captive rival Jamuqa? What did Ökodei really feel about his little brother Tolui – and what did Tolui think about Ökodei? In this sense, the *Secret History* exemplified what Erich Auerbach has written about narrative in the biblical Primary History: 'their speech does not serve, as does speech in Homer, to manifest, to externalize thoughts – on the contrary, it serves to indicate thoughts which remain unexpressed.'[14]

But this is also true at a much lower discursive level. The *Secret History*'s language is very articulate, but generally not explicit. The pervasive parataxis noted above, the tendency to simply place clauses together on the same level, rather than subordinate one to another, means that the logical interrelations between events, thoughts and words are usually implicit, left for the reader to surmise based on the evidence presented rather than explicitly stated. Although the *Secret History* made extensive use of written sources, it was produced overall within an oral culture, one where parataxis produced a narrative voice that was additive not subordinative, aggregative not analytic, relatively copious, situational not (overtly) abstract, and close to the realm of human daily life.[15]

The situational nature of the language often seems to beg for explicitation. When Ong Khan exclaims, *Ai soyiluq*, or literally 'Alas . . . culpable!' in §178, it is left implicit whether the culpable one is Chinggis Khan, who is now his enemy, Ong Khan's son Ilqa Senggum, who provoked the rift, or Ong Khan himself for listening to Ilqa Senggum. Similarly, in §245, when Chinggis Khan's little brother Otcigin Noyan comes back into the *ger* after having Father Mönglik's son killed, Father Mönglik 'understood' (*uqaju*), with no object specified, and laments how for so long he had been a 'friend' (*nökor*). The reader might ask, 'Understood what, exactly?' and 'A friend to whom, exactly?'

In such cases, the translator has to walk a fine line – explicating enough to bridge the gap in the situational understanding between the modern reader's radically different context and that of the original audience, but not so much as to fundamentally change the very nature of the discourse. In the examples above, I resolved the lower-level ambiguities, thus translating, 'Alas, how culpable *of me*!' and 'friend *to the khan*' (explicitation in italics). But I leave the exact object of Father Mönglik's understanding unstated, precisely because it is so open-ended. Certainly, he understands that Otcigin Noyan has killed his son, but how much more does he understand? What conclusions is he drawing about the family he married into and served for decades? About his real position in the new order? We can only guess.

Given the relatively poorly understood nature of the Middle Mongolian language and the vast numbers of idiomatic phrases and vocabulary items whose exact nuances cannot be specified, most translators have opted for a relatively literal translation – it seems risky to translate for the meaning rather than the words when you are more certain of the individual words than of the exact import of the phrase as a whole. Igor de Rachewiltz pushed against this trend – he made tremendous progress in actually understanding the idiomatic meaning of the phrases – and I learned much from his commentary and example. But my awareness of how the peculiar role of parataxis and speech in expressing and hiding motives is essential to the effect, and meaning, of the *Secret History* has prevented me from going too far along that path to dynamic equivalence – not to mention lingering uncertainty in a number of places over what certain phrases actually mean.

POETRY

Mongolian rhyme is head-rhymed, or alliterative: the syllables of the first word in each line have the same onset, as is also found later on in the first word after the caesura. One of the drivers of the tremendous richness of the *Secret History*'s vocabulary is the poetry, which relies very heavily on parallelism, that is, saying the same thing twice or thrice but slotting in different head-rhyming vocabulary in each line. This genre constraint drove much, although not all, of the Secret Historian's delight in obscure word choice.

As was discussed in the Introduction, the prevailing view up to now has been that poetry in the *Secret History* is primary and prose secondary; source-critical research shows that this is the opposite of the reality. The Secret Historian structured the history around vast verbatim quotations from sources that were almost purely prose, and only then added the verse. The verse thus adds little or nothing to the narrative, but is also some of the purest expression of the author's style, and crucial for making the author's larger points.

This translation attempts to create something poetic, in the sense of having a scannable metre, of the original verse and therefore employs, to the greatest extent possible, alliteration and similar wordplay in translations of the verse. The poetry of the *Secret History* can be divided into two broad types. In some cases, it is a matter of a couplet or two inserted into a speech or decree as a kind of proverbial expression. In many cases, such couplets can be found in other sources from the Mongol empire. Such probably proverbial poetry I have not set off as verse and have translated with a strong alliteration of several words in the line to make a memorable phrase: thus, for example, 'woman in every wagon and a damsel in every dray' to express the idea that in English would be carried by the phrase 'there are plenty more fish in the sea' (see §55).

There are also much longer poetic passages, sometimes put in the voice of the narrator, but more often in the voice of a character, which summarize the narrative situation in a lengthy descriptive passage. For these cases, I have set the verses off as separate lines, and in my translation followed a kind of Germanic-style alliteration, as seen in modern translations of *Beowulf* or skaldic poetry, based not on the first word but on two or three prominent words before and after the caesura. In any case, with the poetry, perforce, I have had to go for dynamic equivalence; many specific nuances have been changed, although I have aimed to keep the equivalence tight at a higher semantic level.

Appendix A: Alternative Mouse Year Theories and the Question of the *Secret History*'s Unity

In the Introduction, I set out the arguments for the 1252 date of the *Secret History*, arguments which presume that the *Secret History* was completed in substantially the same form we have it in now. A few other dates have been proposed. Some of these proposals likewise treat the text as a unity, with at most short, interpolated passages. Others, however, divide the *Secret History* into two or more strata of composition, treating a significant percentage of the text as a later addition to the original *Secret History*. The main alternative proposals are considered below, together with the reasons for rejecting them.

THE 1264 THEORY

William Hung proposed a date of 1264. This dating he based on certain minor features of the Chinese names given in §247, features which are, however, due to readings by the creators of the Hanlin recension in the 1380s, not original to the text. Later, Gari Ledyard pointed out that the campaign of Yisuder Qorci against Korea mentioned at the end of §274 actually took place in 1258; this too would speak for a date of 1264. However, it is likely that this passage is an interpolation; it is out of place chronologically and geographically; there were many campaigns against Korea, but the Secret Historian elsewhere mentions none of them. Under Qubilai Khan and his successors, who ruled from 1260 on, Korea became increasingly important in the world of the Mongol empire, and this passage is best read as one of the few, probably interpolated passages from the Qubilai era.

Another, more deeply embedded, passage possibly evidencing a post-1252 date is that relating to Chinggis Khan's sole surviving uncle, Dāritai. While the *Secret History* text in §§154 and 242 presumes that he was spared despite having sided with Ong Khan in 1203, Rashiduddin reports that he was executed and his family given to Chinggis

Khan's nephew Alcidai as 'slaves'. During Qubilai Khan's reign, how-
ever, around 1260–62, they distinguished themselves in battle for the
khan, and the family was restored to membership in the imperial fam-
ily (Rashiduddin/Thackston, p. 96; see also Funada). Eventually they
received a territorial appanage in far north-eastern Mongolia and a
revenue appanage in Ninghaizhou prefecture at the tip of the Shan-
dong peninsula (Funada).

It may be argued that the *Secret History*'s version would only have
been plausible after 1262, when Dāritai's family was restored to
imperial membership. But we know that Dāritai's family still main-
tained a corporate existence, despite being attached to the kingdom of
Alcidai in a subordinate position. Stories of their ancestors having
been really spared, intended to relieve their shame, would presumably
have begun to circulate as soon as a long enough interval had passed
after Dāritai's death to make the reality less clear. Even so, the pres-
ence of this passage may well be another case of an interpolation or
revision by the author of a Möngke-era draft to add in certain Qubilai-
era 'updates' on the status of the members of the imperial elite.

The main problem with positing a Qubilai Khan-era date for the
Secret History is that we know what kind of history of Chinggis Khan
was being written at Qubilai Khan's court and it is very different from
the *Secret History*. The 'Authentic Chronicle of Chinggis Khan', pre-
served in the Chinese of the *Campaigns of Chinggis Khan* and the
Persian of Rashiduddin's history of Chinggis Khan in the *Compendium
of Chronicles*, gives a very different, officially approved account of the
founding of the Mongol empire. The sharp contrast with the stories
and approaches taken by Mongolian-language history writers under
Qubilai Khan makes it clear that if Qubilai Khan-era writers did revise
the *Secret History*, any such revisions were sporadic and unsystematic,
and left the basic 1252 view of, for example, the Mongol empire's
foreign policy tasks untouched.

THE 1228 THEORY

By contrast to William Hung, Francis Woodman Cleaves and Igor de
Rachewiltz took a very different position and identified the Year of the
Mouse as 1228. The basis of this viewpoint is very simple: the *Secret
History* itself speaks of a great *quriltai* that takes place on the Kherlen
in the Year of the Mouse of 1228 – the *quriltai* that elected Ökodei as
khan. Since this *quriltai* is in the right place and at the right time, it
should be the one meant by the author in the colophon, they argue.

Although the viewpoint of two such great scholars of Middle Mongolian carried great weight, this viewpoint was problematic from the first and has become only more untenable with the expansion in our knowledge of the period.

Despite its simplicity, the first great problem with this theory is that while the Secret Historian mentions a 1228 Mouse Year *quriltai* that elected Ökodei as successor to Chinggis, every other source, without exception, makes it clear that Ökodei was elected at a great *quriltai* in the following Year of the Cow, or 1229. Moreover, the period from Chinggis Khan's death on 25 August 1227 to the election of his son and successor Ökodei on 13 September 1229 was a period of great uncertainty and caution, when any unauthorized activity was liable to be punished once the new khan was elected. Several sources say explicitly that the princes stayed at home in their own territories during the period between the three-month mourning for Chinggis Khan in the autumn of 1227 and the great *quriltai* of summer 1229. Thus, we can be quite sure that no one was completing any history in a 1228 Mouse Year great *quriltai*, because no such 1228 great *quriltai* ever occurred.

The second big problem is that this theory demands that much of the existing text must have been interpolated after the completion of the work. Such extensive interpolation is not in theory impossible, or even implausible; many chronicles have later entries by the author or by 'continuators' that post-date the stated date of composition.[1] In this particular case, however, such an assumption generates insoluble problems in understanding the text.

1. Such continuation is more typical in works that were composed in a genuine chronicle format, that is, which treat events in a year-by-year fashion, without any guiding organizational structure beyond that provided by the advance of years. Although it does have a few short year-by-year entries, overall the *Secret History* is very far from being such a year-by-year account. Instead it is grouped around key episodes, many covering more than one year, which are told in a way that often sacrifices exact chronology for narrative coherence.

2. Events that post-date 1228 in the *Secret History* do not just occur in the parts relevant to the reign of Ökodei. Even in the *Secret History*'s sections on Chinggis Khan there are numerous references to events that we know only took place under Ökodei. The reference cited above, to Yalavach becoming the chief overseer or *daruġaci* in Zhongdu (see

§263), which took place in 1241, is just one of many. If the work was finished in 1228, the author or a continuator did not just update the text with entries on later events but actually went back and rewrote the Chinggis Khan sections to make them include 'teasers' on later Ökodei-era events.

3. The Secret Historian's account of Chinggis Khan's reign contains not only references to specific events that took place under Ökodei, but also whole themes and concepts that look forward to Ökodei's reign and to Möngke Khan's seizure of power in 1251. Thus, a central episode in the *Secret History*'s account of Ökodei's reign is the death of his little brother Tolui and the widowing of his wife Sorġoqtani Beki as a sacrifice to save Ökodei Khan's reign. But the language in this episode is presaged by that used to describe the widowing of Alan the Fair and Mother Ö'elun, the death of literal or figurative brothers, Bekter and Jamuqa, and the quarrels over succession to the empire with Teb-Tenggeri and then among Chinggis Khan's sons. Could such pervasive and skilful foreshadowing really be the result of a later editor 'updating' the text? As another example, the treatment in the *Secret History* both of the final conquests of North China's Jin dynasty and of the 'eleven foreign folk' of eastern Europe is extremely idiosyncratic, differing from all other sources, yet consistent across the reigns of Chinggis and Ökodei. Did the later updater go back and massively change a previously mainstream text to reflect the scribe's own highly individual understanding of the history?

4. Finally, source criticism has shown that there are large chunks of the *Secret History*'s account of Chinggis Khan which derive from pre-existing sources, some of which, such as the biography of Jürcedei, the lengthy decree on the *kesikten* and the collection of three narratives known as the 'Indictment Narratives', are known to have been written under Ökodei.

For all these reasons, cutting the *Secret History* up into a main text composed in 1228 and a later continuation is untenable; the unity in theme and language is too clear to allow such a procedure.

Proponents of the 1228 date have attempted to bolster their case with arguments drawn from the current situation of the text in its two recensions, the Hanlin version and the *LAT* recension. The Hanlin recension, the version transcribed in the 1380s by sound into Chinese graphs with a word-by-word translation into the Chinese language, has two forms, one in twelve *juan* (or Chinese-style fascicles) and one in fifteen *juan*. The older twelve-*juan* edition designates the first ten *juan* as the main text and then the last two *juan* as 'additionally compiled fascicles' (Ch. *xuji juan*). The dividing point comes with §247, where Chinggis Khan's invasion of the Jin dynasty begins.

Others pointed to omissions in the *LAT* recension, the version of the *Secret History* that was incorporated into the seventeenth-century chronicle *Altan tobci* compiled by Lubsang-Danzin. This recension does not contain the section on the reign of Ökodei and also omits the part in §§254–5 that covers the succession debate. Those two parts, it was argued, represented the material added after the 1228 Mouse Year edition was completed, but which the *LAT* recension's base copy never added.

Neither of these arguments is convincing, however. First of all, there is the fact that they are inconsistent with each other – if there is a clear distinction of main text and continuation, the two recensions do not agree on where it is, with one putting it between §246 and §247 and the other between §268 and §269. Second, within the supposedly original parts of both the Hanlin and *LAT* recensions there are numerous passages which are flatly incompatible with any date before 1241 and are very hard to envision before 1251. Thus, we know for sure that the two recensions certainly have a common ancestor post-dating 1241, and probably 1251 as well.

In addressing the question of proposed divisions in the text, it is important to remember that neither the Hanlin recension nor the *LAT* recension preserves the original form of the *Secret History*. The Hanlin recension was transformed into a language textbook in a completely different script, and the *LAT* recension was incorporated centuries later piece by piece into a much larger work with a very different paper format. As a result, it is impossible to say exactly what, if anything, these divisions in their version of the *Secret History* text corresponded to in their original *Secret History* manuscript. How did the Hanlin recension's manuscript mark the section after §247 as being a continuation? It is impossible to say. It could well have been simply a decision by the Chinese transcribers based on a consideration of the contents. In any case, when the Hanlin recension was included in the 'Yongle Encyclopedia' a few decades later, it was redivided into fifteen *juan* without any reference to a division between main text and continuation. Similarly, the *LAT* recension contains numerous other omissions, unrelated to any posited later editing, some of them seeming to be mechanical oversights, others perhaps related to the sensitivity of the topic. Thus, in this case too, it is hard to tell the significance of any given omission. In short, neither witness offers us any convincing reason in the format for distinguishing a main text from a continuation.

Appendix B: Socio-political Organization of the Pre-Chinggisid Mongols

MOIETIES AND HOUSES OF THE MONGOLS

The *Secret History* organizes the various houses of the Mongols in the Onon-Kherlen and Hulun Buir steppes in a genealogy, a familiar method for the Mongols of conceptualizing political and social distance and closeness. The Persian historian Rashiduddin, writing in his *Compendium of Chronicles* around 1304, used lists and chapter divisions to organize his account of these houses, a method probably more immediately comprehensible to modern audiences. Below I have synthesized their data into a table. Rashiduddin divided his account of the aristocratic houses of the Mongolian plateau into three groups as follows:

- Those who were not originally called Mongols but who are now (after the unification under Chinggis Khan) called Mongols. This group includes Merkit, Tatars and Siberian forest peoples.
- Those who have monarchs and were not originally called Mongols, but who are similar to them in language and appearance. This group includes the Kereyit, Naiman, Öng'ut, Uyghur, Tangut and Yenisey Kirghiz kingdoms. (In fact, of these only the Kereyit and in part the Naiman were Mongolic-speaking. The rest were Turkic-speaking, except for the Tangut, who spoke a language very distantly related to Burmese.)
- Those who were originally called Mongols: this includes those houses found in the *Secret History*'s long genealogy, in addition to their marriage partners and subjects.

This third category he divides into two categories or moieties, which he calls either the *Niru'un* ('Backbone') and *Dürlugin* ('Ordinary')

Mongols, or else the Kiyan and Negus respectively. Of these two groups, the *Niru'un* or Kiyan were seen as the higher-status moiety from which the pre-Chinggisid rulers were drawn; only they are included in the *Secret History*'s genealogy. The *Dürlugin* or Negus were supposed to be the lower-status group, who could achieve power only by marrying into the *Niru'un* or Kiyan (see §§64–5 and 176), although in reality many of the *Dürlugin* houses were powerful players in the politics of the steppe.

The two sources are broadly consistent in their classification. Most groups are either clearly *Niru'un*/Kiyan or else clearly *Dürlugin*/Negus in both the *Secret History* and Rashiduddin. Others, however, are treated inconsistently either between or within the sources. The following table summarizes the information, while pointing out inconsistencies. At the top left is Chinggis Khan's own Borjigin. Below that in increasing order of social/genealogical distance are the other *Niru'un*/Kiyan houses. To the right are the *Dürlugin*/Negus houses given in Rashiduddin's order. In between are those whose status is ambiguous or treated differently in the two sources.

Niru'un or Kiyan moiety (in order of closeness to Yisukei's lineage)	Ambiguous or disputed status	*Dürlugin* or Negus moiety
Borjigin		Uriyangqan* – under Kiyat
Kiyat		Qonggirat†
Cangśi'ut		Ikires†
Yörkin		Olqunu'ut†
Tayici'ut		Qaranu'ut
Hartagin[1]		Qongli'ut
Cinoas		Gorulas†
(Besut)* – under Tayici'ut		Eljigit
Noyagin	Oronar~Ornat[2]	Hü'uśin* – under Yörkin
Barulas	Qongqotan†	Suldus* – under Tayici'ut
Buda'at	Arlat†	Ildurkin
Adarkin	Kilinggut*	Baya'ut* – under Cangśi'ut

Uru'ut	*Nünjin*[3]	
Manġġut	*Keniges~Keniget*†[4]	
(Siju'ut[5]) – under Tayici'ut	<u>Sö'eken</u>[6]	
(Doġulat)	<u>Kinggiyat (Qingqiyat)</u>	
(Je'uriyet)		
(Jadaran/Jajirat)		
Ba'arin		
Suqai'ut		
Menen Ba'arin		
Salji'ut	*Sönit*†	Jalayir* – under Borjigin, Yörkin
Qatagin	*Qabturġas*	
Belgunut		Tarġut* – under Tayici'ut
Bügunut		Saġayit†
Dörben		

(Besut): Clan names in parentheses given as of dubious paternity in the *Secret History*, but treated by Rashiduddin as legitimately *Niru'un*/Kiyan.

*All or most of this surname are known to be subjects or servants of the *Niru'un/Kiyan* lineages.

†*Dürlugin* or Negus lineages known to be autonomous, 'wife-giving', lineages among the Mongols.

Italics: Treated in *Secret History* genealogy as part of Borjigin but listed by Rashiduddin either as *Dürlugin*/Negus or as not part of the original Mongols at all.

<u>Underlined</u>: Listed by Rashiduddin as *Niru'un*, but not included in the *Secret History* genealogy.

THE THIRTEEN WAGON-FORTS OF TEMUJIN'S FIRST BATTLE WITH JAMUQA

Another view of the social structure of the original Mongols is provided by the order of battle in Chinggis Khan's battle with Jamuqa. The first battle of Chinggis Khan and Jamuqa described in §§128–30 was known as the Battle of the Thirteen Wagon-Forts. The 'Authentic Chronicle of Chinggis Khan', compiled under Qubilai Khan, contained a complete order of battle for Chinggis Khan's side, preserved in Chinese translation in the *Campaigns of Chinggis Khan* and in Persian translations in the *Compendium of Chronicles*. Despite certain differences, comparison of the two enables the original to be accurately reconstructed. The order of battle is given as a sequence of wagon-forts (Mongolian *küre'en*; Persian *kūrān*), translated into Chinese as *yi* or 'wings' (of a battle formation). Despite some slight discrepancies in spellings, most of these persons can be identified with those who appear in the *Secret History*.

1. Mother Ö'elun and Chinggis Khan's older and younger brothers were one wagon-fort;
2. Sam-Qaculai's son Bultacu Ba'atur with Muqur-Qauran of the Tübügesüt and others commanding the Adarkin and Caġurqan's Ġorulas folk were one wagon-fort;
3. Sorġoqtu [*or* Sengkun] Noyan's sons Derengkei and Qoridai and the Buda'at were one wagon-fort;[7]
4. Sorġatu-Yörki's sons Sece Beki and Taicu commanding the Jalayir *Aqa* [seniors] folk was one wagon-fort;
5. Uġucu's sons Ġodu and Ardanggi were one wagon-fort;[8]
6. Mönggedu Kiyan's boys, the Cangśi'ut and the Baya'ut of Önggur were one wagon-fort;
7. Dāritai and Qocar, together with the Doġulan, Negus, Qorġan, Saġayit and Nünjin folk formed one wagon-fort;
8. Qutuqtu-Möngner's son Möngge-Kejiger was one wagon-fort;
9. Qutula Khan's son Coci Khan was one wagon-fort;
10. Altan was one wagon-fort;
11. Qulan and Töde'en were one wagon-fort;
12. Tagi Ba'atur of the Kinggiyat commanded the Sö'eken *Jala'u*s [juniors] as one wagon-fort;
13. The folk of Gendu-Cina and Ölekcin-Cina were one wagon-fort.

Appendix C: The New Aristocracy under Chinggis Khan

THE COMMONER (*QARACU*) COMMANDERS

The four 'steeds' (*külug*, *külu'ut*) – §163

Name	House
Bo'orcu	Arlat
Muqali	Jalayir
Boroġul	Hü'uśin
Cila'un	Suldus

The four councillors – §§210, 216

Name	House
Old Man Üsun	Menen Ba'arin
Ġunan	Keniges
Köke-Cos	Menen Ba'arin
Degei	Besut

The four dogs – §§195, 209

Name	House
Qubilai	Barulas
Jelme	Uriyangqan
Jebe	Besut
Sübe'edei	Uriyangqan

Immune up to nine offences – §§203, 205, 211, 214, 219

Name	House
(Śiki) Qutuġu	Tatar
Bo'orcu	Arlat
Muqali	Jalayir
Jelme	Uriyangqan
Boroġul	Hü'uśin
Sorġan-Śira, Cila'un, Cimbai	Suldus

The four foundlings – §§138, 214

Name	House
Kücu	Merkit
Kökecu	Besut
(Śiki) Qutuġu	Tatar
Boroġul	Hü'uśin

Chief judge (*jarġu*) and scribe – §203

Name	House
(Śiki) Qutuġu	Tatar

Seated at the khan's right
hand – §204

Name	House
Father Mönglik	Qongqotan

Guyang ('Prince of State') – §206

Name	House
Muqali	Jalayir

Presides over army affairs – §209

Name	House
Qubilai	Barulas

Beki (senior priest and
shaman) – §216

Name	House
Üsun	Menen Ba'arin

Received endowment for
orphans – §§217, 218

Name	House
Quyildar	Manggut
Slim To'oril	Negus

Darqat (i.e. those granted special
freedoms for distinguished
service) – §219

Name	House
Sorgan-Šira, Cila'un, Cimbai	Suldus
Badai, Kišiliq	Oronar

The wing commanders – §§205, 206, 220

Name	Position	House
Bo'orcu	right	Arlat
Muqali	left	Jalayir
Naya'a	centre	'Naked' Ba'arin

Captains of units larger than a
thousand – §§202, 207, 208, 210

Name	Unit Size	House
Qorci	10,000	Menen Ba'arin
Gunan	10,000	Keniges
Ala-Quš Digit-Quri	5,000	Öng'ut
Jürcedei	4,000	Uru'ut
Alci	3,000	Bosqur Qonggirat
Botu	2,000	Ikires

Special captains of thousands –
§§212, 221–3

Name	House	Comment
Tolun & Toruqan	Qongqotan	shared command (son & father)
Jebe	Besut	captured subjects
Sübe'edei	Uriyangqan	captured subjects
Degei	Besut	unregistered subjects
Kücugur & Mulqalqu	Besut & Jadaran	shared command

THE IMPERIAL FAMILY

Princes of the centre and right hand
(Chinggis Khan's sons) – §§242, 243

Name	Troops (*Secret History*)	Troops (Rashiduddin)
Joci	9,000	4,000
Caġadai	8,000	4,000
Ökodei	5,000	4,000
Tolui	5,000	–*
Kölgen**	–	4,000

*Rashiduddin claims that Tolui as the youngest son (*otcigin*) received no inheritance in life, but inherited all the undistributed households upon his father's death.

†Chinggis Khan's son by Lady Qulan

Princes of the left hand (Chinggis Khan's younger brothers) – §§242, 243

Name	Troops (*Secret History*)	Troops (Rashiduddin & *Yuanshi*)
Temuke Otcigin	10,000	5,000
Qasar	4,000*	1,000
Alcidai (son of Qaci'un)	2,000	3,000
Belgutei	1,500	3,000**

*Qasar's share later reduced to 1,400

†Figure from *Yuanshi*

Chinggis Khan's mother – §242

Name	Troops (*Secret History*)	Troops (Rashiduddin)
Mother Ö'elun	10,000 (shared with Otcigin)	3,000

Captains of thousands assigned to imperial family members – §243

1) To Joci

Name (*Secret History*)	Name (Rashiduddin)	House
Ġunan	Ġunan	Keniges
Mönggu'ur	Mönggu'ur	Siju'ut
Kete	–	–
	Hü'uśidei Baiqu	Hü'uśin

2) To Caġadai

Name (*Secret History*)	Name (Rashiduddin)	House
Qaracar	Baruladai Qaracar	Barulas
Möngke	Müge Noyan	Jalayir
Idoġadai	–	–
Köke-Cos	–	Menen Ba'arin

3) To Ökodei

Name (*Secret History*)	Name (Rashiduddin)	House
Ilugei	Ilugei	Jalayir
–	Elig-To'a	Tamġaliq Suldus
–	Dayir	Qongqotan
Degei	Degei	Besut

4) To Tolui

Name (*Secret History*)	Name (Rashiduddin)	House
Jedei	–	Manġġut
Bala	–	Jalayir

5) To Mother Ö'elun & Otcigin

Name (*Secret History*)	House
Kücu	Merkit
Kökecu	Besut
Jungšoi	Noyagin
Qorġasun	–

Rashiduddin lists the Oronar, Besut and Jadaran among the folk of Temuke Otcigin and the Ġorulas and Olqunu'ut houses among the folk of Mother Ö'elun.

6) To Qasar

Name (*Secret History*)	House
Jebke	Jalayir

7) To Alcidai

Name (*Secret History*)	House
Ca'urqai	–

Rashiduddin lists folk of the Naiman, Uriyangqat and Tatar houses being in Alcidai's entourage.

Imperial sons-in-law (*küregen*) §§202, 235, 238, 239

Name	House
Olar Küregen	Olqunu'ut
Buqa Küregen	Jedei Baya'ut
Aśiq Küregen	–
Qatai Küregen	Bosqur Qonggirat
Ciku Küregen	Qonggirat
Alci Noyan	Bosqur Qonggirat
Botu Küregen	Ikires
Ala-Quš Digit-Quri	Öng'ut
Arslan Khan	Qarluq
Törolci Küregen	Oyirat
Inalci	Oyirat
Ïduqut	Uyghur

THE IMPERIAL HOUSEHOLD
AND BODYGUARD (KEŚIKTEN)

Chamberlains (Cerbi) – §191

Name	House
Dödei	Sönit*
Doqolqu	Manggut (~Arlat)**
Ögelei	Arlat (~Sönit)**
Tolun	Qongqotan
Bucaran	–
Söiketu	Qongqotan

* Rybatzki, p. 344.

†Rashiduddin says Doqolqu was of the Arlat and
Ögelei of the Sönit house.

Stewards (Ba'urci) – §213

Name	Wing	House
Önggur	right	Baya'ut
Boroġul	left	Hü'uśin

Organization of bodyguard (*keśikten*) under Chinggis Khan –
§§225, 226, 227, 234

Role	Officer	House (senior relative)	Number	Camping position
Nightguards	Big (Yeke) Ne'urin	Jalayir	1,000	centre (?)
Quiver-bearers	Yisun-Tö'e	Uriyangqan (Jelme)	400	right
	Bükidei	(Tüge)	200	right
	Horqudaq	–	200	right (?)
	Lablaqa	–	200	right (?)
Dayguards	Ögelei Cerbi	Arlat (Bo'orcu)	1,000	right
	Buqa	Jalayir (Muqali)	1,000	left
	Alcidai	Jalayir (Qada'an)	1,000	right
	Dödei Cerbi	Sönit	1,000	left
	Doqolqu Cerbi	Manggut (Jedei)	1,000	left
	Canai	Uru'ut (Jürcedei)	1,000	left
	Aqudai	Qonggirat (Alci)	1,000	right
Dayguard-*ba'atur*	Arqai-Qasar	Jalayir	1,000	front

Bold: Shift captains of the guards

This chart presents the *Secret History*'s account of the organization of the *keśikten* under Chinggis Khan. It should be remembered, however, that this account is probably a synthetic one, generated by taking an Ökodei-era document and then replacing some of the names with those which the Secret Historian knew to have been in the *keśikten* under Chinggis Khan.

Organization of bodyguard (*kešikten*) under Ökodei – §278

Role	Officer	House (ancestor)	Number	Camping position
Supervisor	Eljigidei	Tamġaliq Suldus		
Nightguards	Qada'an	Sönit	1,000	
	Qada'an, Bulġadar	–		left
	Amal, Canai	–		left
	Qadai, Qori-Qacar	–		right
	Yalbaq, Qara'udar	–		right
Quiver-Bearers	Yisun-Tö'e	Uriyanggan (Jelme)	400	right
	Bükidei	(Tiige)	200	right
	Horqudaq	–	200	right (?)
	Lablaqa	–	200	right (?)
Dayguards	?Ögelei Cerbi	Arlat (Bo'orcu)	1,000	right
	?Buqa	Jalayir (Muqali)	1,000	left
	Alcidai, Qongqortai	Jalayir (Qada'an), n.a. –	1,000	right
	Temuder, Yeku	–	1,000	left
	Mangġudai	–	1,000	left
	?Canai	Uru'ut (Jürcedei)	1,000	left
	?Aqudai	Qonggirat (Alci)	1,000	right
Dayguard-*ba'atur*	–			

This chart presents the *Secret History*'s account of the organization of the *kešikten* under Ökodei Khan, together with some speculative restorations (marked by ?) of certain names which from internal evidence of the *Secret History* or other sources appear to have been in the *kešikten* under Ökodei Khan.

Appendix D: Chronologies of the Foreign Conquests

CONQUESTS OF THE JURCHEN JIN AND TANGUT XIA DYNASTIES, 1205–34

Early campaigns against the Tangut Xia kingdom (Hexi)

1205: first campaign against the Tangut kingdom.

1207, autumn: second campaign begins.

1207–8, winter: Oroqai (Uraqai) city taken.

1208, spring: return from Tangut kingdom.

1209, April–May: Mongol armies advance and capture Oroqai (Uraqai) again.

1209, August: Mongol armies besiege Tangut capital of Eriġaya (Zhongxing).

1210, January: Tangut ruler makes peace, paying tribute and presenting a princess, given the Mongolian name Caqa, to Chinggis Khan.

First campaign against the Jurchen Jin empire and the Golden Khan

1211, September: Mongol armies cross 'Fox Pass' or Yehu Ridge and decisively defeat a large Jin dynasty army at Huihebu.

1211, October–November: Mongol armies under Jebe advance to the 'Canyon' or Juyong Pass; the defenders flee, Mongol armies pass through Juyong Pass and camp around Zhongdu for the first time.

1212, February: hearing news of large Jin armies arriving, Mongol armies retreat back through Juyong Pass and take Fuzhou and other prefectural seats north of the pass. A large Jin army advances in pursuit, Mongol armies defeat it a second time at Huanrzui.

Second campaign against the
Jurchen Jin empire and the Golden Khan

1212, October: Mongol armies advance through Yehu Ridge a second time. Tolui and imperial son-in-law Ciku take Xuandezhou a second time, and are first up the walls at Dexingfu. Meanwhile, Chinggis Khan is hit by an arrow at Xijing (present-day Datong) and the campaign is called off prematurely.

1213, 5 January: Jebe uses the feigned retreat stratagem to capture Dongjing (Tungging) city.

Third campaign against the
Jurchen Jin empire and the Golden Khan

1213, August–September: Mongol armies advance through Yehu Ridge a third time and take Xuandezhou and Dexingfu. Jin field armies defeated again at Huailai, but Mongol armies unable to take the well-fortified Juyong Pass.

1213, October–November: Mongol armies successfully detour through Zijing Pass, reach the North China plain, and then attack Juyong Pass from in front and behind.

1213, December onwards: Mongol armies fan out to sack the cities of North China. Jin court begins internal discussions on how to make peace.

1213, December–1214, May: Mongol armies in three columns sack cities in Hebei, Shandong, Shanxi and Manchuria. Joci, Caġadai and Ökodei campaign in western Hebei and Shanxi; Chinggis Khan campaigns in central Hebei and Shandong with Tolui and Muqali; Qasar and Jürcedei campaign along the coast in north-eastern Hebei before turning north through Manchuria up into Mongolia.

1214, March–April: Chinggis Khan returns to Zhongdu, begins siege of city. Famine in the city and pestilence among the besieging armies.

1214, 31 March–30 April: peace negotiated between Chinggis Khan and Jin emperor.

1214, 6 May: the Jin emperor (Golden Khan) agrees to terms, including sending a princess to Chinggis Khan.

1214, May: Wongian Fuking (Mongolian *Ongging Cingsang*) escorts the princess (gongzhu) Yaliqai to Chinggis Khan's camp, and accompanies Chinggis Khan's retreat through Juyong Pass and as far as Maoryuzni Spur.

1214, 27 June: the Jin emperor leaves the capital of Zhongdu for Namging (Kaifengfu) in Henan, south of the Yellow River. Chinggis Khan treats this move as abrogating the peace treaty. Revolts then break out throughout the Jin empire.

Further campaigns against the Jin empire

1214, November–1215, January: Mongol forces link up with Kitan rebels to begin operations against the Jurchen Jin around Zhongdu.

1215, 17 February: strategic city of Tongzhou near Zhongdu surrenders to the Mongols, siege of Zhongdu begins.

1215, 31 May: Zhongdu falls to the Mongol forces. Jin treasuries sealed and delivered to Chinggis Khan at his camp in Inner Mongolia.

1215, November: Jurchen commander Wu'anu rebels against the Jin and establishes his own independent regime in Manchuria.

1217, September: Chinggis Khan titles Muqali as the *Guyang* ('Prince of State') and *Taiši* ('Grand Preceptor'), giving him command of all Mongolian and non-Mongolian forces in North China to complete the conquest of the Jurchen Jin dynasty, which is now based in Henan.

1223, April: Muqali dies with the conquest of North China incomplete.

Final campaign against the Tangut Xia

1226, February–March: Mongol armies advance against the Tangut kingdom; Izina city captured.

1226, 29 November: Chinggis Khan lays siege to Döršegei (Lingzhou).

1226, 4 December: Chinggis Khan defeats a relief column near Döršegei.

1227, January–February: Chinggis Khan leaves army behind to besiege the Tangut capital Eriġaya and heads south-west.

1227, February–May: Chinggis Khan campaigns along the Tangut Xia kingdom's borders with the Tibetan plateau and the Jin dynasty territory.

1227, July–August: Tangut emperor surrenders to Chinggis Khan.

1227, 25 August: Chinggis Khan passes away.

Final campaign against the
Jurchen Jin and the Golden Khan

1230, January–February: while besieging Qingyangfu in Shaanxi, the Mongol commander Doqolqu is defeated at Dachangyuan by a Jin relief column commanded by Ila Puwa (Ila), Hû-Šire Yawuta (Qu the Hunchback) and 'Prairie Fire' Eke.

1230, August–September: Ökodei Khan decides to campaign with Tolui against the Jin personally.

1231, February: Mongol forces begin siege operations in Shaanxi; Ila Puwa and Wongian Hada (Qada) adopt a scorched earth policy and move all Jin forces behind Tongguan Pass to protect the Jin dynasty's final redoubt of Henan.

1231, June: stymied by Ila Puwa and Wongian Hada's defence at Tongguan, Ökodei and Tolui devise a new plan to swing through Song dynasty territory and attack the Jin dynasty's final redoubt of Henan from the south. Ökodei sends Jubqan as envoy to request permission for Mongol armies to cross through Song territory, but instead the Song border commander executes him. Tolui is assigned to cross through Song territory anyway with Küikunek Ba'atur as his vanguard commander. Meanwhile Ökodei's army is to cross the Yellow River and attack Henan from the north. Hû-Šire Yawuta (Qu the Hunchback) dies of disease.

1232, 10 January–29 January: Tolui, with Küikunek Ba'atur in the vanguard, crosses the Han River into Henan from the south and Ökodei crosses the Yellow River into Henan from the north.

1232, 8 February: Tolui destroys the last Jin field army at the Battle of Sanfeng Mountain; Ila Puwa and Wongian Hada are captured soon after and executed.

1232, April: Mongol armies begin to besiege Namging (Kaifengfu); Ökodei and Tolui entrust the siege to Sübe'edei, Küikunek and others, and return north. The Jin court sends out the emperor's nephew, Wongian Eke (Prince of Cao), as hostage to the Mongol court.

1232, May–June: Ökodei and Tolui reach Guanshan (Altan Ke'er or Golden steppe) in Inner Mongolia; there Wongian Eke is received by

Ökodei, enrolled in the *kešikten*, and granted the name Tenggeri. Siege of Namging continues.

1232, June–July: Ökodei has serious illness; Tolui participates in a shamanic ritual on his behalf.

1232, September–October: Tolui dies at Alaġa-Diz in Mongolia.

1233, 5 February: last Jin emperor escapes with armed escort from Namging, searching for place of refuge.

1233, 9 March–1 June: after negotiations, Mongol troops enter Namging; entire city population deported north to Hebei.

1233, July–August: last Jin emperor run to ground and besieged at Caizhou near the Song border.

1233, October: Mongol armies capture the Manchurian rebel Wu'anu and crush his regime.

1233, 7 December: Song forces join the Mongol forces besieging Caizhou.

1234, 9 February: Mongol and Song forces storm Caizhou; the last Jin emperor hangs himself. The Jin dynasty ends.

WESTERN EXPEDITIONS
TOWARDS KHWARAZM, BAGHDAD
AND EASTERN EUROPE, 1206–42

Campaigns against the fugitive Naiman and Merkit

1206: Küculug Khan of the Naiman and Toqto'a Beki of the Merkit flee north-west across the Irtysh River into western Siberia.

1208–9, winter: Küculug Khan and Toqto'a Beki's camp raided along the Irtysh; Toqto'a Beki killed, Küculug Khan flees to the Qara-Khitai.

1209: Küculug Khan granted refuge among Qara-Khitai. Toqto'a Beki's sons refused entry into the Uyghur kingdom, flee to Ölberli Qïpchaqs.

1210, August–September: Qara-Khitai defeated by Khwarazm at Talas (Taraz), Samarkand and Bukhara conquered by Khwarazm.

1211, autumn: Küculug Khan captures Qara-Khitai ruler and seizes Qara-Khitai throne.

1217: Joci dispatched with Sübe'edei Ba'atur against Merkit fugitives; Jebe dispatched against Küculug Khan.

1218: Jebe pursues Küculug Khan to Sariqol in the Pamirs where Küculug is killed.

1219, spring–summer: Joci's army destroys Merkit fugitives among Ölberli Qïpchaqs; on the way home, his army encounters and battles a Khwarazmian army at İrġiz in central Kazakhstan.

Conquest of Khwarazmian empire: opening and first campaign season

1219, spring–summer: Mongol trade mission to Khwarazm massacred at Otrar; Mongol envoys sent to demand justice also killed.

1219–20, winter: Chinggis Khan lays siege to and captures Otrar.

1220, 15 February: Chinggis Khan captures Bukhara.

1220, 17 March: Chinggis Khan captures Samarkand.

1220, summer: Chinggis Khan summers at the Khwarazmian sultan's summer residence.

Conquest of Khwarazmian empire: Jebe and company dispatched to the west

1220, May: Chinggis Khan dispatches Jebe, Sübe'edei Ba'atur and Toqucar to cross the Amu River in pursuit of the Khwarazmian Sultan Muhammad and reconnoitre the west.

1220: May–June: passing by Herat, Toqucar captures a fortress and plunders agricultural suburbs. Toqucar killed in the battle; Taġacar Küregen (a son-in-law of Chinggis Khan) and Ni'urkei Noyan take over his command. Herat's military governor Khan-Malik abandons Herat and moves south to Ghaznin in southern Afghanistan.

1220, late summer–autumn: Khwarazmian Sultan Muhammad dies on an island in the Caspian Sea; Chinggis Khan orders Jebe, Sübe'edei and Ni'urkei to continue reconnoitring west. Sultan Muhammad's son Jalaluddin Mengburni takes over resistance to Mongols and joins Khan-Malik in Ghaznin.

Conquest of Khwarazmian empire:
second campaign season

1220, autumn: Chinggis Khan dispatches Joci, Caġadai and Ökodei to capture Urgench, capital of Khwarazm; Chinggis Khan crosses the Amu River with Tolui.

1221, spring: Jalaluddin Mengburni and Khan-Malik gather forces in Ghaznin; Chinggis Khan dispatches Śiki Qutuġu to reconnoitre southern Afghanistan.

1221, 25–6 February: Tolui captures Merv.

1221, 7–10 April: Tolui captures Nishapur.

1221, April: Joci, Caġadai and Ökodci capture Urgench city.

1221, April–May: Tolui plunders south to Sistan and east to Chaghcharan, then lays siege to Herat, accepting surrender under terms. Tolui then rejoins Chinggis Khan at Taliqan in north-western Afghanistan.

1221, summer: Caġadai and Ökodei rejoin Chinggis Khan and Tolui at Taliqan, where they spend the summer.

Conquest of Khwarazmian empire:
third campaign season

1221, late summer–early autumn: Jalaluddin Mengburni and Khan-Malik defeat Śiki Qutuġu at Parvan in central Afghanistan. Chinggis Khan leaves his base camp (*a'uruq*) behind north of the Hindu Kush, crosses the Hindu Kush and advances on Ghaznin; Jalaluddin and Khan-Malik retreat to the Indus River.

1221, 25 November: Jalaluddin and Khan-Malik defeated at battle on the Indus River; Khan-Malik is killed, but Jalaluddin escapes by swimming across the river.

1221–2, winter: Jebe and Sübe'edei cross the Caucasus north into the steppe, attack the Ossetes first, then the Qïpchaqs.

1222, spring: Bala dispatched to find Jalaluddin, attacks Hindu *rana* (king) in the Salt Range.

1222, summer: Chinggis Khan summers at Parvan, where Bala returns to him.

Mop-up and further western campaigns

1222, June–August: Chinggis Khan suppresses a series of coordinated rebellions in the Afghanistan area as far as Badakhshan.

1222, September: Chinggis Khan crosses the Amu Darya north back into Central Asia, appoints overseers (*daruġacin*) there for the region north of the Amu River.

1223, 31 May: Sübe'edei defeats allied Ruthenian-Qïpchaq army at the Kalka River (south-east Ukraine); Jebe is killed in an earlier skirmish.

1223–4, winter: Mongol forces attack the Volga Bulgars before returning to rendezvous.

1223–4, winter: Chinggis Khan dispatches Dörbei the Fierce to strike out against Khwarazmian remnants from Azerbayjan in the north-west to India in the south-east, and capture Jalaluddin. Failing to capture Jalaluddin, Dörbei deserts instead and is taken into the Khwarazmian ranks.

Temporary retreat, reorganization and new expeditions

1225: Chinggis Khan returns to Mongolia.

1227–8, autumn–winter: unauthorized Mongol expedition against Khwarazmian remnants in western Iran.

1228, summer: Ökodei and Tolui agree to send Cormaqan to the west after Ökodei has been enthroned.

1229, September: during his *quriltai*, Ökodei Khan dispatches Kök-edei and Sönidei against Qïpchaqs and Bulgars, and Cormaqan against Jalaluddin in western Iran and the Caucasus area. Mönggedu is dispatched to reinforce Dayir Ba'atur and his *tamaci* (mixed-ethnic resident garrison) armies in Afghanistan.

1230, August: Cormaqan crosses the Amu River, eventually killing Jalaluddin and conquering western Iran, Azerbayjan, Armenia, Georgia, Kurdistan, the Seljuks of Rum (Anatolia); the caliph in Baghdad pays tribute.

Conquests of eastern Europe

1235, spring: Ökodei Khan dispatches the princes Batu, Güyük, Böri and Möngke with the commander Sübe'edei Ba'atur to subdue

Qïpchaq, Bulgar, Ossetian, Ruthenian and Hungarian peoples. Hoqo-tur is dispatched to reinforce the permanent garrison (*tamaci*) armies in Afghanistan, with a mandate to conquer Kashmir.

1236, autumn: Mongol armies sack Biler (Man-Kermen) city of the Volga Bulgars.

1237, spring: Möngke leads Mongol armies to seize main Qïpchaq leader Bachman on an island in the Volga delta.

1238, spring: after a long siege by Batu, armies under Böri and Qadan assist in sacking Kozel'sk.

1239, December: Möngke leads three-month siege, sacks Ossetian capital of Magas.

1240, 6 December: Mongol forces under Batu storm Kyiv (Man-Kermen).

1240–41, December–January: Güyuk and other princes move to return.

1241, 11 April: Mongol forces under Batu defeat the army of the Hungarian king at the Battle of Muhi.

Bibliography

EDITIONS, TRANSLATIONS AND REFERENCE WORKS ON THE *SECRET HISTORY*

Bayar (ed.). 1980. *Mongǧol-un niǧuča tobčiyan*. Höhhot: Inner Mongolia People's Press, 3 vols.

Choimaa, Sharawyn. 2002. *'Mongolyn nuuc towchoon'; Luwsandanzany 'Altan towch' exiin xaricuulsan sudalgaa*. Ulaanbaatar: Mongolian National University and the International Association of Mongol Studies.

Cleaves, Francis Woodman (trans.). 1982. *The Secret History of the Mongols*. Cambridge, Mass.: Harvard University Press.

Kahn, Paul (trans.). 1998. *The Secret History of the Mongols: The Origin of Chinghis Khan*, 2nd edn. Boston: Cheng & Tsui Co.

Kuribayashi Hitoshi. 2009. *'Genchō hishi' mongorugo kanji onyaku, bōyaku kango taishō goi*. Sendai: Tohoku University.

Mostaert, Antoine. 1953. *Sur quelques passages de l'*Histoire Secrète des Mongols. Cambridge, Mass.: Harvard-Yenching Institute.

Onon, Urgunge (trans.). 2001. *The Secret History of the Mongols: The Life and Times of Chinggis Khan*. Richmond, Surrey: Curzon.

Rachewiltz, Igor de. 1972. *Index to the Secret History of the Mongols*. Bloomington: Indiana University.

Rachewiltz, Igor de (trans. and ed.). 2004. *The Secret History of the Mongols: A Mongolian Epic Chronicle of the Thirteenth Century*. Leiden: E. J. Brill, 2 vols, continuous pagination.

Sarengaowa. 2013. *Xizang Ali diqu faxian Menggu wenxian sanye yanjiu*. Beijing: National Library Press.

Wulan [Ulaan]. 2012. *Yuanchao mishi (jiaokan ben)*. Beijing: Zhonghua shuju.

OTHER PRE-MODERN SOURCES

Atwood, Christopher P. 2017/18. 'The History of the Yuan, Chapter 1', *Mongolian Studies*, vol. 39, pp. 35–56.

Atwood, Christopher P. 2019/20. 'The History of the Yuan, Chapter 2, and the Biography of Tolui (from Chapter 115)', *Mongolian Studies*, vol. 40, pp. 2–45.

Atwood, Christopher P., with Lynn Struve. 2021. *The Rise of the Mongols: Five Chinese Sources*. Indianapolis: Hackett.

Buell, Paul D., and Eugene N. Anderson. 2010. *A Soup for the Qan*, 2nd edn. Leiden: Brill.

Cleaves, Francis Woodman. 1949. 'The Sino-Mongolian Inscription of 1362 in Memory of Prince Hindu', *Harvard Journal of Asiatic Studies*, vol. 12, no. 1/2, pp. 1–133.

Dawson, Christopher (ed.), and a nun of Stanbrook Abbey (trans.). 1955. *The Mongol Mission: Narratives and Letters of the Franciscan Missionaries in Mongolia and China in the Thirteenth and Fourteenth Centuries*. Reprint New York: AMS, n.d.

Dunnell, Ruth W., Stephen H. West and Shao-yun Yang (trans.). 2023. *The Travels of Qiu Chuji: A New Translation of the Record of the Perfected Changchun's Journey to the West* (Changchun zhenren xiyouji 長春真人西遊記). Oxford: Oxford University Press.

Gibb, H. A. R. (trans.). 1962. *The Travels of Ibn Baṭṭūṭa, A.D. 1325–1354*, vol. 2. Cambridge: Hakluyt Society.

Jackson, Peter, with David Morgan (trans. and ed.). (1990), 2009. *The Mission of Friar William of Rubruck: His Journey to the Court of the Great Khan Möngke, 1253–1255*. Reprint Indianapolis: Hackett Publishing.

Jinshi, comp. Tuotuo (Toqto'a) et al., ed. Yang Jialuo. 1975. Beijing: Zhonghua shuju, 8 vols.

Juvaini, 'Ala-ad-Din 'Ata-Malik, trans. John Andrew Boyle. 1958. *The History of the World-Conqueror*. Cambridge, Mass.: Harvard University Press, 2 vols.

[Jūzjānī], Minhāj-ud-Dīn, Abū-'Ūmar-i-'Uṣmān Siraj, trans. Major H. G. Raverty. (1881), 1995. *Ṭabaḳāt-i-Nāṣirī: A General History of the Muhammadan Dynasties of Asia, Including Hindustan; from A.H. 194 (810 A.D.) to A.H. 658 (1260 A.D.) and the Irruption of the Infidel Mughals into Islam*. Reprint Calcutta: Asiatic Society.

Khwandamir, trans. and ed. W. M. Thackston. 2012. *Habibu's-Siyar: The History of the Mongols and Genghis Khan*, 2nd edn. Classical

'Writings of the Medieval Islamic World: Persian Histories of the Mongol Dynasties, vol. 2. London: I.B. Tauris.

en-Nesawi, Mohammed, trans. O. Houdas. 1895. *Histoire du Sultan Djelal ed-Din Mankobirti*. Paris: Libraire de la Société asiatique.

Polo, Marco, trans. Nigel Cliff. 2015. *The Travels*. London: Penguin Books.

Qorin nigetu taiilburi toli, ed. Inner Mongolia Language, Literature and History Research Institute. 1977. Zhangjiakou: Inner Mongolia People's Press.

Rashiduddin Fazlullah, trans. and ed. W. M. Thackston. 2012. *Jami'u't-Tawarikh: Compendium of Chronicles (Tome I)*, 2nd edn. Classical Writings of the Medieval Islamic World: Persian Histories of the Mongol Dynasties, vol. 3. London: I.B. Tauris.

Ratchnevsky, Paul. 1985. *Un Code des Yuan*. Paris: Collège de France, 4 vols.

Sagang Sechen, trans. Johan Elverskog. 2023. *The Precious Summary: A History of the Mongols from Chinggis Khan to the Qing Dynasty*. New York: Columbia University Press.

Saghïmbay Orozbak uulu, trans. Daniel Prior. 2022. *The Memorial Feast for Kökötöy Khan: A Kirghiz Epic Poem in the Manas Tradition*. London: Penguin Classics.

Su Tianjue (comp.). 1996. *Yuanchao mingchen shilue*. Beijing: Zhonghua shuju.

Thackston, Wheeler M. (trans.). 2002. *The Baburnama: Memoirs of Babur, the Prince and Emperor*. New York: Random House.

Tekin, Talât. 1968. *A Grammar of Orkhon Turkic*. Bloomington: Indiana University Press.

Xiong Mengxiang, ed. Beijing Tushuguan Shanben zu. 1983. *Xijin zhi jieyii*. Beijing: Beijing Classics Publishing House.

Yuanshi, comp. Song Lian et al., ed. Yang Jialuo. 1976. Beijing: Zhonghua shuju, 15 vols.

MODERN BOOKS AND ARTICLES

Allsen, Thomas T. 1987. *Mongol Imperialism: The Policies of Grand Qan Möngke in China, Russia, and the Islamic Lands, 1251–1259*. Berkeley: University of California Press.

Allsen, Thomas T. 1997. *Commodity and Exchange in the Mongol Empire: A Cultural History of Islamic Textiles*. Cambridge: Cambridge University Press.

Allsen, Thomas T. 2001. *Culture and Conquest in Mongol Eurasia*. Cambridge: Cambridge University Press.

Allsen, Thomas T. 2019. *The Steppe and the Sea: Pearls in the Mongol Empire*. Philadelphia: University of Pennsylvania Press.

Andrews, Peter Alford. 1999. 'The Shrine Tents of Činggis Qan at Eǰen Qoroya', in *Antoine Mostaert (1881–1971): C.I.C.M. Missionary and Scholar*, vol. 1, ed. Klaus Sagaster, pp. 3–30. Leuven: Ferdinand Verbiest Foundation.

Atwood, Christopher P. 2007. 'The Date of the "Secret History of the Mongols" Reconsidered', *Journal of Song-Yuan Studies*, vol. 37, pp. 1–48.

Atwood, Christopher P. 2008/9. 'The Sacrificed Brother in the *Secret History of the Mongols*', *Mongolian Studies*, vol. 30/31, pp. 189–206.

Atwood, Christopher P. 2012. 'Six Pre-Chinggisid Genealogies in the Mongol Empire', *Archivum Eurasiae Medii Aevi*, vol. 19, pp. 5–57.

Atwood, Christopher P. 2014/15. 'Chikü *Küregen* and the Origins of the Xiningzhou Qonggirads', *Archivum Eurasiae Medii Aevi*, vol. 21, pp. 7–26.

Atwood, Christopher P. 2015(a). 'The Administrative Origins of Mongolia's "Tribal" Vocabulary', *Eurasia: Statum et Legem* (Ulan-Ude), vol. 1, no. 4, pp. 7–45.

Atwood, Christopher P. 2015(b). 'Alexander, Ja'a Gambo and the Origin of the Jamugha Figure in the *Secret History of the Mongols*', in *Proceedings of the International Conference on History and Culture of Central Eurasia*, ed. Terigün and Li Jinxiu, pp. 161–76. Höhhot: Inner Mongolia People's Press.

Atwood, Christopher P. 2015(c). 'Pu'a's Boast and Doqolqu's Death: Historiography of a Hidden Scandal in the Mongol Conquest of the Jin', *Journal of Song-Yuan Studies*, vol. 45, pp. 239–78.

Atwood, Christopher P. 2017(a). 'The Indictment of Ong Qa'an: The Earliest Reconstructable Mongolian Source on the Rise of Chinggis Khan', *Xiyu lishi yuan yanjiu jikan*, vol. 9, pp. 267–302.

Atwood, Christopher P. 2017(b). 'Jochi and the Early Western Campaigns', in *How Mongolia Matters: War, Law, and Society*, ed. Morris Rossabi, pp. 35–56. Leiden: Brill.

Atwood, Christopher P. 2021(a). 'Rashīd al-Dīn's Ghazanid Chronicle and Its Mongolian Sources', in *New Approaches to Ilkhanid History*, ed. Timothy May, Dashdondog Bayarsaikhan and Christopher P. Atwood, pp. 53–121. Leiden: Brill.

Atwood, Christopher P. 2021(b). 'Ila, Qada, and Qu the Hunchback: Three Jin Generals in Mongol Historiography', *Central Asiatic Journal*, vol. 64, pp. 133–53.

Auerbach, Erich, trans. Willard R. Trask. (1953), 2003. *Mimesis: The Representation of Reality in Western Literature*. Princeton: Princeton University Press.

Bakhtin, M. M., trans. Caryl Emerson and Michael Holquist. 1981. *The Dialogic Imagination: Four Essays*. Austin: University of Texas Press.

Birge, Bettine. 2017. *Marriage and the Law in the Age of Khubilai Khan: Cases from the Yuan dianzhang*. Cambridge, Mass.: Harvard University Press.

Birtalan, Ágnes. 2007/8. 'Rituals of Sworn Brotherhood (Mong. *anda bol-*, Oir. *and, ax düü bol-*) in Mongol Historic and Epic Tradition', *Chronica*, vol. 7/8, pp. 44–56.

Boldbaatar, Aldar owogt Yündenbatyn. 2008. *Mongol nutag dakhi ertnii nüüdelchdiin zadyn shütleg*. Ulaanbaatar.

Broadbridge, Anne F. 2018 *Women and the Making of the Mongol Empire*. Cambridge: Cambridge University Press.

Bruun, Ole. 2006. *Precious Steppe: Mongolian Nomadic Pastoralists in Pursuit of the Market*. Oxford: Lexington Books.

Chadwick, Nora K., and Victor Zhirmunsky. 1969. *Oral Epics of Central Asia*. Cambridge: Cambridge University Press.

Cleaves, Francis Woodman. 1956. 'Qabqanas~Qamqanas', *Harvard Journal of Asiatic Studies*, vol. 19, no. 3/4, pp. 390–406.

Dunnell, Ruth. 1992. 'The Hsia Origins of the Yüan Institution of Imperial Preceptor', *Asia Major*, 3rd Series, vol. 5, no. 1, pp. 85–111.

Eldengtei, Oyundalai, and Asaraltu, trans. Ardajab and Secengoo-a. 1991. '*Mongġol-un niġuca tobciyan'-u jarim üges-ün taiilburi*. Beijing: Ethnic Press.

Fornara, Charles William. 1983. *The Nature of History in Ancient Greece and Rome*. Berkeley: University of California Press.

Franke, Herbert. 1979. 'Some Folkloristic Data in the Dynastic History of the Chin (1115–1234)', in *Lore, Legend, and Religion in China*, ed. S. Allan and A. P. Cohen, pp. 135–53. San Francisco: Chinese Materials Center.

Fu, Yitao (Doran). 2013. 'A Tactic Study on Cleaves' Translation of *The Secret History of the Mongols*', MA thesis, Minzu University, Beijing.

Funada, Yoshiyuki. 2014. 'Mongoru jidai Kahoku chiiki shakai ni okeru meireibun to sono kokuseki no igi: Dāritai no katsudō to sono tōkaryō ni okeru Zenshinkyō no jigyō', *Tōyōshi kenkyū*, vol. 73, no. 1, pp. 35–66.

Hangin, John Gombojab, with J. R. Krueger, R. G. Service and Wm. V. Rozycki. 1988. 'Mongolian Folklore: A Representative Collection from the Oral Literary Tradition: Part Three', *Mongolian Studies*, vol. 11, pp. 47–110.

Hangin, John Gombojab, with Paul D. Buell, J. R. Krueger, R. G. Service and Wm. V. Rozycki. 1989. 'Mongolian Folklore: A Representative Collection from the Oral Literary Tradition: Part Four', *Mongolian Studies*, vol. 12, pp. 7–69.

Holeščák, Michal. 2018. 'Mongol Archery Equipment through the Prism of *The Secret History of the Mongols*', *Mongolica*, vol. 52, pp. 38–44.

Hsiao, Ch'i-ch'ing. 1978. *Military Establishment of the Yuan Dynasty*. Cambridge, Mass.: Harvard University Press.

Jagchid, Sechin, and Paul Hyer. 1979. *Mongolia's Culture and Society*. Boulder, Colo.: Westview Press.

Kara, György. 1990. 'Zhiyuan yiyu: Index alphabétique des mots mongols', *Acta Orientalia Academiae Scientiarum Hung.*, vol. 44, no. 3, pp. 279–344.

Kara, György. 1995. 'The Bush Protects the Little Bird', *Acta Orientalia Academiae Scientiarum Hung.*, vol. 48, no. 3, pp. 421–8.

Kesigtoġtaqu, C. 2013. '"Mongġol-un niġuca tobciyan"-daki "Yekes-e ġajaru inaru ġaruġsan-dur" gedeg ögülbüri-yin tuqai', in C. *Kesigtoġtaqu-yin ögülel-ün songġodaġ/The Collected Works of Heshigtogtahu/Hexigetaoketao wenji*, pp. 232–49. Hailar: Inner Mongolian Cultural Press.

Kuribayashi, Hitoshi. 2010. *Mōbun sōi: Mongorugo rōmaji tensha hairetsu*. Sendai: Tohoku University.

Lessing, Ferdinand D. (1960), 1982. *Mongolian–English Dictionary*. Corrected reprint. Bloomington, Ind.: Mongolia Society.

Ma, Xiaolin. 2018. 'The Eleven Queens' Qoš Ordos and the Imperial Ancestral Sacrifice under the Mongol-Yuan Dynasty', *Chronica: Annual of the Institute of History, University of Szeged, Hungary*, vol. 18, pp. 226–35.

Marchina, Charlotte. 2021. *Nomadic Pastoralism among the Mongol Herders: Multispecies and Spatial Ethnography in Mongolia and Transbaikalia*. Amsterdam: Amsterdam University Press.

Matsuda, Koichi. 2021. 'Comparing the Depictions of the Mongol Court Created in the Yuan and the Ilkhanate', in *New Approaches to Ilkhanid History*, ed. Timothy May, Dashdondog Bayarsaikhan and Christopher P. Atwood, pp. 176–97. Leiden: Brill.

Molnár, Ádám. 1994. *Weather-Magic in Inner Asia*. Bloomington: Indiana University Press.

Mostaert, Antoine. (1965), 2009. *Dictionnaire ordos*. Reprint Ulaanbaatar: New Polygraph.

Okada, Hidehiro. 1972. 'The *Secret History of the Mongols*: A Pseudo-Historical Novel', *Ajia-Afurika gengo bunka kenkyū*, vol. 5, pp. 61–7.

Ong, Walter J. 1982. *Orality and Literacy: The Technologizing of the Word*. London: Methuen.

Poppe, Nicholas. 1967. 'On Some Military Terms in the *Yüan-ch'ao pi-shih*', *Monumenta Serica*, vol. 26, pp. 506–17.

Pow, Stephen, and Jingjing Liao. 2018. 'Subutai: Sorting Fact from Fiction Surrounding the Mongol Empire's Greatest General (With Translations of Subutai's Two Biographies in the *Yuan Shi*)', *Journal of Chinese Military History*, vol. 7, pp. 37–76.

Ratchnevsky, Paul. 1993. 'Šigi Qutuqu', in *In the Service of the Khan: Eminent Personalities of the Early Mongol-Yüan Period (1200–1300)*, ed. Igor de Rachewiltz, Hok-lam Chan, Hsiao Ch'i-ch'ing and Peter W. Geier, with May Wang, pp. 75–94. Wiesbaden: Harrassowitz.

Róna-Tas, András. 1999. *Hungarians and Europe in the Early Middle Ages*. Budapest: CEU Press.

Rybatzki, Volker. 2006. *Die Personennamen und Titel der mittelmongolischen Dokumente: Eine lexikalische Untersuchung*. Publications of the Institute for Asian and African Studies no. 8. Helsinki: Helsinki University Press.

Saiinjirgal and Šaraldai. 1983. *Altan Ordon-u Taiilġ-a*. Beijing: Minzu Publishing House.

Schlesinger, Jonathan. 2017. *A World Trimmed with Fur: Wild Things, Pristine Places, and the Natural Fringes of Qing Rule*. Stanford, Cal.: Stanford University Press.

Schöning, Claus. 2006. 'Südsibirisch-türkische Entsprechungen von Völker- und Stammesnamen aus der Geheimen Geschichte der Mongolen', in *Exploring the Eastern Frontiers of Turkic*, ed. Marcel Erdal and Irina Nevskaya, pp. 211–42. Wiesbaden: Otto Harrassowitz.

Serruys, Henry. 1984. 'Cacir, Cacar, Cadr: Tent in Mongol', *Zentralasiatische Studien*, vol. 17, pp. 76–81.

Shea, Eiren L. 2020. *Mongol Court Dress, Identity Formation, and Global Exchange*. New York: Routledge.

Shea, Eiren L. 2021. 'Chinese Textiles in Mamluk Tombs: Maritime Trade and Cultural Exchange in the Fourteenth Century', in *The*

Seas and the Mobility of Islamic Art, ed. Radha Dalal, Sean Roberts and Jochen Sokoly, pp. 102–17. New Haven, Conn.: Yale University Press.

Shi, Jinbo, trans. Li Hansong. 2020. *Tangut Language and Manuscripts: An Introduction*. Leiden: Brill.

Shiraishi, Noriyuki. 2006. 'Avraga Site: The "Great Ordū" of Genghis Khan', in *Beyond the Legacy of Genghis Khan*, ed. Linda Komaroff, pp. 83–93. Leiden: Brill.

Shiraishi, Noriyuki. 2013. 'Searching for Genghis: Excavation of the Ruins at Avraga', in *Genghis Khan and the Mongol Empire*, ed. William W. Fitzhugh, Morris Rossabi and William Honeychurch, pp. 132–5. Washington: Arctic Studies Centre, Smithsonian Institution.

Sneath, David. 2007. *The Headless State: Aristocratic Orders, Kinship Society, and Misrepresentations of Nomadic Inner Asia*. New York: Columbia University Press.

Sommer, John L. 1996. *The Kyrgyz and Their Reed Screens*. Fremont, Cal.: John L. Sommer.

Street, John C. 1990. 'Nominal Plural Formations in the *Secret History*', *Acta Orientalia Academiae Scientiarum Hungaricae*, vol. 44, no. 3, pp. 345–79.

Weatherford, Jack. 2010. *The Secret History of the Mongol Queens: How the Daughters of Genghis Khan Rescued His Empire*. New York: Crown Publishers.

Zimonyi, István. 2021. 'The Great Town – Man Kermen in *The Secret History of the Mongols*', *Acta Orientalia Academiae Scientiarum Hungaricae*, vol. 74, pp. 145–57.

Notes

1: The Origin of Chinggis Khan

1. 'Grey Wolf' and 'Fallow Doe': Mongolian *Börte Cinoa* and *Ġoai Maral*. Much ink has been spilled on whether these are intended to be animal ancestors or humans with animal-sounding names. Certainly, ancestry myths involving wolf ancestors were part of the Central Eurasian imperial legend. But Rashiduddin, in his Persian history of the Mongol empire, written under the Mongols of the Middle East, wrote Grey Wolf's name as 'Börte Cinoa' and treated him as a person. My translation is intended to leave the ambiguity unresolved.

2. The sea here is usually taken to mean Lake Baikal, just north of the present-day Mongolian border in Siberia. Lake Baikal freezes solid in the winter and there are many accounts in more recent historical times of Buryat Mongol and Evenki (Tungusic) people migrating across it.

3. As is described in §103, this mountain was a sacred mountain in the Mongol empire. The name may be analysed as *burġan*, 'willow', and *qaldun,* 'craggy height'. As may be seen in §103, where the two names occur separately or in reversed order, the name combines the names of two different massifs to refer to a single mountain chain. These two are the Baga ('Lesser') Khentii and Ikh ('Greater') Khentii Mountains today, where the three rivers of Onon, Kherlen and Tuul take their origin (see §179).

4. 'Marksman': Mongolian *Mergen*.

5. His name means 'Big Eye'.

6. The phrase about Master Borjigin the Marksman being born at the headwaters of Botoġan Bo'orji was added from the *LAT* recension. This river is referenced again in §§106–9, indicating that the reference here likely was part of the original text.

7.   'Master Borjigin the Marksman' and 'Mistress Mongol the Fair': Mongolian *Borjigidai Mergen* and *Mongġoljin Ġowa*. It should be noted that 'fair' (*ġowa*) has the same two-fold meaning in Mongolian as in English, meaning both 'pale' and also 'beautiful'.

8.   'Young man' here is *jala'u*; given the context he is likely a servant in the household.

9.   'One-Eyed' is *soqor*. In Mongolian, *soqor* usually means 'blind', but it can also mean 'one-eyed'; traditional Chinese coins with a square hole in the centre are called *soqor*, for instance.

10.   Covered wagon (*qara'utai terge*) is glossed in Chinese as 'black-coloured wagon'. However, the sense of it in Mongolian appears to be not that the wagon is black-coloured, but that, being covered without a smoke hole, it is dark and shady inside.

11.   Deep Barguzin Hollow: Mongolian *Köl Barġujin Tökum*.

12.   This is the first of many puns that the Secret Historian uses to establish folk etymologies for Mongol surnames; 'banning each other' is *qorilalduju,* which sounds like the surname Qorilar. Surname or *oboq* refers to a family name inherited patrilineally; although it was not used in daily speech like a modern surname, it was usually well known for those of middle or high status. Those subject as slaves or bondsmen to others, however, often forgot their surnames or were known only by that of their rulers.

13.   Sets Up Willows is Mongolian *Burġan Bosġaqsan*. *Burġan* or *burġasu* is 'willow' in Mongolian (the Hanlin recension's gloss as 'elm' in §103 is contradicted elsewhere and likely wrong). Kitans, Jurchens and Mongols practised a ritual of 'shooting willows' associated with rain-making and divination (Franke, pp. 145–51). That practice and the use of 'lords' (*ejet*) suggests Sets Up Willows and Śinci the Rich should be understood as spirit-masters of the mountain. The term 'Uriyangqai' was a general Mongol word for native peoples of the north-west forests, indicating here the native people of the mountain.

14.   'Elk' or Mongolian *buġu* is the same as the North American elk or wapiti, *Cervus canadensis*. Traditionally, Mongolian *buġu* has been identified with the West Eurasian and North African *Cervus elaphus*, known in British English as the red deer. However, recent biological work has confirmed what is obvious at a glance: that *C. canadensis* and *C. elaphus* are different species and that the large deer of Siberia and northern Mongolia is identical to the North American elk (*C. canadensis*).

15. The common practice of taiga hunters was that hunted meat must be shared with anyone who passed by.

16. *Ger* is the Mongolian word for the yurt, a mobile dwelling made of felt covering a willow-wood lattice framework. Today, *gers* are collapsible and disassembled when nomadizing, but at this time most *gers* owned by the wealthy and powerful were non-collapsible and were moved on large wagons.

17. 'sheep from the winter provisions': Mongolian *köngsimel qonin* or *köngsimel*, sheep. In the Hanlin recension, the word *köngsimel* is glossed as 臘 in Chinese, which can be read as either *xī*, 'dried meat', or *là*, 'sacrifice of the twelfth moon'. The word is emended to *ügüce kögsimel* in the *LAT* recension, meaning 'old meat kept as winter provisions'. The meaning appears to be meat slaughtered early in the winter and kept frozen and dried as provisions into the spring of the new year. That the meat was offered in sacrifice is a possible implication as well.

18. The Mongolian here has the singular *inu*, 'his' or 'her', not the plural *anu*, 'their'. Perhaps this is an early example of the singular-plural distinction breaking down. Another possibility is that the story is being told particularly from the point of view of Bodoncar.

19. The phrase 'black-headed', like the *limin*, 'glossy-black commoners's of Chinese and the 'black-headed people' of Sumerian, derives from the view of people with black hair as seen from above, by a lord addressing them. The subordination is relative, not absolute; in §123, Chinggis Khan's uncles refer to their own 'coal-black heads' to indicate their submission to his orders.

20. The fable of the five arrow shafts (or sticks) is widely known; it appears in European tradition as an Aesop's Fable and among the Scythians. It also appears elsewhere in histories of the Mongol empire, although in different historical contexts. The Persian historian Juvaini, writing around the time of the *Secret History*, has Chinggis Khan give this object lesson of the arrows to his four sons at the beginning of his conquests (Juvaini/Boyle, pp. 41–2). Fifty years later, Rashiduddin repeats the story with the attribution to Chinggis Khan, but places it under the reign of Möngke Khan, who came to power by holding his brothers together and purging his cousins (Rashiduddin/Thackston, p. 290).

21. Female goshawks are rather larger than the male; the brown colour, as opposed to the grey of the adult, indicates this is a fledgling.

22. *Keru* describes the north-north-western side of mountain slopes, which in Mongolia are frequently wooded, while the southern slopes or *ölke* are drier and with grass cover.

23. *Esuk* was the Middle Mongolian name for what is today called in Mongolian *airag* or fermented mare's milk. It is called *qumiz* in Kazakh and other Turkic languages, whence the koumiss of European languages. It is produced by pouring mare's milk into a skin bag and then churning the bag with a plunger.

24. The first two syllables of Bu'atu-Salji's name are written here in both recensions as Buġu-. I have assumed this is a confusion with the 'Buġu' immediately above.

25. That is, his legitimate descendants from his married wife mentioned immediately below.

26. This is a sacrifice glossed as 'hanging meat on a pole to sacrifice to Heaven'.

27. Other sources refer to her as Mother Monolun.

28. Qaracar, a captain of a thousand from the Barulas house, joined Chinggis Khan's camp and was later assigned to Chinggis Khan's second son Caġadai as an adviser (see §§120, 243). Qaracar became the ancestor of Temur the Lame (1336–1405), known in Europe as 'Tamerlane', who displaced the descendants of Caġadai in Central Asia and built another empire stretching from Ankara and Damascus in the west to the borders of Muscovy in the north and Delhi in the south-east. He died while planning an invasion of China's Ming dynasty. His descendant, Prince Babur (1483–1530), was eventually driven out of Central Asia and founded the Mughal empire in India.

29. Literally 'from Caraqai Lingqu's *bergen*' or older brother's wife. The Mongols practised levirate marriage, by which junior men (sons, younger brothers and nephews) inherited the wives of their seniors (fathers, older brothers, uncles) upon the latter's death. (In the case of fathers, the son's own mother would be excluded of course.) Besudei's mother was thus originally Bai-Śingqor-Doqśin's wife, who had been inherited by his younger brother Caraqai Lingqu on Bai-Śingqor-Doqśin's death.

30. The Hanlin recension here has Sem-Secule; the *LAT* recension has Qam-Qacula. Comparison with the parallels in other historical sources shows that the name is Sam-Qacula; S and Q are written similarly in the Uygur-Mongolian script and are often confused.

31. 'The Authentic Chronicle of Chinggis Khan' records that in Chinggis Khan's first battle with Jamuqa (see §129), Bultacu Ba'atur

commanded a wagon-fort (*küre'en*) on behalf of Chinggis Khan. See Appendix B.

32. This sentence is found only in the *LAT* recension.

33. That is, 'the blessed one of the Yörkin'. *Qutuqtu* is Mongolian for 'blessed' and was often used as a euphemistic way to refer to those marred by smallpox scars. His name is given as Sorġatu-Yörki in §§122, 139; Sorġatu means literally 'pockmarked'.

34. The sentence about Madame Süjigil or Süjigil Üjin comes from the *LAT* recension and is not found in the Hanlin recension. The Tarġut were a family that was subject to the Tayici'ut house, so that the woman was genealogically a member of the commoner Tarġut but politically under the Tayici'ut.

35. This story will be told later.

36. He appears as Coci Khan in the list of the Thirteen Wagon-Forts fighting for Chinggis Khan in his first battle with Jamuqa (§129). See Appendix B.

37. Altan appears alongside Qocar as one of the two leaders who first helped enthrone Chinggis Khan. According to the list of the Thirteen Wagon-Forts cited in the 'Authentic Chronicle of Chinggis Khan', Altan and Qocar formed separate single wagon-forts in Chinggis Khan's first battle with Jamuqa (§129). See Appendix B.

38. This sentence is found only in the *LAT* recension.

39. A *darqan* by this time was a commoner who was exempted from taxes due to some special service to the ruler. The story of their service will be told later.

40. This term, *Qamuq Monġġol*, translated here as 'all the Mongols', is often taken in Mongolian scholarship to be a specific designation of the Mongol khanate.

41. Before the rise of Chinggis Khan, Tatar was the usual word that outsiders used for all the people of the Mongolian plateau. After his rise, however, the term was limited to the Mongolic-speaking people living mostly in what is now Inner Mongolia, and who served the Golden Khan or Jin dynasty ruler of China.

42. The Hulun and Buir lakes (Middle Mongolian *Kölen* and *Buyur*) define the area of the Hulun Buir steppe in north-eastern Inner Mongolia. It was and is a very lush grazing area, but was controlled at this time by the Tatar allies of the Jurchen dynasty's Golden Khan, then ruling in Zhongdu (present-day Beijing).

43. 'Chinese' here is *Kitat*, the Mongolian plural of the name 'Kitan'. The Kitans, based in Inner Mongolia, built the Liao dynasty that

ruled the present-day areas of Beijing and Datong as well as Manchuria and much of Mongolia. Over time, then, *Kitat* became the Mongolian term for North China and its inhabitants in general, most of whom were Han or ethnic Chinese. In the Turco-Persian form *Khitay*, it became the origin of Marco Polo's 'Cathay' and Russian *Kitay*, 'China'. It should be understood here that *Kitat* refers only to North China; South Chinese were referred to as *Nangqiyas*, a term that does not appear in the *Secret History*.

44. Rashiduddin mentions that the Golden Khan ordered, 'as was their custom, that [Hambaġai] be nailed to a wooden donkey until he died' (Rashiduddin/Thackston, pp. 32, 70, 93). The Jin rulers used the same method of execution, nailing to a wooden donkey with iron spikes, for Chinggis Khan's great-uncle Ökin-Barqaq and the ancestor of the Kereyit khan Marġuz Buyuruq Khan (Rashiduddin/Thackston, pp. 33, 44, 89). This form of execution was an escalation of the practice of humiliating those guilty of misconduct by parading them around the community on an unsaddled mount (*Yuanshi*, p. 2.33; Atwood 2019/20, p. 20). In the twentieth century, abusive officials would be placed on a gnarled wooden log, jocularly called an 'isabella horse', and so paraded about (Mostaert 2009 [1965], p. 160a, s.v. *duġ"ilaŋ*). If the offender's breeches were removed and he was handled roughly enough, rubbing the skin of his groin and thigh against the gnarled wood could be an exquisite torture. Nailing the offender to the log was merely the ultimate degree of punishment.

45. *Qubi* is defined in the Chinese as a dun horse. But *qubi* is evidently the feminine of *quba*, hence a mare.

46. The word translated as 'Madame' here, *üjin*, is of Chinese origin.

47. A valley or *jubur* seems to be a broad valley with lush grass and wooded slopes (it is the 'valley' in the 'wooded valley' phrase of §56 above).

48. *Saqlaġar* or 'bushy' (modern Mongolian *sagsgar*) is defined in the eighteenth-century Mongolian dictionary *Qorin nigetu taiilburi toli*: 'A tree whose branches and leaves are dense and grow down as ground cover is called *saqlaġar*' (p. 529b; cf. de Rachewiltz 2004, p. 317).

49. The ritual on this occasion was described in 1302 by the Mongol minister Bolad *Chengxiang* to Ghazan Khan of the Mongols of the Middle East: 'Qutula Qa'an, [Ghazan Khan's] forefather's

uncle, was the ruler of several tribes in his time, and he was so
heroic and manly that he had become proverbial for heroics and
much poetry had been composed about him. His voice had been
so loud and terrifying that it could be heard across seven hills.
One day it happened that he had mounted to do battle with the
Merkit. While on the road he came across a tree, dismounted,
and spoke to God, asking him for victory and swearing that, if
he triumphed over his enemy, he would make that tree a shrine
for himself and decorate it with pieces of coloured cloth. God
did give him victory over his enemy, and afterwards he returned
to the tree, which he decorated as he had sworn, in gratitude to
the creator. He and his soldiers danced beneath that tree, and
they stomped so hard that the area around the tree sank a yard
into the earth.' See Rashiduddin/Thackston, p. 456 (cf. p. 293).
Despite the Islamization of the terminology, the dedication of
trees and animals with coloured ribbons (*jalama*) is an old Cen-
tral Eurasian ritual practice. See §174.

50. The following story centres on the theme of the *quda* relation.
Quda is a term that men from lineages related by marriage
would call each other (women from such lineages call each other
qudaġai). Presumably Yisukei wished to renew this tie with
Temujin's mother's family, despite the violence of their marriage.
But in the end he was induced to form this tie instead with the
family of Deyi Secen of the Qonggirat. During the Mongol
empire, the Mongol khans entertained such relations above all
with the family of Deyi Secen and his son Alci Noyan.

51. Deyi Secen lived near the border with the Jin dynasty; his name
Deyi appears to be a Mongolization of the Chinese *de*, 'virtue'.
Secen is glossed as 'intelligent'.

52. Deyi Secen addresses Yisukei as a (potential) *quda* or man allied
to him by marriage.

53. The *sülder* is the personalized supernatural spirit that guards the
heavenly-destined, much like the *genius* of a family or ruler in its
original Latin sense. In modern Mongolian, as *süld*, it is often
embodied in a concrete form as a banner or standard represent-
ing the majesty of Chinggis Khan or the state. See §201.

54. As Hidehiro Okada has noted, this picture of the Qonggirat as
pacific and uninterested in contending for power is anachronis-
tic. In fact, up until Chinggis Khan's unification of Mongolia, the
Qonggirat were active players in power politics. But with the
unification, the Qonggirat acquired their identity as the classic

quda or marriage-ally people. In 1227, Chinggis Khan's sons entitled Alci Noyan (Börte's brother) as the 'dynastic maternal uncle' and in 1237, they issued a decree: 'A girl born of the Qonggirat surname will be made an empress in each generation; a boy born of them will be granted a princess in each generation. Four times a year, in the first month of the season, there shall be a reading aloud in session of this decree with which they have been favoured; to the seed of the seed, this shall not cease' (*Yuanshi,* p. 118.2915). It is quite possible that the poem here was composed for just such a ritual occasion. Note the references to not disputing the 'kingdom' (*ulus*) and the 'nation' (*ulus irgen*), which would fit better the context of the Mongol empire. Historically, however, Deyi Secen's people were not the main body of Qonggirat but a side branch, the Bosqur. Chinggis Khan placed Alci Noyan over the main Qonggirat only when a projected marriage alliance with the main body of Qonggirat under their commander Dergei Amal failed. The Qonggirat leadership was then transferred to the more supportive Bosqur commander Alci Noyan. See Atwood 2014/15.

55. 'To place as a son-in-law' (*küregete talbi-*) was to have a boy work for and be trained by his future father-in-law, often with the idea of replacing the bridewealth payment by the groom's family. But as here, it was also seen as a method of training a child more strictly, away from the overindulgent care of his parents.

56. Reading here *oyisulaldun*, 'to plot; conspire against', with Ulaan's text, and *gujirlaju* with de Rachewiltz as a back version of *güjirle-*, attested in Ordos dialect as 'to do violence to someone'.

57. The reference to 'your widowed sister-in-law' (*belbisun bergeniyen*) shows that Yisukei is treating Mönglik like his younger brother. (*Bergen* means elder brother's wife.) By the Mongol custom of levirate, the younger brother would then be expected to marry his elder brother's widow as part of his practice of taking care of her. And indeed, although it is not mentioned in the *Secret History*, Mönglik did eventually marry Ö'elun, although exactly when is unclear. For that reason he is later referred to as 'Father Mönglik'.

58. Mongolian *qatut* (singular *qatun*) refers to high-born married women of various ranks from empress to the wife of a petty nobleman. I have thus translated it as 'lady'.

59. 'Ancestors' here is literally 'great ones' (*yekes*). This ritual of burnt offering is glossed in Chinese as 'sacrifice to the ancestors'

and as 'sacrificing burnt food in the ground'. This custom of burning food offerings to the deceased has ancient roots among Mongolic-speaking peoples and is well attested as part of the funerary customs of the Mongol emperors in China; see Kesigtoǧtaqu. The 'burnt offering' is actually not in the text, although it was added into the Chinese gloss. Kesigtoǧtaqu thought that the verb *tülešileget*, 'to make a burnt offering', must have been accidentally omitted from the Mongolian text, but I follow de Rachewiltz in seeing *ǧajaru inaru*, literally 'To this ground, to here', as being the opening phrase of the invocation offered with the burnt offering, which gave its name to the whole ritual, just as the initial words of the Christian Lord's Prayer, 'Our Father', gave their name to the prayer as a whole.

60. Sacrificial meat is *bile'ur*, glossed in Chinese as 'left-over sacrificial meat', and 'liquor' is *sarqut*. *Sarqut* is also glossed as sacrificial meat, but this must be a mistake as the term is well attested in later Mongolian sacrificial vocabulary as the term for liquor offered to the ancestors or deities. To consume them was to participate in the blessing or favour (*kešik*) of the ancestors, embodied in the meat and drink, and was a mark of full membership in the community.

61. The reference to 'women' is the first hint that Ö'elun was not Yisukei's only lady, that he had another wife, and children by her, who were Temujin's half-brothers. There was also at least one servant woman in the camp.

2: The Youth of Chinggis Khan

1. The *boqta* or *boqtaq* was a high and elaborate hat worn by married Mongol women. It was admired by virtually all the visitors to the Mongol court, even those otherwise quite hostile, and is sometimes thought to have inspired the hennin of European ladies of the fifteenth century.

2. Bekter and Belgutei are introduced for the first time here; they were Yisukei's sons by his other wife who, as will be seen later, was also in the camp together with Ö'elun and her sons.

3. Here I follow de Rachewiltz in inserting the *bütugei*, 'stop' (literally 'don't'), from the *LAT* recension.

4. A *ǧodoli* was an arrow with an ellipsoid head and often with holes in it that whistled when fired. Since it did not have a sharp point it would stun, rather than cut, and hence was appropriate

for small animals which might be mutilated beyond use by a full-fledged arrow. Here the verb form *ġodoliduqsan*, literally 'hit with a *ġodoli*', is used.

5. Isabelline (Mongolian *širġa*) is one of the many Mongolian terms designating subtle differences in horse pelages or colours.

6. Hearth or *ġolumta* was the symbol of the lineage or family. Here it is doubly significant because in Mongol polygamy each wife kept her own hearth. The 'hearth' here then is a reference to the children of the nameless other wife of Yisukei Ba'atur.

7. Dhole or *cö'eburi* refers to the Asiatic wild dog (*Cuon alpinus*).

8. From the beginning, accounts of Chinggis Khan's life tell of him spending a time captive among his enemies, although they differ very radically about who captured him and for how long. The Song envoy Zhao Gong, who visited the Mongol camp in North China, wrote, 'Chinggis, when small, was taken prisoner by men of the Jin and held as a slave. Only after more than ten years did he escape and return; thus, he has a thorough knowledge of Jin affairs' (Atwood and Struve, pp. 73–4). The Catholic missionary William of Rubruck says that he was captured by the Tanguts and only obtained release by pledging temporary submission to them (Jackson and Morgan, p. 158). Rashiduddin tells two stories about his captivity that are much closer, but not identical, to the *Secret History*'s account. In one he was captured by the Merkit, not the Tayici'ut (Rashiduddin/Thackston, p. 37) and in another he was captured by the Tayici'ut, but at an age when his youngest son Tolui by his main wife Börte was already a child old enough to speak (Rashiduddin/Thackston, p. 66).

9. His name in Mongolian is Tarġutai Kiriltuq. The epithet Tarġutai may be a reference either to his association (presumably on his mother's side) with the Tarġut ('Fatties') people, one of the subject clans of the Tayici'iut, or to his own weight, i.e. 'Fatty Kiriltuq'. From the reference to him being unable to ride in §149 it seems that the Secret Historian understood it in the second sense and so I have translated it thus here.

10. Dayguards or *turġa'ut* were one of the two types of bodyguards in Central Eurasian institutions. The other ones were nightguards or *kebte'ul*. The *Secret History* will later quote at length the regulations for the day- and nightguards of Chinggis Khan and his son and successor Ökodei Khan. The reference to the dayguards is a clue, alongside the reference to the 'nation' (*ulus irgen*, literally the 'subject folk of the kingdom') below in §81, that the Tayici'ut

were more formally organized than the *Secret History*'s narratives might lead one to believe.

11. Belgutei and Qasar here show the talents for which they would later be famed, Belgutei as a wrestler with powerful arms, and Qasar as a strong and accurate archer. The other three children were still too small to play a part.

12. What was the 'issue' (*kerek*)? Simply that a potential rival had grown up, as the alliterative couplet suggests or, as some commentators have argued, the murder of Bekter? This later interpretation would imply that the Tayici'ut brethren had some jurisdiction over the Mongols. For what it is worth, Fatty Kiriltuq himself later avers in §149 that he was merely trying to reform and educate Temujin.

13. This Mongolian *qošiliq* was a conical tepee-style tent covered with felt. Such conical tents among native North Americans, Siberians and Sami in northern Europe are all similar in appearance and structure: three or more long branches for stability, with other branches added as a framework, a covering of skin, bark, felt or canvas, and a smoke hole in the centre. They differ, however, in certain ways, such as the covering, the smoke hole arrangements and the height. (Those of Siberia and Europe tend to be squatter in shape.) The Siberian equivalent of 'tepee' (that is, a word of native derivation, but used widely in the settler-colonial language) is *chum*; in Sami it is *lavvu*.

14. This kind of knife is called an *onubci* in §178.

15. 'Subject people' is Mongolian *ulus irgen*, literally 'common folk of the kingdom'; in Ökodei's decrees in §279, this term is used in ways that approach English 'nation' – the political collectivity for whose good the policies of the ruler are directed. Here this binome seems somewhat anachronistic.

16. Such a practice of rotating prisoners occurred until the twentieth century. 'Because the nomads moved continually, it was not possible to put a person in a cage [or other such prison] and abandon him; therefore, it was common, up to modern times, to put a criminal in stocks, chains, or a cage and place him on an ox cart that was sent on a circuit [about the jurisdiction]' (Jagchid and Hyer, p. 363).

17. Despite being called a 'day', this 'Red Disk Day' (*hula'an tergel üdur*) appears to be connected to the first full moon of summer. See also §118 and §193.

18. *Buġa'u* or cangue: in Rashiduddin (Rashiduddin/Thackston, p. 66), this is called a *dushakha* or a heavy forked branch with

the ends of the two forks chopped off. In this simple style of cangue or yoke, the prisoner's neck was placed inside the fork and the ends of the forks were secured by a strap or chain. The prisoner's arm could also be shackled to the branch by the same method. In this case, however, Temujin's arm was left outside and he thus had some free play to pick up and move the cangue and could twist it around his head to let the branch go in front, to the side, or back.

19. The word *tün* refers particularly to the mostly willow groves that grow by the side of rivers in the Mongolian steppe.

20. The Suldus, like the Tarġut and the Besut, was one of the subordinate houses under Tayici'ut control (see Appendix B). As is mentioned in §§146 and 219, Sorġan-Śira was one of the subjects attached to Tödo'e, one of the leading Tayici'ut brethren (not to be confused with the Töde'en Girte of §72). Thus he was part of the gathered Tayici'ut feasters, but was not in the inner circle and not entirely loyal to them.

21. They are Temujin's brethren, because they are all of the line of Bodoncar; even though Sorġan-Śira is politically subject to the Tayici'ut league, he is not genealogically of their noble line.

22. Rashiduddin refers to an old woman known as 'Aunt Tayichu' (Tayicu Egeci) who 'used to comb Chinggis Khan's hair and wait on him. Every time his neck was irritated by the *dushakha* [cangue], she placed a bit of felt on it and consoled him' (Rashiduddin/Thackston, p. 66).

23. On *esuk* (fermented mare's milk) and its manufacture, see the note at §28.

24. *Tel* refers to a lamb that has been nursed by two ewes. Thus it would be fatter than normal.

25. Rashiduddin notes that 'no matter how much obligation they admit, [Mongols] still blame [Sorġan-Śira] somewhat for not having given him some tools and a flint' (Rashiduddin/ Thackston, p. 66).

26. The detailed geography of this place name is related to its later spiritual importance. Kürelgu was the place, apparently a mountain valley, where Chinggis Khan and virtually all of his successors were interred. In 1252, Chinggis Khan's grandson Möngke Khan performed sacrifices to his ancestors and Heaven and Earth at a sacred mountain that should be Kürelgu; in 1254, he performed sacrifices to Heaven at this same Köke Na'ur. Köke Na'ur or 'Blue Lake' is one of the most common place names in Mongolia; Mongolians today identify Qara Jiruken's Köke Na'ur or 'Blue

Lake of the Black Heart' with Lake Khangal in Khentii province's Ömnödelger county. (A 'heart' in Mongolian is a mountain with an oval-shaped top.)

27. The biography of Bo'orcu in the *Yuanshi*, pp. 119.2945–6, says this was a wagon-fort of the Yörkin who appear later; it also adds that Bo'orcu was thirteen years old at the time and that Bo'orcu's father, Naqu the Rich, had previously camped near Yisukei and was friendly with him. On the institution of the wagon-fort (*küre'en*) or *ger*s and wagons placed in a circle to make a fortified camp on the steppe, see the Introduction.

28. 'Red coat' (*hula'an de'el-tu*) here and below is added from the text in the *LAT* recension.

29. The Mongolian *uurga* (Middle Mongolian *u'urga*) is a long wooden pole with a rope at the end of it. The rope can be tied back on the pole to use the *uurga* as a lariat to lasso livestock, or untied to use it as a whip to drive them.

30. This is the famous 'Parthian shot', fired while riding away, at which Central Eurasian nomads excelled.

31. Here we see the ambiguity in the word 'friend' or *nökor*. On the one hand it refers to those united by a strong bond of attachment; on the other, it refers to those in an intimate relationship of service and protection, like patron and client. Bo'orcu had previously had a bond of affection with Temujin, but now he becomes an intimate companion or client of Temujin.

32. The coat or *daqu* is more specifically a fur coat with the fur worn outside.

33. The Kereyit kingdom in central Mongolia along with the divided Naiman kingdom to the west were the major political powers on the Mongolian plateau at this time. These stable and wealthy kingdoms actively sought to employ captains originating from the more anarchic and restive Tatar, Merkit and Mongol peoples to their east. These captains likewise eagerly entered the service of Kereyit and Naiman rulers.

34. The term *anda* referred to a wide variety of sworn brotherhoods that bound together people of different family or social background into a relationship that combined emotional closeness with shared politico-economic benefit.

35. Note here the use of 'Ong Khan' for To'oril, a title the granting of which will not be explained until §134, set in narrative time about ten years later, and the use of 'Khan' (*qa'an* or *qan*) for Yisukei. The title 'Khan' is used for Yisukei only in three linked sources, the 'Indictment of Ong Khan', the 'Indictment

Narrative' and the 'Indictment Narrative Continuation'. This terminology indicates that this particular narration of Temujin and Ong Khan's first meeting was reworked from a written narrative of Chinggis Khan's relations with Ong Khan that actually set the meeting a decade or so later.

36. 'Lift up' here is *seku'ul*, which I read following the *LAT* recension as opposed to the *negu'ul* of the Hanlin recension.

37. I follow de Rachewiltz in connecting *böken* with Kalmyk *böku*, 'humpbacked; knobbly', but interpret it as a reference to the shape, rather than as 'ragged'.

38. 'Willow laths' here translates *burġasun*, which the Hanlin recension glosses as 'elm sticks'. *Qalqasun*, translated as 'willow wands', is glossed as 'broken willow sticks'. The identification of *burġasun* as 'elm' is not corroborated elsewhere. Eldengtei, Oyundalai and Asaraltu, p. 294, note that such an incident of Chinggis Khan hiding in a wagon-*ger* of plaited willow wands is referred to in the liturgy associated with his later cult.

39. Mongolian ritual practice often used anointing with butter (*mal-iya-*) as a form of blessing.

40. 'Libations' is *saculi* or sprinkling with milk.

41. 'To'oril' was actually his personal name, from Turkic *toġril*, 'falcon'. 'Ong' is the Middle Mongolian pronunciation of Chinese *wang* or prince, a title that was granted to To'oril by the Golden Khan, but not until later on in the story.

42. 'Young' here is *de'u*, literally 'younger brother', but often used for the younger in any close relationship or someone of lower status.

43. A *tümen* or 'ten thousand' was a common unit in the decimal organization of armies, roughly equivalent to a brigade. But the term was often used in a very loose way, to indicate a community usually smaller, but sometimes larger, than 10,000 households.

44. As will be explained below, Temujin and Jamuqa had made a relationship of *anda* with each other during their adolescence, a relationship that is being recalled here now. The *Secret History* is somewhat inconsistent in its use of the term *anda* for Jamuqa, although there is no record of his being *anda* with anyone other than Chinggis Khan.

45. Mongolian *dabcitu qor* or 'bow case for a bow with a slack bow-string'. In later Mongolian *qor* is quiver and *qoromsaġa* is bow case; in Middle Mongolian there is no attested word for bow case and it seems a single word was used for both.

46. The Orkhon and Selenge.

47. 'Blessed portal' or *qutuq e'ede* alludes here to household spirit guardians which would be hung by the doorway.

48. Jamuqa's own base was well to the east, in Qorqonaq valley near the lower Onon and in the Ergune-Gen River area in northern Hulun Buir. Thus, he will come upstream along the Onon while To'oril, whose base is on the Tuul River, will follow the Tuul upstream near to where it approaches the Kherlen. Here in the parenthetic phrase the Secret Historian gives a very brief explanation of where the people of Yisukei Ba'atur who had run off with the Tayici'ut in §§73–4 had been all this time – they had been with Jamuqa *Anda* and Jamuqa is now returning them to Temujin. This explanation is necessary narratively since Temujin will be, for the first time in the story, a commander commanding an army.

49. Ja'a Gambo, who appears here for the first time, was To'oril's younger brother, and an independent political actor in the Kereyit kingdom. The title Gambo is of Tangut origin, and Ja'a Gambo spent a lengthy period in the Tanguts' Western (Xi) Xia kingdom as an exile.

50. The title *beki* was used among the less centralized Oyirat, Merkit and Mongols for a leader who combined genealogical seniority with priestly and shamanic functions. It is not to be confused with the homophonous title *beki* which was used for princesses. It is unclear if there was any relationship between the two words.

51. 'Junior kinsman' here is *de'u* or literally 'younger brother'; in this case it is unlikely to be literal.

52. As explained by Igor de Rachewiltz, the knob-headed arrow or *ġodoli* was blunt-headed and by itself would not kill. The whistling sound it made and the bruise it would leave would mark the person for Belgutei's men to execute as they followed behind him.

53. To 'go in the door' (Mongolian *e'uden-dur oro'uldaqun*) refers to being put to domestic service, although not as explicitly in a sexual sense as in the previous phrase.

54. 'Mink' is *usun buluġan*, literally 'water sable'. Igor de Rachewiltz translates this as 'otter', but otter is attested in Middle Mongolian as *qali'un*. The only other semi-aquatic dark fur-bearing mustelid is the mink.

55. This term, literally meaning something like 'lost and found', carries with it the implication of something that the finder has long desired, and which hence the finder has an implicit right to.

56. See the note in §28 above.

57. *Ġaca'uratu Sübcit Huliyatu Sübcit*: these may be specific places, but since their location is unknown, more is gained for the reader by translating them.

58. When doing a ring, or battue, hunt (*abala*-), hundreds of people were marshalled to beat the game in a vast circle stretching across miles until eventually all the game was contracted into a small space and slaughtered. Such hunts were used throughout Central Eurasia as practice for coordinated formations in war.

59. I follow here de Rachewiltz in adopting the meaning of *cinggul-tuktu si'a* that is given in the Chinese gloss: '[hollowed out] knucklebone poured with [molten] copper'. The copper would make the knucklebone heavier and more durable.

60. Mongolians play a wide variety of games with the knucklebones of sheep and goats to this day. Some involve flicking the knucklebones at a target, while others involve rolling them like dice.

61. Zoologically, these horns are like those of Alexander the Great's famous 'horned' horse Bucephalus: small bumps on the forehead that look like the emerging horns of a calf. But the archaeology of the Mongolian plateau also shows that the idea of horses being truly horned, with ibex-like horns, was an important part of equine mythology. 'Kid-white' (*ünugun caġān*) indicates a horse as white as a goat-kid; it was later corrupted to *öndegen caġān*, 'egg-white', used for the sacred horses in the Chinggis Khan cult.

62. The Besut surname was of relatively low status. Like the Suldus, those of that name lived under the rule of the Tayici'ut, so that their range was in the Tayici'ut territory.

63. In this section, the Secret Historian assembles two lists of Chinggis Khan's early followers. In the first list, in §120, we see followers who came as individuals or small families. In the second, in §122, we see those who rallied to Chinggis Khan leading whole *küre'en* or wagon-forts, that is as organized communities, each with several hundred or more families. They are separated by the account of the Qorci of the Menen Ba'arin and his story of the signs portending Temujin's coronation. This first list, in particular, mixes a number of people like Sübe'edei Ba'atur who in their own biographical literature are given a separate and much later story of joining Chinggis Khan's standard. The second list of those who joined by whole wagon-forts shares many names with a list of Chinggis Khan's thirteen wagon-forts during his first battle with Jamuqa. See §129 and Appendix B.

64. The title *cerbi*, meaning 'chamberlain', was one that Doqolqu and the others so named acquired afterwards in the service of Chinggis Khan, not one they held at this time. See §191.

65. In later Mongolian, a *ja'arin* (plural *ja'arit*) refers to a high-ranked shaman, and that shaman's spirits. Some interpreters have read it this way. Others, such as Igor de Rachewiltz, have read *ja'arin* here as the content of the prophetic message, and thus translate it as 'foretoken' or 'heavenly sign'. My own interpretation is that *ja'arin* here designates the spirit or spirits who give visions.

66. *Gerluge* is glossed as 'stake under a *ger*', but this term is otherwise unknown, and the gloss may be mistaken. I have instead read it as *ger* with the comitative particle *luge*, accidentally written as one word.

67. 'Great wagon road' is *yeke terge'ur*, that is, a road level enough for the great *ger*-wagons to travel along.

68. *Qo'ocaq* and *odora* are glossed as types of arrows, probably differing in size; see Holeščák, p. 42. The flight of an arrow is a common metaphor in the Mongol empire for the service of a messenger or envoy, and that is the position these four have been appointed to.

69. As has already been mentioned, the biographical accounts of Sübe'edei indicate that he did not join Chinggis Khan's banner until much later in 1203. See Pow and Liao, pp. 50–52, 69.

70. Other versions of the rise of the Mongol empire place either Bo'orcu and Boroġul or else Bo'orcu and Muqali in this exalted position.

71. This last sentence of Chinggis Khan's recalls several common phrases from the administrative language of the Mongol empire. The motto of the empire that headed all letters and decrees was 'By the Power of Eternal Heaven; by the Protection of the Majestic Imperial Fortune'. Similarly, 'elders' (*ötogus*) who will become 'fortunate friends' (*ölje-ten nökot*) recalls the phrase *ötogu bo'ol*, 'elder slaves', which was used in the empire to refer to those who had been of commoner lineage before the founding of the empire and who joined Chinggis Khan in the establishment of the empire.

72. This speech of Jamuqa's anticipates the one which Chinggis Khan himself will make later to Altan and Qocar, accusing them of poisoning To'oril Ong Khan's mind against him, and ironically wishing them to be good companions of the one they chose to serve.

3: The Early Battles of Chinggis Khan

1. The thirteen wagon-forts on the two sides represent the clans or aristocratic houses, organized for separate defence, allied with each leader. When they joined for battle, however, they would be organized as a centre (*gool*) with two wings, right and left. The centre and two wings would each nominally number ten thousand, with one soldier from each militia household. The exact numbers were, however, almost certainly much smaller; perhaps a total of three or four thousand actual soldiers on each side. The thirteen wagon-forts of Chinggis Khan with their commanders and constituent peoples were listed in the 'Authentic Chronicle of Chinggis Khan' as cited by Rashiduddin and the *Campaigns of Chinggis Khan*; see Appendix B. The Secret Historian reproduces many of the names on this list in §122.

2. The name element *quwa*, said by Rashiduddin to mean 'bravo; bandit', is also read *u'a*.

3. The Uru'ut and Manggut houses were closely linked but also fierce rivals. Later in the history of the empire they competed for privilege, each promoting a version of their history that glorified their own founder, Jürcedei for the Uru'ut and Quyildar for the Manggut, in the rise of the empire. See Atwood 2015b, pp. 167–70. The Secret Historian used as a source the biography of Jürcedei's family but not that of Quyildar, so the *Secret History* favours Jürcedei over Quyildar. Here, for example, Jürcedei is seen as joining Chinggis Khan first; the biography of Quyildar's house, however, says that he was *anda* of Temujin from his childhood.

4. The main political actors each received a large *tüsurge* or skin sack for storing and serving *esuk* which they would share with their followers. One may see here that Mother Ö'elun and Qasar, alone among Chinggis Khan's family members, had separate political identities from him. On these skins and arrangement of the court, see also §213 and the note below.

5. Sece Beki's little mother (*ücu'uken eke*) was his stepmother, the surviving widow of Sece Beki's father, probably much younger than Sece Beki's own birth-mother.

6. Mongolian *kirü'ese*. These hitching posts were a regular part of all Mongolian assemblies and were closely regulated. See Jagchid and Hyer, pp. 57–9.

7. This practice is still virtually de rigueur among Tibetan and Mongol men of the Tibetan plateau and not uncommon in rural

Mongolia as well. The Mongol horseman on the front cover is demonstrating the same practice.

8. Belgutei's language here is highly colloquial, containing a number of words that have taxed the ingenuity of scholars.

9. These sacks or *ituge*s were used for mixing the *esuk* or fermented mare's milk. Each sack had a wood plunger for stirring the *esuk*.

10. Ongging *Chengxiang* (*Ongging Cingsang*) is 'Grand Councillor Ongging'. *Ongging* is Mongolian for the Jurchen name *Wongian* (Chinese Wanyan), the surname of the Jurchen imperial family then ruling the North Chinese (Mongolian *Kitat*). *Chengxiang* (Mongolian *Cingsang*) is Chinese for 'grand councillor'. Dynasties in China at this time had two grand councillors who headed the government. This particular grand councillor was Wongian Xiang (1140–1202). A member of the imperial family, he served as junior *Cingsang* from 1188 to 1196, when, in the wake of the battles described here, he was promoted to senior *Cingsang*, in which position he served until his death.

11. This sudden intrusion of international politics into the brawling of the Yörkin and the Borjigin is the first specific event in the *Secret History* which is corroborated by outside sources. The campaign was part of the Jin court's response to a lengthy border crisis for the Golden Khan's Jin dynasty. This crisis lasted from 1193 to 1198, involving not just the 'outer frontier' events described in the Mongol sources but also rebellion among the Kitans and other 'inner frontier' peoples. This specific campaign mentioned in the *Secret History of the Mongols* began in late spring 1196 and was completed by July 1196. However, neither To'oril nor Me'ujin-Se'ultu, let alone Temujin, is mentioned by name in connection with this campaign outside the *Secret History*.

12. These names mean 'Birch Fastness' and 'Pine Fastness'; they have not been located, and were probably only very temporarily occupied places.

13. *Tana*-pearls were sourced sometimes from the Persian Gulf, and sometimes from rivers of Manchuria. They were considered more valuable than the *subut*-pearls usually sourced from China; see the note to §238. Freshwater Manchurian pearls are probably meant here.

14. This meeting of Grand Councillor Ongging and his local allies took place in July 1196, and was commemorated in a bilingual Chinese-Jurchen inscription which still stands at Serwen Khaalga, south of the Kherlen River near Öndorkhaan, the capital of Khentii province.

15. The exact meaning of the title *ca'ut-quri* is disputed. *Quri* (or *quru*) is the Kitan word for 'commander; officer' but some see in *ca'ut* a plural of Mongolian *ja'un*, 'one hundred'. More likely, *ca'ut* is the plural of *ca'ur*, 'soldiers', so the whole would mean 'commander of soldiers' rather than 'commander of a hundred'. Either way, it is quite a minor title.

16. *Ong* is the medieval Mongolian pronunciation of the Chinese title currently pronounced in modern Mandarin as *wang* 'king; prince'. This was obviously a vastly higher rank than that granted to Chinggis Khan.

17. The Chinese title *Zhaotao*, or more fully *Zhaotaoshi*, meaning 'bandit-suppression commissioner' (Mongolian *ceutau, ceutauši*), was given to border commanders responsible for enforcing dominance over the people of Mongolia. (In imperial thinking anyone resisting the empire was a 'bandit'.) The Jin dynasty appointed three such commissioners, for the south-west, the north-west and the north-east, situated along the frontier of Inner Mongolia from present-day Höhhot to Baicheng. Granting Chinggis Khan this title would of course only have been nominal, but it would have confirmed him as a trusted ally of the Jin court in Mongolia.

18. On this term *sauġa*, a 'long-lost article of value', see §114.

19. The *Secret History* rather exaggerates the importance of Qutuġu. *Šiki* or 'Little Šiki' (Mongolian *Šikiken*) is actually a nickname; it appears to be the same as the Tekechuk found in Juvaini's Persian history of the Mongols. If so, it is likely a Tatar or Qonggirat dialect version of *teke,* meaning 'wild goat; ibex'.

20. The base camp or *a'uruq* (plural *a'uru'ut*) was a mobile baggage train where women, children, old men and other non-combatants would stay during a campaign. On a long campaign, such camps would travel fairly close to the intended battlefield to provide food, rest, recuperation and many other services to the fighting soldiers, but would keep at least a day's ride from the enemy.

21. This location was an important one, where the coronation assembly for Ökodei Khan would be held in 1229 and where the *Secret History* itself would be first composed in 1252. That the Yörkin held it was a sign of their previously dominant role among the people of the Onon-Kherlen valley.

22. The Jalayir were a commoner lineage that had been subjugated by the ancestors of the Borjigin-Kiyat lineage. Their members were thus found among the subjects of all the branches of that lineage, including the Yörkin and Chinggis Khan's Kiyat.

23. Muqali's significance is rather slighted in the *Secret History*, but he was often paired with Bo'orcu as Chinggis Khan's two supreme commanders. He belonged to the branch of the Jalayir.

24. Boroġul was actually of the Hü'usin surname, one of the commoner subjects of the Yörkin. The *Secret History* rather diminishes his accomplishments, but in some versions of the Mongol rise he exceeds even Bo'orcu in rank.

25. I.e. 'Poxy One of the Yörkin': *sorġa*, 'track, mark, trace', was a euphemism for smallpox scars. In the genealogy in §49, this fearsome disease was further euphemized as Qutuqtu-Yörki, 'Blessed Yörki'. I follow de Rachewiltz and the *LAT* recension in deleting the second *Yörki bolurun* as an accidental scribal duplication.

26. I follow here the *LAT* recension and the discussion of de Rachewiltz in which *yorgimaq* is derived from the verb *yorgi-*, 'to be wilful, boastful' (cf. modern Mongolian *yorgio*, 'bumptious, show-off').

27. I read *urida* here from the *LAT* recension, and from the *xian*, 'previously', of the Chinese running translation (p. 4.29r).

28. Then, as now, Mongolian wrestlers wore a short, tight leather jacket today called a *zodog*. Belgutei, by grabbing the two sides of this jacket's collar, would have been able to pull Böri's back up as far as he wanted.

29. His name is given as Qutuqtu-Mönggur in the genealogical section in §§48, 50.

30. This account of the second battle with Jamuqa was pieced together by the Secret Historian from three different sources, each of which is separately quoted in the *Campaigns of Chinggis Khan* and in Chinese summary in the *Yuanshi*. Aggregating these other accounts, two of which may have been historically the same event and the third of which certainly is not, created a large and elaborate battle narrative. This benefit was secured, however, at the cost of considerable geographical incoherence, some of which the Secret Historian was able to finesse, some of which could not be hidden.

31. Here I follow the *LAT* recension in reading *Irkidei Ba'atur* while emending the Chinese transcription in the Hanlin recension from initial *chi* to initial *yi*; the characters are very similar and commonly confused.

32. This person may be the same as the Jali-Buqa of §58.

33. The title *Gür Khan* was understood in Middle Mongolian to mean 'Universal Sovereign', but in the original Kitan it may have meant only 'Sovereign of the Realm'.

34. This double assembly, first at Alǧui and then at the Gen River, was due to the Secret Historian's harmonization of two different accounts, one of which had the coronation at Alǧui and the other of which placed it on the Gen River. Rather than abandon data from either account, the Secret Historian combined them to produce a more event-packed narrative.

35. This weather-magic is referred to in Mongolian as *jada* and in Turkic as *yay*, both of which mean 'weather-stone' (the verb 'to perform weather-magic' is *jadalaqui*). Weather-stones used today in Mongolia consist of bezoars or prehistoric stone tools. Probably the most famous and effective instance of weather-magic's military applications came in the Battle of Sanfeng Mountain, in Henan province, where the last Jin dynasty field army was destroyed in February 1232, in part through a snowstorm generated by a *jada* weather-stone wielded by a Qangli soldier.

36. The Oyirat were one of the 'Forest Folk' (*Hoi-yin Irgen*) with their homeland in the taiga of present-day Mongolia's northernmost province, Khöwsgöl. Here the Secret Historian envisions them hacking their way home through thick woods, although in reality the forests of the taiga are not that dense.

37. This is in the indefinite form *qa* of the term *qan*, 'sovereign; ruler; khan'.

38. Here the Secret Historian links the battle against Jamuqa with the final battle against the Tayici'ut. In fact, none of the three sources which the Secret Historian used for the previous battle account made any such link; the placement of the battle with the Tayici'ut here is the Secret Historian's own guess at the sequence of events.

39. As Paul Ratchnevsky and Igor de Rachewiltz have emphasized, Jelme was worried that the wound might have been made by a poisoned arrow, so it was important to suck the blood away from it rather than let it clot. Bo'orcu's descendants attributed this episode of personally sucking the poisoned blood from Chinggis Khan's wound to their house's founding father, Bo'orcu, rather than to Jelme.

40. The *Secret History* here uses an obscure honorific second-person pronoun, *dan-tur*, 'to you [honorific]'.

41. Here is the first instance in the *Secret History* of the phrase *jarliq bolba*, literally 'It became a decree (or statute).' As may be seen

also from the 'bygone day' (*erte üdur*) for a day that was in the *Secret History*'s narrative context not so long ago, this speech of Chinggis Khan must have been taken by the Secret Historian from another context. It was likely derived from a biography of Jelme, itself written quite likely after Chinggis Khan's death, where Chinggis Khan reviews all the help which this 'old slave' rendered to him in his childhood. The placement of this episode in the midst of the Tayici'ut battle was the Secret Historian's best guess as to when it might have taken place – as de Rachewiltz noted, it seems incompatible with Chinggis Khan's pursuit the very next morning. In fact, a quite similar story of a companion of Chinggis Khan risking his life by going into the enemy's camp is found in Bo'orcu's Chinese-language biography in the *Yuanshi* (p. 119.2946), summarized from the Mongolian: 'In a battle with the Merkit, they also lost their way in the ranks of battle due to a snowstorm, and [Bo'orcu] went back in among the enemy looking for [Chinggis Khan], who had disappeared. He rushed urgently through the enemy's baggage train, but by then, the emperor had already returned and was sitting down to rest in a wagon. When he heard that Bo'orcu had come back, he said "This was Heaven protecting us."'

42. Michal Holeščák, p. 42, speculates that *jebe* or 'weapon' may designate more specifically an arrow with a wide, ivy-leaf-shaped, three-pointed head, possibly used to fell horses.

43. On him and his name, see above in §79.

44. Here we meet for the first time Naya'a, who will be given an importance by the Secret Historian that no other empire-era historian accords him. Naya'a survived into the 1250s and claimed to have eaten at the wedding feast of Chinggis Khan and Madame Börte; the story here is likely to be based on Naya'a's own recollections, which the Secret Historian probably learned of from interviews. But it was probably also intended to counter other versions of Old Man Širgu'etu's surrender, in which his release of Fatty Kiriltuq was not seen as the commendable reticence of a commoner to betray his own sovereign but rather as a culpable vacillation between loyalty to Chinggis Khan and loyalty to the Tayici'ut.

45. 'Sons and junior kinsmen' (*kö'ut de'u-ner*); later on in the *Secret History* this phrase is used to refer to the sons of Chinggis Khan (the princes), and his younger brothers and their descendants (little brothers).

46. The idea of 'taking a pillow' (*dere ab-*) meant killing one of one's killers so that one's body would have a cushion to lie on in the grave.

47. A *nu'u* or *nuġu* (modern *nuġa*) in Mongolian is a meadow within a loop of a meandering river. It is not recorded which river this meadow was along.

4: Chinggis Khan and Ong Khan

1. This word *el* is a common Turkic word meaning realm or people submissive to a single ruler; its opposite is *bulġa*, 'hostile; rebellious'. The appearance of these terms in this section is a sign that the Secret Historian has begun relying fairly closely on the 'Indictment Narrative' text, a text composed by an Öng'ut or Kereyit scribe who was bilingual in Turkic and Mongolian. The language of the 'Indictment Narrative' is thus heavily influenced by Turkic usage.

2. This is the same title, 'Universal Sovereign' or 'Sovereign of the Realm', which Jamuqa was granted in §141. Here, however, it seems to be used as a personal name and hence is not italicized.

3. 'Subject households' translates the Mongolian binome, *irge(n) orġa*, another characteristic usage of the 'Indictment Narrative'; the Chinese translators gloss it as 'common people and households'. In Persian it is variously glossed as 'kingdom', 'nation and army', 'army and possessions' and 'houses and belongings, herds and flocks'.

4. Qara-Khitai is the Turkic pronunciation of Mongolian *Qara Kitat* or 'Black Kitans'. This Turkic version entered English usage via Persian and Arabic sources. But in the Mongolian of the time it literally meant the 'ethnic Kitans'; black was a colour associated with the Kitan people as the colour of the north and of water. *Kitan* (singular) or *Kitat* (plural) had come to be used for all the peoples of North China, but the Qara-Kitat were the 'true Kitans' as opposed to the ethnic Chinese.

5. Requisitions here are *ġubciri*, meaning any ad hoc tax collected in kind on behalf of an army or party of envoys passing by. Later on, in the Mongol empire, this kind of tax was commuted into a regular silver tax.

6. *Hümekei helige*, literally 'stinking liver'. Mongols saw the liver as the seat of family feeling; to have a stinking liver was thus to lack all feeling of kinship solidarity.

7. 'Sart' was a term used widely in Central Asia up to the twentieth century, meaning sedentary, Muslim and usually Tajik or Persian speaking peoples, as opposed to Turkic and nomadic peoples. The Mongolian equivalent *Sarta'ul* had an even wider use in the Mongol empire. Sart and Sarta'ul originally meant 'caravaneers'; by this time it meant all the broadly 'Caucasian' people to the west and south-west of Mongolia, including Muslims, Middle Eastern Christians and Jews, Hindus and Roma. Rashiduddin translates it as Tajik, while Chinese sources translate it sometimes as 'the west' and sometimes as *Huihui*. Only later in Chinese history did *Huihui* come to mean 'Muslims' in the purely religious sense.

8. In the case of Ja'a Gambo this statement is technically correct, but very misleading. In fact, as far as we know, Ja'a Gambo did not flee to the Naiman at this time, but only much later. In between, he maintained good relations with Chinggis Khan and, when his elder brother Ong Khan was overthrown in autumn 1203, served briefly as Chinggis Khan's co-ruler over the Kereyit. Only after Chinggis Khan accused him of conspiring with the Merkit and Naiman in the summer of 1204 was Jürcedei sent to attack him and, if possible, capture and kill him. It was at that point, so far as we know, that Ja'a Gambo fled to the Naiman. See Atwood 2015b, pp. 164–7.

9. The parallel accounts unpack these cryptic words to say that Ong Khan and the conspirators had sworn loyalty to each other when they were coming back from the Qara-Khitai; Ong Khan then claims that he, unlike them, would not break faith.

10. That is, issued a law together with the other Mongol leaders, including Altan, Qocar and Dāritai. This is the first reference to Chinggis Khan pronouncing laws or *jasaq*, meaning decisions taken on particular occasions that had the status of binding precedents. Eventually these *jasaq* would form a sort of code of the empire, known in Uyghur as *yasagh* and in Persian as *yasa*, both cognates of the Mongolian *jasaq*.

11. Mongolian *yeke eye*; in Mongolian 'great', like 'golden', often has the connotation of 'imperial', i.e. involving the personal participation of the khan/emperor.

12. How high were such linchpins (i.e. pins that held the wheel on to the axle) on the great Mongol hordes or mobile palaces? In Otog, a rural 'banner' or district in the Ordos region of Inner Mongolia, one wheel of such a wagon has been preserved; its radius puts the linchpin about 3 feet 9 inches off the ground (see

Saiinjirġal and Šaraldai, pp. 226–7). The cut-off between life and
death would thus have been at about the age of six.

13. It may seem unbelievable that Belgutei would reveal such a plan
to the intended victims, but Big (*Yeke*) Cāran was a marriage ally
of Chinggis Khan's. Presumably Belgutei assumed that Cāran
would not be subject to the policy and as a man on the Mongol
side would not reveal the secret. (This Big Cāran is presumably
different from the Big Caran mentioned in §51 and §169 as a
senior cousin of Chinggis Khan. It is possible that this Big Cāran
of the Tatars is actually a confusion with the Big (*Yeke*) Qutuġut
whose story is told in Rashiduddin; see Rashiduddin/Thackston,
pp. 35, 210.) In the *LAT* recension of the *Secret History*, Cāran's
name is consistently written as Caru; perhaps the Hanlin recen-
sion's text here is faulty.

14. In Belgutei's biography in the *Yuanshi* (p. 117.2905), Belgutei's
duties as judge (*jarġu*) are described entirely as an honour to
him, without any reference to him being excluded from the
imperial councils.

15. *Ötok* was a ceremonial liquor the drinking of which marked the
conclusion of great *quriltai* or assemblies. Its nature is not
described, although it was probably a milk liquor.

16. In the later empire, from 1203 onwards, it is described how all
the Mongols were assigned to units of ten, a hundred and a thou-
sand, with Bo'orcu commanding those of the right wing and
Muqali commanding those of the left wing. In the *Secret His-
tory*'s plot structure, however, this institution did not yet exist,
although it seems presumed in the narrative here.

17. The Naiman kingdom was divided into two halves ruled by
two brothers. The western Naiman, ruled by the elder brother
Buyruq Khan, were called the Kücugut Naiman and the east-
ern Naiman, ruled by the younger brother Tayang Khan, were
called the Betegin Naiman. The two brothers were frequently
hostile to each other, and it becomes clear in the narrative that
Ong Khan and Chinggis Khan must have made an agreement
with Tayang Khan to pass through his Betegin half of the
Naiman kingdom in order to attack Buyruq Khan's western
Kücugut half.

18. Uluġ Taġ is 'Great Mountain' in Turkic and Sogog River, or
Soġuq Usun, is 'Cool River' in mixed Turco-Mongolian. The
mountain corresponds to the peak now known as Taldagiin Ikh
Uul or Great Mountain of Talda. They are located in Mongolia's
far-western Bayan-Ölgii province.

19. Comparison with the 'Authentic Chronicle of Chinggis Khan' shows that the Secret Historian has combined here two campaigns against Buyruq Khan. The first, with Yeti-Tobluq being captured at Qïzil-Baš, took place at this point in Chinggis Khan's career. The second, involving the Sogog River, Uluġ Taġ, and Ulungur River by the Qum-Seng'ir Dunes and the destruction of Buyruq Khan, took place much later.

20. A *belcir* is a place where two roads or two rivers meet. It is unclear whether a road or river confluence is meant here.

21. Mongol empire-era interpreters differ on whether this is a mountain or a river. The *Campaigns of Chinggis Khan* and the Hanlin recension's translators call it a river, but Rashiduddin calls it a mountain.

22. Despite the existence of several medieval translations and glosses of this passage into Chinese and Persian, the precise identification of the two types of birds, in Mongolian *qayiruġana* and *bildu'ur*, is still not clear. From the context it is obvious that the first is resident year-round and the second is migratory. My translation follows the most likely interpretation, that two types of larks are meant. The first is the Mongolian lark, which is resident year-round and has white flashes on its tail, and the second is the skylark or the short-toed lark (modern *byalzuumar*), which is quite similar in appearance but migratory.

23. This is a reference to the funerary practice of burning food in the ground to the deceased seen in §70. Since it was a funerary practice done for the already departed, Chinggis Khan is charging that Ong Khan's sudden departure is like saying, 'You are dead to me.'

24. This dismissive (and rather inaccurate) statement was taken from an account of the ways in which Qasar harmed and helped Chinggis Khan. The passage from which it is taken is quoted in greater length in the 'Authentic Chronicle of Chinggis Khan'.

25. Reading *qo'or* with the *LAT* recension and Choimaa.

26. This word 'champion' (*külü'ut*) also means a champion steed. The phrase 'four champions' was more often used for Chinggis Khan's four sons that he had by Madame Börte. See §254.

27. 'To ascend to the heights' or 'to the craggy heights' means to pass away and be buried. It stems from the practice of burying the bodies of shamans and other great figures on high spots overlooking the territory that they had ruled while alive.

28. One can see here how the status of senior (*aqa*) in a group of brothers or other men of roughly equal status was not something

determined wholly by chronological age, but was a social status which the father of the group could determine according to his judgement.

29.   This sentence builds on the spacing of prestige in the Mongol *ger* ('yurt'). The *ala'un* or place by the door is of low prestige and the space for servants and workers. The *qoyimar* or wall opposite the door is the place for the master and mistress of the *ger* as well as, in modern times, pictures of deceased family members, Buddhas, or other honoured images.

30.   This name has a masculine suffix attached to the name of the Hartagin clan. Together they could mean either 'man of the Hartagin clan' or else just a man named 'Hartagidai'. (It was not uncommon for a man to have this type of clan or ethnic name even when belonging to a different group.)

31.   It is unclear if Ebugejin Noyagin is one name or two. It might be 'Old Man Noyagin' or it might be 'Ebugejin and Noyagin'.

32.   The Berke ('Tough') Sands may be identified with Candmani Sands, a stretch of alluvial sands in western Darkhan county, Khentii province, of Mongolia.

33.   Here we see that Ilqa Senggum as crown prince was given control over an army of his own. In Mongolian political practice such princes were often stationed in a sensitive border region, and Ilqa Senggum is to the east of the Kereyit political centre, able to monitor the newly conquered eastern frontier.

34.   *Eji'e turuq*; this phrase reappears in §207 and appears to be a special idiom unrecognized by the glossators.

35.   Literally 'choke on the white and gag on the black'; in Mongolia, foods are often divided into 'white' or dairy, dominating the summer diet, and 'black' or meat, especially lean meat. The idea is that as he ages he will no longer be able to eat any form of food. I have chosen 'cheese' and 'grease' from among the dairy and meat foods to make the phrases alliterate.

36.   Mongolian *bu'ulcar*; the key element to the feast was the sharing of some form of alcoholic drink (presumably a milk-based liquor).

37.   This Big Cāran was last mentioned in §51 and is not to be confused with the Big Cāran of the Tatars in §§154-6. That so many relatives of Chinggis Khan were there at Ong Khan's court to participate in the upcoming attack shows that Ong Khan in his rise had drawn virtually all of the Onon-Kherlen elite into his orbit. Chinggis Khan was not a general leader or focus of loyalty of the Onon-Kherlen Mongols so much as the one whom Ong

Khan had appointed to administer the area on his behalf. As will be stated below, most of the Onon-Kherlen Mongols went with the great patron Ong Khan, not their uppity kinsman Chinggis Khan, in the split.

38. Merkit White was presumably a white horse that Big Cāran had at some point plundered from the Merkit.

39. This tent or *qoš* was a kind of small temporary tepee, not a well-built *ger*.

40. Most interpreters have taken the reference to 'travelled by night' and then getting to Chinggis Khan's camp 'one night' to indicate that they arrived the same night. This, however, cannot be correct. Badai and Kišiliq took great pains to conceal that they were killing and cooking a lamb; obviously they were preparing rations for a long trip. This would make no sense if they arrived the same night. The Mongolian does not require that the night they arrive be the same as the night they left and I have not translated it as such.

41. Rather than be admitted to Chinggis Khan's *ger* during the night, those bringing news would stand on the northern or rear side and speak their message. As Charlotte Marchina, p. 123, has noted, 'Felt, which covers the wooden structure of the yurt [or *ger*], is a powerful insulator against cold and heat, yet it also allows sound to pass through. As a result, herders can continue to listen for suspicious sounds on the encampment, even when in bed at night.' See the regulations for the imperial bodyguards or *kešikten* in §229 and §278, where these rules are prescribed. (It may be remembered that Mongol *ger*s are pitched with the door to the south or south-east, so the master and mistress sleep in the honoured portion opposite the door on the northern or north-western side.)

42. This name in Mongolian means 'Bad Heights'. Other histories, however, have Mo-Ündur, which would be Kitan for 'Great Heights'. Undoubtedly the Kitan is original and the Mongolian version is a folk etymology.

43. 'Red Willows'.

44. 'Uncle' (*ebin*) here is not to be taken literally; it means any kinsman in the senior generation, related in the male line, but of a junior status to the speaker's own father. As may be seen in §46, the Secret Historian related the Uru'ut to Chinggis Khan's lineage.

45. *Enggeske* is 'rouge', but whether the Secret Historian's Senggum used rouge or his cheek was naturally very ruddy is disputed by commentators.

46. *Inggircaq*: a special pack saddle with no stirrups.
47. A kind of arrow. Inner Mongolian scholar Choiji identifies this type with the *aqjam* arrow, described as '[an arrow] without iron in it, the head of whose shaft is bulging'. See *Qorin nigetu taiilburi toli*, p. 17a; cf. the Onon translation, p. 148, n. 387.
48. *Elbesun jalama*; the attaching of ribbons to trees or animals as a way of dedicating them to Heaven was a common part of Mongolian and other Central Eurasian peoples' spiritual practices. See §57 and the note above.
49. The meaning of these words, unglossed, has been much debated by scholars without any firm conclusion.
50. That is, they have no wagons or *ger*s to dwell in or carry their possessions, only horses to ride.
51. Collecting dung for fuel was a common practice in the Eurasian steppe. The Arab traveller from Morocco, Ibn Battutah (Gibb, p. 470), once observed, 'This wilderness [of the Eurasian steppe] is green and grassy, with no trees nor hills, high or low, nor narrow pass nor firewood. What they use for burning is animal dung (which they call *tazak*), and you can see even their men of rank gathering it up and putting it in the skirts of their robes.' *Tezäk* is the Turkic term for dung; Middle Mongolian for dried dung is *junda'ul* (horses') or *argali* (cattle's).
52. The Uru'ut and Manggut were moving exactly along the site where in 1939 the Battle of Khalkhyn Gol (Khalkh or Qalqa River) would take place on the eastern border of Mongolia between the Soviet Union and Japan and their Mongolian and Inner Mongolian allies.
53. Placing honoured bones on a high place made them protector spirits for the living members of their community (see §201). A *nu'u* or *nuġu* (modern *nuga*) in Mongolian is a meadow within a loop of a meandering river (in this case the Khalkh River).
54. The Hanlin recension takes Dergei (also read as Terke) as one name and Amal as another; the transcribers also read the latter name as Amel. Scholars have sometimes taken Amel as Emel, 'saddle'. Historical sources, however, make it clear that Dergei/Terke is actually a title meaning son-in-law and Amal is a surname; Dergei Amal is thus 'the son-in-law of the Amals'.
55. This adverbial phrase is elsewhere unattested; I follow de Rachewiltz's guess at its meaning.
56. Reading *qo'or* based on the parallel text in §162.
57. I adopt Igor de Rachewiltz's interpretation of *soyiluġ* (2004, p. 643) as a word of Chinese origin with Turkic-style suffixation.

Other Turkic words that appear in Kereyit and Naiman speech include *torluq* and *torulmiśi* (see §§189–90). Turkic was the language of high culture in medieval Mongolia, and I have attempted to reproduce the impression these words made by using strongly Latinate terms.

58. A small pointed knife, the same as the *sumuci kituġai* or 'knife for whittling arrows' of §80. See Holeščák, p. 43.

59. This is a *cung*, which seems to be a technical term for a type of goblet or chalice, but of unclear nature.

60. As many commentators have pointed out this statement is contrary to the genealogy presented in §§49–50. The Secret Historian is here citing verbatim the 'Indictment of Ong Khan' which followed a shorter genealogy in which there were only seven generations from Bodoncar to Temujin Chinggis Khan. The Secret Historian followed a different genealogy, but did not revise this passage to accord with it. See Atwood 2012.

61. This was the title Chinggis Khan had received from the Golden Khan in §134.

62. These are the Onon, the Kherlen and the Tuul. Their headwaters are the sacred mountains of Burġan and Qaldun.

63. 'Boy' here is *de'u*, literally 'junior' or 'younger brother'. Here, however, Chinggis Khan gives the term a very strong caste twist, best captured by the English 'boy'.

64. The Hanlin recension reads Söbekei. However, comparison with the *Campaigns of Chinggis Khan* and *Secret History* §120 makes it clear that the name is Sö'ekei. So, either the Hanlin recension's *b* here is a mistake for *g* (the two are written similarly) or else the *b* is also intended to be elided in pronunciation, thus becoming identical with Sö'ekei.

65. 'Forefather' and 'paternal ancestor' are here *borqai* and *elincug*, literally 'sixth-degree ancestor' and 'great-grandfather' respectively (both in the paternal line). These terms were used for alliteration, however, and are not to be taken literally. Rashiduddin (Rashiduddin/Thackston, p. 102) actually gives Qabul Khan as Chinggis Khan's *elincug*, and Qaidu Khan as his *borqai*; Tumbinai, who enslaved Noqta, was Chinggis Khan's great-great-grandfather or *bodatu*.

66. This is not Chinggis Khan's little brother, but Qaci'un Beki of the Dörben house; see §141 and §166.

67. As Igor de Rachewiltz has commented (2004, pp. 652–4), this must refer to some story or legend, probably comic, which is

now lost. But pinning a tail on a man as a humiliation is mentioned again in §275.

68. The scheme that Senggum understood was that Chinggis Khan intended to use the further exchange of envoys to learn more about the other side's location, their order of battle, and potential rifts between commanders in Ong Khan's coalition. Thus he sends no envoys but instead prepares war.

69. This To'oril is the 'Boy To'oril' referred to in §180. Sö'ekei Je'un was 'Boy' To'oril's brother, them both being sons of Jegei-Qongtaġar.

70. The present-day Greater Khingan Mountains, running roughly north–south in eastern Inner Mongolia. The Khalkh and other rivers originate in its eastern slopes.

71. Mongolian *itegemji*. In the version in the *Campaigns of Chinggis Khan*, following the original 'Indictment Narrative', the 'surety' is the little bucket filled with blood, which the Secret Historian repurposed as a sign of Ong Khan's regret (see §178). The *itegemji* or surety being sent with Iturgen in §184 is a trace of this.

72. Mongolian *Altan terme*; *terme* was a special term, associated with the Kereyit and the Tangut (see §§265–6), for a vast woollen tent. The wooden frame was covered with gold foil; the golden appearance was thus only visible from inside.

73. This passage reflects the concept of hierarchy and patrilocality practised by the Mongol aristocracy. Qadaq Ba'atur and his Jirkin will be hereditary subjects of Quyildar. Their sons will stay with Quyildar's house in perpetuity, but their daughters, rather than being married by their parents, will follow the daughters of Quyildar's family as their dowry servants (*injes*) when those daughters are married off into other families.

74. This 'endowment for orphans' (Mongolian *önecid-un abliġa*) was also given to Slim To'oril, the son of Caġān-Quwa who also died in Chinggis Khan's service (see §§129, 218). There is no explicit definition of the term, but the assignment of Qadaq Ba'atur's descendants as the personal servants of Quyildar's descendants described immediately above is probably the crux of it. Moreover, the offices of men who had passed away in the khan's service were reserved for their designated son and heir; until the heir reached majority, the unit would be governed by that deceased's widow. Quyildar's son finally succeeded him during Ökodei Khan's reign (*Yuanshi*, p. 121.2988; Atwood 2015b, p. 170); until that time, presumably, Quyildar's widow

governed the Manggut. Other examples of this practice include Lady Youri serving as widow-regent for Yêrud Liuke until his son Sece succeeded him (*Yuanshi*, p. 149.3514) and Lady Xiao serving as widow-regent for Xiao Chounu until his son Qing-shan succeeded him (Atwood and Struve, p. 124 n.). Both Yêrud (Yelü) Liuke and Xiao Chounu were Kitan generals in Mongol service.

75. 'Strip bare' or *tala'ul-* refers to a much more systematic process of expropriation than *dauli-*, 'to plunder'. When a city was 'stripped bare', the inhabitants would be marched out into the surrounding fields and divided up among the army, with each ten-man unit of soldiers supervising a particular number while other troops entered the homes and systematically stripped them of everything valuable. In less densely inhabited rural areas, the population would be surrounded by a vast hunting circle (Mongolian *jerge* or Kitan *ñerge*) which would then be drawn tight, and the rural people would be captured, stripped of all their belongings, and assigned to their captor's unit for the duration. In Mongolia, the first method could be applied to the wagon-forts and hordes, if captured, and the second to the herders living in dispersed house-holds. The numbering and assignment of the captives to the units could finally lead to either massacre, as with the Tatars, or else permanent attachment of the captives to the captors' units, as here. Either way, to be 'stripped bare' was a prelude to more or less total disappearance as an independent people.

76. For this metaphor see §177. One may notice that, in the story of the break between Ong Khan and Chinggis Khan, Ja'a Gambo was never mentioned; in fact, he appears to have opposed his elder brother and stood aside when Chinggis Khan overthrew Ong Khan at Jeje'er Heights. From that victory in autumn 1203, through to the summer of 1204, Ja'a Gambo and Chinggis Khan then ruled in effect as co-monarchs, with Ja'a Gambo as the ruler of the Kereyit lands in the west and Chinggis Khan as the supreme monarch in the east. Their alliance was then solidified by the marriage alliance just described. In the end, Chinggis Khan would send Jürcedei to capture and kill Ja'a Gambo on charges of conspiring with the Naiman and the Merkit, and this episode of co-regency would be forgotten except in the family history of Jürcedei, from which this passage is taken. See Atwood 2015b, pp. 164–7.

77. This term refers to bodyguards-cum-household staff that watch over a khan's horde or tent in shifts (*kesik*, hence the name). The

most famous body of *kešikten* or 'shift servers' was that of Chinggis Khan which will be described in great detail below. However, this was not an invention of Chinggis Khan, and as the Mongol empire expanded, princes, empresses and other figures in the ruling class also acquired such protection, as here.

78. The high throne here is the throne in the Golden Tent (*altan terme*). Although the Secret Historian chose to magnify the coronation assembly of 1206 as the date of Chinggis Khan's formal enthronement, most other historians in the Mongol empire dated his coronation from 1203, when he conquered the Kereyit and ascended Ong Khan's old throne. Since the Golden Tent and its Onggojit staff were given into the care of Badai and Kišiliq, Chinggis Khan and his descendants would always see them when they sat on this throne.

79. Desert (Mongolian *cöl*) in Mongolian designates genuinely uninhabitable country, and as such is distinguished clearly from the *gobi* or habitable desert with its sparse, but regular, human population. The desert here is the land along borders of southwestern Mongolia south of the Gobi-Altai Mountains.

80. 'Khulan' is the name, of Mongolian origin, of the wild ass of the Central Eurasian steppe, *Equus hemionus hemionus*.

81. The Secret Historian leaves the impression that Senggum died in the desert. But the *Campaigns of Chinggis Khan* records that he successfully reached the border city of Izina (the present-day ruins of Khar Khot) in the Tangut country. The Tanguts took him in – they were always friendly to Kereyit rulers in trouble – and he eventually tried to rebuild a following among the Böri-Tibetan nomads around Kökenuur. Driven out from there, he fled west to Kucha, where he tried again to build a following among the Cerkesmen nomads in the Tianshan. The Kuchean ruler, however, eventually captured him and sent his head to Chinggis Khan.

5: Completing the Unification of Mongolia

1. Gürbesu's name is a variant of Mongolian *gürbel*, 'lizard'. Already in the *Secret History* we see her beginning to transform into the femme fatale which she became in later Mongolian legend. In contemporary sources she is sometimes said to be Tayang Khan's mother, and sometimes his wife. Undoubtedly, she was a very young junior wife of Tayang Khan's father Ïnanc Bilge

Khan whom Tayang had inherited according to the Mongolian practice of levirate marriage; such young wives of older men played a large role in the erotic imagination of young men in polygamous societies.

2. Glossed in Chinese as a 'large felt rug'; it was used for ceremonial purposes.

3. *Noqan* here is the plural of *noqai*, 'dog'; as Street has pointed out (p. 373), it is probably a feminine plural, a fact confirmed by the feminine gender of the verb *bolbi*, 'has become'.

4. For the related words 'debilitated' (*torluq*) and 'debilitation' (*torulmiśi*), I follow de Rachewiltz's interpretation (2004, pp. 681–2). Both are pure Turkic words in root and suffixation, as is common in Kereyit and Naiman dialogue; see the note for *soyiluġ* under §178.

5. The quiver (Mongolian *qor* or Turkic *kes*) was a symbol of manhood; see Holeščák, pp. 42–3. Working through Turkic translators, Rashiduddin (Rashiduddin/Thackston, p. 142) confused Turkic *kes* 'quiver' with *kiš* 'sable' and misunderstands this passage as Tayang Khan threatening to seize the Mongols' 'sable'.

6. The hunting season lasted from the seventh moon to the lunar new year, roughly from the end of August to the beginning of February. The message came near the close of the hunting exercises, when livestock were also generally weak due to lengthy grazing on the poor winter pastures. Mongolian campaigns followed the same seasonality as hunting and were initiated virtually without exception during the autumn moons.

7. 'Chamberlain' or *cerbi* had a much wider significance than would appear at first glance. The *cerbi*, like the *hajib* or 'chamberlain' in the Turkic and eastern Islamic world of the time, was responsible for the provisioning of the royal or imperial household. Since such households numbered in the thousands, if not more, and were more or less perpetually in motion and usually on a war footing, a *cerbi* or *hajib* necessarily had the functions we would normally associate with an army's quartermaster or staff officer. The *cerbi*s' authority overlapped with that of the 'shift elders' who governed the *keśikten*; it appears that as the *keśikten* increased in importance, the role of the *cerbi* declined, eventually disappearing by the fourteenth century.

8. Or 'with Qutus and Qaljan'.

9. The two sources for this account of the Battle of Naqu Qun had different names for the great mountain range, the modern Khangai, on whose eastern slopes the battle took place. In a

biography of Dödei Cerbi the mountain is called Qangġar-Qan – *qan*, 'sovereign; ruler; king or khan', is a common title attached to mountain names. In the 'Indictment Narrative Continuation' the mountain is called *Qangġai*, the ancestor of the modern name Khangai.

10. The term Altai or 'Golden' was applied to many high mountain ranges in Mongolia. Here it is being used for the Khangai Mountains in central-western Mongolia.

11. Küculug alludes here to a fact that is made more explicitly in other histories and in the *Secret History* below, that Chinggis Khan was fighting here not just the Naiman but all the remaining opponents of his new order, from all over the Mongol plateau. The *Campaigns of Chinggis Khan* lists those assembled as: Tayang Khan and the Naiman, Toqto'a and the Merkit, Ja'a Gambo and Alin Taiši with the remaining Kereyit, Qutuġa Beki and the Oyirat, and Jamuqa with the Dörben, Tatar, Qatagin, Salji'ut and all the other remaining anti-Chinggis Mongols.

12. In both of these sentences the verb ending is feminine (*bolbi*), seemingly referring to the feminine influence on the Naiman exemplified by both Lady Gürbesu and 'old woman Tayang' Khan's lack of manliness.

13. The caragana is a type of pea bush, common in Mongolia. What these technical battle formations might mean is unfortunately unclear; the most plausible explanation is that of Cleaves: 1) caragana-style march: 'to march with the troops massed in close order in the manner of the caragana, a thorny shrub which grows in thick clumps on the steppe'; 2) lake formation: 'to deploy with the troops widely scattered in the manner of the water of a lake which spreads over a wide area'; 3) chisel battle array, 'to engage the enemy with a thrust at his centre in the manner of a chisel which is thrust into a piece of wood'. See Cleaves 1982, p. 124 n. 49.

14. A *tebene* is a kind of large needle used for sewing leather and other tough material.

15. An *anggu'a* is an arrow with a forked tip; see de Rachewiltz 2004, p. 713, and Holeščák, p. 41.

16. A *keyibur* is a long and thin arrow shaped so as to travel far and fast and so used to hunt either very dangerous game, such as tigers or bears from a safe distance, or else very swift game such as buck; see de Rachewiltz 2004, pp. 713–14, and Holeščák, pp. 41–2.

17. The term *manggas* or python is here modified with *gürulgu*, glossed as 'a kind of python' but without further details. My interpretation here follows that of de Rachewiltz (2004, pp. 715–18). True pythons are found no nearer to Mongolia than India and southern China, but they were well known in Central Asia through translated Indian texts. There is also the Tartary sand boa (*Eryx tatarica*), which is found in the Gobi Desert and can grow up to three feet in length; see Khayankhyarvaa Terbish, Khorloo Munkhbayar and Munkhbayar Munkhbaatar, *A Guide to the Amphibians and Reptiles of Mongolia*, 2nd edn (Ulaanbaatar, 2013), pp. 58–9.

18. This image of 'until they stood like rotten snags' (*hünji'u bayitala*) is used several times to describe dead soldiers. Although those familiar with commercial lumbering might naturally think of logs from a clear-cut forest lying in heaps, which is the image the Chinese translators went for, the Mongolian actually seems to be rather an image of a ghost forest, that is, mostly standing trunks of trees killed by rising water, parasites, drought or climate change.

19. As above, this is actually the present-day Khangai Mountains.

20. Literally, 'Let us make it a *jasaq*.' The *jasaq* was a set of ad hoc judgments made into binding precedents for later times.

21. Töregene is elsewhere said to have been a Naiman woman; since the Naiman and the Merkit were politically allied, she was probably married to Toqto'a's son as part of their alliance. Rashiduddin tells of how she became Ökodei's bride: 'It is related that when they seized the brothers Qudu, Chibuq, and Chila'un, they brought the wives of all three and stood them opposite. "Let's go take them by force," said Ökotei to Chaghatai, but Chaghatai did not approve of this. Ökotei, however, went haughtily and took Töregene Khatun by force. Chinggiz Khan approved and gave the other two ladies to others' (Rashiduddin/Thackston, p. 216). Despite these horrific details of how Töregene became Ökodei's wife, ones which the Secret Historian does not repeat, she lived to serve as regent over the Mongol empire from 1242 to 1246 when her son Güyuk was elected as third khan. Even her political enemies acknowledged her intelligence and competence.

22. The Altai here is the modern Altai roughly along the border of present-day Mongolia and Xinjiang.

23. This mountain range in the Turkestan region is not to be confused with the Altai Mountains.

24. 'Shower of arrows' (*śiba-yin sumun*) refers to the Central Eurasian technique of opening battle with a dense spray of arrows intended to disorient the enemy and provoke him into some rash response. See de Rachewiltz 2004, pp. 731–2.

25. The Qangli and Qïpchaqs were two closely related Turkic-speaking pastoralist people, nomadizing in the steppe from eastern Kazakhstan to the Carpathian Mountains and the Danube. The Qangli were in the eastern part of this range, in eastern and central Kazakhstan. The Qïpchaqs' country extended from western Kazakhstan to the Danube. However, those Qïpchaqs allied with the Merkit in particular were the royal Ölberli house in the eastern part of this range centred on the Zhayiq (Ural) River valley, whose sway extended from the Zhem (Emba) valley in the east to the Volga (Etil) River in the west.

26. The base camp or *a'uruq* was a mobile base camp, where non-combatants maintained the preconditions of military mobilization. Such *a'uruq*s were mobile, but would as a rule stay at least a day's ride away from any expected battle and were too large to move in very rugged terrain.

27. Actually, comparison with the 'Authentic Chronicle of Chinggis Khan' and the biography of Sübe'edei (preserved in three Chinese translations) shows that it was not in the Year of the Cow of 1205, but the next Year of the Cow, 1217, in which Sübe'edei was dispatched to hunt down and kill the last Merkit fugitives. (Jebe was sent to hunt Küculug Khan at the same time, as is mentioned in §237, albeit with the same erroneous identification of the year.) See Pow and Liao, pp. 52–3, 70.

28. It is likely that the following text is cited directly from a source document which purported to give the actual decree issued at the time. The reference to having the decree recited (Mongolian *da'u bari'ulur-un*) indicates that even though the Uyghur-Mongolian script and Uyghur scribal practice had already been adopted at the Mongolian court at this time, transmission of the khan's orders was still frequently done orally, to be memorized by the commander so addressed.

29. That is, a wooden pole with a looped rope at its end, used as a lariat to lasso livestock.

30. This phrase about a game animal with the Mongols' arrow in it appears in the biography of Tutġaq, a Qïpchaq who was descended from prisoners captured in Sübe'edei's campaign: 'When the Great Founder [Chinggis Khan] conquered the Merkit, their ruler Ġodu fled to the Qïpchaqs. A messenger was sent to

deliver a message to Ïnas, saying: "Why do you hide the moose we marked with our arrow? Give it back this instant, lest the disaster reach you as well." Ïnas replied to the messenger saying, "The sparrow that flees the falcon hides in the underbrush as if it can save its life; could I then be less than any plant?"' See Su Tianjue, pp. 3.47–8. As György Kara (1995) has shown, the metaphors of the bush and the bird and the game animal with an arrow in it are commonly used in the Turco-Mongolian tradition as contrasting metaphors for asylum and extradition.

31. This distinction between high-status or long-serving persons known to Chinggis Khan, who could only be judged by the ruler himself, and those of lower status or from among the newly adhered masses, who were to be judged, up to and including capital punishment, in the field contrasts with the principle, expressed in §277, that affairs of the steppe are to be judged on the steppe.

32. Like Mostaert and Cleaves, I follow the Chinese gloss and understand the verb root *möse-* as meaning 'to separate' (here 'split into squads'), rather than Poppe and de Rachewiltz (2004, p. 739) who take it to be a cognate of Manchu *muse-*, 'to lose courage; to be disheartened'.

33. Although the Secret Historian was not really familiar with the geography, this campaign, of which Chinggis Khan's eldest son Joci was the titular leader, involved crossing from central Mongolia to western Kazakhstan, a journey of over 3,000 miles. The fugitive Merkit took refuge among the Ölberli Qïpchaqs, a powerful aristocratic house inhabiting the steppes along the Zhem (modern Emba) River between the Ural Mountains and the Caspian Sea. As is implied with the separate references to people and soldiers, we know from other sources that the expedition took a year or more and involved not just soldiers but a whole *a'uruq* or base camp of non-combatants: women, children and old men. See Atwood 2017b.

34. As may be seen from the past-tense reference to the Year of the Cow, the decree being cited here must have been issued on a later occasion. We know that when the Merkit were caught and destroyed there were questions at first about whether all of them should indeed be executed, as well as also an unexpected conflict with the Khwarazmian sultan that broke out as they were returning home in the spring or summer of 1219. This particular decree might have been attached to an account of one or another of these two episodes.

35. As with Jamuqa's pivotal statement in §118, this statement has been subject to many interpretations. As there also, its ambiguity seems to be part of the narrative point.

36. Although unglossed, the *qarambai noġosu* has been identified, tentatively, with the mandarin duck, although that type of duck is not found in Mongolia today, summering no nearer than Manchuria. In any case, the males of the common ducks of Mongolia, such as the mallard or the ruddy shelduck, are also fairly colourful, if not quite as colourful as the mandarin duck.

37. The bird name *borcin sono*, glossed as 'a kind of drake', has not been securely identified; some identify it with the teal (de Rachewiltz 2004, p. 744).

38. That is with the various comparisons which Jamuqa made in describing the Mongol army.

39. Previous translators Onon (p. 187n.) and de Rachewiltz (2004, p. 749) survey some of the explanations offered for this idiom, not attested elsewhere. Is the undigested food gold dust swallowed by men swearing *anda*-hood? Is it the blood of the pledge of *anda*? Is it an unforgettable meal, corresponding to the unforgettable words? Are the unforgettable words positive words of pledge of *anda*, or negative words of hatred? I would interpret both 'food that would never be digested' and 'words that would never be forgotten' in a positive sense – shared food that would leave an obligation until it is digested, which will be never, and shared words that would leave an obligation until they are forgotten, which is never. However, this is but one example of idioms found in the *Secret History* which are not attested elsewhere, and whose interpretation is a matter of speculation.

40. Just as the number of one's mothers in polygamous Mongolia would include all the wives of one's father, so one's grandmothers would include all the wives of one's two grandfathers.

41. To kill without shedding blood was an honourable death, given to rulers.

42. 'Bare bones' is *ölük yasun*, literally 'dead bones'. Mongols practised secondary burial whereby the body of a deceased person was first disposed of provisionally in a way for the flesh to rot or be removed, and then the bare bones would be collected and placed in a more permanent burial site.

43. The supernatural spirit protector or *genius* (in the original Latin sense) of a person; see §63.

6: The New Regime

1. It may seem peculiar that Chinggis Khan is here being given the title of ruler (*qan*) when he had already been 'khan' a decade or more previously. Of course, the scale of the coronation would have been different; in the earlier case, Chinggis Khan was being crowned as the ruler of the Mongols in the narrow sense, around the headwaters of the three rivers, Onon, Kherlen and Tuul at the holy mountain of Burġan-Qaldun (see §§123–4, 179), while here in 1206 he would be crowned the ruler of all Mongolia. This is evidently the Secret Historian's intended interpretation. However, no other source explicitly mentions the earlier coronation, and other sources from the Mongol empire preferred to see his Pig Year or 1203 conquest of the Kereyit as marking the beginning of his rule as khan, leaving the Tiger Year coronation also unmentioned.

2. This title, derived from the medieval pronunciation of Chinese *guowang* or 'prince of state' as *gui ong*, was actually given in 1217 when Chinggis Khan made Muqali his viceroy in North China. However, we know that other sources confused the date as a Year of the Tiger (1218), when it should have been a Year of the Cow (1217); the Secret Historian then must have assumed that this appointment had taken place in the same Year of the Tiger when Chinggis Khan was enthroned.

3. Numbering has been added to the list. As may be noted, the sequence of names is quite different from that in the following text of the grants of favour (*soyorqal*) – evidently, the Secret Historian has incorporated a separate list of the commanders of a thousand that embodied a somewhat different understanding of who was important from the Secret Historian's own. It is also notable that this list contains at least two persons who had already died by this time: Caġān-Quwa of the Negus (see §129) and Quyildar (see §175). The list thus records not the actual commanders of a thousand in 1206, as has often been taken to be the case, but rather those figures whose service to Chinggis Khan in establishing the empire was rewarded with a grant as commander of a thousand. Their descendants would then govern the thousand in the name of that founder.

4. The title *küregen* here and below means simply 'son-in-law', but in this context refers to an imperial son-in-law, that is, the husband of a princess descended from Chinggis Khan.

5. As with the list of commanders, this account of the grants of favour (*soyorqal*) given by Chinggis Khan presents itself as a record of the 1206 coronation, but in reality was compiled by the Secret Historian largely on the basis of various biographical materials, the datable examples of which come from the 1230s, during the institutionalization of administration under Ökodei. It is thus more of an idealized portrait of the new regime's Mongol ruling class as it would eventually develop, rather than a documented picture of the 1206 situation.

6. In the Secret Historian's narrative, this would be Mother Ö'elun, who in §135 serves as Śiki Qutuġu's foster-mother. Historically, however, he was fostered by Chinggis Khan's wife, Madame Börte.

7. One may wonder, since no previous services or efforts by Śiki Qutuġu have been recorded in the history, what the Secret Historian is referring to. This puzzlement would be increased by the reference below to a grant of 'the cities with earthen walls' since no such cities had yet been conquered by Chinggis Khan. In fact, Śiki Qutuġu's first known politico-military task came eight years later in the siege and administration of Zhongdu (the Golden Khan's capital in North China) in 1214–15. Nor was he made a judge (*jarġu*) and administrator of sedentary lands until the reign of Ökodei in the Year of the Horse (1234). The Persian historian Rashiduddin already records an alternative version to that presented here, in which Śiki Qutuġu was not raised by Mother Ö'elun to be Chinggis Khan's little brother, but rather by Madame Börte to be an extra son. Most likely, the Secret Historian took decrees from Ökodei's time, and, presuming that Śiki Qutuġu was an extra son of Mother Ö'elun, thought he must have been prominent earlier and so inserted them into an account of the 1206 coronation rewards.

8. The imperative here is somewhat awkward, and like similar such instances of awkwardness may indicate that this text was repurposed from one originally in a different narrative context.

9. Such a grant of favour up to 'nine offences' will feature commonly in this list of favours. One may wonder how such a level of immunity was compatible with any regular governance. In practice, by this time and up to his death Chinggis Khan's power was unquestioned enough and his judgement in choosing his commanders good enough that we have no instance of any of these figures testing the limits of his favour (but see §246). The

autobiography of Babur, a sixteenth-century prince of Mongol descent and founder of the Mughal empire in India, records a case where he gave such a promise to a powerful ally, but later came to regret it: 'Ever since Baqi Chaghaniani had come and joined us ... no one had held such authority. Whatever was said, whatever was done, it was his word and his deed, notwithstanding the fact that no service worthy of mention or civility one might expect had ever been seen of him. Indeed I had received from him all sorts of discourtesies and ill treatment, and he was a niggardly, coarse, envious, spiteful, and ill-natured bully ... [After many incidents] [h]e had gone too far with his complaints and his absences. Sick to death of his manners and his deeds, we dismissed him, after which he changed his mind and began to agitate. It was no use. He had a letter written and delivered to me, saying "You stipulated that I would not be called to account until I had committed nine offences." I had Mulla Baba write a memorandum enumerating eleven offences one by one and sent it to him. That got him' (*Baburnama*, trans. Thackston, pp. 187–8).

10. 'Junior kinsmen' and 'princes' here are literally 'little brothers' (*de'u-ner*) and 'sons' (*kö'ut*) respectively. In the empire, these kinship terms doubled as status terms.

11. 'felt-walled people [*sisgei tu'urġa-tan*] ... plank-door people (*qabdasun e'ude-ten*)'. That is, for those dwelling in *gers* (yurts) whose walls are skirted with felt and for those dwelling in houses which have wooden doors. Although Mongolians dwelling in *gers* today have wooden doors, in the empire time doors were made of hanging felt (see for example §§77, 97 and 167).

12. On these Blue Registries (*Köke debter*), see Allsen 1987, pp. 116–19. In Chinese during the Mongol empire they were known as the *hukou qingce* or 'Blue Census Registers' (*Yuanshi*, p. 22.503) and listed the households of the empire along with the service categories to which they belonged. The title 'Blue' is probably from the colour of the registries' cover.

13. According to all other sources, Qutuġu Noyan, as he is usually known, did supervise the census in North China, the administration of justice, and the distribution of households as shares to the princes, princesses, imperial sons-in-law and major commanders. This happened, however, not in 1206, when the Mongols were still years away from having 'cities with earthen walls' under their control, but in 1234, under Ökodei. See Atwood and Struve, pp. 110–11, 145, 146, 174.

14. As Rashiduddin recorded (Rashiduddin/Thackston, p. 63), 'this side' was the right hand of Chinggis Khan, where Father Mönglik sat above all others, next to the khan himself.

15. As with Old Man Üsun in §216 below, whose privileges are quite similar to those accorded Father Mönglik, this discourse on the year and the month is probably a reference to astrological prediction. When Chinggis Khan's grandson, Möngke, under whom the *Secret History* was written, was born on Moon XII, day 3 of the Year of the Dragon (10 January 1209), the later Chinese annals of his reign recorded, 'At the time, there was one of the Qongqotan tribe who understood the celestial phenomena, and he said the emperor would later certainly be held in great honour, so, therefore, he was named Möngke' (*Yuanshi*, p. 3.43). Father Mönglik was of the Qongqotan house, as was his son Kökecu, whose rise and fall as a charismatic shaman is narrated in the *Secret History* later. One or the other should be the one who made the prediction of Möngke's future glory.

16. The Altai here is the modern Altai in western Mongolia. Bo'orcu followed Chinggis Khan's campaign in Central Asia, and according to his biography in the *Yuanshi* was appointed to tutor Caġadai (*Yuanshi*, 119.2946). Note that the units of the decimal organization were peacetime units as well, and Bo'orcu's position of 'governing' (*medetugei*) the right-wing *tümen* was as much or more about civilian administrative as about military command.

17. This supernatural sign seems to be the one described in a fourteenth-century Chinese-language biography of Muqali and his descendants as follows: 'His Grace was born east of the Onon River. At the time of his birth, a white vapour filled the tent and there was a miraculous shaman who saw it and said, marvelling, "This is no ordinary boy."' See Su Tianjue, p. 1.1. On the term *ja'arin* see §121; here it seems to be the same as the figure called in Chinese a 'miraculous shaman'. Likewise, 'east of the Onon River' seems to indicate the valley of Qorqonaq Jubur. The description of how Muqali entered Chinggis Khan's service in §137 is much more mundane.

18. The present-day Greater Khingan Mountains. As with Bo'orcu and the western *tümen*, Muqali's rule over the eastern one combined civilian and military aspects. When Chinggis Khan finished his campaigns in North China in 1214, Muqali remained, campaigning in the area of eastern Inner Mongolia and Manchuria, until he was appointed as Chinggis Khan's

viceroy over the whole of the Jin dynasty territory in 1217; see Atwood and Struve, pp. 78–80, 90–92.

19. Reading the phrase *eji'e turuq* as an idiom, unrecognized by the glossators, as also found in §167.

20. The Telengut are a Turkic-speaking people found today as Teleuts in central Siberia's Kemerovo district, and as the Telengits in Russia's southern Siberian Altay Republic. The Tölös (Mongolian Tö'eles) are another Turkic-speaking people, today closely associated with the Telengit of the Altay.

21. This passage is cast as a speech from Chinggis Khan to Jürcedei. However, we know from a Chinese summary of the Mongolian original, preserved in the *Yuanshi*, pp. 120.2962–3, that it was originally taken from a biography of Jürcedei, mostly telling of his episodes in the third person, with only a few first-person passages of approbation spoken by Chinggis Khan about Jürcedei. See Atwood 2015b, pp. 167–70. I have given the quotation marks only for those passages which in the original were evidently meant as direct speech, leaving the rest, which the Secret Historian left in the third person, outside the quotation marks.

22. As may be recalled from §186 and the note thereon, Chinggis Khan's temporary alliance with Ja'a Gambo, by which his half of the Kereyit kingdom was preserved, had been sealed by the marriage of Ja'a Gambo's two daughters, Ibaqa Beki to Chinggis Khan and Sorġoqtani Beki to Chinggis Khan's son Tolui.

23. These two sentences refer to a campaign mentioned nowhere else in the *Secret History*, but summarized in Jürcedei's *Yuanshi* biography. The campaign took place in spring or summer 1204, after the first declaration of war against the Naiman. The Kereyit allies under Ja'a Gambo, who would have been an important part of the campaign against the Naiman, suddenly grew restless and conspired with the Merkit and Naiman. Chinggis Khan entrusted the suppression of this sudden and highly menacing sedition to Jürcedei. See Atwood 2015b, pp. 164–7.

24. High-born Mongolian ladies upon marriage each received a horde (Mongolian *ordo*) or mobile palace with a staff derived partly from her own people who had accompanied her into marriage as dowry servants (*injes*) and partly from those granted her by her husband from among people he had newly conquered. Ibaqa's 'throne' here thus refers to her seat of command over this horde and its attached staff. This position was heritable most often by the husband's next wife coming from the same family, although the details of its inheritance are unclear and were

probably very complicated. As we see immediately below, however, such staff were coveted resources and were often stripped away from the control of the lady or her successors. See Broadbridge.

25. This care to defend Ibaqa's reputation probably relates to the charge that she, through a steward in her entourage, had poisoned Ökodei Khan. Rashiduddin relates: 'Ibaqa Beki, Sorqaghtani Beki's sister, [whom Chinggis Khan] had given to Ke'etei Noyan [that is, Jürcedei], had a son who was a *ba'urchi*. Every year Ibaqa Beki used to come to court from Cathay [North China], where her yurt [territory] was, to consult with Sorqaghtani Beki. When she came she always gave a banquet at which she offered a cup to the Qa'an. In the thirteenth year of the Qa'an's reign, she came as usual and, together with her son the *ba'urchi*, offered a cup to Ögödäi Qa'an. That night the Qa'an died in his sleep from overindulgence in wine. The next morning the khatuns and amirs [ladies and commanders] accused Ibaqa and her son of having poisoned the Qa'an with the cup they offered' (Rashiduddin/Thackston, p. 234). Alcidai, a captain in Ökodei's *kesikten*, defended her and noted that the emperor had obviously died of alcohol poisoning.

26. These two decrees seem to refer to Moci-Bedu'un of the Dörben, who appeared once in §120, and apart from this cryptic reference is never mentioned again. Evidently the Secret Historian included this titbit more as a comment on Qubilai's ability to govern than due to any interest in Bedu'un.

27. The obvious implication is that Toruqan is Tolun's father and the two will share command over the thousand together, as Chinggis Khan feels is appropriate for father and son. However, Rashiduddin (Rashiduddin/Thackston, pp. 63, 208, 209) says that Tolun Cerbi was one of the sons of Father Mönglik. There is no clear solution to this contradiction.

28. Outside the horde or court, less honoured guests were kept at least a bowshot away; when Chinggis Khan tells Önggur and Boroġul to 'ride off and issue food for all the other people', he is asking them to go out and see as well to the supply of food for those gathered outside but not allowed admission to the horde's precincts. See the account of John of Plano Carpini (Dawson, pp. 61–3), who witnessed this at the 1246 coronation of Güyuk Khan.

29. The Chinese translation of Chinggis Khan's last command is free but helpfully fills in some of the implicit cultural background:

'When sitting, you two be separate to the right and left of the liquor things; with Tolun and the others both sit facing north' (Wulan, p. 280/ix.10v). The great skins (*yeke tüsurge*) are the great sacks of skin used to hold *esuk* (see also §130). A bench with such a great sack was placed at the entrance to the *ordo* or horde. The entrance faced south or south-east and those responsible for dispensing sat to the south of the bench with its great skin, facing north, towards the khan and his lady, who were seated facing south at the *qoyimar* or honoured position on the northern side of the horde. As William of Rubruck described it, 'At the entrance [to the court or horde] stands a bench with a skin full of milk, or with some other beverage, and some cups' (Jackson and Morgan, p. 76, cf. pp. 132, 177). Later on, in the Mongol Yuan dynasty, the skin sacks were replaced with a 'liquor sea' made of lacquered wood, 18 feet high and able to hold 5 tons of liquor. The attendants had multiplied and those sitting south of the liquor things facing north now numbered twenty *daraci* or masters of grape wine, twenty *qaraci* or masters of clarified *esuk*, and twenty *ba'urci* or stewards; the last was the position which Önggur and Boroġul held at the court in Chinggis Khan's time. See Matsuda, pp. 185–6, 191–2.

30. In Mongolia, the pluck or *jüldu* (modern *züld*) consists of the head, throat, lungs and heart of a slaughtered animal and is given at banquets as the choice portion to the honoured guest.

31. This seems a strangely brief reference to the rich grants which we know Chinggis Khan bestowed on his daughters and their descendants, who, due to the rules of exogamy and patrilineal inheritance, would not have been of the imperial Borjigin lineage. Jack Weatherford (pp. xi–xii) has speculated on what may have been omitted from this passage and why.

32. *Beki* was a title granted to the senior members of ruling houses among the decentralized peoples of the Mongolian plateau, those without the title of *qan* or *qa'an*. It seems to have combined priestly and political functions, although with the rise of khans among the Mongols the political functions disappeared, leaving only the priestly and shamanic functions seen here.

33. As with Father Mönglik of the Qongqotan (see §204), whose privileges have parallels to those of Old Man Üsun, discoursing yearly and monthly probably refers to offering astrological predictions about the coming year and month. Given that Old Man Üsun was supreme over the shamans, this interpretation is confirmed by the statement of William of Rubruck: 'Some of [the

shamans] are familiar with astronomy – especially the chief – and forecast the eclipse of the sun and the moon' (Jackson and Morgan, p. 240).

34. The name Negus had a broader and a narrower meaning. In the broad meaning, it designated all those of the *Dürlugin* or 'Ordinary' moiety of the Mongols, as opposed to the noble Kiyan or *Niru'u* moiety (see Appendix B). Within the Negus moiety, the term also designated a particular house, one to which To'oril's father, Caġān-Quwa, belonged (see §§120, 129).

35. 'Free rights to the territory' (*nuntuq darqala-*) means the right to nomadize without reference to the territorial boundaries established with the decimal organization. The thousands, like later systems of administration in Mongolia, had particular localities within which they were required to restrict their movements to various seasonal pastures. Sorġan-Śira and his family, however, would not have to observe such limits and could choose the territories from those of any of the neighbouring thousands in which to make their seasonal camps.

36. *Ötok* was a kind of ceremonial liquor, probably milk-based, which was drunk at the high point of *quriltai*s or assemblies. As may be seen in §154, only those with the right to hear the most confidential deliberations were allowed to drink it.

37. Skylark or *bilji'ur* appears to be the same as the *bildu'ur* of §160, where Jamuqa uses it as a migratory bird to be a symbol of a fair-weather friend. Rashiduddin tells us that Naya'a was also known as *jusur*, 'flatterer'; *bilda'uci*, probably related to *bildu'ur*, is another Mongolian word for a flatterer or insincere friend.

38. The two phrases about Bo'orcu and Muqali are missing in the *LAT* recension, and may have been added by a later scribe to explain how this appointment for Naya'a, found nowhere else, is reconcilable with the previously noted decrees.

39. That is, *tümen*s.

40. As will be mentioned below, the punishment for persistent delinquency in the bodyguard was thirty-seven blows of the cane.

41. These four shift commanders of the quiver-bearers are listed in the exact same positions under Ökodei Khan, narratively thirty or so years later. Actuarially, this is of course quite impossible. Most likely, they were the shift commanders for the quiver-bearers under Ökodei, but in the process of using an Ökodei-era decree to describe the imperial bodyguards under both reigns, the Secret Historian accidentally let this anachronism stand.

42. Following the *LAT* recension's 'shift' (*kesik*) for the Hanlin recension's incomprehensibly repetitive 'thousand' (*minggan*).

43. The reference to 'elders' (*ötogus*) supervising highlights how the *kesikten*'s role was by no means exclusively military. In fact, by forming the household of the khan, those serving among the *kesikten* were the nucleus of the khan's civil administration. By the time of Qubilai Khan, in fact, the *kesikten* were no longer much used in a military role. In 1289 one of Boroġul's descendants, Öcicer, complained to Qubilai that by serving as a shift elder he was not able to win merit as a military commander. Qubilai responded, 'Believing that [Muqali's descendant] Hantum and the rest had exactly the same merit in the founding as your family did, all having won many victories, you, my liege, are ashamed of yourself for not keeping up with them. Yet in personally tending to the bow cases and quivers, respectfully guarding Us day and night and enabling me, the one man [i.e. the emperor], to never meet anything untoward, your merit is not small. Where is the need to join the army yourself? Cut off the ears of the affairs at hand as a trophy. Why don't you begin to set your heart on this?' See Su Tianjue, p. 3.44. Since cutting off cars was the usual East Asian custom of generating a body count after battle, here it is being used as a metaphor for successfully handling civilian affairs.

44. In this particular passage, the ambiguity of *kesikten*, which could be interpreted either as 'those on my shift' or 'the ones favoured by me', is particularly clear. *Kesik*, meaning both 'shift' and 'favour', is the root here.

45. The doors were made of felt and were long enough to trail on the floor when let down. By standing on the skirts the guards would both guarantee the security of the *ger* and keep it well sealed and those inside warm during the night.

46. On this practice of speaking through the felt walls of the *ger*, see the note to §169.

47. The phrases 'superior to' here and 'behind' below are in relation to the position of the khan. 'Superior to' means closer to the khan and 'behind' means that they were closer to the back of the khan's *ger* than the nightguards who would be facing away from the *ger* to the north.

48. This sudden reference to an otherwise unknown episode involving Eljigidei is repeated in §278 under Ökodei's reign. It is one of the indications that these regulations for the imperial lifeguard actually derive from a decree of the time of Ökodei, one

subsequently taken by the Secret Historian and projected back to Chinggis Khan's reign.

49. To prolong the life of the *gers*' felt, they are often protected by reeds (*śiltesu*, Mongolian *süldes*, 'bamboo'). See Sommer's *The Kyrgyz and Their Reed Screens*.

50. 'Swaddled *ger*' (*irgetei ger*) refers here to the band of extra felt (*irge*) placed around the bottom of the *ger* where it meets the ground as a splash-guard.

51. Freshly butchered meat was dried for jerky in the summer and hence was not necessarily ready to cook.

52. Surveyors or *nuntu'ucin* were men appointed from the thousands (see §279) or from the horde, as here, to assign places to camp for both the great hordes and the herders in the thousands.

53. The Secret Historian cites the same regulations about the night-guard not going off to war without the khan in briefer form under the reign of Ökodei (see §278). In fact, Chinggis Khan participated personally in all the major campaigns of conquest to come and thus his *keśikten* participated with him. The biography of Caġan, commander of Chinggis Khan's personal hundred, for example, records battles in North China, Central Asia down to the banks of the Indus, and then against the Tanguts (see *Yuanshi*, p. 120.2956). It is thus strange to hear Chinggis Khan sound so defensive about not allowing his elite nightguards to participate in war. This is one more indication that this passage, like the entire text about the *keśikten*, was actually cited from a decree dating to the reign of Ökodei Khan. In the later part of his reign, from 1234 to his death in 1241, Ökodei Khan remained in Mongolia, hunting and travelling the regular round of seasonal camps while some of the largest ever campaigns of the Mongol empire were taking place in eastern Europe, central China and the frontiers of South Asia. In this context one can well imagine that Ökodei had to respond to implicit criticism of keeping the empire's crack forces out of combat during such a time. The Secret Historian, convinced by Ökodei's own insistence that he was merely reiterating his father's regulations, had felt free to cite large passages from it and attribute them to Chinggis Khan. In a few cases, as here, however, the historical anachronism is visible.

54. As the reference to nets makes clear, the various weapons and armour are envisioned to be used for hunting, not for war. Breastplates would be helpful as tigers, wolves and other dangerous game would often be caught in the ring hunts. See Juvaini/Boyle,

p. 27, where preparation for the hunt includes the distribution of appropriate arms to those conducting it.

55. Previous translators have rendered *a'urasu* as 'satins'. This translation is, however, based on a misunderstanding of the Chinese gloss *duanpi* or *duanzi*. In fact, satins were a South China speciality only popularized in the Mongol empire during the fourteenth century; see Shea 2021. That, and the fact that Mongolian *a'urasu* both here in context and in later usage means simply 'possessions', indicates that generic fabrics are meant. Mongol court dress did involve various luxury textiles which were first gained through tribute and then produced by deported artisans. Robes made of these luxury textiles were issued to the *keśikten* to enhance the splendour of court occasions. As Marco Polo observed when he himself was serving among the *keśikten* of Qubilai Khan, on special occasions they all wore robes of a single colour, called *jisun* (from the Mongolian word for colour), of gold for the khan's birthday, of white for the Lunar New Year and of thirteen different colours for each of the different monthly feasts (including one for the intercalary month). See Polo/Cliff, pp. 111, 112 and 114. See also Shea 2020, pp. 29–30, 63–5, 88–9 and Allsen 1997, pp. 19–22, 25–6, 77–9. On the particular luxury fabrics presented to the Mongols in tribute see §§238, 252 and 274 and notes.

56. 'What the herds leave' here is *qoq*. In modern Mongolian (*khog*) it means 'garbage', but here it is glossed in Chinese as *sùi cǎo* 'broken up (or trampled) grass'. Since Dödei will be travelling behind the horde as it nomadizes, his mounts will always be eating grass which has already been trampled and cropped by those ahead. Similarly, *qoma'ul* or horse manure is the worst fuel among the various livestock droppings, disliked for its smoky burn. Again, as the horde progresses, those in front get first pick of the more valued dried cow plops (*arġal*) and the sheep and goat pellets (*qorġal*) valued as kindling, leaving only the horse manure for those in the rear.

57. The Secret Historian here groups a number of campaigns which historically took place between 1207 and 1219. What they have in common is that the targeted rulers, while not Mongols, were culturally and geographically relatively close to the Mongols and were eventually integrated as tributary rulers, the most prominent of whom were made 'son-in-law' states of the new Mongol empire. The organization throughout is thematic, although it has often been misinterpreted as chronological.

58. The Qarluqs were a mostly nomadic, Turkic-speaking and Muslim people ruling over a mixed population of Muslim and Christian farmers and city folk in the Ili valley and Junggaria, along the borders of present-day Kazakhstan and Xinjiang. The Qarluqs were organized into several small khanates; that of Arslan Khan or 'Lion Khan' was the oldest and most powerful.

59. 'Not rebelled' (Mongolian *ese bulġaba*) is from the point of view of the Mongol imperial ideology, in which resistance to conquest is rebellion against Heaven.

60. The Chüy River (Shū in Kazakh, Chu in Russian) rises in the mountains of Kyrgyzstan and flows into south-east Kazakhstan. Actually, Sübe'edei's campaign from 1217 to 1219 went much further west; the final battle where the sons of Toqto'a were killed took place on the Zhem or Emba River, in far-western Kazakhstan.

61. The Secret Historian's Sariġ-Qol or 'Yellow Valley' is more correctly Sariqol or 'Head of the Valley'; the Hanlin recension further corrupted it to Sariġ-Qun or 'Yellow Cliff'. This is the medieval designation for the region of high-altitude desert valleys around the Pamir Mountains where the present-day borders of Afghanistan, Tajikistan and Xinjiang meet.

62. The Uyghur kingdom was centred on the Turpan oasis, in the eastern part of present-day Xinjiang. The kingdom's established majority religion was Mahayana Buddhism, although there were both Muslim and Christian minorities. Uyghurs became tutors (literally and figuratively) for the Mongol imperial family in the ways of civil administration. Ïduqut or 'Holy Glory' was the Uyghur ruler's official title.

63. A version of the same couplet appears in a Chinese translation of the Mongolian biography of Botu in the *Yuanshi* (118.2921). In it, Botu sends a messenger to announce his allegiance to Chinggis Khan, saying, 'it is as if the clouds opened to show the sun and spring winds blew to melt the ice'.

64. *Subut* and *tana* may be translated as 'standard pearls' and 'exotic pearls' respectively. The word *tana* (plural *tanas*) comes from Persian *dānah*, and appears here to designate larger, finer pearls sourced ultimately from the Persian Gulf. See Allsen 2019, pp. 50–51. By contrast, *subut* appears to designate pearls commonly found in China from the South China Sea, which were less valued. Elsewhere in Mongolian writings, *tana* also referred to the finest freshwater pearls from Manchuria, while *subut* (or *nicuhe* in Manchu) referred to lower-quality pearls from China or elsewhere.

The pearls found in §133 may be such fine Manchurian river pearls. See Schlesinger, pp. 47, 70–71.

65. *Našiš* (plural *našit*), from Perso-Arabic *nashīj*, was one of two Middle Eastern-style gold brocaded fabrics that were coveted by the Mongols (the other was *naq*, mentioned in §274 below). *Našiš* is the gold-woven lampas found among surviving Mongol-era fine textiles. William of Rubruck received a bolt of this silk cloth and described it as 'a piece of cloth as broad as a bed-cover and extremely long'. See Jackson and Morgan, pp. 190–91, 237. After their conquest of North China, the Mongols established colonies of deported Middle Eastern weavers in the hill country north-west of present-day Beijing. See Shea 2020, pp. 30–32, 41, 47, 82, 90, plates 9 and 10, and Allsen 1997, pp. 2–3, 11, 28–9, 96. The Mongolian spelling here is the plural *nacit*, but this is a case where written *c* was pronounced according to the Öng'ut dialect reading as *š* (just as in English we see 'chivalry' and say 'shivalry').

66. *Darda* (plural *darda*s) is glossed as 'gold-woven fabric' or 'brocaded fabric'. The fabric described appears to be Chinese and continued in use into the eighteenth century, when dictionaries define it as 'decorative silks' or 'silks glittering with a scattered fine flower pattern'. These may be 'the tabby or twill ground silks woven with repeat patterns in a supplementary gold weft' found among surviving Mongol-era fine textiles; see Shea 2020, p. 30, plates 3, 4 and figure 1.6.

67. The Forest Folk (Mongolian *Hoi-yin Irgen*) was a broad designation of the people of the Siberian taiga. They had a distinctive way of life described by many writers of the Mongol empire. Rashiduddin, mixing descriptions of many separate peoples, described how they never herded ordinary cattle or sheep, but instead only yaks or reindeers, how they used birch-bark tepees, not felt *ger*s, dressed in animal skins, not cloth, and used skis to hunt and sleds to carry game (Rashiduddin/Thackston, p. 42). One anonymous Chinese source, referring particularly to the Qabqanas (see below), pictures them as mostly hunters and gatherers with a few domestic livestock, living in birch-bark tepees, using reindeer as pack and dairy animals, gathering pine nuts and roots of lilies and peonies, and hunting in the winter on skis. See *Yuanshi*, p. 63.1574, translated in Cleaves 1956, pp. 401–2.

68. Here we have the first list of seven peoples of the forest. 1) On the Oyirats, see above. 2) The Buryats here refers specifically to

the Nizhneudinsk Buryats; they were forest-dwelling Mongolic speakers. After the Russian conquest, the term 'Buryat' was later extended to all the Mongolic speakers in Siberia. 3) The Mongolic-speaking Barġut occupied the Barguzin valley. 4) The Urs (plural Ursut) were an originally north-east Iranian-speaking Saka people, known in ancient times as the Aorsi, who had migrated north to Siberia and become a component of the Kïrghiz confederation. 5) The Qabqanas were probably Samoyedic or Kettic speakers in the Tozha Basin along the Bii-Khem of north-east Tuva. 6) The Qangqas dwelled in a town built where the Kem or Yenisey River meets the Angara; their language was a non-Turkic one. 7) The Tuvans occupied the main basin of Tuva today. The Ursut, Qabqanas, Qangqas and Tuvans all traditionally paid tribute to the Yenisey Kïrghiz (see below).

69. These Kïrghiz are not to be confused with the Kïrghiz or Kyrgyz of present-day Kyrgyzstan. The Kïrghiz here are the ancestors of the present-day Khakas people of the Minusinsk Basin in southern Siberia. At present, the Khakas are purely Turkic-speaking, but during the time of the Mongol empire the Minusinsk and Tuvan Basins were inhabited by a potpourri of Turkic, north-east Iranian (Saka), Samoyedic and Kettic speakers. Turkic speakers had been politically dominant for centuries, however.

70. Comparison with the parallels in Rashiduddin, the *Campaigns of Chinggis Khan*, and the *Yuanshi* shows that the *Secret History* text had contracted *Yeti Orun[-u] Urus İnal* to *Yeti İnal*. The Yenisey Kïrghiz at this time were a league of petty principalities, divided into the Seven Thrones (*Yeti-Orun*) and the Six Lands (*Alti-Er*). The Seven Thrones were each ruled by an *ïnal* and hence were also called the Seven İnal (*Yeti-İnal*); the Six Lands were each ruled by a *beg-tegin* (commander-prince) – all of these names and titles are purely Turkic. In the surrender to Joci, the Seven Thrones were represented by Urus İnal, while the Six Lands were represented by Öre (also known as Ör-Bo'oci) Beg-Tegin. The confusion of the text may be responsible for the repetition of the 'commanders of the Kïrghiz' phrase, which sounds as clumsy and repetitious in the Mongolian as it does in the English.

71. The people in this second list of seven are mostly in central and western Siberia, although not all of them can be identified. 1) Sibir is the Ibir-Sibir of Rashiduddin, which he places in the far north near the Angara and/or lower Yenisey River. The name may also be related to Mongolian *śiber* (modern *shiwer*),

referring to densely wooded land in marshes or along river-banks. 2) Keštimi is a Siberian Turkic term designating 'tribute-payers; dependants' and appears to refer to the outlying Turkic population under Kïrghiz rule. 3) Bayit or 'Rich Ones' is a common Turco-Mongolian ethnonym. They may be ancestral to the Bayad Mongols of Uws province in modern Mongolia, but they were found at this time much further to the north-west along the Imar (Ob'). 4) The Tuqas may be related to the Dukha or Tuvan reindeer herders of far northern Mongolia. 5–6) On the Telengut and Tölös (Mongolian Tö'eles) see above under §207. 7) The Taz are a clan among the Kazakhs today, around the mouth of the Zhayiq (Ural) River valley. See Schöning. A Chinese administrative encyclopedia of the early ninth century, the *Tongdian*, gives a description of the Keštimi that would probably apply to many of these people. They are said to have had few sheep and cattle but many horses, a common pattern reported by ethnographers in the Siberian taiga. They had similar marriage customs as the steppe Turk empire, their land had many pine and birch trees and every year they paid tribute to their chiefs in sable and otter pelts.

72. The Bashkir (Mongolian plural *Bajigit* of singular *Bajigir*) or Bashkort people lived on the western slopes of the Urals in the Belaya valley in the present-day Republic of Bashkortostan in European Russia. The Bashkirs of modern and early modern times are a Turkic-speaking people, but European travellers at the time of the Mongol empire knew their kingdom as 'Greater Hungary' and found that Magyars from Hungary were able to converse with the Bashkirs. Likewise, Volga Bulgars used the name 'Bashkir' both for their neighbours in Bashkiria and for the Magyars in present-day Hungary. The Turkicization of the population of Bashkiria only began in the wake of the Mongol conquest. See Róna-Tass, pp. 289–308. The Bashkirs appear to have been mentioned just to mark the westernmost extent of Mongol knowledge before the foreign conquests; it is very unlikely that Joci actually reached their land at this time.

73. This paragraph from the Hanlin recension has no parallel in the *LAT* recension and is geographically out of place. It is quite likely an interpolation in the Qubilai-era text, originally a parenthetical note inadvertently incorporated into the text. (For other such possible interpolations see §§264 and 274). Alaqa (more usually Alaqai Beki) was the daughter of Chinggis Khan originally to be given in marriage to Ala-Quš Digit-Quri. In the event,

Ala-Quš was killed before the marriage could be consummated, and Chinggis Khan married her to Ala-Quš's nephew Cingui.

74. Tayidu'ul Soqor and Botoqui Tarġun. It should be noted that although I translate *soqor* as 'one-eyed' (as with Du'a the One-Eyed in §§3–4, 11), it more usually means 'blind'. It should also be noted that fatness in women was seen as a mark of beauty among the Mongols at this time.

75. 'Bison' (Eurasian bison or wisent) is Mongolian *hula'an buqa*, literally 'red bull'. Cleaves (1982, p. 174n.), de Rachewiltz (2004, p. 861) and Onon (p. 224n.) all consider this animal most likely to be an elk or a moose. However, the elk (*Cervus canadensis*) and the moose (*Alces alces*) are both well known in Mongolian as *buġu* and *qandaġai* – indeed, both words are attested in the *Secret History* (see §§12–16, 103 and 199 for *buġu* and §§103 and 255 for *qandaġai*). No one has yet explained why what were referred to in §103 as elk and moose trails (translated as 'trails of hands' and 'moose's trail' for alliteration) would be referred to as 'red bull trails' in §240. The main reason for considering the animal to be some kind of deer is the conviction that no wild bovines have inhabited southern Siberia for thousands of years. However, although the Eurasian bison (wisent) and the aurochs (wild bull) are not found there today, the bison has been documented in southern Siberia at least to the tenth century AD and the aurochs to the eighteenth century; see T. Sipko, 'European Bison in Russia – Past, Present, and Future', *European Bison Conservation Newsletter*, vol. 2 (2009), pp. 148–59. Of the two, the bison is much more likely to be the 'red bull'. The bull aurochs is black and prefers warmer, lower and wetter habitats, often marshes and river banks, while the bison is reddish-brown, avoids wet, marshy lands and easily adapts to drier pine-spruce forests and very cold and high mountainous terrain; see Cis van Vuure, trans. K. H. M. van den Berg, *Retracing the Aurochs: History, Morphology and Ecology of an Extinct Wild Ox* (Sofia: Pensoft, 2005), pp. 235–6, 243–4, 247–51. Bison in the forests of eastern North America were responsible for many of the trails over the Appalachian Mountains, still known today as 'buffalo traces'.

76. Translators have taken this to mean either that each man carried ten canes that were to be used for beatings (e.g. the Hanlin recension's running translation, Cleaves, de Rachewiltz) or else that carrying ten canes was the punishment for cowardice (e.g. Onon). Neither understanding makes much sense, however – one would

not need ten canes per person to beat them, and carrying ten such canes would not be a harsh punishment. Moreover, neither interpretation takes account of the fact that we have here not the *beri'e* or cane used as a tool of judicial punishment but *müsut*, literally 'shafts', elsewhere used for arrow shafts, which are, as per the fable of Alan's sons and the five arrow shafts (§§19–20), individually easily broken. I take 'bearing ten switches' to be a metaphorical reference to taking ten relatively light blows across the back. Regular judicial canings were given on the buttocks and/or thighs and would disable a man for days, so for men on the march, blows of ten switches bundled together on the back, stinging and humiliating but not disabling, would be substituted instead. The use of ten strokes with ten branches tied together as an alternative to a crippling beating is found in Khwandamir (trans. Thackston), p. 41.

77. As in the instructions issued to Sübe'edei in §199, the distinction between the duties assigned to the people (*kü'un*) in the numbered ranks in general and the men (*ere*) indicates that the army contained whole families and that women were also counted on (literally and figuratively) as part of the expeditionary force.

78. Rashiduddin, however, tells a rather different story: Dāritai was executed and his son Tainal Yeye, with two hundred of Dāritai's men, were given to Chinggis Khan's nephew Alcidai as slaves. However, when Dāritai's grandson Kökecu fought for Qubilai Khan, both in his battles with Ariq-Böke and against Li Tan's 1262 rebellion, the family was rewarded with restoration of their membership in the imperial family and establishment as a separate thousand. Dāritai's family in the Ilkhanate were likewise restored to membership among the imperial family (Rashiduddin/Thackston, p. 96; Thackston's reading as 'Tanyal Biy' is incorrect). Eventually they received a territorial appanage in far north-eastern Mongolia and a revenue appanage in Ninghaizhou prefecture at the tip of peninsular Shandong province (see Funada). But the descendants of Dāritai, like those of Belgütei, still suffered for their ancestors' faults by not being allowed to participate in the most confidential imperial councils, during which the special *ötok* wine was drunk (§154).

79. The text here seems to be missing a verb of speech, and the pronoun 'I' (Mongolian *bi*) in a context where it can only be Chinggis Khan speaking. The editors of the Hanlin recension assigned the pronoun to §243 and thus treated the appointments in §243 as being spoken by Chinggis Khan. The *LAT* recension

suppressed the *bi* and thus left both the conclusion of §242 and §243 as third-person narrative. I have emended the text here to treat the *bi* as pertaining to the previous section and thus taken the appointments in §243 as third-person descriptions.

80. The name Möngke here is found in both the Hanlin and *LAT* recensions. However, Rashiduddin (Rashiduddin/Thackston, p. 212) gives Müge Noyan of the Jalayir as Caġadai's second captain of a thousand. Since the name Müge, but not Möngke, appears in the list of commanders of a thousand in §202, it is likely that the Secret Historian here confused the two names, which are spelled similarly in Middle Mongolian.

81. Teb-Tenggeri is a kind of shamanic title, probably meaning 'Most Heavenly'; Kökecu was his personal name. (This Kökecu is not to be confused with the Kökecu of the Besut clan who became a commander of a thousand.) The Persian historian Juvaini, writing around the same time as the Secret Historian, records of him: 'I have heard from trustworthy Mongols that during the severe cold that prevails in those regions he used to walk naked through the desert and the mountains and then to return and say: "God has spoken with me and has said: 'I have given all the face of the earth to Temüjin and his children and named him Chingiz-Khan. Bid him administer justice in such and such a fashion.'"' They called this person Teb-Tengri, and whatever he said Chingiz-Khan used implicitly to follow' (Juvaini/Boyle, p. 39). Elsewhere in the *Secret History* the Secret Historian has eliminated this shamanic role entirely, although it is alluded to below.

82. This phrase, 'The Nine-Tongued Folk', is not attested elsewhere. It is unclear if it is referring to the whole empire (nine is a traditional number of completeness in Turco-Mongolian folklore) or else refers to a particular people. If the latter, it may be significant that Otcigin's people were in the eastern part of the Mongolian plateau.

83. This phrase, 'From when . . .', is common in Mongolian ritual and folk poetry. It establishes mythic time, like the phrase 'Once upon a time' or 'Long ago in a galaxy far, far away'. See, for example, Hangin et al., 1988, p. 73.

84. This tepee (Mongolian *qośiliq*) here is a conical felt tent related to the *qoš* or travelling-tent of §169. See also Ma, pp. 227–9.

7: The Foreign Conquests

1. The *Secret History*'s account of Chinggis Khan's campaigns in North China from 1209 to 1215 is a strange mixture of precise detail and extraordinary chronological and geographical confusion. Evidently, the Secret Historian was writing well after the conquest and had never visited North China yet had also recorded a number of precise details from participants. These probably included Qutuġu Noyan (Śiki Qutuġu) and someone associated with Qasar's horde. Rather than tryug to sort out the exact sequence in the footnotes, I refer the reader to Appendix D, 'Conquests of the Jurchen Jin and Tangut Xia Dynasties, 1205–34'.

2. Mongolian *Hünegen Daba'a*. This was the Mongolian name of the pass named Yehu Ling or 'Wild Fox Ridge' in Chinese. Traditionally it marked the dividing line between North China and the Mongolian plateau.

3. Mongolian *Cabciyal*. This was the Mongolian name of the Juyongguan or Juyong Pass north-west of Beijing.

4. 'Kitans' here and below is literally 'Black Kitans' (*Qara-Kitat*). With the original Mongolian word for Kitans, *Kitan* (singular) or *Kitat* (plural), turning into a general word for the people of North China as a whole, ethnic Kitans were distinguished by adding the descriptor 'black' (*qara*); in the colour symbolism of the Kitans, black was the colour associated with the north, with water and with power.

5. Eight years later, the Daoist patriarch Changchun and his entourage passed the site and saw 'white bones scattered on the fields of battle' and agreed to hold Daoist services for the shades of the otherwise unmourned dead. See Dunnell, West and Yang, p. 30. On the simile of rotten snags, see §196.

6. Mongolian *Śira Dektur*. The early Ming translators identified this with Longhutai, a village a mile south-east of Nankou, the town at the southern gate of Juyong Pass ('the Canyon'). It was thus at the northern edge of the plain that stretched to the Jin capital of Zhongdu.

7. Zhongdu (Mongolian *Cungdu*) or the 'Central Capital' was the main one of the Jin dynasty's six capitals. (The other five were ruled by viceroys as military-political centres.) It was on the location of present-day Beijing.

8. This Ongging *Chengxiang*, i.e. Grand Councillor of the Jurchens' imperial Wongian surname, was Wongian Fuking (d. 1215),

a distant relative of Wongian Xiang, the Ongging *Chengxiang* of §§132-4.

9. Gongzhu (Mongolian *Gungju*) is in fact simply the Chinese word for 'princess'. Her actual name is recorded in later Mongolian sources as Yaliqai and in Chinese as Yanli; both derive from the Jurchen Yali.

10. The Tangut kingdom had adopted Buddhism in the Tibetan tradition and identified their ruler as an incarnation of a Buddha. Thus they called him 'Buddha' (Mongolian *Burqan*) and 'Victorious Buddha' (Mongolian *Iluġu Burqan*); 'victorious' (Sanskrit *jina*) was a standard epithet of the Buddha.

11. *Caqa* is a Mongolian word meaning 'child'; this was evidently the name she received after being married to Chinggis Khan.

12. On the *sülder*, see §§63 and 201.

13. Feather grass or *deresu* grows from 1½ to as much as 8 feet high in thick tussocks. Not only does it provide good fodder, but also 'feather grass . . . provides shelter for livestock from cold wind and provides favorable conditions for early growth of young vegetation'. See Sodnomdarjaagiin Jigjidsuren and Douglas A. Johnson, *Mongol orny malyn tejeeliin urgamal/Forage Plants in Mongolia* (Ulaanbaatar, 2003), p. 49.

14. Woollens were used for the distinctive court ceremonies, called *jisun* (Mongolian for 'colour') or *jama* (Persian for 'robe'), in which all the *kešikten* present were granted robes of the same colour to wear. See Shea 2020, p. 64.

15. Zhaoguan (Mongolian *Ceugon*) was the Song emperor, then holding only South China's Yangtze valley and south-east coast. In fact, Jubqan (or Subqan in more standard Turkic) had actually been detained and killed by Song officials while an envoy to them in 1231 to request right of way to attack the Golden Khan from the south.

16. These generals are Ila Puwa (Chinese Yila Pu'a), Wongian Hada (Chinese Wanyan Heda) and Hû-Šire Yawuta (Chinese Heshilie Yawuta), respectively. They were associated with a final revival of Jin military fortunes from 1227 until their final catastrophic defeat at the Battle of Sanfeng Mountain (8 February 1232). See Atwood 2021b.

17. This military unit was called the 'Red Patch Army' (*Hongnajun*) in Chinese or the Red Jackets (*Hula'an degelen*) in Mongolian. It was formed of Central Eurasian, mostly Turkic, deserters from the Mongol army and commanded by Ila Puwa. See Atwood 2021b and 2015c.

18. Modern Kaifeng in Henan province. Namging means 'Southern Capital' as it was the southernmost of the six capitals of the Jin dynasty. I use here the Mongolian version of the name to distinguish this city from present-day Nanjing, which at the time was part of Song territory.

19. A *liushou* was a high politico-military commander who ruled in the other Jin capitals, apart from the one occupied by the emperor himself.

20. This Qada, who was appointed *liushou* or viceroy in place of the emperor, is not to be confused with the military commander Qada above. It is striking that the Secret Historian in telling this story forgot to mention the crucial part, that Zhongdu was actually surrendered to the Mongols by this Qada after the original viceroy, Wongian Fuking, killed himself. The official Qada's full name in Jurchen was Ñêmha Hada (Chinese Nianhe Heda); after surrendering to Chinggis Khan, he sent his son Cungšai to the Mongol court. He was a vice-minister of revenue for the Jin dynasty around 1205 and in 1214 held concurrent posts in the provincial administration and in the capital garrison armies, in which he argued for appeasement to deal with the Mongol threat (*Jinshi*, pp. 132.2833, 122.2675).

21. These are probably the *darda*-brocades mentioned in §238 above, that is 'a tabby or twill silk featuring repeat patterns in a brocading weft of metallic thread' (Shea 2021, p. 112).

22. Tenggeri or 'Heaven' was his Mongolian name. This Tenggeri should be the only member of the Jurchen imperial family known to have entered the ranks of the *kešikten*: Wongian Eke, also known as the Prince of Cao. He was the grandson of the Jin emperor ruling in 1214 and was not sent out as a hostage until shortly before the fall of Namging to the Mongols, in the spring of 1232. At that time, he was the nephew of the last Jin emperor. Although the other members of the Jin imperial family were all executed either when Namging fell that summer or when the fugitive emperor was finally captured in February 1234, Wongian Eke received good treatment as part of the Mongol elite. Note also how the dayguards were, in fact, serving as hostages for the good behaviour of the rulers, and in earnest of their surrender.

23. Biiging city is now ruins in the area of Ningcheng county, Inner Mongolia. It was the 'Northern Capital' (Chinese *Beijing*) of the Jin dynasty, although it is not to be confused with present-day Beijing.

24. By this time, the 'Great Base Camp' (*Yeke A'uruq*) was stationed more or less permanently along the Kherlen River in eastern Mongolia. After Chinggis Khan's death the hordes of his four great ladies were stationed there more or less permanently, becoming a shrine to the imperial founder; in the reign of Qubilai Khan, the khan's son Gamala built a shrine there. This site, called Awraga in modern Mongolian, has been excavated; see Shiraishi 2006 and 2013.

25. 'Golden halter' (*altan arġamji*), like the 'golden reins' (*altan jilo'a*) below (§256), is a metaphor for the sovereign's control over his subjects; just as a rider controls his horse by the halter and the reins, so the sovereign controls those under his rule.

26. This phrase, read by the transcribers as *cul ulja'ur*, is of uncertain meaning, but that it contains some reference to Joci's illegitimacy is clear from the ensuing conflict. My translation here follows de Rachewiltz's suggestion that it may be *cöl ūlja'ur*, 'something randomly found in the desert'.

27. Other interpreters take this to be referring specifically to Madame Börte ('She went not by her . . .' etc.), but there is no subject and the verb ending here is not feminine as are other verbs where she is the subject just below. Thus I take it to be the general experience of Köke-Cos's generation, as indeed it was.

28. 'Figure' here translates *buy*, which is Turkic for 'body'; the usual Mongolian word is *biy-e*. One can see here how Turkic functioned as a resource for supplying recondite synonymous vocabulary useful for a poet.

29. 'It won't do' (*ülu boli*) here and above has the feminine ending; Caġadai seems to be implicitly judging Joci as not even meeting a girl's level of masculinity.

30. 'Training of the hat' (Mongolian *maġalai-yin bauliya*) is a metaphor for the exercise of authority. A traditional saying attributed to Chinggis Khan and preserved in the seventeenth-century *Altan tobci* of Lubsang-Danzin describes the hat as the ultimate symbol of authority: 'The Holy Chinggis Khan spoke in reverence to Heaven above, "By your own authority, you have not made anyone on Mother Earth higher or more powerful than me; indeed only my hat is above me." He took off his hat, hung it at the rear [*qoyimar*] of his *ger* and, having bowed down to it on that day, he feasted on grape wine until he felt hot and flushed' (see *LAT* recension, p. 93v). Similarly, a Mongolian biography from the time of the empire records how a Tangut boy in Mongolia, finding himself alone, took off his hat, placed it on his staff and

'worshiped it with song and dance'. When Chinggis Khan came across him doing this and asked him, he said that as a man had to have something to honour, he honoured his hat, thus practising for when he would serve a man of high office. Chinggis Khan was impressed by this spirit and took him into his service. See Atwood 2021a, pp. 88–91. To be 'familiarized with the great training of the hat' is thus to become conversant with how to receive such obeisance and direct it to the purposes of the empire.

31. In other words, every one of Chinggis Khan's sons will have some of Altan and Qocar's disgraced family members in their entourage; the humiliation and degradation experienced daily by these persons will be an object lesson for Chinggis Khan's sons to avoid ever failing to live up to their words and so be subject to a similar penalty.

32. The Secret Historian thus attributes to Chinggis Khan the idea that, even if Ökodei rightfully succeeds him, the rulership would not inhere among his descendants but would devolve to the best of the Chinggisids in that generation. In fact, however, this phrase dates from the coronation of Ökodei's son Güyuk in 1246, where it was deployed in the exact opposite sense: 'After the commanders insisted [on enthroning Güyuk], he said, "I will accept on condition that henceforth the emperorship remain among my offspring." All agreed to this and gave *möchilge*s [written pledges], saying, "So long as there remains of your progeny a piece of flesh a dog wouldn't take if it were wrapped in fat and a cow wouldn't accept if it were wrapped in grass, we will give the khanate to no other."' (Rashiduddin/Thackston, p. 278). A written guarantee or *möcilge* was a contract which those electing the khan were expected to observe on pain of death. In the end, only five years later in 1251, the commanders of the empire broke their pledge and enthroned Tolui's son Möngke instead of one of Güyuk's sons. The Secret Historian was a partisan of this change (see the Introduction) and as a service to the new regime wrote into the history this same phrase as found in the *möcilge* required under Güyuk, but this time with an 'escape clause' attributed to Chinggis Khan himself.

33. 'Golden reins' (*altan jilo'a*) like the 'golden halter' (*altan arġamji*) above (§§254, 256) is a metaphor for the sovereign's control over his subjects.

34. The Secret Historian's account of the campaign against 'the sultan' is even more confused than his or her account of that against the Golden Khan. The events may be compared with the timeline in

Appendix D, 'Western Expeditions towards Khwarazm, Baghdad and eastern Europe, 1206–42'. Evidently, the Secret Historian had never been west of Mongolia, any more than south of it. In this case, however, the Secret Historian appears to have used written sources almost exclusively, so this narrative lacks the vivid touches of that of the conquest of the Golden Khan. Comparison with parallel texts, particularly the *Campaigns of Chinggis Khan*, indicates that the Secret Historian used two primary sources. These can be distinguished from the spelling they use for the Persian city of Nishapur, one spelling it *Nicabur* (the C Source) and one spelling it *Nišabur* (the S Source).

35. The Daoist sage Changchun met Otcigin Noyan there in late April 1220, while travelling to an audience with Chinggis Khan in Afghanistan. Changchun's disciple described Otcigin Noyan's camp as follows: 'A wedding celebration was in progress, and all the chiefs within 500 *li* [175 miles] had brought mare's milk to contribute to the festivities. Black carts and felt tents by the thousands stood arrayed in rows' (Dunnell, West and Yang, pp. 33–4).

36. As mentioned in the Introduction, 'the sultan' refers to the ruler of the empire of Khwarazm, specifically the father Ala'uddin Muhammad (1169–1220) and his son Jalaluddin Mengburni (1199–1231). Like other Mongol historians of the conquest, the Secret Historian makes no mention of the death of one and the succession of the other.

37. This Qangli commander in Khwarazmian sources is variously found in Persian sources as Malik-Khan, Khan-Malik or Yamin Malik. Although Malik and Khan were both titles used for provincial commanders in the Khwarazmian empire, here the combination is being used as a personal name.

38. The Secret Historian alludes to how Jebe, the former Jirġo'adai, was renamed as Chinggis Khan's 'weapon' (Mongolian *jebe*), from §147.

39. That is, a *jasaq* or a judgment that serves as a precedent in similar cases.

40. Urgench (Mongolian Örunggeci), in present-day Turkmenistan, was the capital of the Khwarazmian empire. Sultan Muhammad, however, had abandoned it, and only his wife, Terken Qatun, was holding it.

41. Taking *hon* in the same sense as its cognates *fon* and *po* have in Manchu and Kitan respectively.

42. Reading *üjen meljen*, as opposed to Kuribayashi's *öcen meljen* or de Rachewiltz's *öcin meljen*. The Chinese gloss *bu fu*, 'not obedient', supplies the general sense.

43. Following de Rachewiltz's emendation to read *maġayiju* as *ma'asayiju*, 'smiling happily'.

44. The Tibetan dog is a large, shaggy-coated mountain dog, bred to guard livestock from predators and known in Tibetan as the *'dogs-khyi* or bandog (dog tied up during the day and only released at night). It is often called the Tibetan mastiff, although it is not a true mastiff and is more closely related to the St Bernard, Old English Sheepdog or Rottweiler among European breeds. As can be seen in this passage, Tibetan mountain dogs were already famous in the Mongol empire for their ferocity. Later a version of this breed was nativized in Mongolia as the *bankhar* dog.

45. Historically, we know from many other sources that it was not until early in the reign of Öködei that three *tümen*s were dispatched under Cormaqan to conquer the west (western Iran, Azerbayjan, Armenia, Georgia, Iraq and eastern Turkey), where Jalaluddin Mengburni was stirring up opposition, and where the caliph of Baghdad was also hostile. We also know that in the interregnum between Chinggis Khan's death and Öködei Khan's enthronement, an early razzia was dispatched against western Iran, which was later publicly repudiated by the newly enthroned Öködei as having been unauthorized. This passage about the three quiver-bearers offering to go on an expedition against the caliph as a way of relieving the khan's anger appears to have originally been based on a document in which the three quiver-bearers had led the unauthorized expedition and then appeased Öködei Khan's wrath by offering to go on a larger, potentially more lucrative expedition. The Secret Historian evidently took this document and repurposed it to be about appeasing Chinggis Khan's anger over the division of spoils after the sack of Urgench, leaving many marks of the editing process.

46. On the Qangli and Qïpchaqs, Turkic-speaking pastoralists and former allies of the Merkit, see §198.

47. On the Bashkirs, who at this time were a Hungarian-speaking forest and steppe people probably also formerly allied with the Merkit, see §239.

48. Along with the Turkic-speaking Qangli and Qïpchaqs and the Magyar-speaking Bashkir, who were familiar to the Mongols

from even before the empire, the Secret Historian adds another eight peoples who only came into the Mongols' ken from the time of the empire. 1) The Ruthenians (Mongolian *Orosut*, singular *Oros*, from East Slavonic *Rus'*) designates the East Slavic peoples, ancestors of the Russians, Ukrainians and Belarusians of today. 2) Magyar (Mongolian *Majar*) are Hungarian-speaking peoples, found at this time in two separate places, the kingdom of Hungary in central Europe and between the Urals and the Volga. The former were also called the Kerel and the latter were also called the Bashkir by the Mongols. 3) Ossetes (Mongolian *Asut*, sing. *As*) or Alans are the remnants of the Sarmatian people of the western steppe, speaking a north-east Iranian language. Today, they are found in the two Ossetian republics straddling the Caucasus, although at the time of the Mongol empire they dwelled in a wider area of the steppe between the Caspian and Black Seas. 4) The identity of the Saxons (Mongolian *Sasut*, singular *Sas*) is disputed. One identification, followed here, is the large settlement of Saxon Germans, known in Persian as *Sās*, plural *Sāsān*, that existed in Transylvania, many members of whom were deported following the Mongol invasion of Hungary due to their skills as miners and metalworkers. The other potential identification is with the city of Saqsin on the lower Volga River. 5) Circassians (Mongolian *Serkesut*) dwell in the north-western Caucasus area, concentrated today in the Adyghe, Cherkess and Kabardinian republics of Russia, and speaking a language of the north-west Caucasus family. With the Russian conquest of the nineteenth century, however, vast numbers resettled in the Middle East. 6) Kashmir is of course in South Asia (currently divided between India and Pakistan) and far from the Caucasus – it is unclear why it is placed in this list. 7) Bulgars (Mongolian *Bolar~Molar*) here are not the Bulgarians of the Balkan peninsula but the Volga Bulgars who in the ninth century established a Muslim state in the area of present-day Tatarstan and Chuvashia. Linguistically, they spoke a Turkic language of the distinctive Chuvashic type. 8) Finally, *Kerel* derives from the word for 'king' in Hungarian (*király*), derived in turn from *Carol(us)*, Charlemagne's personal name in Latin (cf. German *karl*, 'free man, warrior'). The title of the Hungarian king, *Király*, then became the title of the whole people.

49.   The Etil is the modern Volga and the Zhayiq is also known as the Ural River.

50.   Man-Kermen or 'Great City' was the local Turkic name of Kyiv, and it has often been taken to be simply the same as Kyiv. However,

it was also the name of Biler, the capital of the Volga Bulgar king-dom (the present-day village of Bilyarsk), which the Mongol armies took after a long siege; it is likely that that city was intended. See Zimonyi.

51. 'Overseers' is Mongolian *daruġaci(n)* or more commonly *daruġa(s)*. They were specially appointed officials chosen for their early loyalty to the Mongol cause who supervised local offi-cials with administrative knowledge, but suspect loyalty.

52. The first sentence uses *daruġacin* for 'overseers' and is probably taken from the S Source, an outline history of the Mongols' western expeditions. The later sentences, where 'overseers' is *daruġas*, are from a separate source, probably written among the Mongols in Caġadai's realm. This source must post-date 1241 when Mahmud Yalavach and Mas'ud Beg (to give them their names as they appear in Persian sources) were appointed to over-see North China and Central Asia respectively.

53. Here the *LAT* recension contains what seems to be an early Qubilai-era interpolation: 'And when the seventh year came and Chinggis Khan was returning from taking the Sart folk, he sent an envoy to the hordes to say, "Let Sorġoqtani come and bring the princes." Once he crossed over Otar Pass, he sent an envoy again to tell the western princes to come at once, and they set out at once. They reached Chinggis Khan when he was at the place called Qara-Jayir. Nine separate times, Chinggis Khan gave to the princes boys and geldings of the Sarts that he had had brought for them. Since he didn't count the princes as they advanced, Prince Qubilai came up every time and the great part of the booty from the Sarts was given to Prince Qubilai. Then he moved on and in the autumn of the Year of the Chicken . . . '. The western princes were the sons of the princes on the right hand, i.e. the sons of Chinggis Khan's sons. (The eastern princes were the sons of Chinggis Khan's younger brothers.)

54. This hunt of the khulans, or Mongolian wild asses, at Arbuqa was famous among the Mongols. The Persian historian Juvaini wrote that Chinggis Khan had ordered a vast herd of wild khu-lans there 'like so many sheep': 'It was said that the hoofs of the wild asses had become worn out on the journey and that they had been shod with horseshoes. When they came to a place called Arbuqa, Chingiz Khan, his sons and the soldiers mounted horse to disport themselves, and the wild asses were driven before them. They gave chase, but from excess of weariness the wild asses had become such that they could be taken by hand.

When they had grown tired of the chase and none but lean ani-
mals remained, each branded those he had taken with his own
brand and let them go free' (Juvaini/Boyle, p. 140). (The AWT-
WQA of the Persian edition should be emended to ARBWQA,
i.e. Arbuqa.) Juvaini places this hunt in the context of Chinggis
Khan's return from the west and combined it with a story about
his last meeting with his estranged son Joci at Qulan-Baši ('Khu-
lan's Head'). The Secret Historian here places it in the context of
his campaign against the Tanguts and the injury that led to
Chinggis Khan's death. This is a good example of how striking
anecdotes could be attached by historians to different framing
narratives.

55. 'Woollen tent' is Mongolian *terme ger*. The word *terme*, for a
vast woollen tent, is used also for Ong Khan's Golden Tent
among the Kereyit. See §§184–5, 187.

56. It is likely that this last quotation is from a decree on the dispos-
ition of captured people, in which 'this and that' (*eyimu teyimu*)
originally had a more detailed specification of which categories
of Tanguts were to be spared slaughter and instead divided up as
booty among the people in the army. This detailed specification
would then have been omitted in the Secret Historian's citation.

57. The exact location of this place (Mongolian *Casu-tu*) is
unknown, but from the name it should be somewhere in the
present-day Qilian Mountains along the border of Gansu and
Kökenuur (Qinghai) provinces today. The same term was used
by the Mongols (and Chinese in their service) for the Hindu
Kush in Afghanistan.

58. Muqali had actually died several years before in 1223. This
anachronism and the reference to the 'Chinese' (*Kitat*), the
Inner Mongolian Jüin auxiliaries and the Golden Khan show
that the Secret Historian took this passage from a decree which
originally was not associated with the Tangut conquest at all,
but rather with the conquest of the Jurchen Jin dynasty. Assum-
ing it was dated to the Dog Year, it would therefore be 1214
rather than the Secret Historian's 1226. Bo'orcu and Muqali
were the supreme commanders of Chinggis Khan's right and left
wings respectively.

59. The Hanlin recension here has *Dörmegei* but the Persian of
Rashiduddin has *Durshakāy* consistently for the same place
(Rashiduddin/Thackston, pp. 186, 199). Given the relative similar-
ity of *š* and *m* in Uyghur-Mongolian, the Hanlin recension's reading
was evidently corrupted by attraction to the *dörmegei*, 'inferior;

lower-level' found in §276. Ironically, Thackston 'corrects' Rashiduddin's correct reading based on the incorrect reading in the Hanlin recension.

60. Travelling palace or *ne'uku qarši*: this refers to a kind of pavilion for temporary travel, rather than a Mongolian-style horde or permanently mobile *ger*.

61. Here I adopt de Rachewiltz's nice translation of this phrase *muquli musquli* which is not found elsewhere and is unglossed but seems to mean literally something like 'to be blunted and twisted'.

8: The Reign of Ökodei Khan

1. This date is incorrect; Ökodei was certainly raised as khan in the Year of the Cow of 1229. Moreover, the Year of the Mouse of 1228 was an unusual one in which the regular annual assemblies of the princes and commanders to plan the coming autumn's campaigns did not occur as the empire's ruling class tried to figure out how to move on after the death of the great founder, Chinggis Khan. After the mourning ceremonies were completed, wrote Rashiduddin, 'The princes and amirs held council together concerning the kingship and then went to their own places of residence. For nearly two years the throne remained unoccupied. Then they thought that if anything happened and there was no leader or ruler, orderly kingship might suffer. It behooved them therefore to make haste to install someone as qa'an. On this sensitive mission they sent emissaries to each other and made preparations for a *quriltai*. When the severity of winter had been broken and the beginnings of spring were apparent, all the princes and amirs came from all directions to the ancient *yurt* and great *ordu*' (Rashiduddin/Thackston, p. 221).

2. This list of the participants in the great assembly (Mongolian *qurilta* or *quriltai*) that enthroned Ökodei neatly summarizes the basic organization and ruling class of the new empire. The empire was divided into a right hand (from the Altai Mountains to the steppes of Kazakhstan), a left hand (from the Khingan or Qara' un-Jidun to the forests of Manchuria) and a centre (Mongolia between the foothills of the Altai and the Khingan ranges). The ruling class was divided into the family of the founder (Chinggis Khan) and the commanders (*noyat*) of the rank of thousands (*minggat*) and ten thousands (*tümens*). The family of Chinggis Khan was divided into princes (literally, 'sons', Mongolian *kö'ut*),

princesses (literally, 'daughters', Mongolian *ökit*) and sons-in-law (Mongolian *küreget*). As was stipulated in §§242, 243 and 255, the four sons of Chinggis Khan and the four sons of his younger brothers each founded a separate 'kingdom' (*ulus*) or princely house with its own territory (*nuntuq*), staff and designated head of the family. The older sons of Chinggis Khan and Madame Börte, Joci, Caġadai and Ökodei, the princes or 'sons' in the strict sense, held the territories in the right hand, while the descendants of Chinggis Khan's younger brothers, the juniors (Mongolian *de' u-ner*) or fraternal princes, had their territories in the left hand. Tolui, along with the princesses and imperial sons-in-law directly subject to the ruling khan, had his territory in the centre. By this time, among the sons of Chinggis Khan, Joci had passed away and his second son Batu had been appointed in his place. Among Chinggis Khan's younger brothers, only the youngest, Otcigin Noyan, remained alive; Yeku and Yisungke were Qasar's two surviving sons.

3. As may be seen here, this passage must be citing a written decree issued in the time of Ökodei. The actions described by Ökodei in his own words were cited in the third person by the Secret Historian, but the pronouns were not completely changed to fit.

4. Mönggedu and Hoqotur were actually dispatched not to reinforce Cormaqan's *tamaci* (mixed-ethnic resident garrison) troops in the area of the caliph of Baghdad, but to reinforce Dayir Ba'atur's *tamaci* troops in Afghanistan. Mönggedu of the Besut, nicknamed Sa'ur and attached to the entourage of prince Tolui, was dispatched in 1229 ([Jūzjānī]/Raverty, p. 1109; cf. Rashiduddin/Thackston, p. 35), and Hoqotur in 1235 (Rashiduddin/Thackston, pp. 35, 230). Hoqotur sacked cities in Kashmir sometime in the late 1230s.

5. Magas was the capital city of the Alans or Ossetes, on the northern slopes of the Caucasus Mountains. While a number of sites have been proposed, that of Il'ichevskii in Krasnodar territory in the western part of the Caucasus Mountains best fits the archaeological and historical evidence. See John Latham-Sprinkle, 'The Alan Capital *Magas*: A Preliminary Identification of Its Location', *Bulletin of the School of Oriental and African Studies*, vol. 85, no. 1 (2022), pp. 1–20. On the other places listed here, see §262.

6. Batu, Böri, Güyuk and Möngke represented the next generation of the Jocid, Caġadaid, Ökodeid and Toluid branches of the family respectively.

7. The phrase 'princes who govern a kingdom' (Mongolian *ulus medekun kö'ut*) designates those princes who ruled the eight branches of the Chinggisid family, founded by the four sons of Chinggis Khan and his four younger brothers. The emphasis that they are to send the 'eldest son of their own sons' indicates that the chronologically eldest one, regardless of social seniority, was dispatched. In the case of the Jocids, for example, Batu was the head of the family, but his brother Hordu was the eldest son, so both participated in the campaign.

8. This is one of the ten places where the Secret Historian uses the phrase 'This [or that] was the way in which ...' (... *yosu [t] eyimu*) to conclude a dramatic narrative episode. In this case it is followed by the phrase *bui j-e*, which indicates certainty in the face of possible doubt. One may surmise in this instance that the Secret Historian had less direct evidence and had to resort to plausible speculation.

9. Olda'ur was of the Jalayir surname; Rashiduddin confirms that he 'was the *shahna* [Persian for *daruġaci* or overseer] to Chinggis Khan's four great hordes and commanded a company of a hundred in the imperial thousand' (Rashiduddin/Thackston, p. 30).

10. The following account of the final campaign against the Golden Khan is the apex of the Secret Historian's geographical confusion over the campaigns in North China. The text envisions Ökodei Khan having to repeat his father's footsteps, capture Juyong Pass again and camp in front of Zhongdu (modern Beijing), with Jebe once again in the vanguard. In reality, Jebe was dead and Zhongdu had been taken by forces under the Mongols sixteen years earlier and was already the administrative centre of Mongol rule in North China. The focus of Mongol campaigns this time was the Henan area, south of the Yellow River and east of the Tongguan Pass, which the Jurchen Jin had made their final redoubt. But Ökodei's illness actually occurred after he and Tolui had completed their campaign and were returning north through Inner Mongolia.

11. See §247.

12. Examine the entrails (*abitla-*) is the Mongolian term for the examination of the entrails of a sacrificed animal, usually the liver, to seek signs of the future. See Mostaert 1953, pp. 358–60.

13. This sentence (*ya'un bolbi*) ends with the feminine form of the verb. Elsewhere this form is used when the subject is a woman, or when the speaker wishes to lament or mock insufficiently masculine behaviour (see §§194, 255). No translator, either medieval or

modern, has suggested any explanation for this feminine ending here, however.

14. This term, *sutu* in Mongolian, a classic epithet of Chinggis Khan, is found elsewhere in the *Secret History*, in §74 (*sutan*, 'majestic', plural) and §111 (*sutai*, feminine singular).

15. *Jöb ese bol-* is a euphemism for 'to die'.

16. This must refer to Sorġoqtani Beki, Tolui's famous widowed wife, mentioned in §186. However, the name she is given here, Berude, is mysterious and has not been explained.

17. 'Slave Boy' (Mongolian *Seuse*) derives ultimately from Chinese *xiaosi*, 'little slave', but that it was a nativized Mongolian word is clear from its use as a common noun immediately below.

18. 'Resident garrison troops' translates *tamaci* (plural *tamacin*). These units were permanent garrisons stationed in areas outside Mongolia. They were formed by selecting one or two from every decimal unit in a broad region of the empire, and then assigning them to go and permanently occupy a particular area. Due to the way they were formed they were of mixed ethnicity, but with a Mongol officer corps. Whatever their origins, they usually lived a fully mobile-pastoralist or ranching lifestyle in the area they occupied.

19. This famous capital of the Mongol empire was built under Ökodei Khan. Other sources describe the palaces and pavilions Ökodei Khan built in Qara-Qorum and its vicinity in great detail, but this topic was not of interest to the Secret Historian.

20. 'Resident garrison' or *tama*; see above in note 18.

21. *Naq* (plural *naqut*), from Arabic *nakh*, was one of the 'Tartar cloths' (Italian *panni tartarici*) that were of Middle Eastern origin, but spread throughout Afro-Eurasia as a result of the Mongol empire. It was similar to the *našiš*-brocade immediately following; exactly how it differed is unclear. See Shea 2020, p. 123; Allsen 1997, pp. 3, 29. Marco Polo, who passed by the colonies of deported *našiš* and *naq* weavers north-west of Zhongdu (modern Beijing), thought the two types of fabric were different, however. See Polo/Cliff, p. 80. But the Arab traveller Ibn Battutah, who received a robe of *naq* and saw it on several ladies in the Golden Horde, defined it as 'a robe of silk gilt' and said that *našiš* was just a different name for *naq*. See Gibb, pp. 445, 485, 503.

22. On these luxury fabrics and *subut-* and *tana*-pearls see the note to §238.

23. The Mongolian lists several words, *güring elö'üt ta'uśi kicidut*, which are all glossed as names of types of camels, but which are

otherwise unknown. My very tentative rendering follows the commentary of Igor de Rachewiltz.

24. Magas was the main city of the Ossetes; see §270. Etil and Zhayiq are mentioned earlier in §§262 and 270, not as cities but as rivers. It is quite possible that a word or more was omitted from the text, in which case the translation would read 'then crossing the Etil and Zhayiq and sacking the city of Magas'. However, there was a Saqsin city on the Etil (Volga) River and a Saraychik city on the Zhayiq (Ural) River, and this may be a reference to the Mongol sacking of these cities. For the other geographical terms in this paragraph see §262.

25. This note is out of place not only geographically but also chronologically, as Yisuder was sent to assist Jalayirtai Qorci only in 1258. It is probably a Qubilai-era interpolation in the text. For other such interpolations see §§239 and 264.

26. The phrase 'to draw in the golden reins' (Mongolian *altan jilo'a tata-*), used here and in §256 in slightly different forms, has more literal and more metaphorical meanings. More literally as here, it refers to turning back home from that conquest when it has been completed. Metaphorically as in §256, it refers to controlling subjects as a rider controls a horse.

27. Pavilion (Mongolian *cacir*) is a loan word from Turkic and refers to a tent of cotton fabric with a ridgepole and a square plan; the larger ones, as here, had vertical walls, much like the large tents or *maikhan* set up today in Mongolia on the Naadam games or other festive occasions. See Serruys.

28. The ceremonial liquor, probably milk-based, which concluded great assemblies.

29. The Mongolian verb here is plural, *u'uqun büle'e*. The following insults also all have a plural object. This is a sign that while the Secret Historian has taken this scorn to be directed at Batu alone, in its original context it was probably directed at the Jocid princes as a whole, several of whom were also on this campaign. Böri, like many Caġadaid princes, resented the rich lands which the Jocid princes had received in the division of the inheritance by Chinggis Khan. William of Rubruck, writing a few years later, explained the controversy as follows: '[Böri's] pasturelands were inferior, and one day while drunk he said to his men: "Am I not of the stock of Chingis Chan like Baatu?" (He was Baatu's nephew or brother.) "Why should I not move along the banks of the Etilia [Etil or Volga] like Baatu, and graze there?"' (Jackson and Morgan, pp. 144–5). Later, one Caġadaid prince complained

that while 'Our other princely relatives possess great cities and happy grazing grounds', they had only 'this miserable little *ulus*' (Rashiduddin/Thackston, p. 370).

30. Later on, when Möngke Khan seized power and purged the Ökodeid and Caġadaid families in 1251–2, the same treatment was applied to the wife of Böri's brother and ally Yisu. They were handed over to Qara-Hüle'u, a rival prince of the Caġadaid family, who supported Möngke: 'As for Toqashi Khatun, she was tried by Qara-Hülegü in the presence of [her husband] Yesü: he ordered her limbs to be kicked to pulp and so assuaged an ancient grudge which he had cherished in his heart' (Juvaini/Boyle, pp. 588–9).

31. To flog with hot sticks (Mongolian *jorġalda-*) was a special punishment for women criminals. During Möngke's purge of the hostile Ökodeid and Caġadaid families, this punishment was applied liberally: 'Their womenfolk were also sent for and were all beaten with burning brands to make them confess; and once they had confessed they were put to death' (Jackson and Morgan, p. 169).

32. Pinning a tail on someone as a humiliation is referred to also in §181.

33. *Busu helige-tu*, literally 'with a different liver'. The liver was the seat of emotions in Mongolian thinking, particularly those of love and loyalty.

34. That Güyuk had returned from the campaign is not mentioned by the Secret Historian, but the *Yuanshi*, p. 2.37 (trans. in Atwood 2019/20, p. 35), does say that he was summoned by the emperor in Moon XII, or December 1240–January 1241.

35. This image of Harġasun filling up his mouth with insolent words against the Borjigin lineage presages his eventual fate in Möngke's 1251–2 purge. He was dispatched to Batu's court for punishment, along with his father Eljigidei and another, unnamed, brother. For Harġasun and his brother, their 'mouths were stuffed with stones until they died' (Rashiduddin/Thackston, p. 289). This punishment of any official not of the blood who dared speak ill of a member of the imperial Borjigin family had already been applied to Körguz, a Uyghur official who in a quarrel had spoken insulting words to a member of Caġadai's family. When he was remanded to Caġadai's court for trial, the Caġadaid prince 'ordered his men to fill his mouth with stones and so put him to death' (Juvaini/Boyle, p. 505).

36. Judging from the description of Güyuk fighting as an outrider (*alginci*) and as a soldier in a *tamaci*-type permanent garrison army, Ökodei was evidently planning to send Güyuk and Harġasun off to the Song dynasty front. On that front from

1235 on, with few interruptions, an inconclusive border war of sieges, slaughters, water-borne raids and malarial disease was going along the Huaihe River. This was also where, as the *Secret History*'s original readers undoubtedly were aware, several of the main princes in Ökodei and Caġadai's families would be exiled after Möngke's 1251 coup. See Juvaini/Boyle, pp. 591–2; Rashiduddin/Thackston, p. 290.

37. 'Möngke' here and below is written as *Möngkei*; this appears to be simply a variant of the more usual spelling – it is certainly the future khan who is in question. The use of a variant form should indicate that this section §277 is of separate origin from the other passages where Möngke is mentioned.

38. This contrast between Güyuk and Böri feeling confident of themselves as able commanders and despising Batu as weak seems to have derived particularly from the siege of the Ruthenian town of Kozel'sk (Mongolian *Kosel-iske*). Rashiduddin writes: 'After that, they turned back from there and held a council, deciding that they would proceed *tümen* by *tümen* in *jerge* [hunting circle] formation and take and destroy every town, province, and fortress they came to. Along the way, Batu came to the town of Kozel'sk. He besieged it for two months but was unable to take it. Then Qada'an and Büri arrived, and it was taken in three days. They camped in the houses and rested' (Rashiduddin/Thackston, p. 232).

39. Those reading or hearing the history at this time would know, however, that far from Güyuk, Harġasun and Böri having been punished, in fact all three of them remained among the leading contenders for power after Ökodei's death in December 1241. Since it was well known that the end of the great Qïpchaq campaign and the summons for Güyuk to return took place late in his reign, the Secret Historian must have thought that while Ökodei had planned these punishments, in fact they were forgotten in the chaos after his death. Güyuk would go on to be elected khan in 1246 and reign for a short time before his death of disease in 1248 cut short a projected western campaign (whether against the caliph or against Batu was never clarified). After the 1251 coup brought Tolui's son Möngke to power, Böri and Harġasun would be handed over to be executed by Batu. See Jackson and Morgan, pp. 144–5; Juvaini/Boyle, pp. 587–8; Rashiduddin/Thackston, pp. 261, 289.

40. This section, with its lengthy preamble, was evidently taken from the written decree which formed the Secret Historian's major source not just for Ökodei's organization of his *keśikten*,

but for the section on the *keśikten* under Chinggis Khan as well. It will thus be noted that the following decrees are almost all verbatim repetitions, with some minor simplification, of those already cited for Chinggis Khan.

41. As in §229, the phrases 'above' here and 'superior to' below are meant not just physically, but also in terms of status. 'Superior to' or 'above' the nightguards refers to being closer to the khan than the nightguards, thus endangering the khan's security.

42. This reference to an otherwise unknown episode involving Eljigidei was already given in §229 under Chinggis Khan's reign. It is one of the indications that these regulations for the imperial lifeguard of Chinggis Khan's reign were actually divided up by the historian from a single decree that 'announce[d] anew the service of the nightguards, quiver-bearers and dayguards ... who had served my father Chinggis Khan'.

43. This passage copies more briefly that in §233 above. There the khan responds to implicit criticism that not allowing the elite nightguards to go to war apart from the khan was depriving the empire of some of its best-trained warriors in the midst of battle. This criticism made little sense in Chinggis Khan's reign, when the khan participated with his nightguards in all the major campaigns. It was, however, much more understandable in the second half of Ökodei's reign when he remained in Mongolia while the great campaigns in the west already described were going on.

44. The text here and immediately below has 'Amal and Canar'. At the end of a word, *-i* and *-r* are, however, frequently confused in the pre-classical Uyghur-Mongolian script. The names Canai and Canar are both extremely rare, and it is highly unlikely that there was both a Canai and a Canar active at Ökodei's court and employed on court missions with Bulġadar (see §279). It is virtually certain, therefore, that Canar is a mistake for Canai.

45. As was noted in §229, this refers to covering the felt skirts of the doors trailing on the floor of the horde cart to guarantee the security of the tent and keep it well sealed during the night. It is noteworthy, however, that, in that passage, nightguards lie around the horde and stand on the door, whereas here it is the opposite. It is unclear if this is a citation from a different part of the decree outlining a different stage of service or if the citation under Ökodei's reign, which contains numerous small errors I have corrected without comment, simply reversed the two accidentally.

46. These are the same four shift commanders of the quiver-bearers listed under Chinggis Khan (§225), supposedly at the time of the

1206 coronation. In fact they were Ökodei's quiver-bearers and their presence among Chinggis Khan's *keśikten* is the accidental result of the Secret Historian's use of a single decree dating from Ökodei's time to describe the organization of the imperial bodyguard under both reigns.

47. This term *acit* is glossed as *tieban*, 'entourage'. Cleaves 1982 and de Rachewiltz translate as 'bodyguards' and Onon as 'sentries'. As in Poppe, pp. 507–8, this term is a plural of Mongolian *aci*, 'sons; nephews'. The *keśikten* were the sons and nephews of the officials and were in training, thus matching the sense of 'cadet'.

48. The text here has *Qongqortaġai*. In light of the reference to him and Alcidai having 'been previously governing', which seems to be a reference to their previous prominence at the court, I identify them with the Alcidai and Qongqortai of §277 and so emend the text.

49. In later usage of the Mongol Yuan dynasty, the cane was about 3.6 feet long, with a handle end from a third to over half an inch thick and a striking end from a fifth of an inch to over two-fifths of an inch thick. Blows were given on the buttocks or on the buttocks and thighs. See Ratchnevsky 1985, vol. 1, pp. 343–4; *Yuanshi*, p. 103.2635.

50. This practice of creating dedicated mare herds to supply fermented mare's milk was applied not just to the khan's table but also by the princes. William of Rubruck observed this at the court of Batu: 'Baatu has thirty men stationed around his encampment at a distance of one day's journey, each of whom furnishes him every day with milk like this from a hundred mares (in other words, the milk of three thousand mares daily) . . . For just as in Syria the peasants yield a third of the produce, so these men are required to bring to their lords' camps the mares' milk for every third day' (Jackson and Morgan, p. 82).

51. 'Ingots' in Mongolian is *sükes*, literally 'axes'. Empire-era ingots of silver were shaped like double axes, hence the name. In Persian and Uyghur, however, they were called 'pillows' (*balish* and *yastuq* respectively).

52. 'Nation' (Mongolian *ulus irgen*) is a binome combining the idea of a kingdom (*ulus*) or a people and place under one ruler, and a folk (*irgen*), that is, a community of common people. From the context, Ökodei Khan is clearly limiting this claim of a nation in whose interests he is ruling to the Mongols.

53. 'deep desert' is Mongolian *cöl* which, unlike the *ġobi*, is uninhabitable by humans, although, as stated here, it still may have

game. The desert in question is to the west of the Altai Moun-
tains, in the Junggar Basin of present-day south-west Mongolia
and northern Xinjiang.

54. 'Post-station' here is *jam* (plural *jamut*); 'post-staff' is *jamuci(n)*.
This was the famous post-road system of the Mongols. It is
widely known in Persian as *yam*, from the Uyghur pronunciation
of the word. The relay riders or *ula'acin* were those who actually
rode as attendants on the envoys using the post-roads.

55. Literally 'Oceanic Khan' or *Dalai-yin Qa'an (~Qan)*. This title is
also found on the seal of Ökodei's son Güyuk.

56. The Hanlin recension here has a character *qian* that is read *tsien*
or *dzien* in Early Mandarin. The sound *dz-* does not occur in
Middle Mongolian, but characters with that sound are routinely
used to represent the Uyghur *z-*, as can be seen in the Chinese
representations of Tangut and Persian words such as *Izina*,
Taziku and *Diz*. Thus, *Arazen* should be intended here; the name
is Tangut.

57. These two sentences are very repetitive in the Mongolian; it is
not unlikely that this repetition is the result of the Secret Histor-
ian having deleted lengthy material in between that was not
considered relevant.

58. The meaning of this quatrain is much disputed. Some think it is
referring to corporal, or even capital punishment for those guilty
(cutting off the nose or the 'noggin' or head), while others take it as
referring to confiscation of half the guilty person's property. Even
within the Hanlin recension, the interlinear translation seems to
adopt the first view, while the running translation adopts the
second. It is possible that 'noggin' (literally 'crown of the head')
and 'nose' here are slang words for informants, who by the empire's
laws would also receive a share of a guilty person's property.

59. Many writers have remarked on this assessment of his reign
placed in the mouth of Ökodei Khan. The most important thing
to note is that while the positive items are all things which were
discussed previously by the Secret Historian, the four negative
ones are all things which, while very well known at the time, are
not ever discussed by the Secret Historian. As with the supposed
punishment of Güyuk, Böri and Harġasun, which the work's
restricted circles of readers and listeners would have known in
the end had never happened, so here the author is appealing to
knowledge about Ökodei's failings that would have been widely
whispered in the ruling-class circles to whom the history was
addressed.

60. 'China' is *Jauqut*. While *Kitat* or 'Chinese' is used for the people, *Jauqut* is the geographical term. Like *Kitat*, however, *Jauqut* is actually restricted to North China. South China is referred to as *Manji* (the country) or *Nangqiyas* (the people); neither term is found in the *Secret History*, however.

61. Grape wine (*bor darasun*) was first introduced to the Mongols by a shipment from Ala-Quš Digit-Quri of the Turkic-speaking Öng'ut, accompanying his surrender to Chinggis Khan (see §190). As Christians, the Öng'ut had patronized vineyards in neighbouring Shanxi province for Communion wine, in addition to their regular fermented mare's milk. See *Yuanshi*, p. 118.2924. The similarly Turkic-speaking, but mostly Buddhist and only partly Christian Uyghurs also produced much wine, which Mongol connoisseurs came to appreciate even more than Shanxi wines. See Polo/Cliff, p. 143; Buell and Anderson, p. 498. The word *bor* is Turkic for grape wine. Many sayings against liquor and grape wine (Mongolian *darasun*) are attributed to Chinggis Khan, such as 'If one must drink, then let one drink thrice a month, for more is bad. If one gets drunk twice a month, it is better; if one gets drunk once a month, that is even better; and if one doesn't drink at all, that is the best of all' (Rashiduddin/Thackston, p. 203). Ökodei's own weakness for liquor was well known. When he died, there were accusations that he had been poisoned, accusations directed against a steward (*ba'urci*) in the service of Lady Ibaqa. But one of the late khan's *kešikten* commanders, Alcidai of the Jalayir (mentioned in §§226–7, 234, 277, 278), pointed out: 'The Qa'an always drank too much. Why must we badmouth our Qa'an by saying he was assassinated by others? . . . Since he was an intelligent man, he realized that the death had been caused by drinking too much' (Rashiduddin/Thackston, p. 234).

62. This episode happened in July 1237. The *Yuanshi* (p. 2.35; cf. Atwood 2019/20, p. 30) refers to it as follows: 'The units on the left wing spread false stories about the selection of girls from the people. The emperor was angered by this, and therefore gave those selected as rewards to his men.' Juvaini/Boyle, pp. 235–6, has a lengthy description of how a rumour arose that girls would be drafted for the imperial court, and families quickly married off their daughters. In retaliation, Ökodei gave orders that 'all the girls over seven years old should be gathered together and that all who had been given that year to husbands taken back from them'. Four thousand girls are said to have been gathered.

'[He] ordered those who were daughters of [commanders] to be separated from the rest; and all who were present were commanded to have intercourse with them. And two moonlike damsels from amongst them expired.' The remaining girls were then distributed to the various court personnel, with the remainder being assigned to the brothels attached to the *jam* stations near the capital to service envoys.

63. The exact manner in which Ökodci conspired to harm Doqolqu is unknown, but the khan was retaliating against Doqolqu for his defeat by a Jin dynasty army in January–February 1230, at Dachangyuan in Shaanxi province. This defeat led to Ökodei's personal expedition against the Jin, which resulted in the defeat of the Golden Khan and eventually the extinction of the Jin dynasty. Presumably it was on his return from the expedition that he secretly took revenge on Doqolqu, for his humiliating defeat that had injured Mongol prestige. See Atwood 2015c.

64. Rashiduddin describes this wall for corralling game, but in an entirely favourable manner: 'At his winter quarters in Ongqin [Ongi] he had ordered a wall built. It was a two-day journey long and was made of wood and clay, and it had gates. He called it a *chihik*. When a hunt was held, soldiers in all directions would be informed, and they would form a circle and head for the wall, driving the prey towards it. From a one-month's distance away, taking all precautions and keeping the circle intact at all times, they drove the prey to the *chihik*, and then the soldiers would form a circle and stand shoulder to shoulder. First Ögödäi Qa'an and his elite would enter the circle, watch for a time, and then hunt.' Killing would then be done by ranks until animals would be separated, a few for breeding and most for delivery as meat to the table by ranks. After paying homage to the khan, and feasting for nine days, they would disperse. See Rashiduddin/Thackston, p. 234. Far from being an occasion of resentment of his brothers, the earlier Persian historian Juvaini records that 'In the region of Almaligh and Quyas, Chaghatai constructed a hunting ground in the very same manner' (Juvaini/Boyle, p. 29).

Colophon

1. This colophon resembles the usual format of the close of a Mongolian imperial decree, giving the date in the twelve-animal cycle and then the place where the decree was written.

2.   The Roebuck Moon (*ġuran sara*) was Moon VII in the Mongo-
     lian lunar-solar calendar. On the date see the Introduction and
     Appendix A.

3.   Other decisions taken at this *quriltai* under Möngke Khan are
     recorded in the *Yuanshi* (p. 3.46): 'Qubilai was ordered to con-
     quer Dali [present-day Yunnan], the prince Turġaq-Sali was
     ordered to conquer Sindh, Ket-Buqa to conquer the Mulahidah
     ['Heretics' or the Nizari Ismailis], and Hüle'u to conquer the
     [caliph] sultan in the west. A decree was issued summoning the
     generals of the Song defending Jingnan, Xiangyangfu, Fancheng
     and Junzhou to surrender.' It is probably not a coincidence that
     the Secret Historian treats all of these peoples, and especially the
     caliph and the Song, as having been already subdued; encourag-
     ing further conquest was far from the historian's agenda.

4.   A place name seems to have been omitted from the text here.

Afterword: The Transmission and
Translation of the *Secret History*

1.   Mongolian *Erten-u qa'ad-un ündusulugsen töro yosun-u jokiyal-i
     tobcilan quriyaġsan Altan tobci kemeku orosibai*.

2.   The earliest surviving Mongolian-Chinese glossary is the *Zhiyuan
     yiyu* or 'Translated Vocabulary of the Zhiyuan Era'. (The Zhiyuan
     era designated the main part of the reign of Qubilai Khan or
     1264–94.) On this vocabulary see Kara 1990. On the system of
     literal translation see Birge, pp. 67–72.

3.   Chinese emperors would give particular designations to the
     years in which they reigned.

4.   It was subsequently acquired by the Manchu aristocrat Shengyu
     and is currently kept in the National Library of China.

5.   It is usually called the Han Taihua manuscript, from the sub-
     sequent owner. It was eventually acquired by the Russian
     monk-scholar Archimandrite Palladius and is currently kept in
     the library of St Petersburg University.

6.   Linguists call this sound change 'lenition'.

7.   It should be noted that Ökodei later in his life changed his
     preferred form of his name to Ögedei, from Mongolian *ögede*,
     'upwards; ascending'. These two were easily confused and in
     later Mongolian Ögedei became standard.

8.   As in Turkic and Manchu-Tungusic languages, prefixes are virtu-
     ally unknown in Mongolian.

9. Ernest Hemingway, *The Complete Short Stories of Ernest Hemingway* (New York: Scribner, 1987), p. 168 (from 'Big Two-Hearted River: Part I').

10. Jane Austen, *Pride and Prejudice* (London: Penguin Books, 1996), p. 5.

11. See Peter Jordan, 'Hemingway and Parataxis', TSS Publishing (2020), at https://theshortstory.co.uk/hemingway-and-parataxis-by-peter-jordan/ (accessed 5 November 2022).

12. Bakhtin, pp. 133–6; Auerbach, pp. 13–23. In the *Secret History* we find that on two occasions (§§229, 245), a suspect's 'word' or 'words' (*üge[s]*) are said to be 'interrogated' (*asaq-*) or 'questioned' (*asa'u-*) in a context where the 'words' can only be the person's intentions, spoken or not.

13. *Iliad*, ix.312–13, translation by Richmond Lattimore (Chicago: University of Chicago Press, 1951), p.206.

14. Auerbach, p. 11.

15. See Ong, pp. 36–57. Yet in other respects it differs quite strongly from the supposed oral features outlined by Ong – the *Secret History*'s world is far from homeostatic and compared to the *Iliad* or the Manas epic of the Kyrgyz, for example, has little celebration of raw physical violence.

Appendix A: Alternative Mouse Year Theories and the Question of the *Secret History*'s Unity

1. A good example is given by the anonymous continuator who continued Gregory Bar Hebraeus's *Chronography* or world-historical chronicle up to the year 1295 after the author's death in 1286.

Appendix B: Socio-political Organization of the Pre-Chinggisid Mongols

1. Mistranscribed in Thackston's translation as 'Härigän' or 'Örtägin'.

2. Mistranscribed in Thackston's translation as 'Oriyat'.

3. Mistranscribed in Thackston's translation as 'Qirjin', 'Onjin' or 'Qujin'.

4. Mistranscribed in Thackston's translation as 'Kinggiyat' and confused with the real Kinggiyat~Qïngqïyat below.

5. Mistranscribed in Thackston's translation as 'Sanchi'ut'.
6. Mistranscribed in Thackston's translation as 'Sügän'.
7. The listing for Sengkun Noyan originally had Sorgoqtu Noyan. The names Sorgatu and Sorgoqtu both refer to smallpox scars (*sorgan* or *sorgoq*); such names were given to drive away the possibility of the feared disease (so-called apotropaic names). But since the very word 'smallpox' was frightening and unpleasant, such names were commonly replaced later. In this case, Sengkun appears to be the replacement for the taboo form.
8. Rashiduddin says he is the son of Ugucu, the brother of Qodu, and his group was 'from among the Kiyat and people who were loyal and attached to them' (Rashiududdin/Thackston, p. 115). Ugucu here is likely the Agucu of the *Secret History*.

Glossary of Names

This glossary, which also serves as an index to the translation, identifies the names of persons, places, ethnic groups and certain distincive Mongolian terms found in the translation. Entries are alphabetized in the form they are found in the translation; where that form differs from the Middle Mongolian, that form has been inserted in italics in parentheses following, thus: **Kherlen** (*Keluren*). For persons, their clan name or kingdom where known is also added in plain text, thus: **Qoridai** (Ġorulas). Where the name has a significant meaning in Mongolian, that meaning is giving in quotation marks, thus: **Ala'ut-Turġa'ut** ('the mottled ones and the sentinels'). All locations of place names are given in terms of modern boundaries.

Abji'a-Köteger, upland in the plains of southeastern Mongolia: cxix, 80, 84

Aciq-Širun (Tübe'en), Kereyit commander of ten thousand: 67, 68, 70, 76

Adangqan, sub-branch of the commoner Uriyangqan people: 8

Adarkidai (Adarkin), eponymous ancestor of the Adarkin clan: 9

Adarkin, noble (*niru'un*) house of the Mongols: cxiii, 9, 104, 141, 192, 194

Adġiraq (Uyghur), envoy sent to deliver message of the Uyghur ruler to Chinggis Khan: 120

Aġucu Ba'atur (Tayici'ut): commander of the Tayici'ut, hostile to Chinggis Khan; probably the same as the Uġucu in the early battle order of Chinggis Khan: 48–50, 53, 194

Ajai Khan (Tatar), early Tatar khan, hostile to the Kereyit: 57

Ajinai: captain of a thousand: 100

Alai Mountains, same in name as the Alai Range of Kyrgyzstan and Tajikistan, but probably designating one of the several ranges in southern Siberia, Xinjiang, Kazakhstan and Kyrgyzstan known today as *Alatau*: cxxii, 92, 93, 139

Al-Altun (Borjigin), daughter of Chinggis Khan betrothed to the Uyghur ruler: 121

Alan the Fair (Alan Ġowa), ncestress of the noble (*niru'un*) families of the Mongols: cxi, cxii, 4–6, 18

Alaq Noyan (Naked Ba'arin), brother of Naya'a and captain of a thousand; his grandson Bayan commanded the conquest of South China: 54–55, 99, 111

Alaqa (or **Alaqai**) **Beki** (Borjigin), daughter of Chinggis Khan, betrothed to the Öng'ut ruler: 122

Alaq-It, wife of Mongol commander Big Cāran: 65

Ala-Quš Digit-Quri Küregen (Öng'ut), regent (*digit-quri*) of the Öng'ut or White Tatar people in south-central Inner Mongolia and later a son-in-law (*küregen*) of Chinggis Khan: 77, 83, 100

Alašai Mountains, Helan Mountains on the border of Ningxia and Inner Mongolia: cxxiii, 144

Ala'ut-Turġa'ut ('the mottled ones and the sentinels'), mountains along the Onon valley in northeast Mongolia: 42

Alci, captain of a thousand: 100

Alci Küregen (Bosqur Qonggirat), brother of Madame Börte; in the Secret History he is called a 'son-in-law' (*küregen*), but other sources know him as Alci Noyan: 100, 114, 133

Alci Tatars ('Crafty Tatars' or 'Lucky Tatars'), common name for the largest body of Tatars, said by Rashiduddin to be divided into seventy factions: 48, 58

Alcidai (Jalayir), commander in the *kešikten* (imperial guard corps): 114, 115, 119, 151, 152, 154

Alcidai (Borjigin), son of Chinggis Khan's brother Qaci'un, said to be Chinggis Khan's favorite nephew: cxiv, 66, 123, 138

Alciq, steward (*ba'urci*) in the entourage of the Kereyit princess Ibaqa: 105

Alġui (Qonggirat), commander of one of the Qonggirat houses, hostile to Chinggis Khan: 48

Alġui Spring (*Alġui Bulaq*), spring in the Hulun Buir area of northeast Inner Mongolia: 48

Alin Taiši, one of four supreme commanders under Ong Khan: 58

Altai Mountains, modern Altai range of far-western Mongolia: cxx, cxxiii, 50, 61, 74, 90, 92, 103

Altai, term in Middle Mongolian also used for the modern Khangai mountains in west-central Mongolia: cxviii, 86

Altan Otcigin (Borjigin): youngest son (*otcigin*) of Qutula Khan, initially supportive of and later hostile to his cousin Chinggis Khan: cxiii, 10, genealogy; 38–39, 41, enthrones Chinggis Khan; 49, 58,

submitting to Chinggis Khan and becoming a *küregen* (imperial son-in-law) in the Mongol empire: 120

Aša Gambo (Tangut), high official at the Tangut Xia court and of Aša (Azha or Tuyuhun) ancestry: 138, 144

Ašiq (Menen Ba'arin), assigned with Qorci to rule a *tümen* (ten-thousand) of Forest Folk: 104

Ašiq Küregen, imperial son-in-law (*küregen*) of unknown family: 100

Ašiq-Temur, steward (*ba'urci*) in the entourage of the Kereyit princess Ibaqa: 105

Aspen, Passes of (*Huliyatu Sübcit*), passes in the mountains north of Ulaanbaatar: 34

A'ujam-Boro'ul, early ancestor of Chinggis Khan: cxi, 3

A'uruq: see Base Camp

Awadh City (*Abtu Balağasu*), major city in northern India, also known as Ayodhya and Oudh: cxxiii, 141

Ayil Qarağana ('Caragana Bush by the Camp'), place in Khentii mountains: 31, 38

Ayiri'ut Tatars, a petty Tatar house along the Orshuun river: 10

Ba'aridai (Ba'arin), eponymous ancestor of the Ba'arin clans: 8

Ba'arin, one of the most numerous of the noble (*niru'un*) families of the Mongols, with many sub-branches: cxii, cxxiii, 8, 37–38, 104, 110, 193

Ba'atur, brave warriors assigned to the front ranks of the army center, often translated as 'hero': lxxxix, 67, 80, 84, 118, 120

Badai (Oronar), common wrangler who delivered news of the Kereyit attack to Chinggis Khan and was rewarded with *darqan* (immune) status: 10, 65–66, 80, 100, 111

Badakhshan (*Batkašan*), kingdom in northeast Afghanistan, famed for its precious stones: cxxii, 139

Bağaci (Tayici'ut), Tayici'ut commander in league with Yisukei Ba'atur and hostile to Fatty Kiriltuq: 72

Baghdad (*Baqtat*), major city of Iraq and capital of the Abbasid Caliph: cxxii, 141, 146, 150

Baidrag Belcir (*Bayidaraq Belcir*), *belcir* (confluence or crossroads) along the Baidrag River on the southern slopes of the Khangai Mountains: cxviii, cxx, 61, 74

Bai-Šingqor-Doqšin (Borjigin), Chinggis Khan's fifth generation ancestor: cxii, 9

Bala Noyan (Šingqot Jalayir), son of Sece-Domoq, appointed to Tolui's entourage: 37, 99, 123, 139, 140, 142

Bala Cerbi, presumably one of Chinggis Khan's early 'chamberlains' (*cerbi*), although he is not found in the list of six *cerbis* in §191 or mentioned in the organization of the *kešikten* (imperial guard corps): 99

Balaġaci (Besut), envoy of the Tayici'ut khan Hambaġai: 10

Baljun Isle (*Baljun Aral*), spit of land between the Balj and Onon rivers in northeast Mongolia: cxix, 6

Baljuna, Lake (*Baljuna Na'ur*), muddy water-hole in the eastern Mongolia plain: cxix, 77, 78, 104–05

Baqu-Corogi (Qatagin), commander of the Qatagin house: 48

Barġu the Fair (*Barġujin Ġowa*), eponymous ancestress of the Barġut: cxi, 4

Barġu the Marksman (*Barġudai Mergen*), eponymous ancestor of the Barġut people: cxi, 4

Barġut, Mongolic-speaking people of the forest belt, east of Lake Baikal: cxxi, 121

Barguzin Hollow (*Barġujin Tökum*), steppe valley in the taiga northeast of Lake Baikal, described as the northern limit of the Mongol empire east of Lake Baikal: cxviii, cxxi, 4, 32, 60, 73, 74, 125

Barim-Ši'iratu Qabici: see **Qabici Ba'atur**

Bartan Ba'atur (Borjigin), Chinggis Khan's grandfather: cxii, cxiv, 10, 48, 75

Baruladai (Barulas), eponymous ancestor of the Barulas clans: 9

Barulas, noble (*niru'un*) clan of the Mongols, with several subbranches: cxiii, 9, 37, 192

Base Camp (*a'uruq*), large camp supplying the logistical needs of an army and housing its women, children and elders while on campaign: 45–46, 93

Bashkirs (*Bajigit*), people along the western slopes of the Ural Mountains, Turkic-speaking today but in Mongol empire still speaking a dialect of Hungarian language: cxxii, 121, 142, 146, 150

Bataci-Qan, early ancestor of Chinggis Khan: cxi, 3

Batu (Borjigin), son of Chinggis Khan's eldest son Joci and founder of the 'Golden Horde': cxiv, 146–47, 150–52, 157

Ba'urci ('Steward'), household official responsible for the preparation and distribution of food and drink to all those in the khan's horde (*ordo*) and assembly (*quriltai*): 39–40, 43, 84–85, 105, 107, 116

Baya'ut ('The Wealthy Ones'), a commoner (*dürlugin*) clan among the Mongols: 5, 37, 107, 192, 194

Bayit ('The Rich Ones'), Forest People found along the Imar (Ob') river: cxx, 121

Beder Spur (*Beder Qoši'un*), ridge in the Khentii mountains: 22

Bedu'un, Moci (Dörben), early adherent of Chinggis Khan who after some unnamed fault was placed on probation under Qubilai Noyan: 37, 106

Beki, title used variously for 1) genealogically senior members of clans with priestly and shamanic functions; and 2) daughters of khans and other rulers: 32, 63, 79, 110, 121

Bekter (Borjigin), half-brother of Chinggis Khan, son of Yisukei Ba'atur by a minor wife: cxiv, 18

Belgunudei (Belgunut), son of Alan the Fair and Dobun the Marksman: cxi, cxii, 4–6, 8

Belgunut, noble (*niru'un*) clan of the Mongols: cxi, cxii, 8, 193

Belgutei Noyan (Borjigin), half-brother of Chinggis Khan, later famed as a wrestler: cxiv, genealogy; 18, rivalry with his half brothers; 19, 22–29, 31, 103, in young Chinggis Khan's camp; 33, losing his mother; 40, 43, manages the hitching post; 47–48, wrestler; 59, indiscreet; 59, made judge (*jarġu*); 84, defies Naiman; 123, 138, assigned subjects and advisors

Berke Sands (*Berke Elet*), stretch of alluvial sands south of the Kherlen River: cxix, 63

Berude: see **Sorġaqtani Beki**

Besudei (Besut), eponymous ancestor of the Besut clan: 9

Besut, a noble (*niru'un*) clan of the Mongols, attached to the Tayici'ut: cxiii, 9, 36, 37, 47, 192

Betegin Naiman, eastern half of the Naiman kingdom ruled by Tayang Khan: cxx

Big Barula (*Yeke Barula*; Barulas), one of the eponymous ancestors of the Barulas clans: 9

Biiging City (*Biiging Balaġasu*), from Chinese 'Northern Capital', a regional capital of the Jin dynasty, now in ruins in southeastern Inner Mongolia: cxxi, cxxiii, 133

Bilge Beki (Kereyit), vanguard commander and envoy of the Kereyit court: 49, 76–77

Black Forest (*Qara Tün*), forest along the Tuul River, mostly of willows: cxviii, 25, 28, 49, 62, 73, 142

Bodoncar the Simple (or the Holy) (*Bodoncar Mungqaq, Bodoncar Boqda*), son of Alan the Fair and a heavenly spirit and ancestor of Chinggis Khan and the Borjigin lineage: cxi, cxiii, 5–8, 38

Böken, captain of a thousand: 99

Bo'orcu (Arlat), Chinggis Khan's earliest friend (*nökor*) and most honoured commander; 23–25, 102–03, befriends Chinggis Khan; 26, 27, in Chinggis Khan's camp; 40–41, 60, 69, 101, 102, 103, 122–23, 134–35, 140, 144, trusted services; 62, 74, 106, one of 'four champions'; 98, captain of a thousand; 103, 112, commander on the right (west)

Böri (grandson of Caġadai), illegitimate son of Caġadai's favorite son Mö'etuken; known for his boldness in battle and violent speech when drunk: cxiv, 147, 150–52

Böri the Brawny (*Böri Böke*; Yörkin), famous wrestler killed by Belgutei: cxiii, 10, 43, 47–48

Böri-Bulciru (Jadaran), grandfather of Jamuqa: 8

Borjigin, name of the imperial lineage of Chinggis Khan, synonymous with 'Kiyan': cxi, 8, 191

Borjigin the Marksman (*Borjigidai Mergen*), eponymous ancestor of the Borjigin lineage: cxi, 1

Boroġul Noyan (Hü'uśin), one of four foundlings raised by Mother Ö'elun, who later became one of Chinggis Khan's most honoured commanders: 47, 108–09, foundling; 62, 74, 106, one of 'four champions'; 69–70, 109, trusted services; 99, captain of a thousand; 107, steward (*ba'urci*); 121–22, death in Siberia

Boroldai (Ikires), messenger from Botu of the Ikires who warned Chinggis Khan of Jamuqa's impending attack: 42

Boroldai Suyalbi, servant in the ancestral household of the Borjigin: 3

Boroqcin the Fair (*Boroqcin Ġowa*), early ancestress of the Borjigin: cxi, 3

Börte, Madame (*Börte Üjin*), first wife of Chinggis Khan, mother of his four main sons: cxiv, genealogy; 14, betrothed; 24–25, married to Temujin (Chinggis Khan); 26, 28–29, 32, kidnapped by the Merkit; 36, 126, advises Chinggis Khan; 135–36, maternal hardship

Botoġan Bo'orji, tributary of the Onon River flowing from the southern slopes of the Khentii Mountains: 3, 31–32

Botoqui the Fat (*Botoqui Tarġun*), widow of Tayidu'ul the One-Eyed and ruler of forest-dwelling Tumat folk at the time of the Mongol conquest: 121–22

Botu Küregen (Ikires), captain of the two Ikires thousands and husband first of Chinggis Khan's sister Temulun and then of his daughter Qoajin Beki: 37, 100

Bu'atu-Salji (Salji'ut), son of Alan the Fair and a heavenly spirit and eponymous ancestor of the Salji'ut clan: cxi, cxii, 5–6, 8

Bucaran Cerbi, one of the original six chamberlains (*cerbi*): 84

Buda'at, noble (*niru'un*) house of the Mongols: cxiii, 9, 192, 194

Buddha–Images, Golden (*Altan sümes*): although the word *sümes* later means 'temples', context and the Chinese gloss show it is images used for Buddhist worship: 145

Buddha Khan (*Burqan Qan*), Mongolian title of the ruler of the Tangut Xia kingdom. The Tangut rulers were famous for their patronage of Tibetan Buddhism: 131, 138, 143, 145

Bügunudei (Bügunut), son of Alan the Fair and Dobun the Marksman: cxi, cxii, 4–6, 8

Bügunut, noble (*niru'un*) clan of the Mongols: cxii, 8, 192

Buġu-Qatagi (Qatagin), son of Alan the Fair and a heavenly spirit and eponymous ancestor of the Qatagin clan: cxi, cxii, 5–6, 7, 8

Buir, Lake (*Buyur Na'ur*), large shallow fresh-water lake on the border between eastern Mongolia and Inner Mongolia's Hulun Buir region: cxix, cxxi, 10, 71

Böcek Ba'atur (Borjigin), son of Tolui by a minor lady, titled Ba'atur under Möngke in recognition of his battle prowess: 152

Börte Cinoa: see **Grey Wolf**

Bujir (Uru'ut), captain of a thousand and junior kinsman of Jürcedei: 99

Bukhara City (*Buqar Balaġasu*), great city of oasis Central Asia, ethnically 'Sart' (i.e. Tajik or Persian speaking), but ruled by the Khwarazmian empire: cxxii, 139, 140, 142

Bükidei, commander of 200 quiver-bearers (*qorci*) in the *kesikten* (imperial guard corps): 114, 118, 119

Bulġadar, shift-commander in the *kesikten* (imperial guard corps) and organizer of the post-road system under Ökodei: 154, 157

Bulgars (*Bolar*), Mongolian term both for the Turkic-speaking Muslim kingdom on the Middle Volga and the Slavicized, Christian kingdom in the Balkans; both kingdoms were originally founded by Bulgar Turks: cxxii, 142, 146, 150

Bultacu Ba'atur (Borjigin), commander of a wagon-fort in support of Chinggis Khan, associated with the Adarkin: cxii, 10, 194

Buluġan, captain of a thousand: 99

Buqa (Ca'āt Jalayir), brother of Muqali and officer in the *kesikten* (imperial guard corps): 46, 114, 115, 119, 121

Buqa Küregen (Jedei Baya'ut), one of Chinggis Khan's sons-in-law: 100

Buqadai, messenger between Chinggis Khan and Ong Khan: 65

Buqa-Temur (Kereyit), younger brother of Ong Khan: 72

Buqtyrma (*Buqturma*), river that rises in the Altai Mountains and flows into the Irtysh, also known as Bukhturma in Russian: cxx, 92

Burġan: see **Burġan-Qaldun**

Burġan-Qaldun, medieval name for the Khentii Mountains in northeastern Mongolia, sacred mountain of the Mongols and source of the Onon, Kherlen and Tuul rivers: cxviii, cxxi, 3–4, 22, 25, 26–28, 31, 32, 33, 34, 52, 76, 94, 103, 107

Bürkh (*Bürki*), small stream in Mongolia's Central province, flowing into the Kherlen River: cxviii, 25–26, 31, 73

Burqan Qan: see **Buddha Khan**

Buryats (*Buriyat*), Mongolic-speaking people of the forest belt, west of Lake Baikal and along the Angara River; today the term is used for all the Mongolic-speaking peoples of Southern Siberia: cxx, 121

Bushy Tree (*Saqlaġar modun*), type of tree that often treated as a landmark. It is unclear if the 'Bushy Tree' of Qorqonaq Jubur is the same as the Bushy Tree of Quldaqar Cliff; Mongolian tradition records another 'Bushy Tree' by the Tuul: 12, 35, 103

Buur steppe (*Bu'ura Ke'er*; 'Bull Camel Steppe'), area of steppe also known today as the Jonon Valley in Mongolia's Selenge Province, near the modern border with Russia: cxviii, 30, 57

Buyiru'ut Tatars, a petty Tatar house along the Orshuun river: 10

Buyruq Khan (Kücugut Naiman), ruler of the northwestern, Kücugut, half of the Naiman kingdom: 48–50, 61, 73–74

Ca'alun (Merkit), woman of Toqto'a Beki's family, variously said to be either his wife or his daughter: 60

Caġadai (Borjigin), second son of Chinggis Khan, famed for his adherence to the ordinances (*jasaq*): cxiv, genealogy; 123, assigned subjects and advisors; 123, character; 134–37, in succession debate; 140–41, in siege of Urgench; 146, enthrones Ökodei as Khan; 146–148, 151, 152, 157, advises Ökodei

Caġān-Quwa (Negus), early adherent of Chinggis Khan, killed by Jamuqa after the battle of Dalan-Baljut: 37, 42, 99, 110

Cakirma'ut ('flints' or 'pale stones'), land formation in the eastern Khangai Mountains: 87

Caliph Sultan (*Qalibai Soltan*), Mongol title of the Abbasid ruler of Baghdad, combining 'caliph' (a religious title) with 'sultan' (a political title): 141, 146

Canai (Uru'ut), shift-commander in the *kešikten* (imperial guard corps) and supervisor of wells and post-roads: 114, 119, 154, 156, 157

Canar: see **Canai**

Cangśi'ut, branch house of the ruling Borjigin or Kiyan lineage, closely associated with the commoner Baya'ut folk: 37, 107, 192, 194

Canyon Gate or **Pass** (*Cabciyal-un Qa'alġa, Cabciyal-un Daba'an*), Mongolian name of Juyong Pass or Juyongguan, northwest of Beijing city in China: cxxi, 129–30, 132, 133, 148

Caqa ('Child'), Mongolian name of the Tangut princess given by the Tangut ruler to Chinggis Khan: 131

Cāran, Big (*Yeke Cāran*; Borjigin), cousin of Chinggis Khan who remained loyal to Ong Khan after the two khans became hostile: cxiii, 10, 65–66, 111

Cāran, Big (*Yeke Cāran*; Totoqli'ut Tatar), Tatar whose two daughters became wives of Chinggis Khan; he seems to be the one named Big Qutuġut in other sources: 59–60

Caraqa, Old Man (*Caraqa Ebugen*; Qongqotan), follower of Chinggis Khan's father Yisukei Ba'atur: 14–15

Caraqai Lingqu (Tayici'ut): successful commander and ancestor of the Tayici'ut rulers: cxiii, 9, 76

Ca'ujin Örtegei, son of Qaidu and ancestor of the Oronar, Qongqotan, Arlat and other Mongol clans: cxiii, 9

Ca'ur Beki (Kereyit), daughter of Ong Khan and sister of Ilqa Senggum: 63, 64–65

Ca'urqai, captain of a thousand, assigned to the entourage of Chinggis Khan's nephew Alcidai: 100

Ca'urqan (Uriyangqan), junior relative of Jelme and messenger of Chinggis Khan: 37, 41, 77–78

Ca'ut-quri, low-ranking military title used in the Jurchen Jin empire, granted to Chinggis Khan: 45, 76

Ceceyiken: see **Seceyiken**

Cekcer, hill in the steppe of southeastern Mongolia: 13, 24, 49

Cerbi, title literally meaning 'chamberlain', responsible for supervising supplies for the khan's household, but also having the function of military quartermaster: 84–85, 106, 119

Chaghcharan City (*Coqcaran Balaġasu*): the capital of Ghor Province in the mountains of central Afghanistan: cxxii, 140

China (*Jauqut* or *Jaqut*): translation of the Mongolian geographical term for the northern part of China proper, including the provinces under the Jurchen Jin dynasty and the Tangut Xia: 158

Chinese (*Kitat*): translation of the Mongolian term for the inhabitants of the Jurchen Jin dynasty, especially the Han or ethnic Chinese of northern China: 10, 44, 129–132, 142, 144, 148–49

Chinggis Khan (*Cinggis Qa'an, Cinggis Qan*), title given to Temujin upon becoming ruler of the Mongols in the narrow sense and renewed when he conquered the entire Mongolian plateau: cxii, cxiv, 12, genealogy and birth; 12–19, childhood; 19–22, taken captive; 22–26, 35, early friendships; 12–14, 24–25, 59–60, 91–92, marriages; 26–34, first campaign; 35–36, 42–43, 48–50, 61–64, 67–68, 88–90, 94–97, friendship and conflict with Jamuqa; 37–41, first coronation; 43–55, 58–60, 70–71, 77–80, 82–93, campaigns in Mongolia; 56–57, 60–65, 66–70, 71–77, friendship and conflict with Ong Khan; 98–120, 123, second coronation; 93–94, 120–22, campaigns beyond Mongolia; 124–28, rivalry with Teb-Tenggeri; 129–133, 138, 142–45, conquests in China; 134, 139 42, conquests in Central Asia; 134–38, debate over succession; 143, 145, illness and death

Chüy River (*Cüi Müren*), large river rising in the Tian Shan mountains of Kyrgyzstan and flowing northwest into the plains of southeastern Kazakhstan, where it disappears in the Moyïnqum Desert: cxxii, 57, 73, 93, 120

Ciduqul the Brawny (*Ciduqul Böke*; Borjigin), ancestor of the Menen Ba'arin clan: 8

Ciġurqu, hill in the steppe of southeastern Mongolia: 13, 24, 49

Cikidei ('Big Ears'), wrangler under Chinggis Khan's nephew Alcidai: 66

Ciku Küregen (Qonggirat), son of Dergei Amal, who succeeded his father when Dergei Amal was executed for rejecting Chinggis Khan's daughter Tümelun as being too ugly to marry: 100, 132

Cila'un (Uduyit Merkit), son of the Merkit leader Toqto'a Beki; his mother was Madame Huja'ur, daughter of Ong Khan: 60, 62, 74, 91, 92, 93, 120

Cila'un Ba'atur (Suldus), minion (*aran*) of the Tayici'ut, who helped Chinggis Khan in his early captivity, became one of his 'Four Champions' and was rewarded with immune (*darqan*) status: 21–22, 62, 74, 106, 110–11

Cila'un, Scissors (*Cila'un Qayici*; Ca'āt Jalayir), minion (*aran*) of the Yörkin who presented his sons as slaves to Chinggis Khan: 46

Ciledu, Big (*Yeke Ciledu*; Merkit), original husband of Mother Ö'elun, from whom Yisukei Ba'atur kidnapped her: 11, 27, 32–33

Cilger the Brawny (*Cilger Böke*; Merkit): younger brother of Big Ciledu to whom Madame Börte was given by the Merkit lords in revenge for Yisukei Ba'atur's robbing of Big Ciledu's wife: 33

Cilgutei (Suldus), minion (*aran*) of the Tayici'ut who joined Chinggis Khan and served as his executioner: 40

Cimbai (Suldus), minion (*aran*) of the Tayici'ut, who helped Chinggis Khan in his early captivity and was rewarded with immune (*darqan*) status: 21–22, 92, 93, 110–11

Cinoas ('Wolves'), noble (*niru'un*) house of the Mongols: 42, 104, 192

Circassians (*Serkesut*), present-day Adyghe and Kabardian peoples, living on the northwestern slopes of the Caucasus mountains: 142, 146

Coci Khan (Borjigin), son of Qutula Khan and cousin of Chinggis Khan; sources outside the *Secret History* treat him as a major ruler among the Mongols during Chinggis Khan's childhood: cxiii, 10, 194

Coci-Tarmala (Dolanggit Jalayir), one of Chinggis Khan's subjects; he had many sons and his descendants later ruled the Jalayirid dynasty in post-Mongol Baghdad: 42, 97

Coci-Qasar: see Qasar

Co'orġat ('The Locks'), mountains probably in the region of the Ongi River in southern Mongolia: 143

Co'os-Caġan (Ġorulas), ruler of the Ġorulas house, initially hostile to Chinggis Khan, but later submitted: 48, 77

Cormaqan Qorci (Ötegen Sönit), commander of a mixed-ethnic resident garrison (*tamaci*) army in the Caucasus area; Cormaqan is a diminutive ('Little Corman') of his original name Corman: 141, 146, 150

Cotan (Bosqur Qonggirat), mother of Chinggis Khan's main wife Madame Börte: 25

Cülgetei, captain of a thousand: 98

Dalan-Baljut ('Seventy Waters'), site along the Onon where Jamuqa and Chinggis Khan fought the Battle of Thirteen Wagon-Forts: cxix, 42, 97, 110

Dalan-Nemurges ('Seventy-Mantles'), site in the forests of the Khingan Mountains in far-eastern Mongolia, where Chinggis Khan fought a major battle with the Tatars: cxix, 58, 70, 103

Darda (plural *dardas*), type of Chinese-style brocade made with twill ground silk woven with patterns in a supplementary gold weft: 120–21, 150

Dāritai Otcigin (Borjigin), Chinggis Khan's only surviving uncle, he was first allied with Chinggis Khan, but then punished for disloyalty: cxii, cxiv, 10, 11–12, 38, 49, 58, 59, 123, 194

Darqat, plural of *darqan* ('ones with free rights' or 'immune ones'), status conferring exemption from taxes or other requisitions, right to choose the spoils of battle and freedom of movement outside the regular assignment of pastures in the decimal organization. It is also related to the immunity from punishment for up to nine offenses: 10, 38, 80, 104, 111

Da'un, captain of a thousand: 100

Dayguards (*turġa'ut*), members of a *keśikten* or khan's guard corps who guarded and served the khan during the day, of lower status than the nightguards: 19, 67–68, 84–85, 104, 112, 114–15, 116, 118, 119–20, 127, 146, 152, 154–55

Dayir Ba'atur (Qongqotan), captain of a thousand and commander of a mixed-ethnic resident garrison (*tamaci*) troops in Afghanistan: 99

Dayir-Usun (U'as Merkit), Merkit leader, initially hostile, but later father of Chinggis Khan's fourth wife Lady Qulan: 27, 30, 32, 35, 91

Degei (Besut), captain of a thousand, appointed to supervise the khan's supply of mutton soup, as one of four councillors and as advisor to Ökodei: 40, 98, 106, 110, 112, 123

Deli'un Boldaq, lone hill or *boldaq*, along the Onon River, where Chinggis Khan was born. Traditionally identified with Staryy Chindant in Russia, it is placed by Mongolian scholars in Binder County in Mongolia's Khentii province: cxix, cxxi, 12, 26, 107

Derge Amal: see **Dergei Amal**

Dergei Amal (Qonggirat), leader of the Qonggirat people who was first hostile to Chinggis Khan and then submitted to him; he was eventually executed after rejecting the khan's daughter Tümelun as being too ugly to marry: 48, 71

Deyi Secen (Bosqur Qonggirat), father of Chinggis Khan's first wife Madame Börte: 13–14, 15, 24–25

Digit-Quri (Turkic *digit* 'prince' and Kitan *quri* 'officer') title among the Öng'ut to designate a regent ruling on behalf of a minor: 83, 100

Dobsaqa (Dörben), commander of a thousand: 100

Dobun the Marksman, husband of Alan the Fair, ancestor of the Belgunut and the Bügunut: cxi, 3–5

Dödei *Cerbi* (Sönit), one of the first six chamberlains (*cerbi*) responsible for supervising the provisioning of the court and shift-elder among the *kesikten* (imperial guard corps): 40, 84, 85, 106, 115, 119, 120

Doġuladai (Doġulan), eponymous ancestor of the Doġulan clan: 9

Doġulan (plural Doġulat), noble (*niru'un*) house of the Mongols: cxiii, 193, 194

Dolo'adai, captain of a thousand: 99

Dolonggir, plural Dolanggit: a branch of the commoner Jalayir clan: 141

Dongġayit, Teaming (*Olan Dongġayit*), an elite vanguard (*ba'atur*) unit of the Kereyit army: 56, 67–68, 80, 104

Dongjing: see **Tungging**

Doqolqu Cerbi (Mangġut or Arlat), one of the original six chamberlains (*cerbi*) and an officer in the *kesikten* (imperial guard corps), he was covertly killed by Ökodei in retaliation for his defeat by Jurchen Jin forces: 37, 39, 84, 106, 114, 115, 119, 159

Dörbei the Fierce (*Dörbei Doqsin*; Dörben), late adherent to Chinggis Khan, who campaigned in Siberia, Iran and India; he later deserted and joined the Khwarazmians: 122, 141

Dörben ('The Four'), noble (*niru'un*) house of the Mongols who resisted Chinggis Khan until the final battle of Naqu Qun: cxi, 4, 37, 48, 91, 193

Dori-Buqa, captain of a thousand: 100

Döršegei, Mongolian name of Tangut city; present-day town of Lingwu in Ningxia: cxxiii, 145

Du'a the One-Eyed (*Du'a Soqor*), man with a single Cyclops-like eye and supernatural vision; he is ancestor of the Dörben: cxi, 3–4

Düiren, a mountain in the Khentii-Daur highlands of Transbaikalia, across the present-day border from Mongolia: 6

Dusky (*Dayir*), a horse of the Borjigin lineage's eponymous ancestor: 3

Ebegei (Yörkin), minor wife of Qutuqtu(or Sorġatu)-Yörki and stepmother of Sece Beki: 43

Ebugejin Noyagin, either one person, or two persons (the Mongolian is ambiguous) who conspired with Jamuqa and Ilqa Senggum against Chinggis Khan: 63–64

Eke Stream (*Eke Goroqan*), place somewhere between Parvan and Badakhshan in Afghanistan: 139

Envoys (*elci*), highly responsible position used to communicate with both friends and enemies, demanding knowledge of routes, ability to gather intelligence and eloquence: 10, 40–41, 44, 57, 61, 74, 76–78, 87, 120, 125, 131–32, 134, 143, 156–57, 158

Eljigidei (Tamġaliq Suldus), supervisor of the *kešikten* (imperial guard corps) under Ökodei Khan and commander in the Middle East under Güyuk Khan; he was executed with his son Harġasun in Möngke Khan's purge of 1251: 117, 153, 155

El-Qotor (Kereyit), commander under Ong Khan; he was the son of an earlier Kereyit ruler, Sariq Khan, by a minor wife: 58

Enegen Güiletu, hill in the steppe of southeastern Mongolia: 49

Erdemtu Barulas, branch of the Barulas, a noble (*niru'un*) house of the Mongols: cxiii, 9

Ergune River (*Ergune Müren*), large river flowing between Lake Hulun and the Amur River, forming part of the current boundary between Russia and China: cxix, cxxi, cxxiii, 49, 50, 77

Eriġaya, capital of the Tangut Xia kingdom, variously known in Chinese at the time as Xingzhou or Zhongxing; present-day city of Yinchuan: cxxiii, 144

Erije'u, major city in the Tangut Xia kingdom, present-day Wuwei city in Gansu: cxxiii, 144

Erke-Qara (Kereyit), younger brother of Ong Khan and rival for the Kereyit throne: 56, 72, 73

Eternal Heaven (*Möngke Tngri*), supreme deity in Mongol religion, whose primary role is to grant political and military success: 3, 5, 20, 50, 51, 64, 69, 75, 80, 91, 94, 97, 101, 104, 112, 122, 124, 128, 138, 143, 144, 145, 150

Etil, Turco-Mongolian name of the present-day Volga River: 142, 146, 150

Fallow Doe (*Ġoai Maral*), ultimate ancestress of the Borjigin lineage: 3

Forest Folk (*Hoi-yin Irgen*), general Mongolian name for the peoples of the Siberian taiga: cxxiii, 101, 104, 121–122

Four Champions (*Dörben Külü'ut*), term, literally meaning 'four steeds', used for Chinggis Khan's four greatest commanders, but also used for his four son by Madame Börte: 61, 74, 106, 134

Fox Pass (*Hünegen Daba'a*), northernmost pass over the mountains northwest of Beijing, seen by Chinese travelers as the beginning of the Mongolian steppe; known in Chinese as *Yehu Ling* or 'Wild Fox Ridge': cxxi, 129

Friend (*nökor*), translation of a Mongolian term that carries the sense of mutual affection, especially between a leader and his most intimate followers. It can also be used to designate a worthy opponent, in which case it is translated as 'contender': xc–xci, 4, 18, 23–24, 25, 29, 41, 48, 53, 55, 67, 76, 77, 79, 95–97, 103, 107, 108, 113, 127, 137 (friend); 67–68, 84, 87, 127, 145 (contender)

Fuzhou (*Wucu*), walled town founded by Jurchen Jin to control the Inner Mongolian approaches to the mountains north of their main capital, Zhongdu (present-day Beijing): cxxi, cxxiii, 129

Ġaca'uratu Sübcit: see **Spruce, Passes of**

Ġal (Uduyit Merkit), son of the Merkit leader Toqto'a Beki: 93

Gambo, Tangut title used for regional military commanders and also adopted by the Kereyit rulers: 31, 56, 105, 138, 144

Gen River (*Gen Müren*), tributary of the Ergune River, in the northern Hulun Buir area: cxix, cxxi, 49

Ger, Mongol name for the 'yurt' or mobile home of the Central Eurasian pastoralists, made by covering a wooden framework with felt: xviii–xx, 5, 21–22, 26, 30, 32, 33, 40, 58–59, 63, 108–09, 117, 118–20

Geuki, commander of a thousand: 100

Ge'un Stream (*Ge'un Ġoroqan*; 'Mare Stream'), place somewhere between Parvan and Badakhshan in Afghanistan. Although Ge'un is labelled in the *Secret History* as a 'stream' (*ġoroqan*), other sources call it a 'fort' (*qorġan*), which is more likely to be correct: 139

Girma'u (Borjigin), son of Qutula Khan: 10

Ġoai Maral: see **Fallow Doe**

Godu (Tayici'ut), early follower of Chinggis Khan, despite being of the generally hostile Tayici'ut house: 40, 194

Godu (Uduyit Merkit), eldest and most important of the sons of the Merkit leader Toqto'a Beki: 48–50, 60, 62, 74, 91, 92–93, 120

Godun-Hürceng (Je'uriyet), leader of the Tayici'ut confederation, although probably of the affiliated Je'uriyet house: 48, 50, 53

Golden Fort (*Altan Qorġan*): a place probably the hills north of the Qashqadaryo River near Shahrisabz in Uzbekistan, 140

Golden Khan (*Altan Qan, Altan Qa'an*), Turco-Mongolian title of the emperor of the Jin dynasty, which was founded in northern China by the Jurchen people; *Jin* means 'Golden' in Chinese: cxxiii, 10, 44–45, 129–33, 144, 148–149

Golden Tent (*Altan terme*), vast tent of wool with gold foil-plated pillers that housed the Kereyit court: 78, 80

Gongzhu (*Gungju*; Chinese 'princess'), daughter of the Golden Khan given as bride to Chinggis Khan; her name in the *Secret History* is just the Mongolian version of Chinese 'princess': 130

Gorulas, commoner house of eastern Mongolia, related to the Qonggirat: 37, 48, 49, 77, 192, 194

Great Base-Camp (*Yeke A'uruq*), logistical center of the early Mongol empire where eventually Chinggis Khan's hordes (mobiles palaces) were stationed: cxviii, cxxi, 119, 133, 139, 148

Grey (*Boro*), horse of the Borjigin lineage's eponymous ancestor: 3

Grey Wolf (*Börte Cinoa*): ultimate ancestor of the Borjigin lineage: 3

Gunan Noyan (Keniges), wagon-fort commander and later commander of a thousand and advisor to Joci: 38, 98, 106, 110, 123

Gunan (Tayici'ut), Tayici'ut commander in league with Yisukei Ba'atur and hostile to Fatty Kiriltuq: 72

Gungju: see **Gongzhu**

Gurban-Talasut ('Three Plains'), place in southern Mongolia, perhaps in or near the Gurwan-Saikhan Mountains of South Gobi Province: 73

Gür-Khan (*Gür Qan*; Kereyit), younger brother of the Kereyit ruler Qurjaqus Buyiruq Khan, who opposed his nephew Ong Khan's fratricidal policies: 56, 72

Gür Khan (*Gür Qa, Gür Qan*), Kitan title meaning 'Sovereign of All', used by the Qara-Khitai as well as by various rulers on the Mongolian plateau: 48–49, 56, 57, 73, 93

Guyang, Mongolian title derived from Chinese *Guowang* ('Prince of State'), designating the viceroy of eastern wing of the realm: 98, 104, 112

Güyük (Borjigin), eldest son of Chinggis Khan's son and successor, Ökodei Khan, and himself third khan of the Mongol empire (1246–1248): cxiv, 147, 150–52

Hambaġai Khan (Tayici'ut), prince of the Tayici'ut and one of the pre-Chinggisid khans killed by the Tatars in alliance with the Jin dynasty: 9, 10, 12, 15

Harġasun (Tamġaliq Suldus), son of Eljigidei, executed in Möngke Khan's purge of 1251 for insulting Batu: 151, 152

Hariltu, Lake, lake in eastern Mongolia: 45

Hartagidai, conspirator with Jamuqa and Ilqa Senggum against Chinggis Khan; either an ethnonymic description ('man of the Hart-agin') or a personal name: 63–64

Hartagin, noble (*niru'un*) house of the Mongols, affiliated with the Tayici'ut: 192

Hasan: a Muslim merchant trading in Mongolia who early joined Chinggis Khan's camp: 77

Heaven, see Eternal Heaven

Heaven and Earth (*Tngri Ġajar*), politico-religious conception of the Mongols, responsible for Chinggis Khan's success: 34, 38, 41, 62, 73, 105, 112, 130, 141, 159

Herat (*Hiru* or *Haru*), major city in northwestern Afghanistan: 140, 141

Hexi (*Qaśin*; Chinese 'West of the [Yellow] River'), roughly modern Gansu province; used in Mongolian as a name for the Tangut territory: 56, 73, 131

Hindus (*Hindus irgen*), Hindu people of South Asia; the Muslim Delhi Sultanate was the dominant political power of northern India, but Hindu kings still ruled in the Salt Range, Rajputana and elsewhere: 141, 142

Hö'elun: see Ö'elun

Hökortu valley (*Hökortu Jubur*), *jubur* or wooded valley on the northern slopes of the Lesser Khentii Mountains: 34

'Honest' (*Śidurġu*), derisive nickname given by the Mongols to the Tangut ruler, Buddha Khan: 145

Hoqotur, commander of reinforcements for the *tamaci* (mixed-ethnic resident garrison troops) in the Afghanistan area: 146

Horde (*ordo*), mobile palace of Mongol emperors with its attached *keśikten* (imperial guard corps) and support staff: xxiii, lxxxviii, 116, 117, 118–20, 153–54

Horqudaq, captain of 200 quiver-bearers (*qorci*) in the *keśikten* (imperial guard corps): 114, 154

Huanrzui, Spur of (*Qonji-jui-yin qośi'un*), site between Fox Pass and Fuzhou, where the Mongol armies decisively defeated the Jurchen Jin forces in February, 1212. The name was corrupted in the manuscripts into a second reference to Xuandezhou: 129

Huihebu (*Qui-Qawu*), fort in the Huai'an County area of Hebei Province along the Yanghe River and site of the first great battle between Mongol armies and the Jurchen Jin forces in September, 1211: cxxi, 132

Huja'ur, Madame (*Huja'ur Üjin*), daughter of Ong Khan given in marriage to Toqto'a Beki and mother Toqto'a Beki's son Cila'un: 72

Hula'an-Burġat ('Red Willows'), willow-clad hills in the Ulagai-Seyelji area of Inner Mongolia, in the Üjumucin (Üzemchin) district: 66–67, 70

Hula'an-Qut ('Red Cliffs'), site of a battle between Kökse'u-Sabraq of the Naiman and Ilqa Senggum of the Kereyit who was later joined by Chinggis Khan's forces; probably on the southwestern slopes of the Khangai Mountains: 62, 74

Hula'anu'ut Bolda'ut: see **Red Hills**

Huliyatu Sübcit: see **Aspen, Passes of**

Hulun, Lake (*Kölen Na'ur*), large lake in the Hulun Buir region of northeastern Inner Mongolia: cxix, cxxi, 10

Hünegen Daba'a: See **Fox Pass**

Hû-Šire Yawuta: see **Qu the Hunchback**

Ibaqa Beki (Kereyit), older daughter of Ja'a Gambo, wife first of Chinggis Khan and then Jürcedei: 79, 105–06

Ider-Altai Valley (*Eder-Altai-yin Belcir*), valley where the Ider River goes between the present-day Tarbagatai and Bulnai ranges of the Khangai mountains: cxviii, 74, 61

Idoġadai, captain of a thousand and advisor to Caġadai: 100, 123

Iduqut ('Holy Glory'), title of the Uyghur ruler in Beš-Baliq and Turpan: 120–21

Ikires, commoner (*dürlugin*) house among the Mongols living near the Ergune River, which later becoming a major marriage ally family for the Mongol imperial clan: 37, 42, 48, 100, 192

Ila, Kitan commander of the Jin dynasty's last-ditch resistance to the Mongols. In Mongolian he is known by his Kitan surname Ila; his full name was Ila Puwa (Chinese Yila Pu'a): 132

Ilqa Senggum (Kereyit), son and heir of the Kereyit ruler Ong Khan: 49, as Kereyit commander; 62, 74, rescued by Chinggis Khan's four champions; 63–65, 77, 102, plots against Chinggis Khan; 68–70, injured in battle of Qala'aljit Sands; 70, conceived by prayers; 76, accused by Chinggis Khan; 79, 80–81, flees from Mongols; 102

Ilugei (Jalayir), captain of a thousand and senior advisor to Ökodei Khan: 98, 114, 123

Iluġu Burqan: see **Victorious Buddha**

Imperial Son-In-Law: see *Küregen*

Ïnalci (Oyirat), son of the Oyiraat ruler Qutuġa Beki and husband of Chinggis Khan's daughter Seceyiken: 121

Ïnanc Bilge Khan, ruler of the unified Naiman kingdom in the days before Chinggis Khan and father of Tayang Khan and Buyruq Khan who divided the kingdom: 72, 73, 82, 87

Indus River (Sin Müren), great river of South Asia and the limit of expansion first of the Khwarazmian empire and then of the Mongol empire: cxxii, 139, 142

Irkidei Ba'atur (Salji'ut), leader of the Salji'ut house: 48

Irtysh (*Erdis*), great river of Siberia, rising in the western slopes of the Altai Mountains: cxx, cssiii, 92, 104, 142

Iturgen (Kereyit), member of the entourage of Ong Khan: 74, 78

Ja'a Gambo (Kereyit), Ong Khan's younger brother, who vacillated between supporting Chinggis Khan and Ong Khan: 31, 49, 56, 58, 79, 105

ja'arin (plural *ja'arit*), shamanic term that today refers to a high-ranked shaman but which the Chinese translation glossed as *shen gao* "spirit message." In context it appears to refer to the spirit who possesses and speaks through the shaman: liv, 38, 104, 124

Jadaran (or Jajirat), noble (*niru'un*) house of the Mongols, centered in the Ergune River and lower Onon River area: cxii, 8, 38, 42, 48, 90, 112, 193

Jajiradai (Jadaran), eponymous ancestor of the Jadaran (also known as Jajirat) clan: 8

Jajirat: see **Jadaran**

Jalaluddin Sultan (*Jalaldin Soltan*), last of the Sultans of the Khwarazmian empire, finally killed while in flight from Cormaqan's armies: 139, 142

Jalama, hill or mountain, probably near the eastern Sa'ari Steppe: 42

Jalayir, important commoner (*dürlugin*) clan among the Mongols, divided into ten sub-branches and supplying many distinguished commanders under Chinggis Khan: 37, 46, 193, 194

Jali-Buqa, Jalin-Buqa (Tatar), Tatar leader; the name appears twice under slightly variant forms and is probably the same person: 12, 48

Jam: see **post-stations, post-staff** and **relay-riders**

Jamuqa Anda (Jadaran), sworn brother (*anda*) and rival of Chinggis Khan for position of ruler over the Mongols under Ong Khan's suzerainty: 8, genealogy; 29–32, 34, campaign against the Merkit; 35–36, 38, 41, alliance and break with Chinggis Khan; 42–43, 48–50, battles with Chinggis Khan; 61, 63–64, conspires against Chinggis Khan; 67–68, 70, 75, 76, 87, 88–91, in the Kereyit and Naiman camp; 94–97, captured and executed

Janggi, commander appointed by Ökodei Khan as advisor to his son Güyuk: 151, 152

Jarci'udai, Old Man (*Jarci'udai Ebugen*; Uriyangqan), black smith from the mountains of the Khentii who gifted his son Jelme as servant to Chinggis Khan: 25–26, 107

Jarci'ut ('servants'), branch of the Uriyangqan, probably the same clan as that of Old Man Jarci'udai: 8

Jarġu: see **Judge**

Jasaq: see **Ordinances**

Jebe ('Weapon'; Besut), Mongol captain of a thousand and commander with Sübe'edei of the famous expedition around the Caspian Sea: 52–53, 140, originally named Jirġo'adai; 58, 85, sent as outrider (*alginci*); 88, 106, one of the 'four dogs'; 98, 120, 139–40, western campaigns; 99, 112, captain of a thousand; 129–30, 132, 148, China campaigns

Jebke (Ca'āt Jalayir), commander of a thousand donated as a child to serve Qasar: 46–47, 90, 123

Jedei Noyan (Manġġut), commander of a thousand and advisor to Tolui: 37, 39, 99, 109, 123

Jeder: commander of a thousand: 100

Jegei-Qongtaġar (Sö'eken), descendant of Slave Noqta captured by Tayici'ut and Mongols: 37, 76

Jeje'er Heights (*Jeje'er Ündur*), high ground near the Berke Sands, south of the Kherlen river: cxix, 78

Jelme Quwa (Uriyangqan), one of Chinggis Khan's earliest companions and most honoured commanders: 26, 107, donated as servant; 26, 27, in Chinggis Khan's camp; 40–41, 50–51, 66, 109, trusted services; 88, 106, one of 'four dogs'; 98, captain of a thousand

Jer Gully (*Jer Qabciġai*), gully or ravine in the Jeje'er Heights: 78

Jerene Gorge (*Jerene Qabciġai*), gorge along the Onon River: cxix, 42, 97

Je'uriyedei (Je'uriyet), eponymous ancestor of the Je'uriyet clan: cxiii, 8

Je'uriyet, noble (*niru'un*) house of the Mongols, affiliated with the Tayici'ut: cxiii, 8–9, 193

Jirġo'adai ('Number Six'), original name of Jebe: 53, 140

Jirġo'an (Oronar), early adherent of Chinggis Khan: 37

Jirkin (Kereyit), small force, one hundred strong, serving as Ong Khan's foremost *ba'atur* (elite vanguard) company: 67–68, 79, 80, 104

Joci (Borjigin), eldest son of Chinggis Khan and Madame Börte, assigned territory in the Kazakhstan steppe: cxiv, genealogy; 63, marriage engagement; 106, 123, assigned subjects and advisors; 121, conquers Forest Folk; 134–37, denied the succession as khan; 140–41, in conquest of Urgench city

Jorġal Qun, craggy mountain south of the Tuul river: cxviii, 71

Jubqan (Öng'ut), high ranking envoy of the Mongol empir who was detained not, despite the *Secret History*, by the Jurchen Jin, but by the Song dynasty; his name is more usually written as Subqan: 131

Judge (*jarġu*), judge of lawsuits and violations of the ordinances (*jasaq*), authority variously vested in Belgutei, Śiki Qutuġu and judges in the nightguards; sometimes written *jarġuci*: 59, 102, 119

Jüin, term used for Inner Mongolian pastoralists, mostly Tatars and Kitans, enrolled as auxiliary soldiers to patrol the frontier for the Jurchen Jin dynasty: xxxvii, 10, 129, 130, 144

Jungšoi (Noyagin), commander of a thousand and advisor to Mother Ö'elun and Otcigin: 37, 99, 123

Jürcedei (Uru'ut), captain of a thousand and commander of the highly respected Uru'ut fighters: 42, joins Chinggis Khan; 68, 104, in battle of Qala'aljit Sands; 71, subdues Qonggirat folk; 78, 105, outrider (*alginci*) against Ong Khan's camp; 98, 106, captain of a thousand; 105–06, granted Ibaqa Beki as wife; 133, in campaigns against China

Jurchens (*Jürcet*), Manchurian people, speaking a Tungusic language and ancestors of the later Manchus; the dominant people in the Jürchen Jin dynasty. The Chinese dynastic name *Jin* means 'Gold' and the Jurchen ruler was known to the Mongols as the 'Golden Khan': xxxv, xxxvii, cxxiii, 129, 130, 133, 150

Juyong Pass: see **Canyon Gate**

Kashgar (*Kišġar*), principal city of the Tarim Basin in present-day southern Xinjiang: cxxii, 142

Kashmir (*Keśimir*), Srinagar valley, now divided between India and Pakistan and at the time a Buddhist kingdom: cxxii, 142, 146

Ke'en, Slim (*Narin Ke'en*; Borjigin), son of Chinggis Khan's cousin Big Cāran and participant in Ong Khan's attack on Chinggis Khan: 65–66

Keltegei Cliffs (*Keltegei Qada*): line of cliffs along the right bank of the Khalkh river, near the Mongolian border with Inner Mongolia: cxix, 71, 84, 85

Keniges, Mongol clan of midling status, later assigned to Joci's rule; also written as Keniget: cxiii, 9, 38, 106, 193

Kerel, Mongol term for the Magyars of the kingdom of Hungary in central Europe, as opposed to those in the Ural region; derived from Hungarian *király*: cxxii, 142, 146

Kereyit, major kingdoms of twelfth–century Mongolia centered on the Orkhon, Tuul and Ongi river valleys: xxviii–xxx, 25, 41, 45, 56, 68, 79–80, 105, 123

Kešikten ('those serving in shifts' or 'the fortunate ones'), imperial guard corps; the *kešikten*'s function was as much political and administrative as purely military: lxxxix–xc, 80, 84–85, 112–20, 146, 152–56

Keštimi, Turkic-speaking forest folk who paid tribute to the rulers of the Yenisey Kïrghiz in the Siberia's Minusa basin: cxx, 121

Kete, captain of a thousand and advisor to Joci: 99, 123

Ketei, captain of a thousand: 100

Keyibur, thin, dart-like arrow used for penetrating, distance shots: 89

Khalkh River (*Qalqa*), river in far eastern Mongolia, flowing from the Khingan mountains into Lake Buir: cxix, cxxi, 70–71, 84, 85, 104

Khangai Mountains (*Qanggai*), high wooded mountains in west-central Mongolia, also known as the Qanggar-Qan Mountains: cxviii, cxx, 85–86

Khan (*Qa'an*, or more rarely *Qan*), Turco-Mongolian title of monarchical rulers over kingdom-or imperial-sized domains: lxxxvi–lxxxvii, 10, 12, 13, 25, 39–41, 44–45, 48–49, 98, 148

Khan-Malik (*Qan-Melik*; Qangli), military governor of Herat in the service of the Khwarazmian empire; nephew of Sultan Jalaluddin's mother: 139–40, 142

Kherlen River (*Keluren Müren*), long river in Mongolia, flowing east from the Khentii Mountains to Lake Hulun: cxix, cxxi, cxxiii, 24–25, 26, 31, 46

Khilok River (*Kilgo Müren*), river in the Buryat Mongolian region of Siberia: cxviii, cxxi, 30, 32

Khotan (*Odan*), major city of the Tarim Basin in present-day southern Xinjiang: cxxiii, 142

Khwarazm (*Qurumsi*), oasis in the delta of the Amu River, today divided between Uzbekistan and Turkmenistan, and center of a powerful Muslim empire: xliv–xlvi, cxxii, 142

Kimurqa Stream (*Kimurqa Goroqan*), small tributary of the Onon River, running through the steppe south of the Khentii Mountains, probably to be identified with the present-day Khurkh River: cxviii, 22, 31, 38

Kinggiyadai (Olqunu'ut), early adherent of Chinggis Khan and captain of a thousand: 37

Kinggiyat (or **Qïngqiyat**), Mongol clan of midling status, closely associated with the Sö'eken: 193, 194

Kiratai, in the *Secret History*, messenger along with Buqadai; in other sources, *kiratai* corresponds to Buqadai's title, *kišat* or *kicat*, the Naiman word for 'steward': 65

Kïrghiz (*Qïrqisut*), Turkic people of the Minusa Basin in Siberia, ancestors of today's Khakas people; not to be confused with the modern Kyrgyz of Kyrgyzstan: cxx, cxxiii, 121

Kiriltuq, Fatty (*Tarġutai Kiriltuq*; Tayici'ut), son of a Tayici'ut khan and powerful among the Tayici'ut but denied the succession to the position of khan: 15, 19–20, 48, 53–55, 111

Kišiliq (Oronar), common wrangler who delivered news of the Kereyit attack to Chinggis Khan and was rewarded with *darqan* (immune) status: 10, 65–66, 80, 100, 111

Kitans (*Qara-Kitat*), pastoralists speaking a language related to Mongolian, some ruled by the 'Golden Khan', others ruling the Qara-Khitai empire: xxxvii, xlii, cxxii, cxxiii, 129, 130

Kiyan (plural **Kiyat**), name of the imperial lineage of Chinggis Khan, synonymous with 'Borjigin': 14, 192

Knob-headed arrow (*ġodoli*), arrow with a blunt head made of horn, often with holes to produce a whistling sound: 28, 33, 35

Köde'e Isle (*Köde'e Aral*; 'Steppe Island'): alternative name of Küte'u Isle: 161

Köiten ('Cold'), battle site in the Khingan Mountains of Inner Mongolia: cxix, 49, 53

Köke, captain of a thousand: 99

Köke Na'ur ('Blue Lake'), small lake in the hills south of the Khentii Range near the Kherlen River: cxviii, 22, 39

Köke-Cos (Menen Ba'arin), captain of a thousand and advisor for Caġadai: 37, 99, 106, 110, 123, 135

Kökecu (Besut), one of the 'four foundlings', commander of a thousand and advisor to Mother Ö'elun: 36, 47, 99, 108, 123, 124

Kökecu, Jamuqa's groom (*aqtaci*), executed by Chinggis Khan for abandoning his master: 80–81

Kökecu: see **Teb-Tenggeri**

Kökecu-Kirsaqan (Sö'eken), descendant of Slave Noqta captured by Tayici'ut and Mongols: 76

Kökse'u-Sabraq (Betegin Naiman), Naiman commander under Tayang Khan; Kökse'u is said to mean "chest-pain" and that he was so called because of his deep voice: 61–62, 74, 82–83, 87

Koreans (*Solangġas*), Korean kingdom under Goryeo dynasty; after many invasions they submitted to Mongol rule under Qubilai Khan: 150

Köten-Baraqa (Tatar), leader of the Tatars allied with the Jurchen: 12

Kucha-Tarim (*Küsen-Tarim*), Kucha is a city in present-day Xinjiang; the Tarim Basin is the vast desert basin in southern Xinjiang. Kucha-Tarim designates the city of Kucha: cxxiii, 142

Kücü (Merkit), one of the 'four foundlings', commander of a thousand and advisor to Mother Ö'elun: 34, 47, 99, 108, 123, 124

Kücugut Naiman, northwestern half of the Naiman kingdom, extending from the Aluy-Saras area to the upper Irtysh; Kücugut is plural of *kücugur* 'jerboa': xxix, cxx, 48, 61, 73

Kücugur, Carpenter (*Kücugur Moci*), captain of a thousand, responsible for the upkeep of the *ger*-wagons: 37, 40, 99, 112

Küculug Khan (Betegin Naiman), son of Tayang Khan who after the conquest of the Naiman realm fled to the Qara-Khitai; he managed to take over rule of that kingdom before being pursued and killed by Jebe: 86–87, 90, 92–93, 98, 120

Küikunek Ba'atur, vanguard commander of Tolui's invasion of the Jurchen Jin's last redoubt in Henan Province, mistakenly transposed in the *Secret History* to the initial 1211 invasion of the Jin dynasty: 129

Küre'en or *küriyen*: see **Wagon-Fort**

Küregen, ordinary Mongolian term for 'son-in-law', also used in the empire for imperial sons-in-law: xcii, 100–01, 146, 147, 157

Kürelgu, sacred mountain in the Khentii mountain range where many of the Mongol khans, including Chinggis Khan are said to have been buried: cxviii, 22, 25, 39, 42, 49

Kürin Ba'atur (Obciq), Kereyit commander; some accounts say that *obciq* is not his clan name, but rather the name of a red fruit which was used of him because of his red cheeks: 61

Küte'u Isle (*Küte'u Aral*), island or peninsula in the Kherlen River, also known as Köde'e Isle: cxviii, cxxi, 46, 146

Kü'un-Quwa (Ca'āt Jalayir), subject of the Yörkin who paid allegiance to Chinggis Khan and devoted his two sons Muqali and Buqa to his service: 46, 103–04

Kyiv (*Kiwa, Keyibe*), capital city of the Ruthenian principalities and then seat of the Orthodox Church among the East Slavs; called Man-Kermen or 'Great City' by the Qïpchaqs and other Turkic speaking nomads: 142, 147, 150

Lablaqa, captain of 200 quiver-bearers (*qorci*) in the *keśikten* (imperial guard corps): 124, 154

Lady: see *Qatun*

Lingqu, title derived from Chinese *linggong* 'Lord Director', granted by Kitan Liao and Jurchen Jin courts to friendly Tatar and Mongolian commanders: 9, 76

Liushou (*Liusiu*), Chinese title for the viceroy appointed in the Jurchen Jin system to govern one of the capitals in the emperor's absence: 132

Little Barulas (*Ücuken Barulas*), branch of the Barulas, a noble (*niru'un*) house among the Mongols: 9

Ma'aliq Baya'ut, branch of the commoner Baya'ut clan: 5

Madame (*üjin*), translation of a Chinese term, *furen*, for a wife of a high official: lxxxvii–lxxxviii, 10, 11, 17–18, 24, 33, 72

Magas City (*Magat Balaġasun*), capital city of the Ossetian people in the forested northern slopes of the Caucasus: cxxii, 147, 150

Magyars (*Majar*), Hungarian-speaking peoples found both in the kingdom of Hungary between the Volga (Etil) and the Urals: cxxii, 142, 146

Mandahari folk (*Mandaqari irgen*), Mandahar clan of Rajputs based in Kaithal and claiming origin in Ayodhya (Awadh). The name was corrupted in the manuscripts to *Madasari*: cxxii, 141

Manggudai (Manggut): eponymous ancestor of the Manggut clan: 9

Manggudai, dayguard commander in the *kesikten* (imperial guard corps) of Ökodei Khan: 155

Manggut, noble (*niru'un*) house of the Mongols, famous for their battle prowess: 9, 37, 42, 67–68, 70, 88, 106, 193

Man-Kermen, name meaning 'Great City' among the Qïpchaqs and other Turkic speakers, designating both modern Kyiv, capital of the Ruthenian principalities and Biler, capital of the Volga Bulgar kingdom: cxxii, 142, 147, 150

Maor-yuzui (*Mauji-yujui*; Chinese 'Cat Valley Spur'), place in the valley leading from Juyong Pass to the Dushikou Pass, elsewhere called *Maoryu* 'Cat Valley' or Morling 'Quern Ridge'. The name was corrupted in the manuscripts into a reference to Mozhou (Renqiu, south of Zhongdu) and Fuzhou: 130

Maral, captain of a thousand: 99

Mas'ud Khwarazmi (*Masqut Qurumsi*): son of Khwarazmian merchant Mahmud Yalavach and the Mongol empire's overseer (*daruġaci*) over local officials in Central Asia: 142

Mau-Ündur ('Bad Heights'), highlands hills in the Ulagai-Seyelji area of Inner Mongolia, in the Üjumucin (Üzemchin) district: 66–67, 70

Megetu, commander of a thousand: 100

Menen Ba'arin, largest and most senior branch of the Ba'arin houses: 8, 37, 193

Menen-Tudun (Borjigin), eighth-generation ancestor of Chinggis Khan, treated by the *Secret History* as the ancestor of many non-Borjigin clans as well: cxiii, 9

Mergen ('Marksman'), term for a good archer, also used metaphorically for a clever man: 3–5, 125

Mergen Secen (Borjigin), son of Bultacu Ba'atur, otherwise unknown: 10

Merkit, Three (*Gurban Merkit*), Mongolian-speaking confederation of three 'hundreds' or houses dominating the rich steppes of the lower Selenge River: xxxi, 111, 191, location; 11, start of the quarrel with the Mongols; 27–35, 52, 103, 134, kidnapping of Börte and first campaign against them; 47, foundling from them; 48–49, 56, 60, 62, 73, 74, 105, further campaigns against them; 57, 72, early relations with Ong Khan; 91–94, final conquest; 120, remnants destroyed

Merkit White (*Merkidei Caǧān*), one of Big Cāran's riding horses: 66

Merv (*Maru*), major Persian-speaking oasis-city, currently in Turkmenistan: cxxii, 141

Me'ujin-Se'ultu (Tatar), wealthy and powerful Tatar leader involved in the widespread Tatar resistence to their Jurchen Jin overlords: 44–45

Moci Bedu'un: see **Bedu'un**

Mönggedu Sa'ur (Besut), commander placed in charge of two *tümen*s of mixed-ethnic resident garrison troops in the Afghanistan area: 146

Mönggedu Kiyan (Cangśi'ut), commander of a wagon-fort formed of Cangśi'ut and their Baya'ut subjects: cxii, 10, 194

Mönggu'ur (Siju'ut), captain of a thousand and advisor to Joci: 99, 123

Möngke: see **Müge**

Möngke (or **Möngkei**) **Khan** (Borjigin), eldest son of Chinggis Khan's fourth son, prince Tolui, and Sorǧaqtani Beki and fourth khan of the Mongol Empire (1251–1259): cxiv, 147, 150, 151, 152

Möngge-Qalja (Mangǧut), eldest son of Quyildar, commander of a separate thousand under Muqali's administration and later participant in Qubilai Khan's conquest of the Song dynasty: 100

Mönglik, Father (*Mönglik Ecige*; Qongqotan), son of Old Man Caraqa, born into the service of Chinggis Khan's family and married by Chinggis Khan to his widowed Mother Ö'elun: 14–15, 43, 65, 98, 102, 124, 126–28

Mongol the Fair (*Mongǧoljin Ǧowa*), eponymous ancestress of the Mongols: cxi

Mongols (*Monggol*), ethnic name used in the *Secret History* in somewhat different senses but usually centered on the Chinggis Khan's immediate relatives and his subjects: xxxi, cxxi, location; 10, 12, 'all the Mongols' (*qamuq Monggol*); 31, 82, 86, 91, character; 41, 87, 98, 101, 110, 130, political identity; 49, 70, 86–87, against Chinggis Khan; 82–83, 86, 89, against the Naiman; 130, 144, 149, against the Chinese, 144, against the Tangut; 149, 'teeming Mongol kingdom' (*olan Monggol ulus*)

Morici (Tayici'ut?), early adherent of Chinggis Khan: 40

Moroqa, commander of a thousand: 100

Mother Earth (*Etugen Eke*), name of earth as sacred, shared with earlier Turkic empires: 34, 137,

Müge Noyan (Jalayir), commander of a thousand and advisor to Cagadai; his name is also, probably by scribal error, written as Möngke: 99, 123

Mülke-Totaq (Ikires), messenger from Botu of the Ikires, sent to warn Chinggis Khan of Jamuqa's approach: 42

Mulqalqu (Jadaran), early adherent of Chinggis Khan and the only one of the Jadaran to be considered eligible for the command of a thousand: 38, 40, 112

Muqali Guyang (Ca'āt Jalayir), viceroy (*guyang*) and commander of the left wing under Chinggis Khan: 46, 103–04, gifted by his father to Chinggis Khan; 60, 101, 102, 103, 106, 122, 123, 134–35, 140, 144, trusted services; 62, 74, 106, one of the 'four champions'; 98, 104, entitled as *Guyang* and viceroy on the left; 98, captain of a thousand

Müruce Se'ul, western spur of the Qadingliq Mountains in the present-day Buryat Republic of Siberia: cxviii, 73

Nacin Ba'atur, ancestor in the *Secret History* of the Uru'ut, Manggut, Siju'ut and Dogolat; in other sources, he plays a different role: cxiii, 9

Naiman: large kingdoms occupying western Mongolia and neighboring areas of western Siberia, Kazakhstan and northern Xinjiang. Divided into eastern and western halves, ruled by Tayang Khan and Buyruq Khan, respectively: xxix, cxx, 191, location; 48–50, campaigns against Chinggis Khan; 56, 57, 58, 63, 72, 73, relations with Ong Khan; 61–62, 74, Chinggis Khan and Ong Khan's joint campaign; 80, 82, kill Ong Khan; 83–84, 105, conspire against Chinggis Khan; 85–91, 96, battle with Chinggis Khan; 92–93, 94, 120, fugitives tracked down

Naked Ba'arin (*Nicukut Ba'arin*), relatively small branch of the Ba'arin, allied to the Tayici'ut: 53

Namging City (Namging Balaġasu), from Chinese *Nanjing* 'Southern Capital', a regional capital of the Jin dynasty, now Kaifeng in Henan Province. After 1214, the Jin court moved its main capital there: cxxiii, 132, 133, 149

Naq (plural *naqut*), type of Middle Eastern-style gold-brocaded fabric: 150

Naqu Qun, site of the largest battle of Chinggis Khan's wars to unify Mongolia, fought in Spring, 1204, between Chinggis Khan's Mongols and the Naiman and their allies: cxix, 87–90

Naqu the Rich (*Naqu Bayan*), wealthy father of Bo'orcu and friend of Chinggis Khan's father Yisukei Ba'atur: 23, 24, 103

Naratu-Šitu'en ('Pine Fastness'), temporary fort built along the Ulz River: 45

Našiš (plural *nacit* or *nacidut*), Middle Eastern-style gold-woven lampas silk: 120–21, 150

Naun River (*Na'u Müren*), large river in northwestern Manchuria that flows into the Songhua; known today in Chinese as the Nen or Nenjiang River: 133

Naya'a Noyan (Naked Ba'arin), captain of a thousand and commander over the center *tümen*: 54–55, 91–92, 99, 111–12

Negus, general name for commoner Mongols as well as a specific commoner clan: 37, 110, 192, 194

Nekun River (*Nekun Usun*), river in southwest Mongolia flowing south from the Khangai Mountains: 80

Nekun Taiši (Borjigin), uncle of Chinggis Khan and leading figure among the Mongols of his generation: cxii, cxiv, 10, 11, 38, 43, 75

Ne'urin, Big (*Yeke Ne'urin*), commander over the nightguards the *kešikten* (imperial guard corps): 114

Nicukut Ba'arin: see **Naked Ba'arin**

Nightguards (*kebte'ul*), members of the *kešikten* or imperial guard corps who guarded the khan during the night, of higher status than the dayguards: 84–85, 112–15, 116–17, 118–20, 146, 152–54

Nilqa Senggum: see **Ilqa Senggum**

Nine-Tongued Folk (*Yisün keleten irgen*), people supporting Teb-Tenggeri's challenge to Chinggis Khan. The reference is unclear, but nine is the usual Turco-Mongolian number of completeness: 125

Nishapur (*Nišabur*), main Persian city, in northeastern Iran: cxxii, 140

Nomolun, Mother (*Nomolun Eke*), ancestress of the early Mongol khans; other sources call her Mother Monolun: 9

Noqta, Slave (*Noqta Bo'ol*; Sö'eken), man captured and enslaved in a campaign by Caraqa LIngqu and Tumbinai, 76

Noyagidai (Noyagin), eponymous ancestor of the Noyagin clan: 9

Noyagin, noble (*niru'un*) clan of the Mongols: 9, 37, 192

Noyan (plural **Noyat**), title meaning '(military) commander, captain' or '(civil) official': xcii–xciii

Nünjin, commoner (*dürlugin*) house of the Mongols, closely associated with the Saġayit: 38, 193, 194

Obciq, probably a clan of the Kereyit, but said by Rashiduddin to be a kind of berry with a red color: 61

Ocean (*Dalai*), in §253, the Bohai gulf, the first body of ocean reached by the Mongols: 133

Odora, heavier arrow used for shorter distances: 40

Ö'elun, Madame (or **Mother**) (*Ö'elun Üjin, Ö'elun Eke*; Olqunu'ut), mother of Chinggis Khan, captured and forced into marriage with Chinggis Khan's father Yisukei Ba'atur: cxiv, 12, 13, position in genealogy; 11–12, 27, 32, captured by Yisukei Ba'atur; 15–16, expelled by Tayici'ut; 17–19, maternal hardship; 26, camp raided; 34, 36, 45, 47, raises foundlings; 36, 43 and Chinggis Khan; 89, 124–25 and Qasar

Ögelei Cerbi (Arlat), one of the six chamberlains (*cerbi*) and dayguard commander in the *kešikten* (imperial guard corps): 84, 114, 119

Ökin-Barqaq ('Girl Barqaq'; Borjigin), son of the early Mongol khan Qabul, supposedly called 'Girl Barqaq' due to his beauty; captured and executed by the Jin court: cxii, 10, 47, 48

Ökodei Khan (Borjigin), Chinggis Khan's second son and successor, ruling 1229–1241: cxiv, genealogy; 69–70, 109, rescued in battle; 92, marries Töregene; 123, assigned subjects and advisors; 137–38, appointed successor; 140–41, leads siege of Urgench; 146–47, enthroned as khan; 148–49, campaigns in China; 150, appoints commanders in the West; 151–52, rebukes Güyuk; 152–58, proclaims regulations; 158–59, self-assessment

Olar Küregen (Olqunu'ut), captain of a thousand and imperial son-in-law. He is said in other sources to be the father of Mother Ö'elun and it is possible that the *Secret History* here actually means Ö'elun's brother, Taicu Küregen: 100

Olda'ur Qorci (Jalayir), overseer (*daruġaci*) of Chinggis Khan's four great hordes: 148

Ölegei Spring (*Ölegei Bulaq*), spring near the Jalama hill or mountain, probably in the eastern Sa'ari Steppe: 42

Olqunu'ut, commoner (*dürlugin*) house and branch of the broader Qonggirat clan; 11, 13, 37, 192

Ong Khan (*Ong Qan* or *Ong Qa'an*), title granted to the To'oril, ruler of the Kereyit and patron of the rising Chinggis Khan: 25, 28, 57,

62–63, 71–72, 73, alliance with Chinggis Khan; 28–34, campaign to rescue Börte; 41, approves Chinggis Khan's enthronement; 44–45, joins attack on Tatars; 45, entitled as Ong Khan; 49–50, attacked by coalition under Jamuqa; 56, 62, 72–73, alliance with Yisuekei Ba'atur; 56–58, 72–73, court conflicts; 60, 73, campaign against the Merkit; 61–62, 73–74, campaign against the Naiman; 64–65, 102, induced to attack Chinggis Khan; 67–69, 70, battle of Qala'aljit Sands; 75, regret over harming Chinggis Khan; 78–79, ambushed by Chinggis Khan's forces; 80, killed; 82, sacrificed to by the Naiman

Onggirat: see **Qonggirat**

Ongging Chengxiang (*Ongging Cingsang*), 'Ongging' is Mongolian for the Jurchen imperial clan Wongian (Chinese Wanyan); *cingsang* is Mongolian for Chinese *chengxiang* or 'grand councillor'. This designates two different grand councillors who came from the imperial clan and served as high officials in the Jurchen court: 44–45, Grand Councillor Wongian Xiang (Chinese Wanyan Xiang); 130, Grand Councillor Wongian Fuking (Chinese Wanyan Fuxing)

Onggojit Kereyit ('Vessel-Bearer Kereyit'), those among Ong Khan's *kešikten* (royal guard corps) responsible for the liquor service, vessels and bowls of the court: 80

Önggur Ba'urci (Baya'ut), designated successor of his master, Mönggedu Kiyan, who joined Chinggis Khan's camp and became captain of a thousand and steward (*ba'urci*): 37, 39, 98, 107, 132–33, 194

Öng'ut, Turkic-speaking, Christian people of central Inner Mongolia, serving the Jurchen Jin as border wardens: xxxvii–iii, cxxi, 77, 83, 100, 121

Onon River (*Onan Müren*), river flowing from the Khentii Mountains northeast through the Mongolian plateau and Trans-Baikal steppe, eventually flowing into the Amur River: cxviii–cxix, cxxi, cxxiii, 3, 6–7, 11, 12, 15, 17–18, 20–22, 31, 35, 42, 43, 50, 98

Or Meadow (*Or Nu'u*), meadow within a meander of the Khalkh River in eastern Mongolia, near the Keltegei Cliffs: 71, 84, 85

Örbei Lady (*Örbei Qatun*), widowed wife of the Tayici'ut ruler Hambaġai Khan: 15

Ordinances (*jasaq*), binding precedents eventually recorded in writing and treated as the imperial constitution: 58, 82 86, 91, 94, 115, 119, 140, 155

Öre Beg-Tegin (Kïrghiz), a leader of the Yenisey Kïrghiz of Siberia, representing the 'Six Lands' (*Alti-Er*). Beg-Tegin 'commander-prince' is a title; his personal name is also given of Ör-Bo'oci: 121

Orkhon (*Orqan*), river flowing north from the Khangai Mountains into the Selenge River: cxviii, cxxi, 34, 87

Oronar, Mongolian clan of midling status: cxiii, 9, 37, 192

Oronartai, captain of a thousand: 99

Orshuun River (*Orśi'un Müren*), river flowing between the Buir and Hulun lakes: cxix, 10

Ossetes, Ossetia (*Asut*), descendants of the Sarmatian nomads who by the time of the Mongol empire were mostly Christian-ized and living in the northern steppes and foothills Caucasus Mountains; also known as 'Alans' in European sources: cxxii, 142, 146, 150

Otar Pass (*Otar Daba'a*), unidentified pass probably in the mountains along the frontier between Kazakhstan and Xinjiang: 287

Otcigin, Turkic term, meaning 'prince of the fire' and designating the youngest son; he would inherit his parents' *ger* with its hearth while the elder sons would receive a new *ger* and portions of livestock and move away: 10, 12, 38, 90, 123, 139

Otcigin: see **Temuke Otcigin**

Ötegen, clan to which Cormaqan belonged; since Cormaqan is else-where said to be a Sönit, it is likely a branch of the Sönit: 141

Otrar City (*Oturar Balaġasu*), now ruined city along the Sïr Darya River in southern Kazakhstan. The Mongolian name comes from the Turkish folk-etymological name 'Sitting City': cxxii, 139, 140

Outriders (*alginci*), rider or body of riders sent out ahead of the main body to reconnoiter and, if advantageous, to engage the enemy. Compared to scouts (*qara'ul*), outriders had a more offensive role: 7, 32, 39, 75, 78, 85, 105, 149

Overseers (*daruġa, daruġaci*), officials appointed over populations of sedentary people, sometimes directly administering mobilized non-Mongol populations, but more usually supervising local officials whose loyalty they monitored. Overseers were commonly non-Mongol in origin and appointed to areas in which they were not native: 142, 149, 150

Oyirat, Mongolic-speaking Forest Folk, living in the area of Mongo-lia's Khöwsgöl Province and the eastern part of the Tuvan Republic: cxx, cxxiii, 48–50, 121

Parvan steppe (*Baru'an Ke'er*), high valley in the Hindu Kush moun-tains north of Kabul in Afghanistan: cxxii, 139, 140

Post-staff (*jamuci*), all the staff responsible for the upkeep of the sta-tions: 157–58

Post-stations (*jam*), post-stations and the system of post-roads in gen-eral: 157–58

Prince (*kö'un*, plural *kö'ut*), literally meaning 'son', 'prince' refers to those of a royal or imperial family, such as the sons of Chinggis Khan or his brothers. As such it is often opposed to 'commanders' or 'captains' (*noyat*), who were not of the imperial family: xcii, 21, 42, 102, 118, 122–23, 134, 140–41, 143, 146–47, 149, 150, 151, 157

Princess (*ökin*, plural *ökit*), literally meaning 'daughter', but here meaning daughters of Chinggis Khan or his brothers: 109, 146, 147, 157

Qa'at Merkit, one of three 'hundreds' of the Three Merkit confederation, dwelling in the Qaraji steppe: 27, 29, 30, 32

Qa'atai Tarmala (Qa'at Merkit), one of three leaders of the Three Merkit: 27, 30, 32, 33

Qauran (Adarkin), captain of a thousand: 100, 194

Qabici Ba'atur, Barim-Śi'iratu (Borjigin), son of Bodoncar the Simple and ancestor of the Borjigin: cxiii, 8–9

Qabqanas, people in the Tozha Basin of the Tuvan Republic in Siberia, primarily hunters and gatherers, herding reindeer and living in birch-bark tepees: cxx, cxxiii, 121

Qabturġas, Mongol clan of midling status, probably a branch of the Sönit: cxiii, 9, 193

Qabul Khan (Borjigin), first ruler of the Mongols to bear the title 'khan': cxii, 10, 47, 48

Qaci-Külük ('Qaci Champion'; Borjigin), son of Menen-Tudun, husband of Nomolun and ancestor of the Borjigin: cxii, 9

Qacin (Borjigin), son of Menen-Tudun and ancestor of the Noyagin: cxiii, 9

Qacir River (*Qacir Usun*), small river running north from the Khangai Mountains, probably the present-day Khanui: 86, 87

Qaci'u (Borjigin), son of Menen-Tudun and ancestor of the Barulas: cxiii, 9

Qaci'un (Borjigin), son of Menen-Tudun and ancestor of the Adarkin: cxiii, 9

Qaci'un Beki (Dörben), elder and priest-shaman (*beki*) of the Dörben: 48, 63–64, 76

Qaci'un Elci (Borjigin), one of Chinggis Khan's younger brothers, who died early: cxiv, 12, 19, 26, 124

Qaci'un-Toġura'un (Toġura'ut Jalayir or 'Crane Jalayir'), early adherent and quiver-bearer (*qorci*) for Chinggis Khan: 37, 39, 40

Qacula (Borjigin), son of Menen-Tudun and ancestor of the Barulas: cxiii, 9

Qada (Jurchen), great commander of the Jin dynasty's last-ditch resistance to the Mongols; his full Jurchen name was Wongian Hada (Chinese Wanyan Heda): 132

Qada Liushou (Jurchen), high official in the Jurchen court and advocate of appeasement towards the Mongols, known as Ñêmha Hada in Jurchen (Chinese Nianhe Heda): 132–33

Qada'an (Sönit), captain of a thousand in the nightguard of the *kešikten* (imperial guard corps): 100, 154

Qada'an (Suldus), younger sister of Cila'un Ba'atur and Cimbai: 22, 52, 110

Qada'an (Borjigin), one of the younger sons of Qabul Khan who died childless: 10

Qada'an Taiši (Tayici'ut), son of Hambaġai Khan, subject of many stories of his strength and prowess; after the defeat by the Tatars, he sought support from Gür-Khan, ruler of the Kereyit, but was poisoned by him instead and died: 10, 12

Qada'an-Daldurqan (Targut), early adherent of Chinggis Khan: 37, 39, 70

Qadai, shift commander in the *kešikten* (imperial guard corps) of Ökodei: 154

Qadaq Ba'atur (Jirkin), commander of the Kereyit's vanguard unit: 67, 79

Qadingliq Range (*Qadingliq Niru'u*), the present-day Malkhan mountains in the Buryat Republic of Siberia: cxviii, 73

Qaidu (Borjigin), common ancestor of the Tayici'ut and the Mongols (in the narrow sense): cxii, 9

Qala'aljit Sands (*Qala'aljit Elet*), site of the famous battle in Spring, 1203, between Chinggis Khan's Mongols and Ong Khan and his allies; location probably at present-day Qaljan Dunes in the Ulagai-Seyelji region

Qaldun: see **Burġan-Qaldun**

Qali'udar (Je'uriyet), man in Qasar's retinue sent by Chinggis Khan on mission to Ong Khan: 77–78

Qangġar-Qan, alternative name of the Khangai Mountains: 85–86

Qangli, Turkic-speaking pastoralists of the central and eastern Kazakhstan area, many of whom took service in the Khwarazmian empire: xlvi, cxxii, 93, 142, 146, 150

Qangqas, non-Turkic, probably Yeniseyan-speaking people of Siberia, centered on a town at the confluence of the Angara and Yenisey rivers: cxx, 121

Qaracar (Barulas), captain of a thousand and advisor to Caġadai; he was the ancestor of Temur the Lame ('Tamerlane'): 37, 99, 123

Qara-Dal ('Black Dal'), river also known as the Tar or Der River, probably the present-day Delgermörön, a tributary of the Selenge river: cxviii, cxx, 91

Khan; 43, 47, 61, ally of Chinggis Khan; 77–78, breaks with Ong Khan; 87, in battle of Naqu Qun; 89–90, 124–25, character; 123, 125, assigned subjects and advisors; 124–25, 126, suspected by Chinggis Khan; 133, in campaigns against China

Qaśi (Ca'āt Jalayir), boy given as servant to Chinggis Khan by his father: 46

Qaśin: see **Hexi**

Qatagin, noble (*niru'un*) house of the Mongols, originally dwelling in the foothills of the Great Khinggan Mountains: cxi, cxii, 8, 43, 48, 90, 193

Qatai Küregen (Bosqur Qonggirat), son of Deyi Secen's brother and husband of Chinggis Khan's daughter Qoru: 100

Qatun ('Lady'), Turco-Mongolian term for a wife particularly of a high-status man, from emperor to captain of a thousand: lxxxvii–lxxxviii, 27, 43, 59–60, 82, 87, 91, 134, 136, 139, 143

Qïpchaqs (*Kibca'ut*), Turkic-speaking pastoralists, particularly those dwelling from western Kazakhstan west to the Danube; called Cumans in Greek sources: xlvii, cxxii, 93, 142, 146, 150, 152

Qïzil-Baš, Lake (*Kisil-Baš Na'ur*; Turkic 'Red Head'), present-day Lake Ulungur in northern Xinjiang: cxx, 61, 74

Qo'aqcin, Granny (*Qo'aqcin Emegen*), serving woman in young Temujin's (Chinggis Khan) camp: 26–27, 32

Qoajin Beki (Borjigin), Chinggis Khan's daughter, offered in marriage first to Ilqa Senggum's son and later married to Botu of the Ikires: 63

Qocar Beki (Borjigin), first cousin and early supporter of Chinggis Khan, later turned hostile: cxii, 38, genealogy; 38–39, 41, enthrones Chinggis Khan; 49, 58, 194, fights for Chinggis Khan; 58, 128, 137, punished; 63–64, conspires with Jamuqa; 70, 75–76, leader of anti-Chinggis Mongols

Qoluyiqan (Borjigin), daughter of Joci, married to the Oyirat commander Törolci: 121

Qonggiran (singular of Qonggirat), captain of a thousand: 100

Qonggirat, large commoner (*dürlugin*) clan, one house of which became the classic marriage ally (*quda*) family in the Mongol empire: 13–14, 24, 48, 71, 91, 100, 192

Qongqai Qorci (Adarkin), quiver-bearer (*qorci*) in the *keśikten* (imperial guard corps): 141

Qongqortaġai: see **Qongqortai**

Qongqortai, commander under Ökodei, appointed to shift commander in the *keśikten* (imperial guard corps): 151, 152, 153, 154

Qongqotan, midling-ranked clan of the Mongols: cxiii, 9, 14, 37, 43, 124–28, 143, 192

Qongtaġar Qorci (Dolanggir), quiver-bearer (*qorci*) in the *kešikten* (imperial guard corps): 141

Qo'ocaq, lighter arrow used for longer distances: 40

Qorci, quiver-bearer, an important element in the *kešikten* (imperial guard corps): 39, 80, 84–85, 111, 112, 114–15, 116, 118–19, 127, 141, 146, 152–54

Qorci Noyan (Menen Ba'arin), shaman who had a vision of Chinggis Khan's coronation and was rewarded with command of a *tümen* in Siberia: 37–38, 98, 104, 122,

Qorcuqui Hill (*Qorcuqui Boldaq*), hill by the Kimurqa Stream in the Khentii Mountains, 22

Qorġasun, captain of a thousand and advisor to Mother Ö'elun and Temuke Otcigin: 99

Qori, Border Guard (*Qori Sübeci*; Naiman), border officer of the Naiman; his image in the *Secret History* vacillates between that of a low-ranking commander and that of a high-ranking general: 80, 82, 87

Qori-Buqa, Tatar captured by Chinggis Khan's father, Yisukei Ba'atur: 12

Qoricar the Marksman (*Qoricar Mergen*), early ancestor of Chinggis Khan: cxi, 3

Qoridai (Ġorulas), man who warned Chinggis Khan of the attack from Jamuqa and his allies: 49

Qorijin, Lady (*Qorijin Qatun*; Yörkin), widowed step-mother of Sece Beki: 43–44, 46

Qorilar, Forest Folk from the Irkutsk area; Qorilar appears to be the ethnonym Qori, with the Turkic plural suffix -lar: 4

Qorilar the Marksman, Master (*Qorilartai Mergen*), eponymous ancestor of the Qorilar people: cxi, 4

Qori-Qacar, shift commander of nightguards in the *kešikten* (imperial guard corps) of Ökodei Khan: 154

Qori-Šilemun Taiši (Kereyit), captain of Ong Khan's thousand dayguards: 67–68, 104

Qori-Tumat, Forest Folk from the Irkutsk area, probably a coalition of separate Qori and Tumat people; the Qori is likely the same as the Qori of the Qorilar: 4, 121

Qorqonaq valley (*Qorqonaq Jubur*), *jubur* or wooded valley, probably the present-day Aga Valley: cxix, 12, 29, 34–35, 96, 103

Qu the Hunchback (*Qu Bögetur*; Jurchen), commander of the Jin dynasty's last-ditch resistance to the Mongols; his name in Jurchen is Hû-Šire Yawuta (Chinese He-Shilie Yawuta): 132

Quba-Qaya ('Light Yellow Rock'), mountain in the steppe somewhere south of the Kherlen River: 53, 57

Qubilai, Prince (*Qubilai Kö'un*; Borjigin), second son of Chinggis Khan's fourth son Tolui, later famous as khan (ruled 1260–1294) who conquered South China and hosted Marco Polo: cxv, 287n. 53

Qubilai Noyan (Barulas), captain of a thousand, one of the 'four dogs' and enforcer of discipline in the Mongol army: 37, 40, 58, 85, 88, 98, 106, 120

Qudu'udar (Tayici'ut), Tayici'ut leader defeated by Chinggis Khan: 53

Qulan Ba'atur (Borjigin), son of Qabul Khan and father of Big Cāran: cxiii, 10, 104

Qulan, Lady (*Qulan Qatun*; U'as Merkit), Chinggis Khan's second-ranked wife: 91–92, 139

Qul-Bari Quri (Kereyit), lower ranked officials in Ong Khan's court who remained loyal to the khan: 58, 74

Quldaqar Cliff (*Quldaqar Qun*), cliff or crag near the Bushy Tree in the Qorqonaq valley.

Qum-Seng'ir (*Qum-Singgir*; Turkic 'Sand Spit'), zone of dunes along the Ulungur River in the Gurban-Tünggüt desert of northern Xinjiang: 61

Quril, captain of a thousand; his name is the Turco-Mongolian version of Greek 'Cyril': 100

Quriltai (or *qurilta*), assembly held annually in summer during which affairs of the realm are discussed, including, but not limited to, enthronement of a new khan: lv–lvi, 161

Qurjaqus, captain of a thousand; his name is the Turco-Mongolian version of Cyriacus: 100

Qurjaqus Buyiruq Khan (Kereyit), ruler of the Kereyit kingdom and father of Ong Khan: 56, 57, 64, 72

Qusutu-Śitu'en ('Birch Fastness'), temporary fort built along the Ulz River: 45

Qutuġa Beki (Oyirat), ruler of the forest-dwelling Oyirats, initially hostile to Chinggis Khan, but later submissive and enrolled as imperial son-in-law: 48–50, 121–22

Qutuġu, Śiki (Tatar), chief scribe and judge of the early Mongol empire: 45, 47, 101, 108, one of four foundlings; 99, captain of a thousand; 101–102, 123, 132–33, 140, trusted services; 102, 119, chief judge; 102, chief scribe; 139, defeated at Parvan

Qutula Khan (Borjigin), pre-Chinggisid khan, famed in legend for his loud voice, immense strength and huge appetite: cxiii, 10, 12, 75, 103

Qutuqtai Qatun (Merkit), woman of Toqto'a Beki's family, variously said to be either his wife or his daughter: 60

Qutuqtu-Mönggur (or **Qutuqtu-Möngler** or **Qutuqtu-Möngner**) ('Blessed Birthmarks'), son of Qabul Khan and father of Böri the Brawny; his name is probably a euphemistic reference to smallpox scars: cxiii, 10, 48, 194

Qutuqtu-Yörki or **Sorġatu-Yörki** ('Blessed One of the Yörkin' or 'Poxy One of the Yörki'; Yörkin), founder of the Yörkin house: cxii, 10, 47

Qutuqul Meadow (*Qutuqul Nu'u*), meadow within a meander of a river, from geographical context probably the Onon or one of its tributaries: 55, 111

Qutus (Barulas), captain of a thousand: 37, 99

Qutus-Qaljan, officer in Chinggis Khan's early *keśikten* (imperial guard corps): 84

Qu'urcin, Lady (*Qu'urcin Qatun*), widowed step-mother of Sece Beki: 43–44, 46

Quyildar Secen (Manġġut), commander of the Manġġut who first volunteered for a desperate charge at the Battle of Qala'aljit Sands: 42, joined Chinggis Khan; 68–69, 104, charge in Battle of Qala'aljit Sands; 71, died; 79, 110, endowment for orphans; 99, commander of a thousand; 106, trusted service

Red Hills (*Hula'anu'ut Bolda'ut*), hills of reddish rock in the uplands south of the Tuul River: 71

Red Jackets (*Hula'an degelen*), Mongolian name of a crack force in the Jurchen Jin formed mostly by Turkic deserters from the Mongol army. Known in Chinese as the 'Red Patch Army' (*Hongnajun*): 132

Red-Earth Grey (*Josotu Boro*), one of Chinggis Khan's riding horses: 143

Relay-riders (*ula'aci*), riders on the post-roads who accompany envoys from station to station: 157–58

Resident garrison troops (*tamaci*), permanent garrisons stationed outside of Mongolia and drawn from diverse units in the decimal organization, including locally mobilized non-Mongolian units, but all under Mongol command: cxxii, 149, 150, 151, 158

Ruthenians (*Oros, Orosut*), translation of the Mongolian term for the East Slavs, the later Belarusians, Russians and Ukrainians: 142, 146, 150, 152

Sa'ari steppe, type of black-soil steppe with a surface in small bumps, called *sa'ari* from a type of shagreen with similar granulated surface The Sa'ari steppe of the *Secret History* covers at least two such separate steppe areas, an eastern one between the Tuul and the Kherlen and a western one in the Orkhon valley: cxviii, 42, 131, eastern; cxviii, 61, 74, 85–86, western

Saġayit, commoner (*dürlugin*) house of the Mongols, closely associated with the Nünjin: 38, 193, 194

Sali-Qaca'u, early ancestor of Chinggis Khan: cxi, 3

Salji'ut, noble (*niru'un*) house of the Mongols, originally dwelling in the foothills of the Great Khinggan Mountains: cxi, cxii, 8, 48, 90, 193

Samarkand city (*Semizkent Balaġasu*), great city of oasis Central Asia, ethnically 'Sart' (i.e. Tajik or Persian speaking), but ruled by the Khwarazmian empire. The Mongolian name derives from a Turkic folk etymology meaning 'Fat City': cxxii, 139, 140, 142

Sam-Qacula (Borjigin), son of Qabul Khan and father of Bultacu Ba'atur: cxii, 10, 194

Saqal-bayan ('rich in beard'), plant used for making rafts. Mongolian interpreters identify this with the modern *sakhal öws* 'beard grass' or brown galingale, while Chinese translators glossed it as *zhuzong-cao* 'pig-bristle grass' or Venis-hair fern: 30

Sariġ-Qol (Turkic 'Yellow Valley'), extremely high, cold steppe in the Pamir Mountains, today divided between Afghanistan, Tajikistan and Xinjiang: 120

Sarīġ-Qun: see **Sariġ-Qol**

Sarts (*Sartaq, Sarta'ul*), Mongolian term for broadly Middle Eastern people. The term is often translated as "Muslim" but was not religiously specific and could include Jews, Christians and Hindus from the Middle East as well: xliv–xlv, 57, 73, 93, 134, 139–42, 143, 287n. 53

Saxons (*Sasut*), Saxons of Transylvania, an autonomous community in the kingdom of Hungary: cxxii, 142, 146, 150

Sauġa, Mongolian term for something which the finder has long desired and hence which once found, ought to be given to the finder: 34, 45

Scouts (*qara'ul*), soldiers stationed to watch a border or army encampment. Compared to 'outriders' (*alginci*), scouts had a more defensive role: 49, 61, 80, 85–88, 122

Secen ('wise'), epithet particularly for those able to find the right word for an occasion: 9, 10, 13, 37, 68

Sea (*Tenggis*), term for the largest inland bodies of water known to the Mongols, such as Lake Baikal or the Caspian Sea: 3

Sece Beki (Yörkin), senior member of the Borjigin lineage and head of the Yörkin house with his brother Taicu: cxii, 10, genealogy; 38,

194, command of a wagon fort; 39, 43, alliance with Chinggis Khan; 44, 46, punished for disobedience; 75, nominated as khan

Sece'ur (Gorulas), captain of a thousand: 37, 100

Sece-Domoq (Śingqot Jalayir), early supporter of Chinggis Khan: 37

Seceyiken (Borjigin), daughter of Chinggis Khan married to the Oyirat commander Inalci: 121

Selenge (*Selengge*), widest Mongolian river, receiving many tributaries such as the Orkhon and Tuul and flowing into Lake Baikal: cxviii, cxxi, 32, 34, 50, 57, 62, 72, 111

Sem-Soci, early ancestor of Chinggis Khan: cxi, 3

Senggum or *sengkun*, title derived from Kitan *seng'un*, itself from Chinese *xianggong* 'lord minister'. *Senggum* with an *-m* is a Turkic possessive form of address, meaning 'my lord': 9, 49, 62, 194

Senggum, Senggum Anda: see **Ilqa Senggum**

Senggum-Bilge (Tayici'ut), early Tayici'ut prince: 9, 10,

Senggur Stream (*Senggur Goroqan*), small river flowing south of the Khentii, probably to be identified with the present-day Tsenkher ('Azure') River: cxviii, 22, 24, 25, 39

Sets Up Willows (*Burgan-Bosgaqsan*; Uriyangqai), one of two 'masters' (*ejet*) of the sacred Burgan-Qaldun Mountains, probably a spirit or shaman figure: 4

Seuse: see **Slave Boy**

Seven Hills (*Dolo'an Bolda'ud*), hills in the area of the Küte'u (or Köde'e) Isle by the Kherlen River: 46, 161

Seyelji: see **Ulagai-Seyelji**

Shishged (*Śišgis* or *Śiqśit*), river in the taiga forests of northern Mongolia, flowing into the Tuvan Basin: cxviii, cxx, 50, 121

Sibir ('dense wood'), area along the middle Irtysh and Ob' (Imar) rivers, often found as Ibir-Sibir; origin of the Russian word 'Siberia': cxx, cxxiii, 121

Siju'udai (Siju'ut), eponymous ancestor of the Siju'ut clan: 9

Siju'ut, noble (*niru'un*) clan of the Mongols: cxiii, 193

Śiki Qutugu: see **Qutugu, Śiki**

Śiki'ur, Steward (*Śiki'ur Ba'urci*), steward (*ba'urci*) in the service of Chinggis Khan's extended family: 43, 46

Śilgincek, one of the Seven Hills in the Köde'e (or Küte'u) Isle: 161

Śiluqai: captain of a thousand: 99

Śinci the Rich (*Śinci Bayan*), one of two 'masters' (*ejet*) of the sacred Burgan-Qaldun Mountains, probably a spirit or shaman figure: 4

Śiraqan, member of the *keśikten* (imperial guard corps) under Ökodei responsible for entry and exit to the horde: 153

Śiraqul, captain of a thousand: 100

Śirgu'etu, Old Man (*Śirgu'etu Ebugen*; Naked Ba'arin), minion (*aran*) of Fatty Kiriltuq of the Tayici'ut who eventually went over to Chinggis Khan with his sons Alaq and Naya'a: 53–55, 111

Sistan City (*Sistan Balaġasu*), present-day town of Zaranj in southwest Afghanistan: cxxii, 140

Slave Boy (*Seuse*), derisive nickname given to the last Jin emperor ('Golden Khan'), personally named Shouxu (reigned 1223–1234): 149

Snowy Mountain (*Casutu*), name of a snow-capped mountain, most likely the Qilian Mountains in Gansu and Qinghai: 144

Sö'ekei Je'un (Sö'eken), early adherent of Chinggis Khan who served as messenger before defecting to Ong Khan's side: 37, 40, 41, 57, 71, 73, 76, 77

Sö'ekei, Slave (*Sö'ekei Bo'ol*; Sö'eken), son of Noqta, captured and enslaved in a campaign by Caraqa Lingqu and Tumbinai, 76

Sö'eken, Mongol clan of midling status: 193

Sogog River (*Soġoq Usun*; 'Cool River'), river flowing east from the Altai: cxx, 61, 74

Söiketu Cerbi (Qongqotan), captain of a thousand and one of the six chamberlains (*cerbi*): 37, 39, 84, 99

Sönit, Mongol clan of midling status: cxiii, 9, 193

Soqatai, Lady (*Soqatai Qatun*), widowed wife of the Tayici'ut ruler Hambaġai Khan: 15

Sorġan-Śira (Suldus), minion (*aran*) of the Tayici'ut princes, who gave reluctant assistance to a young captive Chinggis Khan: 20–22, 52–53, 99, 110–11

Sorġoqtani Beki (Kereyit): younger daughter of Ja'a Gambo, wife of Chinggis Khan's son Tolui and mother of Möngke and Qubilai khans: 79, 149 ('Berude'), 287 n. 53

Sorġatu-Yörki: see **Qutuqtu-Yörki**

Soqor, envoy in the service of Temuke Otcigin: 125–26

Spruce, Passes of (*Ġaca'uratu Sübcit*), passes in the mountains north of Ulaanbaatar: 34

Steward: see *Ba'urci*

Sübe'edei Ba'atur (Uriyangqan), famous commander of Chinggis Khan, commander of several western campagins: 37, 40, early adherent of Chinggis Khan; 88, 106, one of 'four dogs'; 93–94, 120, pursues Merkit fugitives; 99, 112, captain of a thousand; 139–40, vanguard in Central Asian campaign; 141–42, 146–47, 150, 152, vanguard in western campaign

Subqan: see **Jubqan**

Subut, salt-water pearls sourced from China: 120–21, 150

Suǧu Secen (Barulas), early adherent of Chinggis Khan: 37

Süjigil, Madame (*Süjigil Üjin*), wife of Bartan Ba'atur and grandmother of Chinggis Khan: 10,

Suldus, commoner clan of the Mongols: 20, 37, 79, 192

Sultan (*Sultan* or *Soltan*), title of Muslim rulers, equivalent to khan, king, or emperor: 139–40, 142, Sultan of Khwarazm; 141, 146, caliph sultan of Baghdad

Taǧai (Menen Ba'arin), assigned with Qorci to rule a *tümen* (tenthousand) of Forest Folk: 104

Taǧai Ba'atur (Suldus), messenger and captain of a thousand: 37, 40, 41, 57, 73, 79, 99

Taicar (Jadaran), cousin of Jamuqa, killed in altercation over horse theft: 42, 97

Taicu (Yörkin), younger brother of Sece Beki and joint leader of the Yörkin house: cxii, 10, genealogy; 38, 194, command of a wagon fort; 43, alliance with Chinggis Khan; 44, 46, punished for disobedience; 75, nominated as khan

Taiši, title derived from Chinese *taishi* 'Grand Preceptor', used among Mongols and Kereyit for the realm's second in command. Muqali bore this title, although it is not used for him in the *Secret History*: 10, 11, 58, 67, 72, 75

Tai-Temur Taiši (Kereyit), younger brother of Ong Khan who was initially co-ruler with Ong Khan of the Kereyit kingdom, but was later executed by his brother: 72

Talqun Isle (*Talqun Aral*), spit of land between the Orkhon and Selenge rivers and center of the U'as Merkit: cxviii, 30, 34

Tamaca, early ancestor of Chinggis Khan: cxi, 3

Tamaci: see **Resident garrison troops**

Tamaci, captain of a thousand: 100

Tamir River, tributary of the Orkhon River flowing from the Khangai Mountains: cxviii, 87, 90

Tana (plural *tanas*), term used both for the fresh-water pearls of the Manchurian area as well as large pearls from the Persian Gulf: 45, 120–21, 150

Tana Stream (*Tana Gorqon*; 'Pearl Stream'), small river on the southern slopes of the Khentii Mountains, presumably so-called from the presence of fresh-water pearls in it: 31,

Tanguts (*Tang'ut* or *Tang'udut*), people from the Tibetan plateau who founded the Xi Xia or Western Xia kingdom in northwestern China: xxxix–xl, cxx, cxxiii, 56–58, 73, 131, 138, 142–45

Tannu-Ola (*Tanglu*), mountain range separating northwestern Mongolia from Tuva: 94

Tarbai (Uyghur), envoy sent to deliver message of the Uyghur ruler to Chinggis Khan: 120

Tarġut, clan of commoner (*dürlugin*) Mongols, subordinate to the Tayici'ut: 10, 37, 107

Tarġutai Kiriltuq: see **Kiriltuq, Fatty**

Tas: see **Taz**

Tatars, in the *Secret History* used to designate Mongolic-speaking people enrolled as border auxiliary troops for the Jurchen Jin dynasty and usually hostile to the Mongols: xxxi, cxxi, 191, definition and location; 10–11, 12, 14, early conflicts with the Mongols; 44–45, 46, punished by Jin armies; 47, foundling; 48, join alliance against Chinggis Khan; 57, conflict with Kereyits; 58–60, 103, 108, annihilated by Chinggis Khan

Taur River (*Taur Müren*), tributary of the Naun (Chinese Nenjiang) River whose course cuts an easy route from Manchuria through the Great Khingan Mountin into Mongolia: cxix, cxxi, 133

Tayang Khan (Betegin Naiman), khan of the eastern or Betegin half of the Naiman realm and brother of Buyruq Khan who ruled the western, Kücugut, half: 63, 82–83, 86–91

Tayici'ut, noble (*niru'un*) house branched off from the Borjigin lineage, ruling a confederation of subordinate houses: cxiii, 9, 192–93, genealogy; 10, 12, 72, allied with the Mongols; 15–17, 18, 19, turn against clan of Temujin (Chinggis Khan); 19–21, 110, capture Temujin; 25, 36–37, 47, 111, 140, some join Chinggis Khan; 48, 50–53, annihilated by Chinggis Khan; 91, remnant surrender

Tayidu'ul the One-Eyed (*Tayidu'ul Soqor*), former commander (*noyan*) of the Qori-Tumat: 121

Taz, people listed as Forest Folk, probably in the far west, near the Bashkir; the modern Taz are a clan of Kazakhs near the Caspian Sea: cxxii,

Teb-Tenggeri ('Most Heavenly': Qongqotan), shamanic title of Kökecu who originally announced Heaven's nomination of Chinggis Khan, but later challenged his power: 124–28

Tebene ('auger'), large needle used for sewing leather and other tough material: 89

Tegus Beki (Uduyit Merkit), son of Toqto'a Beki, probably the eldest and expected heir apparent of his father: 60

Tele'etu Pass (*Tele'etu Amasar*), unidentified mountain pass, probably somewhere in Mongolia's Bulgan province: 46, 62, 74

Telegetu the Rich (*Telegetu Bayan*; Ca'āt Jalayir), grandfather of Muqali Guyang: 46

Telengut (*Telenggut*), Turkic-speaking people of Siberia, today divided between the Teleuts in Kemerovo and the Telengits of the Altay Republic: 104, 121

Teme'en steppe (*Teme'en Ke'er*; 'Camel Steppe'), steppe area located north of Lake Dar in Inner Mongolia: cxix, 83

Temujin Öke (Tatar), Tatar commander captured by Yisukei Ba'atur, after whom Temujin (Chinggis Khan) was named: 12

Temujin (Borjigin): personal name of Chinggis Khan; see 'Chinggis Khan' for full citations: 12, named; 39– 41, Temujin becomes Chinggis Khan; 52, 54, 64, 65–66, 70, 74, 124–25, called Temujin by childhood acquaintances; 57, 62, 67, 73, 'Prince Temujin'; 61, 63, 88–89, 'Temujin *Anda*'; 64, 'Temujin's kingdom'

Temuke Otcigin, youngest brother of Chinggis Khan; the title Otcigin is his as youngest son of Yisukei Ba'atur and Mother Ö'elun: cxiv, 12, genealogy; 19, 26, in Chinggis Khan's early camp; 83, 87, in Batle of Naqu Qun; 90, 124, character; 123, 138, assigned subjects and advisors; 125–27, humiliated by Teb-Tenggeri; 139, supervises Great Base Camp; 146, 157, supports Ökodei Khan; 159, marriageable girls in his kingdom requisitioned

Temulun (Borjigin), Chinggis Khan's sister, married to Botu Küregen: 12, 19, 26

Ten thousand: see *Tümen*

Tenggelik Stream (*Tenggelik Ǧoroqan*), unidentified stream flowing from the Lesser Khentii Mountains into the Kherlen: 26

Tenggeri (Jurchen), Mongolian name of the Jurchen prince sent as dayguard and hostage to the Mongol court; his Jurchen name was Wongian Eke (Chinese Wanyan Eke): 133

Terge: see Dergei Amal

Tergune Heights (*Tergune Ündur*), deeply forested area in the heights of the Khentii Mountains: 19

Tibetan dogs (*Töbudut noqat*), large, shaggy-coated guard dog, known today as *bankhar*: 141

Titik Ša'al, misunderstood in the *Secret History* as a placename near the Nekun River, other sources treat it as the name (Titik) and title (*ša'al*) of the frontier commander stationed there: 80

To'oril Khan (Kereyit): personal name of Ong Khan; see 'Ong Khan' for full citations: 28, 45

To'oril, Boy (*To'oril De'u*; Sö'eken), conspirator against Chinggis Khan with Jamuqa; he was son of Jegei-Qongtaǧar and the brother of Chinggis Khan's early messenger Sö'ekei Je'un: 63–64, 76, 77

To'oril, Slim (*Narin To'oril*), son of Caǧān-Quwa who inherited his father's captaincy of a thousand: 110

Tobuqa, captain of a thousang: 100

Töde'en Girte (Tayici'ut), treated in the *Secret History* as a Tayici'ut leader, other sources identify him as a quiver bearer (*qorci*) in Chinggis Khan's family entourage. The epithet *girte* may be related to Turkic *qïrt* "short; stingy": 15

Tödo'e (Tayici'ut), either son or younger brother of Qada'an Taiši, who feuded with Fatty Kiriltuq, Baġaci and other Tayici'ut princes: 52, 111

Tödo'en Barulas, branch of the Barulas, a noble (*niru'un*) house among the Mongols; *tödo'en* may be related to Turkic *tödük* 'pure, noble': cxiii, 9

Tödo'en Otcigin (Borjigin), youngest son of Qabul Khan: cxiii, 10

Tödo'en, Pretty (*Sayiqan Tödo'en*; Kereyit), envoy of Ilqa Senggum: 64, 76–77

Toġon-Temur, captain of a thousand: 100

Toġura'un ('crane'; plural Toġura'ut), branch of the commoner Jalayir clan: 37, 107

Toġura'ut: see **Toġura'un**

Tölös (Tö'eles), Turkic-speaking people in the present-day Altay Republic: cxx, 104, 121

Tolui (Borjigin), fourth and younger son of Chinggis Khan and his first wife Madame Börte: cxiv, genealogy; 79, marriage; 108–09, almost killed as a child; 123, assigned subjects and advisors; 132, battle-field heroism; 137, in the succession debate; 140, in the western campaign; 146, enthrones Ökodei; 149, sacrifices himself for Ökodei

Tolun Cerbi (Qongqotan), one of the six chamberlains (*cerbi*) and commander of a thousand: 84, 98, 107, 108, 133, 143, 145

Tongguan Pass (*Tunggon Amasar*), strategic pass near the Yellow River, communicating between China's Shaanxi and Henan provinces: cxxiii, 132

To'ocaq Heights (*To'ocaq Ündur*), high point in the Khentii Mountains: 4

Toqto'a Beki (Uduyit Merkit), leader of the Uduyit Merkit and one of Chinggis Khan's die-hard foes: 27, 30, 32, 35, involved in kidnapping Börte; 60, 62, attacked by Ong Khan; 72, early alliance with Ong Khan; 73, second war with Chinggis Khan; 91, 92, conquered by Chinggis Khan

Toqto'a, Shaman (*Toqto'a Bö'e*), person in an obscure figure of speech attributed by Ilqa Senggum to Chinggis Khan: 77

Toqu (Borjigin), third son of Chinggis Khan's younger brother Qasar, said to have been very short: cxiv, 77

Toqucar (Qonggirat), one of Chinggis Khan's early seventy dayguards and commander in the first western campaign as far as Khan-Malik's territory. The *Secret History* says he survived the ensuing fighting and was punished for violating orders, but other sources say he died in the fighting: 139–40

Toqucar, supervisor of the post-road system: 158

Törbi-Taš, in the *Secret History* an envoy from Tayang Khan to the Öng'üt regent Ala-Quš Digit-Quri; other sources make him the envoy from regent Ala-Quš Digit-Quri to Chinggis Khan, however: 83

Töregene, originally wife of the young Merkit commander Godu, given in marriage to Ökodei; after Ökodei Khan's death, she served as regent over the whole empire from 1241 to 1246: 92

Toroġoljin the Rich (*Toroġoljin Bayan*; Borjigin), early ancestor of Chinggis Khan: cxi, 3

Törolci Küregen (Oyirat), eldest son of the ruler of the forest-dwelling Oyirats, married to Joci's daughter Qoluyiqan: 121

Toruqan, joint captain of a thousand with Tolun Cerbi: 107

Tota'ut Tatars, leading Tatar house, elsewhere known as the Totoqli'ut: 58

Tübe'en, Ten Thousand (*Tümen Tübe'en*; Kereyit), crack vanguard unit in the Kereyit army, nominally ten thousand strong: 56, 67–68, 80, 104

Tüge, captain of a thousand and father of the quiver-bearer (*qorci*) Bükidei: 98, 114

Tügei (Uduyit Merkit), wife of the young Merkit commander Godu: 92

Tüge-Maqa (Ikires), leader of the Ikires and member of the coalition enthroning Jamuqa: 48

Tügu'udei (Jadaran), ancestor of Jamuqa: 8

Tüideger, captain of a thousand: 100

Tülkin-Ce'ut, hills in the Teme'en or 'Camel' Steppe area: 83

Tumat, Forest Folk from the Irkutsk area, in close alliance with the Qori people: cxx, cxxiii, 4, 121–22

Tumbinai Secen (Borjigin), great-great grandfather of Chinggis Khan, often treated as khan: cxii, 9, 10, 76

Tümen ('ten thousand'), in the Turco-Mongolian decimal organization a body of nominally ten thousand soldiers and a community of households capable of producing such a body of soldiers: lxxxix, 29, 31, 38, 42, 56, 103, 104, 106, 112, 118, 121, 123, 146

Tüngge (Ca'āt Jalayir), boy given as servant to Chinggis Khan by his father: 46

Tungging City (*Tungjin Balaġasu*), from Chinese *Dongjing* 'Eastern Capital', a regional capital of the Jin dynasty, now Liaoyang in Liaoning province: 129–30

Tüngke Stream (*Tüngke Ġoroqan*), stream or (according to other sources) lake probably in the steppe southwest of Lake Buir: 71

Tüngkelik Stream (*Tüngkelik Ġoroqan*), stream flowing down the north slopes of the Khentii Mountains: 3, 6–7, 31

Tungquidai, captain of a thousand: 100

Tuqas, people closely related to the Tuvans and possibly ancestors of the Dukha, present-day reindeer herders in the Shishged valley of Mongolia: 121

Turġa'ut: see **Ala'ut-Turġa'ut**

Tusaġa (Kereyit), son of Ilqa Senggum: 63

Tuul River (*Tu'ula Müren*), one of three main rivers rising in the Khentii Mountains and emptying into the Orkhon River: cxviii, 25, 28, 34, 62, 73, 142

Tuvans (*Tubas*), Turkic-speaking people, the main population of the Tuvan basin, and also in surrounding areas: cxxiii, 121

U'as Merkit, one of three 'hundreds' of the Merkit, centered on Talqun Isle, headed by Dayir-Usun: 27, 29, 32, 35, 91

Ücuken Barulas: see **Little Barulas**

Ucumaq, arrow with a long shaft and three-pointed iron head: 70, 104

Udutai, captain of a thousand: 99

Uduyit Merkit, one of three 'hundreds' of the Merkit, centered on Buur Steppe, headed by Toqto'a Beki: 27, 29, 30, 32, 34, 94

Uġucu: see **Aġucu Ba'atur**

Üjin: see **Madame**

Ula River (*Ula müren*; Jurchen 'River'), present-day Songhua River: 133

Ulagai-Seyelji (*Ulġui-Silu'eljit*), area of well-watered steppe along the Ulagai and Seyelji rivers in the Üjumucin (Üzemchin) district of Inner Mongolia: cxix, 58, 70

Uluġ Taġ (Turkic 'Great Mountain'), peak Taldagiin Ikh Uul in the Altai Mountains: 50, 61, 74

Ulungur River (*Ürunggu*), river flowing from the Altai mountains through the Gurban-Tünggüt desert in northern Xinjiang into Lake Qïzil-Baš: cxx, 61, 74

Ulz River (*Ulja*), broad, shallow river running between the Onon and the Kherlen and flowing into Lake Barun-Torei: cxix, cxxi, 44–45

Unggirat: see **Qonggirat**

Uquna ('Billy Goat'), head of a party of envoys and merchants sent by Chinggis Khan to open relations with the Sultanate of Khwarazm.

His name is not otherwise attested and may be a Mongol nickname for a Khwarazmian merchant in Mongol employ: 134

Ural River: see Zhayiq

Uraq Desert (*Uraq Cöl*), apparently an uninhabited desert area on the bend of the Kherlen River, although the Kherlen basin is all inhabited steppe today. This great bend may be the area downstream from Choibalsan city: 25

Uraqai City (*Uraqai Balaġasu*), frontier fortress of the Tangut kingdom, situated north of the great bend of the Yellow River: cxxi, cxxiii, 144

Urgench City (*Ürunggeci Balaġasu*), capital of the Khwarazmian Empire, corresponding to Köneürgenç or 'Old Ürgench' in Turkmenistan, not to be confused with 'New' Ürgench to the southeast in Uzbekistan. The Mongolian name comes from the Turkish folk-etymological name 'Bright City': cxxii, 140–41, 142

Uriyangqai, general Mongolian term for Forest Folk from the northwest: cxxiii, 4

Uriyangqan (plural Uriyangqat), commoner (*dürlugin*) clan among the Mongols, of forest origin and commonly associated with blacksmithing and shamanic skills: 4, 8, 25, 37, 192

Ursut (singular Urus or Urs), originally Iranian-speaking nomads incorporated into the Yenisey Kïrghiz confederacy: 121

Uru'udai, eponymous ancestor of the Uru'ut clan: 9

Uru'ut, noble (*niru'un*) house of the Mongols, famed for their battle prowess: cxiii, 9, 42, 67–68, 70, 71, 88, 105–06, 193

Urus Ïnal, a leader (*ïnal*) of the Yenisey Kïrghiz of Siberia, representing the 'Seven Thrones' (*Yeti Orun*), probably of Ursut origin: 121

Üsun, Old Man (*Üsun Ebugen*; Menen Ba'arin), captain of a thousand, one of four councillors and senior priest-shaman (*beki*): 37, 99, 106, 110

Utkiya, unidentified place name, probably in the Ulagai-Seyelji area: 49, 93

Uurga (*u'urġa*), long wooden pole with a rope at the end of it, usable as either a lasso or as a whip: 23–24, 93

Üye'et, branch of the commoner Jalayir clan, mostly subject to Qutula Khan's sons: 10

Uyghurs (*Uyi'ut* or *Uyiġut*), then Buddhist people in the east of present-day Xinjiang, famed for their literacy and learning: xliii–xliv, cxx, cxxiii, 56–58, 73, 120–21

Vanguard (*manglai*), large units that fought in front of the great center (*ġool*) of the army: 49, 67–68, 129, 132, 139, 148, 149

Victorious Buddha (*Iluġu Burqan*): see **Buddha Khan**

Volga: see **Etil**

Wagon-Fort (*küre'en* or *küriyen*), circular assembly of *ger*-wagons and covered wagons (*qara'un terge*) used to defend people and livestock from raids or attack: xxiv, 23, 34, 37–38, 42, 50–52, 57, 73, 90, 103, 107, 193–94

White Tatars (*Cagān Tatar*), in the *Secret History* designating a Tatar house; in Chinese sources often used as another term for the Öng'ut: 58

White-Muzzle Bay (Aman-Cagān-Ke'er), Big Cāran's riding horse: 66

Wongian Eke: see **Tenggeri**

Wongian Fuking: see **Ongging Chengxiang**

Wongian Hada: see **Qada**

Wongian Xiang: see **Ongging Chengxiang**

Wu'anu (Jurchen), Jurchen Jin commander in Manchuria who rebelled and established a separate Manchurian regime; known as Fusen Wu'anu in Jurchen (Chinese Puxian Wannu): 133

Xuandezhou (*Sönticu*), Chinese prefectural seat in valley between Juyong Pass and Fox Pass: cxxi, cxxii, 129

Yalavach (*Yalawaci*; Turkic 'envoy'), merchant who entered Mongol service as envoy and became overseer (*darugaci*) first of the Central Asian cities and then of North China; known in Persian sources as Mahmud Yalavach: 142

Yalbaq, shift commander in the *kesikten* (imperial guard corps) of Ökodei: 154

Yaliqai: see **Gongzhu**

Yarkant (*Uriyang*), city of the Tarim Basin in present-day southern Xinjiang: cxxii, 142

Yatir, wrangler under Chinggis Khan's nephew Alcidai: 66

Yeke Barulas: see **Big Barulas**

Yeke Cāran: see **Cāran, Big**

Yeke Ciledu: see **Ciledu, Big**

Yeke Ne'urin: see **Ne'urin, Big**

Yeke-Nidun ('Big Eye'), early ancestor of Chinggis Khan: cxi, 3

Yeku, dayguard in the *kesikten* (imperial guard corps) of Ökodei: 155

Yeku (Borjigin), eldest son of Chinggis Khan's brother Qasar: 77, 146, 157

Yellow steppe (*Sira Ke'er*), area in the plains of eastern Mongolia: 14

Yellow steppe (*Sira Ke'er*), plains north of Zhongdu (present-day Beijing): 132

Yellow Terrace (*Sira Dektur*), village of Longhutai just south of Juyong Pass in northern China, 148

Yeti-Orun (Turkic 'Seven Thrones'), one of two leagues of petty principalities into which the Yenisey Kīrghiz were divided: 121